BLOOD FLATS

EDWARD TRIMNELL

1

On the morning that he became a fugitive from justice, Lee McCabe awoke with two persistent sensations in his consciousness. The first was the sound that Apache helicopters make when they land in the desert, and how the dust swirls beneath them as they raise up little tornados of sand. The second was the smell of a woman's strawberry shampoo.

As he struggled awake—alone in the small bedroom of his rented trailer—Lee realized that the sound was not that of an Apache helicopter, but the rumbling of an approaching motor vehicle. Sounds carried a long way this far from town, especially on a Saturday morning.

He resisted the notion that the approaching car or truck might be something to worry about. He was still overly cautious, he knew. What else could he expect after two years of living in a war zone?

The clock on the nightstand beside the bed read 5:32 a.m. In recent months, Lee McCabe had learned to appreciate the small luxuries. It was a luxury to sleep until 5:30 a.m., even on a Saturday. It was a luxury not to have to arise even earlier, to step outside your barracks into the glaring, sand-blown heat of a hostile land, where any man, woman, or child might be bent on killing you.

And it was a luxury to have the regular company of women again. The smell of the strawberry shampoo was on the tee shirt that he had worn to bed. It mingled with the perfume of the woman he had danced with the previous night at the Steeplechase Saloon.

She had been young—and in Lee's estimation—frivolous and carefree. At first it had seemed that she wanted to do nothing but laugh and talk. But after a while she somehow perceived that Lee was still reclaiming that world in which light conversation and laughter were possible. She did not push him beyond his means. She took his hand and led him to the center of the room, where they slow-danced, her head on his chest, her hair on his cheek and his shoulder.

He had taken in the scent of her wild strawberry shampoo then, and now its lingering presence brought back the feel of her firm young body pressed up against his. Before they had parted, she slipped him a matchbook cover that contained her phone number. The recollection made him smile. Perhaps he would call her. *Yes, he definitely would.*

Lee McCabe was twenty-three years old and he had returned from Iraq to Perryston, Kentucky, less than three months ago.

Early sunlight filtered through the curtains of the single window in the bedroom. The few pieces of furniture that surrounded him were scuffed and dented. The furniture was older than he was. *But why would he care?* The furniture was neither green nor camouflage, like practically everything that they gave you in the Marine Corps.

Once again his attention was drawn to the sound of the lone motor vehicle; and he tried to estimate its distance. A mile? A half mile?

What difference did it make, anyway? There were no al-Qaeda in Perryston. No suicide bombers. He was safe here.

Since Lee had come home, not a single person had tried to kill him. Three months without hostile gunfire aimed in his direction. Three months without a booby-trapped car or some maniac hiding a bomb beneath his *dishdasha* at a checkpoint.

The streets of Perryston were free from gunfire and explosions. Walking around town in civilian clothes rather than combat fatigues,

Lee had not once had to turn away from the shrieks of hysterical survivors, or the anguished groans of the dying. Not once in three months.

Lee decided that he had lain in bed long enough. It was the first week of June and the day's heat was already rising, prickling his skin with humidity. He swung his feet out of bed and stood erect, his toes digging into the blue threadbare carpet.

He reluctantly discarded the tee shirt with its pleasant woman's scent and retrieved a clean one from the bureau drawer. He hastily pulled on a pair of jeans, then socks, and then the steel-toed boots that were regulation safety gear at the machine shop where he worked. The boots smelled vaguely of oil.

The distant engine was drawing closer now, crowding the thoughts of the young woman from his mind. This despite his best efforts. He did not want to think about the vehicle but there it was: He judged it to be a pickup truck or an SUV that was coming along the adjacent two-lane highway.

He paused as he heard the vehicle slow down and then come to an abrupt stop. Next he heard the metallic sounds of the vehicle's doors opening and closing. Finally there were several masculine voices—perhaps three or four.

Ease up, Lee, he told himself. *Now just you ease up.*

He *did* have to learn to take it easy. Despite his joy at being home, relaxation no longer came naturally to him. He was still struggling to rid himself of the constant wariness that had kept him alive in Iraq. He did not intend to go through the rest of his life flinching at ordinary sights and sounds.

Some days were better than others. The other day he had been standing in line at the Perryston Wal-Mart when a small boy suddenly ran up to his mother, who was waiting in line directly in front of Lee. Lee had practically jumped, his body tensing from an involuntary reflex. He had scared the boy and the boy's mother, and greatly embarrassed himself.

He had never been prone to that sort of reaction before going to

Iraq. He was back in the world now, and he would have to work to fully retrain himself to the old ways.

Lee continued to lace up his work boots, resisting the urge to investigate what was outside. It was just this thing he had developed about cars while over in Iraq, he told himself. Three men in Lee's platoon had been killed one day when a jihadi detonated a car bomb. Over there you quickly learned to regard every car and truck with suspicion—or you ended up dead even more quickly. In Iraq all unknown vehicles had been potential harbingers of death.

But in Kentucky a lone vehicle at a strange hour was no particular cause for alarm.

It was nothing, he decided.

2

Lee walked through the wood-paneled hallway toward the kitchen of his trailer. The trailer was old. Its flooring creaked and groaned beneath his feet.

The trailer was temporary, of course—just like his present job as a lathe operator at the SJR Machine Shop. He had banked a fair amount of his Marine Corps pay, resisting the temptation to spend it on leave like there was no tomorrow, as so many men did—*since there might well be no tomorrow for any particular person in a time of war*. And the lathe operator job paid decent wages. In the fall he would begin to take evening classes. There was a satellite branch of the University of Kentucky right here in Hawkins County.

It was funny how your power relative to others changed, he reflected, sometimes moving you upward, sometimes pushing you back down the ladder. In the Marine Corps he had been a sergeant, grade E-5, with authority over other men and responsibility for other men's lives. Now he was a lowly lathe operator. That was all right. In Iraq he had given commands that had brought death—mostly to the enemy, but once or twice to men he was leading, through his own misjudgment of the circumstances, the superior tactics of the enemy, or plain and simple bad luck.

God, I have had enough of giving orders for one lifetime, he thought. *From here on out, let me neither take orders nor give them. Let me simply enjoy my freedom.*

This was something that civilians seemed incapable of grasping. They all wanted to know what the war had been like—and how it felt to be back; but they gave Lee slightly embarrassed smiles when he told them that it was simply good to be alive and free in a familiar place where no one was taking potshots at you.

No, civilians *didn't* understand. No matter how circumspect their questions, civilians all wanted to know about the violence. They were practically obsessed with it: *Were you in any shootouts? Did you see any al-Qaeda fighters?* And always that one unspoken question that no one dared to ask: *Did you have to kill anyone?*

Lee avoided these questions as much as he could. He simply wanted to reacclimate himself to the ways of peace. He had gotten to know violence intimately, and he wanted no further part of it. And no, he had no interest in telling war stories. Perhaps he would tell them when he was an old man. But he had no desire to tell war stories now. This, also, was an inclination that civilians could not fully grasp, he supposed.

He was in the kitchen when he heard the heavy footsteps in the gravel outside his front door. His body stiffened. Judging by the heaviness of the crunching noises, three to four men were passing by his trailer. They were walking deliberately without any banter or conversation between them.

Lee made an instant connection between these footsteps and the engine he had heard a few minutes ago. He let go of the notion that he could simply ignore the situation. Rational or not, it was bothering him now.

He stepped to his front window and drew the white ruffled curtain back a few inches. There were in fact four of them. He could see their backs now: each one was wearing either a trench coat or a hunting jacket, which didn't make sense at this time of year. Then Lee noticed an angular bulge inside one of the trench coats. This made the reason for their unseasonable attire immediately apparent.

The men obviously were not planning to pay him a visit. They were headed toward the adjacent lot. The trailer occupied by Tim Fitzsimmons, and his girlfriend, a young woman whom Lee knew only as Jody.

Just past the edge of his own trailer, one of the men briefly turned around, as if making a quick survey of the surroundings. Lee froze.

The man had a dark beard and a bulbous nose. He looked vaguely familiar, though Lee could not place him. When you lived in a small town, there were many people outside your circle of friends and acquaintances whose faces were nevertheless familiar to varying degrees. Probably this man was someone whom Lee had seen around town. He was definitely a local.

The man apparently had not noticed Lee looking out the window. He turned back around and continued walking with his companions.

One of the men pointed to Tim Fitzsimmons' trailer and gestured to the others. Yes, that was definitely where they were going. *Where else would trouble of this kind be headed?*

3

L   ee stood there in his kitchen, thinking about the lights of
        the little pipes that sometimes glowed in the darkness
        outside Tim Fitzsimmons's trailer at odd hours of the
evening. Usually Tim would shoo these more indiscreet customers
away; and occasionally he would brandish a gun at them. *"Get your
sorry meth-head ass away from here before you do that!"* the ex-con
would shout. It didn't take much observation to figure out what sort
of commerce was occurring in the trailer next door. The money and
the little baggies of whitish powder sometimes exchanged hands on
the steps outside Fitzsimmons's front door.

So far, Lee had had relatively little interaction with the other residents of the Tradewinds Trailer Park. Most of them seemed to be
agreeable enough; they were predominantly lower middle-class
working people like himself, for whom the Tradewinds was a way
station along the path to something better. Young couples saving up
for a down payment on a tract house in town. A handful of retirees in
temporary limbo. Some divorcees with small children. Even a few
recently discharged veterans like himself. None of them had much
money; you didn't live in a trailer park if you had real money.

It had not taken Lee long to identify Tim Fitzsimmons as the sort of predatory presence that invariably works its way into low-income environments like the Tradewinds. Fitzsimmons was in his early thirties. He wore the perpetual glare of a man who had long ago accepted the role of a hood, and he wanted everyone he encountered to know it. He also had the authentic credentials: Fitzsimmons had spent most of his twenties in the Kentucky State Penitentiary in Eddyville.

These recollections weighed on Lee's mind as he watched the four strangers disappear around a bend in the gravel path. He had long recognized what was going on next door; and yet he had done nothing about it.

Then he reminded himself that he was a civilian now. It wasn't his job to carry a gun anymore.

But he *should* have called Sheriff Phelps. Many times he had thought about it. Perryston was the Hawkins County seat, and Phelps's office was located in the town proper. Lee could have walked into the sheriff's office and talked to him. For that matter, he could have made a telephone call.

Yes, he *should* have done that. But talking to Sherriff Steven Phelps had never been easy for him. And nothing had changed since he had come back from Iraq. The lawman still gave him an expression that implied a range of emotions: blame, resentment, distrust— as if Lee were responsible for the pathetic way the sheriff's life had turned out.

It was absurd when you thought about it. Unbelievably so. But the sheriff had never let go of his old grudge. The grudge sprung from events that had occurred before Lee had even been born. *But that made no difference, did it?*

Was he imagining the depth of the sheriff's ill will? *No*—Lee still remembered an encounter he had had with the sheriff toward the end of his high school years. The shame and humiliation of the incident still stung—even after all that had occurred since. Even after Iraq.

So you thought you were in love once, huh, Phelps? Lee thought bitterly. *And I guess I'm a reminder of how that worked out for you. I guess I always will be.*

This was a cruel and petty thought, he knew; but Lee could not resist taking a certain degree of satisfaction from it.

4

L ee could hear one of the men banging on the front door of
Tim Fitzsimmons's trailer: *"Hey, Timmy, open up in there.
Let's do this the easy way!"*

His desire to be left alone—to mind his own business—was countered by an opposite emotion: *I did not survive Iraq to come back to this.*
And in some ways, the present situation in the trailer park did
remind Lee of Iraq: Men with guns came into the homes of decent
people and did what they pleased. It didn't matter if the men with
guns were al-Qaeda operatives who wanted to impose their fanatical
ideology, or small-town drug lords who simply wanted to extract a
blood profit. The underlying principles were much the same.

It was clear to Lee that the men who had come to visit Tim
Fitzsimmons were no mere customers. They must be affiliated with
whatever drug network Fitzsimmons used in order to obtain his
product. This was obviously some sort of dispute.

And it might be only a few seconds away from turning violent.

Lee abandoned his plans to make a quick cup of coffee before
reporting for Saturday overtime work at the machine shop. He
stepped across the main section of his trailer into the living room

area. He crouched down and felt beneath his recliner (which still smelled like the previous owner's cat) and retrieved a loaded .45 semi-automatic. He tucked the pistol between his belt and the small of his back and tried to decide what he should do next.

Then he was struck by the absurdity of the actions he was contemplating. If he walked outside with the gun, things could go very badly for him in short order. Wasn't this another example of his inability to adjust to civilian life, his inability to leave Iraq behind him?

This problem belongs to Sheriff Phelps, Lee thought. *Sheriff Phelps the also-ran lawman, the corrupt cop who loved my mother and hated my father.*

Lee knew only the broad outlines of the love triangle that had once existed between his parents and Sheriff Phelps. He knew that his mother had once been with the sheriff, and then she had spurned him to be with his father. Lee did not want to know the details. It both and embarrassed and angered him—especially now that his parents were both dead.

Why couldn't the sheriff let go of the past? Why couldn't he allow the dead to rest in peace?

And why should he help Sheriff Phelps do his job? Let my neighbors complain about our Tim Fitzsimmons problem—maybe it will cost Phelps his job next Election Day.

He knew, though, that he could not simply ignore a meth trafficker who was operating openly next door, endangering all his neighbors. He would have to opt for a middle course.

I'm going to go to work, Lee decided. *And then I'm going to stop by the sheriff's office and file a complaint. I'm a civilian here. This problem isn't my job. It's Phelps's job. So I'll make the complaint and Phelps can do his job.*

Lee placed the .45 down on the kitchen counter. He pulled his cell phone from the key and change tray that he kept on the table where he ate his meals. *Put the damn gun away*, he thought. *You don't even have to see Phelps; all you have to do is call him.*

He put his cell phone in his pocket and told himself that it would be easiest for him to call the sheriff's office during his mid-morning break. He could even ask to speak to one of the deputies.

Lee's mind was made up, and he began to wonder if there was still time for a quick cup of instant coffee. Then he heard the sound of a woman's screams next door.

5

Lee stepped outside with the .45 in his right hand. He took a moment to assess the situation as coolly as possible: The odds weren't in his favor. His Marine Corps training and combat experience gave him a certain amount of confidence when facing the average man; but these advantages had their limits. There were four men and they were armed; they would easily kill him if they chose to make a stand.

Fitzsimmons's trailer was only yards away. The screams had stopped, almost as suddenly as they had begun. Whatever had happened in the trailer mere seconds ago, the aluminum structure now emanated an odd sort of quiet, like a building that has been long deserted.

Lee stood perfectly still on his own stoop and listened for any sounds of movement, any voices. There were no voices and no sounds of movement that he could hear at this distance. Nevertheless, the woman's screams continued to echo in his mind. These had not been mere figments of his imagination.

The grass between the two lots was still wet with dew; the trailer park was still asleep in the deceptive peace of an early Saturday morning. Most of his neighbors would not have stirred yet, thoughts of Saturday morning television and breakfast still an hour away.

The quiet of the morning issued its own challenge: He was the only one who had heard the screams, and the only one who could respond to them now.

A final twinge of hesitation urged him to go back inside his own trailer, to forget this primordial urge to answer men who believed that a gun gave them the right to trample on all rights and all manners of civilized behavior. *The desire to show them that it would not be so.*

Yet he thought that if Perryston was to become like Baghdad or Fallujah, then he truly would have no place to go, and for the rest of his days he would never know peace. *It would be easier to face them now,* he told himself, looking at the men's tracks through the glistening grass. *It would be easier now, while my guard is still up and I have not yet completely relaxed. A few weeks or a few months down the road, things might be different.*

The decision to answer violence—it was like holding your breath and diving into deep water: once you leapt, there was no return.

Lee became aware of the heft of the .45 in his hand, the pace of his breathing, the keenness of his senses. A sudden heightened awareness filled his body. There was no choice, really. That choice had been hammered out of him in the broken cities and villages of Iraq.

Fortunately, the lessons of combat were still close at hand. And something about this most unnatural of actions—moving toward armed men with the intent of possibly killing them—felt more natural than waiting in his trailer and calling the police. As he approached Fitzsimmons's lot, he ducked low, alternately looking ahead, and then to each side. In Iraq many men had been killed by the enemy who should have been far in the distance, but was actually waiting just out of sight and well within gunshot range.

Fitzsimmons's trailer exuded a reek that was part garbage, part beer and cigarettes, and something more besides: an earthy smell of decay and corruption. The door of the trailer had been left open. It was pushed back, ajar on its hinges.

He paused but could still hear nothing. Perhaps the four men had already gone; and perhaps they were waiting to ambush anyone who responded to the screams.

Then Lee realized that he was not alone after all. Someone behind him whispered, *"HEY!"* and he nearly turned and shot the whisperer.

"Don't shoot me!" the cowering figure said. The emphasis on the last word strongly suggested that there was indeed someone who should be shot.

The trailer across from Fitzsimmons was occupied by Hal Marsten, a timid, fiftyish bachelor who mostly kept to himself. Lee could see Marsten standing behind his front screen door. Marsten's eyes were wide with shock and his raised finger was trembling. From where he stood, Marsten had a clear view into Fitzsimmons's home.

Marsten pointed at the gaping mouth of the trailer.

"THEY KILLED 'EM!" Marsten spoke in a loud whisper.

Lee tried to communicate with Marsten through hand signals, to ask him if the men were still in the trailer. He shushed Marsten with a finger raised to his own lips. Lee did not want to speak aloud and alert the other men to his presence.

But of course Marsten did not understand military hand signals. He stared blankly back at Lee. He finally retreated from the screen door, back into the interior of his own living space; he was far too shaken to be of any help.

A stack of concrete cinderblocks had been arranged before Tim Fitzsimmons's front door as makeshift steps. Lee ascended these as quietly and as cautiously as possible, leading with the barrel of his .45.

Once inside, Lee crouched to his knees, in order to make himself a small target. The air inside the trailer was thick, humid, and redolent of the coppery odor of blood. Lee jerked his pistol to the right, and then to left. He scanned the shadows for movement. A dust-filled shaft of sunlight shone on Fitzsimmons's kitchen counter. An old-fashioned cuckoo clock ticked loudly in the living room.

There was no one waiting to ambush Lee in the front part of the trailer. But the space was not exactly empty. Lee took a brief look at the armed men's victims.

They had shot Tim Fitzsimmons in the back of the head, execution style. Their guns must have been equipped with silencers, as he had heard no shots. Tim had not submitted easily: his tee shirt was ripped down the back. He had likely made a run for safety and the men had grabbed him as he attempted to escape through the back hall. Now he lay facedown in his ransacked living room, the blood from his head wound already forming a wide, dark red circle on the carpet.

They had not caught Tim alone, as presaged by the earlier screams. Lee recognized the woman on the floor as Jody, Fitzsimmons's live-in girlfriend. Lee guessed that she was about twenty— certainly no older than twenty-four or twenty-five. He had spoken to Jody once or twice in passing. On those occasions she had been cordial but not exactly friendly. Fitzsimmons's presence had seemed to dominate her, and it had been clear to Lee that he would never be able to draw her out, even if he had been inclined to try.

The men had shot Jody in the jaw, horribly disfiguring her face. There was another bullet wound just above her belt line—an abdominal shot that would almost certainly be fatal. Her chest and stomach were so soaked with blood that Lee could not determine the color of the shirt she was wearing. Her bare legs were smeared with blood down to the knees.

But Jody was not dead yet. Her glazed eyes fixed on Lee as she attempted to make a sound through her shattered mouth.

Lee forced himself to turn away. He could do nothing for her now. And the men who had shot her might still be in the trailer.

He stepped over Tim Fitzsimmons's body and took a few more steps into the back hallway, where the bathroom and bedrooms would be. He immediately noticed that the corridor was filled with sunlight. Then he saw that the back door had been left open.

Lee edged down the hall, pointing the muzzle of his gun into each room as he went. In one of the bedrooms he saw the telltale signs of a miniature meth lab: a jerry-rigged conglomeration of rubber hoses and pressurized cylinders atop a foldable card table. Beneath the table were several boxes of coffee filters, funnels of various sizes, and a coiled length of what looked like a cut garden hose. There were numerous bottles of chemicals. Lee could smell them from the doorway.

He made it to the back door in time to see four men completing a dash up an embankment beyond the trailer park. They were running toward the highway, their gait awkward but fast. Another few seconds and he would have missed them entirely. The men held their guns aloft. The killers were concealing nothing now; they were pumped with adrenalin in the wake of their crimes and focused only on escape.

They made a final sprint toward a waiting black pickup truck that idled on the edge of the road. It was a jacked-up, four-wheel drive version. Probably American; but there was no way Lee could discern the exact make and model from this distance. And as for the license plate—forget it.

The four men hoisted themselves into the back of the pickup truck (*almost as efficiently as real soldiers*, Lee thought). They were seated quickly, and their guns were stowed at their feet, out of sight again.

One of them pounded on the back window of the truck cab: a clear sign to get moving.

The truck sped away, spitting gravel as it went.

Lee walked back into the silent carnage of the now sweltering living room. Fitzsimmons's girlfriend, Jody, was still. She did not appear to be breathing anymore. It seemed that there was no square foot of carpet where Lee could step without placing his foot in blood.

He felt that wave of hesitation return—the hesitation that was showing its true strength five minutes too late. His .45 was useless now. His purported skill at answering violence and killing bad men was useless as well. None of that would mean anything to the young woman who was toppled back against the wall, her dead face a misshapen obscenity.

The real killers were gone and he was alone in this makeshift tomb for the dead. And if he could in fact do no good, then what was he doing here at all?

In the adjacent kitchen, the refrigerator kicked on. Then Lee heard the sound of voices outside the trailer—and the sirens.

6

Perhaps a dozen of Lee's neighbors saw him emerge from the trailer with the .45 in his hand. Faces scanned the interior of the trailer, where the bodies were clearly visible, and then they appraised Lee. It was not difficult for him to imagine what they saw: a quiet, withdrawn veteran who had recently been discharged from a killing zone. Had some of them even picked up on his dislike for Fitzsimmons?

He stood before them in the grass. No one made an effort to speak to him yet. The gun in his hand drew all their attention. When he raised it briefly, several of them flinched—until he tucked it in the back of his pants.

And then the faces seemed to make further connections. Eyes darted nervously back and forth within the little crowd.

They backed away from him, huddling in a semicircle at what they must have perceived to be a safe distance.

And someone said: "He's got a gun."

"Listen," Lee began. "I saw four armed men approaching this trailer." He took a step toward the semicircle of his neighbors. They backed away.

"I didn't see any armed men," someone else said. "The only armed man I see is you."

The sirens were growing louder. A Hawkins County sheriff's vehicle appeared at the far end of the access road that led into the trailer park. There was a second sheriff's car behind it. Both patrol cars were going faster than they should have been in this enclosed space. The red and blue light bars atop their roofs were flashing. Their headlights flashed as well.

Even from this distance, Lee could see Sheriff Phelps in the lead car. Their eyes met, and recognition dawned on the sheriff's face.

As the sheriff's vehicles approached, the group of onlookers spread out and took a few more steps away from Lee. It had the effect of isolating him.

Sheriff Phelps's car came to a halt a short distance away, not far from Lee's own trailer. He spoke into a handheld mike that amplified his voice from a speaker. "Stand where you are!"

Was Sheriff Phelps speaking to the entire crowd, or had he already singled Lee out? The .45 was still stuck in his pants. Phelps could not see it; but there was no way to ditch the gun without the lawman noticing it. Moreover, at least a dozen people had witnessed him exit a murder scene with a weapon drawn.

Then Sheriff Phelps looked directly at him, and repeated the command. There could be no doubt. His eyes met Phelps's stare dead-on, and Lee knew that both of them were gripped by the same question: *What is this man going to do next?*

Lee felt a surge of blood rush to his head. The situation had escalated too fast. Less than thirty minutes ago he had been contemplating a cup of coffee, and the comfortable routine of his work at the machine shop. Now he was at the center of a horrific crime, and a catastrophic misunderstanding had enclosed around him. His neighbors obviously believed that he was responsible for the two dead bodies in the trailer. And what did Phelps think?

That, too, was pretty obvious, wasn't it? Phelps could see him standing there. He would talk to witnesses. And Phelps detested him anyway.

"Hal!" Lee shouted. He believed he remembered the name of the man who lived across from Tim Fitzsimmons—the peculiar old bachelor who kept to himself.

Hal appeared in his doorway. He surveyed the situation: The sirens, the gathered crowd. Hal's face quavered. He clearly found the entire scene overwhelming.

"Tell them!" Lee said. *"Tell them what you saw!"*

Marsten waved him away. The expression on his face seemed to say: *I'm sorry—but I can't get involved.*

Hal Martsen disappeared into the shadows of his trailer. The only witness who could possibly exonerate Lee had just betrayed him.

"Looks like Hal didn't see nothin'" a spectator said.

"Don't be tryin' to trap ol' Hal just 'cause he be a quiet one."

"Likely story, I'd say."

Lee was gripped by a sudden urge to drag Hal from his trailer and wring his neck. But he knew that this would do him no good. There were really only two choices before him: He could stay put as Sheriff Phelps commanded and take his chances. Or he could run and take his chances. Either way, there would be accusatory fingers pointed at him. Either option would put his freedom in jeopardy.

Lee knew what the textbook answer would be: Cooperate with the police and let the system take its course. The wheels of justice would turn; and given enough time, they might very well determine his innocence.

But that would mean the immediate surrender of his freedom. For how long? Weeks? Months? *Years?*

Before Iraq, he would probably have entrusted himself to the impersonal behemoth of the state's justice. Things were different now. Lee had stared down death and he had survived. The Fates had had their opportunity to break him. The state had no right to rob him of that precious commodity of freedom. He had earned it through the survival of his ordeal.

As Sheriff Phelps began to push open the door of his police cruiser, Lee made his decision: He spun on his heels and bolted. He was not even tempted to look back when Sheriff Phelps shouted again.

Driven by a rush of pure adrenalin, he sprinted around the rear of Tim Fitzsimmons's trailer, where the bodies of the two murder victims must now be growing cold. He was vaguely aware of Sheriff Phelps calling out for him to halt, using his name this time.

The trailer park abutted a grassy field that descended into a belt of forest. Lee aimed for the tree line, his legs pumping wildly. He felt the gun against his back and knew that the sheriff, surely out of his car by now, would be able to see it clearly.

The field was high and unmowed, a tangled mass of fescue and bluegrass, dotted with black-eyed Susan and Queen Ann's lace. Lee nearly fell once, when one foot landed in a hole that had been dug by a rabbit or a groundhog. He somehow recovered his balance without significantly slowing down, the shelter of the woods now within sprinting distance. He aimed for a break in the trees that opened into a narrow path used by hunters and local children.

Sheriff Phelps called out his name a final time. The lawman was now likely at the crest of the hill, and Lee wondered if Phelps and his deputy would follow him. But he was unwilling to accept the delay that looking back would cost.

The sunlight gave way to shade, and Lee plunged into the damp, musty cavern of the woods. He had to slow his pace somewhat, as the ground beneath him was uneven, and filled with exposed tree roots and piles of the previous season's leaves. A catbird cried out overhead as Lee bolted past.

After several winding turns, the trail took him further downward. He could hear the trickling of a creek. He inhaled the smells of moss and water with each labored breath. Tiny gnats began to dart before his face. He ignored them.

The creek cut through a little valley. Beyond the creek, the trail would climb upward again, and there would be another break in the woods. Sunlight filtered through the trees beyond him, growing stronger as the land ascended on the far side of the valley. This valley was only a temporary refuge. His present course would take him back out into the open.

Then he would have to hide, evade, and run again.

All because he had responded to a woman's screams. All because he could not trust the sheriff of the county where he had grown up—where his parents had been raised and died. All because a timid old hermit had refused to speak for him in a critical moment.

Lee could sense that these realizations were building into rage, and he tried to suppress them. While rage might give him speed and courage, the emotion lying just beneath the rage would not.

That emotion was fear. Fear for his life, which had become more precious to him over the past three months. Lee thought that he had left real fear—mortal fear—behind him in Iraq. He should have known better: There was more than one way to lose your life; and evil did not always arrive in the form of a hooded fanatic shouting verses from the Quran.

He was thinking too much. There was no time now to ponder the nature of fear and of evil. Probably there would never be, at the current rate.

The cool shade of the forest brought a chill to his sweat-drenched back. He kept running, his breathing loud. The creek came into view: a shallow current gurgling over shale and limestone rocks. The bank was muddy and denuded of thick vegetation. The creek would be passable.

He stepped into the ankle-deep water before him. His feet were suddenly cold and sodden. He exercised caution so that he did not slip on the moss- and lichen-covered rocks.

7

S heriff Steven Phelps watched Lee McCabe disappear into the woods behind the Tradewinds trailer park. He stood at the edge of the grass that had been mowed, the overgrown, downwardly sloping hill before him.

For a moment he considered giving chase down the hill and into the mass of trees; and then he thought better of it. McCabe was more than two decades younger; and he had recently been discharged from the Marine Corps. With McCabe's head start, there was no way that Phelps could catch him—not on foot, and not in that terrain. If the young man wanted to run, let him run for now. Within ten minutes there would be a statewide APB issued for Lee McCabe. The woods and valleys around Perryston offered many hiding places; but one man could only hide so long from canine search teams and helicopters, and whatever other resources Phelps could enlist from the state police.

Hawkins County had a total of four fulltime peace officers, himself included. The involvement of the state police was therefore a given at this point. The sheriff's department was equipped to handle the usual DUIs and domestic disturbances. A multiple homicide call on a Saturday morning was a different matter.

The dispatcher had told him that the residents of the Tradewinds had seen at least two bodies inside the trailer. There hadn't been a murder in Hawkins County since the early 1960s, a few years before Phelps had even been born.

He removed the hand-held radio from his belt and started to call the sheriff's department dispatcher. But first he called Norris, the deputy who had accompanied him here.

"Deputy Norris?" Phelps said into the radio. "Have you secured the crime scene?"

"Affirmative," Norris replied, the word partially broken by static. "Almost, that is. There is only one of me and there is a crowd of residents here."

"Don't let any of them inside that trailer."

"Roger that, Sheriff. Do you want me to help you pursue the fugitive?"

Phelps knew that Norris would be lucky to run across the parking lot in front of the sheriff's department facility. He would be all but useless in a pursuit on foot through hills and woods.

"No, Deputy. I want you to secure the crime scene. I'll be along in a minute."

Next Phelps contacted the sheriff's department dispatcher. Rita Dinsmore picked up immediately. Rita was in her early fifties and she had the gravelly voice of a lifelong chain-smoker.

"What now, Sheriff?" The question was punctuated with a cough. Her tone was anxious. Rita had been a school girl at the time of the county's last homicide.

"I want Deputies Johnson and Hathaway to proceed to the Tradewinds trailer park. Make it a code 10-39, Rita." A 10-39 was the police code for urgent; it told available officers to turn on their sirens and respond with all possible haste.

"Deputy Hathaway called in sick this morning," Rita said tentatively. Deputy Hathaway, the newest and greenest of Phelps's deputies, was already distinguishing himself as a slacker: Since being hired by the department seven months ago, he had called in sick an average of once every two weeks.

"He says that he has a cold," Rita added by way of explanation.

"Well, call him back," Phelps said. "And tell him that we need everyone out today. We're going to need to set up checkpoints."

"Roger that, Sheriff." She had no more faith in Deputy Hathaway than Phelps did.

"What about Deputy Johnson?" Phelps asked.

"She's in supplemental firearms training this morning—down at Frankfort. You remember, Sheriff?"

Phelps cursed silently. Yes, he had told Deputy Johnson that she could sign up for a supplemental firearms training course in Frankfort, the state capital. Darla Johnson was an uncannily good shot. Phelps knew that she wasn't satisfied with the career path that Hawkins County offered. Within a few years she planned to apply for the state's SWAT team.

Compared to Norris and Hathaway, Darla Johnson was an ideal deputy. Phelps planned to support her SWAT application, even though her move would leave him short-handed. This morning, however, he needed every officer he could muster—which was never more than three plus himself. The supplemental firearms training had come at a bad time.

"Well, then, I suppose Deputy Norris and I are going to have to handle this situation, unless you can raise Hathaway on the telephone."

"I'll call him now, Sheriff."

"Thank you, Rita. Over and out."

He turned away from the wooded valley into which McCabe had vanished, and toward the crisis that was unfolding at the murder scene. His one available deputy, Ron Norris, had already pushed the crowd back to a reasonably safe distance. Norris had established himself as a boundary in the space between the doorway of the trailer and the murmuring crowd. Norris was in his late thirties, and he had put on a bit of weight in recent years. His belly protruded over his belt buckle. He was breathing heavily; little beads of perspiration glistened on his cheeks and forehead.

The sight of Norris did not inspire confidence. The deputy was fidgeting: he kneaded the leather of his Sam Brown belt with his thumbs and forefingers. He bit his lower lip and took a few meaning-less paces to his left. Then he paced back to his right before finally standing still. What was the deputy's problem?

As Norris was completing his nervous routine, Phelps noticed one woman in the crowd eying the deputy with concern. She looked at Norris and then spoke to a woman beside her. Both of the women stared back at Norris and they shook their heads.

"I said step back folks!" Norris barked at the throng of gawkers. From what Phelps could see, the folks were not making any real attempts to move closer to the trailer that contained the two fresh corpses. No reason for Norris to shout at them like that. They were curious, of course, as anyone would be when disturbed by violence on a peaceful Saturday morning. The murders had occurred only a few paces from where they ate their meals, made love, and put their children to bed. The fabric of their daily lives had been torn asunder. The first job of the police was to stitch that fabric back together. At a crime scene, the police were supposed to reassure the citizenry they served, to reestablish the sense of security that all Americans took for granted.

Norris was generally a reliable deputy when handling routine calls; but he seemed unusually agitated by the brutal homicides. Had Norris ever handled a truly violent crime before? No, as a Hawkins County Sheriff's Department deputy, he probably hadn't.

The two sheriff's department black-and-whites also formed a barrier of sorts. Their lights were still flashing. The word had spread through the Tradewinds, and a secondary crowd was already gather-ing. But this group stayed behind the black-and-whites.

There was a fresh wave of murmuring from the crowd as Phelps approached. He spoke quietly to Norris, so that he would not be overheard.

"You've been inside, Deputy?"

"Affirmative, Sheriff. Exactly like the 911 calls reported, more or less. Two Caucasian victims: one male, one female. Both with gunshot wounds to the head. Both very much dead. These people here tell me that the male victim was one Tim Fitzsimmons, aged early thirties. I don't know the identity of the female victim."

Phelps raised his brows. "Not *that* Tim Fitzsimmons?"

Norris nodded. "The same. Did time in the state pen. Rumored to be dabbling in the sale and distribution of hillbilly crack."

Hillbilly crack was a slang term for methamphetamine. In recent years the drug had been sweeping through the rural South. Like most small-town law enforcement agencies, Hawkins County wasn't prepared to combat a serious narcotics trade.

"We should have been out here before this," Phelps reflected.

"Yeah, I figured you'd say something like that, Sheriff; but the local rumor mill was all we had to go on. And if we listened to the rumor mill, we'd be shaking down every unemployed redneck for something or other."

That might be true, of course; but they had known that Fitzsimmons had a record.

Then Phelps realized that he was stalling—avoiding the grisly task that lay before him.

I'm one hell of a sheriff, he thought sourly.

Phelps maneuvered around Norris and climbed the stairs of the trailer. He stepped through the doorway.

8

The sight of the two bodies struck him like a sudden physical blow. Phelps had been expecting them, of course; but seeing them was something else entirely.

Fitzsimmons, ex-con and probable drug dealer though he was, made a pitiable spectacle, sprawled on the floor of his living room with half of his head missing. The woman was worse: Phelps stared at her mutilated body and thought of her wasted youth. Whoever she was, she should not have ended up this way.

He looked away, suddenly disgusted—with the scene but also with himself. A sheriff was not supposed to be sensitive. A sheriff was supposed to be insensitive so that regular people would not have to view images such as this.

Phelps had seen corpses before. Nearly twenty years earlier, he had been a young Marine in Operation Desert Storm, the last major American war of the twentieth century. One morning in late February of 1991, Sergeant Phelps had witnessed the aftermath of a vast killing, and he still saw it from time to time in his dreams.

By late February of that year, the short war had been winding down, and Saddam Hussein's ignominious but temporary defeat had been all but a given. Phelps's platoon had been ordered to secure a portion of the northern Kuwaiti desert. This section of the vast dunescape was sundered by the six lanes of Highway 80, the main conduit for vehicle traffic between Iraq and Kuwait.

When the U.S.-led coalition drove the Iraqi forces out of Kuwait, the invaders had exited Kuwait City in a makeshift fleet of military transports and stolen civilian cars. They loaded these conveyances with as much looted property as they could. And so the Iraqis had fled, the rape and plunder of their southern neighbor finally at an end, the U.S.-led coalition pursuing them.

Near a portion of the highway known as the Mutla Ridge, American aircraft had attacked the long Iraqi convoy. Hundreds—perhaps thousands—of Iraqi soldiers were incinerated inside their escape vehicles. Western journalists had wasted no time in dubbing this scene "the Highway of Death."

By the time Phelps and his men had arrived, the charred corpses and blackened machine wreckage had cooled. Phelps had walked among the vehicles, staring into the empty eye sockets of leering skulls. The men inside the stolen BMWs and Mercedes were little more than skeletons now. In the end, their rape of Kuwait and their desperate trek through the desert had been for nothing. *What had they been thinking?* Their delusion had been vast: Some of the Iraqi dead still wore the blackened remains of Rolexes taken from Kuwaiti department stores.

Phelps pushed the memories away. The two corpses before him now troubled him more than those hundreds of corpses from two decades prior. That had been war, after all; and if not all of those men had deserved to die in such a fashion, they had certainly been complicit in their own fate. This was no war zone; it was a residential trailer park in Phelps's hometown, a community that he had sworn to protect and serve. He could not escape the fact that he bore some responsibility for those two bodies on the floor.

Phelps unholstered his pistol. Norris had already made a brief search of the trailer and he believed it to be empty; but he did not want to be killed by that most dangerous of enemies—the one who is not supposed to be there.

He proceeded through the back hallway. He saw a makeshift meth lab in the spare bedroom. Apparently Fitzsimmons had harbored ambitions of being a producer as well as a distributor. That ambition had probably been a factor in getting himself and the woman killed.

The rest of the trailer was clear—and unremarkable. The trailer was filled the usual trappings of lower middle class existence. Even before this morning's carnage, the place could have used a serious cleaning. His criminality excepted, Tim Fitzsimmons had led a mundane and uninteresting life.

Back in the living room, Phelps forced himself to deal with another of the morning's inevitable conclusions: Lee McCabe was the probable killer. Just as the two bodies had made him think of Iraq, the image of Lee McCabe running down the hillside made him think of Lee's mother. Another batch of memories that he would have to suppress if he intended to fulfill his duty conscientiously.

Phelps forced himself to take another look at the dead, lest he allow his personal feelings to crowd out the larger reality of what had taken place here. But for now there was nothing more he could do— not in this trailer. A thorough search would follow, of course, once the county forensics team arrived. He knew that an ambulance was also en route, though there was nothing that a team of paramedics could do for these two people on the floor.

He listened to the voices outside: The residents of the trailer park were anxious and quickly growing agitated. From what he could hear, Norris was doing a clumsy job of handling them.

Phelps returned his pistol to its holster and fastened the snap. For now he would have to focus on the situation outside.

9

Phelps could hear a fresh set of sirens: the county ambulance already. He resisted the urge to look again upon the dead female victim. Tim Fitzsimmons had done time in stir; he was a reputed meth dealer who had consorted with criminal elements for most of his life. No big surprise that he would go out with a bullet to the back of the head. But the girl troubled Phelps: Another woman who had made the fatal mistake of falling for the wrong man. That had been enough to get her killed.

The approaching siren seemed to mock the dead. Fitzsimmons and the girl would leave the trailer in body bags, not on stretchers.

He felt relieved when he stepped outside, leaving the two bodies behind him. But the audience that was awaiting him was not exactly friendly. The people outside were growing anxious. A burly man at the front of the crowd pointed his finger at Phelps and said:

"Aren't you going after him, Sheriff? He's getting' away!"

"You ain't going to catch him in that trailer!"

Phelps quashed the resentment he felt at being told how to do his job. It was a natural question, of course. None of these people had ever pursued a suspect in real life. They had done it only in their minds, vicariously, while watching television shows and movies.

They therefore didn't realize a central truth of police work: that the Hollywood image of the lone officer chasing down a criminal and challenging him in a gunfight was more myth than fact. Actual police protocol strongly discouraged one-on-one confrontations with armed suspects, unless the loss of innocent life was imminent. The man-to-man shootout was a last resort. Sometimes the best choice a cop could make was to hold tight and call for backup.

Phelps believed that he had made the right decision, though there would probably be more than a few citizens here who would disagree. He could not have apprehended McCabe on foot—not by himself, and not with the head start that the young man already had. But it was only a temporary setback. A net would soon be drawing around McCabe. Phelps was confident that he would be in custody soon.

"We saw who did it: It was that Lee McCabe!"

"Why don't you go get him, Sheriff?"

Phelps sighed. You could not treat private citizens like fools just because you were the one with the badge and the gun.

He held up his hand in a gesture that commanded silence. He scanned the faces gathered around him. He knew most of them on a first-name basis.

"Okay, here's what I can tell you now. As most of you already know, there are two corpses inside this trailer. One white male was seen fleeing the scene, and we'll be putting resources in place to apprehend him. I don't think that he will come back here. If he does, dial 911. Do not attempt contact with him yourself."

"If he comes back here, I'll shoot him!" one man said.

"Don't talk like a fool, Mike," Phelps replied. The speaker, Mike Early, was a well-known town roughneck who frequently involved in fisticuffs at the half-dozen bars that sufficed for nightlife in Perryston. "If you see Lee McCabe, you are to leave him alone and call the police."

There, I've said his name, Phelps thought. So much for innocent until proven guilty. But then, Lee McCabe was clearly present at the crime scene with a weapon. *And he had clearly fled from the police.* Lee

McCabe was already guilty of at least one crime, no matter what his degree of guilt regarding the murders turned out to be.

"There is going to be a lot of traffic through here," Phelps continued. "A team of paramedics is going to be inside this trailer in less than two minutes, and a coroner's team after that. There will be a forensics team, too; and you're going to see a substantial state police presence by tomorrow at the latest. As of right now, this is an official crime scene. I want you all to stay back; but I need to ask you to remain nearby. Deputy Norris and I are going to have to interview any of you who saw anything. Thank you all for your cooperation."

He walked away before they had a chance to ask any more questions. There was nothing that he could reveal at this point, and much more that he simply didn't know. With two dead bodies and a fugitive suspect loose in the woods, he could only devote so much time to informing the public. Within the next hour, the media would learn about the shootings. Television stations throughout the state would be talking about the bloodletting in Hawkins County. The murders would make the news in Cincinnati and Nashville as well. By lunchtime the residents of the Tradewinds would be able to learn the latest developments by switching on their television sets or their computers—just like everyone else.

The crowd parted for Phelps as he headed toward his patrol car. He wondered how much ground Lee McCabe had already covered. The terrain of those woods was hilly, rocky, and nearly impassable in many places. Perhaps McCabe was having second thoughts already.

Why did that idiot have to run like that? Phelps wondered if his own past behavior had influenced McCabe's decision to run: *Would McCabe have surrendered to a different lawman?*

He recalled an incident that had occurred a few years ago, when he had treated McCabe in an unprofessional manner. In his mind's eye, he could still see the single taillight of McCabe's beat-up Trans Am alongside the road in the misty darkness of a spring night, the lights of his own patrol car sweeping red beams across its rear window. He could still see the uneasy, but somehow defiant expression on McCabe's face when he handed over his license.

The memory brought a wave of shame: He should never have done what he did. He should never have said what he said.

Phelps had been meaning to apologize to the young man for that. He had been thinking that perhaps he could, somehow, make amends. But then Lori had died, and the idea of an actual conversation with her son had become too unpleasant to contemplate.

Thereafter, Phelps had studiously ignored Lee McCabe, and he had ignored him since he had come back from Iraq. *Did McCabe believe that his county sheriff was out to get him? Well, how could you blame the young man? Wouldn't he be thinking the exact same thing if he were in McCabe's shoes?*

Until the entire truth came out, Phelps resolved to erect a Chinese wall between his feelings and his professional duties. He did not like Lee McCabe, and nothing could be done about that; but he owed him objectivity and fairness.

He decided to discount the crowd's conviction that the young man was solely responsible for the murders inside the trailer. True, the circumstantial evidence against Lee McCabe was substantial; but he would need to learn more before he drew any conclusions.

He was anxious to begin interviewing those people who crowded around Deputy Norris and the trailer. *Had any of them actually seen McCabe kill that couple?* There were many ways that this could play out. For example, Lee McCabe might have been selling meth along with Fitzsimmons. Perhaps a third party had come to the trailer park with the intention of killing both Fitzsimmons and McCabe. Perhaps the two men had been making a stand together; but Lee had survived, while Fitzsimmons and his girlfriend did not. That scenario could still fit with McCabe's decision to flee the scene of the crime.

Behind him, Norris ordered the crowd back again, his voice cracking under obvious stress. A few male onlookers shouted back this time: *By God they're killing people in our backyard*, one of them said. *Don't tell us to stand back but give us some goddamned answers.*

For a brief moment Norris looked like he was going to draw his gun—then thankfully thought better of it. Norris was the wrong man for a crowd like this. One hothead among them—coupled with one miscalculation on Norris's part—and the crowd could easily degenerate into a mob.

Phelps stood just out of earshot as he pulled his personal cell phone—rather than his police radio—from his belt to begin his requests for help and resources. For police calls beyond the county line, the cell phone was his only immediate option. His 700 MHz police radio couldn't patch directly into the Frankfort network. Like all states in the post-9/11 world, Kentucky had plans to make all its local emergency networks compatible and interoperable statewide, with updated equipment and additional radio towers. But that would take more time, more state budget appropriations, and more federal grants.

Phelps was already having second thoughts about his decision to let McCabe run. *Would he have made the same decision ten or fifteen years ago? Would he have done differently if the fugitive had been someone other than Lori Mills's son?*

There was no way of knowing.

He pushed these questions aside when a police dispatcher in Frankfort answered his call. Phelps began to set the wheels of law enforcement in motion.

10

When Lee McCabe stopped running, he found himself on the edge of a large clearing that was dominated by a cornfield. The plants were ankle-high and unmoving in the hot, still air. Cicadas chirped from the adjacent woods.

The little valley lay behind him, and he felt exposed out here in the open. *So this was what the life of a fugitive was like, was it?* You could never feel comfortable in open places, and would instead prefer the shadows—dark places like the little creek valley, where the light of day could not fully penetrate.

There was no going back the way he had come, of course; even now Phelps and his deputy might be wending their way down through the valley, their guns drawn and ready. Then he would be forced either to surrender or to gun down two officers of the law. The thought of those stark alternatives impelled him forward.

On one side of the cornfield was a band of asphalt that Lee thought he recognized as the Seven Mile Road, though he could not be sure. He knew Hawkins County well, but one location was sometimes indistinguishable from another in the rural sectors that were removed from town.

He dared not approach the road; standing in the middle of this clearing was equally dangerous. He could not afford to be seen. Not by anyone if he could help it.

Lee skirted the cornfield and cut across the clearing to the south, finally threading his way back into another band of woods. His escape from the Tradewinds had started him in a southerly direction, and he was continuing a southerly trajectory now. Where would he go? Would he cross the state line into Tennessee a month from now?

The trail that he found was nearly as large as a two-lane roadway, and the trees on either side of him were massive oaks that might date back to pre-Revolutionary War times, when this part of Kentucky had been the land of the Shawnee. It was said that some of these old trails were, in fact, originally Shawnee hunting paths, and that they went on for miles. Somewhere in these woods there probably was a trail that he could follow all the way into Tennessee.

Long before he reached Tennessee, though, he would head deeper into the county. If his memory served him correctly, there was a state campground not far from here. That might be a good place to hide—the woods would be a place to collect himself until he regained his bearings, where he might be able to gain the time and distance he would need to formulate a plan.

The forest canopy was high and it all but blotted out the sky. This dark world of the woods provided a feeling of relative safety, even though that was probably an illusion. How long before helicopters would be searching for him, he wondered. At least the aircraft would not be able to see him if he remained in the forests.

I am already thinking like a fugitive, he realized.

Lee knew that his predicament was dire. He had been seen running from the scene of a double murder. Multiple witnesses had observed him as he emerged from the bloodstained interior of Fitzsimmons's trailer. His neighbors had seen his gun. The police had seen him too—both Phelps and at least one of his deputies.

And now another realization struck him.

He was utterly alone.

11

Lee came upon the family so quickly and unexpectedly that he had no time to hide himself from their view.

He had followed the trail through the woods, and before long he strayed into an area of forest that he recognized as state land: He could tell because the trails were well kept and covered with mulch in many places. He was not worried about game wardens. They rarely appeared in Hawkins County—and then only during hunting season.

He had not expected to come across the campground so soon, though; and the family was a complete surprise. There was no time to avoid them. He stepped into a clearing and there they were: A mother, a father, and two small children—a boy and a girl. The parents looked to be in their mid-thirties. The children were perhaps seven or eight years old. Possibly twins.

All four of them were seated in folding lawn chairs. They were relaxing in the shade of a pull-out awning. The awning was attached to a Northstar camper that had been towed into place by a Ford pickup truck.

Lee had strayed into the family's weekend camping expedition. A scuffed Coleman cooler sat atop a wooden picnic table that was county property. There was also a pitcher of what looked like lemonade. The lemonade had been heavily iced, and the pitcher was coated with condensation.

This was in fact the Shady Pond Campground. The waters of the eponymous pond glittered some distance off to the west. A wooden sign with a silhouette of the state of Kentucky confirmed the name of the campground.

The father of the family started when he saw Lee step out from the trees. He did not appear to feel threatened, only mildly surprised. He obviously did not believe that anything bad would happen to him at the campground on a sunny Saturday morning. He had a day off work. He was with his family and all was right with the world.

Lee noted that the man also had protection: a high-powered hunting rifle stood leaned against the camper. The presence of the gun did not particularly surprise Lee: Guns were a fact of life in Hawkins County. This was Second Amendment country. Practically everyone grew up handling firearms. The opening day of deer season in mid-November was a major local event.

Lee assiduously avoided a second glance at the weapon. His own .45 was tucked in the back of his pants, where none of the family members could see it.

As inconspicuously as possible, Lee untucked his shirt so that it would fall over the grip of the gun. This gesture might arouse some suspicion; but the situation might deteriorate quickly if they glimpsed the gun. He would still need to keep his back to them: the shape of the .45 would be quite noticeable beneath his shirt.

"Whoa! Good morning, mister!" the father hailed.

Lee believed that he recognized the father. Like the dark-bearded shooter at the Tradewinds, he was one of that nameless or half-named mass of Perryston residents whom Lee knew vaguely by sight. He had a goatee, a receding hairline, and the beginnings of a middle-age paunch.

"Good morning," Lee replied. *Did he sound unsteady?* It would be a struggle, he knew, to affect a casual manner after what he had seen and done only a short while ago.

"That's a good way to scare a fella, comin' out of the woods like that."

The delivery of these last words was not unfriendly; but Lee noted that the man had involuntarily looked in the direction of his rifle.

"I'll say," his wife agreed. "I thought we had the campgrounds to ourselves."

"Well, it is a public campground," her husband allowed. Then to Lee: "Where are you parked?"

"Over there," Lee motioned to an unspecified area behind him. "On the other side of the woods. I have a camper too."

"It looks like you've been sleeping in the woods," the woman said.

Lee knew that he probably did look like a mess—even in the unceremonious setting of a campground. He was sweating profusely by now in his jeans and tee shirt—which were less than ideal clothes for a cross-country run. Briars clung to his pants legs. Impolite though her observation was, the woman had a point.

Had the family gotten word of the morning's events at the Tradewinds? Probably not. Lee didn't see a radio or a battery-powered television set.

"Say," the man said. "*Don't I know you?* You're Lee McCabe, aren't you?"

Lee nodded. There was no way he could plausibly deny his identity before a person who recognized him. Not in a small town like Perryston.

"I read all about you," the man continued. "I saw that article in the *Perryston Gazette*. It says you won a bunch of medals over there."

"I wouldn't put it that way," Lee said. *My God, is this going to be another request for war stories,* he wondered.

"Bullshit!" the man said, his smile broadening. "You're a hero. That's what you are." He stood up from his lawn chair. The man was a good four or five inches taller than Lee. He walked over and shook Lee's hand, then clapped him on the shoulder. "I'd be honored if you'd stay and have lunch with us."

"I appreciate the offer," Lee said. "I really do. But I can't."

"Well, give it some thought. My name's Tradd. Tradd Mentzel. Maybe you'd like a beer. I've got some Buds in the cooler."

"It's a little early for beer," Lee said. "But I would be very grateful if you'd give me a glass of that lemonade." And the thought of the lemonade did make Lee grateful: He was dehydrated after his long run through the woods.

"You got it, Lee McCabe!" Tradd said. "Jenny, how about getting Mr. McCabe a cup of lemonade."

Tradd's recognition of Lee—and his identification as a war hero—had resulted in an immediate change of his status within the family group. He had gone from interloper to honored guest. Even Jenny was regarding him favorably now. She wasted no time in lifting herself from her lawn chair to search for a drinking cup among the family's belongings. The children stirred from their chairs as well. The entire family was suddenly on their feet.

"Make it a big cup, Jenny," Tradd said to his wife. "Lee here looks like he's about ready to die of thirst. Use one of the big red tumblers."

Lee expressed more thanks, and then Tradd said: "I was very sorry to hear about your mother. I know it was a few years ago; but well—please accept my condolences."

"Thank you," Lee said.

"How old was she?" Tradd asked gently.

"Forty-two." In that instant Lee recalled the last time he had seen his mother: She had been a small woman to begin with, and the cancer had wasted her away to a state of emaciation. At five-foot-four, she had weighed eighty-two pounds when she died. Lee remembered her staring back at him on that last day in the hospital, barely conscious in the last stages of her disease—and they had filled her with painkillers as well.

"She was a wonderful woman," Tradd said. "She used to babysit my older brother way back when. I've heard nothing but good things about her."

Lee could not think of a suitable response. Talking about his parents was, for him, a bit like talking about the war. It was a subject that he didn't like to discuss—least of all with people whom he did not know well.

Since his mother had died, he had often heard remarks like that:

about how wonderful she had been. No one had ever said as much about his father. Tom McCabe had been born in nineteen sixty-four. Tall and good-looking, he had been a notorious ladies' man throughout most of the nineteen eighties. *You've got your father's good looks*, an aunt of Lee's used to say when he was an adolescent. Her tone was not complimentary, as if a resemblance to his father was not an entirely good thing. Never mind that his father had been so popular with the girls.

Lee's mother had certainly been taken with Tom McCabe—even though they had split up shortly after Lee was born. Throughout Lee's growing up years, when she had been a single mother in her twenties—and then in her thirties—there had been no other serious love interests. Lee could not recall her going on many dates, nor even talking to other men on many occasions.

Lee realized that his mother had been waiting—hoping—for a fairytale reconciliation. *One day your father will settle down*, she used to say. *He'll grow up. Then you'll see: we'll be a real family yet.*

That had been the catechism of Lee's childhood and adolescence. Then one evening his father had run a red light after consuming enough alcohol to intoxicate two men. His car plowed into the grill of a semi at sixty miles per hour. Thus ended the life of Tom McCabe, and Lori McCabe's hope of the fairytale ending.

Snap out of it, Lee thought. *You don't have the time or the latitude to be sorting out your childhood right now.*

Jenny was pouring him a generous portion of lemonade. The red tumbler was in fact large, as Tradd had promised. Lee accepted the cup with a nod and a smile, wondering how fast he dared drink it. He couldn't afford to linger; but the lemonade would provide much needed energy and hydration.

"Zack, this man here is a war hero," Tradd said, addressing his son.

Lee took a long drink of lemonade, and in that instant little Zack darted out of his field of vision. His next words turned Lee's bowels to ice.

"He must be a soldier, Dad. Look—he's even got a gun!"

Zack was behind Lee now and slightly off to the side. He was pointing at the shape of Lee's .45 in the small of his back.

"What are you talking about, Zack? Don't fib or I'll have to tan your hide. And didn't your mother and I tell you that it's impolite to point?"

"He's not lying," Lee said. He had just thought of another way out. It might work. He had a gun. Tradd had a gun. Nothing unusual there. *So what*?

"I saw a wild dog around my campsite this morning. It looked mean. I've been carrying this pistol around just in case."

Tradd nodded. "Got to watch those strays," he said. Something about his tone—and the expression on his face—suggested that he was not wholly convinced by Lee's explanation. Lee couldn't blame him. From Tradd's perspective, Lee supposed, this scenario didn't entirely add up. A man comes out of the woods into your family's campsite, dirty and disheveled. Next you discover that he's carrying a gun.

Then they were all distracted by the sound of electronic chimes playing the William Tell Overture. Tradd reached into his jeans pocket and pulled out a cell phone.

"My sister," he said, examining the number on the screen. "Hold on a sec, okay?"

Tradd put the cell phone up to his ear. "Yep. No, I haven't heard..." And now a shadow of real concern darkened his face. "At that trailer park?....How many killed?....Who would...?"

He stared directly at Lee. They locked eyes. Then Tradd dropped his stare as if nothing had happened. He made a great show of not looking at Lee.

"Well, okay, sis. Thanks for telling me," Tradd said. "Say hi to the kids for me, too." Tradd closed the cell phone and pocketed it.

"Would you excuse me for a minute, Mr. McCabe? I'll be right back." Tradd swallowed awkwardly, then turned on his heels and spun in the direction of the camper. He was making a beeline not for the door, but for the high-powered rifle.

"Stop," Lee said.

Little Zack cried out and Jenny gasped.

When Tradd turned back around, halfway to the camper, Lee was holding the .45 at waist level. "Step away from that gun."

Damn it! Lee thought. Standing here before this family, the gun felt like a diseased and filthy thing in his hand. He tried to reconcile this feeling with the realization that there had been no other choice: Tradd paused and looked guiltily back at his firearm. He had been going for the rifle. That would have meant another set of unworkable alternatives: Maybe Tradd was planning on making a citizen's arrest, and maybe he was—in the heat and fear of the moment—planning to simply gun down the murder suspect who had come among his family under false pretenses.

In all probability, it would have been a gunfight—a gunfight that the father of two would surely have lost.

Lee had not ordered Tradd to raise his hands, but he raised them nonetheless. His Adam's apple bobbed as he swallowed. "Please don't hurt my family, McCabe. Oh, God, if you hurt my family I swear I'll track you down and I'll kill you, marine or not, I'll-"

"Shut up!" Lee snapped. "I'm not going to hurt anyone. I haven't hurt anyone, though someone's obviously given you the idea that I've killed some folks." He turned to Jenny: "Bring your kids and stand over there by your husband."

Jenny was trembling. She did not move.

"Do what he says, Jenny!" Tradd said.

Jenny summoned the kids to her in a series of frantic, whispered words. There were tears in her voice. The daughter started crying; and little Zack—who had been so interested in Lee's gun a moment ago—was now whimpering softly.

The entire family was huddled together. Tradd was doing his best to look brave but he made a poor job of it.

I mean them no harm but I feel like a son-of-a-bitch, Lee thought. He wondered how many times this scene had played out during the Sunni-Shiite violence, and the sundry internecine bloodshed that had so plagued the American occupation of Iraq: A man holding a gun on unarmed civilians—men, women and children.

He knew that his intentions were nothing like that; but he could not ignore the analogy. Tradd, Jenny, and their two children were obviously terrified, wondering what was going to happen next.

"Listen," Lee said. "I'm not going to hurt you. I simply couldn't let you grab that gun. That's all."

Lee walked over to the rifle where it stood leaning against the side of the camper. He plucked it away with his left hand.

"I'm going to take your gun," he explained. "But I'm not stealing it. I'll place it somewhere in the grass back there." Lee gestured to the grassy field between the pond and the woods. "You'll be able to find it. Do you understand?"

Tradd nodded. A response seemed to be beyond Jenny's capabilities at the moment. The children continued their sobbing.

"Now I want you all to turn around." Lee said.

"You're going to shoot us in the back!" Jenny said.

"No I'm not. If I was planning to shoot you, I would have done it by now. Just do as I say."

Tradd grabbed his wife's shoulder in remonstrance. "Do as he says, Jenny. Come on."

Lee was looking at the backs of the family. A family that had been enjoying a pleasant Saturday morning at a campground until he had crossed their path.

"Count until one hundred before you turn around," Lee said, as he backed away, holding the .45 in his right hand and Tradd's high-powered rifle in his left.

The family kept their backs turned to Lee while he departed. He did not want to look at them, but it was necessary. Tradd might attempt to rush him when his guard was down. Some men were like that, Lee knew. They had a childlike obsession with being heroes; and they could not resist the doomed, heroic gesture—even if it would serve no purpose.

Once back in the field on the other side of the pond, Lee laid the rifle down in the grass.

Little Zack furtively turned around and spied Lee hunkered down near the ground. Lee smiled and waved at the boy: He did not want

Zack to be emotionally scarred by what had occurred here this morning, though he knew that the boy would never forget the strange man who had come from the forest bearing not gifts but a gun.

Zack did not return the wave or the smile. He turned his back on Lee again, and wrapped his arms around his mother.

12

B ack into the woods again. Lee had no idea where he was
going now—except that he was still traveling south. It would
be about noon: He allowed himself a brief glance upward
and saw that the sunlight filtering through the tree leaves was
intense, burning the outlines of branches into negative images across
his retinas.

Perhaps he had made a mistake in leaving Tradd's gun where the
young father could find it. Tradd might be tracking a short distance
behind him even now, as the law was surely tracking him.

He passed a deer blind that was suspended about a foot off the
ground. There would be no hunters in June but the deer blind
spooked him nonetheless: It reminded him of a machine gun pillbox
on four wooden legs: He imagined Sheriff Phelps taking aim at him,
sliding a rifle out from the wooden structure's firing slit.

Was the image a premonition? Was that how this was all going to end?
A bird darted across a shaft of sunlight in the middle of the trail and
Lee started, expecting Tradd or Sheriff Phelps or perhaps someone
else.

Calm down, he told himself. *You have to think. You have to get your
wits about you.*

Lee also found that he was haunted by the parting look that the boy, Zack, had given him. He pictured the young boy telling his grandchildren about the incident someday, the way that old-timers sometimes told stories about chance encounters with famous outlaws from the 1920s. He knew that he was no John Dillinger or Baby Face Nelson; and at this exact hour much of the county still regarded him as a war hero. But that collective opinion of him would surely change —just as Tradd's opinion of him had shifted in the flicker of an instant. The false accusations and the circumstantial evidence would be enough to damn him in most people's minds.

Whatever Lee's true motivations, whatever the truth of what had happened in the trailer, the young father would recall only one fact: that Lee had held a gun on him and, by extension, his family. And when the law learned of the incident it would only add to the weight of his apparent guilt. He was going to end up dead or behind bars —*and probably dead*—through a series of his own miscalculations and plain bad luck.

The trail descended and rose again and the woods abruptly ended. Beyond the woods was not the uncut meadow or cultivated field that he might have expected, but a stripped landscape of dirt and uprooted trees. The land had been cleared in a wide semicircle, and the uncomfortable fantasy of being an outlaw in the woods gave way to an even more uncomfortable reality: He was an outlaw in the open daylight.

Lee heard the sounds of the heavy equipment before he saw the men working: A county work crew was adding an extension to Route 257: The new road would pass by the campground where Lee had been an unwelcome guest at the campsite of Tradd and his family.

He sensed that he was walking into a bad situation; but once again going back the way he had come was not an option. Lee walked forward, trying his best to appear nonchalant, hoping that he would be able to make his way without attracting attention. It was a hope that soon proved futile.

"Hey, you can't cut through here!" the leader of the work crew shouted at Lee above the rumbling of a road grader. He was in his early fifties, and he had a considerable paunch. He badly needed a shave. A cigarette dangled from his lips.

The crew leader had been talking to the crewman operating the grader when he noticed Lee. The massive yellow machine was about to transform a strip of this bumpy field into a more level surface that would become the next increment of the Route 257 extension. Black smoke belched from the machine's vertical exhaust pipe.

The crew leader signaled for the crewman operating the road grader to hold on for a moment. He came jiggling over to Lee, shaking his head and muttering beneath his breath—no doubt cursing this fool who didn't have the sense to stay away from a construction site.

"You can't cut through here!" the crew leader said. He was close enough for Lee to smell the man's sweat and the cigarette.

The .45 was tucked in the waistband of Lee's pants at the small of his back. Lee did not think that any of the county work crew members were close enough to notice the outline of the gun beneath his shirt. But they were pausing their tasks and gawking now, as men engaged in tedious work will do in the presence of any unexpected diversion.

"I'll stay away from the equipment," Lee said. He knew that these words would not placate the man even before they were out of his mouth.

"No, you don't understand," the crew leader said. "This is a restricted area. You get hurt here and the county is liable. That would mean my ass and probably my job. I'm not going to lose my job because some fella wants to take a hike through the woods."

"I'm just passing through," Lee said.

The operator of the road grader had now killed the engine of his machine and was climbing down from the cab.

The crew boss removed his cigarette from his mouth, turned his head and spat in the dirt. "I can't let you through here. Look—we've got pits and trip hazards all over the place. This is a dangerous area."

I've witnessed a double murder, for which I'm now on the run, and this guy wants me to concern myself with "trip hazards" Lee thought.

Nevertheless, Lee was now facing a potential confrontation with two men, as the crewman from the road grader was beginning to walk toward him. He was a large man who looked like he had a temper—the sort of guy who regularly engaged in knock-down-drag-out bar fights on Friday nights—just for fun.

"What's the matter, dude? You hard a hearin'?" the road grader driver called out. "You're in a restricted area."

A few more exchanges of words and there might be a real confrontation, Lee realized. He had the .45 of course, and the crew boss would back down in an instant if he saw it. But that would expose his presence to yet another set of witnesses. And the crewman from the road grader might call Lee's bluff. Some men were daring and stupid enough to charge a loaded firearm.

"Tell me where I *can* go," Lee said.

"Now that's the spirit," the crew boss said. "You got two choices: Go back in the direction you came from, or take that road outta here." He jabbed a thumb toward a gently declining hill at the edge of the construction area. Lee could see pavement through the breaks in the trees.

Since Lee could not retrace his steps in the direction of Tradd, he would have to go down the hill, then.

He eased his way backward, taking short steps so that he would not take a pratfall and then roll down the hill. The road crew probably interpreted this maneuver as fear of an attack. In reality, this was the only way Lee could keep them from seeing the .45.

"Show's over!" the crew boss shouted to his subordinates, seeing that Lee was going. "Back to work!"

Lee walked through a short band of trees and undergrowth and came out on a two-lane highway. His first impulse was to head for the grassy expanse on the opposite side of the road. Another forest lay beyond it.

Then he heard the *thucka-thucka* of the helicopter.

13

For Lee the sound of helicopters would forever have an association with Iraq, But the helicopter was no Marine Corps bird. This was a Kentucky State Police helicopter. It was making wide circles across the fields and forests, following a general trajectory down the highway.

Perhaps Phelps had not pursued him into woods, after all. The sheriff had chosen to work smart rather than hard. Lee could appreciate the reasoning of his adversary. The sheriff would have looked more heroic if he had engaged in a foot chase. But that would have ultimately been fruitless. Lee was both younger and fitter. He had had a head start on the lawman. Phelps had no doubt taken these factors into account. He was thinking strategically rather than emotionally.

And now Lee had to control his own emotions if he intended to keep his life and his freedom.

There would be two men—possibly three—circling above him in the helicopter. He imagined them looking down on him through a pair of binoculars. *Yes, that's the man*, they would be saying. *He's the one who killed those two people in that trailer.*

If he fled across the field into the woods, he would draw the helicopter down upon him. A lone man racing across an empty field would not go unnoticed from their vantage point. They would descend upon him and call in more units and drive him into a noose.

Nor could he go back the way he came. And yet, he would draw attention if he merely walked down the highway.

A short ways down the road was a feed and agricultural supply store. Surely the general citizenry would not be alerted of his fugitive status yet. He could go in there and mill about for five or ten minutes, pretending to be another shopper. By that time the helicopter would be gone.

The aircraft made another circle in the general area above him. *Had he already caught their attention?*

He began to walk toward the agricultural supply store, his steps as deliberate and natural as he could manage them. There was a sign in the parking lot that advertised special pricing on herbicides. Another sign declared a deal on a device that captured carpenter bees.

Lee was within a few yards of the parking lot when he realized that the .45 was still jammed in his belt.

A pickup truck rolled past him from behind, slowed, and idled into the parking space near the front entrance of the store. What a damn fool he had been; the gun would have been clearly visible from the front seat of the truck. Lee was lucky if the driver had not seen it, in fact; hopefully he had not been paying attention.

A sunburned man clad in jeans, a stained tee shirt, and a John Deere cap climbed out of the parked pickup truck and walked through the front entrance of the supply store without giving Lee so much as a glance. He *had* been lucky; but he had to do something about the gun before another vehicle drove past.

The sound of the helicopter's engine seemed to grow louder as it roared overhead again. He risked a brief glance at the sky: The chopper was moving away from him now, though he knew it would circle back, sweeping the area in a series of wide, gradually shifting arcs.

There was a culvert at the edge of the parking lot. Lee did his best to ascertain that no one was watching him. Then reached behind his back and removed the gun from his belt. He knelt and pretended to tie one of his boot strings. He slid the gun into the mouth of the drainage pipe, and pushed it far enough into the corrugated steel opening so that no one would notice it.

Then he stood up. The police helicopter was growing louder again. Hopefully the men above him had not noticed the lone figure stooping to push an object into a drainage pipe.

Lee crammed his hands into his pockets and walked toward the main entrance of the store. Two other shoppers walked past him, exiting the store: one with a bag of seed slung over his shoulder, another carrying a newly purchased shovel and hoe. Neither man was familiar.

The automatic glass door slid open and Lee stepped into the air-conditioned interior. The floors were bare concrete and the main area of the store was a maze of pallets: Many of the items that farmers bought were packaged in bulky sacks, bundles, and buckets. The pallets were stacked waist-high or shoulder-high. Along the outer perimeter of the main room were shelves of smaller items: hand tools and containers of insecticide, work gloves and spare parts for farm equipment.

At the back of the customer area was a television mounted near the ceiling on a steel frame. A group of three men and one woman were gathered around the set.

I need to kill about five or ten minutes in here, Lee thought. *Just enough time for the police helicopter to move on.* Lee prayed that none of the shoppers would recognize him. Of course, he had many friends and acquaintances in the county, and his picture had recently been in the paper following his return from Iraq.

Lee buried his face in a newspaper-sized promotional circular that was lying on an adjacent stack of boxes. The boxes contained a chemical fertilizer that was—according to the words printed on the cardboard—specially formulated for use on soybeans. The circular had been printed by the Burpee seed company.

He pretended to divide his attention between the circular and the television set. This strategy, he decided, would make him less noticeable than a deliberate and obvious effort at seclusion. He stood just outside the gaggle of shoppers watching the television.

The broadcast was a news magazine talk show of some sort. The show's host was interviewing a middle-aged, bearded author. When the camera panned on the interview subject, the man's name and source of distinction were identified by electronically generated letters: "Brett St. Croix, author of *The Death Factory: How the U.S. Military Turns American Youths into Killers*"

The interview had apparently been underway for a while, and St. Croix was in the middle of making a particular argument.

"Militant Islam is nothing more than a reaction against Western interventionism!" St. Croix declared. The camera angle shifted from the author and the host to the studio audience. The author's comments elicited a few groans from the crowd—but these groans were drowned out by a larger volume of cheers. "And we shouldn't be intervening in the Middle East!"

Lee was in no mood for politics at the moment; but he found himself, ironically, welcoming the distraction from his more immediate predicament.

By God, I agree with you, Lee thought, repeating the author's last statement in his own mind. *Though for an entirely different set of reasons.*

Hawkins County was red-blooded patriot territory; but Lee knew that the war in Iraq had been less than popular in many quarters of the country at large. He had seen the protesters on television and on the Internet. In fact, he had watched more than a few news reports of these protests while in Iraq. There was a television in the rec room of the fortified compound that had been his home in Iraq. On more than one occasion, he had subjected himself to the irony of these televised protests against the war, only hours or minutes before the Marine Corps subjected him to the real thing.

The protesters don't get it, Lee thought. *Even when they are right, they are right by accident.*

There were perspectives on militant Islam and great power intervention that the media mostly chose to ignore. Lee remembered one particular Iraqi village that he and his fellow marines had entered during an anti-insurgent sweep. They had found no al-Qaeda in the village; but they had found something else that made Lee question the ultimate success and meaning of the U.S. mission in Iraq.

In the center of the village a group of men had been gathered around the body of teenaged girl. Her arms were bound around her waist. To Lee's horror, the girl had been buried up to her waist in the sand so that the men could more easily pelt her to death with rocks.

The girl had already been dead by the time the marines arrived. The village men were in the last stages of their rock-throwing. A few members of Lee's squad had fired in the air to make them stop. The marine interpreter had shouted at the male villagers, demanding an explanation.

There was much shouting, and more than a few threats hurled in both directions. Gradually the story came together. The sixteen-year-old girl had been married off to a man three times her age. Her father had wanted a choice patch of land that belonged to the prospective groom, who already had two middle-aged wives and four children who were older than his new bride.

Apparently the young girl had been quite beautiful, and she had attracted many admirers. Trouble had arisen when the girl's husband had decided that she was too flirtatious with a young man in the village. Nothing had ever been proven; but there were damning accusations. The young man had fled one night in terror. The girl had remained to face the summary justice of the Quran. Her father and her estranged husband were among the men who had thrown the stones.

There was nothing about the girl that looked flirtatious or beautiful now, with half of her torso buried in the sand, her hair matted with blood, her face a mass of contusions.

Is this the society that we are fighting to preserve? Lee had thought, as he looked at the smashed concavity that had once been the nose of the young girl. *Is this what I am risking my life for?*

Standing in the feed store now, Lee recalled the dark, violent impulse that had seized him in that moment, as he had looked from the crushed, swollen face of the teenage girl to the sullen faces of her male executioners. He had wanted to gun down all of those men who had thrown the stones, to slaughter them in a righteous fury of the Old Testament variety. In the end he had restrained himself; but there had been moments since then when he had wished he had killed them—every last one of them.

These reminiscences came to an abrupt stop when there was a sudden change in the programming. The talk show was interrupted by a news bulletin.

Lee didn't wait to hear if the news broadcaster mentioned his name, or to see if they flashed a photo of him across the screen. No doubt that would come with time. He turned as soon as soon as he heard the words "multiple shootings" and the name of the trailer park.

On the way out he bumped into a man who looked familiar. He greeted Lee with a smile. "Say aren't you?" he began—for this man had not seen the images on the television.

Lee nodded and brushed past him, then out the main entrance of the store. He scanned the sky: there was no helicopter in the burnt blue haze, and its sound was gone as well.

He knelt by the culvert and quickly pulled the gun from the drainage pipe. He shoved it into his belt and stepped onto the two-lane highway. There was the screech of brakes, and a horn blared. Lee leapt aside as the driver of an old Ford Mustang shook his fist and accelerated again. *Watch where the hell you're going* he shouted, mouthing the words through his windshield as Lee, more than a little dazed, silently stared back at him.

14

Hal Marsten pulled the curtains of his kitchen window back a few inches. He saw Sheriff Phelps and his deputy talking to some of his neighbors. They did not notice him looking —which was just fine with him. The other residents of the Tradewinds were obsessed with the violent events that had occurred less than an hour ago.

But he was the only one who had actually seen the shootings.

Hal Marsten spent a lot of time watching the world through his window. He had never been much of talker. Tense social situations made him anxious. Sometimes his neighbors made him anxious— the way they looked at him and asked him awkward questions. Often it wasn't the spoken questions themselves, but the subtext behind them that made him nervous. For example, when they said, "Watcha doin' Hal?" they really meant: "How come you live all alone, Hal?" "How come you don't have a wife or girlfriend at the age of fifty-one?" The years had made him an expert at deciphering these meanings.

Women had always made him anxious. Especially the much younger ones—like Jody White, the young woman who had lived with Tim Fitzsimmons. *Why would she take up with a guy like that?* Hal asked himself. On a few occasions he had dared to nod hello to Jody

White, but most of the time he averted his glance when she came into his range of vision. Where Jody was, Tim Fitzsimmons was never far behind; and Hal could tell that Tim was a mean one. He glared at you like he would just as soon kill you as say hello.

Hal knew that men like that were best avoided. Trouble was best avoided. If you avoided trouble, you could keep things simple, and people would leave you alone. Most of the time.

This morning, though, Hal had seen some real trouble. He had seen the four armed men enter the trailer across the road. He had seen the struggle that had ensued after they burst inside. The way they grabbed Tim Fitzsimmons as he was trying to run away, and without so much as saying another word they shot him in the head.

He wasn't sorry to see them kill Tim Fitzsimmons—not really, being the sort of man that he obviously was. But then they shot Jody once in the face and once in the abdomen. He figured that they had probably shot Tim Fitzsimmons because of a dispute over drugs— but why did they have to go and shoot Jody, too? Why the hell would anyone—even bad men—do a damned thing like that?

He stepped away from his window and slid into a chair at his kitchen table. The buzz of voices went on unabated outside. He stared at his hands and saw that they were trembling. This was all too much. Things had happened too fast for him to process.

He didn't know why he had failed to speak for Lee McCabe when the young man called to him. A part of him wanted to come to the ex-marine's rescue, to tell his neighbors what he had seen—that McCabe was completely innocent and had had no part in the killings.

But then he had felt his chest seize up and his throat go dry. A dozen little scenarios began running through his head: What if his neighbors laughed at him, as his grade school and high school class-mates so often had? (*Good God, Hal was thankful that those days were long in the past.*) What if they challenged him, calling him a liar? Then he might end up in a world of trouble along with McCabe.

Well, maybe that last thought was far-fetched—and maybe it wasn't. But he couldn't take any chances right now. Lee McCabe might have problems, but he wasn't the only one. Hal had a big problem of his own—and it wouldn't go away, no matter what happened to Lee McCabe.

His eyes darted to the telephone mounted into the kitchen wall near his refrigerator. (Hal Marsten did not own a cell phone. He did not make or receive enough calls to justify the expense.) And he thought about his mother: The only person who had ever been nice to him.

Hal's father had taken off when he was two years old. He had no memory of the man. His parents were both originally from Arkansas —so he had never gotten to know his extended relatives. And after the hell of his school years, he had never overcome his social anxiety to make many friends or acquaintances in the world at large.

It was only him and Mamma. And soon that might be at an end. It would be only him—alone against the world.

He paused to consider the enormity of this and he decided: Someone else would tell the police about the armed men. Someone else would have to take care of the matter for Lee McCabe.

Mamma was in the hospital. Not just the local hospital in Perryston, but the big university hospital in Lexington. She was in her early eighties now, and the doctors had been warning her for years about her bad habits: She ate too much salt and too many sweets. Worst of all, she smoked. A whole pack of Virginia Slims each day. Sometimes a pack and a half.

He felt a warm, familiar shape brush up against his calf. It was Bullet, the neutered tomcat that he shared the trailer with. *Well*, he thought ironically, *I guess I do have one additional friend:* The cat had been very loyal—and Bullet, unlike people, never asked him awkward questions or stared back at him in a way that made him self-conscious and uncomfortable. The cat nuzzled against his leg again, and he rewarded it by leaning over to rub the soft, silky hair on the feline's head.

Yes, he had plenty to manage without becoming involved in this trouble.

At the same time, though, he knew what Mamma would say. If she were here and in better health, advising him, she would tell him to overcome his fears and talk to the police. You've got to find the courage to do what's right, Hal, she always said. And he had to grudgingly admit that this would indeed be the right thing to do. The ex-marine was in a real predicament. A word from Hal might be enough to save him—if no one laughed at Hal or accused him of telling tall tales to get attention

It was a real dilemma, and Hal sorely wished that the matter would all simply go away. He was too worried about Mamma. And getting involved in trouble would only lead to more trouble. Wasn't that the way things usually worked? Hadn't his fifty-one years taught him that he could best avoid problems by maintaining a low profile—by keeping to himself?

Hal had nothing against the young man who had gone to investigate the shootings in the trailer. (He couldn't help thinking, though, that Lee McCabe was at least partially responsible for his own predicament.) But he did not want Lee McCabe's problems to become his own.

He had to keep his priorities straight. Mamma needed him right now.

She needed him more than Lee McCabe ever would.

15

After dodging the Mustang, Lee loped into the field on the other side of the road. The driver of the Mustang had stopped again and was shouting curses, yelling for Lee to come back.

Lee had doubly offended the man, apparently: First he had stepped into the Mustang's way, and then he had turned his back on the driver's shouts of confrontation.

He was dimly aware of the car accelerating again, the roar of all eight cylinders accentuating its driver's anger. People were like that: They might be spoiling for a fight—but not badly enough to chase a man across a field.

As he ran through the high grass, he did not bother to look behind him. He knew that he would attract attention out in the open. People did not normally exit stores and then arbitrarily head for vacant land. If any customers in the parking lot had noticed him, he had no doubt aroused their suspicions. There was nothing that could be done about it.

A cluster of trees beckoned him, promising at least temporary cover. He permitted himself a brief glance upward just before he completed the final running steps into the shelter of the massive, grey-brown trunks. The helicopter might circle back at any moment, after all.

But for now he had outwitted his pursuers. He did notice a vulture gliding silently overhead, scanning the field and the highway for its rancid nourishment. While the carrion-feeder's significance as an omen was obvious, he forced himself to dismiss it.

This was too much—to be hunted from the air as well as from the ground. In Iraq the enemy had not possessed helicopters. All aircraft had been friendly. On numerous occasions help had in fact arrived from the skies. This was a new feeling—to fear the sky and a mechanical bird of prey that was stalking him there.

This was not a trail through a great woods, but merely a belt of forest between two areas of cleared land. Lee had to navigate his way through a nasty patch of thorns that were flourishing in the undergrowth. He broke through the briars and his right foot came down on a pile of sticks. One of the sticks bolted and slithered quickly away in a zigzagging pattern. He had disturbed a black snake.

Lee was not afraid of snakes; and the non-venomous reptile might even be a favorable omen—certainly a more auspicious one than the vulture.

Immediately beyond the trees he came to a fence that consisted of three horizontal strands of rusted steel wire strung between rotting wood posts. Thankfully the landowner who had erected the fence some decades ago had not thought to use barbed wire.

As he grabbed a fence post and hoisted one leg over the wire, he was all the more aware of his vulnerability. He had heard that a lot of men had been killed in battle while climbing over fences in fields such as this one—though probably in those days they would have been made of split rails rather than rusted wire.

He was thinking not of Iraq this time, but of a more chronologically distant conflict: During the War between the States, the Army of the Mississippi and the Army of the Ohio had briefly clashed in Hawkins County. Confederate General Braxton Bragg and his Union counterpart, Major General Don Carlos Buell, had each been tasked with taking the area for their respective sides. There had been a series of skirmishes nearby that local residents still referred to as the Battle of Perryston. Lee had heard that it was still possible to find the occasional Minié ball in the forest, though he had never met anyone who actually claimed to have come across one.

Lee had barely touched ground on the other side of the fence when a shot rang out. He instinctively hit the ground, his chest pressed into the warm grass.

Then he realized that the shot had been fired several miles away, and it had probably not been fired in anger. An off-season hunter maybe, or a farmer shooing deer or vermin away from his field.

There was no danger from the shot but he was faced with yet another empty field and yet another road beyond it. Lee stayed down while a pickup truck passed along what he believed to be Route 168. Despite the wide open view the field afforded, the highway was a good distance away. The driver did not appear to have noticed him; the truck continued to chug away. Lee could hear its thirty-year-old engine rattle.

And then, overhead, he heard the *thucka-thucka* of the state police helicopter.

Would this never end? Lee pressed his body against the ground, knowing that his prone position really gave him no protection from the men in the helicopter. If they flew directly over him, they would easily spot him.

The sound of the helicopter's engine and turning rotor drew closer. At least his tee shirt was a drab color. *But would that really offer him any protection?* He lay perfectly still, and even held his breath, convinced that his flight from the state was about to come to an end.

His present situation reminded him of one occasion in Iraq. He had been separated from his unit during a firefight in a little town seventy kilometers west of Baghdad. For more than two hours Lee had crouched behind the demolished façade of a clay brick building. The building had been a store of some sort before a tank round or a mortar had destroyed it. Lee deduced this fact from the remnants of merchandise he had noticed in the rubble: candy bars smashed to shapeless masses of stiff, hardened brown goo, punctured cola cans, and shattered CD cases.

On the other side of the street, two young men—Lee did not know if they had been al-Qaeda jihadis or Iraqi fedayeen—had been firing at him from the second-story windows of a fully intact building. The fighters appeared to be even younger than he was, probably no older than sixteen or seventeen.

Lee later concluded that the Arab fighters had not realized their advantage. Lee had been the only U.S. Marine in a three-block area. If they had grasped the degree of his isolation, the fighters could have descended from their perch and attacked him from two opposing positions, enveloping Lee in a crossfire that would have been virtually inescapable.

But the two young men in the plaid headscarves had remained in the building across the street. They were able to pin Lee down but they were unable to sight him for a direct shot. Apparently they had possessed no RPGs either. So they had fired almost randomly into the rubble of the demolished store, hoping for a lucky ricochet. Lee, meanwhile, made his body small against the cover of the rubble, radioed for help, and returned fire conservatively: his ammunition had been running low.

Help had finally arrived in the form of a light armored vehicle equipped with a 25-millimeter Bushmaster chain gun. When he saw the LAV, Lee knew that the fight was all but over, and his life was no longer forfeit. The LAV's cannon took out the front wall of the building that sheltered the two Arab fighters. The young men's bodies fell to the street in a shower of brown, dusty debris.

In the present circumstances, Lee was even more isolated than he had been that day in Iraq. Today there were no fellow marines to come to his aid. Having landed himself on the wrong side of the law, he had more in common with the two young men in the plaid headscarves than he did with his former comrades-in-arms.

Miraculously, the helicopter veered east rather than passing directly over him. He watched its tail rotor disappear over a high, thickly wooded knob of a hillside. But the helicopter would be back.

There was a simple way of ending this. He could hike back to town now, walk into Phelps's office, and turn himself in. Phelps wasn't going to shoot him, after all. He would be treated humanely, in accordance with the law. Yes, he would lose his freedom—for a while. But what choice did he really have?

There would be an investigation, of course. Forensics teams would comb the trailer for fingerprints and fiber samples. With all Fitzsimmons's drug-related traffic, that would result in a list of dozens of unidentified visitors. Would that help him or damn him? He didn't know.

The inevitable ballistics test was also an open question. The shots that killed Tim Fitzsimmons and Jody White would not be traced to Lee's .45; but how could Lee prove that he had not discarded the actual murder weapon after fleeing the trailer park?

There were so many angles and directions that an investigation could follow; and he knew next to nothing about actual police procedure. He couldn't possibly figure it all out.

He removed his cell phone from his pants pocket and dialed the emergency number for the Hawkins County Sheriff's Department. He still recalled the number from his childhood. He had memorized it when he was nine years old, as part of a fourth grade exercise in local citizenship.

He was about to push the cell phone's send button when he heard the police siren.

16

Deputy Ron Norris's patrol car sped along Route 168, heading south, in the general direction of the town of Blood Flats—a little burg that lay within the orbit of the county seat of Perryston. In the nineteenth century Blood Flats had been home to a substantial meatpacking industry, and the smell of blood had been said to hang in the vacant fields near the slaughterhouse district, filling the countryside with a charnel stink. Hence the name. But by 1880 competition from the meatpackers in Cincinnati had been too severe. The slaughterhouses had left Blood Flats but the name had stayed. Then a few decades later the Cincinnati houses had themselves been bankrupted by meatpackers in Chicago—proving, perhaps, that nothing of this world lasts forever.

The thought of Blood Flats made Norris's field of vision turn red; and this was no play on the town's name. In one way or another, Blood Flats was the source of all his troubles, the reason for the task that lay before him. Or rather, his problem was one man who polluted Blood Flats with his very presence.

Norris knew the woods into which Lee McCabe had escaped; he had hunted and fished in those same woods numerous times since childhood. If Lee behaved like the typical fugitive, Norris would have a chance of intercepting him. True—it was a long shot. But he could either try to capture McCabe, or he could simply stand around and wait for his entire life to implode.

How many hours had passed since Norris and Phelps had first arrived at the Tradewinds earlier that morning? Norris wasn't sure. From the beginning, though, he could sense that his boss was out of his depth in this case. Norris realized that he was edgy himself; but he had a damned good reason to be edgy, didn't he?

Midway through the second witness interview, Phelps had seemed to realize that the good citizens of Hawkins County would feel reassured if a police car was out looking for Lee McCabe—even if it was only burning gas. A double homicide had taken place, after all. So he had told Norris to make a run of the roads in the direction that Lee had fled.

Norris had eagerly agreed. And for once, he was not disturbed by Phelps's incompetence—by the fact that he was far better suited for and more deserving of the sheriff's office himself. For once he forgot about his lingering ambition to challenge his boss in the next election. Sheriffs in Kentucky were elected to four-year terms, and Phelps had one year to go before the next Election Day.

If he could get this problem sorted out, he would still have a chance of moving on, of trouncing Phelps on Election Day one year from now. And by then he would also find a way to take care of his Blood Flats problem.

Oh my, Ronnie boy, you're getting ahead of yourself there, aren't you? he thought. Norris gunned the police cruiser's engine. The Crown Victoria P71 Police Interceptor surged to the rise of an oncoming hill that afforded poor visibility. *Well, he had the sirens on, didn't he?* It was the local citizenry's job to get out of the way.

Norris knew that the average fugitive was driven by the desire to put as much distance as possible between himself and the scene of his crime. Most fugitives traveled in a more or less straight line in the direction in which they originally fled. That meant that Lee McCabe's trajectory would likely intersect Route 168 at some point.

Norris did not know exactly where. He did not know if Lee

McCabe had already passed over the road, or if McCabe would behave atypically, holing up somewhere in the woods. He might even change his direction.

Removing one hand from the steering wheel, Norris unsnapped his holster and fingered the grip of his service-issue pistol. It was a 15-round, .40 caliber Glock 22. To date, Norris had never fired the weapon in anger. The Austrian-made pistol was a fine gun, the standard-issue weapon of thousands of law enforcement agencies throughout the world. But this was not the gun that Norris planned to use if he caught up with Lee McCabe. If he used the Glock, he would have to account for every round fired. This, too, was standard police procedure. It was one of the methods that governments everywhere employed to maintain control of their police. And the task that lay before Norris was not exactly police business.

Norris barely slowed down as he opened his glove compartment and removed another weapon—a 9 mm Beretta. He had purchased the pistol at a gun show in Tennessee several months ago. It was unregistered and untraceable.

He removed his police-issue Glock from its holster and placed it on the passenger seat beside him. Then he placed the Beretta inside the holster.

Norris took a deep breath. A part of him actually hoped that he would not find Lee McCabe, that the young man would have enough sense to stay in the woods until he could flee the county, and eventually, the state. Then he would not have to take this step. In time, perhaps McCabe would decide to spirit himself away to Mexico or Canada. The whole problem might go away, and Norris could get on with his life.

But no, that was his own foolishness talking. Sooner or later Lee McCabe was bound to be caught. And when he was finally caught, his initial interrogation would likely turn the investigation in an entirely different direction.

Lee McCabe had probably seen the men who had in fact killed Tim Fitzsimmons and Jody White. Those men would inevitably be ferreted out, and then there would be more revelations. Revelations that would eventually turn Ron Norris the sheriff's deputy into Ron Norris the convict.

He shuddered at the thought. Prison life was notoriously brutal for that handful of cops who were stupid enough to turn to crime—and then both unlucky and stupid enough to be caught. They became the immediate and constant prey of their fellow inmates. Ex-cops were given no peace if they landed in stir; they were marked for violent death the moment they were issued their orange jumpsuits and prisoner numbers.

He remembered hearing of an especially nasty case that had occurred a few years ago. A state trooper who had been caught selling stolen property had been sentenced to five years at the Little Sandy Correctional Complex. A dozen of his fellow inmates had cornered him one night and stabbed him to death with homemade shanks. The prison coroner later reported that the murdered ex-trooper had been stabbed one hundred and eight times.

Norris fingered the imitation wood grain on the grip of the Berretta as a field of soybeans flew by. He would kill himself, he decided, before he would expose himself to a fate like that. And he would kill Lee McCabe before he killed himself. He bore no particular malice toward the ex-marine. But if he had to choose between his own life and the life of McCabe, then the young man would come up short.

He happened to glance to his right, and he noticed a male figure standing in an open field. Unbelievably, it was McCabe. And McCabe did not appear to be taking any sort of evasive action at the approach of the crusier. Quite the opposite, in fact: McCabe was waving him in. The young man's arms were raised over his head in a V-pattern. He looked vaguely like he was signaling to an airplane.

Norris couldn't believe his luck—and he didn't dare trust it. At the same time, the object of his pursuit was standing right in front of him. He hadn't expected it to go down this way, but he couldn't simply walk away from a gift that was so openly being handed to him. Didn't he deserve a lucky break, for once?

Still, his heart pounded at the thought of what he was about to do.

17

"Hands up, McCabe!" Norris shouted. The command was superfluous. McCabe's hands were up even before Norris had stepped out of his cruiser.

The deputy held the Beretta leveled at McCabe. He had not imagined the encounter taking place like this, with McCabe surrendering. Norris had imagined that McCabe would attempt to flee, or perhaps put up at least some token resistance.

"I'm surrendering," McCabe said, confirming Norris's impression. "I'm turning myself in."

"Are you armed?" the deputy asked. "Don't lie to me. I saw that gun you were carrying at the trailer park."

"Yes," McCabe acknowledged. "In my belt. Behind my back."

In that instant Norris almost pulled the Beretta's trigger. But he was profoundly disturbed by the thought of killing McCabe while the young man was looking at him. That would make it too personal, and there was really nothing personal about any of this business. Norris was simply trying to save his own life from complete and total ruination.

He knew that he could not have explained this to the young man who was standing there with his hands raised. McCabe would be bound to take it personally, and how could you blame him, really?

Norris decided that he would have to get his prisoner turned around before he shot him. But first he would have to relieve him of that gun. McCabe might figure out the score in the final seconds and draw the weapon.

Norris had no way of knowing for sure if McCabe was right-handed or left-handed—and of course he could not rely on a truthful response if he asked him. So he decided to rely on the most likely of the two: the ex-marine was probably right-handed.

"Okay, McCabe. Now I want you to use your left hand and—very slowly—I want you to reach behind your back and pull that pistol out of your pants. Drop it on the ground. Toss it away from you—to your left. Try anything—and I do mean anything—and I'll blow a hole in you a mile wide."

Norris watched as Lee McCabe followed his instructions to the letter. McCabe's pistol fell into the long grass.

Norris held his own gun aloft, aimed at his prisoner's face. McCabe stared back at him impassively.

"Now I want you to turn around. And keep your hands up, McCabe!"

McCabe seemed puzzled by the command but he complied. He probably believed that Norris was going to approach from behind and cuff him before moving him to the backseat of the cruiser. Even now, McCabe apparently had not an inkling of the truth.

Norris decided that he would put three rounds into McCabe any second now—two in the back and a final kill shot to the head. Then he would walk calmly back to his cruiser and drive away. Before he returned to his duties, he would toss the Beretta into the nearby Chickasaw Creek.

It wouldn't take long for McCabe's body to be found, of course. But no one would trace the shooting to him.

Norris was taking aim at the spot between Lee McCabe's shoulder blades when the radio on his belt crackled.

"Deputy Norris—over. Pick up if you're out there!"

Norris knew in that instant that he should disregard the radio and take McCabe down without further delay, while the young man's back was still turned. But the sound of Sheriff Phelps's voice rattled him. He removed the radio from his belt and pressed the transmit button.

"Norris here," he said. He desperately hoped that the quavering in his voice was not detectable.

"Where are you, Norris? Have you seen anything?"

"That's a negative. I'm in the woods right now—out near the Farm Pond Road. I saw some movement in the trees and I decided to check it out. But I think it may have been a false alarm. Probably just a deer."

Norris was still holding his walkie-talkie to his mouth with one hand, the Beretta with the other, when Lee McCabe turned around. McCabe's motion was slow and steady. He kept his hands in the air. His eyes bored into Norris.

"What are you talking about?" Lee said. McCabe had obviously overheard him lying. "The Farm Pond Road is a good five miles from here."

"What did you say, Norris?" Phelps asked.

"Nothing. Nothing. Listen: I'm climbing through some awkward terrain right now. The reception is bad. Too much static. You're breaking up. I'll report in when I make it back to my cruiser, okay?"

Without waiting for a response, Norris killed the radio and replaced it on his belt clip. He motioned emphatically at McCabe with the barrel of the Beretta.

"Who told you to turn around?"

Lee McCabe ignored the question, though he kept his hands in the air. "You were lying, Deputy." McCabe uttered the last word with more than a hint of sarcasm. "What the hell is going on?"

Do him now, a silent voice told Norris. *Take him out while you still have the advantage.*

"Get down on your knees, McCabe," Norris ordered.

"What?"

"Do it!" Norris screamed. *"Get down on your knees!"*

McCabe shook his head and complied.

"Now fold your hands behind your head!"

Once again McCabe did as he was told, though with visible reluctance. Norris noticed that his own right hand—the one that held the Beretta—was shaking.

Then he heard what sounded like the approach of a distant motor. *And why not?* They were beside a highway. Vehicles traveled down highways, didn't they? Within a matter of seconds, they might not be alone anymore. If he was going to do what had to be done—then he would need to do it now.

Norris felt his nerves tingle as he tried to steady the pistol. His entire body seemed to be shaking. He squeezed the trigger once and the shot went wild. The boom reverberated like that of a cannon.

In the next instant Lee McCabe threw himself to the ground, where he quickly rolled over and retrieved his own pistol.

Norris tried to take another shot. But he could not force himself to stop shaking. He had never been in a firefight before. This was the first time he had ever fired a shot with the intention of doing harm.

Now Lee was lying on the ground in a prone shooting position, his elbows braced on the earth. Norris could look directly into the muzzle of McCabe's pistol.

"Are you going to shoot an officer of the law?" Norris asked pleadingly, because he could think of nothing else to say.

McCabe leveled the gun at him. Norris held the Beretta at his side. He became suddenly aware of the substitute pistol, the weapon he had procured specifically for illicit violence—violence that now proved to be beyond the capacity of his nerves and experience.

"I'm going to drop my gun, McCabe," Norris said. "Okay? I'll drop the gun and I'll go back to my squad car. We can both pretend this never happened."

McCabe laughed bitterly. "Yeah, let's forget the whole thing. I'll forget that I've been made a suspect for two murders that I didn't commit. I'll also forget that an officer of the Hawkins County Sheriff's Department just tried to kill me in cold blood."

"It's more complicated than it looks, McCabe."

"Yeah, I imagine it is. Drop the weapon, Deputy. And walk back to your squad car before I change my mind."

Norris dropped the gun—no, *flung* it—away from himself. He breathed a sigh of relief for the fact that McCabe was going to let him live. And in the same instant, he realized that his larger problem persisted: McCabe would also survive this encounter; and he might live to reveal information that would bring the world crashing down on Norris's head. This temporary reprieve meant nothing, not in the long run.

"I'm going back now," Norris said. McCabe climbed to his feet. The aim of the pistol never wavered. Norris briefly considered rushing McCabe and immediately thought better of it: He would be dead before he had taken two steps in the direction of the ex-marine.

"Turn around," McCabe ordered him. "Walk slowly in the direction of your cruiser."

Norris did as McCabe commanded him. He turned around and took one deliberate step after another through the ankle-high grass and weeds. Once when he quickened his pace, he heard McCabe shout, *"I said slowly."* He wanted to turn around; but he knew that like Lot's wife, he would doom himself if he did.

As the cruiser came within sprinting distance, Norris began to weigh his options. There was a shotgun in the vehicle's gun rack, a double-action Remington 12-gauge with a 14-inch barrel. If he could simply get the weapon in his hands and get it pointed at McCabe, he couldn't miss. Not with that gun. And he still had his Glock as a backup.

Maybe that was the best way. Engage McCabe in a firefight. The cruiser would give him adequate cover. McCabe would be stranded out in the open field.

Even as he began to formulate the rudiments of an action plan, Norris realized that the whole idea would likely lead to his own death. It was a classic catch-22: If he attempted to take McCabe in a shootout, he would probably end up dead; if McCabe escaped, his life as he knew it would be over.

Unless he saved McCabe for another day. If he waited long

enough, he might be able to take another shot at McCabe—later and under different circumstances. And the next time he would not waver. Or miss.

He would have to make certain, though, that McCabe would not turn himself in to Sheriff Phelps, or any other Hawkins County sheriff's deputy.

"Listen, McCabe!" Norris summoned all his courage and then took the biggest gamble of his life. He turned around and faced McCabe. The young fugitive held his gun outstretched in a two-handed grip.

"You are one foolhardy son-of-a-bitch," McCabe said softly. "Give me one good reason why I shouldn't shoot you now."

"This wasn't my idea!" Norris protested, the outlines of a plan coming together in his mind. "Sheriff Phelps put me up to it. He wants you dead, and he told me to snuff you. The sheriff threatened to kill me and every relative of mine he could find if I didn't go through with it."

Having committed himself to this story, Norris tried to gauge the expression on McCabe's face to see if the young man holding the gun had taken the bait. Norris knew that there had been a history between Phelps and McCabe's late mother, and he suspected that Phelps might be pining over the woman even now. Norris had known Lori Mills McCabe, of course, and he had never quite understood the sheriff's preoccupation with her. She had been attractive enough, but certainly no Helen of Troy. And in the final years before the cancer took her she had looked tired, prematurely old, and world-beaten, as people often do when their expectations for their own lives go radically awry. But Phelps might have tossed him a lifeline with his old romantic obsession. Norris was willing to grasp at any straw at this point.

"Then tell me," Lee said. "Tell me why you lied to the sheriff just now."

Norris was barely able to choke out his response. He was transfixed by the muzzle of McCabe's pistol, and the realization that it could bring death in an instant.

"All police broadcasts are monitored," Norris explained unsteadily. "The sheriff told me to take care of it quietly. He wanted— what do you call it? *Plausible deniability*."

He could not tell if McCabe believed him or if he recognized the lie.

Then McCabe said: "Turn around Norris. Turn around before I change my mind."

"What?" Norris felt his knees turn to jelly. McCabe was planning to shoot him in the back. Just as he was planning to kill McCabe only a few minutes ago.

"Do it," McCabe said. "Don't push me, Deputy."

Norris did as he was told.

"Now put your hands over your head and count to one hundred. Count loudly. Loud enough so that anyone within a mile could hear you."

Still shaking, Norris began to count: *"One! Two! Three! Four!"*

When he reached the number twenty-eight it occurred to him that he had not heard from McCabe in a while. But then, he would have had difficulty hearing him above his own voice—unless McCabe himself was also shouting.

He stopped his count on number twenty-nine.

"McCabe?"

Norris turned around, and found himself alone in the field.

18

It was now mid-afternoon—the hour at which Deputy Norris customarily ate lunch—but he was not the slightest bit hungry. As he steered his cruiser through downtown Perryston, he passed the McDonald's and the Hardee's entrances without a second glance. All he could think about was McCabe. McCabe might as well have been sitting beside him in the cruiser's passenger seat.

Norris could still see the mixture of astonishment and anger on the young man's face when he had first reckoned the lie. That was before Norris had fired the wild shots and lost the physical advantage; but McCabe had actually won the encounter in that instant. The rest of their encounter had seemed almost preordained.

For a moment Norris had believed that Lee was going to shoot him. Norris almost wished that McCabe had in fact pulled the trigger —a gunshot wound to the back of his head would have at least put him out of his misery.

The Beretta was hidden inside the glove compartment. Before he left the field, Norris had at least had the composure to retrieve the gun from the spot where he had dropped it. The stowed pistol seemed to mock him, reminding him of how he had failed to do what had needed to be done. He should probably dispose of the gun now, as it could be used as evidence against him. *Or would it be better to keep it—just in case he had a need for it again?* He wasn't sure. Norris was used to being on the winning side of the law. He wasn't accustomed to the thought patterns of those on the wrong side of justice.

For days his stomach had been roiling in anticipation of the Fitzsimmons hit. Now that the big event had actually occurred, his stomach felt even worse. And the one-sided gunfight with McCabe had completely unhinged him. He reached into the change tray in the cruiser's center console for a roll of Tums. He had gone through three rolls of the damned things this previous week.

Norris had never needed antacids until a few months ago, when a smalltime hood named Lester Finn had entered his life, bearing some incriminating photographs and a fistful of demands. Since then, he had been fighting a constant war with his anxiety, which escalated into outright terror at least once daily.

He was a police officer, after all. *What the hell was he doing?* He was taking numerous risks—risks that he would have never even considered a few short months ago. He cringed when he thought about the potshots that he had fired at Lee McCabe. And that was, arguably, not even the most reckless act he had undertaken in recent weeks.

But another way of looking at it was: *What choice did he really have?*

Norris drove his police cruiser east on Main Street, past Perryston's business district. He stopped at a little park that lay on the edge of town. The park was dominated by a Civil War memorial, a bronze-plated statue of a Union soldier holding a bayoneted rifle. Kentucky had been divided territory during the war—literally brother against brother—and the legacy of this division was an abundance of Civil War memorials that exceeded the tally of any other state. Farther south, most of the state's memorials honored the Confederates; but Perryston had been mostly Union territory.

Norris parked his vehicle and walked past the picnic tables and cinderblock bathrooms, to the edge of an encircling woods. He heard a dog barking somewhere in the distance, but there were no human voices within earshot. When he had looked in all directions and made sure that he was completely alone, he removed a cell phone from his pocket. This was not his regular cell phone, but a disposable one that he had purchased solely for his communications with Lester Finn.

He knew that Finn would probably be in his bar in Blood Flats. Conversations with the tavern owner were always unpleasant. There was no way he could avoid talking to him this time, though.

Norris dialed Finn's number and the two-bit mobster answered on the third ring.

"Ah, my old friend Deputy Ron Norris," Finn said, in that infuriatingly ingratiating, condescending tone of his. "Always good to hear from Hawkins County's finest."

"You stupid son of a bitch," Norris responded without preamble. "Do you think that any part of this situation is *funny*?"

"Deputy Norris," Finn said, the cheerfulness suddenly gone from his voice. "My mother was a God-fearing woman. You will respect her memory. You don't have the protection of your badge anymore. You lost that the minute you took that girl into your car. Are we clear on this?"

Norris stifled an even harsher reply. He thought briefly about the girl—the one who had brought Lester Finn into his life in the first place. She had been no more than sixteen. The girl had been an unfair tactic. Her memory made his loins feel warm, even as thoughts of Lester Finn's blackmail scheme filled him with rage.

"My apologies to the sainted Mrs. Finn," he said. "But we have more immediate problems. Your boys botched it."

"I don't think so, Deputy Norris. That's not what they told me. In and out; a clean hit."

"No," Norris said. He felt a rush of stomach acid surge into his lower throat. "It was *not* a clean hit. For starters, they killed the girl. The woman Fitzsimmons was living with. That wasn't part of the deal, Lester. She was innocent."

Lester laughed on the other end of the line. "Jody White was *not* innocent. She was *involved*, Deputy. She was shacking up with a known meth dealer. She was in the wrong place at the wrong time, and she had no one to blame but herself. My men tell me that Jody White tried to pull a gun on them, and I believe them."

"*There was no gun anywhere near her body!*" Norris said, in a far louder voice than caution dictated. He looked around again and verified that he was still alone. "I saw what was left of Jody White's face after your 'clean hit', but I didn't see any gun that she could have pulled on them."

"I wasn't there," Finn acknowledged, as if addressing a child. "But all wars have collateral damage. This will blow over."

"If you believe that, then you're more deluded than I thought. It's one thing to kill a meth-head dope peddler with a twenty-year rap sheet. But your men stepped over the line."

"So what do you want me to do, Deputy? Resurrect the dead? Bring back Jody White?

Norris ignored the question. "And you've got bigger problems still."

"Such as?"

"A witness."

Finn paused. "I don't think so. My men went in there early this morning. They assured me that no one saw them. No witnesses."

"That's because they didn't *see* the witness. Which might be traced to the fact that you obviously hired a bunch of idiots. But *he* saw *them*, or at least he might have."

Lester Finn now seemed genuinely interested, though he continued to preserve that devil-may-care pose of his. "And who, pray tell, is this witness—whom not one of my four men happened to see?"

"His name is Lee McCabe. A local boy. Got back from Iraq a few months ago."

"Lee McCabe," Lester repeated the name.

"You know him?"

"No, but I could find him if I needed to. Hawkins County is a small place."

"You're absolutely clueless." Norris snorted. "Jesus, what a piece of work you are."

"Watch it, Deputy."

"Don't you tell me to—"

"So where is this Lee McCabe right now?"

"I have absolutely no idea."

"What the hell do you mean by that?"

"I mean, I have absolutely no idea. When we pulled up to Fitzsimmons's trailer he was there. Then he took off and ran. And now half the state is looking for him."

Norris was about to relate his subsequent encounter with McCabe but stopped himself. Nothing could be gained by telling Finn about that. In fact, Lester would probably find a way to use that knowledge to his advantage. *Of course he would*, Norris thought. His failed attempt on McCabe's life raised his complicity in the murders at the trailer park to a new level.

McCabe and Lester had him completely trapped, didn't they? Before his failed attempt on the ex-marine's life, there had been a slight chance that Norris could have skated out of this, even if McCabe was captured, and the wanted man's testimony uncovered his own connection to Lester Finn.

Norris figured that the photos of him and that girl would probably have come out—but that would have meant a misdemeanor at the end of the day. The rest of his involvement might have been hidden, buried—if only he had possessed the foresight to take preventative actions. How much material evidence against him had really existed, before today? It might have come down to little more than his word against the word of a small-town drug lord. *Who would the system have been more likely to believe?*

But now he had gone and taken a shot at Lee McCabe. That glaring mistake would be his undoing in the end.

"What did this McCabe see, Norris?" he heard Finn ask him.

But what he saw was the image of another young woman—not the young girl whom had he had been caught with, but the dead one he had seen this morning. Jody White's death pose—her shattered jaw and gaping abdominal wound—was a madman's movie that kept playing in his mind's eye. He had the sudden sense that some discorporate form of Jody White was pursuing him even now, seeking vengeance for the wicked act that Norris had abetted through his own weakness and venality.

The air was simultaneously thick and short of oxygen in his lungs. Stars swam before Norris's eyes. A mixture of terror, confusion, and self-despair closed in on him, squeezing his chest like a giant vise. It was all going to hell in a handbasket, and there seemed to be no way to halt the downward spiral.

This abundance of tension had to be directed outward. Norris's hand tightened around his cell phone. He forced himself to relax his grip when he heard the first crack of the phone's hard plastic casing. He paused to wipe the perspiration from his forehead with the back of his free hand.

Norris coughed loudly, tasting bile in his mouth and throat. Then he answered Finn's question.

"McCabe was inside the trailer. We saw him as he was walking out. I don't know exactly what he saw. But there's a good chance he saw your men."

"I wonder what that sorry bastard was thinking," Finn said. "Probably trying to play the hero."

"If that was his aim, it backfired. Right now he's the lead suspect."

"It sounds like McCabe put himself in the perfect position, at least from our perspective."

How could this man have gotten such leverage over me? Norris wondered. Didn't the small-town gangster understand what a liability McCabe actually was? Didn't he see where this was likely going?

"No, not perfect, dumbass," Norris said as calmly as possible. "How could you think there is anything perfect about this? Phelps has asked the state police for assistance. And it's only a matter of time before the feds become involved. This is a double homicide we're talking about, with an obvious connection to drug trafficking. Do you realize the significance of what I'm saying?"

"Of course I do," Finn said. Norris could imagine Finn speaking through clenched teeth.

"No, I don't think you do. So let me explain it. I assume you know what a dragnet is. Right now there is a large, multi-force dragnet closing around Lee McCabe. And that means it's only a matter of time before he ends up in custody. And *that* means that Lee McCabe will be talking to law enforcement before long. Now, would you like to guess how long it will take him to lead the investigation to your men?"

Lester paused on the other end of the line. He treated Norris to a long, exaggerated sigh before he spoke again:

"And that will inevitably expose your involvement in this little matter. Correct, Deputy Norris?"

"Stop calling me that!" Norris shouted. He had told Lester Finn not to call him Deputy Norris over an unsecured line. But the hoodlum seemed to take a perverse delight in addressing him as such. No doubt it brought Lester Finn a perverse sort of delight, reminding them both that he held a police officer at his beck and call. Norris paused and made another visual scan of the park. He was still alone. "I've told you a thousand times not to say that over the line. You're screwing me over badly enough as it is."

Finn laughed "Don't get nervous on me now. Let's be methodical about this: Do you really think McCabe saw anything at all? Other than Tim Fitzsimmons and the girl?"

Norris wanted to scream but he restrained himself.

"Do *you* really think we can take the chance? Do you think we can afford to just sit around and wait to find out? McCabe is a liability. To both of us."

"Ah, Norris," Finn said. At least he omitted the "deputy". "You know what this means, don't you?"

"Of course I know. And it makes me sick, as it would make you sick, if you weren't a dope-peddling lowlife. But what other choice is there?"

"Save your self-righteousness for the bums in the drunk tank, Norris. A fine specimen you are. A few minutes ago you were turning into a bleeding heart humanitarian over a drug dealer's dead girl-friend. And now you want to me to eliminate a veteran who has recently returned from Saddam Hussein's little hellhole in the Middle East. You'll forgive me if I find that ironic, *Mr.* Norris."

Norris sighed. "I don't care *how* you find it. I only want you to take care of it."

"That's what I do, Mr. Norris. I take care of things. I took care of Tim Fitzsimmons; and I'll take care of this problem as well."

"Well," Norris said. Maybe this would work out, after all. There was still a chance. "Alright, then. But do it quickly."

"I'll do it when I decide to do it. You don't give the orders in this relationship, Norris. You still don't seem to understand that basic fact."

Norris found himself squeezing his cell phone again. He couldn't believe that Lester Finn was such a misguided fool. McCabe might have knowledge that could send them both to prison for life, and Finn seemed more concerned with posturing.

Nevertheless, Lester Finn was the only ally he had at the moment —the only person in the universe who had roughly the same stake in this outcome. He would deal with Finn later; but he needed him for now.

"Whatever you say, Lester. Now tell me: Are you going to take care of this or not?"

"I'll do it. Get me a photo of this Lee McCabe."

"You can get yourself one. The *Perryston Gazette* ran a story on him when he got back from Iraq. It included a photo of him in his dress blues. It's still online. You can Google it."

"I understand. Good day, Mr. Norris."

"Wait, when exactly are you going to—"

But Norris was talking to a dead line.

19

L ester Finn pressed the call termination button on his cell phone while the cop was still talking. He laid the phone down on the dark hardwood counter of the empty bar before him. He was trying to get his arms around the fact that a young veteran named Lee McCabe would have to die. That would be regrettable. He would much rather put a bullet in Norris, though Norris had proved himself to be a useful—if unwilling—tool. And the deputy would likely turn out to be even more useful in the future, now that he was an accomplice to murder. The Tim Fitzsimmons hit had been carried out based on information provided by Norris. The deputy had fingered Fitzsimmons as the distributor in the trailer park.

All the same, it *would* be a shame about the marine.

Lester's daddy had been a decorated marine in Korea. The elder Finn had deserted Lester and his mother when he was only five; and his father had taken his own life while Lester was still in high school. He had absolutely no respect for his long-dead father as an individual. But blood was blood. He didn't relish the idea of killing a man who had some connection to his father, however tenuous.

Nevertheless, it would have to be done. And it would have to be done carefully—not botched like the hit on Tim Fitzsimmons.

Lester noticed his reflection in the shiny surface of the bar: the long, grey hair tied back in a single ponytail, the network of wrinkles that lined his face. He had not made it to the ripe age of fifty-two by being careless. But the four men he had charged with the task at the Tradewinds had obviously made a lot of mistakes; and now he would have to scramble and take more risks in order to undo the damage.

Lester's bar, The Boar's Head, was deserted at this hour on a Saturday, except for Lester himself and two of his "associates": Luke and Dan. Luke and Dan were both strapping young men who had already done a combined six years in the Kentucky state penitentiary system. The two of them were seated at a table in the far corner of the tavern, playing cards for dollar bills. Judging by their respective facial expressions, Dan seemed to be doing most of the winning. That was the usual course of events, given Luke's arrested level of mental development: Lester wondered if the big man could read and perform arithmetic at even a fifth-grade level.

Not that either one of them was exactly a walking brain trust. There was one aspect of criminal enterprise that persistently vexed Lester, and he supposed that it also vexed men in other lines of enterprise, though in different ways and for different reasons: *It was simply hard to find willing and competent help.* Brutal and violent men were a dime a dozen; but a man who could think for himself and take initiative was rare.

"Hey Dan," Lester called out.

Dan ignored him.

"Hey, *Dan.*"

"What?" Dan did not even look up from his hand of cards.

"Do you think you could stop taking that oaf's money for a while and actually earn the good money I pay you?"

"Whadaya need?" Dan asked. He still did not remove his attention from the deck of cards.

"I want you to round up some men. I'll give you the names and numbers. They're guys we've worked with before. I've got a little something that needs to be done."

"What about the men we just hired for the Perryston thing?"

"No, they won't be a part of this. We need to engage some more competent ones. Like I said, I'll write down the names for you. I'll want them all here in town by tomorrow afternoon at the latest."

Dan sighed and pushed his chair back from the table. He laid his cards face down beside his growing pile of dollar bills.

"All right, I'll get on it."

"What's an oaf?" Luke asked.

"Never mind," Dan said. "This here card game's over."

"But you took all my money!" Luke shouted.

"So? That means this is a lucky break for you. We need to quit now, before you lose even more money."

Luke silently shook his head. Lester could discern the big man's internal gears working laboriously behind his irritated stare: He was halfway to convincing himself that what Dan had just said was true.

Idiots, Lester thought, shaking his head. *I'm surrounded by idiots.* He watched Dan scoop his winnings into a pile and group them into a neat little stack. *If only my granddad were still around*, Lester thought. *Wouldn't the two of us be able to kick some ass for real?*

The Boar's Head had belonged to Lester's grandfather—his mother's father. (Such a place could never have come from the line of worthless drunks that had produced his father.) Lester's granddad had opened the bar during the final years of World War II. During the war there had been an army depot just south of Blood Flats, and the Boar's Head had hopped every weekend with randy soldiers and victory girls.

The army depot had closed with postwar demobilization, and the Boar's Head had reverted to a local bar. Things were never the same after the war, although the place crept along, supported by local clientele—as well as various sidelines.

But ah, the war days. Lester had not been alive during the war; but he had heard the old stories. Sometimes he still imagined his grandfather moving about the Boar's Head's dark interior. In these daydreams, Granddad was wearing his black dress pants, white shirt, and suspenders. He walked about with his dust rag, polishing the mirror behind the bar and the handles of the antique taps.

The old man would still feel at home here. Much of the interior of the bar was still in its vintage state, exactly as Lester's granddaddy had envisioned it.

That was then, and this was now. The noble generation that had produced his grandfather had passed from the scene, and younger, degenerate generations had inherited the earth. His two associates—Luke and Dan—were prime examples of the substandard people that had sprung from American loins in recent decades.

Luke and Dan were now engaged in another line of banter, his instructions to them already forgotten. It was no wonder that the Coscollino family ran circles around him. He couldn't even manage his people anymore. *Was he losing his touch?*

The real problem here was Dan, not Luke. Luke was a pliable fool who would go whichever way he was led. Dan, on the other hand, was a born smartass. He had accepted a position on Lester's payroll, but he didn't want to follow orders. If this had been an ordinary business with ordinary employees, Lester would have simply fired him weeks ago. But it wasn't as simple as that when your main lines of business were dope and whores. A fired employee was bound to be disgruntled; and a disgruntled man could easily become a snitch.

And so Lester had not really done much of anything. He had been hoping that the ex-con would see the light on his own. Instead, Dan was taking even more liberties, and his attitude threatened to infect the other men in Lester's employ. Lester had let this situation get out of hand. He had allowed Dan's insubordination—and the arrogance behind it—to fester and grow for weeks now.

Sometimes the best tactic was to force a confrontation. Lester leaned forward and said loudly over the bar: "I believe I gave you an order."

Yelling really wasn't in his nature. Lester sometimes imagined that he could run his organization like a normal business. He occasionally allowed himself to page through books written by Donald

Trump and Mark McCormack—the guy who had penned those
books about what they don't teach you at Harvard Business School.
Lester wasn't the idiot that he knew many people believed him to be.
As a young man, he had completed six semesters at the University of
Kentucky, though he had never earned a degree.

*What good was any attempt at real management, though, with
employees like this?*

"*I believe I gave you an order,*" Dan said in a mocking falsetto. He
poked Luke on the arm, in a clear attempt to incite him to join in the
joke.

Luke looked back at him uncertainly. "Gee, Dan, I dunno. Maybe
we ought to go ahead and do what Mr. Finn says."

"Shut up!" Dan shouted at Luke. Then to Lester: "Let me tell you
one thing, old man: You ain't no better than anyone else in here. Just
because you own this dump of a bar and run dope for a bunch of
wops up in Chicago." He was pointing at Lester. He accentuated his
words with little jabs in the air. "Don't be thinking you can give me
orders, or you'll learn real quick where you really stand."

Then Dan gathered up the playing cards into a perfect rectangle
and began shuffling them. "Come on, Luke. We're going to play one
more hand." Luke was silent as Dan dealt a fresh hand of cards.

Lester sighed with the realization that his next course of action
was inevitable. It had been a long time since he had taken this sort of
step with a member of his crew—perhaps *too* long.

He grabbed an object from beneath the counter and lifted the
little hinged partition that was used for access to the area behind
the bar.

He walked slowly toward the two men seated at the little table.
When Luke and Dan noticed him, their talking ceased.

With the end of the conversation there was near silence. In the
center of the room, an ancient, dusty ceiling fan spun slowly and
creakily overhead.

Luke asked: "Hey, Lester, what are you doin' with that baseball
bat?"

Lester did not answer him. He merely kept walking closer.

A smirk appeared on Dan's face. He leaned casually back in his chair to accentuate his disregard of the threat.

So that's the way you want to play it, Dan? Lester had been prepared to accept an act of contrition; but Dan's insolent smile told him that this particular ex-con was beyond redemption.

Then Dan spoke—not to Lester—but to Luke:

"Why lookie here, Luke, Lester gonna come teach me a lesson!"

As Lester raised the baseball bat, the smile disappeared from Dan's face. *He actually thought I was bluffing,* Lester realized. Dan frantically reached for a .38 that he kept in a calf holster beneath his jeans. He simultaneously lifted another hand to deflect the blow that he knew was coming.

Lester swung the bat.

The baseball bat struck Dan in the forearm, shattering both his radius and his ulna. He screamed. The excruciating pain caused him to forget all about the .38. His attention was now entirely focused on the wounded arm. He grabbed his forearm—now jointed where it should not be jointed—with his remaining good hand.

"*You sonofabitch!*" he cried. "*You sonofabitch!*"

Then Lester swung the bat again.

This time the bat struck Dan a glancing blow across the head. His eyes rolled, and he fell backward out of his chair, and sprawled upon the hardwood floor—the same floor that Lester's granddaddy had laid down for his jitterbugging and Lindy Hopping war-era clientele.

And what had Dan called The Boar's Head?

He had called it a dump.

20

Lester took a moment to appraise Dan's condition: he was out cold but the blow had most likely not been fatal.

He began to raise the bat again, but then he looked at Luke.

"Come on, Luke. Help me move him into the back."

Luke had watched the bat-swinging maneuver with bug-eyed shock. "Lester, I—"

"Do as I tell you!" he shouted. Then, in a quieter voice: "Wait. First go and turn the sign in the window around so it says that the bar is closed."

Luke nodded and stood immediately. Perhaps he was simply eager to move away from the shattered form of his friend—if that was what Luke and Dan had been. Lester frankly doubted that men like Dan and Luke were capable of forming any bond that approached true friendship.

Luke lifted the sign that hung from a string and a suction cup in the tinted glass window at the front of the bar. He turned the sign around so that the "*Yes...We're Open*" side faced the inside.

"Good, now lock the front door, too. Then get your ass over here and help me."

Once the front entrance of the bar was secured, Lester hoisted the top half of Dan's body by the armpits.

"Grab his feet."

In this way they lifted Dan off the floor and carried him toward the rear storage room behind the bar. Dan was a big man, and his inert bulk was heavy. Even with Lester and Luke both carrying him, the seat of his jeans bumped across the floor. All in all it was a clumsy operation.

They did not have far to go, and the door to the storage room was a free-swinging type with no latch. Once they were well inside, Lester ordered Luke to halt. He abruptly dropped the top half of Dan's body. Dan's head thudded onto the bare concrete floor. Luke waited about five seconds before dropping Dan's feet. Dan's cowboy boots—one of his small-town tough guy affectations—clattered onto the floor.

Lester silently pointed to Dan. It was an unspoken command to Luke that even the big dumb man could understand: *Watch him and make sure that he doesn't wake up.*

Lester rummaged around in an adjacent alcove and removed a folded plastic tarp. He tossed the tarp onto the floor just above Dan's head. He walked past Luke and back into the bar area. He returned with the baseball bat.

Lester laid the bat on a stack of cardboard boxes that bore the imprint of a well-known Kentucky distillery. Luke seemed transfixed by the sight of the bat, as if it were some sort of talismanic object.

At Lester's instruction, they spread out the tarp and lifted Dan once again. They edged him over the unfolded tarp and dropped him for the second time.

Lester lifted the bat by its fat end and extended it to Luke.

"Take it."

Luke showed no sign of taking the bat. The big man looked at the bat, then down at Dan's figure on the floor. Dan's head was cocked to the side. His breath was going in and out in an irregular wheeze.

"What?" Luke asked.

"Finish him," Lester said.

"Aw, Lester, I—"

Lester knew that Luke had killed before. In fact, Luke had been imprisoned for killing a man during a bar fight. But there was a difference between a man who had killed, and a killer. Thus far, Luke was only a killer of the accidental variety. Even the prosecuting attorney in his case had agreed that the barroom killing had been unintentional and mitigated by extenuating circumstances. Otherwise, Luke would still be behind bars.

Lester knew the sort of men he needed if he was ever going to hold his own against the Coscollino's. If providence was determined to deny him men who could think, then at the very least he needed to have men who would *obey*.

"Luke, you've got to do it."

"I-"

"Here. Take it."

Luke reluctantly took the bat. Lester took a few steps backward. He leaned against a stack of boxes and folded his arms, his gaze boring into Luke.

Luke gripped the bat with both hands and raised it over his right shoulder. After hesitating briefly in midair—perhaps grappling with last-second thoughts—he swung the bat downward in a mighty arc, connecting squarely with Dan's head. The blow produced a cracking sound, and beneath that a more solid thud of both firm matter and wetness.

"Again!" Lester said. "Do it again, Luke!"

Lost in a sort of trance now, Luke raised the bat and brought it down a second time, then a third, and a fourth. Lester noted the glassy look in Luke's eyes, the face pinched up in fury. *Where does a fool like that get such sudden anger*, Lester wondered. *What inner source does he draw it from?*

When the bat was wet and red, and Dan's head was no longer recognizable, Lester called out for him to stop.

Luke looked down at the object in his hands, which was now no longer a baseball bat but a gory tool of murder.

"Drop it on top of him," Lester said. "It's no good for anything anymore."

Luke dropped the bat atop Dan's chest. Dan's shirt was now covered with blood and little flecks of brain matter.

Luke shook his head. "I didn't want to do that. No, I sure didn't."

Lester clapped him on the shoulder. The gesture had a quality about it that was almost gentle.

"You did what you had to do," Lester said. "Dan was a danger to us all, with that bad attitude of his."

"If you say so, Lester."

"And there's more to it than that, isn't there Luke?"

"Hmm?" Luke stared dumbly back at him.

"Dan used to make fun of you all the time, didn't he? He used to bully you around, even though you're bigger than him."

"Well, yeah, but—"

"I don't think you liked that very much. In fact…"

"What, Lester?"

"I think it felt pretty good for you when you slammed that bat into his head. That's what I think."

"Aw, I—"

Looking into Luke's tense face, Lester saw a glimmer of understanding. Then the glimmer went out again. Luke was dumb, all right —but perhaps he was not as dumb he seemed to be. Perhaps a portion of that apparent stupidity was actually subterfuge. In some environments, an outwardly stupid man could get away with a lot. He would be consistently underestimated and forgiven. For a moment he even wondered if the big man was going to cry. Or maybe Luke would pick the bat up again, and make him, Lester, the second victim of the bloody tool.

But Luke did neither; and Lester issued his next set of instructions. There was a lot of work to be done; and in the big scheme of things the Dan situation was little more than a sideshow.

Lester patted Luke on the shoulder again.

"Wrap him up in this tarp and put him in the freezer for now."

"We're going to put him in the freezer?"

"Only for a little while. After dark we'll put him in the back of the van. We'll take some chains and some cinder blocks with us. Then we'll drive down to the reservoir near Mosteller Falls. I know a place where the water is almost a hundred feet deep."

21

Sheriff's Deputy Ron Norris sat alone in his squad car beneath a little overhang of tree branches that mostly obscured the few remaining traces of daylight.

He had turned off the vehicle's headlights and taillights, and he hadn't turned on the rooftop LEDs or the front strobes. He did not want to be recognized, didn't want some Joe or Jane citizen slowing down to gawk at him, or worse, stop to make an inquiry: "Hello, Officer Norris, is there anything I can help you with?" In a small town like Perryston, civic-minded citizens still made gestures of that sort.

Norris held the muzzle of the Beretta against the soft fleshy area between his throat and his chin. This was the same weapon that he had used in his unsuccessful attempt to kill Lee McCabe.

It would be easy to pull the trigger. The world wouldn't long wonder about the reasons for his suicide. It wouldn't remain a mystery. Sooner or later either Lee McCabe would be captured or Lester Finn would be otherwise exposed for the miscreant that he really was. Either way, the trail would eventually lead to him, and his involvement in the events at that trailer park.

As Norris hesitated, he wondered how he could have been such an idiot. He had been given an opportunity to end all of this, and he had faltered.

Lee McCabe, of course, wouldn't be as cooperative in the future. Never again would the young ex-marine stand passively still so that Norris could take a shot at him.

The metal of the Beretta's muzzle was cold and hard against Norris's skin. His mind drifted. Maybe he should switch targets. Kill the source, so to speak.

He could easily kill Lester Finn. He could walk right into Finn's tavern and gun him down.

But that would pose complications. Despite his many sins, Lester Finn was not currently a suspect for any specific crime. If Norris killed him, the tavern owner's death would have to be explained or hidden.

And that still wouldn't prevent the whole thing from unraveling when Lee McCabe was caught. He still didn't know exactly what McCabe had seen in that trailer. But even that didn't make any difference now. McCabe would recount the events in that field. And he would be able to back up at least part of his story. He had heard Sheriff Phelps call in over the radio. He had overheard the conversation, heard the lies that Norris had told. McCabe could simply mention that radio transmission, and his story would have immediate credibility.

Norris's wrist was beginning to ache from gripping the pistol. And then a realization hit him: Despite all of his problems, he didn't really want to die. Not yet. Not here.

Norris sighed and laid the Beretta on the car seat beside him.

He reflected on the duplicitous and methodical way in which Lester Finn had wormed his way into his own (mostly) law-abiding life. This recollection only amplified his rage—both at Lester Finn as well as at Lee McCabe. These two men were both causing him a lot of trouble. No—trouble was an understatement. Hadn't he been ready to end his own life only a moment ago?

22

L ester Finn had caught Norris with his pants down—quite literally. Somehow the smalltime hood had found out about his clandestine trips to Louisville. This debacle could be partially attributed to his own carelessness; but Finn's acquisition of this highly damaging personal knowledge had not been random. Probably Finn had kept him under surveillance for quite some time before finally catching him.

Norris occasionally liked to make trips to the less savory neighborhoods of Louisville, where young girls often sold themselves for a pittance in order to make money. These weren't high-class whores— not by any stretch of the imagination; and Norris spurned many of them. But a young jewel could occasionally be found among the chaff of the older, the worn-out, and those in the advanced stages of meth, crack, or heroin addiction. And even the young and pretty ones could be purchased on a rural sheriff's deputy's salary. Drug-addicted prostitutes did a poor job of maintaining price floors or assessing their actual worth.

On the day that everything changed, Norris had driven to his customary haunt: a rundown section of Louisville that was only a few blocks from the muddy waters of the Ohio River. This was a bad neighborhood where cars were frequently stripped and left abandoned for weeks, and where local youths openly sold drugs in vacant lots and on street corners. He had reflected on that day—as he often did—that he was probably the only cop within miles. No one would know this, of course: He always made these runs in his personal vehicle and in civilian garb. He always kept a gun beneath the driver's seat in case he ran into serious trouble: usually the Beretta.

He saw the girl leaning against the dusty façade of a brick building that was probably built in the 1920s. She fulfilled his primary criteria: she was young, reasonably thin, and white. A low-cut yellow tee shirt, blue jeans shorts, a nice pair of come-fuck-me high-heel shoes.

As Norris approached in his car, she seemed to be anticipating him. (Norris would later reflect that she almost certainly *had been* anticipating him.) She stepped away from her haunt and strolled forward to the sidewalk. When Norris got a better look at her, his excitement peaked: This was a rare find indeed. There was hardly a blemish on her, and she was definitely young: The ink was likely still drying on her high school diploma (though Norris knew that over half of these girls had never, and would never, graduate from high school.)

Norris dropped all pretense of window-shopping and brought the car to halt alongside the curb. He pressed the automatic window button for the passenger's side. She leaned forward. He could smell her perfume and from this distance she looked even younger. She gave him a smile that suffused him with warmth and nearly made him speechless.

"You lookin' for some company, sweetie?"

Staring into the dark cleft between her breasts, which were made more visible by the angle of her stance, Norris felt himself stiffen. Yes, he was definitely in the market for company.

The negotiations did not take long. Norris quickly brought her to agreement on a price, and she slid into the front passenger seat of his car. He removed two bills from his front pants pocket and laid them on the dashboard.

Her hands moved expertly across his lap. She worked his zipper down, and Norris bucked his hips upward against the pressure of her hands.

"Easy, boy," she said, pausing briefly to stare up into his face. "Why are you in such a hurry?"

Norris might have given her any number of reasons for being in a hurry: the dangerous neighborhood and the threat of arrest were chief among them. But in an odd way, the element of danger always heightened his arousal when he made these little pilgrimages into the land of his darker inclinations.

Like always, he knew that this transaction would be followed by a period of shame, and even a brief period of resolve to never return to Louisville again. And then the frustration and the heat would gradually build up in him, and he would come back to begin the cycle anew.

But these inhibitions and concerns seemed a million miles away as the girl worked him loose from his pants and took him in her mouth. In that instant, he wasn't a middle-aged small-town cop who would never make more than fifty grand per year. He felt powerful, beyond the limits of his daily life, with all its restrictions and drudgery. In that moment, as he felt the girl's mouth close around him, he might have been Genghis Khan, taking his pleasure with a nubile slave girl whom he had ripped from the tent of a defeated enemy.

And that was when he heard a metallic click.

His first thought was that the click had been made by a round being chambered in gun—or perhaps the click of a safety being turned off. He opened his eyes and his head jerked upright. What greeted him was not a gun, but a digital camera.

A few seconds passed before he fully grasped the situation: Two men standing on the driver's side of his car. One of them clicking away at a small silvery camera.

The other man did have a gun.

With a quickness that surprised him when he reflected on it later, Lester pushed the girl away. She gave out a little grunt. Lester reached for his own gun.

And now one of the men held a pistol just below Lester's ear, directly against his carotid artery.

"Don't even think about it," he said. He had a receding blond crew cut and a little mustache that looked like a caterpillar. An elaborate swastika pattern was tattooed on his neck: probably the mark of the Aryan Brotherhood. That told Norris that he had mostly likely done time.

The other man continued to click away at his digital camera. Now he was walking around the front of Norris's car. He stopped at the passenger side and took some more pictures: Norris and the girl, a tableau that would cost him his job at a minimum—and possibly his freedom. There was a strong chance that the girl was underage.

In a sudden fury Norris pushed his manhood back into his pants. This occasioned laughter from both of the men.

"Aw, Deputy, you lost your mojo in a hurry there. You know you can buy Viagra on the Internet, don't ya? Dirt cheap, they tell me."

They continued to laugh as Norris frantically closed his zipper: How many pictures had been taken? At least a dozen, he thought, from a variety of angles.

The prostitute had now shrunken away from Norris. She was leaning against the door, her head and shoulders scrunched back to an angle that did not interfere with the last few clicks of the digital camera. Was this girl in cahoots with these men?

"Why are you lookin' at me like that?" she asked, as if reading Norris's mind.

"You bitch," Norris said. "You set me up, didn't you?"

"You're scarin' me baby. I didn't do nothin' to you. You drove here. You stopped at the curb. Don't give me none of that—"

"Shut up." The man with the digital camera said, and the young whore was instantly silent. He yanked open the passenger side door.

"Get out," he said.

The girl risked one final, offended glace at Norris. She plucked up the bills that he had placed on the dashboard. Then she slid out of the car and walked quickly away, her heels clicking on the pavement.

The man with the camera gave Norris a smile that revealed at least one missing tooth. Norris noticed that this one, too, had Aryan Brotherhood tattoos.

"Say cheese," he said, before he clicked the camera tauntingly at Norris for the final time.

"Give me your right hand," the other one said. He was still standing just outside the driver's side door. He still held the gun.

"What?"

"Give me your right hand. And don't make me repeat myself again."

Norris had no choice. He obeyed.

Norris had to twist his body around in order to extend his right arm out the window. The gunman grabbed his wrist and yanked it high into the air. Still brandishing the pistol, he somehow managed to close one half of a pair of handcuffs over Norris's wrist. He leaned into the car and closed the other half of the cuffs over the steering wheel. Norris was awkwardly tethered to his own car.

The gunman removed a small key from his pocket. He held the object aloft so Norris could see it. Then he flicked the key past Norris's face. It ricocheted off the passenger seat, bounced against the door of the glove compartment, and finally came to rest on the floor.

"We'll be in touch," the gunman said. He reached out and took Norris's earlobe between his thumb and forefinger. Norris arched his back and howled. The man with the camera laughed, held the camera to his eye, and snapped another picture.

"That one was just for fun," he said, finally pocketing the camera.

It took Norris about half an hour to retrieve the key from the floor of his car. By that time, of course, the men were long gone, and the whore, he imagined, was far removed from the scene as well.

Trembling with leftover fear and building rage, Norris assessed the situation. Genius-level analytical skills were not required to figure out that he had fallen prey to some sort of a blackmail scheme. The operative questions were: *Who* was blackmailing him—and what did they want?

23

Norris did not have to wait long for his answer. Within a few days, the humiliating pictures began to show up in his personal email bin, sent from an anonymous Yahoo email account. These were accompanied by no messages, no demands—but Norris knew that these were coming.

At least the blackmailers had not sent the photos to his sheriff's department email account; but he knew that this could be next. If they were able to acquire his personal email, then acquiring his work account would be even easier. In fact, there was a personnel email directory on the department's website. This had been Sheriff Phelps's idea—he had wanted to make the department more "accessible" to the public.

Two days after he began to receive the emailed photos, Norris received a phone call on his personal cell phone from an unfamiliar caller who had a local accent, the gravelly voice of a lifelong smoker, and an infuriatingly presumptuous tone.

"Deputy Norris," the male caller said. "Hawkins County's amateur porn star."

"Who the hell is this?" Norris snapped.

"I don't believe we've had the pleasure of an in-person meeting,"

the called said. "But we will soon. You're going to swing by my bar.
Nice little place in Blood Flats. The Boar's Head. You've heard of it, I
believe. You're going to come by on your personal time and you're
going to arrive in your personal vehicle. You aren't going to tell
anyone about this call or about our meeting. Otherwise, the sheriff,
the state police, and every media outlet in the state is going to receive
a copy of those photos."

"You son of a bitch!" Norris screamed. He wouldn't realize until
later that he had been crying.

The caller—who Norris had now identified as Lester Finn (the
mention of the Boar's Head made this much obvious) was unper-
turbed. "Don't worry, Deputy Norris; I'll pick the best shots. I particularly like the first few—the ones where the whore still has you in her
mouth. You seem to be enjoying yourself. I like to see a man take his
pleasures in such an unabashed manner."

This was Norris's first actual conversation with Lester Finn. Prior
to this, he had been aware of Finn's presence, of course: The tavern
owner had been on the radar of the sheriff's department for years. He
had long been suspected of various illegal activities, drug trafficking
and the promotion of prostitution chief among them. But these suspicions had been rumors. They had never crystallized into any
evidence that could be fashioned into actual charges. The department had been vaguely watching Finn; but he had never been the
target of a formal investigation. Once or twice a year they sent a Finn-
related memo to the state cops and the Louisville police, where Lester
was rumored to have criminal contacts. Officially, though, Lester Finn
was a law-abiding citizen who owned a bar in the town of Blood
Flats, about twenty miles south of the county seat of Perryston.

Norris knew better than to dismiss Lester Finn's blackmail threat
as idle bluster. After all, it wasn't as if the tavern owner would have to
commit murder in order to ruin his life. He would need to do nothing
more than send a few emails. And so Norris had presented himself at
the Boar's Head, exactly as Finn instructed him.

At first Norris believed that he was going to get off easy. His worst
fear had been that Lester would try to compel him to use the cover of

his badge to commit acts of violence. But Lester did not try to draft him into the role of enforcer. He seemed to want nothing more than mere information: Finn was especially interested in intelligence about the local meth trade: Not only the local dealers—but also the distribution networks above them, most of which were based in Louisville, Nashville, or Atlanta.

Norris figured that Lester was feeding this information to someone else: Whatever his pretensions of being a local godfather, Lester Finn at the end of the day was nothing more than a small-town hood. He must be working with one of the large organized crime outfits—no doubt another out-of-state group. This alarmed Norris, because that increased the stakes of the game in which he had become an unwilling participant.

Nevertheless, there was always a chance that Lester Finn might get in over his head, and incur the wrath of the wrong person. The bar owner was arrogant and overconfident. If Norris were lucky, Finn would eventually end up in a ditch somewhere, his hands bound behind his back and half his head blown away. Another underworld statistic.

And so Norris had not objected strongly when Lester Finn demanded specific information about dealers in the local meth trade. For Norris the paramount concern was the continued confidentiality of the photos of him and the teenage whore. If Lester wanted local names, he would give him local names. He went out and shook down a few junkies, detained them on vague charges, then hauled them out to some secluded back road for one-on-one discussions.

Norris was amazed to discover how quickly a disoriented meth addict will reveal his sources after a few strategically placed baton blows. A few of them, of course, had dared to accuse him of police brutality. They seemed to regard this expression itself as some sort of magical incantation. Perhaps they expected an ACLU representative to walk out of the woods; or maybe they thought that the ghost of Johnnie Cochran was going to materialize and craft a defense for them. If that was the case, they were all sorely disappointed. They dropped this line of argument quickly after Norris did a little xylophone routine on their kneecaps.

He had never engaged in any forceful interrogations before; and he had to admit that it did afford a certain power rush. He believed that he now understood how the men of the KGB, the Iranian SAVAK, and the Iraqi Mukhabarat had kept up their work day in and day out. That sort of thing wasn't as disagreeable as one might think.

In all of these conversations, one name had emerged consistently: Tim Fitzsimmons.

"What are you going to do with this information?" Norris had asked the tavern owner, just after he revealed the name during a cell phone conversation. Finn had recently refused to allow Norris to deliver his clandestine intelligence in person. He had insisted that Norris communicate via cell phone or email. Norris knew that this was Finn's way of implanting his hooks even deeper, creating an extensive electronic record of communications between himself and the proprietor of the Boar's Head.

"I only want to have a little business chat with him," Lester Finn had said.

Norris had thought that he had grasped the subtext: Finn would threaten Tim Fitzsimmons—possibly rough him up a bit, possibly cut him a deal. Norris was familiar with the ways of small-town roughnecks and hoodlums. They threatened, they occasionally committed petty acts of violence. So Norris had been half-prepared for trouble.

He had not been prepared for a double homicide—Fitzsimmons and the woman murdered in their living room, execution style. This was more than Norris had bargained for, even when he had submitted to the blackmail scheme. If you were careful, there were certain things that you could hide: Risky though it was, it might have been possible for Norris to have complied with Lester Finn's demands without linking himself to misdeeds that would not escape notice. As Norris knew from a lifetime in law enforcement, a great amount of evil takes place each day without most of the world caring one iota.

But now things were completely different. Even in the final hours before the hit, when Norris had suspected that Fitzsimmons might not be long for this world, he had not anticipated a brazen massacre in a residential area.

The situation with Finn had exploded into a veritable bloodbath —the kind for which everyone, from the local taxpayers right up to the governor of the state, would demand to have answers.

And Norris knew that he was one of those answers.

His life now depended on keeping that answer hidden. And that meant that Lee McCabe—who could now incriminate him from multiple angles—would have to die.

24

The last traces of the dying day provided little light beneath the canopy of the forest. To the west, an orange sun burned here and there through a silhouetted latticework of trees. The shadows were long, and Lee knew that soon the forest would be completely dark.

Lee had never been frightened in the woods at night; and there was no reason for the uneasiness he felt now. There were no monsters in these woods, after all. The monsters were all in town; they walked on two legs and assumed human form, though they were not quite human in fact. They had killed Tim Fitzsimmons and Jody in cold blood, shot them in the head and in the face at point-blank range. That had not been a shootout—but a pair of executions.

And this was not even the worst of it, at least not from Lee's own perspective. He had always known that Sheriff Phelps detested him. He had realized that Phelps would give him the benefit of no doubts; and he could even have imagined Phelps allowing him to be framed for murders that he did not commit.

Nevertheless, he would have supposed that there was a line that Phelps would not cross. That assumption no longer held. Today

Phelps's deputy had attempted to gun him down after he had already surrendered. Although Phelps had not fired the shots, those shots would not have been fired without the sheriff's approval. Deputy Norris would have had no personal motivations for killing him. Phelps had to be behind it—more or less as Norris had asserted.

He shuddered at the depths of the sheriff's hatred. Phelps had loved his mother—but in the end she had spurned him for another man. That man—Tom McCabe—had become Lee's father. Since his father was now dead, he supposed that meant that the sheriff had simply transferred his rage to the next generation.

Apparently the sheriff had never gotten over the rejection, or the heartbreak, or whatever it was. The dark emotions inside of him had grown over the years, metastasizing. What was once a young man's bitterness was now a middle-aged man's openly murderous intent.

The rough forest pathway ahead of him sloped upward. At the crest of the hill, Lee could see a break in the trees and a pale orange wall of twilight. He paused for a moment when he heard a twig snap on the far side of the hill. For a full minute he stood there, listening. When he was satisfied that he had heard nothing more than a random forest sound, he continued walking.

His thoughts returned to the sheriff and the man's unrelenting anger. He had almost died in that field. If Norris had been a steadier shot...

Lee shook his head at his own naivety. He should have seen it coming. After all, he had glimpsed into the depths of Phelps's ill will once before, when he was still in high school. He remembered the spring night when Phelps had pulled him over on a flimsy pretense, then ordered him out of his car.

Lee had not been drinking that night—and the sheriff knew it. Nevertheless, he had forced Lee to step out of his vehicle and walk the line like a common drunk.

"I haven't been drinking," Lee had protested.

"Well, it's not like you haven't been taught to be a drinker," Phelps had said, in obvious reference to Lee's father.

Up until that point Lee had maintained a polite veneer. But then he had snapped, telling Phelps that he was pathetic—a loser who could not get on with his life. Then Phelps had snapped, too, telling Lee that he was no better than the man who had sired him.

Phelps had never said as much, but he had been wanting Lee to take a swing at him. He had been hoping for the blow and the license to violence that such an act on Lee's part would give him. He had been praying for it, Lee thought.

But Lee had controlled himself, resisting the urge to escalate the verbal conflict into a physical one. In the end Phelps had found nothing to charge him with, so he had simply ordered Lee back into his car with a vague warning to "keep an eye on his speed."

That was in the distant past now, a minor adolescent blip compared to the troubles of the present. But he might have seen the present troubles coming, based on what he had seen that night.

Lee silently cursed the sheriff: How could a man remain bitter for all these years over an unrequited love? Now—when both of his parents were dead?

These thoughts were interrupted by a shadow that blocked the path ahead of him. Lee started: This was no mere shadow; the shadow quickly assumed the shape of a man—a man bearing a rifle.

"Whoa," the unknown man said. "Who are you?"

Lee made a split-second decision: His pistol was tucked behind the small of his back. To reach for it would imply threat. Lee stopped in the middle of his path and raised his open hands to shoulder level, so as to demonstrate that he was carrying no weapons and intended no harm.

"My name is Lee. And I'll tell you right now that I have a weapon; but you have nothing to fear from me. I'm simply passing through. Excuse me for startling you."

After taking what seemed like an interminable moment to ponder these words, the man who blocked the pathway finally nodded. He slung his rifle over one shoulder and removed a small flashlight from the front pocket of his jeans. He turned it on so that they were both illuminated by a little pool of light, which appeared to be very bright in the darkness of the forest. For the first time, Lee got a good look at the man's features: He had broad shoulders, cold blue eyes and blond hair that was fringed with white. This man was much older than Lee—much older than Steven Phelps, for that matter.

"Very well, my young friend," the stranger said in a tone that struck Lee as patriarchal—almost Biblical. "I can see that you intend me no harm. But you have to be careful, creeping through the woods alone at night. I might have shot you where you stood."

"I might have shot you," Lee replied.

The man turned away, as if he felt absolutely no threat from Lee's presence. "You would not have shot me," he said. "And if you had tried, you would be dead by now." He switched off the flashlight. "But enough of that. Follow me."

"Wait a minute," Lee protested "I'm only passing through. I have to get moving."

The flashlight came on again. The man turned back to him, a half-smile on his weathered face.

"Where could you be going at this place and in this hour that is so important?" And when Lee did not answer he said, "You're wandering. That is what you're doing."

The man turned back around and continued forward, the beam of the flashlight bobbing ahead of him

"I can tell that you are tired and hungry," the man said. "And these woods are not friendly to a man late at night. It's your choice, of course. But you should follow me."

He switched the light off once again, and Lee could only discern his presence by sound. But the man moved more quietly than most, like one who is experienced at maneuvering his way through hostile environments.

The stranger's implied promise of food and a place to rest swelled, large and inviting, in Lee's mind. How long had he been walking, driven by fear and adrenalin but steadily depleting his inner resources?

Lee knew that he would have to go now, or he would lose the stranger; and he did not think that the man would come back for him later, were he to change his mind and call out for the unknown man in the darkness.

So before he could change his mind, Lee walked after the muted sounds of the stranger making his way through the forest.

25

B y the time they reached the stranger's camp, Lee had figured out who the man was—or at least roughly who he was.

This stranger in the woods was a local legend of sorts, though not one who inspired any particular degree of awe or dread. Lee could not recall the last time he heard him mentioned, though he had certainly heard him mentioned at some unspecified time in the past.

They called him the Hunter. Whether or not the Hunter actually hunted anything was not known. What was known was that he lived in the woods, or in a cabin or a trailer at the edge of the woods. He was not regarded to be dangerous or sinister; but nor was he a man to be trifled with. He kept his distance from others. And others afforded him a similar courtesy.

"James Hunter," the man said, when they finally reached a little clearing in the woods. Lee gripped the Hunter's rough and calloused hand and said his own name once again. Lee omitted his last name; but this was probably a meaningless bit of subterfuge. If the Hunter had heard of the earlier events in town, then he would be able to grasp Lee's identity with the information that he already had. But nothing about the Hunter's manner suggested that he recognized Lee to be a fugitive.

The minimal formalities of introduction concluded, the Hunter squatted down before a circle of smoldering coals that was surrounded by a barrier of odd, randomly shaped rocks that had been culled from the forest, and a little trench that might have been scraped from the earth with a camper's shovel. The Hunter laid some twigs and other kindling on the coals and began to blow into the few embers that were still glowing orange. Soon there was the crackling sound of the fire taking hold, and the flames shot up to knee height.

The clearing thus illuminated, Lee was able to take in the outlines of the Hunter's campsite: There was a crude tent strung on a clothes-line between two trees, several duffel bags of supplies hung from large, low-hanging branches, and a rucksack leaned against a fallen log.

"I'm going to make dinner now," the Hunter said. "You're welcome to stay if you'd like. The choices on the menu are beef stew or beef stew."

"Beef stew sounds great," Lee said, "And thank you for your hospitality."

For the first time since he had arisen that day, Lee allowed himself to relax. He sat down on the ground before the fire and watched the Hunter prepare the food over the fire. While he was cooking, the Hunter dismissed Lee's few attempts at conversation with peremptory grunts.

The Hunter ladled their dinner onto two plates, drawing the stew from a metal cooking pot that was suspended over the fire by a tripod. They drank lukewarm water from tin cups. This was basic fare even by military standards; but Lee thought that it was the most delicious meal he had tasted in a long time, given the circumstances.

"I suppose you're wondering about me," the Hunter finally said at length, having spooned and eaten the last of his beef stew.

Lee had been so lost in his own troubles that he had given the Hunter's biographical information little more than a passing thought. But he nodded nonetheless. If the Hunter were to talk about himself, that would delay questions about Lee's full identity, and why he had been trekking alone through a remote part of the woods at such an odd hour.

"I grew up around here," the Hunter began. "But there are few details from my earliest years that you or anyone else would find extraordinary. My life did not begin in full until I left home. There was a war on those days; and so my chance to see the world was ready-made. I considered it to be an opportunity. Little did I know back then what awaited me.

"In 1968 I was an eighteen-year-old marine stationed at a fire base in the Khe Sanh valley. I was attached to an artillery battery. We had rows of Howitzers—both the towed as well as the self-propelled kind. We were fighting a peasant army that was pulled from the rice paddies and grass huts of a Third World nation. We should have felt safe and confident. But that was not the way things were.

"The Viet Cong made sandals from pieces of old tires. At night they would walk into the perimeter around our base, and in the morning we would walk out into those areas that had been cleared of vegetation, and see their tire-tread footprints in the mud and loose earth. Sometimes they launched mortar attacks on us at night. At other times, their snipers killed some of our number from a distance.

"For a little more than a year, I lived constantly in the shadow of death. But I did not face death passively. During that year, my god was Ares. And I was faithful to the doctrine of that god of war. Marxists are pure materialists, you know. They do not believe in hell. But I do. And I dispatched as many of them as I could. Somewhere in the darkest corner of Hades, I liked to think, there was a gathering of Marxist devils who were there because of me."

"Devils?" Lee asked. "Aren't you exaggerating a bit? Did you ever consider that some of them were there for other reasons? They might not have even been Marxists at all."

"I killed only true Marxist believers, my friend. That was what I told myself."

"I see."

"When I returned to the States," the Hunter continued, "A crowd of peace protestors was there waiting for us at the airport in San Francisco, with signs calling us baby killers and whatnot. So much for the gratitude of the American public. I was quite sure that I had killed not one single baby during my tour of duty; every man I had killed was firing back at me. So their signs angered me, of course; but I would have let them go, all but one of them.

"One of the protestors—a young man about my age at the time—strode forward from the crowd and directly approached me. I could tell that he had decided to make an example of me. He was going to use me to make his mark, to cement his reputation as the bold one among the group. I knew immediately that I was not going to be able to simply walk away from this. Most of the peaceniks were passive, you see—but this one was different. He was not a true believer in their cause—not a pacifist by nature. Like so many of them, he had joined the movement because it kept him out of the war, and provided constant access to drugs and compliant women. This young man was as big as me and almost as strong; and despite his long hair, peace medallion, and colored beads, I believe that he was a killer in his mind.

"But he was not a killer in his heart, and that proved to be his undoing. You see, I had actually taken men's lives over the past year, and it was obvious that this fellow never had. He made his move for me, and he might have taken me down had I been the person that I was several years before; but now he hesitated whereas I did not. I struck him, and he fell at my feet and then I was upon him. And I was in no mood for mercy—not after all that I had been through.

"You've heard that old expression about seeing red. And most of the time it is nothing but an exaggeration. But in that moment, I truly did see red. Blood filled my eyes as I was suffused with pure rage. I began to pummel the young man with my fists. I was in a daze. Until finally they pulled me off of him.

"And then I saw what I had done. The young man's face was bloody. His blood was on the collar of my dress shirt and the sleeves of my uniform jacket. There were police at the airport; but they simply smirked and looked away; they pretended that it not happened. Then the other protesters saw what I had done to this one of them that was apparently their leader. One by one they lowered their signs and they shrank away. I walked through that terminal of the airport unaccosted. It was a silence unlike any I had heard before —or since.

"After my discharge from the Marine Corps, I was in no mood to return to Hawkins County—not yet. So in an odd turn of identity, I grew my hair long and moved among the numbers of the hippies themselves. For a brief while I even lived in a commune on the West Coast. And I knew women. Many, many women, my young friend. I was tall and strong and quite good-looking back then, if I do say so myself.

"You should not think, though, that I completely abandoned myself to hedonism. I also developed my mind. I read many books in those days. Many, many books. In keeping with the times, Hermann Hesse was one of my favorites. His writings had quite an influence on me. I can't say for sure, in those days, if I was more of a Siddhartha or a Steppenwolf. Perhaps I was a bit of both.

"But finally I had had enough of the women and the communes and yes, even the books. I returned home. And one day I met that one woman who made me forget all the rest. Have you met that woman, my young friend? No, something tells me that you have not."

The Hunter paused only briefly in his monologue, as a courtesy. It did not seem necessary for Lee to answer. *Somehow*, Lee thought, *he already knew the answer to the question. As crazy as that sounds.*

The Hunter went on: "And so I married her. And within a few years we had a daughter. She was beautiful and kind like her mother, and headstrong and defiant like me. Meanwhile, I prospered in business. I owned a business that once existed in town—Hunter Concrete. Have you heard of it?"

Lee stopped to consider this. Hadn't he heard of a company by that name, from sometime in his distant childhood? "Yes," Lee said. "You owned—"

The Hunter finished his thought for him. "That big building and storefront just east of town. You see? "You remember more than you think you do."

"Then why," Lee began. He could not think of a tactful way to phrase the inevitable question.

"You want to know why I am living here in these woods, if I had a wife and a daughter who loved me, and a successful business. Is that correct?"

"Something like that."

"Very well. I never speak of these things that follow, but I will make an exception in your case. Because I can see that we are alike in various ways. For example, you've been to war, haven't you?"

"How did you—"

"How I know is not important. When you are older, you'll be able to see things in a man's eyes that he doesn't put into so many words. But anyway, the rest of my story:

"One day—it was more than twenty years ago—when my daughter was a young woman, and my wife was no longer so young, but still very beautiful, at least to me. My wife was driving along Highway 168. My daughter was in the passenger seat. They didn't see the truck coming at them from the other direction. They had no time to react. Do I need to tell you what happened, or can you piece the rest together by yourself?"

"Yes," Lee said quietly. "I understand."

"After that, I wanted no more part of the world. I sold my business, and I purchased a cabin on a small piece of property in the woods. I spend most of my nights in the cabin. But sometimes I like to head out, as is the case tonight. On those nights I feel the need to sleep under the stars, to be alone with myself and look up into the face of God."

26

Lee said nothing for a while after the Hunter finished his story. And then the inevitable moment came—when the Hunter asked him to give his own account. Lee had no inclination to lie; it seemed unthinkable, after listening to the Hunter lay bare his past as he did.

He therefore told the complete tale of how he had happened upon the aftermath of the murders earlier in the day, how he had run, and how he had wandered through the forest.

"You and this Sheriff Phelps," the Hunter said after Lee's story was complete. "It reminds me of Saul and David. When the two men returned from their battle with the Philistines, the women sang, 'Saul hath slain his thousands and David his ten thousands.' And thereafter Saul, the older man, hated David, the younger. David was a reminder to him of all that he could not be."

"I don't think it's exactly like that with the sheriff and me," Lee said. He recalled just enough of the Old Testament story to grasp the Hunter's metaphor. "Phelps isn't envious of me personally. He loved my mother; but in the end she would not have him."

"Yes," the Hunter said. "And you are a constant reminder of what the sheriff views as his own failure—or the way fate cheated him. Just like David reminded Saul of the warrior that he would never be. A woman gives a man many things. Life on this earth would be worthless without them. And one of those many things is immortality. Through the children he begets with her. Your mother—for whatever reason—denied that to the sheriff. And now he seems to hold you accountable."

"Wait a minute," Lee said. "My mother didn't deny him any of that. This whole business about 'immortality' and whatnot, well, it seems a little bit melodramatic to me. What you're talking about is simply a part of life. So my mother broke things off with the sheriff and went with my father instead. It happens to almost everyone at one time. He had a choice: He could have simply accepted the situation and moved on."

The Hunter gave Lee a half smile. "You're making a rational argument, my young friend. But that part of the self is irrational. It taps directly into the animal self—what Freud referred to as the 'id'. Have you heard of Sigmund Freud?"

"I've heard of Freud," Lee said, a trifle defensively.

"This moving on that you're talking about. Some people can't—or won't—move on. Or perhaps they simply choose not to. In any case, it would seem that this Sheriff Phelps is one of these men. So all of your dealings with the sheriff will be colored by what went before you even existed. You are the child he never begot—a living reminder of his failure."

"Thanks a lot," Lee said. "Is this supposed to cheer me up?"

"I'm not trying to cheer you up. I'm trying to help you assess the predicament you've found yourself in. If I can."

"I still don't understand why the sheriff couldn't just let it go," Lee said, shaking his head. "All that happened more than twenty years ago—before I was born. About the same time that—" Lee stopped himself, shocked at what he had been about to utter.

"About the same time that I lost my wife and daughter, you were about to say. No, don't deny it, my young friend. That is what you were thinking. And don't be naïve enough to believe that time heals all wounds. It doesn't. I will say this to you once again: You are the child that the sheriff never begat. That another man begat with the woman he once loved. Still does love, if all that you tell me is true."

"So what are you saying? Does that mean that the sheriff will never stop hating me? That he'll end up killing me? Or arresting me, so that I will go to prison for the rest of my life?"

"These outcomes are possible. But not inevitable. One thing is certain, though: You have a battle in front of you."

"It seems that I have a life of hiding ahead of me. Or death. Or prison."

"So you are going to keep running?" the Hunter asked.

"You tell me."

"No—*you* tell *me*. What do you intend to do? Wander around these woods until they finally come in and hunt you down?"

"What other choice do I have?"

"You might try going on the offense. Give it some thought, my young friend."

Lee stared into the crackling fire: What the Hunter was saying was crazy; and what the Hunter was saying made the most perfect kind of sense. There was no percentage in this acting and thinking like a fugitive. He had to take matters into his own hands, somehow —Sheriff Phelps, Deputy Norris, and the gunmen who killed Fitzsimmons and Jody be damned.

The question was: *How?* He knew that this answer would be complicated. And it would, in all likelihood, not come to him tonight. Nevertheless, this seemed to be his only real choice. He knew that his temperament would not allow him to passively flee forever.

Then he said to the Hunter: "Would you be willing to help me? You seem like a capable man."

This was an enormous presumption, Lee realized. But you could never tell with people. Sometimes strangers did grant you unexpected favors. Not often, but sometimes. And the Hunter had turned out to be anything but typical so far.

However, the older man shook his head. "I wish that I could help you. In another time and place, it might have been possible. But not now. That world out there is not for me anymore. I cannot leave these woods."

This struck Lee as stranger yet. Apparently the Hunter was still brooding over events that had happened a lifetime or two ago. Well, it had been worth a try; he would not push the issue.

"It is getting late," the Hunter said. "And time for an old man to turn in. Feel free to make your bed here if you would like. I'll keep the fire burning. It should drive away whatever wild beasts still reside in these forests."

"Thank you for the dinner," Lee said. "But I don't believe that I'll impose on your hospitality any further."

"As you wish. Take care, my young friend. And find a way to go on the offense. No matter how much your instincts may tell you to run. Sometimes the world is as dark as this forest, son. It doesn't just seem that way—it *is*. But you have to find a way to fight it—both for yourself, and for those who cannot fight for themselves."

Lee only nodded in reply as he stood up and brushed off his pants. He felt the urge to get moving, to continue his journey. For some reason that he did not fully understand, he did not want to stay here with this man who seemed to have an unobstructed view into his soul.

27

The inside of his townhouse was pitch-black by the time Phelps called it a day and returned home. Although June was the season of long days and leisurely evenings that seem to last forever, it was full dark at eleven-ten p.m., the time reported by the digital readout on Phelps's cable television box.

He flicked on the overhead light switch in the main foyer of the townhouse, and the entire room was bathed in artificial light. Phelps lived alone; and he had no pets. His abode was clean, well maintained, and decorated with the requisite minimum of wall hangings and bric-a-brac; but something about the townhouse looked barren. This was arguably an inevitable characteristic of all bachelor pads, though Phelps reflected that the term "bachelor pad" was probably intended to describe the lairs of prowling twenty-five year-old men just out of college—not those of middle-aged men who were already thinking in terms of aching backs and prostate exams.

He had spent most of the afternoon with a borrowed canine unit, combing the long swath of woods between the Tradewinds and Highway 168. No luck. Not a single sign of Lee McCabe.

Phelps had anticipated a faster response from the state police. He had expected actual assistance in the form of boots on the ground, as that was what was needed to find a man on the run in dense forests.

While manning a roadblock, Phelps had heard the *thucka-thucka* of a helicopter, and looked up to see a Kentucky State Police airborne unit pass overhead. He had known right then that this would be mostly a waste of time. The canopies of the surrounding forests were thick with early summer foliage, and the airborne unit's approach could be heard from a long distance. McCabe would have had no trouble evading the helicopter. The young man was a former marine, after all. He had only recently spent months in the role of pursuer, ferreting al-Qaeda terrorists from their hovels and secret bunkers in Iraq. He would know all the best strategies of the fugitive.

Walking into the kitchen, Phelps opened his refrigerator and removed a chilled brown bottle from an open case of Samuel Adams Boston Lager. He would stop at one, he told himself. Two at the most. He would not get drunk tonight.

He knew that his mood—his focus—was all wrong. Two people in the county had been murdered today. And his only suspect was on the run. He should be thinking about the case, about how he would capture Lee McCabe.

But instead he was thinking about Lee's mother—Lori McCabe. Or Lori *Mills*, as Phelps preferred to think of her. The Lori who had not yet met Tom McCabe.

Moving to the living room, he placed his beer on a glass-topped coffee cable, barely taking the time to set a coaster beneath the dripping bottle. He knew that his next course of action would do him no good; but he felt drawn to it nonetheless. He supposed that this was how junkies must feel. They know better: but sometimes even bad medicine seems preferable to the impulse that won't let you rest.

He walked into this bedroom. The shoebox was at the bottom of his closet. Exactly where it always was.

He carried the shoebox back into the living room and let it rest on the cushion adjacent to him on the couch. This was his Pandora's box, a shoebox full of memories that would be better left covered and stored away. Or better yet—discarded completely. He knew, though, that he wasn't up to this latter option. It was enough of a struggle for him to maintain the first.

The shoebox contained mostly photographs—relics from a few decades ago, a time when no one had thought in terms of photographs as bits of electronic data to be stored on computer hard drives and posted in cyberspace—another term that was completely alien to that time. These were photographs that bore the words PRINTED ON GENUINE KODAK PAPER on their backs in faded red lettering. Or they were Polaroids taken on bulky squares of instant film, the kind that had developed within a few minutes of taking the shot.

He shuffled through the pictures, and the odd assortment of concert ticket stubs and letters that also filled the box. Lori had often written him letters in those days; which was kind of silly, since they had lived in the same town, their houses separated by no more than a few miles. Then he remembered how her letters abruptly stopped not long after he had moved away.

One particular photograph caught his attention and he removed it from the shoebox: It was a picture of himself and Lori Mills. They were seated on a sofa at a friend's house. Phelps remembered the moment that the photograph had been taken as if it were yesterday. Lori's arms were wrapped around him and her mouth was pressed against his cheek. Phelps had seen the camera but Lori had not, so Phelps's gaze was on the person taking the picture, and Lori's attention was focused on him.

She was wearing faded jeans and a pullover top with black-and-yellow horizontal stripes. A lock of her hair—she had worn it loose and shoulder length in those days—had fallen across one of her cheeks. The photo made Phelps's heart ache.

The two of them had gone to a concert that night at Rupp Arena in Lexington. The headline band had been Foreigner—one of the big pop-rock acts of the 1980s. Phelps had always been lukewarm toward the group's music but Lori had loved them. He remembered the way she had gyrated during one of the band's fleshier songs, her body occasionally brushing against him in rhythm with the drums and bass onstage.

His mental image of Lori was young and immortal, nothing like that of the early middle-aged woman who had wasted away from cancer.

Enough was enough. Phelps turned the photograph over to its white paper side and dropped it into the shoebox.

Phelps did not want to look at any more old pictures. Before he could change his mind, he stood and carried the entire box back into his bedroom. He felt relieved when he closed the closet door, the shoebox safely stowed in the rear corner.

He paused in the middle of his bedroom, thinking. Nothing could be accomplished by focusing on these old memories. Phelps knew better. He realized that he was chasing ghosts—quite literally, in the case of Lori. She was gone now; and she had been gone to him even before she had died. Years before, in fact.

He also knew that despite his best efforts, he would always think about Lori Mills. He had become resigned to that defeat long ago. Connections to Lori's son were another matter, though. There had been some good times with Lori. But no good had ever come from any of his connections to Lee McCabe.

He recalled that flashback he had in Fitzsimmons's trailer— remembered glimpses of the Iraqi dead on the highway in Kuwait. How old had Lee McCabe been then? He would have been a mere child.

Phelps had not known then, of course, that Lori McCabe's young son would enter this same hot, dusty land as a U.S. marine nearly two decades later. Nor could Phelps have predicted that he would one day be the Sheriff of Hawkins County, and that this role would make him Lee's pursuer.

He thought again about those burned Iraqi soldiers. Phelps had been unable to find much pity for them at the time: he had known what the Iraqi army had done in Kuwait. As the years passed, though, he had gradually adopted what he considered to be a more philo-sophical view. He concluded that not all of those men could have been heartless killers who murdered and raped and tortured. At least a few of them must have been innocent men who had been compelled to take part in the invasion. Their innocence had not saved them, though. They met the same fiery deaths as the guilty.

Phelps had seen Lee McCabe run from the trailer. He had seen the young man's gun. All the circumstantial evidence was aligned against him. And yet, there was something about the scenario that didn't make sense. McCabe had been trained in military tactics and he had survived a war and its unsettled aftermath. Phelps had to assume that he had some tactical sense and a degree of street smarts. If McCabe had gone to Fitzsimmons's trailer to commit murder, he would have planned it more carefully; he wouldn't have gone about it in a way that was guaranteed to place him at the crime scene with a dozen witnesses.

Had McCabe suffered some sort of a breakdown and snapped? Possible, but still a stretch. When men broke and went amok with guns they usually took many innocent lives. The violence at the Tradewinds had been narrowly targeted at Fitzsimmons and the unfortunate Jody White.

For Phelps personally, the path of least resistance was to assume that Lee McCabe had committed those murders, and then to direct all his energies toward apprehending him. Then the justice system would do its work and Lee McCabe would either go free or to prison —perhaps even to the lethal injection table. Kentucky was a death penalty state.

Perhaps that last option would be best for all; it would provide a bit of closure. With Lee's death, he could forget that Lori had betrayed him all those years ago, forget about the man who was Lee's father.

Damn you, Steve, he cursed himself. *Damn you for even entertaining thoughts like that.*

Not for the first time, Phelps reflected that his own life might have had more meaning if it had ended somewhere in the Iraqi desert in 1991; then he cursed himself for that thought as well.

He whirled around, stood before the closet and pounded his fist twice on its closed door. Then he resolved to do what he should have done years ago: He opened the closet door and retrieved the shoebox again. He would throw it away, all of it.

He carried the shoebox outside and placed it in the back seat of his police cruiser. He permitted himself one last look at the snapshot of him and Lori: *Yes, he was chasing ghosts, and his obsession with the past would only cloud his judgment in the present.* That might get him— or someone else—killed in the days ahead.

28

His name was Terrence James Anderson; but everyone had always called him TJ—even in prison. TJ was a late riser; and he regarded the late morning sunshine with a touch of irritation. He had always preferred the nighttime.

He was cleaning his gun: a 9 mm Bersa Thunder semiautomatic. The gun had a thirteen-round magazine and could be easily concealed inside a piece of clothing, or even inside a boot. The gun was stolen, and his possession of it would have violated the terms of his parole in any case. But TJ wasn't worried about anyone seeing it— not this far out in the country. He leaned back in the rocking chair and let the nickel plating on the gun's barrel gleam in the sunlight. He was proud of the way that barrel gleamed. He gave it a few more rubs with the cloth in his lap before declaring the job done.

He saw a crow land in the front yard. The bird jabbed its beak into the grass and pulled out a squirming, living thing that might have been a small toad or a frog. TJ was tempted to take a shot at the crow; he had shot at birds before from the front porch and had even hit a few. But that would be a waste of ammo; and he didn't want to antagonize any of the neighbors in the adjacent farmhouses. Word traveled fast—even in rural districts like this. By now, all of his neighbors would know that an ex-con had taken up residence in the rental house atop the hill.

He heard the front screen door squeak open. Tammy was leaning just inside the doorway, her long, bare legs looking so inviting in a pair of gym shorts. To think that he had lived in an institution with only nine hundred men for company until a few months ago.

She walked out onto the front porch and approached the rocking chair from behind. Then she began to massage his bare shoulders. He felt himself stir when her fingers dug into his skin: Tammy Lynn Davis—twenty-one years old and damn easy on the eyes.

"What are you doin' out here, TJ, when I'm inside?"

"I won't be much longer," he said.

Tammy didn't seem to mind the fourteen-year difference in their ages, nor the fact that TJ had done time behind bars. This did not completely surprise him—he had long known that some women liked their men older and harder, particularly spoiled princess types like Tammy here. Her father was the sales manager at the John Deere dealership in town, and the old guy no doubt laid awake at night agonizing over the fact that his precious daughter was shacking up with a thirty-five-year-old ex-con. He wanted her to date Biff the Football Jock, or some promising young egghead who planned to study law or engineering.

TJ realized that Tammy was, in her own way, using him as an instrument of her private rebellion against her parents. That was all right with him, though—a man could be used in worse ways.

"You're always polishing that gun," she observed.

"Well, like I said, I won't be much longer. Why don't you go inside and make us a couple of sandwiches for lunch?"

"TJ, you're bein' a jerk," she said. But she did as she was told when she saw that he was serious and not in the mood to talk.

And TJ didn't have time to talk to Tammy right now. He needed time to think about the money, and what he would need to do in order to get it: Lester Finn had called him late last night with an offer: lead a team of men and kill Lee McCabe. Finn had offered him a princely sum if he achieved this—more money than he had ever seen in his entire life. Six figures. In cash.

TJ had done one small job for Finn since his parole from prison. Lester Finn seemed to contact all of the ex-cons in the area sooner or later. That one job had been easy work: TJ had shaken down a john who had failed to pay one of Lester Finn's hookers. The payment for this minor service had eased TJ's financial concerns for several weeks.

TJ knew that Lester Finn was full of himself—he apparently fancied himself to be a big-time gangster. Pure bullshit. But Finn had indeed paid for the last job in cash. He had been good to his word so far. And if he was promising six-figures to kill Lee McCabe, then TJ was willing to assume that old Lester must have access to that kind of money. And if Lester turned out to be a liar, he would be a dead man, of course. The proprietor of the Boar's Head would not be stupid enough to promise what he could not deliver.

He grasped only the rudiments of Finn's beef with McCabe: Something about McCabe being a witness to some other act of violence: Probably those killings at the trailer park yesterday. The whole county was talking about those murders. Hell—even the Cincinnati and Lexington stations were talking about events in Hawkins County now. TJ did not give a damn about the Internet; but Tammy had told him that the killings had made the national online news sites—CNN, Fox, and MSNBC.com, no less.

So Lee McCabe would have to die because he was in the wrong place at the wrong time. Too bad for him—plenty of people had died for far less.

The crow, having devoured its first kill, resumed its hunt through the grass. TJ sighted the bird down the barrel of his pistol. He did not want to spend the rest of his life as a scavenger, subsisting on meager funds from payoff to payoff. He had a lot in common with that crow, now that he thought about it.

But not for much longer. He would have to act quickly in order to catch McCabe before he left the area. The young ex-marine was going to put a permanent end to his money problems.

29

I f one watched carefully from the street, it was possible to catch an occasional glimpse of one of the armed guards who loitered about the front porch and foyer of the house at 2130 Montpellier Avenue.

These guards did not wear the blue uniforms of a security company. Instead they wore dark blazers and dress slacks, silk shirts and expensive penny loafers. They leaned against walls, sometimes smoking, sometimes speaking in low, smirking whispers with toothpicks protruding from their mouths, with their hands in their pockets. They did not have the bearing of conventional security guards. They watched, but they watched furtively.

Nor did the men carry their guns openly in hip holsters. They kept their weapons tucked discreetly in clandestine holsters beneath their blazers. They would not identify themselves as guards when visitors arrived at 2130 Montpellier Avenue. And of course they wore no badges. There was no need for such trappings. Everyone knew their function. Everyone gave these men a wide berth.

This was one of the most exclusive neighborhoods in Chicago. Manicured ivy crept up the fieldstone facades of houses that regularly exchanged hands for seven figures, even in the currently depressed real estate market. Mexican and Salvadoran gardeners labored to maintain the early summer lawns in an immaculate state of weedless green. Unlike so many sections of the great city, this neighborhood had never decayed into ghettos and tenement housing. It had started out as a realm of money and influence when the foundations of its first mansions were laid in the mid-nineteenth century. And it remained so more than a hundred and fifty years later.

The house at 2130 Montpellier Avenue belonged to the Coscollino family. Everyone knew the nature of the Coscollino family's business —though spokespersons for the Coscollinos publicly insisted that it comprised nothing more than a passel of legitimate concerns: a trucking firm based in Cicero, a wholesaling business that had locations in various points throughout Chicagoland. The Coscollinos also owned a string of convenience stores, and an airport restaurant that sold hot lattes and fresh sandwiches to travelers at O'Hare. The family even owned a jewelry shop in Naperville, a suburban enclave located thirty miles west of Chicago, where few people gave much daily consideration to the criminal enterprises of the teeming, smoking, insular city on the shore of Lake Michigan.

The people of Chicago had lived with organized crime since the 1800s, when *La Mano Nera* had begun running extortion rackets in Italian-American neighborhoods. The Five Points gang had been operating gambling dens and prostitution rings in the city when the American frontier was still being settled, and there were still living men who were awakened at night by memories of the bloodshed that had occurred at Gettysburg and Shiloh. Organized crime was as much a part of the city as its streets and towering skyscrapers. The city's residents had long since learned when and how to look the other way.

No one would have been surprised to learn the full extent of the Coscollino family's other, less public enterprises. But few people would have dared to openly talk about them, either. More than one crusading journalist at the *Tribune* or the *Sun-Times* had dared to make accusations in print against the Coscollinos over the years.

These men had quickly learned the limits of the Freedom of the Press. Threats had been sufficient to silence all but one of these men. The one who had defied the Family's threats had suffered an unfortunate accident. His drowned body had been pulled from the lake days after he had apparently slipped and fallen from a pier. The journalist did not own a boat; and his widow told police that he had hated the water.

In one of the three living rooms of the Coscollino house, an elderly man sat alone before a 72-inch Toshiba flat-screen television. He was watching a reporter who was employed by a CNN affiliate in central Kentucky. The reporter was an attractive woman in her mid-twenties. She had long blond hair and a pronounced southern accent. She was interviewing a Perryston resident regarding local reactions to the murders at the Tradewinds trailer park. The interviewee was a much older woman. She responded to the reporter's inarticulate questions with even more inarticulate platitudes. *What was the world coming to, when people were gunned down like animals in the heartland of America?*

The onscreen image of the reporter and the random Kentucky woman was replaced by a brief still shot of the trailer where Tim Fitzsimmons and Jody White were killed. Alfonzo had learned their names by now.

He had also learned the name of Lee McCabe. His was the next image to flash across the surface of the Toshiba: a young marine in dress blues, solemnly standing at attention, an American flag in the background.

Alfonzo Coscollino was seventy-two years old. Though he bore the dark, Romanesque features of southern Italy, Alfonzo had been born in America. His Italian was poor, barely adequate for basic conversational purposes. It had been the language of his grandparents, after all; and Alfonzo was now a grandfather himself. He did not wear the expensive European fashions that characterized the mafia dons of the *Godfather* movies and their numerous imitators (though he had in his younger years.) Nowadays he dressed for comfort—not style. Most days he wore a warm-up suit. Two years after surgery for prostate cancer, his bladder still plagued him at times; and the warm-up suits facilitated his frequent trips to the bathroom.

Alfonzo had cut his teeth in the family business during the glory days of the organization, when the Sicilian clans controlled everything worth controlling, from influence pedaling in the longshoremen's unions, to the seedier venues of narcotics and prostitution. Now he ran the family business himself, the sole survivor of the last generation to come of age in a more dignified time, before the dons had become the fodder of tabloid magazines and made-for-TV movies. A time when even public officials still uttered the words, "There is no mafia" with a straight face.

Now the pundits were saying that the old Italian underworld was all but finished, defanged by savvy federal prosecutors armed with aggressive RICO statutes and modern, technologically driven law enforcement practices. They called the families anachronisms, and said that the Sicilians were bound to go the way of the dinosaurs. They were gutted, dying. On their last legs.

As usual, Alfonzo knew, the pundits were largely full of shit. Nevertheless, Alfonzo was savvy enough himself to realize that the federal government had been sporting a hard-on for *la Cosa Nostra* since the Kennedy Administration. Their cumulative efforts had not driven the families out of existence, but they had certainly driven them into a corner. Times had changed. The families had to be careful nowadays, just like the management teams of large corporations. No one swallowed the line that there was no mafia—and that had been the case for more than thirty years. When a judge seemed to be on the take, or a renegade union leader ended up floating in Lake Michigan, the mob was the first place people looked. Any misstep could bring unwanted attention, and ultimately ruin.

Which was why Alfonzo was so concerned about events in Hawkins County, Kentucky. He seethed as he reflected on the stupidity that had created this mess: Stupid to hit a small-time hood like that in broad daylight, in a way that was practically guaranteed to attract wide attention. Even stupider to leave a probable witness alive, a man who would eventually be nabbed by the police, who could then spin a tale that might eventually lead the authorities to the room in which Alfonzo now sat.

He balled his hand into a fist. The hand was liver-spotted and arthritic now, but it had once been a hand that had dealt vengeance to the Family's enemies. Twenty-three men and one woman had died by this hand.

He knew that something had to be done. If the feds ever established a link between the Coscollinos and the events in Kentucky, they would take his scent and pursue him like the merciless, baying hounds that they so often were. How the FBI and the Justice Department would love to see him sent to prison, doomed to live out his remaining years behind bars.

This thought filled him not only with anger, but also with dread. He had done a two-year stint in prison many years ago. But he had been much younger and much more resilient then. He had been looking forward instead of looking backward. If they sent him to prison now, he would never survive. He would take his own life first.

He should have known that something like this would eventually happen. He should never have entrusted the work in Kentucky to subordinates. The family had long known how to navigate its way through the big-city unions, the casinos, and the Chicago city council. The family had no experience in Hicksville. Yet the family had taken Hicksville lightly, based on the assumption that everything in Hicksville would be a pushover. And Hicksville might end up taking the entire family down.

What had his nephew Paulie said? *"We're talking about Kentucky, Uncle Alfonzo. They mate with goats down there. We'll run circles around them."*

He would have to deal with his nephew; and he would have to rethink the Family's strategy for handling Kentucky.

The family had been able to ignore places like Kentucky a mere twenty years ago. Even with the feds already nipping at the family's heels, there had been plenty of opportunities in Chicago and the northern Midwest. But competitors had arisen since the mid-1980s. First the Columbians and the Mexicans, then the Russians in more recent years. In one area after another, these upstarts were squeezing the family's traditional profit centers.

Take women, for example. The Coscollino family had once dominated the sex trade on the south side of the city. Then the Russians had come in, with a seemingly inexhaustible supply of doe-eyed farm girls from the former USSR. Alfonzo had heard that habitual south-side johns were now buying Russian-language phrasebooks along with their condoms.

So when the methamphetamine trade had exploded in the rural south, the family had taken notice. Here was an untapped market: Rural America had not been a target for serious contraband since the moonshine running days of the Prohibition.

Moreover, this was an area that the foreign gangs were unlikely to crack, due to linguistic and cultural barriers. A Russian or a Columbian would have a difficult time blending in and establishing networks in the states below the Mason-Dixon Line. But a third-generation Italian would be relatively inconspicuous.

And the Coscollino family's strategy had hinged on using locals for enforcement and distribution. That meant local dealers and local muscle. The Coscollinos' plan had been almost corporate in its calm methodology: Begin by establishing a monopoly: Frighten off the less competent local dealers who were already selling meth, hire the rare few who were found to be talented and pliable. Then fill the pipelines with cheap, mass-produced methamphetamine from Mexico. Sit back and watch the profits roll in.

That had been the plan for Hawkins County, until a stubborn small-time dealer named Tim Fitzsimmons had decided that he was too good to work for the Coscollino family. Alfonzo felt no remorse for the man's death—not a single iota. Fitzsimmons had been offered a buyout before threats were used. He had been given a choice between life and death. And he had opted for death.

But the Coscollino family's local operative, this Lester Finn, had botched the hit, and now all hell was poised to break loose.

Lester Finn's incompetence was obvious. Finn required constant supervision. He was an amateur, after all, a yokel who had been barely getting by before the Coscollinos had made him an offer—which Finn had so eagerly accepted.

Alfonzo was dismayed and puzzled, though, by the fatal negligence of his nephew Paulie. The Hawkins County operation had been Paulie's responsibility. He was supposed to be watching Lester Finn, making sure that the Kentuckian didn't pull something stupid.

But Paulie had not even known about the hit before Alfonzo had summoned him to this house. The young man had failed. He had been negligent in his duties.

Now Paulie would have to make things right, or he would suffer the consequences.

A don of the Coscollino family had never ordered the execution of his own flesh and blood; and this was not a prospect that Alfonzo relished. But if Paulie continued to demonstrate gross indifference to the family's concerns—*if his negligence actually brought down the family...*

Hopefully it would not come to that. He would give the young man a chance to clean up his mess. As bad as this looked, it could still be salvaged. More deaths might be required to assure the secrecy of the first deaths. Yes, more killing would be inevitable. This Lee McCabe, for one, would almost certainly have to die.

If the situation became too ugly, the family might need to resort to something like a scorched earth policy in Hawkins County. That would mean aborting the whole operation. So be it, if it came to that. There were other depressed counties in other Southern states. But the family's interests—let alone its survival—could not be compromised. No matter what.

Alfonzo reached inside his breast pocket and withdrew a pack of cigarettes and a lighter. He coughed violently on the first puff. He covered his mouth with one hand and felt relief when he examined the open palm: no blood. He had been hospitalized twice in the past year for emphysema. He kept a tank of oxygen beside his chair, though he usually did not need to resort to it this early in the day.

His doctor had warned him to stop smoking. *Prostate cancer is one thing,* the doctor had counseled him. *It has a ninety-five percent survival rate. Lung cancer is another. Only fifteen percent survive that. And for a man of your age and health...*

Alfonzo sighed. If it was not one thing, it was another. He seemed unable to rest. He would have to remain vigilant and preoccupied even in his final days. Alfonzo had been shot three times. He had endured the years in prison, and for most of his life, any number of people had wished him dead. Death he could face—but not an ignominious farewell in a federal prison cell. Nor would he endure the humiliating circus of a drawn-out public trial, with puffed-up journalists and officials exposing the Family's secrets in open court. There would be too many of them to silence with either threats or bribery.

He would tell Paulie to go to Kentucky, to look into the situation.

He would tell Paulie to take care of it.

30

Phelps looked up from his desk as he heard a soft rap against the metal frame of this office door. The door itself was open. Deputy Justin Hathaway stood in the doorway. He was not wearing his uniform. He looked like he was preparing for an afternoon at a shopping mall or a casual outing with friends: jeans and a red golf shirt. Phelps could not see the young deputy's shoes; but he knew that these, too, would be non-police issue. Probably Nikes or loafers.

The uneasy expression on Hathaway's face made Phelps feel equally uneasy. He had always questioned his newest and youngest deputy's dedication to the job. Hathaway was chewing on his lower lip, nervously shifting his bodyweight from one leg to the other.

Nevertheless, Phelps decided to play the situation straight.

"Hathway!" Phelps said. "There you are. We could have used you yesterday. Did you hear what happened?"

Hathaway nodded.

"Well, get your uniform on. From now until the foreseeable future, we need everyone on the job. That means no more sick days."

"That's what I wanted to talk to you about," Hathaway said.

"We'll talk about that later," Phelps replied. "Right now I need you in uniform."

Hathaway took a deep breath and said: "I'm afraid that won't be possible."

It was now clear that some version of Phelps's worst misgivings about Hathaway was about to materialize.

"What are you talking about?"

"Well," Hathaway said. "I've told you about my uncle before. The one who owns the chain of nightclubs in Florida."

Phelps nodded. He had indeed heard about Hathaway's entrepreneurial uncle who lived in Florida. From what Phelps had discerned, the "chain of nightclubs" was actually just a pair of rather seedy bars on the outskirts of Daytona Beach. Hathaway had always seemed very impressed with the uncle, though, as if he were some sort of mogul.

"You see," Hathaway went on, "my uncle has offered me a position at one of his nightclubs. I'll be assistant club manager and director of security. That's what my business card will say. My uncle even said."

Phelps sighed.

"You couldn't have picked a worse time, Justin."

"I realize that. I'm sorry."

"You couldn't wait until we get our hands around this? Most people give two weeks notice when they quit, you know."

"My uncle says he needs me right away," Hathaway said quickly. "And it will take me a good week to move down there."

Phelps suspected that the uncle's urgent need for Hathaway's assistance was mostly a fabrication. It was difficult for Phelps to imagine anyone having an urgent need for the young deputy—though the young man's presence would be sorely missed in the midst of the crisis in Hawkins County.

More likely, Phelps suspected, Hathaway had been made skittish by the carnage at the trailer park. He had been talking to the uncle about a job in Florida for a while, no doubt. The killings had compelled him to make his move sooner rather than later.

"Anyway, Justin, what the hell do you want to go to Florida for?"

"Kentucky gets damned cold in the winter," Hathaway said. "And there's nothin' goin' on here. Except—" he amended. "Except for those murders. And I think I can miss out on that."

With an attitude like that, Phelps thought, *I'm better off being short a man.* If Hathaway stayed, he might get himself killed. Or his negligence might lead to the death of another officer.

"Alright, Justin. Go ahead and clean out your locker. Before you leave, write a formal letter of resignation for the file, and give us the address where we should send your last paycheck."

31

Lee was aware that at least two sets of hands were probing his pockets and various points on his body. He had been asleep as the probing began, and the sensations of it merged with the fading traces of a dream.

Lee had been dreaming that he was back in Iraq. The enemy had taken him prisoner, and they were binding his hands before his execution. This was a recurring nightmare that he had experienced with regularity since his return from the Middle East. The details of the dream varied slightly, but the primary scenario was always the same: He was surrounded by a small group of hooded men. One on the men held a huge, curved, beheading sword. Another operated a digital camcorder.

The dream abruptly dissolved as Lee was flipped onto his stomach. He was aware of sunlight—and men's voices. They were not speaking the language of the enemy, but his own tongue.

"Look, Malcolm, he's got a gun!" And this voice came unmistakably from the waking world.

"Well, grab it!" Another voice said.

"Forget about the gun, get his wallet!"

Lee was righting himself as the .45 was removed from the back of his jeans. At almost exactly the same moment, he felt his wallet slide out of his rear pants pocket. He could feel a man's thick, bony fingers worm their way into the pocket and pluck out the billfold.

He was now on his haunches. He could see them. His attackers were both thin and shabbily dressed. He thought he might have recognized the man closest to him. He had reddish hair, and a long mustache. Perhaps two weeks worth of beard growth covered his jowls.

The man with the reddish hair was wielding a fragment of a two-by-four. It appeared to be partially rotted.

"Give 'im a whack, Malcolm!" his scrawny companion urged. Lee could see that this man was clutching Lee's wallet. The other one, named Malcolm, had jammed Lee's gun into his own front pants pocket.

Then he recalled the name of the red-haired man: Malcolm Taylor. Malcolm was about ten years older than Lee. He drifted from one minimum-wage job to another, and hung around the bars a lot. Lee believed that he had seen Malcolm once or twice at Tim Fitzsimmons's trailer. His face bore the pockmark sores of a meth user. This was also true of Malcolm's accomplice.

"Whack him one, Malcolm!" the accomplice repeated.

Lee wondered for a moment why two men who possessed a loaded .45 would bother to use a rotting two-by-four as a weapon. They both appeared to be intoxicated, so perhaps the use of the gun was beyond them. Perhaps they were merely too stoned to recognize their more lethal alternative.

The two-by-four descended toward Lee's head. Malcolm was not a very skilled attacker, and the piece of board missed Lee's head by a good six inches. This gave him time to stand up.

Malcolm raised the board to take another swing. Lee drove his fist into Malcolm's stomach. Malcolm dropped the board, grabbed his stomach, and teetered on his feet. Then he doubled over and vomited vilely onto the ground.

"Give me my wallet!" Lee shouted at the other man.

The other man looked at Lee dully, still holding the wallet in both hands. He opened his mouth to speak when Lee snatched the wallet away and shoved him backward.

He turned and ran.

Lee then remembered that Malcolm still had possession of the .45. Lee turned around and stared into the raised barrel of his own weapon. Malcolm leveled the weapon at him. His hands were shaking—either from fear, or from drugs, or both.

"Give me the gun," Lee said as steadily as he could.

"No, no you don't," Malcolm said. "I think I'll be takin' that wallet now. And I'll take this gun, too."

Lee dropped his wallet onto the ground and took a step toward Malcolm. Malcolm looked at the wallet on the ground, then back at Lee. Without further hesitation, Malcolm's finger tightened over the trigger. But there was no shot. He looked down at the gun, and, panic rising on his face, squeezed it anew.

"What the hell?" he shouted.

Lee backhanded Malcolm across the face and simultaneously wrenched the gun out of his hand. Malcolm swung a fist in a wild arc and Lee tackled him.

It was no contest. Lee expended little effort in taking Malcolm down and pinning him to the earth. He sat atop Malcolm's chest.

Malcolm struggled desperately; but Lee held him down without difficulty. Malcolm might have been reasonably strong at one time. Now, however, he was obviously in the advanced stages of meth addiction. His face was not only marked by sores; it also bore the bony appearance of malnutrition. Lee could feel Malcolm's ribs through his shirt.

Lee thought about revealing the mistake his attacker had made. But there was never anything to be gained by taunting a defeated opponent. Moreover, there was nothing to be gained by telling the addict about the pistol's safety button. Lee did not want to increase Malcolm's knowledge of guns. Malcolm was dangerous and reckless enough as he was.

Malcolm might possibly prove useful, though. He was high on meth, and he could not have obtained any from Tim Fitzsimmons in the past twenty-four hours. He therefore must have another source. And that source might be connected to the parties that had killed Tim Fitzsimmons, and were thereby responsible for Lee's current predicament.

It was a point from which to start. The only starting point Lee had.

"Where do you get your meth?" Lee asked the pinned man.

"No! I ain't telling you nothin'!" Malcolm cried out. He renewed his feeble struggle against Lee's grip. "I already done three months in stir. I ain't never goin' back there again. Please! It'll kill me, I tell ya."

"If you don't want to go back to jail, then tell me where you get your meth."

"Yeah, but then I'll be kilt!"

"No you won't. Because this here conversation is going to be our little secret."

Malcolm paused in his struggle.

"Yeah? How do I know I can trust you?"

Lee considered this. He could think of only one satisfactory answer. "You don't. You simply have to trust me because I have no reason to hurt you, and you have no other choice."

Malcolm seemed to realize that he was trapped. He let out a wail, and a waft of his rancid breath struck Lee squarely in the face. There were flecks of spittle on his lips.

"You really promise you won't tell?"

"Yeah. I already promised you. So tell me. Tell me now, dammit!"

Malcolm sighed wearily. He could see that he was trapped.

"Jimmy Mack," he said at length. The words came out in a wheeze.

"Jimmy Mack? You mean the guy who runs the gas station down on Dark Hollow Road?"

"That's him," Malcolm said. "Now please get offa me. I can't breathe with you on toppa me like that. Yer killin' me, I tell ya. Whatcha' doin' that fer?"

Lee shook his head and stood up—but not before he had picked up the .45 and placed it securely in his back pocket. The gun had fallen to the ground when Lee had tackled Malcolm. Perhaps the addict actually knew what a safety was, perhaps he did not. Lee did not intend to risk his life on this uncertainty a second time.

Malcolm dug his hands into the earth and pushed himself backward, away from Lee. He clambered to his feet. He looked at Lee and bit his upper lip.

"*Sonofabitch!*" he muttered. "And all I wanted was a little money to score a little crank. *Damn it!*"

Then, without giving Lee another glance, he bolted toward the nearest line of trees.

Lee watched him run. Then he bent down and retrieved his wallet. Somehow the junkie had been offended by Lee's resistance of an unprovoked assault, and his determination to hold on to all of his possessions.

He reflected on the fragment of knowledge that he now had, and how he might use it. This bit of intelligence seemed incredible, even after the incredible events of the past day: *Jimmy Mack a meth dealer?* Malcolm's claim surprised him; but at the same time it seemed an unlikely fabrication. If Malcolm had simply wanted to spout a random name, he would have picked someone from among the drug-and-party crowd that occupied the fringes of Hawkins County society.

Jimmy Mack struck Lee as a businessman, not a partier—and certainly not a drug dealer. He knew the name well. Lee had driven by Jimmy Mack's gas station on a number of occasions, though he could not recall having ever stopped there. Nor did he recall any meeting between Jimmy Mack and himself. The gas station owner and Lee had simply never crossed paths.

However, Lee planned to introduce himself to Jimmy Mack in the very near future.

32

Phelps watched Justin Hathaway—now a civilian—exit his office. A part of him envied the young man. This was a part of himself that he despised, although his self-reproach was tempered by two realizations: One, he knew that he would never—could never—abandon the citizens and taxpayers who had elected him. No, he could not leave them in the lurch with so much violence afoot. He also knew that his second thoughts about law enforcement were inevitable.

Phelps had gone to Iraq with a sense of fatalism. He was by no means seeking death; but he was seeking absolution for what he perceived as his own weakness. Lori Mills had already spurned him by then. Phelps had believed then that Lori's rejection had placed him in Iraq, though that was unfair. She had been an excuse for him to run away to what he hoped would be an adventure consisting of black-and-white lines. Pure good against pure evil. At the time, that had seemed preferable to facing the implications of Lori's recent announcement.

Phelps stopped himself from journeying any farther down that particular branch of memory lane. He did not want to untangle the events and ill-considered decisions that had caused him to drop out of college all those years ago and enlist in the Marine Corps. He knew well enough that his life could have been—should have been—much different. But that was the oldest story in the world, wasn't it?

There were more current matters that demanded his thought and attention.

He had barely made this decision when the phone on his desk rang. A call to his direct line. He lifted the receiver and it was Jim Ferris, asking him how the hell he was holding out.

Lieutenant Colonel Jim Ferris headed the Operations Division of the Kentucky State Police. Ferris reported directly to the state's Police Commissioner. If anyone in the state could secure more law enforcement resources for Hawkins County, it was Jim Ferris.

"Well," Phelps said in response to his question. "I've got two dead bodies and a suspect loose in the woods. One of my three deputies just resigned."

"Oh."

"I've seen better days. But I'm working on it."

"Well, you've done all you can with limited resources, Sheriff. You won't be working alone much longer, though."

"Good." These were welcome words, indeed. "I appreciate the assistance from the state helicopter yesterday. But what I really need is more manpower. Our only suspect is somewhere in Hawkins County. I sorely need a state police team here. We need to search every barn and every patch of woods in the area. We need to knock on every door."

Simply describing this task reminded him how herculean the challenge was—even in a sparsely populated place like Hawkins County. Phelps had arisen at four in the morning. He had spent several predawn hours driving the local roads and stopping by some of the obvious places where a fugitive might hide. Beginning at seven-thirty, he had knocked on some doors. But it was truly like looking for a needle in a haystack. No one seemed to have seen Lee McCabe.

Ferris said nothing in response, and Phelps wondered if he had said something wrong. Perhaps he had overstated the obvious. Of course a lieutenant colonel of the state police would understand the details of a manhunt. Ferris wouldn't need someone to draw him a picture, as Phelps had just done.

"Help is on the way Sheriff, but not from the state. At least not for a few days."

"I see," Phelps said noncommittally.

"I've taken the liberty of asking for federal law enforcement resources on your behalf," Ferris said. "Two agents from the FBI's Louisville field office will be in contact with you. Very soon."

The FBI. This was not the help that Phelps had been expecting. Nor did he believe it was the help he needed. He knew that a county-level sheriff could count on the state police—they shared the same concerns, spoke the same language. But the FBI was part of the Washington morass, and that often meant a different agenda.

"I had thought that this would escalate according to a certain pattern of progression," Phelps said. "I want to find out who killed two local citizens. I believe that will have a local answer. I don't want to spend valuable time trying to connect a local crime to whatever happens to be on the FBI's top ten list at the moment."

"What happens in Hawkins County is on the feds' top ten list now," Ferris said. "Have you been keeping up with the reports from around the region? There's been a string of homicides just like this—two-bit meth dealers gunned down for no apparent reason. Just last week a meth dealer fifty miles east of Cincinnati was found in the cab of his pickup truck with this throat cut ear-to-ear. Two more small-timers were gunned down in Nashville less than a month ago. One of them right in front of his family, I might add."

"And you think that what happened here is somehow connected? It's not like drug dealers never kill each other."

"The federal government believes that someone outside the region is trying to consolidate the meth market in the middle southern states. And that theory, quite frankly, makes a lot of sense. Why do you think that young man—an ex-marine of all things—gunned down two of his neighbors in cold blood? Neighbors who happened to be engaged in the manufacture and distribution of methamphetamine, by the way. Do you think that was a crime of passion?"

"I don't think we'll know for sure what happened until we apprehend Lee McCabe and question him."

"That's exactly what the FBI is going to help you with. For the record, Sheriff, I would like nothing better than to send a state police team down to Hawkins County this minute. But we're bleeding from budget cuts, and record crime rates in Lexington and Louisville. Every marginal character who *isn't* doing meth seems to be busy with other sorts of criminal activity at the moment. Car theft in both cities is up by more than thirty percent. I'll have some state personnel freed up later in the week."

"I understand," Phelps said. "And of course we'll appreciate whatever help the FBI can provide in the meantime."

"Hold that thought, Sheriff. If you take a moment to consider the situation, I think you'll find that FBI involvement will actually work to your advantage, both in terms of solving the crime as well as politically."

Politically? Phelps didn't see this is a political issue. There was nothing political about the carnage he had seen in that trailer.

"What are you getting at, Colonel?"

"I'm sure you know about the criticism you've been receiving from certain quarters," Ferris said. "An editorial in the *Louisville Sun* gave you some very sharp criticism. Sad to say that wasn't the only source of criticism, Sheriff. Our constituents and politicians consume a lot of cops-and-robbers movies, you know. There were a lot of folks out there who were expecting a little more of a chase."

Phelps felt his cheeks turn red. He had not read the editorial in the *Louisville Sun*—but he could imagine the recriminations. He had seen something similar in some of the faces at the trailer park.

"There was no practical way we could have apprehended the suspect at that moment in those woods," Phelps said. "There were only two of us, and we had a crime scene with two corpses to secure. When we first arrived, we didn't know if there were more gunmen in the vicinity. I had to decide how to allocate minimal resources in a very unusual situation, for Hawkins County."

"You have the support of everyone in this office," Ferris said. "We catch our share of flak from the papers and politicians too, by the way. It comes with the job. I'm simply saying, Sheriff, that it might not be a completely bad thing if the FBI ends up with primary jurisdiction here. Those murders might be the tip of the iceberg. If the feds are right, things may get a whole lot worse in your part of the world before they even think about getting better."

"And when will this federal help be arriving?" Phelps asked.

"As a matter of fact, I believe they are in transit to Perryston even as we speak."

33

The call from Jim Ferris complete, Phelps gathered the materials that he would need to show the FBI. He looked at the pictures from the crime scene: Whoever had fired the shots in that trailer was remorseless. Objectively speaking, such a person deserved to die.

But how convenient for him to draw such a conclusion, given the identity of the prime suspect.

A judge can recuse himself from a case, Phelps thought. *Why can a sheriff not do the same?*

Who was guilty, and who was innocent? When the moment came to give Lee the benefit of a doubt or take him down with a bullet, which course would he take?

And since the young man seemed hell-bent on resisting arrest—intent on running—Phelps realized that this stark choice was a distinct possibility.

Why had McCabe returned to Perryston after his discharge from the Marines? The young man no longer had any family here, and there was little economic opportunity in Perryston. McCabe should have gone to Lexington or Louisville or Cincinnati, where he could start anew.

He realized that a part of him wanted Lee McCabe to be guilty of the double homicide. And this was an internal voice that was difficult to resist. If Lee was guilty, after all, then his own past mistakes would be partially vindicated. If Lee McCabe was in fact a murderer, then his own behavior at the traffic stop some years ago would seem petty by comparison.

Phelps had never apologized to Lee McCabe for what he had done; and Lee McCabe had become a reminder of his own weaknesses. He had already been that for years before the incident at the traffic stop: Lee stared back at Phelps through eyes that were both Lori's eyes and Tom McCabe's eyes. Tom McCabe had never been worthy of a girl like Lori Mills—and look how her life had turned out after she had taken up with him.

These were petty thoughts. *Cruel* thoughts. But they were thoughts that he could not resist.

That night had been a particularly bad one for him, when his solitary condition had struck him as especially lonely and pathetic. He had gone for dinner at the Wrangler Steakhouse in Perryston. Every table in the restaurant seemed to be filled with happy families —devoted wives and smiling, cherubic children. Contented, well-obeyed fathers, many of whom were more or less his own age.

He had realized that this was only half of the truth, of course. Those families had problems of their own. No one was living in a paradise on earth, despite the outward appearances that they often struggled desperately to maintain. Nevertheless, the fathers of those families had looked a lot happier than he was—eating a steak-and-fries dinner by himself before finishing his duty shift and going home to an empty bachelor residence.

As he left the restaurant, he had thought: That could have been Lori and me. *We would have had children of our own by now—if only she had not taken up with Tom McCabe.*

It was in this frame of mind that Phelps happened to see the late eighties-model Pontiac Trans Am with one burned-out taillight. The car was making a right turn onto State Street from Martin Luther King Avenue. The single taillight burned red and blurry in the mist of an early March drizzle. The driver might have been going a tad too fast for the center of town; but nothing that couldn't be addressed with a verbal warning. Phelps turned on his overhead blinkers with the intention of giving the driver a friendly small-town-cop admonishment to maintain his vehicle and watch his speed while in town. He hadn't known at the time that Lee McCabe was the driver.

The Trans Am pulled obediently to the curb after Phelps pulled up beside it. He didn't recognize McCabe behind the wheel until he walked up to ask for the driver's license and registration.

There was a moment—when Phelps saw McCabe and the young man saw him—when the encounter might have gone either way. Phelps might have ended it exactly as he had planned, despite his discomfort at encountering Tom McCabe's son. He might have let the matter go, and remembered that sons are not responsible for the sins and trespasses of their fathers.

But then Phelps saw—or thought he saw—an expression of sullen defiance on the face of Lee McCabe. Lee's father had stolen the love of his life—did the son have to do his part to add insult to injury, sneering from behind the wheel of his beat-up car?

Phelps had never talked much to Lee McCabe. But the young man would have known the general outline of the history—parents often talked about those things among themselves, and McCabe would have overheard.

Was he inwardly laughing, as he gripped the steering wheel of the Trans Am—this young man who was half Lori Mills and half Tom McCabe? Was he reveling in the fact that while the sheriff might have a gun and a badge and the authority to stop drivers in town—he had lost the girl he loved to another man?

And that was when Phelps had snapped. "Step out of the car," he had said, doing his best to sound like a dispassionate public official.

"What?" Lee McCabe had asked. "I wasn't even speeding."

"You were weaving," Phelps had shot back, loathing himself for venting his rage against a seventeen- or eighteen-year-old boy. But unable to hold back the bitter tide. "Now please step out of the vehicle."

Then more angry words had followed, including Phelps's thinly veiled reference to Lee's profligate father. Phelps had made McCabe run through the standard street-level intoxication tests that are well known by every patrol officer, and every inebriated driver. McCabe dutifully walked a straight line on the sidewalk, touched the tip of his nose while standing on one foot, counted backwards from one hundred to ninety. He passed with flying colors, of course, as both of them had known that he would.

34

The two FBI agents seated across the table from Phelps had introduced themselves as Special Agent Amanda Porter and Special Agent Jack Lomax. They had arrived in Perryston less than thirty minutes ago, shortly after Phelps's disquieting phone call with Jim Ferris. Phelps had hastily ushered them into one of the cramped conference rooms in the sheriff's department building.

Lomax was fortyish and balding. Phelps knew that the Bureau hired a lot of accountants; and Phelps would have bet his last paycheck from the county that Lomax was an accountant. Porter was of indeterminate age but considerably younger than Lomax. She moved and spoke with a feline deliberateness that pegged her as an athlete and a classic overachiever. She could probably have taken any man in the room in a game of raquetball.

Deputy Ron Norris occupied the chair beside Phelps. Since Norris was assigned as the lead deputy on the Tradewinds case, Phelps had pulled him into the meeting too. And now Norris was fidgeting, shifting around in his chair and tapping his fingers on the tabletop. The deputy seemed agitated by the presence of the two FBI agents. This was understandable to some degree; but the situation was tense enough as it was. Phelps sincerely wished that Norris would calm down.

The table space between the local cops and the federal cops contained a variety of materials related to the shootings—including crime scene photos of the bodies of Tim Fitzsimmons and Jody White.

Phelps fought the urge to think of the crimes in personal terms. *Remember that Chinese wall*, he thought. *This isn't about you—and it isn't about Lori.* But the images of those bodies, and their brutal manner of death galvanized him. Was Lori's son in fact responsible for those corpses? *Is this what Lori ultimately brought into the world when she dumped me and started sleeping with Tom McCabe?*

These were thoughts that stubbornly refused to go away.

"Well," Lomax began. "We've ascertained the timeline thus far and examined the crime scene data that we have. It's still early. We don't have ballistics data or autopsy reports yet. Those'll take a day or two more, I'd guess. Now let's talk more about this Lee McCabe." He opened a manila folder that he had brought with him and removed a paper that contained information about Lee McCabe. "He was recently discharged from the Marines, correct?"

And here, Phelps knew, was his opportunity to be certain that fairness ruled the day, to counterbalance his internal biases against McCabe.

"Lee McCabe is more than just a former marine," Phelps said. "He was awarded a distinguished service medal—not to mention a purple heart—for courage under fire during a particularly bad firefight near Fallujah. He charged a house that contained three al-Qaeda fighters. They had pinned down another marine who was wounded and it was only a matter of time before they would have killed him. Lee saved his fellow marine, and took some shrapnel wounds in the process."

Lomax paused to scan his paper. "That's what my report says." He gave Phelps a tight, almost grudging smile. "Admirable. But his more recent actions sort of tarnish the hero image, don't they?"

"It looks bad for McCabe," Phelps acknowledged. "But I want to at least question him before I convict him in my own mind. Deputy

Norris and I interviewed numerous witnesses at that trailer park. We have established McCabe's presence at the murder scene beyond a reasonable doubt. But no one saw him shoot anyone. I also want to wait on the ballistics results. Two civilian witnesses who have a good knowledge of firearms observed that Lee McCabe was carrying a .45. The state database indicates that he purchased a weapon of that caliber at a nearby pawnshop shortly after his discharge from the Marine Corps. If the ballistics report indicates another caliber of weapon, then we'll need to take that into account."

"No one's convicting anyone here," Lomax said. "We're simply trying to tally up what we know so far. And right now all the evidence that we have points to McCabe."

"The circumstantial evidence is against him," Phelps allowed. "But there is still a lot we don't know. I want to move forward with an open mind."

"I'll keep an open mind here, Sheriff," Lomax said. "I'm going to ask you to do the same. "

"Fair enough," Phelps said. "But I have a hard time imagining Lee McCabe doing something like this. There has to be more to this— something we don't know yet."

"We agree," Special Agent Porter said. "Maybe you don't know this: There is a very real possibility that these shootings were orchestrated by outside forces. The same forces that are orchestrating similar crimes in nearby states."

"I suppose that's why the two of you are here," Phelps said. "I spoke with Ferris at the state office. He told me about the possible organized crime link."

Special Agent Porter nodded. She lifted a Styrofoam cup full of steaming coffee to her mouth and took a sip. "Exactly. The meth trade in rural America is expanding every day. There's already too much money there for the big syndicates to ignore. And when organized crime moves into the hinterlands, they typically don't send in an army of outsiders. They recruit locals: local distributors, local dealers, and local enforcers."

Phelps caught the implied slight in Porter's use of the term "hinterlands" to describe Hawkins County, but he let it slide.

"Let me get this straight," he said. "You believe that Lee McCabe may have been acting in concert with—*at the behest of*—outside organized criminal elements?"

"We're saying that it's a distinct possibility," she said.

"Look at it this way," Lomax said. "Lee McCabe is a recently discharged veteran of a war that has turned unpopular. Like a lot of young Americans, he probably joined up with the best of intentions. He wanted to punish the men who had masterminded 9/11. All fine and good. But he ends up in Iraq instead, and that whole thing goes south. Then when he returns, the economy is shot to hell. There are no good jobs, even for veterans. He's disillusioned, and why shouldn't he be? But the U.S. military did give him one unique commodity: combat skills. Then someone comes along and offers him a lot of money to apply those skills as a freelancer. Can you see how that could happen?"

Phelps leaned back in his chair and rubbed his chin. "I can't believe it. I could maybe accept that Lee McCabe had some sort of a conflict with Tim Fitzsimmons and it escalated to murder. I could even accept that Lee was somehow involved in the drug trade. But I don't see him as a cold-blooded contract killer." *Or perhaps you simply don't want to see Lori's son as a cold-blooded contract killer*, he thought to himself. *Or on the other hand, perhaps you do—when you remember who Lee's father was.*

Agent Porter interjected: "We can't dismiss the possibility that Lee McCabe was somehow connected: He would definitely have the skills needed to be a contract killer."

"That much is true," Phelps said. "The question is: was McCabe inclined to market those skills to that end? Based on what I know of him, I find that scenario a bit difficult to accept."

"You may find it difficult to accept, Sheriff," Porter said pointedly. "But it may very well be true, nonetheless. You implied that you've already been briefed about the other killings of small-time meth dealers in Lexington, Louisville, and Cincinnati."

Phelps was about to respond when Norris burst out: "*Yes!*"

Phelps slid around in his chair to see Norris staring at him with reddened cheeks. A vein on the deputy's forehead was bulging.

"What's wrong, Norris?"

With a visible effort, Norris steadied himself and spoke.

"Sheriff, I respect the fact Lee McCabe has served his country. I'd like to believe that Lee McCabe is what we thought he was: a local hero. *Wouldn't we all like to believe that?* But we can't ignore the facts before us."

Phelps took a quick assessment of the room: He might be the sheriff of Hawkins County; but his own deputy was now openly disagreeing with him. And the FBI *definitely* disagreed with him.

Maybe these other law enforcement officers were right: Were his own emotions clouding his judgment? Was his present insistence on keeping an "open mind" nothing more than a self-deceiving attempt to avoid a greater moral hazard—the risk that he would pronounce Lee guilty because that one malignant part of him *wanted* Lee to be guilty? Was he really being fair, or simply using this as a means to regain his self-respect as a lawman—the self-respect that he had lost when he misused his power in order to humiliate Lee at that traffic stop?

"We won't ignore the facts we have," Phelps said. "And we're going to gather more facts while we're at it."

He addressed Special Agents Porter and Lomax. "Norris and I are going to conduct a second round of witness interviews at the Tradewinds. We should have ballistics and other forensics data soon. Lee McCabe—whatever his level of involvement turns out to be—is the target of a statewide manhunt."

Phelps gestured to the crime scene photos. "We're working this thing from every possible angle, and we're going to keep working it until we apprehend whoever shot those two people."

35

Dawn Hardin leaned against a wrought iron gate that enclosed—of all things—a cemetery. It was an old graveyard that had been constructed when this part of Louisville was still mostly farmland, rather than the run-down industrial outskirts that it now was.

The metal felt cool against her bare shoulder. She happened to glance down and noted the garbage strewn along the edge of the curb: cigarette butts, an empty bottle of Mogen David—better known as Mad Dog 20/20—and a wadded up newspaper. At least there were no used condoms. Those could sometimes be seen in the back alleyways and gravel parking lots of this area.

She smiled weakly as a car driven by a lone middle-aged man passed by. She did not thrust out a leg or make any obvious gestures, as some of the working girls did. That was too much of a provocation for the police, especially in the middle of the afternoon, when there was still a fair amount of run-of-the-mill citizen traffic. Since she had arrived here a number of months ago, she had not been bothered by the police; but she was more careful than most of her colleagues. The remnants of her past life—the intelligence that she had once been so proud of—remained with her.

When she was alone, she sometimes allowed herself the satisfaction of affirming that she was not like the other women and girls out here. None of them could boast a nearly perfect score on the SAT. None of them had ever been awarded scholarships.

But this realization only made matters worse. Her past meant that she had fewer alibis. When the great craving came at its regular hourly intervals, her pride and her intelligence both counted for naught. In those moments she was just another streetwalker, just another junkie who would do practically anything to score another hit of crank.

A crow cawed from somewhere back in the cemetery. Dawn felt vaguely guilty for doing business so close to the dead. But then again, she supposed that the dead would not really mind so much. And anyway, *their* problems were over. Dawn had passed her twenty-second birthday only last week. There had been no cake and no candles; but one of her regulars had given her an extra wad of bills that was fastened with a paperclip. Within twenty-four hours the bills had all gone to meth; and Dawn had hated herself anew, swearing that she would put an end to her current path, even if it meant joining the denizens of the graveyard behind her.

Now a pine green Ford Taurus was approaching and she knew that this was a likely prospect. She could tell by the way the driver was alternately glancing at her and then glancing from side to side, making sure that no city police cars were in the vicinity. Dawn knew that the police were not that dumb—when they set up a surveillance sting they usually took some effort to hide their presence. But of course an apparent first-timer like this guy would not know that.

He flicked on his turn signal as he slowed down. Dawn could not see his face clearly yet because of the sunlight glare on the windshield, but she could see that he was a man in his late thirties or early forties. Most of them fell into that age range—men who were still young enough to have appetites, but often not young enough to satisfy those appetites through more socially acceptable channels. Many of them were married, too. These men often felt compelled to tell Dawn about their marital problems, as if she were a therapist of some sort.

As the Taurus came to a stop along the curb, Dawn approached. She wanted to get this over with, and then take the money to buy another hit of the white lady. She was already craving the pipe, craving the feel of the dopamine rush that would accompany it.

Nevertheless, she forced herself to slow down and make the proper observations, listen to the proper hunches. A street woman who didn't do that might end up dead pretty quickly.

He rolled down the automatic window and she leaned one hand on the sill. He did not look like an axe murderer or a serial killer. He looked like a middle-aged office worker who was using an early lunch hour to quench unsatisfied urges. His nervousness was palpable. In the early days, the nervous ones had bothered Dawn: She had often found herself caught in an anxious feedback loop; and she had ended up backing away from some tricks that were actually quite harmless but self-conscious men. Since then, she had learned the patter of the street ladies, learned how to calm down the Nervous Neds. This typically involved making an appeal to their male egos.

"Looks like someone is in the mood for little fun this morning," she said.

She watched the guy take a good look at her and something in his face shifted. She knew that expression: It was a form of buyer's remorse, or pre-buyer's remorse. She knew what the crank was doing to her physical appearance; but there was no way around that. She could only hustle harder and lower her prices.

Then he spoke: "You're skinny. You sure you're okay?"

"Do I look okay?"

He shrugged. "You haven't got AIDS, do you?"

"No," Dawn said. This was the truth as far as she knew. "I haven't got AIDS. Listen, do you want to go through with this or not? Because if you don't, I'll step away and you can just go about your business."

She felt a wave of the old pride returning, the person she was before the crank had entered her life. It was galling: There was a time, not so long ago, when men of all ages used to stare at her as she walked by. Back then, this man would have tripped all over himself just saying hello to her. And now she faced the daily humiliation of trying to convince johns like this that she was worth a few paltry twenties from their wallets.

But the pride and the recollections were quickly overwhelmed by more immediate urges. The presence of the urges made her humble. She realized that this man wasn't to blame for her physical deterioration. And this venue—the one she had placed herself in—had its own code of conduct. She was a streetwalker and he was a john. He was critically appraising her as she was critically appraising him. Her anger at the trick passed. She had a lot in common with this man in the Ford Taurus, pathetic and nervous though he might be. They were both driven by hungers that they could not control. And she wondered: *Did he hate his desires as much as she hated hers?*

"I want to go through with it," he finally said. "How much?"

Dawn felt a sudden rush of anxiety and the beginnings of a sharp headache. It wasn't the trick that was getting to her—but the craving. She needed to get this done and over with.

"Sixty," she said.

For a moment the man behind the wheel of the Taurus looked like he might try to bargain. But then he nodded.

"Okay. I have a room nearby," she said. "Meet me around the corner in ten minutes. First turn on your right. Plum Avenue. The motel is called the Riverside Suites. I'll be in room one-sixteen."

Before he could object Dawn stepped away from the car. Many of the johns were wary about following her to the room. She partially understood their misgivings: This was a classic ploy used by hookers who robbed their customers. Once a john was inside a motel room in the wrong neighborhood, he was vulnerable. It would be easy to rob him if a woman had a bit of help. She had heard of girls who worked in cahoots with male accomplices to perpetrate this sort of crime. But she didn't know any girls who admitted to doing this; and she certainly had no intention of doing it herself.

In her peripheral field of vision she could see the Ford Taurus pull away from the curb. It drove past her up the street, then made the turn onto Plum Avenue. The man was going along with her instructions.

She took a shortcut to the motel, through an alley that was largely filled with the discarded crates and cardboard boxes of a wholesaling business, and one abandoned car. A pile of loose bricks, partially covered with weeds and moss, rose in one corner of the alley like someone's bad attempt at a pyramid.

This route took her into the motel's side parking lot. She didn't see the green Taurus yet; but she couldn't see the entire parking area from this vantage point.

The Riverside Suites fulfilled all the clichés of a seedy motel: It was a long, boxlike two-story sandstone structure that had been built in the Eisenhower era, when this section of town had been newer and more prosperous. Paint peeled from the externally facing doors of the rooms. The metal railing on the second-story balcony, which ran the length of the building, was all but denuded of paint, and flecked with rust in many places. On the scrubby front lawn of the Riverside Suites there was a fountain in the form of a cherub; but no water had flowed from the cherub's stone water pitcher for many seasons. The innocent nature of the old statue mocked the current function of the place.

Almost no one used the Riverside Suites as a conventional motel anymore. Everyone here was on the lam, on drugs, or turning tricks. Once in a while Dawn noticed what appeared to be an adulterous couple ducking into one of the rooms; but the Riverside Suites was a less than ideal place for an afternoon extramarital tryst.

The selling point of the Riverside Suites was its pricing: Dawn rented a room here at a weekly rate that was a fraction of what she might have paid even at one of the extended stay chains. She changed her room number every week. This was a safety measure: Sometimes prostitutes rolled johns; but sometimes it was the johns who returned to rob, rape, or strangle the ladies who serviced them.

She opened the door to room 116, sighing aloud when the lock stuck on the first try. The room was cramped and threadbare; its only redeeming feature was a seascape painting that Dawn liked. She had never been to the ocean.

Inside, she turned on a single overhead light and sat on the bed, waiting for her customer. A few minutes later there was a tentative knock at the front door. She stood, and after verifying his identity in the peephole, welcomed him into room 116.

"Hey," he said. He brushed past her, looking nervously around the room as he entered.

"What's your name?" Dawn asked.

"You don't need to know my name."

"Well, what do you want me to call you?"

He was silent for a few seconds before he answered. For a moment Dawn thought the man was going to say "Dick" or "John," either of which would have been a crude pun.

"Call me Robert," he said finally.

"Okay, Robert it is. And you can call me—"

"I didn't ask your name."

Dawn shrugged, suddenly more eager than usual to get this trick over with. There was of course nothing to be gained by antagonizing Robert. If Robert didn't want to call her by any name, then he could simply make due with the second person pronoun.

"What do you want, Robert?"

"Just lie down on the bed," he said, loosening his tie. "Take off your clothes first," he added.

Dawn did as Robert instructed. She pulled off the sleeveless tee shirt she was wearing and dropped it on the floor. Then she stepped out of her denim skirt and panties.

Robert looked at her and said: "Damn, you're skinny." His present tone suggested that this might be either a compliment or a complaint. Robert didn't elaborate, and she didn't ask.

She lay down on the bed, feeling the coarse material of the bedspread on her bare skin. The mattress beneath it was hard and lumpy. The room's air conditioning—an old wall unit with a noisy fan—kicked on. The sudden rush of cold air chilled her. She felt goose bumps.

By this time Robert had managed to shed almost all of his attire. Dawn watched him nearly trip as he untangled his pants from his shoes. Why hadn't Robert removed his shoes first? Well, Robert was nervous about this—that much was as plain as day.

"Do you have a condom?" Dawn asked.

"Right here," Robert said, tearing open the little vacuum-sealed foil package.

Robert was no more eager to engage in foreplay than he was to know her name. He slid the condom over his now erect penis and unceremoniously crawled on top of her. There was absolutely nothing erotic about it, Dawn thought. Robert might have been demonstrating a wrestling move.

She felt his belly grind against her, smelled the onions of the sandwich that had been his lunch. Robert's skin was slick and moist against hers. There was a locker room smell about him—the chemical scent of Speed Stick deodorant mixed with the more pungent funk of sweat, agitation, and masculine desire.

But finally his grinding and his movements stopped. He lifted himself with both arms and pushed himself away, backing off of her. He stood at the foot of the bed. The condom hung like an absurd balloon on his abruptly flaccid appendage.

"What's the matter?" she asked.

"I can't go through with this," Robert said.

"You're married, aren't you?" Dawn asked softly. "You feel guilty."

"No, to tell you the truth, I've been divorced for five years; and my ex-wife hauls me into court to bust my balls every chance she gets. I'm not ever going to feel guilty over *that* woman."

"What is it then?"

"It's you."

Dawn did not ask for any elaboration; but Robert seemed more than willing to provide it.

"There's no easy way to say this, darling. But well, you need to take better care of yourself. Frankly speaking, you're a bit on the rough side."

Dawn turned her face away from Robert, looked at the wall.

"I shouldn't be messing with you street whores," Robert said. "Sorry," he said, when she turned back to him. "And you can keep the money. You followed through on your end. Fair is fair."

"Thanks."

"You know, I used to be quite a ladies' man in my day," Robert informed her, as if this tidbit might possibly be of any interest.

Dawn laughed humorlessly. "And I used to be a straight-A student. I was studying to be a doctor."

Robert merely shook his head. It was obvious that he did not believe her, although it was true. She *had* been a straight-A student, premed, no less.

36

The door clicked shut behind Robert, and Dawn went into the motel room's tiny bathroom. She turned on the tap and splashed cold water onto her face, noting her sunken cheeks, and the dark circles beneath her eyes. Robert's words still stung her: he might only be a middle-aged trick; but scorn was still scorn. Perhaps the sting was even greater *because* he was only a middle-aged trick.

She could not blame Robert for doubting her parting claim. The gaunt apparition staring back at her did not look like a straight-A student, and certainly not a straight-A student who was on the path to becoming a doctor. In fact, she very much looked like someone who *needed* a doctor: Her face and arms were marked by the little scabs that meth addicts give themselves in their opiate fits, as they endlessly scratch the nonexistent insects that that they believe to be crawling on their skin. Dawn forced a smile before the mirror and her heart sank: her gums were beginning to rot and recede—another tell-tale sign of the crank junkie.

Her past life as a premed student seemed like ancient history now—like someone else's life, even though it was not long behind her.

A few short years ago that world of promise had indeed been

opened up to her. She had been third in her class at South Hawkins County Consolidated High School. (She had narrowly missed being salutatorian, a fact that had enormously frustrated her at the time.) But third in your graduating class wasn't bad—even if you graduated from a rural district like South Hawkins County. Number three had been good enough for a generous partial scholarship to the University of Louisville. It was heady stuff. There had never been a doctor in her family—not even a college graduate.

She had decided on the premed track because it seemed to be the logical course, given her pattern achievement up to that point. It was a mountain worth climbing. She could make something of herself and maybe give something back to the world at the same time. What more could you ask for?

Of course, the premed grind entailed lots of study. At South Hawkins County, Dawn had stood out as one of the very brightest kids. In her classes at the U of L she was perhaps in the middle of the pack. Everyone in this race was a brain; and they all studied as if every exam was a matter of life-and-death.

And so Dawn had thrown herself into study as well. She arose at 3 a.m. to pore over biochemistry texts with a highlighter. She fell asleep with calculus books in her lap.

She also worked two part-time jobs, to cover the expenses that were not covered by her scholarship. She made sandwiches at a Subway restaurant near campus two evenings per week, and the remaining three weeknights she re-shelved books in the university's main library.

When money was tight, she worked extra shifts at one or both of these jobs on the weekends. Between her classes, her homework, and her part-time jobs, she seldom had a spare moment—and she *never* had enough sleep. Dawn would later realize that her chronic exhaustion had been her exploitable weak point—the Achilles' heel that convinces every junkie to try smack or crank or coke for the very first time.

Late one night she had been studying for an organic chemistry test in the dorm lobby. This had enabled her to avoid the constant noise of her roommate's cell phone and television. The first floor of the dorm had been arranged into a study area: there were several clusters of comfortable couches and beanbag chairs. This area was generally deserted after about ten p.m., and therefore, quiet.

Dawn had needed quiet that night. Organic chemistry was the bane of every premed's existence. It was analytically difficult like a math course, and it required more memorization than any humanities class. Organic chemistry was also a premed weed-out course: It was the class that convinced many aspiring physicians to settle for a career in insurance sales or corporate middle management instead.

Dawn was determined that organic chemistry was not going to beat her. But she would need to stay awake long enough to study for her exam.

She was highlighting a chapter on benzene ring reactions when the young man approached her. He had been hanging out in the first-floor common area of the dorm as if he belonged there; but he did not have the air of a student. Something about his smarminess suggested that he *didn't* belong there. This had not particularly alarmed Dawn at the time. She had been focused on organic chemistry.

The young man sat down in the couch opposite her. "Sleepy?" he asked, in a tone that was openly presumptuous. She assumed that he was hitting on her. She was not interested—but she decided to play along. She was too tired to play the ice queen—a role that had never really suited her, anyway.

"Yeah," she said. "But I've already had three cups of coffee. One more cup and I'm going to have to study in the ladies room." She vaguely hoped that this oblique reference to urination would send him packing. Many men did not like to be reminded of the bodily functions of women, as if they really believed all that bull about little girls being made from sugar and spice and everything nice.

But this one was more interested in a discussion about the relative merits of various stimulants. "Coffee just doesn't cut it," he said.

"Do you have a better idea?" Dawn asked, thinking that his next suggestion would be over-the-counter caffeine tablets. She had already tried these, and they upset her stomach.

"As a matter of fact, I do," he replied. After glancing about to make sure that no one was observing them, the young man partially removed a baggy that was concealed in the pocket of his jacket. The baggy contained a whitish, powder-like substance.

"What the hell is that, cocaine?" Dawn asked.

The young man sniggered. "Cocaine is so nineteen eighties. This is better and cheaper. And it will keep you awake. Awake all night."

Dawn now realized that the young man who was posing as a flirt was actually a drug dealer. He was trying to sell her drugs.

"Give it a try, why don't you," he said. "This first one's on me."

"Get the hell away from me," Dawn said. She waved him away with a brusque hand gesture.

The young drug dealer shrugged. "Have it your way." He stood up.

Dawn returned her attention to her textbook, trembling slightly over the fact that she had just been approached by a drug dealer—a first for her.

There was only one problem: she couldn't get her cognitive gears to work. She was simply too tired. The details of the open pages before her—the Lewis structures of various carbon-based molecules —swam before her eyes.

Would it really hurt to take something special to stay awake just this once? She knew that some of her classmates were popping pills that were marginally legal, at best. In the game that she was struggling to play, you needed every competitive edge that you could get, even if you had to bend the rules once in a while.

"Wait a minute," she said. She did not even have to look for him. The young man had been hovering near her, as if he knew that her capitulation was inevitable. "You say that this stuff will keep me awake?"

"I guarantee it," he said, with a wide, ingratiating grin.

"And you say that you're willing to give me a—free sample this time?"

"Didn't I already tell you that?"

Dawn pulled an all-nighter; and she wasn't even drowsy when it was time for her test at 9:00 a.m. the following morning. She didn't score an A on the test, as she had hoped for; but the B that she did score was sufficient to maintain her G.P.A.

She wasn't happy about the compromise she had made. She wasn't the sort of person who took drugs. Nevertheless, there was no denying a simple fact: The B would not have been possible without the methamphetamine. She hadn't taken the drug recreationally; she had taken it for a specific, performance-related purpose. That was *different*, wasn't it?

Besides keeping her awake, the white powder had given her an edge of confidence as she entered the exam room. She experienced none of her usual jitters. The meth had made her feel euphoric and powerful.

In the premed track, most of the students came from moneyed backgrounds. They had had lifelong advantages: access to expensive tutors and private schools. Some of their parents were even doctors themselves. If a simple white powder could give her an advantage, why shouldn't she take it? Some people might view it as cheating. But what about all the advantages that those wealthier undergrads had? How in the world were *those* things fair?

She knew about the dangers, of course; but she also believed that she could handle them. She wasn't the sort of person who became a junkie. She was simply an overworked premed student who needed an extra boost.

For a while, her compact with the white powder had functioned, but that equilibrium did not last a single semester. The craving for the drug grew into a rampaging monster, a relentless demon that blotted out all other considerations. First her grades began to slip. Then she found that all of her money was going into meth. (She hadn't had to seek out the drug dealer when it came time to purchase her first hit following the initial free sample: the young man had made it his business to find *her*.)

Then she found herself unable to focus on anything except the meth. Thinking back on it now, her downward spiral had been surprisingly fast.

Her descent into addiction had produced some new memories, some of which were even more unpleasant than servicing men like Robert. She thought of her parents, and how proud they had been when she set out for the university, ready to conquer the world. They weren't proud of her anymore. And her father now wanted to deny that she even existed.

That particular memory was still an open wound. She might be dead soon. As difficult as it might be, she would have to go back to Hawkins County, and the little house in Blood Flats where her parents and younger sister still lived.

The thought of Blood Flats stirred the realization that Lester Finn would be there. He waited for her like a drawn blade. She had not heard from Lester for a while; but if she returned to Blood Flats, he would either find her or their paths would somehow cross. Then Lester would find a way to use and torment her—maybe even break her for good.

Perhaps that did not matter now. She took a final look at the skull-like angles of her face and was struck by the same premonition that had been haunting her for weeks now: She might not have much time left to find her redemption.

37

Jimmy Mack's garage was located at a sharp, downwardly sloping bend on Dark Hollow Road. The gray cinderblock building was surrounded by debris: a pile of old tires, another pile of pallets. A rusted dumpster overflowed with the discarded guts of machinery and miscellaneous garbage.

Lee walked along the southbound lane of Dark Hollow Road. As the gas station drew closer, he jumped the ditch and walked through the high grass. From this position, he would not be visible from the windows of the gas station's front area, where Jimmy Mack doubtless spent most of his time. He planned to enter through the front door; but he would still rely on the element of surprise. He did not want to give Jimmy Mack time to form any conclusions. The .45 was tucked in the back of his jeans.

As Lee crossed the property line of the gas station, he discreetly maneuvered himself behind the dumpster. An ancient tow truck sat in the parking lot. It was half-covered with dust, and one of the tires appeared to be flat. Lee walked behind the tow truck and passed the service area of the gas station. The door to the service area had been rolled down into the closed position. Its glass panes were nearly as dusty as the windows of the tow truck. Nevertheless, Lee could see inside: the station's single service bay was absent of both vehicles and people.

When Lee walked through the front customer entrance of the gas station the proprietor was seated behind the cash register counter. Jimmy Mack was a big man. He was wearing a pair of grease-stained blue coveralls. He was perched atop a barstool with his arms folded.

"Lee McCabe." Jimmy Mack said. When Lee got a good look at Jimmy Mack his blood turned to ice. Lee was almost certain that he recognized Jimmy from the previous morning at the Tradewinds. Jimmy had been one of the four gunmen who had murdered Tim Fitzsimmons and Jody White. Lee had only gotten a fleeting look at him; but Jimmy's large frame, dark beard, and bulbous nose had formed a memorable profile. Jimmy was the gunman who had briefly turned around.

And now Jimmy was grinning. "Well, I suppose I should be honored. It's not everyday that a wanted felon pays me a visit."

These words were yet another blow. Lee knew that his own name and face were plastered throughout the media by now, so anyone, including Jimmy, might have recognized him. But something else was at work here. Jimmy's face registered no surprise at his presence. In fact, he was acting as if this were *his* show, as if he somehow had the advantage.

Nevertheless, Lee decided to ignore Jimmy's opening gambit. "It's illegal to deal meth, you know."

Jimmy laughed and shrugged. "It's also illegal to murder two innocent people in cold blood. That was quite a job you did on that poor Fitzsimmons and his little piece. Really hard core. Channel 5 says that you shot the girl in the face."

Lee reached behind his back and withdrew the .45.

Jimmy held up his hands and showed Lee his palms. "Whoa, don't be drawing any guns on me. As you can see, I'm unarmed."

"Listen to me," Lee said. "Listen very carefully. I know you're dealing meth. I also know that you were one of the men who killed Fitzsimmons and Jody."

"Let's see you try to prove that." Jimmy Mack's smile did not waver.

This encounter was not working out as Lee had hoped. Jimmy Mack was obviously unimpressed with Lee's drawn weapon. Lee had anticipated that Mack, as a bit player and small-time drug dealer, could be manipulated with a little pressure. But Mack was holding to a pattern of defying Lee's expectations.

"You're working for someone," Lee continued. "The same person who is supplying your meth. And you're going to tell me who this person is so I can clear my name."

Jimmy Mack chuckled. "Is that a fact? You think you can simply barge in here with a gun and make demands, huh? I'll give you this: you've got a pair of brass balls. But Malcolm told me you were full of yourself."

"Malcolm?" Lee said aloud. Suddenly the situation was clear to him.

Lee was startled by the sound of scuffling feet behind him. He whirled to see Malcolm, charging in his direction with a large object raised as a club. This time the addict was wielding a large wrench rather than a rotting piece of lumber. Lee ducked, and the wrench sailed past his head, narrowly missing his temple.

Jimmy took advantage of this moment to reach beneath the counter. Lee was grappling with Malcolm; but he saw the shotgun pointed in his direction. Malcolm knocked the .45 from his hand.

Lee shoved Malcolm away at the last second before Mack pulled the trigger. This placed Malcolm squarely in the line of fire. The shotgun made a deafening boom in the enclosed space of the garage office. A second later, Lee smelled the coppery stench of blood, though not his own.

Fired at nearly point-blank range, the shotgun blast shredded a large portion of Malcolm's body. His chest cavity was instantaneously collapsed and then scattered outward behind him—lungs, bone, and viscera. It made a horrific sight; but Lee knew that he could not allow himself to be distracted, even by this.

Lee ducked low, and Jimmy Mack shifted the barrel of his weapon downward. Another blast erupted from the shotgun. Jimmy Mack pumped the handgrip on the shotgun's barrel and ejected an empty shell. Lee threw himself to the floor and retrieved the .45. He scooted himself toward Jimmy Mack, where the counter would prevent the armed man from aiming at him. He knew that this protection would only be temporary. He extended his own weapon just as Jimmy Mack was leaning over the counter with the shotgun raised at an unnatural angle, away from his body. Holding the gun this way, Jimmy Mack would risk breaking one of the bones in his arms from the recoil. But this would be no compensation to Lee: it would be another point-blank shot. He would end up like Malcolm.

Lee fired twice, barely taking time to aim the pistol. He was showered with a spray of Jimmy Mack's blood. The shotgun clattered to the floor, and he heard the big man fall behind the counter, knocked back from the two pistol rounds.

Lee leapt to his feet and leaned over the counter, holding the .45 at a ready position. Jimmy Mack was sprawled on his back. His chest was covered with blood, so that the blue of his coveralls could barely be discerned.

Lee lifted himself onto the counter and slid across it, without taking his attention away from Jimmy Mack. For Mack was still alive. He regarded Lee wrathfully from the floor. The owner of Mack's Gas and Garage looked incapable of taking any action against him; but Lee knew from his Marine Corps training that countless men had been killed by the enemy they believed to be incapacitated.

Lee knelt down, and he and Jimmy Mack exchanged stares. Lee now knew without a doubt that Jimmy Mack had taken part in the murders of Tim Fitzsimmons and Jody White. There could be no doubt that Mack was the man whose face he had noticed as he turned around.

Unfortunately, this was an answer that only led to more questions: Who had Mack's accomplices been? And more importantly, who had given the orders that had placed Mack and the other three men at the Tradewinds the previous morning?

Lee knew from his experience in Iraq that wherever there was an organized gang of gunmen, there was a puppet master behind the scenes. The men who actually pulled the triggers were usually the tools of other men with influence and money. In this case—as in Iraq —there might be multiple factions pulling the strings.

"I know what you did," Lee said. "And you know that I know. Whether or not I can prove it....That doesn't matter now, does it?"

Jimmy Mack said nothing. He continued to stare at Lee through a haze of pain, and what was surely a recognition that his own death was imminent. Lee knew that evil men sometimes made deathbed statements of contrition. Jimmy Mack was a drug pusher and a contract murderer. But did that mean that he was thoroughly evil? Perhaps Lee could appeal to whatever sense of decency might remain in this man.

Jimmy Mack took a deep breath, and Lee heard the air suck through the holes in his chest. One of Lee's bullets must have struck a lung. Mack shifted his weight. A large quantity of blood was released from the wound. The movement had dislodged a mass of blood that had been collected near the opening. The color of the blood suggested that one of Lee's bullets had also struck an artery.

"You know you're not walking out of here," Lee said in a faltering voice. For some reason, he thought about the man he had met in the woods the previous night—the Hunter. The Hunter would probably have known exactly what to say in this situation. That man was full of words, a seemingly endless well of pithy aphorisms and reflections. Lee knew that his own words would be inadequate, but they were his only resource at the moment.

In the same faltering voice, he continued.

"So why don't you tell me who ordered you to do it? This is your last chance to make it right. Tell me who is behind all this and I will do my best to stop them from doing more harm. And maybe that will enable me to make it right for both of us."

A broad, pained smile appeared on Jimmy Mack's face. His chest began to spasmodically shake. Lee realized that Mack was laughing.

"Go to hell!" he said, his words half-drowned in a gurgle. One of Mack's hands shot forward and reached for Lee's gun. Lee knocked the hand aside and stood up. Mack fell into a coughing fit. The smile disappeared and was replaced by a clenched expression of pure agony.

"Who ordered the hit?" Lee shouted, his willingness to engage in subtle maneuvers gone now.

"I hope you do find him," Mack said from the floor. "And I'll be laughing..." Mack arched his back and coughed. The cough sprayed blood upon his black beard. "I'll be laughing while he kills you."

And then Jimmy Mack was gone. This was not the first man Lee had watched die, of course. Nor was it the most gruesome of deaths. Tim Fitzsimmons's trailer had been a far more shocking death scene. But there was something about Jimmy Mack's parting words that raised the hairs on Lee's spine. The man had cursed him with his final breath.

38

Lee recalled his grandmother, and how the old woman used to tell him tall tales of banshees and ghosts—stories and superstitions that she had heard at the knee of her own grandmother. Almost reflexively, Lee crossed himself, as if the gesture might ward off whatever evil that Jimmy's Mack's last utterance portended. A part of him felt foolish for giving himself the blessing, after all that had happened. But in his current position, Lee was willing to grasp at whatever blessing he could.

He backed away from the corpse of Jimmy Mack, and exited the space behind the counter. He was alone with two dead bodies. If he wanted answers, he was going to have to find them for himself.

He noticed a darkened room off to the side of the customer service area. He could make out a desk and a computer monitor in the shadows. This was Jimmy Mack's office space. If there were any answers to be found here now that Mack was dead, he would probably find them there.

Lee glanced out at the front window of the gas station as he walked toward the office. There were no cars, nor any customers. Probably Jimmy Mack didn't have a very thriving business, which might partially explain why he had turned to running meth in the first place.

The nearly eviscerated body of Malcolm Taylor lay on the floor. His mouth was partially open; his final gasp of surprise and pain had followed him to his death. Malcolm's eyes were wide open—and Lee felt the chill again. The gas station had become an evil place because of what had happened here this afternoon. When all of this was over, they would bulldoze the building and the site would take its place in the local body of dark folklore as a little patch of unhallowed ground.

He flipped the wall switch in the office. It was an unkempt room of dark green carpet and walls of painted cinderblock. It smelled of cigarettes and stale coffee.

The bookshelves on the surrounding walls were packed with automotive manuals, hot rod magazines, and sundry spare parts—spark plugs, air filters, and a wire harness that had apparently been slit open with a razor blade. The bookshelves also contained thick blue binders, the generic kind that could be purchased at any office supply store. The spines of the binders were not labeled.

Lee sighed wearily. It would take him hours to search the office thoroughly, and he knew that he should not linger here for more than a few minutes.

He turned his attention to the desk. Jimmy Mack had been a disorganized sort, so perhaps he had not gone to extraordinarily lengths to conceal the evidence and records associated with his activities. His involvement had been betrayed by Malcolm Taylor, after all, an even more disorganized junkie. This meant that Mack had been somewhat careless. He had lacked the instinct for subterfuge that a professional criminal requires.

There was a ledger book on the desk blotter. It might be nothing more than an account of some automotive parts that Mack had recently purchased; but Lee suspected otherwise.

Lee opened the book. Each page contained two columns of numbers with dollar signs. The numbers were alternately three, four, and five-figure amounts. At the top of the left column were written the initials JM in blue ink: It was reasonable to assume that this was Jimmy Mack's reference to himself. Atop the right column were the initials LF —most likely the initials of the supplier who provided Mack's meth.

Lee paged through the ledger. This accounting went on for a good twelve to fifteen pages. Mack had written dates in parentheses beside some of the numbers. The earliest date indicated that he had been distributing meth since the previous January.

Any doubts about the nature of the ledger were removed when Lee noticed an entry at the bottom of the most recent page, scribbled in the lefthand column: "TW: $2,000 received from LF"

In the adjacent column was Saturday's date. Could "TW" refer to anything other than the Tradewinds? So Mack had received two thousand dollars for his part in the murders.

Lee pulled open the bottom desk drawer. If he had been a junkie himself, he would have just hit the jackpot. The desk drawer contained small bundles of white powder wrapped in clear plastic. Mack had apparently had no qualms about mixing his drug trade with his automotive-related business. Well, the figures in the ledger suggested that the former had become far more profitable than the latter.

Lee noticed a closed cardboard box on the floor behind the desk. He bent down and pulled the box open. More meth. He noticed that the packets containing the drug were coated with a thin layer of sawdust. The coating was irregular and much too sparse to provide any protection. It must be inadvertent, then, picked up from the environment in which the meth had been packed.

He took another look at the meth packets in the drawer. These, too, were lightly coated with sawdust. Lee made a mental note to remember this. The presence of the sawdust might ultimately be significant to him—and then again, it might mean nothing.

Jimmy Mack had left his cell phone atop the desk. Lee lifted the phone and scrolled through the navigation panel. He noticed a lot of calls to and from a mobile number that was identified in the phone menu as LF.

Without hesitation, Lee selected the menu link to call this number.

The phone rang three times before it was answered. The voice on the other end was male and late middle aged.

"Jimmy Mack," the voice said. "I'm surprised you've got the nerve to call me after that colossal clusterfuck you were part of yesterday."

"How so?" Lee asked.

"Have you been watching the news, you idiot?" the far voice asked.

Then there was a pause.

"Wait a minute. You're not Jimmy Mack."

"I'm not."

"Then who the hell are you?"

Lee realized that there was a certain danger in revealing himself. But then again, that might be the trigger that would spur the man on the other end of the call to reveal his own identity—and perhaps additional information. All the evidence—the initials in the ledger, the notation about the Tradewinds, and this man's inadvertent reference to yesterday's violence—added up to one conclusion: This was the man who had ordered the murders of Fitzsimmons and his girlfriend.

"I'm the one who is currently taking the rap for what you had done yesterday. But I won't be taking that rap much longer."

"Lee McCabe?" the man asked. "Is that who I am speaking with? Why are you calling me on Jimmy Mack's cell phone?"

"Never mind that. I know what you did."

"You don't know shit. Nothing that you can prove, anyway. But I would like to talk to you. I don't want anyone having the wrong impression of me—least of all a young war veteran. This is simply a misunderstanding. Nothing that two reasonable men can't sit down and talk about. Why don't you pay me a visit? Or tell me where you are, and I can send one of my associates to pick you up."

"Why don't I come to you?" Lee asked. "Where would I find you?"

"You can find me in the Boar's Head. A nice little family bar in Blood Flats. But don't try anything stupid. Marine or no marine, I've got men who will make you sorry if you try to come in here with guns blazing."

"Who should I ask for?" Lee asked, though he had already pieced the answer together. "Is this Lester Finn I'm talking to?"

A dry laugh on the other end "I'm glad to know that my reputation precedes me, as does yours. I'm sure it will be a memorable meeting for both of us."

Lee was about to respond when he heard the sound of someone moving around in the customer service area, where the bodies of the two dead men still lay.

39

Phelps wanted the FBI agents to leave so that he could get busy. There was much to do: He needed to call the state crime lab to see if there were any results from the evidence collected at the murder scene. And he needed to return to the Tradewinds to conduct more witness interviews.

He wanted an opportunity to talk to Norris one-on-one. The deputy had always been a bit high-strung; but Phelps had never seen Norris agitated to this degree. Phelps noticed the dark perspiration stains beneath Norris's armpits—despite the cold air that the sheriff's department's air conditioner was churning out. Phelps was actually chilly himself. And the deputy continued to drum his fingers, scuff his feet on the floor, and rub the space between his eyebrows with the pad of his thumb. Something was up with Norris—but Phelps didn't want to pursue the matter while in the presence of two federal agents.

Most all, Phelps needed time to think. He had never been very good at group-based brainstorming. He required a certain amount of time and space to assemble and reassemble what he already knew, to try and figure out how all of the various factors might fit together. Then he would decide how to run with his conclusions. But Special

Agents Lomax and Porter showed no signs of terminating the meeting.

Phelps wanted to pound his fist on the table. In the middle of an urgent murder investigation, Special Agent Porter was giving him a mini-seminar on the scourge of the rural meth epidemic.

"The number of meth addicts in the rural South has more than doubled in the past ten years," she said. "At present, a user can buy a gram of meth for less than $100. This makes it attractive to the lower-income, blue-collar market. Meth also proliferates in rural areas because there are so many isolated and abandoned buildings where it can be made."

"And where there are abundant supplies of anhydrous ammonia," Lomax interjected. "One of the key ingredients for manufacturing meth."

Lomax was talking about fertilizer, of course: Anhydrous ammonia had long been used to fertilize crops. Pressurized tanks of it were a common sight in farming environments. Anhydrous ammonia was ammonia from which the water had been removed. When released into the air, molecules of the compound sought moisture. This characteristic made it one of the most dangerous chemicals used in agriculture. Every human tissue—skin, eyes, lungs, and mucous membranes—contained moisture. Anhydrous ammonia reacted with these tissues, causing severe burns and permanent damage upon exposure. Pressurized tanks of anhydrous ammonia were also unstable and given to explosion if the external temperature was not carefully monitored.

Now Agent Porter was glibly reciting data on ambient temperatures and psi settings: "When the air surrounding a tank of anhydrous ammonia is 60 degrees Fahrenheit, the psi inside the tank is roughly 93 psi," she said. "When the temperature rises to ninety degrees, the pressure inside the tank can nearly double. This is why there are so many explosions in amateur meth labs—especially during the summer months."

Like most peace officers outside the big cities, Phelps was already familiar with this story. He had known about the hazards of anhydrous ammonia before he had even become a lawman; and he knew all about the demographics of the meth epidemic. With methamphetamine, the purveyors of illegal drugs had finally discovered a product that could extract revenue from the pickup truck and gun rack crowd. You couldn't convince the average Southerner to snort cocaine or inject heroin. Meth was different, though. It had taken hold in places like Hawkins County, where the customer base was mostly white and mostly blue collar.

Phelps kept his response low-key. "Thank you. I know all about the rural meth problem, Agent Porter. And after what happened out at that trailer park, I don't need to be told that we've got it here, too. But you may be wrong about the involvement of outside organized criminal elements. Meth trafficking in Hawkins County is small-scale and fragmented. Confined to local players, as far as we've been able to determine. We've made some meth busts over the past several years; and invariably they turn out to be amateurs with their own homemade labs, like Tim Fitzsimmons."

"The cartels and the big crime families are absorbing that end of the business," Special Agent Lomax said. The overhead lights reflected off the dome of his bald head. "They're consolidating the markets and the distribution. This Tim Fitzsimmons represents a dead business model." Lomax paused, as if considering what he had just said. "No pun intended," he added humorlessly.

Phelps compared this information to what he had heard and read from other sources. Yes, the rural narcotics market was changing, along with the narcotics market everywhere else. The drug traffickers, like Wal-Mart and General Motors, now had their own global supply chains. It all came down to economies of scale. Small-time operations, like the one that had been run by Tim Fitzsimmons, were inefficient in a mass-production world. Anyone with a minimal amount of knowledge could set up a meth lab in a corner of their garage or a spare bedroom. But the real money was made by outsourcing the production to so-called "superlabs" in countries like Mexico. In these nations, anti-drug enforcement measures were comparatively lax, and the police were more corruptible.

Large-scale manufacturing operations were far riskier inside the U.S. Superlabs required warehouse-sized facilities, where industrial-grade equipment could be employed. A set-up like that wouldn't escape scrutiny in Midwest suburbia, or even in a comparatively rural location like Hawkins County.

If what these FBI agents were saying was true, then he had another issue to contend with: Somehow he had missed the signs that he should have seen. He had thought that he was up against a disorganized collection of local criminals. Was his true adversary, in fact, a national—or even a global—crime syndicate?

That would mean a lot more meth in the county, and probably a lot more violence as well.

He listened as Agent Porter continued to drone on, reciting her data and statistics. He knew that he would have to play ball during this phase in order to have the FBI's support when he really needed it. But how many more deaths would there be among the community that depended on him? And would he ever have a chance to redeem his many mistakes?

40

"I know who you are!" the old man said. "You're that fella on TV. The one who killed all those people!"

The elderly man who stood in the customer reception area of Jimmy Mack's was more than just old—he was ancient. Lee would have guessed him to be in his nineties. He addressed Lee as he exited Jimmy Mack's office. It seemed that the old man had been waiting for him.

As was often the custom of the elderly, the old man was over-dressed for a visit to the local garage: He wore a fading suit that hung limply on his thin body, worn but polished black shoes, and the sort of hat that most men had stopped wearing in the 1950s. He also held a cane, and he aimed it at Lee in one quivering hand.

"Go ahead and kill me, too, if that's what you're goin' ta do. I ain't afeared of ya."

Lee held up his empty hands in a gesture that was intended to display his lack of harmful intentions. The .45 was behind his back.

"I'm not going to hurt you, sir. You have nothing to fear from me."

The old man slowly, deliberately surveyed the carnage about the room—Malcolm's horribly disfigured body, Jimmy Mack's blood on the counter, the shelves of automotive components that had been upended during the struggle and gunfight. Lee also noticed that their earlier gunfire had taken out one of the front windows. That particular damage must have been caused by some stray pellets from Mack's shotgun.

The man stared back at Lee. It was almost absurd for Lee to suggest that he should calm down—that this scene really shouldn't be viewed with an exaggerated eye. If this wasn't pure bedlam, what was?

"Is that what you said to this poor fella here on the floor?" the old man asked. "Did you tell him you weren't going to hurt him?"

"Listen mister," Lee said. "I was attacked. But I promise you that you have nothing to fear from me. Now if you'll just let me by you, there, I'll be on my way."

The old man did not move. Lee might have been speaking to him in a foreign language. Nevertheless, Lee knew that there was nothing he could accomplish by remaining here. It wouldn't be long before a Hawkins County patrol car would show up—*and what then*? If it was Deputy Norris, then the deputy would almost certainly take another shot at him, or force him into gunfight in which he would become guilty of murdering a police officer. And Lee expected no better of Sheriff Phelps.

As carefully as he could, Lee sidestepped past the old man, simultaneously giving Malcolm's corpse a wide berth. The old man's trembling increased when Lee moved by him. He kept his cane aloft, following Lee with the tip of it, aiming it like a gun.

At the exit, Lee felt the urge to utter more words of vindication at this man, who would be the first witness at the crime scene. The old man did not appear to be in a listening mood.

"Git!" he told Lee, shaking the cane. Then, in a more pleading tone: "Please git outta here."

41

Phelps had the feeling that the meeting with Special Agents Porter and Lomax was finally drawing to a close.

"You said you have some more witness interviews to conduct, Sheriff?" Agent Porter asked.

"That's right. Norris and I are going to make another trip out to the Tradewinds trailer park. We interviewed about a dozen witnesses right after we secured the crime scene. They basically told us the same story. When we go back, we'll be knocking on doors. There might be a witness out there who saw something that the others didn't. If there is, we'll find them."

"Why don't you take Agent Porter and I with you?" Lomax suggested.

Phelps shook his head. He had been afraid of this. "With all due respect, Agent Lomax, I think that we would get more information if Deputy Norris and I went out there alone. We're locals, you see. These people are our neighbors. They'll talk to us—or at least there's a better chance that they'll talk to us."

Lomax laughed. "Let me guess—independent-minded South-erners who have a collective hang-up about the federal government."

"Now, now," Phelps said with a measured degree of levity. "This is

Kentucky in the twenty-first century—not Mississippi in 1964. We have high-speed Internet and running water out here, you know. And despite what you might hear over coffee when you visit the Hoover building, we don't marry our sisters and our cousins."

Lomax chuckled and waved his hand. *Do it your way,* he seemed to be thinking. But Agent Porter obviously didn't see the humor in the situation.

"We've found that it often helps to approach witnesses from a variety of different angles," she said. "We respect your local perspective, of course." She tapped her pen on her legal pad, and Phelps had the distinct impression that Agent Porter did *not* respect their "local perspective". He remained silent, and Agent Porter continued talking.

"But Special Agent Lomax and I have been trained in some of the latest interrogation and witness interviewing techniques. We've done joint training with law enforcement agencies from around the world. I've personally trained with Scotland Yard and MI-5. Special Agent Lomax did cross training with the *Police Nationale* in Paris only a few months ago." She pronounced the name of the French law enforcement agency with what sounded to Phelps like an exaggerated French accent. "We may be able to provide a perspective that you *don't* have locally," she concluded.

"I appreciate that," Phelps said. "And if we were going to interview al-Qaeda suspects or members of some German Baader-Meinhoff cell, I would be grateful to have you along. But we need to keep in mind the unique characteristics of the witness we'll be looking for. Norris and I established a very noticeable police presence at that trailer park yesterday morning. We were quite visibly talking to people and conducting interviews. What I'm getting at is—if someone saw something and was inclined to talk to the police, they would have stepped forward then and there. They had every chance, you see.

"When we go back out, we'll be looking for the witness who *didn't* feel comfortable talking to law enforcement, for whatever reason. Maybe they were afraid of some sort of retaliation. Maybe they were paranoid about the government, as you suggest. But the way to get that person to talk is take a low-key approach, through local, familiar contacts."

"Provided that such a witness even exists," Lomax said.

"Yes," Phelps reluctantly agreed. "Provided that such a witness exists."

42

Phelps confronted Norris as soon as Lomax and Porter had departed.

"What the hell's wrong with you, Norris?"

"You're angry because I contradicted you," Norris said guardedly. He clasped his hands together atop the table. He was rubbing them together, interlacing his fingers, as if lathering them with some invisible substance.

"No, of course not," Phelps replied, though he secretly wondered if he was in fact angry at having been contradicted by his subordinate in front of federal agents. "The point of a meeting like that is to exchange ideas. You don't have to agree with me. Agreeing with me all the time isn't a part of your job description—except when I give you a direct order in tactical situation."

Norris looked up at him, saying nothing.

"What I'm talking about, Deputy, is your bearing. You've been acting strange ever since this all started."

Norris sighed and made an appealing gesture, his palms open now on the tabletop "Okay, Sheriff, I'll tell you, if you really want to know."

"Yes, I really want to know."

"You see," Norris began shakily. "All of this has been just a bit too much for me. Fitzsimmons and Jody White—" It appeared to Phelps that Norris was struggling to prevent himself from trembling. "The way they were killed, you know. I could see Fitzsimmons's brains, right there on the carpet. And that woman—what those men did to her face."

Norris buried his face in his hands. When he looked back up at Phelps, his eyes were red and moist. "I've never seen anything like that—not as a sheriff's deputy in Hawkins County. I never thought I would."

Phelps looked away, suddenly embarrassed for Norris. On one hand, it would be easy to make the case that Norris should never have gone into law enforcement if he could not handle the aftermath of death. On the other hand, Phelps knew from his own experiences in the Gulf that many men could not handle those sights. And many of them had no advance knowledge of this inability. They simply crumbled when facing it for the first time.

"Well, I'm going to need you to pull yourself together," Phelps said, because he could think of nothing else to say. "When this is over, the two of us can sit down and talk. Maybe you'd like to consider another line of work over the long term. If you want to try something like corporate security, I'd be glad to write you a letter of recommendation. You can make a good income there, and real violence is extremely rare."

"Thank you, Sheriff. I appreciate that."

"But for now, you have to refocus. I'm sure you realize that this department is hurting for resources: Hathaway has resigned. That leaves you, Deputy Johnson, and me. I need you, Norris. And I'm going to need you until this is over."

Norris nodded solemnly at Phelps. "Don't worry, Sheriff. I'm feeling better already, just knowing that I have your support. You can trust me. You can count on me."

43

Phelps started the engine of his cruiser as the heat of the day began to bear down in earnest. Sun glinted off broken glass in the parking lot of the sheriff's office. Today would be a hot one. Phelps turned the knob of the cruiser's air conditioning to the maximum setting.

Less than ten minutes had passed since his conversation with Ron Norris. Phelps found himself unable to feel reassured by Norris's professions of confidence. He would have to keep his eye on the deputy. This was all that he needed—following Hathaway's unexpected departure. At least Darla Johnson was still reliable, he told himself.

After speaking with Norris, Phelps had felt the need to escape the confines of the sheriff's department office. His current mission was part police work, part personal therapy. He had not wanted to remain in the same building with Ron Norris—not for a while, at least. The deputy's shame had become his own.

Phelps edged the cruiser onto Market Street—one of the main thoroughfares of Perryston, and set a course for the farmlands immediately south of town, in the direction of Blood Flats.

Phelps figured that if Lee McCabe was still in Hawkins County, he was likely not hiding in the woods. If they found him nearby—*and Phelps had no doubt that the young man would eventually be found*—they would find him taking refuge with a friend or an acquaintance. Possibly a distant relative located on some obscure branch of the McCabe or the Mills family tree.

Or maybe with a woman. *Yes*, Phelps thought sourly. *If McCabe was anything like his father, he would probably find a way to drag some hapless female accomplice into this mess.*

Possibly, though, they would find McCabe in another county or another state. He might con a woman into driving him to Nashville, or into giving him enough money to buy a clunker that could serve as a getaway vehicle. For that matter, he could have hopped a train or hitchhiked. As a combat veteran himself, Phelps did not doubt McCabe's resourcefulness.

Nevertheless, the due diligence of law enforcement was an engrained habit. Phelps had already combed most of the obvious hiding places in and around Perryston: the abandoned houses and seldom-used barns, a handful of winter cabins scattered throughout the nearby woods.

He had not yet searched Fischer's Gorge.

Located in a shallow valley that was cut by the Chickasaw Creek, Fischer's Gorge was actually not much of a gorge at all, at least compared to the gorges one saw in the Western states. It was topographically daunting, though, and inaccessible even to four-wheel drive vehicles. The site had also been used as an unofficial dump for years: It was littered with the shells of rusted automobiles and discarded farm implements. Inhospitable though it was, the gorge might appeal to a fugitive looking for a hiding place.

No road led all the way down to Fischer's Gorge; but there was a gravel access road that branched off the Tarker Farm Road. The gravel road ended a hundred yards or so short, where the downwardly sloping hillside became a steep declivity.

Phelps parked the cruiser where the gravel road terminated. Before he exited the vehicle, he removed a Remington 870 shotgun from the cruiser's gun rack. He considered strapping on the bulletproof Kevlar vest that he kept in the trunk. But his instincts told him that if Lee McCabe had made a camp at the dump, the young former marine would hear him coming down the steep hillside. McCabe would flee. He would not be walking into a firefight with the son of his ex-girlfriend. Not here, at least.

As the ground sloped downward, the air became cool and moist beneath an overhead canopy of branches. There was a path that led down to the dump, but the terrain of the gorge prevented any trimming of the treetops or undergrowth. This was, Phelps thought, the countryside as the Native Americans would have known it.

He found the path and followed its winding course downward. It was a serpentine, zigzagging route, owing to the steep angle of the land. Within a few minutes he could hear the gurgling waters of the Chickasaw Creek.

He rounded another bend and the exposed roots of hundred-year-old oak trees became visible on the opposite side of the gorge. On the far side of the Chickasaw there was no pathway to the water, only a precipitous drop into the shallow rapids and the jagged rocks below.

On the near bank, the final length of the hillside was occupied by the remnants of garbage—some of which had been here for decades. The rusted-out cab of an old pickup truck poked out of the earth. Most of the truck had been buried by the process of erosion. The windows had long since been busted out and stripped of glass. The contours of the vehicle suggested the late 1950s.

Old tires, too, were everywhere. There were tractor tires as well as car and truck tires. Phelps could see one of them on the water's edge. The next rainfall would push it into the Chickasaw. It might eventually end up in the Mississippi River.

Phelps held the shotgun at the high port position and scanned the uneven mountains of metal, earth, and rubber that comprised the hillside. He could see no sign of fresh tracks—and no single item or pile that could be effectively used as a hiding place. If McCabe had even been here, he had likely not stayed long. The hillside was dangerous—even for a trained marine like McCabe. McCabe would have slid into the Chickasaw if he had tried to erect a shelter of any sort.

Phelps gave the far bank a final look and sighed. He noticed a hawk soaring high above the distant woods. When the hawk disappeared behind the edge of the tree line, he turned around and began walking back up the path.

44

From a knoll on the same side of the Chickasaw Creek, Lee McCabe watched Sheriff Phelps make his way down the twisting pathway toward the old dumping ground and the white-frothed shallows. His ears were still ringing from the gunshots that had been fired inside Jimmy Mack's garage. He could still see the face of the old man he had encountered on his way out—and the fearful yet determined way the old man had pointed his cane at him.

He had a clear view of Sheriff Phelps from where he crouched, and a miraculously clear shot through a parting in the tree trunks. He withdrew the .45 as Phelps paused above the metallic tangle on the hillside. The heft of the gun felt deadly and powerful in his hands.

He knew, though, that he could not do this. He could not kill the sheriff in cold blood, even after the sheriff's deputy had taken those shots at him in that field. He looked at the gun angrily, then shoved it back into the waistband of his pants.

Lee was on higher ground looking down at Phelps. He crept backward through the underbrush, being careful to make no sound that might alert the sheriff. He ducked low and found a pathway of soft earth that was nearly bare of dead leaves and fallen branches. He made his way silently upward, away from the Chickasaw.

Finally he stepped out into the clearing, and saw the sheriff's cruiser, white and black and gleaming chrome beneath the glare of the afternoon sun. Phelps had apparently come alone, unaccompanied by any of his deputies.

Lee McCabe examined the cruiser and then glanced back in the direction of Fischer's Gorge. Even if he started back this moment, the sheriff would need five minutes or more to ascend the curving trail.

Unsure of his exact plans and intentions, Lee approached the cruiser. He walked to the rear driver's door of the vehicle, which would be obscured from view in case the sheriff surprised him by coming back sooner than expected.

Lee pulled on the door handle and the door swung open with a click.

The sheriff had left the cruiser unlocked. Of course that would figure, wouldn't it? They were in an isolated area and the sheriff would not have planned on being long at the gorge.

What the hell was he doing? He realized that this foray into enemy territory entailed a certain risk; but he could not resist the sense of power that it gave him. Over the past day and a half, his adversaries had made him feel weak and vulnerable. This incursion reminded him that the other side, too, had its vulnerabilities.

He made a quick perusal of the interior. The sheriff's nightstick was lying on the front seat, along with what appeared to be a can of mace. Neither of these items would be worth taking. He noted that the gun rack was empty; and of course the sheriff had taken his sidearm with him.

Then he noticed an item that did not fit: a shoebox lying on the floor in the backseat area on the passenger side. He leaned into the vehicle and pulled the shoebox toward him.

When he opened the shoebox, he found what appeared to be a collection of the sheriff's personal possessions: old letters inside envelopes that were stiff and yellowed with age. An athletic ribbon that probably dated to the sheriff's days as a high school athlete. Lee vaguely remembered hearing that Sheriff Phelps had been something of a jock in his day.

The box also contained a number of photographs—snapshots that dated back to the eighties, judging from their contents and visual quality. A much younger version of the sheriff in a baseball uniform. Ticket stubs from a rock concert that had taken place several years before Lee had been born. More random photos.

One photo in particular caught his eye, for reasons that became immediately obvious: A photo of a young couple seated on a sofa. The girl had wrapped her arms around the teenaged boy. She was planting a kiss on the young man's cheek. Despite the couple's embrace, the overall affect of the photo was wholly innocent: These people were young and celebrating a simple and joyful stage in their lives. No doubt they had believed themselves to be immortal in that instant.

Lee recognized the two long-ago young people in the photograph as Steven Phelps and his mother. The photo seemed horribly out of place, the last thing Lee would have expected to find in a police vehicle. Why was Phelps carrying this around in his squad car—a snapshot of himself and a dead woman, a moment that had been frozen in time more than a quarter-century ago? Why did it haunt Phelps so?

The photo was personal for him, as well. He felt a wave of mourning for the young woman in the picture—whom he had had known so well later in her life. The memory of his mother's passing buffeted him, an unexpected surge of grief that he had to struggle to control. He had a mental image of her wasting away in her hospital bed at Hawkins County General, the cancer taking her life well before her forty-third birthday.

This resulted in a fresh burst of anger toward Phelps. The sheriff had already turned him into a fugitive for a crime that he did not commit. Did he have to confront him with images of his dead mother as well, as if to pour salt on those old wounds?

And part of him felt embarrassed for the lawman. This was an emotion that approached pity. How pathetic could Phelps's life be now, that he was so attached to these old memories?

Lee suddenly realized that he had dallied too long. The sheriff would return at any moment. Lee removed the photo of Phelps and his mother from the shoebox and tucked it into his wallet. Then he replaced the lid on the shoebox and returned it to where he had found it.

He withdrew himself from the cruiser and gently closed the door. He wondered if Sheriff Phelps was emerging from the pathway even now—if he had heard the click of the latch.

Lee permitted himself a quick look in the direction of the gorge. He did not see the sheriff; but he did hear the sound of a branch snapping as Phelps ascended the pathway.

He looked behind him—away from the squad car—at an opening in the surrounding woods. It seemed to Lee that his life had become a series of episodes in which he darted in and out of the forest.

Ducking low so as to use the police cruiser for cover, he ran once again.

45

P helps returned the Remington to the cruiser's gun rack and started the vehicle's engine. He had just placed the car in gear when Rita Dinsmore contacted him on the radio to tell him that there was a double homicide at Jimmy Mack's garage on Dark Hollow Road.

That was not far from his current location. He turned on the sirens and gunned the engine, his tires spitting gravel until he reached the pavement of the Tarker Farm Road.

Two more deaths, Phelps thought. These would almost certainly be related to yesterday's shootings. The odds of two unrelated double homicides occurring in Hawkins County on two consecutive days were simply too small.

He reminded himself again that the ongoing events were not the product of his own past. And yet—given the identity of the primary suspect, it was impossible to deny at least a tangential connection.

A number of years ago Phelps had seen a documentary about the phenomenon known as the "the butterfly effect." The butterfly effect was based on a short story by Ray Bradbury of the same title. In Bradbury's eponymous tale, a time traveler journeys to the distant past and accidentally kills a butterfly. When he returns to his own time, he finds the world a vastly different place—all because of his own inadvertent actions in the altered past. The time traveler had literally changed the world by killing a butterfly.

The premise was simple yet overwhelmingly complex: Seemingly inconsequential causes lead to consequential results. If Lee McCabe was in fact responsible for the bloodbath in the county, then the current tally of four deaths—and any that might yet come—could be traced to a butterfly that he had killed himself, a long time ago.

In 1985 the Perryston High School baseball team had made it all the way to the state finals; and Steven Phelps had received no small amount of acclaim as the team's star pitcher. All the same, everyone had been surprised when Phelps had won a full-ride scholarship to the University of Kentucky.

His life had been perfectly on track: The scholarship had given him the means to escape from his current surroundings. Hawkins County had provided him with a not unpleasant childhood; but he knew that his prospects would be limited if he remained here. He would end up like his father: working a dead-end job at one of the handful of factories in town.

Heading into the spring of his senior year, he didn't even know what he was going to study once he arrived at the university. But he knew two things: He was going to make a success of himself, and he was going to marry Lori Mills.

He had met Lori Mills the year before, though she had caught his attention two years before that, when they were both freshmen at South Hawkins County Consolidated High School. He had noticed her almost immediately, and her grip on his imagination had never flagged. Throughout the first two years that they were classmates, she was the heroine of the imagery that played in his mind with every rock ballad on the radio. Phelps couldn't listen to a song that was even mildly romantic without thinking about Lori, picturing the ways in which they might eventually get together, mentally scripting the dialogues that they would someday have.

When he saw her in the hallways talking to other boys, he was seized by fits of almost uncontrollable jealousy. Once he had seen her give a junior—her then current boyfriend—a long, arms-around-each-other kiss in front of her locker. Phelps had gone into a state of mild depression for the better part of a week.

Although Phelps was only fifteen, he was able to muster the self-observation to see that he was falling for Lori Mills. And falling for her hard. Sooner or later he would have to do something about it.

That might be easier said than done. Lori Mills had been everything that Phelps was not: Whereas Phelps had been the golden boy—an athlete and a member of the National Honor Society—Lori had seemed destined for a life of mediocrity in Hawkins County. Though most of Phelps's baseball teammates would have agreed that she was "hot", Lori had been distinct from the type usually favored by the jock set—the college-bound girls who were on the cheerleading squad or the school's new girl's soccer team.

But there had been something about her—her dark good looks, the way she had of smiling at him crookedly when they passed in the hallway. There was an aspect of her temperament that seemed mildly dangerous. And perhaps for this last reason, she made him nervous.

He knew that his star athlete status would be no guarantee of success if he ever asked her out. As was often the case in rural high schools, there was a line between the college prep kids who were destined to leave, and the blue-collar track kids who were destined to stay in town after graduation. That line was often difficult to cross.

Nevertheless, the day came when Phelps simply decided that enough was enough. He summoned his courage one night, dialed the number of Lori Mills' house, and asked her out.

He was more than a little surprised when she accepted his invitation, and even more surprised when the two of them hit it off. There were some awkward moments at first—they sometimes struggled to find topics of conversation—but that awkwardness disappeared when she pressed her tiny body against his. She was neither shy nor uninhibited. This was one more way in which she complimented him, he often thought. Perhaps it was true what they said about opposites being made for each other.

Two months later, he lay back against the backseat driver's side door of his 1979 Ford LTD, convinced that if he were to die in this moment, he would have lived a complete life. His and Lori's breath, and the heat of their bodies, had fogged up the car's windows.

Their clothes were in a tangle on the floor below them. She lay back in the opposite direction, so shameless and beautiful in the perfection of her seventeen-year-old nudity. She poked him playfully with her foot.

"Are you tired already?" she asked with a smile.

He felt no need to answer her, as he knew the question had been made in jest. Several of his more experienced friends had told him that it was difficult to be much of a man about it your first time. However, he was confident that he had acquitted himself well; and Lori's pleasurable moans and muffled cries—the way she had dug her fingernails into his bare back—told him that he had more than satisfied her.

He also knew that this was not her first time. This did not bother him—not really—but already he could feel a little well of latent jealousy rising up within him. How had it been with her and the previous one? And how many had there been before him? Phelps knew better than to ask such questions.

"Well," she said. "I suppose we'd better get dressed. It's got to be past one in the morning. My parents aren't exactly strict—but we ought to be getting back."

He watched as she slid into her bra, her taut, exquisitely proportioned breasts jiggling as she raised her arms. He allowed himself a moment to do nothing but peruse the contours of her body in the dim light of the three-quarters moon. The mystery was gone—but not the hunger. It had seemed to him that he would never be able to get enough of that act, never be able to get enough of Lori Mills. He wanted her with him always.

He reached across the space of the backseat and clutched her hand—an intentionally innocent act, he thought, after some of the things that they had just done.

"I love you, Lori," he said.

She smiled. "You're sweet, Steven."

"Maybe you don't believe me," he said hurriedly. "Maybe you think I'm just like those other guys." Then he stopped himself, realizing that this had been the wrong thing to say. Moreover, he was on the verge of babbling.

"I—" he began.

"Steven," she said, interrupting him, "Just let it go. Okay? Don't spoil the moment by—overanalyzing it."

"But I meant—"

"Hush," she said, placing an index finger to his lips. She leaned forward and kissed him, then reached behind her back with both hands to fasten the clasps on her bra.

Watching her lift her next garment off the floor, Phelps suspected that while Lori had not exactly taken their coupling lightly, it had not had quite the same gravity for her that it had for him. But maybe that was nothing to worry about. After all, this *was* his first time. And Lori was here with him, right? There was no reason to believe that this would not always be so. He would make sure of it.

When his LTD pulled into her parents' driveway, she kissed him once more. Her skin was still moist from their exertions, and her tongue tasted like the beer they had shared before the act.

"Good night," she said, breaking the kiss to lean her forehead against his.

He watched her traverse her walkway to the front stoop. She turned around to smile at him and wave in the light above the door.

She seemed so light, so carefree. He was now past the point of no return when it came to loving her—past the place where he had any choice in the matter. But did she feel the same way about him? When he had told her that he loved her she had not returned the sentiment. That wasn't the way it was supposed to work, was it? When you made that sort of a vow to someone, they were supposed to repeat it back to you.

As he pulled out of the driveway, he wondered: Was he setting himself up for heartbreak?

"Maybe you *are* dangerous," he said in the solitude of the darkened car. "But I want you anyway."

46

B y the time Phelps reached the railroad crossing, a Norfolk Southern freight train was already barreling through the intersection of the roadway and the rail tracks. Most of the railcars were loaded with coal from the mines of eastern Kentucky.

Phelps tapped impatiently on the dashboard as he waited. The train roared and rattled along, oblivious to the emergency at hand. Bad timing once again.

He didn't want to think about Lori anymore; but he knew that this was somewhat inevitable. This was how it always worked with these memories. Once they got started, there was no easy way to put them to rest.

Phelps had left for the University of Kentucky in the third week of August after he and Lori graduated. By this time Lori was a fulltime employee at the local Kmart. She had worked the afterschool shift at the store throughout most of high school. The transition to fulltime seemed to suggest something inevitable and permanent. It was a scenario repeated by many of their non-college prep classmates. During junior or senior year, they began the low-wage jobs that would become their fulltime vocations after they received their diplomas.

But Phelps knew that it was going to be different for Lori—all because she was going to be his wife. Throughout that summer, he talked incessantly about the business administration classes he had now decided to take, about how he would end up as a partner at a law firm someday—or a top manager at a large corporation.

"Then you'll see," Phelps told her. "I'm going to earn enough money so that I can buy us a big house, and you're going to live like a queen."

When he made pronouncements like this, she used to laugh and shake her head. "Steven, you're crazy. You're going to meet some rich man's daughter at UK and you're going to forget all about me." Then she would kiss him. "It's a nice fantasy, though."

She visited him only once at UK. He made the mistake that weekend of taking her to a party thrown by his business college fraternity. Lori was within earshot when a fellow undergrad named Rick Mulligan approached Phelps and leaned against him in a drunken stupor, gripping Phelps's shoulders as he swayed back and forth.

"Steve, buddy, that's a real little hottie come down to see you from Perrytown or wherever."

"Perryston," Phelps corrected him. Phelps knew that Rick was prone to making untactful remarks when he drank. He also knew that Rick was the son of an insurance executive and had some less than egalitarian notions about social and economic class. Moreover, he had a habit of making remarks that struck many listeners as sexist —even in the pre-political correctness era of the mid-1980s.

Phelps therefore tried to change the subject by asking Rick about a business law exam they had both taken the following week; but Rick would not be diverted from the subject at hand.

"Listen to me," Rick said in a conspiratorial tone. (The words came out *Risten to me.*) "She's cute, that little dime store checkout girl of yours; but it will never work. I can tell that you're going places, buddy. And you'll need a wife who can hold an educated conversation. I overheard her talking to Sheila a few minutes ago. Sheila asked her what she thought about the Reagan-Gorbachev Summit in Reykjavík, and do you know what she said? She asked Sheila if Reykjavík was in Rhode Island or Maine. Sheila didn't have the heart to tell her that there's this place called Iceland, and it's a whole other country... Take my advice Stevie: You've had you're fun with this girl, but she won't be a long-term asset to you."

In the months that followed, Phelps would think about the various actions that he could have taken—should have taken. He could have grabbed that pompous jackass Rick Mulligan by the collar and told him to watch his mouth when talking about the woman he loved and was someday going to marry. He could have sought out Lori at that moment and left the party.

But instead he had merely smiled and nodded noncommittally, taken aback by the mere realization that there were actually men who could not recognize the specialness and uniqueness that he saw in Lori.

Phelps had not seen Lori walk out of the party. But she was nowhere to be found when he searched for her after detaching himself from Rick. He finally found her waiting on the front doorstep of his dingy off-campus apartment.

"I don't fit in here," she said simply when he approached her. "I heard what your friend said."

"He isn't my friend."

"He sure did seem to be your friend."

There was no more open recrimination; but Phelps could see that he had missed an opportunity when he had failed to stand up for Lori publicly. It was as if he had been forced to make a choice of loyalties, and he had chosen this better educated, more moneyed crowd.

That hadn't been his intention at all, of course. Much of his hard work at school was motivated by the desire to create a more comfortable, more prosperous life for both of them someday. And yes, his future success would probably depend to some degree on his ability to get along with people like Rick Mulligan and his friend Sheila— who had been so shocked at Lori's ignorance of the capital of Iceland. These were the sorts of people who held the keys to power and influence outside of Hawkins County, for better or worse. He knew, however, that it would be difficult for Lori to grasp this reality.

In the weeks that followed, Phelps noticed a pronounced chilliness in Lori's phone calls and a slowdown in her letters. Gradually her calls became more and more sporadic, and her letters stopped altogether.

Busy with homework and exams, Phelps determined that a period of reduced contact might actually do them good. It would give her time to get over the incident at the campus party; and she would see that he remained loyal to her over time, even if they weren't writing and calling each other everyday.

However, his resolve began to crumble when a new trend emerged: He would call Lori's house, and Mrs. Mills would evasively inform him that Lori was "out." This, combined with the long gap in their communications, could only mean one thing.

He drove home one weekend in May, just before final exams. He walked into the Kmart where she worked and found her arranging a display of women's summer attire. When she saw him, the expression on her face conveyed barely restrained dread rather than any degree of joy or affection.

"Hold on a minute," she said. "I'll clock out and go on break."

They walked out to the parking lot together. It was a beautiful late spring afternoon of sunshine, high cumulus clouds, and early summer heat.

"Forget about me," Lori said without preamble. "Go back to college and find yourself someone else. I'm not right for you. I'm not what you need."

"Lori!" he said, turning to face her. "Can't you see that you're *exactly* what I need? *Exactly* what I want? What I'm trying to do right now is become someone who can give you the life you deserve. Remember all those talks we had about living in a better place, in a big house with—"

"Steven," she said. "We didn't have those talks. That was *you* talking at *me*. And yes, I listened. Like I said, it was a nice fantasy—a sweet thing for you to say. But I never said that I...wanted that. You and I—we had a good thing for a while in high school. Let's leave it at that."

"I don't *want* to leave it back in high school," he said. "I want *you*."

"It isn't quite that simple"

"It's simple enough for me. Is there something that's making it less simple for you?"

She looked down at her feet. "Yes. Tom McCabe."

"Tom McCabe?" Phelps had blurted. "The same Tom McCabe who is always getting in fights at all the local bars? The same Tom McCabe who's already been arrested once on a DUI?"

"There's more to him than that," Lori said, her tone suddenly defensive. "And he's very sweet to me. At least he doesn't let his friends insult me to his face."

Phelps felt his cheeks redden. He placed both of his hands on Lori's shoulders. "I'm sorry about that," he said. "More sorry than you'll ever know. But it was just a random comment by some idiot at a stupid college party. It doesn't mean anything. Now I want you to tell this Tom McCabe to get lost, and we'll start over again."

"No," she said, wriggling out of his hands. "I can't do that. Even if I wanted to."

"Why not?"

"I'm pregnant." Lori said simply.

These two words knocked the air out of Phelps. He felt like the Kmart's parking lot was spinning around him. He backed away from her, observed the contours of her body through her jeans, her yellow pullover blouse, and her red Kmart smock. She didn't *look* pregnant. But of course that didn't mean that she wasn't. If she was telling him she was pregnant, then she must be. Moreover, he hadn't slept with Lori in months, so there was no question about the paternity of this baby—this baby who would change everything.

"So now what are you going to do?" he asked.

"I suppose I'm going to marry him," Lori said through tear-streaked eyes. "He's already asked me. Do you have a better idea? Do you want to marry me now?"

The question had been rhetorical but it demanded an answer

nonetheless. Phelps had slowly shaken his head. There were some levels to which pride would not allow a man to stoop—whether or not he was in love. He could not even entertain the notion that he could be a father to the child sprung from Lori's faithlessness—not that he believed Lori was really making such a proposal.

Even then, perhaps, Phelps had realized that there would always be a certain enmity between himself and the child in Lori's womb. It would be better for all concerned if they had as little contact as possible. Ideally, Phelps and that child would never meet.

Phelps walked away from Lori that day, and away from the person that he had been on his way to becoming. Lori's rejection of him prompted a soul-searching process: What had Lori seen in Tom McCabe that she had not seen in him?

Phelps was not personally acquainted with Tom McCabe, though he was aware of him. McCabe was a few years older. McCabe had a rougher edge: He fought. He drank. He had troubles with the law. Phelps wondered: had his own quest for conventional success led him astray somehow? He was on the fast track, sure. But what good would that do him if it did not ultimately bring him the loyalty of the one woman he loved?

He recalled how he had stood there, meekly, while Rick Mulligan mocked Lori. As Lori had suggested, Tom McCabe—despite all his flaws—would have defended her honor, consequences be damned.

In this light, Phelps's classes on dry topics like managerial accounting and econometrics began to lose their meaning. His grades took a sharp downturn during the next academic year. When the guidance office informed him one day that he was on the verge of losing his scholarship, he realized that he was at a crossroads.

In the fall of his second year of college, he happened to drive by a Marine Corps recruiting office in Lexington. On a whim he stopped in, and listened to the recruiting sergeant's spiel about the Marine Corps being the "the few, the proud." There was nothing tougher than the Marine Corps, was there? A marine, it seemed to him, would never allow a puffed up windbag like Rick Mulligan to openly insult his woman.

This was a sort of toughness that competed with what the Tom McCabes of the world had to offer, but it was simultaneously positive. Whereas Tom McCabe was a lawbreaker, he would be a defender of the law. Because of her pregnancy, his break with Lori was irreparable; but a change of direction might absolve him of the weakness that had caused him to lose her in the first place.

With that sentiment in mind, he abruptly left college and enlisted in the U.S. Marine Corps. He went first to Paris Island, South Carolina for basic training, then to Camp Geiger in North Carolina for advanced infantry training. After that, the Marines sent him to South Korea, the Philippines, and Japan.

When he returned home on leave, he occasionally saw Lori around town. By now she had a young child in tow; and her last name was McCabe rather than Mills. Phelps could see traces of Lori in the child's face; but the boy looked more like Tom McCabe—who by now was distinguishing himself as an errant husband, based on what Phelps had heard through the grapevine. There was more drinking, and occasional infidelities.

Phelps was nearing the end of his enlistment when Saddam Hussein invaded Kuwait in the summer of 1990. He was posted to Camp Fuji, in Japan's Shizuoka Prefecture. Fuji was a cushy posting by Marine Corps standards. His primary assignment involved joint training with the Japanese Self-Defense Forces, who were more pleasant to work with than either the cocky, disorganized Filipinos, or the volatile South Koreans. The base included a Shinto *torii* and a spectacular view of Japan's picturesque Mount Fuji, or *Fuji-san*, as the Japanese called it.

From a television in the rec room at Camp Fuji, Phelps watched the images of the Iraqi invasion on CNN. No one needed to tell him that these global events would become a part of his personal story, for better or worse. There was already talk of a UN Security Council resolution against the invasion, and President Bush was hinting at military action if there was no Iraqi withdrawal. Within weeks, Phelps was on a transport vessel bound for the Persian Gulf.

His cachet as a Marine combat veteran had been instrumental in his entry into law enforcement three years later, and his election as Hawkins County Sheriff eight years after that.

As the train finally cleared the intersection and the crossing gate was lifted, Phelps reflected once again on the butterfly effect: Superficially minor events had indeed changed his life: What if he had stood up to Rick Mulligan on that long-ago night? What if he had never met Lori Mills to begin with? He might be elsewhere right now, with a more conventional job, a wife and a family, and no involvement in these sordid matters of life or death. Lee McCabe might still be a killer—but this fact would have no connection to his own life.

With these thoughts in mind, Phelps accelerated over the railroad crossing and continued toward the crime scene at Jimmy Mack's garage.

47

The sole witness on hand at Jimmy Mack's garage—a retired tobacco farmer and postal worker named Earl Carter—was probably in his late eighties. Phelps instructed Carter to sit in the passenger seat of his idling squad car while he gave his preliminary statement. He turned up the squad car's air conditioner to its maximum setting. Then he gave the old man a lukewarm bottle of water to sip. Carter was way past his prime and obviously shaken up. Phelps thought: *If he goes into shock, this old man could become the third casualty here.*

Carter twirled the clear plastic Aquafina bottle in his liver-spotted hands. He looked at Phelps: "It was him," Carter said in conclusion. "The young fella they been showin' on TV. I knowed it the second I seen his face in there."

"Thank you very much, Mr. Carter," Phelps said. "I think that will be enough for now. We may need to contact you for some follow-up questions within the next few days."

"I know what I seen," Carter said, though Phelps had not challenged the accuracy of his statement. "I seen his face and the thought goin' through my head was: It's that fella who done all that killin, and there was two more who he done kilt." Carter took another drink from the water bottle. "And right away I was wonderin': *Is he goin' to kill me too? Do you know how old I am, Sheriff?*"

Phelps would not have been surprised to learn that Carter was over a hundred years old, but he said: "I have no idea."

"Eighty-nine," Carter said. "I already outlived two a muh chil-drun. And there I was, fearin' for my life like I was a young pup. At my age, why should I care? But there I was, hopin': *Oh, please Jesus, not here, not now.*" Carter placed a cool hand on Phelps's wrist. "You live long enough, and there be plenty a things that make you cry. But once you get into this life, you ain't too keen to leave it. You know what I mean, Sheriff?"

Carter removed his hand from Phelps's wrist and drank the last of his water.

Phelps thought: *Yes, I do know what you mean. And I'm determined not to let anyone else leave this life involuntarily because of Lee McCabe.*

The testimony of Earl Carter could not be discounted. He had not seen McCabe kill anyone; but his words were nonetheless damning —from a practical perspective if not from a purely legal one.

Phelps had known that his antipathy toward Lee McCabe was unfair and biased; but he had not denied its existence. When he saw Lee McCabe, he saw the smirking face of Tom McCabe, and he re-experienced the revelations of Lori's unfaithfulness.

In the beginning he had worried that this antipathy would preju-dice him against Lori Mills' son. As the sheriff of Hawkins County, he could not recuse himself from his duties as an officer of the law. He was bound to pursue McCabe and take him into custody. And that might mean killing him, if the young man resisted arrest with violence.

But he could prevent himself from acting as a de facto judge— from prejudicing the evidence against the young man. And so he had compensated for his own weakness by adopting a forced objectivity that minced logic and denied the facts before him. He had taken Lee's side when talking with the FBI, he had made sure that the investiga-tion did not narrowly focus on McCabe.

Now Lee was placed at the scene of two more murders, by a reliable witness who had no motive to fabricate; and meth appeared to be at the center of the bloodshed. Once again there was an irrefutable connection between Lee McCabe, drugs, and violence.

Why was he so steadfastly determined to see around, above, or beyond that connection? He had seen McCabe at Fitzsimmons's trailer with his own eyes. And Earl Carter had seen McCabe step out of Jimmy Mack's office, rummaging around only a few feet away from two fresh corpses. Circumstantial evidence sometimes pointed in the wrong direction; but this was the exception rather than the rule. Two decades of law enforcement had taught Phelps that the elaborate conspiracy against an innocent man was mostly the stuff of detective fiction and movie melodrama. The law was supposed to be unbiased; but the facts rarely were: The suspect who was guilty by appearance was usually guilty by deed as well.

Phelps wondered if Iraq had in fact turned Lee McCabe into a casual killer, as Agent Lomax had suggested. The images of the two men in the garage—one with his chest blown out, the other with his lungs and heart perforated by gunshot wounds—painted the situation in stark terms: Lee McCabe might very well be the sort of monster who could gun down both men and women in cold blood. Phelps reminded himself once again that none of this was about him —his past, or his fizzled ambitions, or his desire to somehow expiate his own sins.

If he prejudiced himself in favor of a killer, he would fail in his duty as surely as if he prejudiced himself against an innocent man.

48

Phelps was not surprised when Agent Lomax showed up in a nondescript Detroit-built sedan with U.S. government plates. The FBI agents had set up shop in a spare office room at the sheriff's department. They would have heard all about the most recent shootout. Phelps gave him an account of Earl Carter's testimony.

"Do you still believe that Lee McCabe is some sort of angel?" Lomax asked.

"I never did believe that he was an angel, Agent Lomax. But I don't like to see a man convicted before all the evidence is in. That's all I'm trying to do."

Lomax nodded. "I hear you, sheriff. But last time I checked, our job was law enforcement. We leave the judgment part to the next people in the assembly line."

"Agreed," Phelps said.

"And let's suppose," Lomax went on. "Just for the sake of argument, that it was your job to judge Lee McCabe. He's now been tied to two crime scenes. The circumstantial evidence is not in his favor, you'd have to agree."

Phelps did agree—and this was exactly what he had been thinking himself. Nevertheless, he felt compelled to maintain a thread of objectivity, if only for his own sake.

"Well, McCabe certainly didn't gun down the family in the campground. In fact, both the husband and the wife said that McCabe behaved almost gentlemanlike, considering the circumstances. You could argue that a cold-blooded killer, already on the run and facing a man with a rifle, would not have hesitated to err on the side of violence in a situation like that."

Lomax said: "When this is over, I need to send you up to Quantico for a profiling course. Mass murderers and serial killers are seldom uniform in their brutality. They all have soft spots. There was a case in Sweden a few years ago, a serial killer who tortured thirteen women and girls to death. He kept them locked in a homemade cell in his basement. He usually raped them for a few weeks before he finally killed them."

"I remember reading about that," Phelps said. "The Butcher of Halmstad."

"That's right. But you may not recall that the Butcher of Halmstad was a twenty-seven-year-old man named Gustav Elofsson, who hated female members of his own species—while retaining a soft spot for cats. When the Swedish national police finally broke the case, they discovered his latest victim in the basement cell. She was only twelve years old. Elofsson had her chained to the wall, sitting naked in her own filth.

"But the thing is, Sheriff, Elofsson's cats were living like little lords in that house, even by the highest standards of the most fanatical animal-lover. They had the best food, the best veterinary care. The cats had obviously never been mistreated. They kept weaving between the policemen's feet while they were freeing that girl from Elofsson's torture chamber."

"I know what you're getting at, Lomax."

"Do you, Sheriff? So Lee McCabe decided to play the kindhearted outlaw prince with that family in the campground. That doesn't mean a damn thing. No more than Elofsson's love of cats meant anything. Remember: violent men are seldom known for consistent, predictable behavior. That's another thing that keeps you and me in business."

49

"Tell us what you saw last Saturday morning. Tell us everything."

Phelps and Norris repeated this question many times that evening. They drove out to *the Tradewinds* and knocked on the flimsy, hollow-sounding doors of more than twenty trailers. The people tensed up a bit at first, as people are wont to do when a policeman shows up at their door. After all, a visit from an officer of the law is never a good thing. You might be in trouble, or a relative of yours might have landed in jail—or worse—the county morgue.

When Phelps informed each resident of the purpose of their visit, he was met by either quick shakes of the head, or long, nodding sighs. The head shakers stated that no, they had not witnessed the horrible of events of that morning; but you might want to talk to so-and-so in the next trailer down. So-and-so had been heard talking voluminously of the killings. So-and-so must have seen *something* that will help you get to the bottom of this horrible business. And oh my, isn't it a shame about that McCabe boy—turning to crime after he only recently returned from Iraq a hero. What is the world coming to when a young man like that can go so thoroughly wrong?

The nodders urgently bid the policemen to sit down before they fell into a conspiratorial tone. *Yes, I saw something that morning. Let me tell you all about it.* This group was generally eager to be of assistance. Phelps discerned that at least a few of them were also eager for the opportunity to be a part of something vast and more important than themselves, if only tangentially. This realization caused Phelps no resentment or ill will. The witness who sought personal validation and recognition was familiar to every cop who had ever investigated a serious crime.

Those residents of *the Tradewinds* who had seen anything all reported the same facts: Lee McCabe had emerged from Fitzsimmons's trailer with a gun. More than a dozen witnesses confirmed McCabe's presence inside the trailer. But no one had seen Lee kill either of the two victims, or anyone else.

When Phelps knocked at the trailer directly across from the home of the late Tim Fitzsimmons, he was disappointed. They knocked and waited, then knocked and waited again.

"No one home," Phelps finally concluded. "Well, we can come back if we have to, Ron. This trailer had the best view of the crime scene. We might not learn anything we don't already know; but we've got to talk to whoever lives here."

"That's Hal Marsten's trailer!"

Both Phelps and Norris turned at the sound of the voice. A middle-aged woman stood in the gravel roadway. She was heavyset and she wore an unflattering pair of shorts and a polka-dot blouse. A little boy of perhaps five years of age held her hand. The little boy wore no shirt. He had evidently been playing hard that day: his bare torso was coated with grime.

"That's Hal Marsten's trailer," the woman repeated. The child fidgeted and she tugged his arm: "Stand still, Tad!"

"Do you know where we might find Hal Marsten?" Phelps asked.

"In Lexington," the woman said. "Hal's mother's in the hospital. She's been in for more than two weeks now, but she took a turn for the worse. Hal got the call around noon and took off right away."

"Any idea when he'll be back?"

"Sure don't. But when he comes back you probably won't have any trouble finding him. Hal's what you'd call a homebody."

"Do you know if Hal was here on the morning of the shootings? We're interviewing all residents who might have been here when the homicides took place." Phelps gestured across the road toward the Fitzsimmons trailer. The front door was covered with crisscrossing strips of yellow POLICE LINE – DO NOT CROSS tape. The trailer wouldn't be here much longer. Tomorrow a truck and crew would arrive to remove the death chamber from its moorings and tow it to a state crime lab in Frankfort.

"Hal was probably here," the woman speculated. "Like I said, he's a homebody, and he's always looking out that screen door. Kind of an oddball, ya know? More than fifty years old and never been married. Keeps to hisself, he does. But he's always lookin' out that door."

"I'll leave a note for him," Norris said, preempting Phelps. His pen was already moving across a Hawkins County Sheriff's Department memo pad. "I'll leave him my cell number, too. If I hear from him late tonight, I'll call you at home."

Phelps nodded at Norris. He thanked the woman for her help and she continued on her way, still tugging at the arm of the unruly child. Apparently little Tad hadn't learned his lesson about the fidgeting.

"Let's go, Ron," he said. "After you tuck that note in his door jamb. We've done all we can here tonight."

Phelps was halfway back to his cruiser before he noticed that the deputy had not accompanied him. Norris stood in the roadway between the trailers of Hal Marsten and Tim Fitzsimmons. His arms were crossed and he was looking intently at first one trailer and then the other, as if running potential scenarios in his head, trying to puzzle out what had occurred on the bloody morning.

ON HIS WAY home Phelps stopped at a campground where there was an outdoor brazier enclosed within a small brick housing. Phelps shut off the cruiser and removed the shoebox from the floor area behind him. Then he withdrew a disposable lighter from the police car's glove compartment.

This was a strange way to go about it, he knew. But dumping the old photos in the garbage would not suffice. If he merely threw them away, they could potentially be retrieved in the subsequent days. His purging of the past required a certain finality.

He dumped the contents of the shoebox into the brazier. Then he applied pressure to the thumbwheel of the lighter and a little flame appeared. It was not much of a flame, but it would do.

He lifted an old envelope from the pile of photos and other miscellaneous documentary evidence of what had once been his life. The envelope contained a letter that he had written to Lori after her pregnancy announcement but had never mailed. He touched the flame to the envelope and it immediately crackled. A two-inch flame leapt from the corner of the paper. Already pieces of the envelope and the letter inside were crumbling to ash.

He placed the envelope into the pile from the shoebox and these materials caught fire quickly. A column of smoke—white, noxious, chemical smoke—rose from the little brazier. Finally he tore the shoebox into strips and fed these into the fire, too.

Phelps stood back and watched the fire burn until the last of it was gone, and the floor of the brazier was covered with a layer of indistinguishable ashes.

So that's what's left, he thought. *It's all gone now.*

After a little while longer—later he would not be able to recall exactly how long—he turned away from the dead ashes and began his ride home for the night.

50

A man wearing only a dark hood approached the bound and gagged woman from behind. She trembled when she felt his fingertips touch the base of her neck. She knew what was coming.

They were in a room that approximated a medieval dungeon. The walls were rough-hewn, grey stone. A single torch was mounted in an iron base in the wall behind them. Torchlight flickered across the woman's face. Her cheeks were heavily rouged. She wore blue eye shadow.

The hooded man slid his hand down from the woman's neck and cupped it around one of her bare breasts. She moaned—at first with pleasure, but then with pain, as the hooded man tightened his grip.

Ron Norris lifted the remote that controlled his DVD player and increased the audio volume. The light from the television set was the sole source of illumination in his living room.

This DVD was new to his collection. It had arrived only last week in the P.O. box that he kept in Louisville—registered under an alias, of course. The dialogue was entirely in a Slavic-sounding language that Norris of course did not understand—probably Russian or Czech, possibly Bulgarian. A certain group of underground filmmakers in Eastern Europe specialized in this type of movie: "rough porn" consisting of simulated violence and cheesy sex scenes.

Technically, there was nothing in this video—or the others like it in his collection—that was illegal. The violence was all faked, and the "actors" were all over the age of eighteen, so far as he could tell. But the DVDs comprised a secret—not unlike his secret activities in the streets of Louisville, which had transformed Lester Finn into his controller.

If you had a secret (and who *didn't* have secrets?) you had to take every possible step to keep those secrets hidden. Your secrets could easily destroy you.

The action onscreen was just getting interesting when he heard his cell phone chirp. He leaned forward and plucked it off the coffee table.

The little readout on the cell phone displayed a local number and the name "Marsten, Hal".

If Hal Marsten had been looking out his front door last Saturday morning, then Hal Marsten was now the latest keeper of Norris's largest, most dangerous secret. Marsten had not asked for this role, of course. It would also be true to say that Marsten possessed only a piece of it: While he might have seen Lester Finn's gunmen enter Fitzsimmons's trailer, there was no way he could piece together the full implications of what he had seen. But those mitigating factors would not absolve the peculiar bachelor from his new responsibility. If Marsten had seen the four armed men enter the trailer before Lee McCabe, then his words would have the power to destroy Norris. This could not be allowed to happen.

The deputy pressed the talk button of his cell phone and steadied himself.

"Deputy Norris here," he said.

51

There seemed to be a voice calling his name. The voice roused Hal Marsten out of an uneasy sleep—one that had been filled with turbulent, half-remembered dreams.

"Hal Marsten?" There came the voice again.

It had to be the voice of a dream. He decided that he was still partially asleep. Sometimes dreams could bleed into waking reality, especially when you awoke in the middle of the night.

Usually he was a sound sleeper, but these were not usual times. For Hal Marsten, the past few days had been filled with turmoil and worry. First that horrible pair of murders across the road, and then the call from the hospital about his mother. The call that had sent him on a frantic drive to Lexington earlier today.

Hal knew that his mother probably did not have long to live. When he stood beside her bed, she had barely recognized him, both because of her condition and because of the pain killers they had given her. She was well into her eighties, and she had multiple health problems. He did not hold out much hope; but the prospect of losing his mother weighed heavily on him. The inevitability of his impending loss did nothing to lessen the blow.

"Hal?"

Again the voice: someone calling him. Now he might be dreaming about his conversation with Deputy Norris. After returning from the hospital, he had called the deputy, as the paper wedged in his door jamb requested. His conversation with Deputy Norris confused him somewhat. First Norris spoke of arranging a meeting with himself and his boss—the sheriff. And then Norris seemed determined to make him describe every detail of what he had seen on Saturday morning. Perhaps it was simply a matter of the police being thorough, he told himself.

Norris had listened silently as Hal told about the four armed men who broke into the Fitzsimmons trailer. He described the screaming, the cursing, and the sounds of struggle, and then the sounds of muffled gunfire.

He told Norris how the young man, Lee McCabe, had entered the trailer after the killing was already done. He knew it was important that Deputy Norris grasp this point.

Hal had reproached himself for not speaking out on Lee McCabe's behalf much earlier—when the young man was being tried and convicted by a kangaroo court of his neighbors. And he had remained hidden inside his trailer when the police knocked on his door yesterday morning.

But today he had finally revealed the information that should exonerate the young ex-marine. And in redeeming Lee McCabe, he had also redeemed himself.

These were the thoughts passing through his mind when he heard his name spoken once again—now in a louder, more emphatic tone. Suddenly Hal was fully awake. This was no dream. An intruder was in his trailer—in his living room, judging by the sound.

Hal kept a loaded and holstered .22 magnum revolver beneath his bed. Taking care to avoid making the box springs of his bed cry out, Hal slowly rolled over on his side and reached for the gun.

The gun was gone.

"Come on out, Marsten," the unidentified male intruder said. "I've got your gun in here, if that's what's keeping you. You can collect it in the living room."

"Who are you?" Hal cried out, his heart pounding.

"Just someone who wants to have a little talk with you."

When Hal did not reply, the man spoke again: "Come on out, Hal. I don't have all night. You have nothing to be afraid of if you simply do as you're told. If my intention was to kill you now, I could have shot you in your sleep."

Now that Hal thought about it, this line of reasoning did contain a certain amount of logic. Moreover, the man was in his living room and he was apparently not going to go away without a face-to-face meeting.

What choice did he really have, then?

Hal hoisted himself out of bed. He walked through the doorway of his bedroom and into the main hall that connected the living room and kitchen to the trailer's two bedrooms and single bathroom.

He was about to flip a light switch when he heard the words: "Leave the lights alone, Hal. We've got plenty of light for our little talk. All the light we need."

There were actually two men in the living room. A late middle-aged man with long hair was seated in Hal's recliner, and a younger, larger man was standing beside him.

Hal struggled to maintain his composure, to take in as many relevant details as he could. Although the light in the trailer was sparse, it was not completely dark. The hulking younger man who was on his feet was completely unfamiliar to him—but there was something familiar about the seated, older man. Where had Hal seen him, though?

Then he noted that the older man was holding a shape in his lap. It was Hal's cat, Bullet. Bullet flicked his tail and nuzzled himself deeper into the stranger's lap, apparently unaware that anything was amiss here. Bullet was like that—unlike so many cats, he took instantly to strangers.

"You ain't gonna hurt Bullet, are you?"

The stranger appeared to be surprised by the suggestion.

"Bullet? I think 'Gullet' would be a better name for this cat. This animal needs to go on a diet. But, no I'm not going to harm your cat.

As it turns out, I'm rather partial to these feline beasts. Cats have dignity. They are loners, hunters. Far superior to dogs, you know. Dogs, on the other hand, are pack animals. Vile creatures."

The man looked down at the contented Bullet and Hal suddenly grasped his identity: He was Lester Finn, the owner of that bar in Blood Flats. Hal didn't hang out in the bars much, but he had visited the Boar's Head several times over the years.

But why was the tavern owner in his trailer like this, and who was the other man? The younger man had yet to speak. He stood beside the recliner with his arms folded across his chest, his head nearly touching the trailer's low ceiling.

Lester Finn patted Bullet's head

"The great masters understood the true natures of dogs and cats. Tell me, Hal, did you ever read *Cyrano de Bergerac*?"

Hal shook his head.

"Have you seen the movie?"

Hal shook his head again.

"Tell me, have you ever *heard* of *Cyrano de Bergerac*?"

Hal Marsten returned a blank stare.

"No," Lester Finn said. "I didn't think so." He paused and quoted the film: "'When I see people going about their business making friends—as dogs make friends, I say to myself: thank heaven, *here comes another enemy*.'"

Hal was about to ask for a clarification—why Lester Finn, a man with whom he had no identifiable business—had shown up in his home in the middle of the night in such a manner. He noticed that Lester's accomplice had a semiautomatic pistol tucked into the front waistband of his pants, not that he really needed one, given his size and the fact that Hal was unarmed.

Lester gingerly lifted Bullet and placed the purring tomcat on the floor. Bullet idled lazily away, his tail swishing behind him.

"No—I'm not going to kill your cat. But—" Lester Finn raised his hand, as if a profound idea had just struck him. "I'll make no such promises about your mother."

Hal started forward, suddenly furious. "If you do anything to Momma—"

The big man standing beside Lester drew the pistol from his waistband. Lester didn't even flinch. Hal stopped when he saw the gun pointed at him. A stray beam of moonlight glinted off the gun's muzzle.

"Then you'll do what?" Lester asked. "It should be pretty clear to you that I didn't come here for a negotiation. Here's the situation: I understand that you saw something in that trailer the other morning."

"Yes," Hal said. "I saw four men burst into that trailer, and then they up and killed that crackhead Tim Fitzsimmons and his girlfriend."

Lester sighed. "Luke, I think what Mr. Marsten here needs is a bit of aversion therapy."

Without warning, the big man lunged forward and drove his fist into Hal's stomach. Hal cried out as his entire torso exploded with pain. He fell to the ground. The giant named Luke towered over him. He knelt and raised his fist to strike Hal again.

"Enough, Luke," Lester said. "I think that's sufficient to give Hal here the lesson he needs. Hal, you are never to speak of those four men—those men who do not exist—again. Do you understand? Answer me, Hal"

Hal gasped for air. His stomach was empty but he felt the urge to vomit. The simple act of drawing breath was a major agony.

"Yeah," Hal wheezed. "Why—"

"Because if you do otherwise, your mother will die. Then you will die. Does that clarify the situation for you?"

Lying on his side, staring up at his attackers, Hal feared that he was going to lose consciousness at any moment. *Why were these men here? Why were they tormenting him so?*

"Buh-but, I already tol' someone. I tol' that Deputy Norris from the county sheriff's department."

"Did you tell anyone else?"

"No," Hal replied, gritting his teeth as a fresh wave of pain buffeted him. This was the truth.

"Don't worry about Deputy Norris," Lester Finn said. "Another thing: I think it would be a good idea for you to leave town for a while. Go to Lexington, be at your sick mother's bedside. Do you think you can do that? Otherwise, we may have to come back tomorrow night for another chat. Or we may decide to go ahead and visit your mother."

"I'll git," Hal said. "I'll git first thing in the morning."

"That's what I like to hear." Lester said, standing up from Hal's recliner. "Oh—another thing: If you tell anyone about our visit here tonight, first we'll kill your mother, and then we'll kill you. If you call the police, we'll know about it."

"I won't tell nobody," Hal said. And once again, Hal was speaking the truth. He had talked to Deputy Norris—hoping to do the right thing and help Lee McCabe. And just look where it had gotten him.

"Good night, Hal." Lester said. "It's been a pleasure talking to you. Why don't you stay there on the floor for a while? It will give you some time to reflect on the bad things that will happen if you fail to follow our instructions to the letter."

The two men walked out of Hal's trailer and closed the front door behind them. Hal lay there in the darkness for a long time, thinking about how foolish and naïve he had apparently been.

52

The radio announcer said that the state and local police were searching the area for twenty-three-year-old Lee McCabe of Perryston. McCabe was considered to be armed and dangerous. The announcer mentioned that McCabe was a Marine Corps veteran who had recently returned from Iraq.

When Dawn heard the name as she drove toward Blood Flats, she nearly slammed her foot on the brake pedal. She took her foot off the gas and her car slowed to a crawl. Another driver who had been following her too closely tapped his horn, then pulled into the left lane and gunned past her. He was a middle-aged man who wore a suit and tie. Dawn saw him briefly interrupt his cell phone conversation to glance in her direction as he accelerated away, shaking his head at another absent-minded young woman who could not drive.

Lee McCabe. Surely it was not *that* Lee McCabe.

But on the other hand, it *had* to be. While McCabe was a common enough name, Perryston was a small town. There might possibly be two Lee McCabes of roughly the same age in Perryston. That was an acceptable, though unlikely, coincidence. But there could not be two such men who were both Iraq war veterans.

It *had* to be that Lee McCabe.

Even as Dawn recognized the name, and she had no trouble recalling Lee's face. The thought of Lee McCabe caused her to feel a little jolt of emotion. It was the sort of feeling she had not felt about men for a long time—and a feeling that was completely alien to her in the presence of men like Robert.

At the same time, it was a little silly for her to feel anything for Lee McCabe at all. She did not really know Lee McCabe—not like she *might* have—though she had definitely met him. It had been only a few years ago. Since that time, she had been unable to decide if Lee McCabe was a man she should have gotten to know better—or simply another small-town arrogant jerk, inflated by a false sense of self-importance.

It had been the summer after her senior year in high school. A pool party thrown by a former classmate named Rhonda Glasser. Rhonda's father owned a successful contracting business; and the Glassers lived in one of the nicer homes in the county, a rural McMansion built on ten acres of converted farmland.

Dawn had been in particularly buoyant spirits that night. Although in the fairly recent past, this seemed a lifetime before she had taken her first hit of meth. She had been in the full flush of early womanhood. Her body was fit and lean from four years of high school track and lacrosse. As she threaded her way through the crowd in the fenced-in enclosure around Rhonda's pool, she detected the glances that she drew from the young men around her. Although she had never considered herself to be either a flirt or a tease, she had to admit that their glances gave her a certain feeling of power. Even if you were a straight-A student who had been awarded an academic scholarship, it still felt good to be openly admired by members of the opposite sex.

Lee McCabe struck up a conversation with her near the Glassers' outdoor wet bar, which was covered by a timber awning and built into an impressive stone foundation. Lee had been wearing civilian attire, but his close-cropped haircut made him easily identifiable as a member of the military.

"Dawn Hardin," he said. "Last time I saw you, you were leaning over one of your textbooks in study hall."

Lee had been several years ahead of her at S.H.C.C.H.S. She was surprised that he remembered her at all.

"And the last time I saw you, you were getting your butt kicked in a wrestling match."

Lee laughed. They both understood what was going on. He was testing her and she was testing him back. "Well, I guess I didn't win all of my matches. But I seem to remember that I won most of them. Too bad that you happened to see me on one of my off days."

After that, the conversation had flowed easily between them. They exchanged small talk for a while. He told her about his training in the Marine Corps, and how he would be shipping out for Iraq in a few weeks. She told him about her scholarship to the University of Kentucky, about her plans to be a doctor.

It came time for the conversation to end, and for it to either terminate completely or end on some promise of future contact. She liked Lee. Their paths had rarely crossed in high school. (*Her claim to seeing him get his butt kicked in a wrestling match had been nothing more than a line.*) Nevertheless, she liked what she saw in him now. Unlike most of the recently graduated high school boys at the party, Lee seemed sure of himself. He didn't appear to be posturing or going out of his way to impress her with transparent lies and exaggerations, like so many of them often did. He was simply being himself, and that was more than enough to hold her attention and interest.

She would have been glad to give him her phone number. They could have exchanged email addresses. U.S. service personnel had access to email, didn't they? And maybe he was going to Iraq, but that wasn't forever, was it? They might stay in touch via email, and in a few years, who knew?

When she hinted about keeping in touch, Lee shocked her with his reply.

"It would never work," Lee said simply. "You're going to UK in a few months, and in a few years you're going to be a doctor. I'm going to be spending the next few years in a desert hellhole. When I come back to Hawkins County—if I come back—I'll be a machinist or maybe a manager at a construction site. We'll be in different worlds by then, and we won't even recognize each other as the people we are right now."

These words were more than enough to change her opinion in an instant. In that moment she had reassessed Lee McCabe as a boy who was simultaneously arrogant and hampered by an inferiority complex.

A number of retorts had been on the tip of her tongue. She was even tempted to make some attempt at rescuing the situation, assuring him that she did not come from money herself, and was not necessarily committed to marrying another doctor or even a rich man. She planned to be with the man she most admired and respected—whoever he turned out to be.

But in the end she had said: "Watch out for yourself in Iraq."

That had been more or less the end of their conversation. In the short span of a few years, circumstances had changed radically for both of them, in ways that neither would have anticipated. She was no longer a med school-bound honors student, but a meth addict who sold herself for money. Lee had indeed gone to Iraq and apparently acquitted himself well there; but now he was a fugitive—and apparently a murderer.

These realizations brought tears to Dawn's eyes as she struggled to concentrate on her driving, fighting the distraction of a sharp pang of meth craving. *How can people go astray so completely?* she wondered. *How can dreams turn into nightmares almost overnight?*

53

Lee found Brett St. Croix exactly where he said he would be, in a little clearing within a patch of woodland that was sufficiently isolated. St. Croix had told him to travel a half a mile north of the Chickasaw Creek, and to then go east until he came to an unusually large, rounded shape rising up from the earth. St. Croix said that he had set up camp on the other side of the massive hill.

"That's an Adena Indian burial mound," the journalist had said over the phone. "Did you know that?"

"I may have heard about it at some time," Lee replied. "I've spent a lot more time than usual in the woods these past few days. And what did you say your name was? 'Brett St. Croix'? Where have I heard of you?"

"I wrote a book about the U.S. military establishment," St. Croix said. "It's called *The Death Factory: How the U.S. Military Turns American Youths into Killers*. I've been interviewed on television a few times recently. I was on just the other day, in fact; but my guess is that you were otherwise occupied."

Of course, Lee thought. The author whom he had seen on the television in the feed store.

Lee had been surprised a few hours earlier when he had received a phone call from an unfamiliar number, with an area code that was definitely not local. He had been continuing his trek through the woods when his phone had chirped. At first he had expected that it would be Deputy Norris or Sheriff Phelps. It would make sense for them to contact him, if only to use the cell phone signal to triangulate his position.

The call, though, had not been the police, but this Brett St. Croix.

"How the hell did you get my number?" Lee asked. "And what do you want?"

"There isn't an investigative journalist worth his salt who can't get anyone's cell phone number within a few hours," St. Croix explained. "And I'm calling you because I saw *you* on television. And I want to tell your story, if you'll let me. I'm going to go out on a limb here and say that you could use a competent spokesperson about now."

Starting from this preamble, St. Croix informed Lee that he was on his way to Hawkins County as he spoke. St. Croix was based in Cincinnati—only hours from Perryston, "where the very shootings took place," St. Croix noted.

"Just let me tell you right off the bat that I didn't do it," Lee said.

He heard St. Croix snort into the phone. "For the time being, Mr. McCabe, it matters not to me whether you killed those people or not. I'm not an attorney and I'm sure as hell not a judge. My mission is to find out what motivates you—what makes you tick."

Lee agreed to meet with St. Croix. While it was possible that the journalist was working in cahoots with law enforcement, Lee did not believe that this scenario was likely: St. Croix was clearly hostile to the military. Most of those types were on equally unfriendly terms with the police as well.

If the man wants to talk, I'll talk to him, Lee had decided. *If he doesn't attempt to screw me over, then he might be able to tell the outside world the truth about what happened in Tim Fitzsimmons's trailer.*

These were the thoughts that Lee McCabe was mulling over as he rounded the top of the wooded hillside that Brett St. Croix had identified as an Adena Indian burial mound. He saw the journalist's campsite in the clearing, and then the journalist himself, seated on a folding camp chair. He was booting up an expensive-looking laptop. An empty, identical chair had been set up across from him, in a conferencing position.

When he heard Lee approach, St. Croix merely smiled and gave a short wave of his hand.

Lee stopped short of the campsite. Something about this entire situation seemed quite unnatural. Lee was literally fleeing for his life; he had been forced to kill one man, and he had seen three more people shot dead. And here this man was, camped out in the middle of the forest, affecting a casual posture that suggested that none of this was as serious as it appeared to be.

"I know you're armed," St. Croix said. "And you have probably already figured out that I'm not. You have two choices, Mr. McCabe. You can either shoot me or sit down and talk. Do one or the other."

He had expected Brett St. Croix to be an effete, timid sort of man. But the journalist's present demeanor belied his short, pudgy stature and pale complexion. Lee had the impression that St. Croix was not afraid of him, and this engendered a grudging respect for the man. It took a certain amount of courage for an unarmed man to stare down another who had a gun.

Lee scanned the nearest hillsides on either side of the clearing, and the woods behind St. Croix's tent. He looked for any sign of movement: a shooter with a scope and a high-powered rifle, or perhaps a group of men who would attempt to force his surrender.

St. Croix momentarily stopped tapping on his laptop. "Oh I get it: You think I'm working as a police decoy. If you've studied my work at all, you should know that I'd never work for them. Or perhaps you think I am in the employ of one of the criminal factions that is involved in this little fray. Ah, yes, I would truly relish the idea of putting myself in the middle of a shootout between yourself and a band of drug traffickers. What a lovely way to meet my maker."

"I thought you were an atheist," Lee said.

"So you've read my work. I'm flattered, Mr. McCabe."

"No," Lee said. "I'd never heard of you until I saw you on TV the other day. It was just a logical assumption. You can't be a proper anti-establishment type if you believe in God. You've got to be able to roll your eyes and act all superior when someone mentions religion at a cocktail party."

"Touché, Mr. McCabe. Touché. Now, are we going to trade clever barbs all afternoon, or are you going to take a seat so that maybe, just maybe, I can tell the world your story and possibly alleviate your current predicament? Or do you enjoy the life of a fugitive? Keep this up, and you might make the FBI's ten most wanted list by the end of the week—if you're not already on it."

"I said I would talk to you and I will," Lee answered.

"Very good. Very good, Mr. McCabe. By all means let's talk." St. Croix made a flamboyant gesture to the chair opposite him. "Have a seat."

Lee stepped forward and took a seat in the proffered chair. He was downwind from St. Croix and he could smell the writer's cologne.

"Excellent," said St. Croix. He pointed to a red Igloo cooler beside his own chair. "Would you like a refreshment? Something to eat?"

"Thanks, I've already had lunch."

"Frogs and possums don't count, Mr. McCabe. Here—" He leaned over, flipped the cooler open, and removed two items: a large granola bar in a red foil wrapper, and a box of Capri Sun. St. Croix tossed both items to Lee.

McCabe caught the juice and the bar. "I said I'd already—"

St. Croix rolled his eyes. "Oh, please, Mr. McCabe. Drop the macho bullshit already. You've been living in the woods. You'd probably sell your mother for a Big Mac right now."

"My mother's dead."

"My condolences. Your wife or your girlfriend then."

"I don't have either at the moment."

Without waiting for St. Croix's next rejoinder, Lee tore open the foil wrapping on the granola bar. He removed the plastic straw taped to the side of the juice box and perforated the drinking hole. He took a bite of the bar and a long drink of the juice.

"Hit the spot?" St. Croix asked.

"It'll do," Lee said.

"A lot better than prison food, I imagine."

"I don't plan to go to prison," Lee said, chewing the granola bar.

St. Croix smiled indulgently but said nothing. He tapped away on his laptop as if he had momentarily forgotten about Lee.

After Lee had finished eating and drinking, St. Croix looked up from his computer.

"Well, Mr. McCabe, I would be willing to bet that you're surprised to see me here."

"Almost as surprised as you must be to see me."

"Not at all, actually. You're a fugitive and I'm a well-known journalist who has volunteered to tell your side of the story. You have much to gain from this meeting, if you handle it right."

Lee let the Capri Sun box and the granola bar wrapper fall to the ground beneath his chair. This one time, he was willing to be a litterbug.

"I'll say this for you, Mr. St. Croix. You've got a brass pair for coming out here."

"Oh, I get it," the journalist said. "I'm supposed to be shaking in my boots, afraid that you'll shoot me."

"What makes you so sure that I won't?"

St. Croix smiled thinly. "Because you're not stupid. At least, I don't think you are. I've read your service record—and all about the medals you were awarded in Iraq. As much as I disapprove of our government's current actions in the Middle East, I have to admit that your ability to stay alive demonstrates a certain resourcefulness. For you to kill me now would be a misuse of resources. I'm worth far more to you alive than dead."

"True," Lee allowed.

"And I'll tell you once more, Mr. McCabe: Drop the macho bullshit. You aren't the most dangerous thing I've ever encountered—not by a long shot. I was a junior correspondent in Rwanda back in 1994, when the country's Hutu majority decided to launch a genocide against their Tutsi neighbors. Do you know how most of the killing was done, Mr. McCabe? With machetes. And a handful of Westerners who got in the way were among the victims. One day, I had to rely on my high school French to talk a Hutu vigilante out of carving me up with a seventeen-inch knife.

"You see this?" The journalist rolled up his sleeve, revealing a long, white scar that was clearly recognizable as a blade wound. "One of the vigilante leader's followers took a swipe at me before the leader shouted him down," St. Croix explained.

Lee nodded. "Close call."

"Yes. Close call indeed. I could also tell you about the Serbian soldier who knocked me unconscious with his rifle butt in 1999, or the Mexican drug lord who threatened to shoot and decapitate me when I contradicted him during an interview. I'm no marine, Mr. McCabe, and I've never won a medal; but I'm no coward, either. Now, you make up your mind: Do you want to tell me your story, or do I fold up my tent and go home?"

Lee folded his hands in his lap and sighed. He wanted to spar further with this pompous journalist, this sanctimonious intellectual who wrote books that portrayed U.S. Marines as robotic murderers. But there was no point in it—no time, and nothing to be gained.

Perhaps he would be wise to accept the journalist's offer, after all. No one from the outside world seemed to be on his side at the moment. Lee had no illusions that St. Croix was motivated by genuine concern for a former marine who had been wrongly accused of a crime. The journalist doubtless had his own angle; he had something to gain from this. But that did not mean that the journalist would necessarily betray him.

And it was possible—just barely possible—that St. Croix's recounting of events would turn the tide in his favor. A long shot, but the only shot Lee had at present.

"Once again," Lee began. "I didn't kill those people in that trailer. Nor did I have any involvement in their killings."

Lee told St. Croix how he had overheard the attack on Tim Fitzsimmons and Jody White, and how he had attempted to intervene—only to find the victims already dead, or dying, in the case of Jody White.

For the most part St. Croix listened patiently, interrupting only to ask for clarifications and more details. When Lee recounted his initial flight from the scene of the crime, St. Croix interrupted him:

"If you were innocent, why didn't you stay put and cooperate with the police? "

"Sheriff Phelps hates me," Lee said.

"The sheriff *hates* you?"

Lee elaborated the history between Sheriff Phelps and a long-ago local girl named Lori Mills. This caused St. Croix to burst out laughing. Lee suspected that the journalist's laughter was genuine, and not merely done for effect.

"Let me get this straight: You ran because you believed the sheriff would try to frame you, all because of some youthful drama that occurred long before you were even born—long before the sheriff was even a sheriff."

"I understand your doubts," Lee said. "But there's a bit more to it. The sheriff's deputy tried to gun me down in cold blood." Lee told the story of his attempted surrender to Ron Norris, and the shots the deputy fired at him.

"I don't suppose there were any witnesses to this encounter, were there? I mean when the sheriff's deputy allegedly tried to gun you down."

Lee shook his head slowly. "No."

"Hmm."

"I suppose that comes across as a little too convenient."

"Some people would say so. But anyway—" St. Croix tapped furiously at his laptop. "Give me a second to catch up."

St. Croix asked a few more neutral questions of clarification: *Exactly where were the bodies positioned in the trailer when you entered? Did the young woman, Jody White, say anything to you before she died?*

He continued to tap on his keyboard. Finally, he looked up from the laptop and said to Lee: "Let me get this straight: You had absolutely nothing to do with those murders. You have absolutely no involvement in the local meth trade. Nor are you working for any faction involved in the manufacture, sale, or distribution of meth."

"No, no, and no."

"In fact, Mr. McCabe—the truth is quite the opposite. Far from being the villain here, you were acting as a sort of gun-toting Good Samaritan. You came upon a scene of dastardly evil, with every intention of playing the hero, even if it meant risking your own life and limb."

Lee was unsure of how to interpret the question. Was the journalist expressing doubt at the story he had just heard? Was he trying to bait Lee into making a transparently false statement? Or—least likely of all—was St. Croix expressing genuine admiration, albeit in a backhanded sort of way?

There was no way to know for sure, but some response was incumbent on Lee.

Lee said as evenly as possible: "What else would you expect of a U.S. marine?"

"Touché once again, Mr. McCabe. What else would one expect, indeed?...Well let's suppose, Mr. McCabe, that I was to take up your cause—sort of act as a proxy for you, if you will. What would you have me do?"

"You could start by telling people the truth."

"Oh, my dear boy," St. Croix began. "Sorry—I know you're not a boy. You've been to war and you've seen some terrible things. But you are still very naïve about the way the world works, aren't you?"

"Suppose you tell me how it works, *Mister* St. Croix."

"Very well. Here's how it works. Let's say I leave these woods and go forth into the world proclaiming, 'Call off the manhunt. Lee McCabe is innocent.' There's a problem there, you see. That would be nothing but my word against the word of various legal authorities, who believe that you are quite guilty. And as you've probably gathered, I don't exactly have a lot of pull among the establishment—law enforcement, the military, that sort of thing."

"So you're basically saying that I'm screwed and there is nothing you can do for me."

St. Croix held up his hand patiently, as if imparting an obvious lesson to a small child. "Not at all. Not at all. Let's say that I was somehow able to discover who really *did* commit those murders in the trailer—and more importantly, the men who paid them to commit them. Then the actual culprits would be charged with those crimes, and your lack of involvement in the crimes would be clearly shown. You would not only be exonerated, but given the—forgive me if this sounds a trifle patronizing—the hero status to which you are entitled."

"I'm not asking to be a damned hero," Lee said. "I just want my life back."

"Well and good. But your acclamation as a hero is inevitable—once the public discovers how you have been the victim here—no less a victim than the two young people who died in that trailer. Trust me, it's *an inexorable outcome.*"

To Lee, it seemed that the pretentious man sitting before him was speaking a different language. His words made sense enough—but St. Croix didn't seem to grasp the essential nature of the "predicament", as he called it. No doubt the journalist espied some opportunity to make himself a co-hero—or to gain publicity for himself at the very least.

Well, that much *was* inevitable, Lee thought. The journalist wasn't camped out in these woods for altruistic reasons. He had something to gain. But if St. Croix was willing to help, then why not trust him? *What other choice did he have?*

"If I become a hero as a result of all this," Lee said. "You can ride beside me in the ticker tape parade. But let me ask you: What makes you think you can get to the bottom of all this?"

"I'm a journalist, Mr. McCabe. That's what I do for a living. I get to the bottom of things. Just tell me where to look and whom to look at."

"Okay," Lee said. "As far as I can tell, you need to focus on two items, one human, one material: a guy named Lester Finn, and sawdust."

Lee told St. Croix everything about his shootout in Jimmy Mack's garage, and the meth that was inexplicably coated with sawdust. Then his brief conversation with Lester Finn.

"Give me a bit of time to work on this," the journalist said when

Lee had finished, closing his laptop. "We might just have something here."

Once again Lee had the feeling that St. Croix's overwhelming concern was the journalistic potential of the situation. "Any advice concerning what I should do in the meantime?" Lee asked.

"Try to remain free, since you can't trust the police," St. Croix said. "And try to stay alive."

54

The second he saw the truck round the bend, Lee realized that he had let his guard down and made a terrible mistake.

After his odd interview with Brett St. Croix, he continued onward. At this point, he was weighing a question: Should he flee or should he fight? The Hunter had told him to fight, of course; but this strange man in the woods had offered very little in the way of practical advice.

Brett St. Croix, on the other hand, seemed to advise that flight would be the better option. With a bit of time and resourcefulness, he could make his way out of Hawkins County. He might go south to Tennessee—or maybe north to Ohio. Wherever he went, the tentacles of the law would follow him. But if he merely stayed out of police custody and away from men like Jimmy Mack and Lester Finn, Brett St. Croix might unravel the connection between Lester Finn and the killers at the Tradewinds, and whatever Deputy Norris had in all of this. The journalist might very well do the heavy lifting for him. In the meantime, he would be able to stay free if he fled and maintained a low profile. He knew how to survive in hostile territory. This was a skill that his time in Iraq had given him.

His momentary distraction with this issue prevented him from noticing that he was approaching a road: A winding, serpentine country road that did not carry much traffic; but a road nonetheless. And roads are dangerous for a man on the run.

The vehicle that came around the bend was not a police vehicle; but Lee immediately recognized that this was no ordinary citizen or family out for a drive. This was a four-wheel drive truck. There were two men riding in the cab, and another two in the back.

The speed of the vehicle, and the postures of the men, suggested wary surveillance rather than mere travel. They looked from side to side as the truck judiciously navigated the downwardly sloping curve. These men were on the lookout, either for quarry or for danger. Such was the bearing of either the hunter or the hunted. This was the way men used to drive about in vehicles in Iraq.

When one of the men in the back made eye contact with him, there was an immediate flash of recognition. And Lee knew: this man not only recognized him, but he had been looking for him, also.

The man whistled and pounded on the rear window of the cab. Then the other men looked at him, and their faces all bore the same mixture of emotions: A tiny bit of fear perhaps, but a stronger intent to capture or kill him. After all, the numerical advantage was on their side.

"Hey, Lee McCabe," the man who had first recognized him shouted. "Hold it right there, buddy. We want to talk to you!" And now the truck was accelerating toward him, rapidly closing the distance.

He saw the two men in the back reach for unseen items on the bed of the truck. Lee knew even before he saw the black barrels of the weapons that they were retrieving their guns.

Lee realized that he had one chance to save himself, for a firefight at close range with four men would be suicide. He drew the .45 and aimed it at the windshield of the speeding truck. He fired two rounds, and the windshield of the truck shattered.

This had the desired effect. The truck careened wildly, tossing one of the men in the back to the bed of the truck. Another was tossed overboard. He cried out as he tumbled into the ditch on the opposite side of the road.

The truck failed to negotiate the next bend. The wheels left the pavement; and the front end of the vehicle plowed into the brush-covered hillside. Lee heard at least one of the men in the cab cry out.

Even in this state, the truck and the men were still dangerous. He caught only a glimpse of the weapons carried by the men in the back; but they did not appear to be mere hunting rifles or shotguns, which were deadly enough. These weapons had appeared to be automatic assault rifles: probably AK-47s.

Lee spun and ran, knowing that he would be vulnerable to their gunfire until he made it to the cover of the trees. When he reached the tree line he did not look back, but kept running.

Finally, he allowed himself to pause to catch his breath. He stopped and remained perfectly still, peering through the woods in the direction from which he had come. If they were actively following him he would be able to hear or see them by now, probably. But it would be wise to increase the distance between himself and the truck, nevertheless.

This was an entirely new development. Up until now, the local and state police forces had been pursuing him. Even if Norris (and probably Phelps) were intent on shooting him on sight, Lee assumed that the state police were only intent on capturing him. Jimmy Mack had drawn a gun on him, but he had deliberately walked into Jimmy Mack's lair.

Now it appeared that bands of armed, irregular gunmen were also pursuing him, and they would be working for whoever was responsible for the murders of Tim Fitzsimmons and Jody White. Surely the men in the truck had not been mere vigilantes or bounty hunters. They were hired killers, like the men who had done the shooting at the Tradewinds.

"Remain free, and stay alive," Brett St. Croix had advised him. This was simple advice, but it was growing more unlikely and difficult with each passing hour.

55

Seated in the driver's seat of the pickup truck, TJ Anderson did an inventory of his limbs and torso. The rounds fired by Lee McCabe had not struck him. He believed that he would know immediately if he had been shot. Nor was he paralyzed, from what he could tell. He was still able to wiggle his toes and his fingers. His chest hurt horribly—he had struck the steering wheel when the truck collided with the hillside—but he had no difficulty breathing. Possibly a broken rib, but probably not.

The man in the passenger seat—another ex-con whom Lester Finn had hired—was groaning, his face contorted in pain and his eyes clenched shut. He appeared to be hurt a bit worse: Blood was flowing from an open wound on his forehead. Not a bullet wound, but a laceration from the broken glass.

"TJ!" one of the men who had been riding in the back of the truck shouted. Judging by the sound, he was somewhere back along the roadside. "You alive?"

"Yeah." He leaned his head out the window. "Did either of you get a shot off at McCabe?"

"Naw. He done got away."

Well, that figures, TJ thought. *It would be too much to ask, wouldn't it —that McCabe would be felled by a lucky shot this early in the game?*

"I think my leg might be broke!" the fallen gunman shouted. "And Delray here is alive but he's torn up, awful bad."

Time to regroup, TJ thought. The truck was stolen so it could simply be scoured of fingerprints and abandoned. They would be able to commandeer more vehicles, if necessary. That was the sort of logistical arrangement that Lester Finn was actually quite good at.

And he would need a fresh crew as well.

TJ began to brush the largest shards of glass from his lap and chest. The front seat of the pickup truck was filled with more glass. There was no time to waste. Lee McCabe would no doubt be spooked by this little incident. He might decide to haul stakes and head out of the county. And if he did that, he would take TJ's big payoff along with him.

56

Dawn pulled into the driveway of her parent's house and turned the ignition off. She sat there for a while, listening to the engine tick. She wanted to go inside the house. And at the same time, she wanted to start the car again, back out of the driveway, and go somewhere else—anywhere else.

This small ranch house, with its weather-faded bricks, uneven blacktop driveway, and weedy lawn, had been Dawn's home for most of her life. It carried the association of Christmas mornings, first days of school, and long, lazy mornings during summer vacations.

She had taken her first steps here—which she did not remember —but which her father had delighted in recounting during the stand-offish, self-conscious days of her adolescent years. Bobby Hartman had nervously kissed her for the first time on this front porch. When she had been four, her father had taught her to ride her little pink-and-white bike in this driveway, walking right behind her with his arms outstretched, in case she should lose her balance.

These were the memories she tried to keep in the front of her mind as she tentatively stepped out of the car and approached the front door. She had grown up here; this was the residence of the only family she had. But now she felt compelled to ring the doorbell before entering. It was still home—and yet it no longer was. And she could no longer cling to the illusion that she was completely welcome here.

Her mother answered the doorbell on the second ring. No doubt she had been actively waiting for Dawn's arrival; perhaps she had been peering through the gauze curtains of the front window.

I'm coming home, Dawn had said to her mother on the phone, as she drove toward Blood Flats.

Oh, Dawn, her mother had said. *You broke your father's heart. Don't expect too much from him.*

But in the end her mother had agreed that she could come, and so here she was.

"Come on in," her mother said. The lines on Marcia Hardin's face were noticeably more pronounced than they had been when she had last visited home. But how long ago had that been? Going on a year now.

Dawn stepped inside, all the possessions she carried in a single gym bag. *Is that all you brought?* Her mother seemed to ask, looking at the little bag. Dawn had once had a shelf full of books and a laptop computer that was her pride and joy. But those days were long gone.

Once inside the house, she recognized the familiar smell of her mother's cooking. What was it? Meatloaf, probably.

In the living room, her father was reading the newspaper. He did not stop reading when Dawn entered. Her father did not look at her; he did not even acknowledge her.

She felt her mother's hand on one shoulder.

"Give him time, Dawn," she said in a low whisper. "I warned you that this is going to be rough for him."

Dawn's life on the streets of Louisville was no secret to her family. None of them approved, of course. But her father—who had been so protective of her during her growing up years, ferrying her to soccer practice and church youth group meetings and whatnot—his reaction had been the most severe and damning. And also the reaction that had stung the most. Dawn knew that every father was protective of his daughter, especially men like Bill Hardin, who had been raised on God and Americana and solid blue-collar values. There would be a part of him that had wanted to preserve her as pure, to let no man touch her until her wedding day. This made her particular fall from grace all the more galling. Bill Hardin knew that his daughter had not only become an addict—she had become a whore as well. She gave herself to unknown men for money, and she used this money to buy drugs.

Walking past the living room, Dawn carried her gym bag down the hall. The house was not very large, and so the main hall was not very long, either.

At least her bed was still there, though it was covered with folded piles of Liz's clothes, which she would presumably move so that Dawn would have a space for sleeping tonight. Liz was lying supine on her own bed. Dawn's younger sister was leaned back on a pile of pillows, earbud headphones in her ears, and her attention absorbed by the tiny keyboard of her cell phone. No doubt sending texts to one of her friends in town. Or maybe to a guy. *Did Liz have a steady boyfriend now?* This was the sort of family information that did not reach Dawn in this current phase of her life.

For years she and Liz had shared the bedroom. Her sister had taken sole possession of it when Dawn left for college. That had been a running joke: Liz finally evicting Dawn from the bedroom. *How nice it will be to be rid of your snoring, and of course to take over your closet space,* Liz had joked.

There had been a good-natured sibling rivalry between them then. That, too, had changed when Dawn's meth addiction became known. Liz was close to her parents; and she seemed to view her older sister's failure as a testament that the Fates would punish those who dared to rise above their preordained stations. Dawn was supposed to have been the one who would lead the way. Instead she had become the one who broke their parents hearts and plunged lower than anyone in the family—or practically anyone else that any of them knew.

Dawn understood Liz's judgment of her—and the revulsion that she now provoked in her younger sister. Liz was determined to escape the dicey blue-collar future that Blood Flats offered her. At eighteen, she had already seen many of her female classmates fall into teen pregnancy and a hasty wedding to a local boy. Others merely fell into teen pregnancy without the wedding part.

Liz and Dawn shared many of the same physical characteristics: the same blonde hair, similar mouth and nose, and high cheekbones. But that similarity was harder to see now, given the extent of Dawn's deterioration. The older sister might have been mistaken for the mother of the younger one.

Liz removed the headphones and did a double take when Dawn walked in, before conspicuously averting her eyes.

"What?"

"Nothing," Liz said without looking at her.

"Go ahead and say it."

"Well, you look like hell," Liz said.

"Nice to see you, too."

"Would it be better for me to lie?"

"No, I guess not." Dawn sat down on a narrow strip of her own bed, between the piles of Liz's clothes.

"So you're going to be staying here for a while?" Liz asked. Something about Liz's tone suggested that her younger sister was less than pleased by this prospect.

"It depends. We'll see how things go with Dad."

"Well, I wouldn't expect too much there," Liz said, oddly echoing what her mother had told her on the phone earlier. "I probably shouldn't tell you this, but Dad has taken to telling new people he meets that he has 'a daughter', and not 'two daughters' as had always been the case. Hey, don't look at me that way, I'm just telling you like it is. Dawn, are you crying? Look, I'm sorry I said anything. But I thought it would be better for you to know the score."

57

After another night spent in the woods, the barn looked like an oasis in the desert. Lee trudged wearily through the dew-soaked grass toward the sagging wooden structure, his feet stirring up eddies in the predawn fog that blanketed the ground. On one side of him was a field of June tobacco; the low, broad leaves drooped with the morning's moisture.

The barn was old; it had probably been built more than a hundred years ago. But that did not matter: It might contain running water, and possibly other useful items if he was lucky.

Lee detested the fact that he was now reduced to living like a scavenger—a common burglar, in fact. At the same time, there seemed to be little choice. He was being pursued by the law; and it was now clear that another group was hunting him—probably the same people who murdered Tim Fitzsimmons and Jody White. The few dollars that he had in his wallet were useless; he could not walk into a store; even a vending machine constituted an enormous risk. Nor could he ask anyone for help.

I'll take no more than I have to, he determined. And when this is over, I'll make whatever restitution I can.

As he drew closer to the barn, he got a better look at the white farmhouse situated a good distance beyond it. There were no lights in the windows, so it was safe to assume that the occupants were still sleeping. Nevertheless, his span of opportunity would be short; he had to get moving.

He forced himself to jog the rest of the way to the barn. The side facing him was dominated by a large painted-on sign that read "Chew Mail Pouch Tobacco." He loped around the corner of the barn and saw a pair of sliding wooden doors.

He stole another quick glance at the farmhouse: Still no lights. He slowly pushed one of the massive wooden doors open, being careful to make as little noise as possible. He opened the door no more than was absolutely necessary. When he had created a gap wide enough to squeeze through, he edged into the murky, musty interior.

The inner space of the barn was filled with the smells of bare earth, oil, and mildew. The darkness was partially alleviated by three windows along the far wall. The light that filtered through the dust-covered glass allowed Lee to make out what he needed to see. There was apparently no livestock in here; Lee looked up and saw the apparatuses that the farmer would use to hang his tobacco later in the season.

And then, in one corner of the vast room, was an item that Lee could only describe as a godsend.

The refrigerator was an old model, probably dating back to the 1960s. Lee heard its ancient motor pumping refrigerant. It had been placed in a little workbench area. The farmer who owned the barn probably used it to store drinks and snacks to consume during breaks in his daily labors.

Doing his best to avoid the considerable debris on the floor, Lee walked over to the refrigerator and pulled the door open. The rush of frosty air was magnificent—but not as magnificent as the sight of the twelve-pack of Coca-Cola that occupied the top tray. There was also an assortment of Hostess snack cakes.

Lee removed a can of Coke and one of the Hostess snacks—a chocolate cupcake that gave off a rich aroma when he tore open its cellophane wrapper. He took a bite of the cupcake and popped open the Coke can. The caramel-scented liquid was cold, gaseous, and wonderful as he chugged it down. He crumpled the empty can and placed it atop the refrigerator. Then he removed another one, and he suddenly realized that he was placing too much sugar-rich food into an empty stomach. He drank the second Coke more slowly, so as to avoid any chance of nausea.

When he had finished a second cupcake and the second can of Coke, he pulled his wallet from his rear pocket and fished out a single dollar bill. He folded the greenback at the center and placed it underneath the twelve-pack of Coke. It would be plainly visible when the refrigerator was opened. Someone had already framed him for murder; no one was going to frame him for petty theft.

Lee was closing the refrigerator door when the semidarkness around him vanished in the glow of overhead electric lights. Lee whirled. He thought of the .45 in the rear of his waistband, but he did not draw it. It would probably only make matters worse.

"If you were hungry, you should have come up to the house and knocked," said the man in the doorway of the barn. He was a large fellow with sandy blond hair and a heavy beard. His jeans and faded denim shirt suggested that he had come to the barn to begin the morning's chores. He held up his empty palms, "Please don't draw that gun on me. I mean you no harm."

Lee shook his head. "Of course not. Listen, I left you a dollar for the food I took. If it's alright, I'll just be on my way, I-"

"I know who you are," the stranger said. "Your name's Lee McCabe. You're the guy they say killed those people in that trailer park. You're in a world of trouble, son."

A statement like that demanded a response. Its very enormity could not go unanswered.

"I didn't do it," Lee said simply. "I haven't killed anyone." Then he amended, "Not since I got back from Iraq."

The man's response surprised Lee. "I believe you. You don't know me; but I used to run around with your father sometimes. Back in the old days. I don't believe that any son of Tom McCabe would be a cold-blooded killer."

"No," Lee agreed. "That I'm not."

It seemed that finally his luck had turned for the better. What were the odds of him trespassing on the property of a man who was favorably predisposed toward him, all because of a past association with his father—the father who had been such a hell-raiser and such a source of agony for his mother?

The blonde man scratched his beard. "I tell you what: Why don't you come back to the house and we can talk about this. I can't promise anything, but maybe the two of us can think a way out of the box you've got yourself into."

"I don't know," Lee said. "I don't want to—"

"It's no trouble. And if we can't think of anything, then you take off again and I never saw you. Let my wife fix you a proper breakfast, at the very least."

Lee capitulated. If this man was willing to help him, then perhaps it would be foolish to turn down the offer.

"OK. Thanks."

The man killed the light switch, turned, and began walking toward the farmhouse. A waving gesture indicated that Lee should follow. "You like scrambled eggs? My Peggy makes the best scrambled eggs in the county."

Lee hurried after the stranger. At this moment, the thought of real scrambled eggs—cooked in salt and butter—was almost as appealing as the potential logistical assistance that this stranger might provide. Yesterday men he didn't know had been shooting at him; and now another stranger was going to have his wife make him eggs. Maybe she would make biscuits and bacon as well. Lee wouldn't ask for either of these, but he would gratefully eat them if they were offered.

"Mister, I really appreciate this," Lee said to the big blonde man's back. He stepped out of the barn and into the pale sunlight.

"Don't mention it. It's the least I can do for a son of Tim McCabe," he said.

Lee stopped, wondering if his sudden sense of misgiving was justified, or simply a product of the recent days' events. When you entered a combat zone, you naturally became suspicious of everything. Often that impulse kept you alive; but sometimes it could be a detriment. This fellow had been nothing but friendly so far. Lee didn't want to overreact. At the same time, he had to answer the anxiety that was now roiling in his stomach.

"Tom," Lee said. "My father's name was Tom."

The big blonde man stopped and turned around. He was now only a few paces ahead of Lee. He rubbed his beard and appraised Lee thoughtfully.

"So it was," he said. "That was my little mistake, wasn't it?"

Without saying another word, the big man closed the short distance between himself and Lee and sucker-punched Lee in the stomach. Lee saw the punch coming at the last second. On another day he might have been able to deflect it; but he had been too weakened by the lack of sleep and food. Lee doubled over and grabbed his stomach, then he straightened up and moved for his .45.

He stopped cold when he felt a round metallic shape jab him in the temple. While Lee had been doubled over, another man had approached from behind the barn. This one was carrying a high-powered rifle of some sort. He had the rifle leveled at Lee's head.

"Easy," the gunman said. "This one has a hair trigger. Could be messy if it were to go off just now."

The big blonde man—the one who had posed as the farmer—moved quickly behind Lee and plucked the .45 from his waistband. Lee now realized that he had been fatally deceived. The man who had surprised him in the barn was no farmer; and there was no wife waiting for him in the kitchen. These two were part of the group that had been pursuing him the previous afternoon. They had apparently seen him enter the barn, and decided to dislodge him with an impromptu ruse rather than a gunfight.

"Should I do it now?" the gunman asked the big blonde man. "I can get it done with right here."

"No. Hold on, and don't be an idiot. We're in the middle of some-one's backyard, for chrissakes. We aren't going to do anything here. We're going to walk him back into those woods. Then we call Anderson, and Anderson will call Lester Finn. Then Lester either tells us to bring him in or to get it done right then and there."

Lester Finn, Lee thought. The ultimate source of the methamphetamine that Jimmy Mack had sold to the addicts in the woods. Now Lester Finn wanted him dead; and he was willing to mobilize an entire army of men to get the job done.

The big blonde man jabbed a forefinger in Lee's face. "Let's get moving. Just follow me. And if you try anything at all, this situation is going to get even worse for you. We can make this very painful for you, you know."

At that moment Lee heard the sound of a screen door creaking open. It was the real farmer, awakened to three strange men—one of them bearing a rifle—in his backyard.

"What the hell is going on out there?" cried a voice that was older but not quite elderly. Lee saw a figure in the rear doorway of the farmhouse atop the back porch. The owner of the farm held a shotgun.

"Hold on!" the big blonde man whispered sharply to his accomplice. Lee could discern that his intention was to talk his way through this situation. He did not want his apparent hothead of a companion to overreact.

But it was too late. The man who held the gun to Lee's head removed it from Lee's temple and swung it in the direction of the front porch.

A gunshot exploded near Lee as the man with the rifle fired at the back porch. The shot went wide of its target, tearing a chunk out of the white wooden exterior of the farmhouse. The man on the porch returned fire. Lee saw a mound of earth erupt directly in front him, blowing grass and wet topsoil across the front of his pants.

Lee knew that he had no more than a few seconds to make his move. He drove his elbow into the ribcage of the big blonde man, just as he was raising Lee's .45 to fire. The gun fell from his hand onto the grass; but the force of the blow caused him to fling it away rather than simply drop it. It landed too far away for Lee to make a move for it.

He still had to worry about his other assailant, who held a high-powered rifle. And then there was his final problem—the home-owner with a shotgun. Under the circumstances, he wouldn't make any distinction between Lee and Lester Finn's henchmen.

The rifle borne by the blonde man's accomplice was a bolt-action weapon, probably a .30-06. He had ejected an empty shell and was about to ram another one into place when Lee propelled his shoulder into his bulk. This caused him to stumble in the opposite direction, though he quickly righted himself. Lee attempted to grab the rifle away, but a few seconds of struggle convinced him that it was a lost cause.

If he could not win a fight, he would have to flee. On the other side of the backyard Lee saw a woodpile: cords of firewood stacked six feet high, forming a long wall. Lee took the only option realistically open to him at the moment: he bolted for the protection of the stacked firewood. Three voices were yelling behind him. Then he heard another round of shots, likely another exchange between the farmer and the other two.

Lee dove behind the woodpile as shots landed in the grass, in a trajectory that would have hit him if he had been a bit slower. Another shot blasted a cord of wood at the top of the woodpile, showering him with fragments of pungent, moldy smelling wood.

58

S heriff Phelps and Deputy Ron Norris surveyed the damage in the kitchen belonging to John Poe. This man, a sixtysome-thing farmer who raised and sold tobacco, was the most recent Hawkins County citizen to have contact with Lee McCabe.

Poe was seated at his kitchen table. He was still trembling from the gunfight that had erupted in his backyard less than an hour ago. Mrs. Poe, a woman of similar age, sat beside him. Their hands were interlaced and Mrs. Poe leaned against her husband.

"I've never been so scared in my entire life," she said. "I was upstairs and I heard all these guns going off downstairs. It was like being in a war zone. I knew that John was down there and I figured that he had to be in the middle of it."

Sheriff Phelps nodded. "I can understand your being frightened, Mrs. Poe. Anyone would be under similar circumstances."

The main kitchen window had been shattered by gunfire, and there were two slugs lodged in the wall opposite the window. Poe informed him that there was also substantial damage to the rear exterior of the house.

Amazingly, the gunfight had left no casualties. All three men had apparently run off when Poe stopped to reload his shotgun.

"And you say that one of these three men was Lee McCabe, the one that we've been looking for?"

"That's right," Poe said. "Of course, I didn't know it was Lee McCabe at the time. But now that you've shown me his picture, yep, I'm sure it was him."

"And you also said," Phelps continued. "That Lee McCabe and the other two men seemed to be involved in some sort of a conflict."

"That's sure what it looked like to me. First the fella with a rifle took some shots at him—this while he was in the middle of shootin' at me. Then that young man, McCabe, was wrestlin' around with the other one. They were fightin' over a pistol. But finally that fella got the best of McCabe. And McCabe, he ran off and the other one grabbed the pistol."

"Could you tell what kind of a pistol it was?"

"Some type of semi-auto," Poe said. "I couldn't really tell for sure. Keep in mind that I'm getting' shot at all this time. But it wasn't a revolver, that I could tell for sure."

"I understand, Mr. Poe. By any standard, it was an extremely high-stress, and very dangerous situation. The information you've given us will be quite helpful in our investigation. If you don't mind, Deputy Norris and I would like to take a look around the rear of the house, as well as in the backyard."

After the interview with the Poes had been concluded, Phelps and Norris finally climbed into their respective squad cars. In the Poes' backyard, they had collected five .30-06 shell casings. They had also dug slugs from the Poes' kitchen wall, and from the rear exterior wall of the house.

"What do you make of it, Norris?" Phelps asked. "It's been a while since I've heard of a three-way gunfight."

"Doesn't really surprise me," Norris said. "It wouldn't be the first time that scumbags turn on each other. We're talking about drug pushers, after all. Maybe it's a money dispute. Or maybe some of Lee's buddies have decided that his new visibility is too much of a liability."

"It's possible," Phelps allowed.

"The world will be a better place when they're all put away," Norris said, climbing into his patrol car. "Put away in jail forever or put six feet under. Ask me—the latter option would probably be a better service to the taxpayers."

59

P aulie Sarzo watched the hardscrabble countryside of central Kentucky roll by through the front passenger's window of a gold-colored Lexus, cursing the day that he had first heard of the town of Blood Flats.

He doubly cursed the two-bit player who ran the operation out of the Boar's Head. If Lester Finn told him one more story about his granddaddy, Paulie resolved, he would put a bullet in the old redneck's forehead, the Family's business interests be damned.

"Yo, check that out," Tony Loscotti said from the driver's seat. Tony was referring to a young woman climbing the front porch of a farmhouse that had already raced by them. The young woman was clad in blue-jean cut-offs and a white halter top that had seen better days. The girl was likely not a day over twenty. Her movements were languid, as if she were in no hurry. *And why should she be in a hurry? Weren't most of these hicks unemployed? Didn't most of them draw welfare checks?*

"Wouldn't mind having some of that Daisy Mae action." Tony briefly decelerated to take a second look back at the girl. Paulie frowned. Tony was a useful tool: a reliable man to have in a fight. Tony also had a knack for intimidating people. However, he was not much older than the girl was, and he occasionally needed reminders about priorities.

Paulie gave Tony's attempt at conversation no more than a grunt in reply, and the car accelerated forward again. Paulie had no interest in Daisy Mae at the moment. He was still focused on the image of pointing his 9 mm Beretta at Lester Finn's forehead, then pulling the trigger.

Paulie had olive skin, a prominent chin with a cleft in the middle, and curly black hair. He was only of average height, but also muscular, thanks to a lifetime of weightlifting. At the age of thirty-five, Paulie could bench-press more than three hundred pounds.

Paulie could use his fists when he had to; but he was ready to leave that role behind. There was no future in the rough-and-tumble role of an enforcer. Sooner or later you were bound to end up dead. That work was best left to the young and dumb ones like Tony here.

The thought of shooting the hillbilly was cathartic, but Paulie knew that Finn was safe from him unless Uncle Alfonzo gave the word. So far his uncle seemed determined to ride out the current troubles with Lester Finn. That could change if this business with the ex-marine wasn't cleaned up quickly and without further incident. Who knew what GI Joe had seen in the trailer? He might be able to identify some or all of Lester Finn's men. If the police nabbed the ex-marine first, he could lead them back to Finn, and that trail would eventually lead them north, to Chicago and the Family.

By that time it would no longer be a local matter. The FBI and the DEA would be involved, and the federal authorities would descend upon the Family like a biblical plague of locusts. Paulie saw a mental image of FBI men escorting his Uncle Alfonzo from his Chicago mansion in handcuffs and leg shackles. The thought alone was sufficient to make Paulie shudder. If that happened his future in the business would be over. Probably his life would be over as well. It was rare but not unprecedented for the Family to kill its own.

Uncle Alfonzo had ordered him to go to Kentucky and make sure that the ex-marine problem was cleaned up. Time was of the essence, of course, he and Tony had been driving south since the previous night.

Lee McCabe, Paulie thought, contemplating the Kentuckian whose name had been on CNN so much in recent days. The cursed name that had caused Uncle Alfonzo so much grief, and caused Paulie so much distress and outright fear.

Before I head north again, Paulie silently vowed to the unseen fugitive, *I am going to see you dead.*

60

Lester Finn tensed up as the two Chicago mafia men walked through the front door of the Boar's Head. Paulie Sarzo was already flashing that arrogant wiseguy grin of his. Paulie was accompanied by a younger man who seemed to exude violence. This one practically strutted; he reminded Lester of the recently departed Dan.

Both of them were wearing expensive sports jackets and white silk shirts that were guaranteed to stand out anywhere in Hawkins County. Their dress, as well as their manner, seemed calculated to mock Lester. The message was: *You're nothing but a pissant country bumpkin, and we all know it.*

Lester occupied his normal place behind the bar. The "Sorry... We're Closed" sign had been displayed in the Boar's Head's front window in anticipation of this meeting.

Luke was seated at a table in a far corner of the room. Lester had ordered him to remain seated and quiet unless called upon while the Chicago men were here. Luke would be a mere prop at this meeting: the Coscollino family was an organization. Lester had to remind them that he, too, had an organization.

Lester nodded as the two men approached. He removed three

shot glasses from the shelf beneath the bar and filled each one half full of Maker's Mark. This was premium bourbon whiskey; and it was made not in some smog-filled Northern city, but right here in the Bluegrass State.

"Lester Finn," Paulie said, his tone openly taunting and infuriating. "The leader of our Kentucky comrades. How are things going in your little neck of the woods these days?"

"We're managing," Lester said neutrally. "Thanks for asking."

"Don't mention it. So what else? Any problems down here that *y'all* can't handle?"

"Like I said, we're managing."

"I see. The stone-cold killers of Hawkins County!" Paulie laughed. The younger mafia man laughed in appreciation of his boss's witticism.

"You might want to ask Tim Fitzsimmons for an opinion on that,"

Paulie accepted one of the proffered glasses of whiskey and took a sip of its contents.

"Oh, yeah. Tim Fitzsimmons. Seems I heard something about that."

"We took care of the situation. Tim Fitzsimmons won't be selling any more product in central Kentucky."

"Hmm." Paulie took another sip of whiskey and regarded Lester contemplatively. "Yeah, I guess you did 'take care' of the 'situation' as you call it."

Lester lifted his own glass of Maker's Mark. "Right. No more competition from Tim Fitzsimmons."

"That's great. Just great. But I think you're leaving out a few details, Lester. And maybe you're giving yourself too much credit. You started with a simple task: You needed to remove one smalltime dealer who was too stupid to listen to simple persuasion. But what did you actually do? You sent four men into a hillbilly trailer park with guns blazing in broad daylight."

Lester smiled: "I wanted to be thorough."

"No, you wanted to be *stupid*. You could have taken out this Fitzsimmons quietly. He was an easy target and no one would have missed him. Ex-cons disappear all the time. Nobody gives a shit. But your men have to go in there and commit *two* murders."

Lester could feel his color rise. This little wop prick had just called him *stupid*.

"Jody White was a junkie, if that's what you're talking about. And I happen to know that she was even turning tricks at one point."

"*I don't care if she was blowing Osama bin Laden!*" Paulie shot back. "Now that she's dead, they'll turn her into Mother Teresa."

"Bullshit," Lester said.

"*Bullshit?* Do you ever watch TV? The media loves a dead white girl—as long as she's young and passably pretty. Did you know that Jody White's picture is already plastered all over CNN? Did you know that FBI agents are harassing my Uncle Alfonzo?"

"I'm sure the turmoil will pass," Lester said primly. "We only need to be patient. And as for your uncle, I certainly regret any inconvenience this affair might have caused him. But when people get killed, it usually makes the news. Surely you know that, Mr. Sarzo, given—well, your particular line of work and all."

Lester was satisfied to see the little dago's face redden. At the same time, he wondered if he had pushed Sarzo too far. For a second the Chicago mobster seemed poised to reach over the bar and throw a punch, or worse—draw his weapon and start shooting. Finally he did not.

No, he wouldn't dare, would he? His family needed Lester, after all. *How else could they run their operations in Hawkins County?*

"You stupid hillbilly fuck," Paulie said quietly. "Do you realize what you did?"

Lester felt his temper snap. "*Damn right!*" he shouted. "*You wanted Tim Fitzsimmons out of the way. I took him out of the way!*"

"*We wanted him out of the way quietly! We didn't want you to make national news!*"

"*Killing is a noisy business, Mr. Sarzo!*"

Paulie snorted out a derisive laugh. "Listen to you: '*Killing is a nasty business*,'" He aped a rural accent as he quoted Lester. "You'd last about two minutes if you had to operate anywhere outside of this bumfuck corner of nowhere."

"If this is bumfuck," Lester asked. "Then why is the Coscollino family so intent on establishing itself here?" Lester asked.

Paulie shook his head.

"You took a hit that absolutely *no one* would have cared about if it had been done quietly. But instead you turn it into a double homicide that turns the world's attention on what you're doing down here—and by extension, what we're doing. Did you know that even Nancy Grace is talking about Hawkins County and your hit at that trailer park?"

"Please, Mr. Sarzo," Lester said in his most placating voice. *I'm a businessman*, Lester thought to himself. *No matter what this puffed-up Chicago peacock may think, I'm the one here with class.*

"At the moment our main problem is Lee McCabe," Lester went on. "He was the only witness, the only one who could possibly lead police to our involvement in the matter. Once he disappears, our mutual problem disappears. Then we keep our heads down for a little while, and it's back to business as usual."

"Alright Lester," Paulie said, draining the last of his whiskey. "Suppose you tell me exactly what you're doing to make sure that Lee McCabe disappears. Then we'll decide if you have a future ahead of you."

61

Brett packed up his camping gear, folded and bagged his laptop, and proceeded to make his way out of the forest.

He did not want to remain in the woods another minute —much less another night. His decision to camp out in the woods had been an unusual one, even for a man who had endured the minimal-comfort environments of sub-Saharan Africa and the Balkans. Brett had reasoned that McCabe would agree to meet him in the woods because here the ex-marine would feel safe and in an advantageous position. McCabe had done as Brett had expected. Now that the interview was concluded, it was time to stop playing Boy Scout.

The entire load comprised a full backpack, plus his laptop case. His legs and back were aching by the time he reached his Acura, parked some two miles away. Luckily, no one had tampered with the vehicle. It was in the parking lot of the campground, exactly as he had left it.

He drove into the town of Blood Flats—even though Perryston was closer to the campground. He had work to do in Blood Flats. Before beginning his work, Brett looked for more civilized accommodations. He knew that this would be a stretch in central Kentucky. There were no Hiltons or Radissons of course—not even a Holiday

Inn or a Motel 6—the poor man's alternative to the better hotel chains.

He finally settled on a mom-and-pop establishment: the Baxter Manor Hotel. *"Manor" indeed*, Brett thought as he removed a gym bag full of essentials from the Acura's trunk. The place looked like it had been built around the middle of the twentieth century. It was a faux plantation-style building with pealing white paint and clumps of weeds in the middle of the parking lot.

Brett signed the hotel registry with the name "Bill Schneider"—a safely anonymous pseudonym that didn't sound *too* anonymous. The woman behind the glass-enclosed counter divided her attention between Brett and a sitcom playing on a dusty portable television set. She accepted Brett's cash and handed him a room key with a plastic red fob that bore the name of the hotel in fading white lettering.

"That'll be room 106, Mr. Schneider," she said.

Room 106 lived up to Brett's low expectations: The carpet was threadbare, the air conditioning was an older style wall unit, and the bathroom fixtures dated back to at least to the nineteen seventies. But there was plenty of hot water, and Brett allowed himself a full fifteen minutes beneath the steamy wet bliss of the shower head.

After he had toweled off and dressed, he sat down on one of the twin beds. There was a dark green rotary dial phone atop the night-stand mounted into the wall between the beds. He did not plan on using the ancient phone; but he did want a phone directory for Hawkins County.

The phone directory was in the second drawer of the nightstand, beneath a copy of the New Testament. He turned to the yellow pages and began looking for any sort of business that would generate sawdust.

After exhaustively searching the yellow pages for the better part of an hour, his efforts yielded nothing. There was a Home Depot just outside Perryston—but that was a long shot that was not even worth investigating. Even these hick hoodlums would know better than to run a meth operation out of a Home Depot. They would use a smaller business for their cover, an establishment that was off the beaten path, and unencumbered by a large stream of customers.

But there was no business that fit this criteria in the phone book.

Well, you didn't expect it to be that easy, did you? Brett thought. And in truth he had not expected it to be so easy—though it was always wise to begin an investigation by looking for low-hanging fruit. Sometimes the answers were right in front of your nose, but more often than not you had to dig for them.

He did find a listing for the Boar's Head, however. The small-town gangster named Lester Finn had splurged a bit in his local yellow pages ad. There was a sketch of a wild boar, and the words, "Good food and drink since 1942!" This meant that Lester Finn was not the original proprietor, unless he was in his eighties or nineties. *Was the Boar's Head a family business? Had Lester inherited it?* The answer did not matter: Now the tavern was somehow involved in a meth distribution ring, though the meth would probably not be stored there.

Once again—the question of the sawdust.

He also located a listing for Jimmy Mack's Garage, just outside Perryston. The owner of this establishment would now occupy a draw in a refrigerated vault at the county morgue. Future editions of the Hawkins County phone book would contain no listings for his business.

Brett glanced at his watch. It was already past eight o'clock p.m. Enough for today. He would start fresh in the morning.

He found his thoughts turning most inappropriately to a young woman. Her name was Michelle Ackerman. She was a junior employee at Queen City Media, where he held a string of titles —*senior creative director* and *senior media editor* among them.

So far, Michelle had shown no inclination to sleep with him, as young women were supposed to do when placed in the presence of older, more experienced men-of-the-world. Michelle—with her Ivy League education and pretensions of future greatness in journalism —was proving to be a frustrating challenge.

Well, maybe she would change her mind when this project came to fruition, when he, Brett St. Croix, became the toast of the news talk shows and graced the pages of *Newsweek* and *Time*. That much was inevitable. This story had all the necessary elements. And then, not even prim Michelle Ackerman would be able to resist him. She would be the icing on a very big slice of cake.

It would make his time spent in central Kentucky worthwhile, he thought. Even if there wasn't a decent restaurant to be found within a hundred miles. Well, he would have plenty of time for fine dining when he returned to Cincinnati.

A fine place, Hawkins County, Brett thought as he finally drifted off to sleep.

The next morning Brett arose early, and dropped his room key off to the same woman behind the registry counter. She was still watching the small battered television set.

First he drove out to the now abandoned garage. The late Jimmy Mack's gas station was boarded shut and festooned with police crime scene tape.

Brett stopped in the parking lot so he could get a closer look. He knew that he would find nothing here, really; but sometimes this sort of reconnoitering helped him drop into the right mindset for an investigation.

He left the Acura's engine running and walked over to peer inside through the building's dusty glass. The main window had been blown out during the gunfight and was now boarded over, so Brett was able to get only an oblique look at the interior: It was a litter of overturned shelving and various debris.

Brett imagined the shootout between Lee, Jimmy Mack, and the meth trafficker's junkie lackey. Lee McCabe might be innocent of the murders in the trailer park; but he was racking up an impressive body count of his own as he did battle with the real killers. How many more men would McCabe dispatch before this was over? Or before his luck ran out and one of them dispatched him?

"Lee McCabe was here," Brett thought whimsically. *That's what someone ought to spray paint on the window of this gas station.* With that thought he cut short his visit. He drove away in the Acura, the imagined gunfight still playing in an endless loop inside his head.

62

Brett left the environs of Perryston and headed south again, back toward the town of Blood Flats. Now he would employ his investigative prowess, the skills that he had touted in his meeting with Lee McCabe.

He arrived in the late morning hours, when foot traffic about the town proper was a mix of elderly shoppers, mothers with small children, and a handful of older kids on bikes. The vehicle traffic that he passed consisted of older cars—mostly American-made, and the Acura stood out like the proverbial sore thumb.

Near the center of town, Brett parked in front of the Carlson Drug and Pharmacy. The drugstore was marked by a neon sign of twisted glass tubing that overhung the sidewalk. The sign portrayed an apothecary's mortar and pestle.

This seemed like as auspicious a place as any for this step in his investigation. Brett put a quarter in the parking meter, summoned the character role that he would need for his task, and walked though the swinging glass door.

It was a small store that had seen better days. There was a lot of merchandise but not nearly enough floor or shelf space to contain it all. A round mirror hung near the ceiling in each of the four corners.

This was how stores had discouraged shoplifting in the days before bar codes and electronic theft prevention systems. In Hawkins County Kentucky, such systems were apparently still state-of-the-art.

An elderly man in a starched white shirt and bowtie was loading cartons of cigarettes from a cardboard shipping container into a clear plastic display case. He had been deeply concentrating on this work, until disturbed by the overhead bell that tinkled when Brett walked through the front door.

"Can I help you?" the man said. He was wearing thick glasses inside thick frames. Brett could see the half-moons of his bifocals.

"As a matter of fact," Brett said. "You can. Or maybe you can."

"You look sunburned," the old-timer observed. "You ought to check out our skin care section. We've got lots of good stuff for sunburns."

"I appreciate that," Brett said. "But first, I'm wondering if you might help me out with a bit of local knowledge."

"Local knowledge?" The old man's tone suggested complete bafflement.

"Yes, local knowledge. I'm a salesman, you see. No—don't worry, I'm not trying to sell *you* anything. I sell equipment for wood processors—electric band saws, planers, that sort of thing."

"Oh," the old man replied neutrally.

"Do you know of any local businesses that might have a use for such items? Is there a sawmill around here? Maybe a company that manufactures wood products?"

The old man paused while he gave this some thought. After a few moments he finally said.

"Naw. Nothin' like that around here."

"I see," Brett said, his disappointment swelling. He could ask other town residents, of course; but this old rube probably knew the lay of the local land as well as anyone. The answer would probably be the same no matter how many locals he asked. And if there was no commercial facility around here that produced large amounts of sawdust—then the next step would be to look for private homes and farms that produced sawdust in significant quantities. This would be highly impractical, the proverbial search for a needle in a haystack.

"But there used to be," the old man said after another pause. "The old Peaton Woods Furniture Company. But they've been out of business for a few years now. Won't be anyone at Peaton Woods buying any band saws."

Brett restrained the rebound in his spirits so as not to stir the old man's suspicions. If he had truly been a salesman, the existence of a defunct furniture manufacturer would be no less disappointing than the total absence of one.

"The Peaton Woods Furniture Company," Brett said thoughtfully. "You know, I've heard of that company. I think I even visited their plant once. It was located on....What was the name of that road again?"

"The Briar Patch Road," the old pharmacist said. "Off State Route 226."

"Thank you!" Brett said. This news didn't conclude the matter—but his instincts told him that he had just inched further toward his goal.

Brett did indeed purchase some analgesic cream for his sunburn before departing. (He might justifiably pride himself as a journalist—but he was no outdoorsman, he realized.) Feeling magnanimous, he also selected a package of gum and a Diet Coke. The old man had been legitimately useful. *Why not reward him by letting him make a few bucks?*

He didn't know the location of either Briar Patch Road or State Route 226; but the Acura's GPS system zeroed in on both roads immediately. There was no specific location in the database for the defunct Peaton Woods Furniture Company: this would have been a bit too much to hope for.

He cruised up Briar Patch Road, scanning both sides of the two-lane highway. The area was a former industrial park in a state of decline. He saw a shuttered trucking company, an abandoned metal fabrication shop, and a several closed restaurants. The latter had served the men and women who had worked in these industrial concerns in more prosperous times.

The Peaton Woods Furniture Company was located atop a rise in the landscape on the left side of the road. Brett drove past the little factory. The driveway was obstructed by a padlock chain; and Brett would not have dared to make such an entrance, anyway. If his hunches were correct, this facility was dangerous.

He slowed the Acura and pulled off the highway at a flat spot where there was plenty of gravel and the ground looked solid. He might have to make a hasty getaway; and he didn't want to die because his tires were stuck in the mud.

Exercising caution so as to make as little noise as possible, he stepped out of the car and gently closed the front driver's side door behind him. He left the door unlocked. He carried only one object of significance with him: a small digital camera.

Brett approached the furniture factory clandestinely, moving back to the edge of the shrub line that skirted the road. Since it was June, there was plenty of foliage in which to take cover. Either the building was guarded—or his guess had been completely wrong and this was all for naught. However, no organized criminal outfit would leave an active meth distribution center unguarded—no matter what the hour of the day.

At last he edged within sight of the abandoned factory. It was a small factory by most measurements, but fairly large by central Kentucky standards. In its heyday it had probably provided paychecks for one or two hundred people. Now it was in all likelihood a source of income for the worst sort of criminals.

Brett paused and contemplated his best line of approach. He crouched behind a cluster of scrub trees and overgrown wild bushes. From his present position, he was safely outside the viewpoint of anyone inside the abandoned factory. That would change very soon, however—as soon as he stepped out from behind the leafy enclosure.

He imagined a man with a rifle and long-range scope waiting inside the factory, perhaps edging the muzzle of his gun beneath the sash of a window that had been opened a few inches. Perhaps they were already alerted to him.

He forced these internal voices to be quiet. The present situation was dangerous—no doubt about that—but certainly no more dangerous than some of his past scrapes. Certainly nothing compared to Rwanda, he told himself.

Across the road from the factory was a two-story farmhouse that he had not noticed when he drove by it in the Acura. It was an old wooden structure that bore the evidence of many cycles of freezing and baking. The peeling paint and broken upstairs windows indicated that the home was abandoned.

Brett briefly considered crossing the road, where he could watch the factory from a position of relative safety. That was no good, though. It wouldn't get the job done. He might spend hours hunkered down in the farmhouse without observing anything conclusive. No—in order to be certain, he would have to get close. There was no way around it.

He thumbed the power switch on his digital camera and noted that the power supply was full. At least he would be able to take plenty of pictures, provided that he didn't get shot before or after taking them.

Brett crept toward the driveway with his body hunched over, so that he would have a low profile. Once he arrived, he dove onto his stomach beside the driveway, in the drainage gulley. The bottom of the ditch was muddy and smelled of decaying vegetation.

Then he made his first significant observation. The posts placed on either side of the driveway were rusted, and probably dated back to the closing of the plant. Ditto for the two lengths of chain, which had both oxidized to a dark brown.

The padlock, however, was brand new. It had obviously been purchased within the last few months. This evidence wasn't conclusive, of course; but it was strongly suggestive.

He saw a route that would allow him to approach the factory by walking up the hillside. If he maintained a low posture, this would enable him to edge close enough to look in the windows, though he would be largely hidden from anyone inside the building.

He rose to his feet, and this time he ran as fast as his legs would carry him. He had to sprint across a section of ground between the ditch and the adjacent hillside. Throughout this stretch, he would be plainly visible and an easy target for anyone with a gun and a decent aim.

He tripped just as he reached the safety of the hillside, but there were no shots or cries of alarm from the factory. The overgrown grass rose up to meet him as he crashed downward. The wind was knocked from his chest and he saw little points of light swimming before his eyes.

Maybe I am getting too old for this, he thought, momentarily paralyzed by his burning lungs, his sudden fear, and an ache that seemed to permeate his entire body. He reminded himself that Rwanda had been more than fifteen years ago. He had been a much younger man in those days.

His next thought was of the camera. Before he hit the ground, he had managed to toss the camera away from his body. He saw the device lying in the grass a few feet away from him.

Lying on his back, he reached out and lifted the camera. The power light was dark. *Damn! Damn!*

Then he toggled the switch and the light lit up red. He was still in business. He could still make this work if he kept his cool and didn't make a stupid, fatal mistake.

He saw the movement inside one of the darkened side windows of the factory immediately after he righted himself. He plunged back to the ground, thankfully exercising enough presence of mind to avoid falling on the damned camera.

There was the sound of a metal click, metal scraping against metal, then the noise of a large industrial-sized door being pushed open. From where he lay, he could see the large brown door swinging wide, and the outlines of two men emerging from within. The glare of the sun prevented Brett from seeing their features clearly, but they looked young and strong, more alert and agile than the type of man who would spend his years laboring over a lathe in a furniture plant.

He could also make out the unmistakable silhouettes of their guns. These were AK-47s, or possibly older style assault rifles smuggled in from Eastern Europe or China. There was one inevitable thing about being a journalist who frequently visited war zones: you learned about guns—even if you *did* consider yourself to be a pacifist.

63

The sign in the front window the Boar's Head read CLOSED, but Paulie ignored it. First he attempted to push the door open, then he began pounding on it.

"Hillbillies," he said to Tony Loscatti, as he cast a disdaining gaze around the unimpressive panorama of downtown Blood Flats. A big flatbed farm truck was idling through the center of town. It was loaded with cages full of chickens.

"I ain't never seen anything like that in Chicago," Tony observed, sneering at their rustic surroundings. "What's next? A dump truck full of cow shit?"

Finally Lester's employee—the big dumb one called Luke—came to the door. He opened the door a crack.

"The tavern's closed," he said.

Don't give me that shit," Paulie said. "I want to see Lester. Open up now."

"Open up *now*," Tony added for emphasis.

A brief series of speculative looks passed between Tony and Luke. Paulie wondered: In a bare-fisted street fight, which of these two would win? They were both large and physically intimidating. Luke had a slight size advantage. But Tony would surely be a better street fighter.

"Hold on a sec," Luke said, closing the door again.

"I'm going to kill him," Paulie said to Tony, thinking of Lester. "All I need is one word from Uncle Alfonzo, and I'll perforate both of their thick foreheads. Then we'll leave this shithole of a town and get back to where it's civilized."

Paulie had barely uttered these words when the door opened again. Luke stood aside to let him and Tony pass. Lester was standing behind the bar.

"What the fuck is this?" Paulie asked. "When we need to talk to you, we need to talk to you. Don't keep us waiting again."

"Gentlemen, gentlemen," Lester said. "What seems to be the problem?"

"We need an update. That's the problem."

"I gave you an update only last night," Lester said.

"Yeah, and now you're going to give another one. In fact, you're going to give me an update every two hours until this ex-soldier is dead."

"Marine," Lester corrected. "Lee McCabe was in the Marine Corps."

"You know, you're not acting like a man with a lot of smarts right now," Paulie said.

"I was only clarifying McCabe's service record," Lester said primly.

Paulie lifted a chair from a nearby table. He flung it over the bar, not exactly at Lester's head, but close enough so that the tavern owner would be compelled to duck and move suddenly to the side. The chair crashed into the shelf behind the bar, sending three or four bottles of whiskey tumbling to the floor. There was a sound of shattering glass.

Lester stood back up, his cheeks reddening. Luke took a step in Paulie's direction.

Tony Loscatti flung his blazer open, revealing an Uzi submachine gun. Paulie had told Tony to bring the weapon, just in case Lester and his hired hick were in uppity spirits. Of course, he didn't plan to shoot Lester—not yet—but he was in no mood to dally with the man.

"Stand back," Lester said to Luke. "Okay, Paulie, no need to escalate things."

Paulie was delighted to see Lester Finn subdued and humiliated in this way. "Now you listen to me, Lester. I don't care if this guy was in the Marine Corps, the army, or the fucking circus. I want him out of the way so that my uncle will stop calling me every hour and I can go back home. Now cut the crap and tell me what you know. Something useful."

This made Paulie think again of Uncle Alfonzo, and the old man's displeasure at the turn of events in Hawkins County. Alfonzo had been calling him at regular intervals. *Paulie, my dear nephew. Don't disappoint me,* he said. *Or this could go badly for you. And that would cause me pain—you, my own sister's dear boy.*

"It's like I told you yesterday," Lester said. "I've hired three teams of men. They're being lead by a very competent local man. Name's TJ Anderson. Anderson's done time but he's ambitious and he's got good sense. The three teams are fanning out throughout the county, tracking him on foot as well as on the road. We're tracking him north as well as south. The county is only so large, gentlemen. Sooner or later we're going to get him. We've had two near misses so far."

"And what if he decides to leave the county?" Paulie asked. "What's your brilliant plan then?"

"If McCabe wanted to hop a train or hitch a ride out of the county, he could have already done that by now," Lester said. "From what I can tell, he's hanging close by. McCabe's a local and he's young. He is probably afraid to leave the area that he considers his comfort zone."

"Yeah, that's more brilliance," Paulie said. "He was in Iraq a few months ago, and now he's afraid to go to Tennessee or West Virginia. Makes perfect sense to me."

Lester shrugged. "He hasn't gone anywhere so far. From what we can tell."

"*From what you can tell,*" Paulie repeated. "That's why I have no confidence in this redneck version of a manhunt. You should have ended this by now, Lester. We shouldn't have to bring our own people in and take over; but we've got no choice if you're all we have to rely on."

Lester was about to protest, until Tony looked down at the Uzi.

"'*Your people*.'" Lester asked cautiously. "All I've seen so far is the two of you."

"We're bringing in some additional resources," Paulie said. "Let's just leave it at that for now. We'll let you know what you need to know, when you need to know it."

Lester nodded. "Alright." Paulie could tell that Finn was seething. It was a pleasure to observe the other man's impotent anger.

Paulie allowed himself a few more minutes of needling Lester Finn. He had never liked Lester, and in the past twenty-four hours Paulie had come to despise him. Lester Finn's screw-up might get him killed any day now.

In all fairness, though, the tavern owner's assessment of the current situation did seem to be correct in at least one regard: *Lee McCabe was likely still in the area*. If he stayed in the area, then the combined forces of the local gunmen and the Family's resources would catch him. There were only so many places to hide.

If only the police didn't catch him first. But Lester Finn claimed to have that angle covered. Paulie looked forward to meeting this Deputy Norris. The story of how Norris had been entrapped—literally with his pants down—had provided a welcome bit of comic relief to the urgency of the past few days.

"We'll see you in two hours," Paulie said, walking out. "And you'd better not make me knock this time."

The light on the sidewalk was harsh compared to the semidarkness of the tavern. Paulie squinted, until something caught his attention.

Paulie noticed a silver Acura pulling up to the curb. He knew immediately that this wasn't a local vehicle. First of all, the car bore Ohio plates. Secondly, there wouldn't be many people in this part of the world who could begin to afford a car like that.

The bearded driver of the Acura saw Paulie at about the same instant that Paulie noticed him. There was a look of recognition in his face—possibly fear.

Which might mean that this man was a problem.

Paulie reached into his blazer. This caused the driver of the Acura to stop, throw his car into reverse and then drive away. It was not quite an all-out act of flight, but there was an unmistakable element of hasty evasion.

Paulie did not withdraw his gun—as the panicked driver of the Acura likely expected. Instead he withdrew his cell phone—which had a built-in camera. As the Acura was pulling away, Paulie snapped several pictures of the rear of the vehicle.

The driver of the Acura was probably someone who was snooping around, Paulie decided. A curiosity-seeker from nearby Ohio, who became spooked when he saw him and Tony step out of the bar. Paulie knew that together, they made quite an impressive pair; and it was easy to imagine a normal Joe Citizen experiencing feelings of intimidation when they made an unexpected appearance like that.

Moreover, the Boar's Head probably didn't have the best reputation around these parts. No doubt there were rumors about Lester Finn and the various "side enterprises" that were conducted from the tavern. Another factor that made Finn a liability.

There was no reason to suspect immediate danger. Better safe than sorry, though. Paulie held up the camera to look at the two photos he had snapped. The license plate was unreadable; but someone on the Family's payroll could likely enhance the images and make the characters legible.

Just in case the driver of the Acura turned out to be more than a jumpy tourist.

64

Brett took his time making his way back to his car. He was relieved to find it exactly where he had left it, parked along the gravel berm of Briar Patch Road.

His glimpse inside the Peaton Woods Furniture factory had been brief. He had not seen any methamphetamine; that would be hidden deep inside the building.

Really he had seen nothing but the men with the guns. But the gunmen had been enough—enough to convince him that the building was not the abandoned factory that it appeared to be from a distance. The men with the guns also dissuaded him from going any further. He had stayed alive all these years partly by knowing when to stop moving forward, because a particular situation had simply become too dangerous.

Luckily, the men had merely been outside for a smoke break. They were unaware of his presence. He waited until they went back inside, then he slowly, cautiously, returned via the same route that had brought him there.

Now, starting the Acura's engine, Brett considered his options for investigating the Boar's Head. The tavern should be easier, because unlike the furniture factory, it was an operating public establishment.

There would be no need to be overly furtive. He could simply walk in the front door and observe whatever there was to observe. If his luck held out, he might also be able to engage Lester Finn in a conversation. This bit of undercover work could enhance his final story—which would hopefully become a bestselling book.

He drove back to Blood Flats imagining how he might break the ice with Lester Finn. If the bar was indeed a family establishment, Finn might be willing to talk about its origins. Most small-town drinking establishments were connected to a unique series of old stories. He could pose as someone passing through on vacation, who was curious about the traditions and landmarks of the local area.

Yes, that strategy could definitely work.

Brett knew from his earlier look at the phone directory that the Boar's Head was located in the center of Blood Flats, on one of the town's main thoroughfares. It shouldn't be too hard to find. He located the tavern after making only a few loops around the town proper: the bar sat on some prime real estate at the center of town—if it was possible to use the term "prime" in regard to any real estate in Blood Flats, Kentucky.

As he pulled up to the curb, he noticed a CLOSED sign in the window. He checked the clock in the dashboard and saw that it was already past 1 p.m. in the afternoon. Brett felt a stab of disappointment: he had hoped that the Boar's Head would be open for lunch. If the bar did not open until the evening, then he might have to spend another night in Hawkins County—a prospect that he did not relish.

Then he thought of a backup plan, one that would get him the information he needed—and also get him out of Hawkins County and back in Cincinnati by nightfall: He would knock on the door and pretend to be a reporter for a regional travel magazine. He would tell Lester Finn that his readers were interested in discovering attractions in central Kentucky. *Would the owner of the historic Boar's Head be willing to talk for a few minutes?* he would ask.

Being a journalist anyway, it would be easy for him to weave together a credible story along these lines. There was, of course, a small chance that Lester Finn might recognize him from his previous television exposure. But this risk was small: He was but one face out of the innumerable mid-list non-fiction authors who were occasionally interviewed on TV. And he knew that his own bearded, somewhat weak-chinned middle-aged face was not especially striking or memorable. The tavern owner would not recognize him.

He was about to kill the engine when the two well-dressed men stepped out of the closed bar: They were both broad-shouldered and fierce-looking, though the younger of the two towered over the older one with the curly hair. They had olive complexions and they were well dressed—definitely not Hawkins County locals.

The glare of suspicion that they cast in his direction caused Brett to make an immediate conclusion: These two must be associated with one of the drug cartels that was funneling methamphetamine into the central Kentucky region. Were they Italian or Mexican? Difficult to tell—for that matter they might have been Chechens or Columbians.

Could he be sure? No. Appearances were sometimes deceiving; but these men could not be idle tourists or agricultural buyers. Not with that attire, on a hot summer day in a rural town. Not with those looks and those postures—men who knew no fear, who were a law unto themselves.

Then Brett saw the unmistakable contours of a small automatic weapon beneath the taller man's blazer. This erased the last shred of doubt: He was being stared down by two extremely lethal characters. Their eyes bore into Brett.

The shorter of the two men reached into his own blazer and Brett's bowels turned to water. Did they mean to gun him down right here in broad daylight? In the middle of town? *Surely they wouldn't dare.* But men like that generally did as they pleased.

He jerked the Acura into reverse, made the fastest turnaround of his life, and sped in the opposite direction. The car's tires screeched on the pavement.

He heard no shots; and he did not look in his rearview mirror to see if the man had withdrawn a gun at all. He was afraid to look back, as if looking back might invite pursuit. He gunned the Acura out of town and sped down the main two-lane highway toward the interstate access ramp.

Brett's hands did not stop shaking until, more than twenty minutes later, he had cleared the interstate on-ramp and was headed toward Cincinnati at seventy miles per hour.

65

A three-quarters moon cast long shadows behind the headstones of St. Patrick's Cemetery. Lee carefully made his way between the grave markers, toward a familiar location that he knew would trouble him as much as it drew him. He kept his senses alert. He did not think there would be any other visitors in the cemetery at this hour of the night. But graveyards were often haunted by the chronically grieving; and they might be drawn here at any time.

St. Patrick's Cemetery was located on one of the many rolling hills that undulated the landscape south of Perryston. It was an old graveyard that contained the bones of Irish settlers who had migrated to the area in the mid-1800s. They had been pushed out of Ireland by the Great Potato Famine, and then pushed once again into the interior of their new country, by an intolerant East Coast establishment dominated by old Anglo-Saxon families and club-wielding Know-Nothings.

Many of Lee's own ancestors were buried right here: But his childhood had been an irregular one, and there had been little time for stories about the old McCabes. His grandmother had occasionally reminisced for him when he was a small child; but now his grandmother was gone—just like those ancestors whom he had never known.

He stood before the two headstones that marked his parents' graves. Tom and Lori McCabe had technically been separated when the first of them passed; but here they were, together again in death.

The dates on both headstones sketched out two lives that had been cut short. They had both been born in the 1960s, and neither had lived long into the new century. His father had died in an automobile accident at the age of forty-one. His mother had died from cancer at the age of forty-two, only a few years ago.

Someday, perhaps after Lee was long gone himself, a member of some future generation would happen upon the two graves and wonder at the bad luck that had brought early deaths to both of them, at different times and for different reasons.

He was not really sure why he had come here. Neither of his parents had provided him with much guidance in life. His father had too often been absent. His mother had tried harder to be a parent; but she had been unable to rise above the pain of her turbulent marriage and her many subsequent disappointments.

Lee's beliefs about the hereafter were still fluid. He was equally uncertain about the nature of God, if indeed such a being existed. It would be nice to believe that a world that contained fanatical jihadis and murdering drug dealers was counterbalanced by good of a supernatural kind. But he simply wasn't sure. How *could* a person be sure, after all?

He was, however, sure of his next course of action. After all his wandering about and uncertainty, he now knew what he had to do— or at least what he believed that he *should* do.

I'm not going to run, Lee thought. *I'm going to stand and fight. And I'm going to take the fight directly to the enemy—to Lester Finn in Blood Flats.*

Lee had reached this conclusion shortly after his escape from the men who had come upon him in the barn, the men who had nearly killed him and who had taken his gun.

Perhaps St. Croix, the journalist, would be able to help him, and perhaps he would not. In any case, he felt weak and helpless running from hideout to hideout, waiting for the bullet that might strike him down at any moment. Nor was he willing to consider trusting any branch of law enforcement. His encounter with Deputy Norris had taught him the folly of that path.

But why should such a resolution compel him to visit the graves of his parents? Being skeptical about religion, Lee was therefore skeptical about the notion of guardian angels. However, the idea was simply too tempting to avoid embracing, as it conveniently dovetailed with his parents' early deaths. He sometimes imagined them as being bigger and better in death than they had been in life—as if the ordeals of their passing had somehow purified them. Lee knew that their earthly imperfections had been glaring; but perhaps they were different now. And if that could be true, then perhaps they might be watching over him, ready to offer some sort of protection or guidance, if only he could fine-tune his senses sufficiently to detect and receive it.

It was probably nothing more than self-deluded nonsense, he knew. Nevertheless, he permitted himself a moment of silence and reflection as he stood there. In the past seventy-two hours, he had witnessed the sort of killing that he had thought he had left behind in Iraq. And men he did not know were trying to kill him once again. Was a bit of protection from God—or at least his deceased parents— too much to ask for?

He briefly knelt down and touched each headstone: first his mother's, and then his father's. Satisfied that he had gained whatever solace might be found here, he arose and began walking back toward the entrance of the cemetery.

On the way out, he passed the gravestone of a young man who shared his birth year. Lee vaguely remembered hearing about the youth's death at the age of sixteen. A car accident. Another statistic.

Lee shook his head and continued on. It was too easy to die young in this world—even if you never went to war.

66

When Alistair Jones was done reading the report that Brett St. Croix had compiled, he shook his head and let out a long sigh. He laid the paper-clipped pages down on the white tablecloth before him.

Two days had passed since Brett had observed the activity at the ostensibly abandoned furniture factory in Blood Flats, and had his wordless encounter with the two men outside the Boar's Head.

He had driven back to Cincinnati without stopping, often pushing the speedometer to reckless speeds. He did not go home. Instead he went directly to his office at Queen City Media in downtown Cincinnati. Laboring through the night, he feverishly typed out a summary brief of his meeting with Lee McCabe, and his discoveries in Blood Flats. Then he worked these events into a book proposal.

This version of the proposal was different than the verbal one Brett had pitched hurriedly over the phone a few days earlier, while he was on his way to meet with Lee McCabe. But in Brett's judgment, this surprise outcome was even more exciting than the original story.

Brett had initially intended to write a book about a disturbed veteran who goes on a killing spree. Now he would write a book about a naïve veteran who was framed for a crime he did not commit

—a crime that he, Brett St. Croix—the author of the book—had effectively solved.

But Alistair's sudden shift of demeanor baffled him. Alistair Jones was an acquisitions editor at Fenton, Stafford, & Brown, one of the largest publishers in the country.

Alistair had seemed very interested over the phone. Now his expression suggested an air of disappointment, though Brett could not fathom why.

Finally Alistair spoke. "This represents a change of direction, doesn't it?" he asked.

The two of them were having lunch in *La Cuisine de Montagne*, one of Cincinnati's few French restaurants. A waiter was clearing away the remains of the soup course. In the far corner of the darkened dining room, three tuxedo-clad musicians churned out light classical music. Lunch at *La Cuisine de Montagne* typically ran about fifty dollars per person.

"A change of direction?" Brett asked, still only mildly alarmed at Jones's tone and the expression on his face. "Well—yes, I suppose it does represent a shift of sorts. But Lee McCabe was not what I expected. Nor were the circumstances surrounding those murders."

"Hmm," Alistair began to smear butter on a slice of bread.

"I mean—a journalist heads out into the field with a certain set of expectations. Sometimes those expectations are overturned by what he—or she—actually finds." Brett feared that he was rambling—because he was. He didn't like the vibes he was receiving from Alistair. Didn't like them at all.

"Yes. Yes of course," Alistair said through a mouthful of bread. "I wholeheartedly support journalistic integrity. Very important."

"I sense a 'but' coming here."

"Well." Alistair laid the slice of bread on a white china bread plate and cleared his throat. "You came to me with one version of this story: the rogue veteran who becomes a killer for profit. Now you're coming to me with a story about a U.S. Marine who is the victim of some convoluted conspiracy. Let's suppose we tell this new version of the story. If McCabe survives all this—and I don't think he will—then he's a hero. If he doesn't—the far more likely scenario—then he's a martyr."

"So what's wrong with that—from a journalistic perspective?" Obviously, Brett reflected, Lee McCabe himself would be unable to look upon the matter quite so dispassionately.

"Nothing at all," Alistair said. "And you might want to pitch that story to Fox or the Military Channel. One of them could make a documentary about it. A solid hero tale. Everyone waves the flag and agrees to vote Republican in the next election."

"I didn't see this as a political piece," Brett said.

"Oh, come on now, Mr. St. Croix. I've read your previous books, you'll remember."

"Sure," Brett acknowledged. "I don't much care for the U.S. military, and I don't trust military types. I'm a throwback—I'll gladly burn the flag if that's what it takes to get my point across."

"Bravo," Alistair said smugly. "I'm not in the business of hiring revolutionaries, though. I'm in the business of hiring authors who can produce the books I need. Your original premise had depth and merit. It might have been a book that academics and journalists around the country would have cited as a call to change the military culture. It would have been received well in Europe, where anti-American pieces sell like hotcakes. What you're presenting to me now is a potboiler, a cliché that will only be of interest to the NASCAR and Wal-Mart crowd."

"I'm not going to lie, though," Brett said. "And it would be worthwhile for us both to remember that a man's life is at stake here."

Alistair waved his hands impatiently. "Lives are at stake all over the world," he said. "And in any event, I'm not telling you what to do here. I'm not going to stop you from going on the air and telling the world that Lee McCabe is the reincarnation of Sergeant Alvin York, if you want to."

"But-"

"That changes the situation where the book is concerned. At least with this publishing firm."

"So the deal will be off? If I tell this version of Lee McCabe's story"

Alistair smiled tightly. "Regrettably, yes. I don't think I can make this new incarnation of the book sufficiently palatable for our acquisitions board."

Brett thought about Lee McCabe, running around like Rambo somewhere in the woods of central Kentucky. Lee McCabe—who had been about to win him a contract for half a million dollars. Now Lee McCabe threatened to take that contract away, with his story about gun-toting hillbilly meth dealers and corrupt small-town sheriff's deputies.

Brett lifted his wine glass, took a long drink, and wondered what the hell he was going to do.

67

For two days Lee spirited himself into the woods, and waited for the networks of his pursuers to thin or slacken the pace of their hunt. It quickly became apparent that they would give him no rest. Several times per day, he saw the helicopters of the state police circle overhead. And twice more he observed roving bands of men in the woods—not police, but irregulars who were in the employ of Lester Finn. These men were less disciplined than real soldiers and clearly untrained. However, there were many of them and there was only one of him. They were heavily armed, and since losing his gun, Lee was unarmed. If they spotted him, flight would be his only option.

He could not stand still, like a hunted animal awaiting the depredations of the hunter. So he found ways to move toward Blood Flats slowly. Often he was forced to take circuitous paths that neither brought him into open land or near any roadways. And even this was not safe, for all of his pursuers seemed to know—or strongly suspect —that he was somewhere in the woods.

Lee's only consolation was that the police and the agents of Lester Finn were not working together. But after his encounter with Deputy Norris, even this possibility could not be entirely ruled out.

On the third day of his off-again, on-again trek toward Blood Flats, he ventured into an open clearing, in plain sight of a road. He determined that the road would not pose an unacceptable risk if he crouched low as he approached it, and threw himself into the grass if he heard the sound of a motor. Then he would cross the road quickly and bolt into the woods on the other side. The road stood between him and the route to Blood Flats. There was no way to avoid crossing it.

With his attention fixed on the road, he did not see or hear the band of men who were coming through the adjacent woods—the men whose path brought them into the same clearing. His first indication that he was not alone was the sound of a man whistling to alert his companions. This act of poor soldiering—a mistake that a professional would never make—was the only factor that saved his life, he would think later, though subsequent circumstances would make it anything but a triumph.

The men were now yelling his name. They were chasing him. And they were firing their weapons.

Tearing across the field, Lee forced himself through the briars, ignoring the thorns, thinking only of the men with guns who were pursing him. His lungs were on fire and his heart was pounding. Still he ran. He let the adrenalin do its work. He aimed for the road, without the slightest idea of what he was going to do once he reached it. At any moment the men might shoot him down; but he could not let that knowledge siphon even a minute fraction of his strength.

The high grass made every stride more arduous. He felt the sun burn his forehead. He was sweating profusely now. A bumblebee collided with his cheek. He batted it away before it could sting. Only a few more yards to the road.

He leapt across the drainage ditch on the near side of the road. Another long step and his feet struck the pavement.

He did not see the car coming. He was aware of the sudden blare of an automobile horn, the screeching of tires on gravelly pavement.

The car came to a stop about eighteen inches from his knees. It was a late eighties or early nineties model Honda Civic with metallic blue paint, a dent near the front driver's side wheel well, and some rust about the lower fringes of the body. Through the dusty windshield he could see the driver: a young woman about his own age. She had shoulder-length brown hair and wore a shocked expression.

He paused to look back in the direction from which he had fled. He could see them coming—his pursuers crashing through the brush and the high grass.

Lee fully grasped the paucity of his choices. On the road he would be an easy target. To follow the pavement would be suicide. And there was no cover in sight—save in the direction from which he had come, which was irrevocably blocked.

Without hesitating further he walked quickly around the front of the car and approached the passenger's side door. He leaned over and said into the open window: "Help me, please."

68

A my Sutter did not know what to make of the figure leaning into the passenger's side window opposite her. He was ostensibly asking for help—and yet he seemed to be already imposing his presence on her.

Her cautious voice (the one that was usually indistinguishable from her mother's) told her to release the brake and gun the engine now. Nothing could be more stupid and reckless than picking up strangers in the middle of nowhere—especially desperate-looking characters like this one.

But this man did not look like an axe-murderer. He was staring at her earnestly, not demanding—as she had originally perceived—but imploring her for assistance.

"Get in," Amy said. The man had already opened the door and seated himself before her words were complete.

"*Now drive!*" the stranger commanded. Then he observed the defiant gaze she shot him and said, "*Please! Please drive now!*"

Amy drove. The Honda lurched forward. The tires squealed and spit gravel. Then came the unmistakable sound of gunfire. The exterior mirror on the driver's side shattered in an explosion of reflectorized glass and chrome. Another bullet tore into the hood of the car.

"I *told* you to drive!" the man beside her said unnecessarily—as if she could have somehow anticipated this outcome.

TJ ANDERSON WATCHED Lee McCabe step into the blue Honda. One member of his crew fired a burst of rounds at the speeding Civic. But within seconds McCabe's escape vehicle was out of range. The car tore down the highway.

Not again, TJ thought. But he knew that McCabe was not out of the proverbial woods yet—not by a long stretch.

He pulled his cell phone from his belt. The three crews under his tactical command had been maintaining close contact. According to TJ's understanding of their current positions, one group of his men would be just a few miles down the road right now.

Where they could lie in wait and intercept the Civic.

He contacted the leader of the other group and issued a quick set of instructions. *Don't screw this up*, he told the other man. Trap the car and Lee McCabe will have no place to go. We'll have him. Get ready. You've got maybe four or five minutes at the most. Call me as soon as it's over.

TJ allowed himself a smile. It was a waiting game for him now, and he would know the outcome within a few minutes.

Lee McCabe, he thought, *you're going to make me a rich man yet.*

69

"I really appreciate this," Lee said. He did not want to distract Amy Sutter from her driving, but he felt that it was incumbent on him to say something.

The young woman in the seat beside him was attractive in a mildly interesting way. She appeared to be athletic. She had long brown hair. She wore blue jeans and a T-shirt with Greek lettering on it—the telltale sign of a college sorority.

"You're that one they're looking for, aren't you?" the woman said, without taking her eyes off the road. Lee noticed that she was gripping the steering wheel tightly. Obviously she was terrified because she had just been shot at; and it now appeared that she might be afraid of him as well.

"Nice to meet you, too," Lee said, with as much levity as he could muster. "Yes. My name is Lee McCabe; and I am the one that certain people are looking for, as you put it."

"I recognized your picture from the Internet," she explained.

"I didn't kill anyone. And no, I don't get shot at everyday."

"My name's Amy. Amy Sutter. I'm from Warwick." Warwick was a town on the far side of Hawkins County.

"Nice to meet you, Amy Sutter. Looks like you go to college. You're even in a sorority."

"You say that like it was a dirty word."

Lee sighed. Even in a situation like this, he realized, he wasn't above feeling a bit of class envy at the kids who had parents who were wealthy enough to send them to college. Hell, he was envious of kids who *had* parents, for that matter.

"I was in a fraternity of sorts," Lee said. "The U.S. Marine Corps."

"You say that like it was better than other fraternities. Like you're better than me."

Lee paused. This girl did have a lot of nerve. He had to give her that. For all she knew, he might be quite dangerous; and there was no question that he was involved in some very dangerous business. And she had presumably never been fired upon until just a few minutes ago. Nevertheless, she had no trouble calling him on the carpet—for a charge that he suspected was at least partially true.

"I suppose you've got a point there," Lee said. "We do have a tendency to think of ourselves as better than others. But I don't want to fight with you. And like I said, I really appreciate your picking me up. I know you didn't have to."

"Well, don't give me too much credit," she said, smiling for the first time. "You didn't exactly give me much time to think about it, did you?"

"No, I guess I didn't. But please believe me: I didn't do what they're saying I did." Lee looked behind his right shoulder. He judged that he was now a reasonably safe distance from the men who were pursuing him. "Now please pull over."

"Why?" she asked. But she lightened the pressure on the accelerator, slowing the car. "Won't those men be coming after you?"

"Exactly," Lee said. "Come on, stop the car."

Amy gave him a dubious look and applied the brakes. Lee opened the passenger door as the Civic slowed to a stop. The *door open* warning chime began sounding.

Lee stepped out of the car.

"I don't want you to have any further involvement in this, Amy

Sutter. You've done enough already. Now listen: I want you to put some distance between yourself and here."

"Now I know that you're not a cold-blooded killer," she said.

"And how's that?"

She gave him another smile. "A cold-blooded killer wouldn't be concerned for my safety."

"Thanks again, Amy."

He closed the door and he watched Amy drive away. *In another time*, Lee thought, *and under different circumstances. I would have liked to have met a woman like you.*

70

Amy Sutter did not see the armed men until it was too late. There were three of them, each man armed with a Chinese-made AK-47. They had responded quickly to Anderson's cell phone call. The armed men were already in place by the time Amy approached the intersection of Highway 178 and Rural Route 1153—their eyes scanning the empty road for a metallic blue Honda. Anderson had not noted the license plate, and this caused no concern. Traffic was minimal: nothing more than the occasional farm truck at this time of day.

The three armed men were all ex-cons, and all killers, though new to the professional business of killing. All three were very much enamored with the Chinese-made AK-47s. As they waited, they speculated among themselves about the potency of their weapons: How would the destructive power of such a gun manifest itself on a car—especially with all three of them firing?

And so they were already primed by the time Amy Sutter's Honda actually came into view. They picked themselves up from the waist-high overgrowth in which they were only half concealing themselves. They strode almost casually toward the road. At this short distance, the driver of the Honda would have no time to turn the car around on the narrow pavement and flee. Nor were there any side roads or drive-ways that might provide a last-second reprieve. Their quarry was trapped: there was no place for the Honda to go.

One of the men, an ex-felon by the name of Henry ("Hank") Peters, was about the same age as Amy—though he did not know this as he released the safety on his weapon. Hank Peters had done three years in one of Kentucky's state institutions. He had landed there after his scheme to steal and resell items burgled from upscale homes in suburban Louisville had gone wrong.

Hank was tense. He felt his knees go liquid as he approached the oncoming Honda. He had never fired a gun in anger before this day. And now he was a real contract killer; his employment in the company of Lester Finn represented a step up to something bigger, he was quite sure. Never again would he have to rifle through the possessions of middle-aged housewives and corporate middle managers, desperately hoping to find some trinket worth stealing.

Burglary, he now realized, was small-time, a crapshoot that hardly ever paid off. He would never go back to such a life again. Now he was playing the game at an entirely different level. Because of Lester Finn, Hank had money in his pocket—while not a fortune, it was more than he had ever had before.

And he also had this amazing gun. He enjoyed the heft of it in his hands. There was something more than a little exotic about it, this piece of steel and high-density plastic. The AK was more than a mere gun. It was an instrument of death. And with it, Hank was an Angel of Death. He was no longer the two-bit con who had been busted by the Louisville police after a nosy suburbanite had observed him squeezing himself into a basement window. Nor was he the baby-faced inmate who had immediately attracted the attention of the sodomites and the bull queers at the Little Sandy Correctional Complex.

Those memories still stung—the way they had forced him to become a part of their own depravities. The shame and the bleeding that followed one of their attacks. After he returned from prison, Hank had confessed his shame to his father. The old man had driven him from the house, shouting that he had no use for a son who was both an ex-con and a queer.

Hank vented the rage these memories brought by squeezing the handguard and the grip of the AK-47.

Suddenly, the Honda screeched to a halt. The glare of the sun prevented Hank from seeing inside the car. He could not make a one hundred percent verification that this was the correct vehicle; but there was really no need for any such confirmation. Anderson had called just a few minutes ago—and anyway, how many metallic blue Honda Civics could there be in this county, and what were the odds that a similar one was on the same stretch of rural highway at this particular time?

Hank and his two companions lowered their guns to their waists and began firing. The sound was beautiful; the gun was beautiful. It kicked and it bucked powerfully in his hands, ejecting metal shell casings onto the pavement. But most of all, the gun rained destruction. The windshield of the Honda shattered. There was a spray of blood and gore as rounds tore into the cab of the vehicle. This caused Hank a brief second of self-doubt. He knew, though, that this Lee McCabe was at war with Lester Finn—the same Lester Finn who had raised him up from nothing and given him this new lease on life and this beautiful gun. Anyway, Lee McCabe was an ex-marine. He should have known that his actions would lead to something like this sooner or later.

"Stop!" the leader of the three-man crew said. Hank obediently ceased fire.

They walked toward the ruined Honda. The leader of the crew looked inside of the car.

"That's not Lee McCabe!" he said. "That's a fucking woman!"

"It *was* a woman," the third man corrected.

Then Hank forced himself to look, too. He could see that yes, indeed, the sole occupant of the car had been a female—probably a teenager or a young adult. Hank tried to imagine what she had looked like only a few minutes ago, but the task was impossible: Their bullets had torn open her chest; the front seat was drenched by what could only be described as an explosion of blood and tissue. Her face was unrecognizable; they had nearly decapitated her.

This was, he realized, his first close look at violent death. No one could fault him if he took it a little hard the first time. Hank turned away from the other two men and retched into the adjacent ditch.

They ignored his convulsions. Hank suspected that the two of them might be having difficulties of their own. But there was no way to know for sure with such men.

The coppery smell of blood filled the warm summer air.

"Well I'll be damned," the leader of the three said simply. He began punching numbers into his cell phone. "I'd better let Anderson know.

71

After hearing the report, TJ Anderson threw his cell phone angrily at the ground—an indulgence that he immediately regretted. If he lost his ability to communicate with the other crew, then he would have no chance of tracking Lee McCabe further.

He picked up the cell phone and saw that it was still working. He called the crew leader back.

"Get away from that car," TJ ordered. "Starting walking in this direction. Stick to the fields. I'm going to come and get you in the truck. Maybe we'll see McCabe along the way. We might get lucky."

However, this did not seem very likely, given the run of their luck so far.

"Come on!" TJ barked at the three men who were with him. "Time to get back in the truck."

This truck was a 1997 Ford F-150, painted cherry red. Also stolen —but stolen from Louisville, not locally. There were a lot of Ford F-150s in the Bluegrass State; and it probably wouldn't be tracked here before the business of killing Lee McCabe was over.

They had left the truck in the driveway of an old farm rental property. They had been completing a circular sweep of the surrounding area on foot when they spotted McCabe. So it was less than a mile away from their current position.

TJ forced the other two men to run the distance to the truck. *Keep your guns low*, he ordered. Ordinarily, a single man with a hunting rifle or a shotgun would not attract undue attention in Hawkins County. Three men with assault rifles were another matter. And how long would it be before some citizen happened upon the bullet-riddled Honda—the one that Lee McCabe had no longer been riding in when his men attacked? The crew leader had said that the driver had been a young woman, and the car bore local license plates. It would not be long before Lester Finn's hunt for Lee McCabe was public information. That would make his own job infinitely more difficult.

"Jump in the back," he told the two men who were with him. They were panting from the run. "I'll drive."

They did as he told them. TJ started the truck's engine and pulled out onto the road. He had travelled less than a mile when a car sped up behind them—apparently just a random citizen in a hurry to arrive somewhere.

This should not have been a problem in itself. But when TJ looked in his rearview mirror, he noted that one of his men was holding his AK-47 aloft, scanning the surrounding fields and fringes of woodlands for Lee McCabe.

The car pulled up behind them. It was a Dodge Charger, driven by a woman. In the rearview mirror, TJ watched her look up at the AK-47 in horror.

Then the Dodge fell back, but not before the woman lifted her cell phone.

She would be calling the police, that much was certain. TJ weighed his options: On one hand, he could reverse direction, run the Dodge down, and gun the woman down. He was about to do this when he reconsidered: Another death would only increase the public outcry over their ongoing manhunt. Moreover, his own liabilities would be exponentially increased. The community would greet the death of Lee McCabe, a fugitive murder suspect, with a certain degree of relief. These other deaths were more problematic. In a worst-case scenario, he would be on the hook for the murder of a local housewife. That would mean a one-way trip to the lethal injection chamber at Eddyville.

So TJ decided to run. He gunned the truck's engine. He would quickly pick up the other crew and get this very distinctive truck off the road. Let Lee McCabe go for now. A tactical retreat.

He still felt sure that he would take McCabe down, sooner or later.

72

Hawkins County Sheriff's Deputy Darla Johnson sped down Highway 143, her lights flashing and her siren blaring. Cultivated fields and bare woodlands sped by on either side of her. She watched her cruiser's speedometer edge slightly above 70 m.p.h., a dangerous speed on a two-lane road like this.

Her heart seemed to race along with her vehicle's engine.

According to the information Rita had provided, the red pickup truck bearing the gunmen should be less than two miles to her north.

At thirty-four, Darla was a ten-year veteran of the sheriff's department. She had never been in a real shootout—that sort of opportunity (not an opportunity at all, really), seldom presented itself in Hawkins County. She had tussled with her share of drunks, of course, and broken up a few fights at the Steeplechase Saloon. During one call to a domestic violence incident a few years ago, an irate, intoxicated husband had taken a swing at her. Darla had pinned the man's arm behind his back, then wrestled him to the ground, where he cried out in pain. The whimpering bully had finally begged her to let him go.

Darla knew that none of these incidents were of the same magnitude as what she now faced. The men who were behind the recent spate of violence were a league apart from the usual small-town hoodlums. These were men who would kill without hesitation. And they might have connections to even more brutal criminal networks from outside the county.

She pushed the accelerator to 73 m.p.h.—as fast as she dared travel on this road. Her car was full of guns and ammunition. She had her personal sidearm and a Remington shotgun. Plenty of rounds for both. And still she was terrified—feeling inadequate for the task before her.

She advanced on a passenger vehicle that was traveling at less than 40 m.p.h. The driver pulled to the edge of the road, but she almost misjudged the clearance. She came within a hair's breadth of clipping the car.

Calm yourself, Darla. Calm yourself.

Darla was a master marksman, thanks to a combination of police training, personal interest, and her childhood. The youngest of four girls, Darla had become the son her father never had. Ralph Johnson had been a dedicated gun enthusiast—and every Saturday, almost without exception, he took his fourth daughter on a firearms-related outing. Sometimes they hunted waterfowl, sometimes rabbits. Deer every autumn. Other times they went skeet shooting or simply banged away at paper targets tacked to tree trunks deep within the innumerable acres of woods throughout the county.

By the time she was sixteen, Darla could handle a firearm better than practically any boy her age—and better than most grown men.

Nevertheless, she had never fired a weapon in anger—and she had certainly never been on the receiving end of hostile gunfire.

Such were her thoughts at the moment when the red pickup appeared on the crest of the hill directly in front of her, traveling in the same direction. It had been obscured until the last moment by the undulating topography. As her cruiser ascended a hilltop, she saw the outlaws' truck at the top of the next hill. There was only a short distance, a dip, and an incline between them.

Darla rammed the accelerator with her right foot. At that instant the driver of the pickup became aware of her presence. A man in the passenger seat gestured at the rearview mirror. The driver looked at the mirror and there was a verbal exchange between the two occupants of the cab. Then the man in the passenger seat began to pound his fist on the rear window of the pickup.

She had not noticed the man in the bed of the truck until now, hidden as he was by the angle and his posture. Now he sat up; and Darla could see that he was armed: He held an AK-47.

Then several more men sat up, all of them similarly armed: The back of the pickup truck contained a total of four armed men. They had been hunkered down—probably to avoid being conspicuous.

The truck came to an abrupt stop. Now the distance between Darla's cruiser and the other vehicle was closing rapidly. The first man in the back of the truck held his gun aloft; Darla could already see the dark opening of the gun's muzzle.

The other three raised their guns as well.

The men in the truck had decided to turn the tables. They were no longer fugitives; but attackers. There were four of them, plus two more in the cab. They had superior firepower; and the men in the back of the truck could simply fire away at Darla while she was occupied with driving.

Darla had already jammed on the brakes when the AK-47s began to erupt, first cracking the bullet-resistant glass of her windshield before finally shattering it.

She instinctively ducked toward the passenger's side. This gesture had at least two outcomes, one preventative, one disastrous: The burst of rounds from the assault rifles did not shatter her head, as her attackers deliberately raked the interior of the police cruiser. She was aware, though, that she had been struck in the hip by a ricocheting bullet. Blood appeared on her thigh—another ricochet wound, by the look of it.

She also lost control of the squad car. The cruiser swerved sharply to the left; both driver's side tires became hooked in the space between the road and the gulley at the edge of the blacktop. Darla pulled the steering wheel to the right when she lunged into the passenger's seat, as glass and steel rained around her. She felt the right side of the car leave the pavement, felt her body whip suddenly backward and upward as the car went airborne in a horizontal roll.

Her head slammed against the steering wheel. In the second before she lost consciousness, she wondered if the men in the truck would let her die in peace. Or would they leave their truck and follow her tumbling vehicle into the grass, intent on finishing her off themselves?

73

From the driver's seat of the pickup truck, TJ Anderson watched the police cruiser go airborne. It rolled over onto its side on the pavement, then made another complete tumble. The cruiser smashed through a barbed wire fence on the far side of the road before finally coming to rest in the grass. The patrol car was upside down; the windshield was completely gone and the roof of the cab was all but crushed by the vehicle's own weight. The underside of the vehicle faced the sky; two of the wheels were bent at forty-five degree angles.

The pickup truck was still stopped. TJ knew he could not afford to linger here for long, but he wanted to take a brief look at the damage. A humbled law enforcement officer was always a sight to behold.

There is one cop car that is never going to trouble anyone again, he thought. The cop herself (TJ was almost certain that he had seen a woman behind the wheel) was going to be out of service for a while, too.

If she wasn't already dead. Another liability for him. One that couldn't be helped, though.

One of the men in the back of the truck—a young guy named Hank Peters—stood up in the bed, held his weapon over his head, and hooted. It seemed to be an attempt at an Indian war whoop. When the youth made as to dismount, TJ leaned out the window and said:

"Where the hell do you think you're going?"

"I got to finish what we started, don't I?"

"You've got to sit your ass down in that truck," TJ said. He released the brake and accelerated. Peters fell back against the rear window of the cab with a heavy thud. TJ felt the sudden need to put distance between himself and the disabled police car. Cops were like insects: where there was one there were sure to be more.

Peters cursed him roundly, jamming his middle finger upward before the rear window.

"Anderson, you're a sonofabitch!" he shouted.

TJ bit back on his anger. The man beside him smiled awkwardly.

"Not a good idea to piss off a man who's holding a gun like that," he said.

TJ grunted. He could not argue with that sentiment; but Peters had been acting like a fool.

The men in his command were becoming bloodthirsty and careless, swollen on the cash and the power that they had fallen into. Before they had been ex-cons, now they were paid mercenaries. The man in the passenger seat had told TJ about Hank Peters' reaction to the death of the young woman. His attempt to "finish off" the female police officer was no doubt an attempt to redeem his own perception of his manhood, to prove that he was the biggest, baddest killer in the bunch.

It was all nothing more than a pointless dick-measuring exercise.

TJ still believed that he could use these men to track down Lee McCabe. But they were also a danger to him, their supposed leader. If he was not careful, these men might get him killed or captured before their mission was complete.

74

Deputy Ron Norris stopped his patrol car. He could not believe his luck.

Perhaps a mile away, at the crest of the horizon, he spotted the figure of Lee McCabe. Lee was walking just inside the tree line. The rolling, open land before the woods—an overgrown field and a cultivated stretch of soybeans—nearly obscured him from view. McCabe probably believed that he was far enough from the road. He believed that he was safe, untouchable.

He believed wrong.

Norris stepped out of his patrol car and quickly opened the trunk. He scanned the highway in both directions. All clear. He would only need a minute or two to assemble the gun and take a shot. And one shot would be all the he would get.

The weapon in the trunk was another from his private collection. Like the Beretta, it was unregistered and untraceable. It was a bolt-action Winchester that fired .308 cartridges. The gun was outfitted with a U.S. Optics S-10 scope.

Norris removed the gun from its case and steadied it on the roof of the patrol car. Once again he noticed that he was shaking; but the shaking was more controllable here than it had been in the field—

when he had stood face-to-face with McCabe and the young man had been pointing a gun back at him.

A stiff breeze was stirring the grass and the soybeans. This was another factor that could complicate the shot, as Norris sighted McCabe in the telescope's crosshairs, he compensated a bit for the direction of the wind.

His first intuition was to attempt a head shot; but that would be difficult at this distance. He reminded himself that he would have only one clear shot.

So instead he centered the crosshairs on Lee's upper torso. With a single well-placed shot in this area, he could shatter McCabe's vital organs or possibly his spinal cord. Either scenario would result in a kill.

Norris's finger was tightening on the trigger as he heard the approach of a large motor vehicle—probably an eighteen-wheeler. For a second he considered waiting. However, Lee was walking at a brisk pace. If Norris waited, his target might disappear into the tree line. Then no shot would be possible.

No time. No time, thought Norris.

The motor was drawing nearer. *How would it look—a sheriff's deputy aiming a rifle into the distance like this? How would he explain the incident if someone reported it?*

He squeezed the trigger. The shot went wild, slamming into a tree trunk that was a good two feet from Lee. As expected, McCabe dove for cover. Norris muttered an expletive and swung the gun off the roof of the cruiser. He opened the rear driver's side door just as the eighteen-wheeler crested the horizon and came into view.

The truck slowed as it passed the parked patrol car. The driver tipped his hat to Norris. Another law-abiding citizen going out of his way to be friendly to the police. Norris briefly fantasized about taking the gun back out and firing on the damned truck.

When the truck had passed out of view again, Norris did retrieve the rifle. This would almost certainly be his last chance to personally take care of the McCabe problem. Such an opportunity would not come along a third time. After this, he would have to entrust matters completely to Lester Finn, whom Norris trusted not at all.

He snatched the rifle in both hands and bounded over the drainage ditch beside the road. He pushed himself to his limit, breaking into a run that turned his lungs to fire and made his heart feel like it was about to explode.

Norris paused at the edge of the soybean field. He had a clear view of the woods now; but of course McCabe was not to be seen. He was hiding. And he probably had a pistol.

Norris realized the magnitude of his mistake. He could not see McCabe. McCabe could see him. He was a target in an open space.

Nevertheless, McCabe had been armed with a pistol, which would not be accurate at this range.

He opted for the middle path. *I might get lucky*, he thought.

Holding the rifle to his shoulder and using the scope once again, Norris fired a succession of rounds into the area where McCabe had been, firing several shots to each side. Norris fired quickly, pausing only to eject empty shells and slide new ones into the chamber.

Finally the gun was empty. No sounds came from the woods, save the cries of some distant crows that had been disturbed. There were no human moans of agony, and no return fire,

For a moment he contemplated walking to the edge of the woods. If one of his bullets had struck McCabe, it might be necessary to finish him off with a large rock or the butt of the rifle. But Norris knew himself, and he realized that he was afraid to proceed any further. The tree line presented too many unknowns.

LEE WATCHED Norris walk back down the hill toward his parked squad car. He lay on his side in a patch of high grass. His left shoulder was on fire.

One of Norris's randomly fired shots had struck him at the highest point of the arm, near the triceps muscle. The bullet had nicked him, so he did not have a hot round in his body, which might have meant a shattered bone and artery. It was only a flesh wound—very treatable in either a civilian or a military hospital—but possibly fatal in situation like this, where he could not seek medical help.

He had been sure that Norris was going to walk back to the woods to finish the kill when there was no return fire. Instead the deputy had left him wounded and unarmed, his prospects bleaker than ever.

75

S ome hours later, Lee forced himself up from his resting place in the woods and made his way down past the soybean field through the empty stretch of grass to the road.

Not only was he muddy and disheveled from his time in the woods; he also now looked like a man coming fresh from a gunfight. He had torn a strip of his shirt to use a tourniquet, but his left arm and much of that side were covered with dried and drying blood.

Now what? he thought. But there was only one immediate option: *He had to get moving.*

He set out along the pavement in the twilight. His shoes scraped in the gravel with each step. The inside of his mouth was sandpaper.

He surveyed the landscape that surrounded him. The shadows from the hills and trees were lengthening, although the heat of the day had not yet abated.

What was this road called? He was not sure; since he had begun his flight, he had seen an endless series of woods and fields and rural roads. Set against a rolling background of trees and hillsides, one nondescript barn or farmhouse looked very much like another. All he knew for sure was his direction: he was still heading inexorably south, toward Blood Flats and whatever form of exoneration or death might wait there.

He brushed away a fly that had settled on the bloody, ragged wound near his shoulder. The gash on his arm might only be a flesh wound; but it would soon become infected in this environment—*if it wasn't already*. The blood loss was also weakening him. His makeshift tourniquet only partially staunched the bleeding. He was still losing blood—and strength.

He would have to appeal to someone for help. He would pick one of the farmhouses on his right or his left. He would select one at random and knock on the front door. Perhaps he would happen upon a good Samaritan who did not watch much television or read the papers—someone who did not yet know about the massacre at the Tradewinds and his fugitive status. If he was lucky and persuasive, he could convince them that he was the victim of a hunting accident. They would give him some antiseptic for his arm—that would at least keep him from losing the limb to gangrene.

He decided that his choice should not be entirely random. He began to look for a house that could be fairly described as friendly-looking. This assessment relied on a vague set of criteria, of course. He would pick someplace that was brightly lit, with a front yard that seemed designed with the welcoming of visitors in mind. Needless to say, that would rule out any dwelling with a NO TRESPASSING or BEWARE OF DOG sign.

After trudging a bit further, he came to a house that appeared to be a good prospect: In the front door was hung a dried floral arrange-ment in the form of a wreath. The wreath was crisscrossed by the word WELCOME in stitched red letters. The house bore a woman's touch. It was the home of a married couple, perhaps a young married couple with children. If the occupants had not yet heard of Lee McCabe the wanted killer—if they had not seen his face on television—then in all likelihood they would help him.

Lee walked up the driveway, trudging past a blue Chevrolet Malibu and a four-wheel drive pickup truck. Before ringing the door-bell, he turned his injured arm away from the door: The sight of all that blood would put anyone off, whether they were basically friendly or not.

Lee pushed the doorbell and almost immediately he heard a commotion in the rear part of the house. There were two voices, a man and a woman. Lee could not make out the words; but their tone was simultaneously muted and urgent. The man's voice was tinged with an unmistakable edge of irritation.

Now there were footsteps, short and quick and suggestive of feminine feet. The door opened, and Lee stared into the face of a woman. She was in her late twenties or early thirties, and a bit on the plump side. She had that sort of round girlish beauty that often softens into plainness by early middle age.

If the woman herself was unremarkable, her choice of attire was another matter. She was wearing only a white bed sheet; with one hand she clutched the sheet across her breasts. Her other hand was on the front door.

She greeted Lee with an expression of surprise: "Who are you?"

Given the publicity surrounding the shootings and his fugitive status, Lee decided that he should not give his name—at least not right away.

"I don't think we're acquainted, ma'am. You see, I've had a bit of an accident, and—"

More stirring at the far end of the house.

"Cheryl, who is it?" an unseen man shouted.

By now Lee had deduced that he had interrupted an act of marital congress in mid-session.

In less dire circumstances, he would have been embarrassed—if he had not been bleeding from a bullet wound, if he had not been on the run from armed thugs, and an equally homicidal sheriff's deputy. As matters stood, however, Lee could not afford any concessions to embarrassment—neither his own nor that of another.

"You see, ma'am, I just need a bit of antiseptic for this arm."

Her eyes grew wide. "Oh my God! You're bleeding!"

"CHERYL, WHO THE HELL ARE YOU TALKIN' TO?"

Cheryl yelled back to the voice down the hall. *"Hold on, Ross. It ain't Danny!"*

"WELL HOW THE HELL AM I SUPPOSED TO KNOW THAT?"

"I told you before: Danny's workin' second shift and he'll be at the plant until two in the mornin'. Now give me a minute. I got a man bleedin' here."

Lee heard Ross's feet strike the floor, and he now had a new assessment of the coupling that he had disturbed.

Then Ross came plodding out of the rear hall and into view. He was shirtless and buckling his belt as he walked. This was a big man —perhaps six-feet-four inches tall and well over two hundred pounds. Ross had large biceps that were incongruous with his nascent beer belly. He had the look of a former high school jock who had since turned to beer and sloth.

Ross was far from friendly. He stared past Cheryl and addressed Lee.

"Who are you?"

"I'm a neighbor. I leave nearby. I'm hurt and need I help."

"You look okay to me."

"Ross, he's got blood all over him," Cheryl interjected.

"Well, he can still walk. Let him go to some other house. What does this look like, a first aid station?"

Cheryl looked at Lee and shrugged as if to say, *What can you do?*

"Please," Lee said. "All I want is some medicine for my arm. I won't take but a few minutes of your time."

Ross shook his head. He was obviously not accustomed to being contradicted to this degree. A rage clouded his cheeks.

"MISTER, YOU EITHER LEAVE NOW, OR I'M GOING TO BOOT YOUR ASS INTO THE MIDDLE OF THE ROAD!" Ross's hands were balled into fists. A single vein protruded from his forehead.

Lee felt a wave of his own rage surge through him, both at his own impotence, and the ever-evolving nature of bad luck. Neither of the illicit lovers was aware that he was a wanted fugitive. But they were not inclined to help him. Cheryl was obviously under the control of Ross; and Ross was impervious to neighborly persuasion. Ross had his nerve. This was obviously not his house; but he had assumed the role of household master while he was cuckolding the hapless, second-shift-working Danny.

Could he simply force his way inside? Lee sized Ross up and he knew that if it came to physical blows, he would have no chance against this opponent in his current state. Moreover, Cheryl was taking her lover's side. Lee would be guilty of trespassing; some would even call it a home invasion. There was no way that such a fight could turn out well for him.

Then he thought of one last card to play.

"I'll tell Danny," he said simply.

Suddenly wide-eyed, Ross and Cheryl looked at each other briefly and then, back at Lee.

"What the hell are you talkin' about?" Ross demanded.

"I'm talking about poor Danny. Danny happens to be a friend of mine. I'm sure he'd love to know what's going on at his house while he's at work."

Ross snorted. "You're bluffin' You don't know Danny. You don't know nobody."

"Do you want to take that chance?" Lee intended this remark for Cheryl more than Ross.

"How about if I just rip your head off for you instead?" Ross countered. "How does that sound?"

Then Cheryl intervened. She removed her hand from the door and placed it on Ross's bare shoulder. "Come on, baby. It ain't worth all that. Let's just get rid of him."

"I think I'd rather kill him!"

"I don't want you killin' nobody, at least not on my front porch."

Then to Lee, she said curtly: "What do you want?"

Lee sighed. "Just give me some antiseptic: Rubbing alcohol, hydrogen peroxide, anything that will kill germs."

"You can stay out on the porch," Cheryl said. As she closed the door, Lee caught a final glimpse of Ross, who did indeed seem ready to rip his head off, or do him some similar act of violence. In one last show of hostility, Ross thrust his body forward past Cheryl into the doorway. Lee thought that a fight might be coming after all. Then Cheryl pushed him back.

"Please, baby. Calm down. For *me*, huh?"

"Son-of-a-bitch thinks he can barge in here like he owns the place," Ross said. "Who does he think he is?"

"Why don't you just go back to the bedroom honey? *Please*. I'll be along soon."

In a few minutes Cheryl handed out a plastic Wal-Mart bag that had been filled with a number of useful items: a tube of polysporin antibiotic ointment, a blister pack of aspirin, some cotton balls and a roll of medical adhesive tape. Cheryl had even thrown in a little bottle of mosquito repellant. Lee had asked for a single item of anti-septic medicine, and Cheryl had given him a poor man's first-aid kit.

"Thank you," Lee said.

But Cheryl had already slammed the door.

"Don't never come back here again!" she yelled.

76

"Is she alive?"

"We'll tell you in a few moments, Sheriff."

Phelps fought back a surge of dread and nausea as the county rescue crew finally extracted Darla's inert form from the wreckage of her patrol car. Night had already fallen. The rescue work had taken longer than it should have—because of the angle of upturned patrol car, and the inadequate equipment on hand in Hawkins County.

There were four members of the life squad—three men and one woman. They placed Darla on a stretcher and began to ferry her across the field toward the waiting ambulance. Phelps walked behind them.

Please let her be alive, he thought.

Phelps had spent most of the day attending to a fresh wave of tragedies: First there was the young woman—a college student who had apparently been ambushed by high-powered automatic rifles. Her bullet-riddled car had looked like the wreckage of a war zone, the sort of thing that exists as part of the ongoing tragedies of certain foreign lands, but not an expected part of life in Hawkins County. Then Amy Sutter's parents had arrived on the scene; and they had resisted all of Phelps's efforts to keep them away from their daughter's body. *You don't want to see her like this,* he had insisted. *Trust me, the best thing for you to do is to stay back.* But finally they had prevailed and they had caught a glimpse of her mangled form behind the wheel of the shattered Honda. Amy Sutter's mother had collapsed by the side of the road, crying and screaming and beating her fists futilely into the earth. The girl's father had sworn impotent oaths of revenge.

And now here was Darla, probably attacked by the same men or their close confederates. Phelps had been unable to do anything for Amy Sutter or her parents; and now he was unable to help Darla in any substantive way, either. He was essentially a bystander.

The paramedics lifted the stretcher into the ambulance, attaching various equipment to Darla's body. Phelps noted several gashes—bullet wounds. She had lost a lot of blood, he was certain.

Now instruments were beeping inside the ambulance. Straps being fastened down and buckled.

The female member of the life squad crew diverted her attention from Darla and said to Phelps:

"She's alive, but she might be in some serious trouble." The paramedic secured Darla's head with a neck brace and then placed an oxygen mask over her face.

Phelps dared not ask any more questions. Now that he knew Darla was alive more questions followed: *Would she regain consciousness? Would she spend the rest of her life as a cripple? Would she slip into a coma from which she would never awaken?*

But Phelps knew that these four paramedics could provide answers to none of these unknowns. The ER doctors at Hawkins County General would have some of these answers, starting much later tonight. The answers would trickle in at an agonizingly slow pace. Phelps was no doctor; but his work in law enforcement had made him intimately familiar with the morbid rituals of hospitals and physicians.

Phelps was standing by the rear doors of the ambulance, watching them work on Darla. He wanted her to wake up before they closed the doors, to show some sign of life. He wanted to be able to give her some nod of encouragement, feeble though the gesture would be. She was his responsibility.

"*Sheriff?*"

Norris appeared out of nowhere in the darkness, startling Phelps. He had arrived on the scene earlier, more or less concurrently. The two of them had set up two road blocks. All traffic on this highway—sparse though it was—was blocked in both directions. They had set up detour signs to route cars around the rescue crew vehicles and Darla's overturned cruiser.

"How's Darla?" Norris asked.

"Alive," Phelps responded. "That's all I know for now."

Norris nodded thoughtfully. "That's good. That's good. Well, we'll give these emergency vehicles a few minutes to clear out, and I'll take down those detour signs."

Norris walked away, humming to himself in a distracted manner. Was he simply worried about Darla? This was the truth as far as Phelps knew. The two of them had never been close. Norris was still behaving oddly, as he had since the beginning of this crisis.

The metallic-trimmed red doors closed on Darla and the paramedics. The sound made Phelps think of the lid closing on a coffin. He was struck by a sense of foreboding that was both implacable and irrational: *At least one of his deputies would die before this was over.*

77

Clutching the Wal-Mart bag, Lee walked a safe distance past the house where Cheryl and Ross had likely resumed their coupling. He found a tree near the road that was large enough to shield him from view. He sat down while he tended to his arm as best he could. Without running water or full daylight, it was an imperfect job. At best, his efforts might have protected him from gangrene or another infection for a little while. Perhaps another eight or twelve hours. The arm stung badly. Lee opened the blister pack of aspirin and chewed two of them before forcing himself to his feet again.

He resumed his walk along the road running south, toward the town of Blood Flats.

He had walked past two more houses before he came to one that had a significance for him. He had never seen this house before, and there was nothing special to distinguish it from the others along the road—except for the name on the mailbox.

The mailbox identified this as the residence of David and Marie Wilson. The latter name had a meaning for Lee—a connection to a childhood that was already fading into a distant memory.

Wilson was a common name, of course; but he believed that this would be the Marie Wilson he remembered. *I have had so much bad luck*, Lee thought. *I am due for a shift of fortune. This will be her house*, he told himself. *Oh, please let this be her house.*

And for the first time that day, at least, Lee was not disappointed. The door was answered by an African-American woman of perhaps sixty-five years of age. Her eyes widened when she saw the apparition on her front porch, battered and still largely covered with blood as he was. There was a moment of tension, when Lee did not know if she was going to turn him away, or perhaps even call the police.

Then, to Lee's half surprise, she recognized him.

"Why...Lee McCabe."

"Mrs. Wilson." Lee said simply.

She beckoned him inside, and the interior of the house smelled both clean and homey at the same time. His shoes left two muddy footprints on her hardwood floor. He started to apologize but she gestured him to be quiet.

Then she took his face in both of her hands. "Lee McCabe, whatever have you gotten yourself into?"

"I want you to know, Mrs. Wilson. I want you to know that I didn't kill those people in that trailer. I was trying to help, and I—"

"Shhhhh. I know you aren't a killer, boy. I remember you. I know you."

"Thank you," he said simply—partly to Marie, and partly to the luck that had brought him there.

Book cases dominated Marie Wilson's living room, as might be expected of a schoolteacher. Lee's gaze wandered across the titles: There was *Great Expectations* by Charles Dickens, *Crime and Punishment* by Fyodor Dostoyevsky, *Tom Sawyer* by Mark Twain, and many others. On the far side of the room he saw an antique console table that was dominated by pictures of a single African-American man at various ages. Most of the pictures captured him in early or late middle-age, a few nearer to the end of his life. Lee noted one in particular: the young man in the photograph was dressed in a Vietnam-era army uniform. An American flag and a blue background were behind him.

"My husband died last year," Marie said by way of explanation.

"I'm sorry," Lee said.

"Mom? Who is it?"

Marie's eldest son, Joe, walked into the room. Joe was about thirty, so he and Lee were not well acquainted. Joe's younger brother, Jeremy, was four years younger. That placed him and Lee in roughly the same peer group—though still too far apart to have attended high school at the same time. Jeremy was now serving in the Army. The last Lee had heard, he was part of the Combat Aviation Brigade stationed at Bagram Air Base in Afghanistan.

"You know Lee McCabe, don't you, Joe?"

Joe took a few seconds to appraise the wounded man standing in his mother's living room. "I know that Lee McCabe is in a heap of trouble, is what I know."

"I didn't do it," Lee said.

"Maybe you did," Joe said. "And maybe you didn't. Why are you here?"

Marie gasped. "Joseph! Where's your sense of Christian decency? I've known Lee McCabe since he was a twelve year-old in my seventh grade class. He's a good boy, I tell you. Do you think I'd welcome a murderer into this home?"

Even in his present state of exhaustion, Lee had no trouble discerning the low-grade hostility emanating from Marie Wilson's elder son. *He's concerned about his mother*, Lee thought. *Can I blame him? I've been a walking case of trouble these past few days.*

Nevertheless, he was no murderer, and that much he would set straight. "I can imagine what you've heard, Joe. But I didn't kill those people in that trailer. And I won't bring you or your mother any trouble. I would appreciate some attention to my injured arm here, and maybe a drink of water. Then I'll be on my way."

"Nonsense!" Marie said. "You'll stay for dinner." She held up a hand before Joe could protest. "And what's more, you'll stay the night. You can sleep in Jeremy's room. He's in Afghanistan tonight and he won't be needing it."

"Mrs. Wilson, I couldn't—"

"Shush!" she said. "Now let me go find something to fix that arm."

As Marie walked purposefully off toward the bathroom medicine cabinet, Joe turned discreetly to Lee.

"I got my eye on you, McCabe," he said. "You do anything to bring my mamma any grief, and I'll kill you."

78

Marie bandaged his wounds and she gave him dinner. The three of them—Lee, Marie, and her son Joe—sat around her large kitchen table, which still had room for two more people.

"It's been a long time since we've had even three at this table," Marie said, more than a little wistfully. "And much longer than that since we've had four." This made Lee recall the two who were missing —Marie's deceased husband David, and her younger son, Jeremy.

At first the dinner promised to be a silent affair, with Joe obviously so distressed at his presence. But Marie shamed her older son: *"What's your problem, Joe? Is your life so uninteresting that you have nothing to say?"* And finally Joe relented, so that the meal was punctuated with at least some conversation. But Lee did most of the talking: Marie and Joe made him retell his story several times.

Afterward, the three of them sat in the living room and watched television. Lee mostly ignored the sounds and images emanating from the screen, lost as he was in his own thoughts. He tried to engage himself in the sitcom that Marie Wilson had selected; but he found this task impossible. He had too much to think about.

Then the programming was interrupted for a special news announcement, and Lee's attention was suddenly riveted to the TV.

"Police are investigating the grisly murder of a female University of Kentucky student early this afternoon...."

Lee had an immediate sense of dark foreboding. He somehow sensed the blow that was coming, even before the sharply dressed and perfectly coiffed anchorwoman revealed the rest of it.

"The body of Amy Sutter was discovered on a rural highway near Perryston late this afternoon. Police say that Ms. Sutter was shot multiple times with a high-caliber weapon. She was driving when she was apparently attacked—"

Lee leaned forward in his chair and put his head into his hands. He now realized that his last-minute attempt at gallantry had been in vain. By exiting Amy Sutter's Civic, he had not spared her—he had only spared himself.

I killed her, he thought, *as surely as if I had pulled the trigger myself.*

Now both Joe and Marie Wilson were looking at him, asking him what was wrong. On the television screen, the image of the anchorwoman was replaced by an image of Sheriff Steven Phelps. A reporter was asking Phelps if Amy Sutter's murder was in any way connected to the recent drug-related murders at the Tradewinds trailer park.

"Like many other rural communities," Phelps said. "Hawkins County has recently seen a sharp rise in methamphetamine trafficking and drug-related violence. At this time we know of no connection between Ms. Sutter's murder and the Tradewinds killings. This new homicide is under investigation. Needless to say, we will inform the public of any new developments as soon as we possibly can."

"Lee, what's wrong?" Marie said.

Since Joe and Marie had taken him into their home and their confidence, Lee felt that he owned them an explanation. He told them about his chance meeting with Amy Sutter along that two-lane highway, and how she had saved his life by giving him a ride. In the end she had traded her own life for his.

And though he was ashamed of his lack of composure, Lee

pressed his palms into his eyes and felt that they were wet. He did not know if these were tears of despair or rage. Perhaps both.

"Poor Lee," Marie said. She leaned over from where she sat and placed one arm upon his shoulders. The spasms of grief and fury moved through his body, an unstoppable force that Lee was powerless to resist.

"My poor Lee," Marie repeated. "And that poor girl."

She removed her arm from Lee's shoulders and sat back in her own chair. Crossing her arms, she listened to the remaining details regarding Amy Sutter's murder. And then she asked a question. Although she spoke it aloud, she must have known that it could not be answered by either Lee or her son.

"I want to believe what the Good Book says. I want to believe that the meek will inherit the earth. But tell me, sweet Jesus, what's going to happen to all of us? What are we supposed to do, with so much evil running loose in this world?"

79

D awn Hardin stared into her father's face. He had awakened her in the middle of the night with a nudge, when her sister and her mother were already asleep. It was the first time he had spoken to her, or acknowledged her presence, since she had arrived from Louisville.

"Wake up," he had said in the darkness of the bedroom she was sharing once again with her sister, Liz.

There had not been much waking up to do, for she was only half-asleep. The tension in the house—tension that she had caused—made restful sleep nearly impossible.

"Don't turn on the light or wake your sister," Bill Hardin said. "We need to talk, just you and me."

And so the two of them went into the living room and talked in low tones in the darkness, Bill Hardin sitting in his armchair that faced the television set, Dawn seated opposite him on the couch.

There was little light in the living room; but Dawn could see the outlines of her father's face: The hard-set lines of his jaw and the overall coldness of his expression. It was as if he did not know her —*like she was an intruder in his house rather than his own daughter.*

For a while he did not speak. Then he said in a low whisper:

"Why are you back here? Is it for money? Your mother and I have nothing to give you."

These words came like a blow. But of course: *what would she expect her father to think?* Didn't junkies always turn to their relatives for money, like the leeches they were? And in the early days of her meth addiction—while she was still hanging on at school—hadn't she in fact convinced her mother to send her several hundred dollars? *Money that she promptly blew on meth?*

"No, Dad. That's not why I'm here. I'm sorry for everything I put you and Mom through. Sorry for what I put myself through."

"I'm thinking most about your sister," Bill Hardin said. "Since you left—since you've kind of kept to yourself—Liz has been doing better. I think she's put all the trouble with you behind her. We still have a chance with her. I think she might turn out alright."

And the implication here was, of course, that Dawn had *not* turned out alright. But how could she argue with her father's assessment on this point?

"I know," Dawn said. "I don't want to do anything to hurt her."

"Your being here hurts her. Hurts your mother and me. Now I'm going to ask you again: *What is it that you want?*"

What she wanted was for her father to wrap his arms around her like he used to do when she was a child—to tell her that he still loved her and that however bad this all was—he would help her to fight her way though it. They would overcome it together.

But this sort of parental sympathy did not seem forthcoming. And she could not bring herself to ask for it. *No—if he did not know that this was what she needed, how could telling him possibly make a difference?* He did not have this reserve of love to give her. Or he was unwilling to give it?

So instead she said: "I came back because I wanted to change."

"*Change?* Does this look like a drug rehab center to you? I have to go to work during the day. Your mother has to go to work. Liz has to go to school. Do you think that any of us wants to come home one day and find that you've sold the television set or your mother's china for drug money?"

"I wouldn't do that, Daddy."

"Tell me, then: *Are you clean? Are you free of the drugs?*"

She wanted to be free of the meth—wanted it more than anything right now. But she knew that a struggle still lay ahead of her, and the final outcome of that battle was unknown. It would have been easy to lie to him. Easy and futile. He would know the truth, either now or later. One way or another he would know.

"Not completely," she said.

"Then there's no place for you here. And frankly, even if you weren't doing drugs anymore, I don't think that this would be the best place for you to stay."

"You're saying I no longer have a home here, then."

He pounded the armrest of the chair once with his fist.

"Don't give me that! You brought this on yourself!"

Yes she had, in a manner of speaking. But did that mean that her father and mother no longer loved her? Did it make her a different person? Was it so easy to fall from grace, to become unworthy of a parent's love?

She began to cry, unable to hold it back any longer. She kept her sobs low. She did not want to awaken her mother and sister.

"You should have thought of that before, Dawn," Bill Hardin said. "You hurt us all with what you did. Me especially. You were my little girl once."

There was an unspoken subtext in these words of his that she dared not openly acknowledge: The shame not only of her addiction —but of the depths to which she had sunk to satisfy that addiction. This was the shame that her father would never be able to forget—to move past—even if she managed to overcome her urges for the white powder.

So she implored him in the only language that might get through —words that harkened back to an earlier time, before she had brought this darkness into all their lives.

"I am *still* your little girl. If you would only let me be."

Bill shook his head.

"You are a dope-taking whore and a shame to this family. You should have stayed where you were."

And this pronouncement broke her—it was proof that her old life —her pre-meth life—was broken beyond repair. Never to return again. She thought about the redemption that she had been hoping for when she left Louisville. Wherever that redemption was—*if it existed at all*—she would not find it here.

"I'll leave," she said at length. "Just give me a few minutes to collect my things, and then I'll be gone."

80

I t was past one-thirty in the morning, and the Boar's Head had been closed since midnight. No point in keeping the place open any later on a weekday night.

Luke was sweeping the floor of the main bar area while Lester arranged clean glasses behind the bar. The big oaf (Lester could rarely force himself to think of the Luke in any other terms) was wearing a Magnum .22 revolver in a shoulder holster.

Lester reflected for a moment on the deal he was getting by employing Luke: He paid the big oaf a pittance: He was making barely more than minimum wage—which would have been perfectly normal if Luke's duties had been confined to odd tasks at the bar. In a town like Blood Flats, work of that sort rarely commanded more.

But Luke was in fact a multipurpose tool: He swept floors or fetched beers when Lester needed an extra hand on the Boar's Head side of his enterprises. And he provided muscle when there was activity on the clandestine side. Even in Blood Flats, muscle work paid better than minimum wage. A lot better.

Lester winced when he considered the princely sum that he was paying Anderson. Anderson had discerned that he was in a jam, and the unemployed ex-con had charged what the traffic would bear. *A pretentious, self-important redneck*, Lester thought.

But not Luke. Luke was too dumb to reckon his own bargaining power, and so Lester could control him. This was one of the key tactics that had allowed Lester to stay afloat for so long. *I know how to manipulate lesser men. I can read them and then mold them to my purposes. I should thank God that I'm something of a genius*, Lester thought, watching Luke meticulously pull the chairs away from the table so he could sweep underneath. *No—I should thank my granddaddy. I know Granddaddy existed. God I'm not so sure about.*

Lester smiled at the big man's back, then crouched below the bar to put the last of the clean glasses from the dishwasher onto the shelf. Technically, this was grunt work; but in this case Lester did not mind. Granddaddy had always been hands-on in the bar area; and working like this gave Lester a sense of connection with the old man's spirit.

But now another task occurred to him: a task that Granddaddy would have appreciated even more, given the old man's affection for cash—especially the tax-free kind.

"I'm going in the back for a while," Lester shouted at Luke's back. Without turning around, Luke raised a hand to indicate that he had heard. He didn't even break the rhythm of his sweeping. *Good boy*, Lester thought, as he headed toward the office and storage area behind the main barroom.

Lester Finn was proud of his private office. Like the portions of the bar that the customers saw, it bore the imprints of his grandfather. The furthermost wall—the one that faced the doorway—was dominated by a mahogany wood desk from the 1920s. Antique Western prints—reproductions of Frederic Remington paintings—occupied prominent places along the three walls that faced the desk.

Atop the basic décor established by his granddaddy, Lester had added imprints of his own: A few avant-garde pieces from the 1950s onward, including a reproduction of Andy Warhol's famous portrait of Marilyn Monroe. Vintage poster of seventies rock acts: KISS and Aerosmith and Peter Frampton.

But Lester's favorite piece was a vintage *Star Wars* poster from

1978. The poster hung protected inside a glass case; Lester had paid a collector two hundred dollars for it at a flea market in Louisville.

The poster featured an image of Darth Vader, extending one gloved hand in an upward grasping motion. Behind Vader, a montage of explosions and streaking starship fighters evinced the ultimate sensation of chaos and destruction.

In his more fanciful moments, Lester liked to imagine himself as somehow in league with the Dark Lord himself, pulling strings and meting out punishment in his own little universe. He realized that the analogy was a bit of a stretch; but a man had to be self-indulgent from time-to-time when crafting his own self-image, Lester had long ago concluded. Otherwise, the world would never take him seriously.

Lester sat down in the padded, high-backed chair behind the desk. He felt along his waist and unsnapped the key ring that he wore on his belt. The key ring was still joined to Lester's belt by a chain, a chain long enough to reach the right middle drawer of the desk. Lester ran his fingers through the multiple keys until he found the correct one and inserted it into the keyhole. The desk drawer slid open, revealing a cigar box: The familiar portrait of the Dutch Masters gathered serenely around a table.

He raised the lid of the cigar box and saw the stacks of bills: Each one-hundred-dollar note bore the image of Benjamin Franklin.

It was a sight that gave Lester a slight, pleasant tingle. He had been dealing meth for several years now; but the money still gave him chills.

His previous ventures on the shadowy side of the law—pot, whores, and gambling—had been lucrative in their own way, but ultimately limited in scope. Pot had become a small-time and low-dollar trade since seeds had become readily available, and anyone could become a grower. Competition had similarly eroded the margins on whores. Gambling required too much administration and oversight.

But ah, meth—just complicated enough to discourage serious competition from amateurs, yet simple enough for a dedicated businessman with the right connections. High margins and a very dedicated customer base. A meth user would gladly exhaust his very life force to satisfy his habit. The same could seldom be said of potheads, johns, or gamblers.

Lester removed the cigar box, bound it with a rubber band from a tray on the desk blotter, and tucked the box beneath his arm. The contents of the cigar box represented weeks—maybe months—of wages for the average man. Lester had made this money easily, without raising a hammer or turning a screw or kissing anyone's ass the way the average man did. But he was not the average man, was he?

He stood and looked at the picture of Darth Vader: No, maybe the analogy between the fictional character and himself was not so far-fetched, after all.

Lester exited the office and walked across the hall into the utility room. He flipped a wall switch and a single overhead bulb barely illuminated a concrete-floored enclosure with blank walls. This room housed the mechanical guts of the Boar's Head: The bar's furnace and A/C unit was chugging and wheezing like the old piece of equipment it was, circulating cool air throughout the building. A water heater stood beside it—a big, old industrial model that might have another three years of life left in it.

On the far side of the utility room was a workbench that Lester purposefully left in a state of studied neglect: The unoccupied surface area of the worktable was coated with a sticky mixture of dust and machine oil. But there was not much unoccupied space with all the clutter: A chipped and dented vise stood amid a jumble of nearly worthless, half-functional hand tools, miscellaneous screws and nails, and two half-unraveled spools of wire. Some of the Boar's Head's fussier patrons would be afraid to approach the workbench without donning a hazmat suit.

The space beneath the workbench was obscured by two layers of debris: Lester had leaned an odd assortment of boards against the edge of the bench—mostly two-by-fours cut at odd lengths. Behind that was a large piece of ragged plywood.

It all looked so random; and yet it was all so very deliberate.

Lester did not keep his safe in the office. That was exactly where a burglar would look. The Boar's Head had never been burglarized to date; but if an intruder ever did enter with an intent to steal, there would be no doubt about his priorities: first the cash register—then the back office.

But a burglar would ignore the utility room; and he would certainly ignore that workbench.

Lester knelt and placed the cigar box on the floor. He did not bother to close the door behind him: he felt quite sure that no one was watching his activities. He was the only person who ever entered the utility room: No patron would ever stray in here. Nor would any of the three bartenders whom he employed. And Luke? Lester smiled at the mere suggestion. Anything mechanical baffled the big oaf. He would never enter the utility room.

He set the two-by-fours and the piece of plywood aside. And there it was: the safe that he used as temporary storage for his drug profits, a depot between the street and the offshore account that Lester had opened in the Caribbean with the assistance of a shady financial advisor in Nashville.

He took a penlight from his pocket and shone it on the dial. The combination was easy to remember: 10-12-24—a slight alteration of his mother's date of birth. Lester's mother had actually been born on 9-11-23. He had increased each number in the date by an increment of one.

The safe now contained many stacks of hundred-dollar bills. When the current patch of troubles was over, he would need to load the bills into his car and make yet another solitary trip down to Nashville. There his financial advisor would convert the money into untraceable, electronic offshore funds. Funds that could be accessed from anywhere in the world.

Lester knew that the day was fast approaching when he would decide that he had finally had enough of Blood Flats and Hawkins County. On that day he would leave the entire place to its own ruin. Let the county sink into the perdition it deserved. He would spend the rest of his days enjoying the good life. He would find someplace tropical—an island where he could while away the afternoons sipping piña coladas on an immaculate beach, and then spend his evenings screwing compliant, bronze-skinned women.

Nevertheless, the plan involved certain risks. Money laundering, Lester had discovered, required meticulous planning and nerves of steel. Cash created many logistical burdens when it became this abundant.

The Nashville runs were the part of the process that always made him the most nervous. He didn't like the idea of carrying around so much money with minimal protection. But there was no way around it. The money was just as unsafe here. He couldn't turn the utility room of the Boar's Head into Fort Knox.

He minimized the transportation problem by converting all street funds into hundred dollar bills before loading the money into the temporary safe. He worked methodically, carrying the sackfuls of odd bills received from junkies to various places of exchange. He went to many different banks so as to avoid drawing attention to himself, often driving as far away as Dayton, Ohio, and Indianapolis, Indiana.

He emptied the cigar box into the safe and closed it again. Yes, the metal container was almost full. There was enough money here to buy several upscale homes or a fleet of new vehicles.

So much money: How many greedy souls within a five-mile radius would kill to grasp it—if only they knew of its existence? This realization made him uncharacteristically nervous. Despite the ingenuity of this hiding place, the money was always vulnerable. The safe had been purchased at Wal-Mart, after all. A strong man could easily slide it out from beneath the workbench and hoist it onto his shoulders. Then it could be opened with a sledgehammer or a blowtorch.

Stop worrying, Lester. No one is going to discover this safe. And soon Lee McCabe will be dead, the wops will be back in Chicago, and life will resume as normal. Get a hold on yourself.

He carefully arranged the wood back into place. He was brushing the dust off his pants when he heard an angry voice calling his name from the main bar area.

81

"*L*ester Finn, where the hell are you? Get your ass out here!*" Paulie Sarzo was shouting.

Lester made an effort to calm himself before he stepped out into the bar area. He was flustered by this unexpected intrusion. Did Sarzo think that he could just barge in here at any hour of the day or night? Apparently so.

The two Coscollino men were standing just inside the front door: that arrogant prick Paulie Sarzo and the younger one, too. What was his name? Tony Loscatti. They were all dressed up like a couple of pretty boys, in their silk shirts and fancy dark blazers. Did they realize that they looked like a couple of dime store dandies? Did they even know that?

Lester realized that his voice was shaking as he struggled to respond nonchalantly. This whole scene was *wrong*. How did the Italians get in? The door had been locked. And where the hell was Luke? The big oaf was nowhere in sight.

Had the Chicago mafia men killed him? No—surely *not*.

Then where the hell was he?

"Gentlemen," Lester said. There was a sawed-off shotgun underneath the bar; but he had absolutely no chance of successfully retrieving it now. If he went behind the bar, the Coscollino men would stop him—*perhaps by shooting him*. Besides, he knew that he was only kidding himself with such thoughts. He didn't want it to come to that. Drawing a gun on any representative of the Coscollino family would mean certain death—if not at the moment, then later.

He noted the bulges beneath the blazers of both men. Were these guys ever unarmed? Did they carry their guns with them to the john? *Did Sarzo shower with a Beretta in the soap dish?*

"The bar is closed," Lester went on. "And it is a bit too late for a business meeting."

Paulie Sarzo darted forward and grabbed Lester by the collar of his shirt. Lester tried feebly to resist; but Sarzo was younger and much stronger.

Paulie pushed Lester against the bar.

"Do you know what your local idiots did today?" Paulie shouted in his face. *"They made more national news, that's what they did! Don't try to tell me that you don't know about that college girl! Or the cop, either!"*

Paulie momentarily released Lester, stepped back, and back-handed him across the face. Many years had passed since Lester had been struck so hard in anger. The blow to his face was accompanied by incredible pain, then the sensation of blood rushing from his head.

He was unaware that he was falling until he saw the floor rushing up at him. He fell on his elbows, but his cheek collided with the polished wood floorboards.

"Get up," Paulie said simply.

Lester was torn between two emotions: Relief that this was apparently not going to be an extended beating; and a welling mixture of shame and rage. *What would his grandfather think of him now?* These two goons were cursing him and slapping him around in his own place of business. And he was powerless to stop them.

Lester pushed himself up. He did not look either man in the eye.

"The dead college girl was unfortunate," Lester said, remembering TJ Anderson's account of the mistaken shooting. "As was the situation with the policewoman. But here is the important point: My men are getting closer. They've spotted McCabe several times. We've had a few near misses. His luck can't hold out much longer. And by the time your people get here—well, maybe they won't even be necessary."

For what seemed like a long while, Paulie did not answer him. Then he removed a pistol from inside his blazer—a gleaming, black semi-automatic—and pointed it at Lester's temple.

"Do you think this is a game, Lester?" Paulie asked quietly. "No—don't say anything. You just listen. Every time you do something that makes the news, you put my family in danger."

Paulie moved the position of the pistol, so that Lester could look directly into its muzzle.

"The next time you screw up Lester. The very next time."

Tony Loscatti stepped toward Lester. Lester flinched, preparing himself for another beating.

But Paulie held up his left hand—the one that was not pointing the gun at Lester's forehead. This gesture stayed Loscatti.

"Don't bother," Paulie said. "We're done with fists. Done with words. The next time Lester screws up, he's done, too."

With that the two men turned and walked out of the bar. Lester did not relax until the front door had swung shut behind them.

A new realization struck him: He might have to move forward his timetable for cashing in and quitting Hawkins County. *He had more than enough money now, didn't he?* And all the money in the world would do him no good if he was dead.

He didn't believe that Paulie Sarzo would simply walk into his bar and shoot him on the spot. The mafia didn't operate like that. Surely Sarzo and Loscatti had been observed in Hawkins County. If they killed him tomorrow or the next day, the authorities would make a connection between his own death and the Coscollino men's presence. They wouldn't be so stupid. So obvious.

But that didn't mean that they wouldn't find a way to kill him in good time, on their own schedule. The hit might come several weeks or months later. He would have to look over his shoulder every time he stepped out of the Boar's Head, every time he started his car.

That was no way to live—and no way to die. Lester had no illusions about the inevitability involved here: If Alfonzo Coscollino ordered him dead, he would die.

He would have to monitor the situation very carefully. Make some preparations to flee in the event that everything went south.

Just then he heard the click of a door being opened. He started, fearing that Paulie and Tony had returned to administer a beating, after all. Then he saw the men's room door open, and out stepped Luke.

Luke. He had forgotten all about Luke.

"And where the hell have you been?" Lester asked.

"In the bathroom," Luke said simply. "Something wrong, Lester?"

"Other than the fact that you weren't available when I could have really used you for backup, nothing," Lester said. "Nothing's wrong at all. And there's also the fact that you left the front door unlocked, even though the bar is supposed to be closed."

"Gee, sorry, Lester."

Lester wanted to scold him further; but he didn't have the energy right now. He did have unanswered questions, though. Lester was almost certain that the big oaf was lying. *Why was he lying?* If he was lying merely to save himself from criticism for a few minutes of indolence, that was one thing. But Luke's disappearance had been a bit too convenient, hadn't it?

He wondered if Luke had heard the humiliating exchange between himself and the Coscollino men. He didn't like the idea of being humbled in front of his own employees. But if Luke had heard and remained hidden, that also raised disturbing questions.

He was even more troubled over the fact that Luke had forgotten to lock the front door, even though the bar was closed for the night. Was that a mere oversight—a mere mistake? Or could he have been working in concert with the Coscollinos?

He didn't think that Luke was smart enough for that sort of machination; but henceforth, he vowed to himself, he would keep a closer watch on the big oaf.

Perhaps he wasn't such an oaf after all.

82

When Lee awoke early the next morning, the figure of Joe Wilson was towering over him. In one hand he held a backpack that Marie had prepared for him the previous evening. It contained a fresh change of clothes (Lee was about the same size as Marie's younger son, Jeremy), a bottle full of water, canned tuna, and an assortment of high-energy snacks.

The one essential item that Marie had neglected to provide was a gun. This was something that he could not ask her for—he didn't even know if she would have one. But he would have to find a replacement for his .45. Men were still hunting him; and he was still unarmed.

The dressing Marie had applied to his arm had put to rest his fears of gangrene and amputation. He might die from a bullet before all this was over (or, more likely, from a hail of them) but this particular bullet wound would do him no further harm.

"Best you be leavin'" Joe said. He dropped the backpack on the floor beside the bed.

"Good morning to you, too."

Lee was struggling to free himself of a foggy sleep, made even foggier by the painkillers Marie had given him, and a sequence of troubled dreams.

Most of these dreams he could not recall now, except for one that had been particularly vivid. In this dream he had relived the previous Saturday morning, retracing the steps he had taken to Tim Fitzsimmons's trailer. In the dream version, however, he did not discover the bodies of Jody White and Tim Fitzsimmons in the trailer. Instead he found the body of Amy Sutter. She was lying on the floor, wearing a pair of jeans and her sorority T-shirt. The top of her head was missing, obviously from a bullet wound. When Lee stepped near her, Amy sat up, slowly opened her eyes, and said: "You thought you had me all figured out—didn't you, Lee? Well, look at me now."

"Hey, are you hearing me, man?"

Lee sat up in bed. "Sorry."

"My mom's left to go into town. I'd prefer you be gone before she gets back."

"I wasn't planning on moving in, you know," Lee said. "And I'm grateful for what your mother—for what both of you—have done for me."

"I didn't have any part in it," Joe said.

"Well, at least your heart's in the right place."

"Look, since my dad died, things have been rough on my mother."

"Rough on you, too, I'd bet. That's nothing to be ashamed of, you know."

Joe stared at the floorboards for a second and clenched his fists.

"Never mind that. My mom's got a lot to worry about. She doesn't need something else to worry about."

"Like me, you mean."

"Like you, I mean."

Lee swung his feet out of bed. "I would never do anything to hurt your mother."

"I bet you felt that way about that Sutter girl, too."

When confronted by Lee's suddenly icy expression, Joe held up his hands and said. "Sorry. That was a cheap shot. I know you never intended for any harm to come to that girl. But sometimes what we plan isn't the same as what we actually get."

"No, it isn't," Lee agreed.

"Anyway, there's a fresh set of clothes on the dresser. They belong to my brother. They should fit you. Just like the clothes in the pack."

Lee nodded. "Thanks."

Joe exited the room and closed the door. Lee put on Jeremy Wilson's clothes. As Joe had predicted, they fit him more or less perfectly.

When Lee walked out into the front area of the house, Joe was sitting in a rocking chair with his arms folded. *He's going to make damn sure I leave, isn't he?* Lee thought.

It was an awkward end to what had otherwise been a brief and pleasant respite from the nightmare. As expected, Joe remained in the chair, watching him. There was no ambiguity in his expression.

"Give my regards to Mrs. Wilson—to your mother."

"Consider it done."

As Lee was lacing up his boots in the foyer, Joe spoke again.

"You know, I didn't want you bringing any trouble into my mother's house. But just for the record, I hope you succeed. I've heard all about Lester Finn."

"Then why don't you come with me? I could use some help, you know."

This request had come on the spur of the moment. It even surprised Lee. Joe Wilson was an odd character in many ways; but he struck Lee as the sort of man who would be good to have in a fight.

But Joe only shook his head and half-smiled. "No, I don't think so. What you got yourself here is a heap of trouble. The kind of trouble I make it my business to stay away from."

Well, Lee thought. *It was worth a try.*

"Okay, then. I'll be on my way."

"Good luck, Lee McCabe."

83

After another day of walking, Lee arrived on the outskirts of Blood Flats. He still did not know exactly how he was going to confront Lester Finn. Right now the main thing on his mind was water. While he was unwilling to resort to outright theft or shoplifting, he had no qualms about borrowing a bottleful of water from a random resident of the town.

Lee stood just inside the perimeter of the forest, staring across a long, wide backyard at a two-story white farmhouse. From this position Lee had a clear, sunlit view of the screened-in back porch. It contained a collection of outdoor furniture, but no people.

He could also see into a window on the first floor—probably the kitchen. No electric lights cut the mid-afternoon shadows.

The house was likely empty. Judging by the position of the sun, it was about three or four p.m.—an hour or two before most local businesses would release their employees, though some factory workers would already be on the way home. Most children would still be engaged in the rituals of summertime play.

The house represented an acceptable risk. And anyway, Lee did not plan to enter the house. He saw what he needed in the middle of the backyard, not far from the screened-in porch: an old-fashioned water pump.

This should be simple, he decided: a short walk to the water pump, about two minutes to drink his fill, then another two minutes to fill the water bottle that Marie Wilson had given him.

He unslung the knapsack from his shoulder and removed the empty water bottle. He placed the knapsack beside a tree, where it would be easy for him to find if he needed to make a hasty retreat.

Lee took his first tentative steps into the backyard. The backyard was semi-wooded, so he was able to mentally plot a path that would keep him out of full view from anyone inside the house—just in case he was wrong about the house being empty.

He heard a sharp crack to his left. He whirled, facing a large maple tree. He quickly scanned the area for any sign of movement.

Nothing. It might have been the noise of some animal, or even a—

He ducked instinctively after he felt the breeze of an object that whizzed past the back of his neck. This was immediately followed by another loud crack. As Lee dove to the ground, he saw something fall, then roll into the grass: a stone that had apparently struck the trunk of the maple tree.

He was under fire yet again—this time from rocks rather than bullets. But this was no one making casual throws at him in a taunting or playful fashion. These rocks seemed to be propelled by more than the strength of his attacker's arm—likely a slingshot.

He carefully maneuvered himself onto his side, so that he could see the direction from which the rocks would have come.

There was a little hillock on the edge of the woods. The hillock was covered with high weeds. That would be a logical place for an attacker to take cover.

Then a portion of the weeds shifted, ever so slightly.

"Who is it?" Lee called out softly. "Please don't wing any more rocks at me. I mean you no harm."

He waited. There was no answer. Whoever it was, the unseen sniper had no intention of revealing himself.

What now? If he continued on to the pump, he would make himself an easy and irresistible target. A slingshot wasn't as deadly as a bullet, of course, but a direct hit from a fast-moving rock could put him in a world of hurt.

It wasn't worth the risk. There would be other pumps in other backyards. His best course of action now was to retrieve his backpack and regain the cover of the woods. From there he might be able to see the person who was launching the projectiles at him. After taking his own cover among the trees, he might be able to negotiate with this new opponent. Perhaps his opportunity at this pump would not be lost, after all.

"I'm going to get up now," Lee said. "And I'm going back the way I came. I'm leaving."

Lee lifted himself to his knees and assumed a crouching position. He plucked the water bottle from the place where he had dropped it when he hit the dirt.

He very carefully arose and stood erect. He ducked low and prepared to sprint for the woods.

THWACK!

The impact plunged Lee into darkness. The pain literally blinded him. He dropped the water bottle again, and placed both hands over the stinging spot on his forehead. Stars swirled inside his closed eyes. Next, a wave of dizziness and nausea. He swayed on his feet.

You need to right yourself and get moving again, he thought. Another rock would surely be flying his way momentarily.

Lee forced his eyes open. The bright daylight, and a panorama of trees and sky gradually coalesced from the dark blur. He was still dizzy, though, and felt as though his body might topple over.

"Stand right where you are, Mister."

The voice surprised Lee—partly because his opponent had refused to speak until now—and partly because of the nature of the voice itself. The voice was unmistakably female. And unmistakably young.

And very close to him.

Lee finally was able to focus on the space directly in front of him:

The outlines of a young girl took shape. She was in late childhood or early adolescence—perhaps eleven or twelve years old. Straight black hair, freckles, and spindly legs, wearing shorts and a T-shirt. The T-shirt bore an image of a screaming American eagle, and the words, "Give' em hell!"

Lee reflected that the T-shirt was an unusual choice for a girl of that age. On the other hand, maybe it was not so unusual, given that she had practically incapacitated a grown man who had of late been enlisted in the U.S. Marine Corps.

"Put your hands up!" The girl had another rock ready in the sling. And she had already proven her willingness to do him harm.

Lee put his hands up, the sad absurdity of this situation fully dawning on him.

"Take it easy, would you?" he asked, not unkindly. "I was only after a drink of water."

Lee's interest in water did not seem to interest her. "I know who you are. I seen yer face on TV."

He figured that this line of discussion would not run to his advantage. "My name is Lee. And I'm telling you, I mean you no harm. What's your name?"

"My name's Isabelle, not that it's any o' yor beeswax. And the TV said you *kilt* a bunch a'people."

The Marine Corps had taught him how to use persuasion on weak-willed terrorist operatives and irate Iraqi civilians. The Corps had not prepared him for anything quite like this.

"Isabelle, no matter what you saw on television, I'm no killer. Now, you're making me kind of nervous, pointing that slingshot at me. Maybe you could lower it for a minute, and we could talk about this—"

Lee heard a metallic click behind him. A few seconds later, he felt a round cylindrical hardness press against his lower back. Judging by the diameter, it was probably a shotgun.

"Keep those hands up," a man's voice said. "If you've got something to say, you can say it to me."

84

"Now turn around, Mister," the man behind Lee said. "Turn around real slow. If you pull anything—if you even look like you're going to pull anything—I'll put a hole in you that'll be wide enough for a goose to fly through."

Lee had no doubt that a North American waterfowl would indeed be able to pass through his innards in the event that the gun went off against his lower back at such close range. It was a theory that he had no intention of putting to the test. He turned around, slowly as the man had commanded, and got his first look at the most recent person to hold a gun on him.

He was a man in his early to mid-forties, by the look of him. He was tall and lanky, and dressed in the sort of attire that one might wear to a job in a garage or on a road crew. He wore a grey baseball-style cap that proclaimed him a veteran of the first Gulf War, the one that occurred in the early nineties, when Lee was still a child.

"Were you in Iraq?" Lee asked, in an attempt to create rapport—an attempt that he knew would likely be futile. "I was in Iraq, too, though a bit more recently."

"According to what the news says, you been in a lot of places," the man said. "And you been a'killin' wherever you go."

"I'm innocent," Lee said. His kept his hands above his head.

The man smiled, not in a particularly friendly way. "Why don't that beat all?" he said. "What we've got ourselves here is an innocent man. They always are, aren't they? The meth-head who killed my wife was an innocent man, too. At least that's what he told the judge. And they sentenced him to twenty years in prison with rehabilitation. That for killing my wife!"

"I'm sorry to hear about your wife," Lee said.

The man ignored him. He said to the girl: "Izzy, go inside and call the police. Dial 911. Tell them that we've got a murderer in our backyard, and we'd appreciate a little help from the county."

As the girl turned in the direction of the house, Lee realized that he was at the end of the road, once again.

"Wait a minute," Lee said, both to the girl and to the man with the gun. "Just hear me out, please. The man who is responsible for these murders is Lester Finn. He's a drug dealer who operates out of a tavern here in Blood Flats. A place called the Boar's Head. I'm here partly because I've been blamed for the murders; and also because Lester is trying to kill me."

"I know all about Lester Finn," the man said. "And the way I figure it, you probably take your orders from Lester Finn."

"Are you kidding?" Lee asked, though the shotgun and the man's comportment to this point made it very clear that he was not kidding at all. "Lester Finn is my enemy. I've never met the man, but he's my enemy all the same. Because of what he's done to me—and to others."

Lee saw something in the man's face waver. For whatever reason, this last argument had struck a chord with his captor.

"Let me get this straight: You're here in Blood Flats to kill Lester Finn?"

This wasn't a completely faithful repetition of what Lee had said, but it was close enough, under the circumstances.

"If it comes to that, yes," Lee affirmed.

"Izzy," the man said to the girl, who by now Lee deduced to be his daughter. "Hold on for just a second on that telephone call." Then to

Lee: "Mister, I'm gonna give you about one minute to convince me not to call the police on your ass. And while you're at it, you can also convince me that you shouldn't be shot trying to escape. If you try any bullshit, I can still put a big hole in you. Try not to forget that."

Lee nodded vigorously, hoping to assure the man that this fact would remain foremost in his mind.

85

L ee told the man his entire story, from his discovery of the
bodies in the trailer, to his gun battle with Jimmy Mack,
through the previous night spent in the spare bedroom of
Marie Wilson.

It was this last item that finally won the man over to his side—or
seemed to win him over.

"Marie Wilson," he said. "I was one of her students, too. If she
trusts you, I guess that I can trust you." The man seemed to waver. "I
don't know—I might be making a mistake here."

"You're not making a mistake," Lee said, realizing that this is what
any man would say under the circumstances—guilty of murder or
not. Nevertheless, he felt compelled to throw in a final plea for his
own defense.

"I'm not a killer," Lee said. "Please. Trust me."

SHORTLY THEREAFTER, Lee found himself sitting at this man's kitchen
table. "Pot roast and potatoes for supper," the man had said, lowering

the shotgun. "And my name's Ben Chamberlain, by the way. I believe you've already met my daughter, Izzy."

This was a turnaround that Lee had not expected. He would have been happy if the man had merely allowed him to fill his water bottle and sent him on his way. But he was in no position to turn down hospitality—however inexplicable its source. He followed the man back to his house, the roughly eleven-year-old girl trailing alongside them.

"My name's Isabelle," the girl corrected her father. "But my friends call me Izzy. Are you my friend?" For the first time the girl smiled at him.

"Yes, Izzy," Lee said. "I'd be honored to be your friend."

Lee said little as Ben Chamberlain removed a pan of pot roast and potatoes from the oven. The kitchen table had been set for father and daughter; but the girl quickly set another place for Lee.

"That's where my momma used to sit," Isabelle said by way of explanation, as she laid down an empty plate and a set of silverware for Lee. Lee looked at the man with an unspoken question: *Is it okay to intrude—to sit in this place where this girl's now dead mother used to sit?* Ben gestured for Lee to sit down.

"Thank you, Isabelle," Lee said simply. "I sure do appreciate your letting me sit here."

In the manner of typical working-class country people, Ben and his daughter did not feel the need to burden their meal with formal conversation. Ben ate ravenously; he had been at work all day, he explained, working first shift at a factory in the northern part of the county. Isabelle ate at a pace that belied the girl's size.

Where does that girl put it? Lee wondered. *She's as thin as a rail.*

Lee was waiting for Ben to say more. He sensed that there was more at work here than simple hospitality. A man does not invite a total stranger to share dinner with him and his daughter—certainly not a stranger who is on the run from the law and other, more murderous factions. This would be folly for a man with a comfortable home and a daughter, even if he believes the stranger to be innocent.

And after he had finished eating, Ben laid down his knife and fork and supplied the missing bit of information—his motivation for helping Lee in his self-appointed mission.

"I have my own reasons for wanting to put an end to Lester Finn," Ben said. "As you have already figured out, Lester Finn is dealing meth around the county. You probably also know what meth does to people—how it turns them into animals and makes them do things that they wouldn't do otherwise."

"More or less," Lee replied.

"Well," Ben took a deep breath. "Two years ago one of Lester's best customers broke into this house early one afternoon, looking for money to buy drugs, or something to sell for drug money. I was at work at the time and Izzy was at school. So my wife was alone."

Lee held up his hand and lowered his head in a sign of respect, signaling that Ben need not go on—that he could piece together the rest. The meth addict had killed Ben's wife—Izzy's mother—during the break-in.

A shadow passed over Isabelle's face, and Lee noted that the little girl's eyes were moist. "Can I be excused now?" she said in a voice that was partially choked by tears. *She's holding it back*, Lee noted, admiring her pluck. *She's not going to cry in front of a stranger.*

Ben gently ruffled his daughter's hair. "There, there. You go on up to your room now. I'll be along to check on you after a while. We've got things to talk about—things that you're better off not hearing."

The girl pushed her chair back from the table, and Ben waited until she had departed before continuing.

"She's still taking it hard," he said by way of explanation, though no explanation was necessary. He stared down at the tabletop and sighed. "Truth be told, I am, too."

"Well," Lee said. "It looks like I'm not the only one here in need of justice. This probably doesn't mean much, but I'll be thinking about you and your daughter. I'll be thinking about your loss."

Lee stood up. "Now I've burdened you enough. I really should take my leave of you now. I want to get started before nightfall."

As Lee spoke, there was an element about his own words that struck him as false bravado. How was he going to start, exactly? What was he going to do? He didn't yet know.

"Whoa," Ben said. "Hold on a sec. You're a stranger in Blood Flats, and a wanted man besides," Ben said. "I've lived here all my life, except for the time I was away in the Gulf. I'm part of the landscape, you might say."

"So what are you saying?" Lee asked.

"I'm saying that we should work together on this. Make common cause, you might say. The junkie who murdered my wife died in a prison knife fight before he was even convicted. He's beyond my reach. But Lester was responsible for his being here."

Lee had half-suspected that this sort of proposal might be forthcoming. The man had lost his wife, after all. In a way, this Ben Chamberlain had as much of a stake in the situation as Lee did.

Lee nodded. "I'll accept your help, but nothing that will put you in danger. That little girl has already lost one parent."

The memory of Amy Sutter and his guilt over her death had not faded. This time he would make sure that he would do nothing to endanger his benefactor.

"Don't worry about me," Ben said. "I can take care of myself. Like I told you earlier, I've been to war, too. I've been shot at. And I know how to shoot back."

Something about this man's manner disturbed Lee. He was almost nonchalant about the dangers involved in confronting Lester Finn and those who were working in league with him. *How long has it been since he's "gone to war?"* Lee thought. *The Gulf War was twenty years ago. All this man is thinking about now is getting his revenge for his wife. And he probably feels guilty as well—guilty that he wasn't here to save her. I can certainly understand that. But I'm going to have to be careful with him. He might have a reckless side that could get one or both of us killed.*

Still, these reservations aside, Lee could not deny that his chance meeting with Ben Chamberlain—thanks to his daughter Isabelle and her slingshot—represented an incredible stroke of good fortune. And this on top of his happening upon Marie Wilson's house. Maybe his luck was starting to turn around. That luck had been long in coming.

Once again I have found a little island of people who are willing to help me, he thought. This was not a thing to turn away from lightly.

"Thank you," Lee said simply. "I sincerely hope that I can clear my own name and we can get justice for your wife. Lester Finn belongs behind bars. In jail."

But this assessment was unsatisfactory for Lee's host.

"Jail?" Ben Chamberlain said. "Lester Finn belongs in the ground."

86

Reconnaissance was what they called it in the Marine Corps. Gathering information about the enemy.

This was Lee's mission the next day. He set out in the late morning, while Ben was at work and Isabelle was being watched by Ben's aunt, a woman whom Ben described as "nice but very set in her ways."

"My Aunt Margaret makes the best chocolate bourbon bundt cake," Ben said.

Lee had never heard of such a concoction; but he had to admit that it did indeed sound delicious. "If I live through this," he said. "I'll have to get your aunt to give me a piece." He sighed. Would he ever be able to give consideration to such trivial matters again?

Ben was skeptical of his plans to spy on Lester Finn. And Lee was half-inclined to agree with him. But he felt a need to observe his enemy up-close; it was a sensation that he could neither deny nor satisfactorily explain to his host.

"I'll be careful," Lee said. "And I won't get too close."

Lee avoided the main thoroughfares of the town, sticking to back streets with long, overgrown trees and bushes. These were crisscrossing lanes of gravel and shoddy pavement. He walked quickly, but not so fast as to attract attention.

Ben had offered to lend him a gun. Like many Hawkins County residents, he had a number of them. But Lee saw no way to carry one without looking conspicuous: Even a snub-nosed pistol would make a distinctive bulge in his pocket. And on this trip, at least, he did not intend to engage the enemy.

He located the street that ran directly behind the Boar's Head. To his disappointment, the rear of the building was enclosed in a high chain-link fence. He could walk in through the front door, of course; but that would be suicide. A man like Lester Finn would be constantly surrounded by armed minions.

Lee felt a fresh stab of dismay. He feared that the task before him might be larger than he had anticipated. The enemies arrayed against him were well-armed, well financed, and numerous. He was one man with no plan and minimal weapons.

Perhaps he had placed too much confidence in his Marine Corps training and his experience of the battlefield. Once again, he was reminded that it was one thing to fight as a member of a team. To fight as a lone warrior, well, that was quite another matter.

He chose an alternate route back to Ben's house. If any Blood Flats citizens had observed him during his trek here, he did not want any of the same citizens to observe him on the way back. He was passing through an alley, reasonably confident that he had avoided all detection, when he discovered that he had, after all, been recognized.

87

"Lee McCabe!"

Lee jerked upright when he heard his name called out. He now cursed himself for his decision to travel into Blood Flats unarmed. He looked around for something to use as a weapon. Or perhaps he should merely bolt.

And then he stopped as the same person repeated his name. The voice did not sound threatening, and it was feminine, besides.

Lee inhaled sharply and scanned the surrounding alley: a dumpster, a pile of half-demolished wooden pallets, an assortment of discarded soda cans and other miscellaneous refuse. Bare brick walls on both sides of him. He could detect no living presence, though, save for a scrawny stray cat that darted for cover when it noticed Lee.

"Lee McCabe!" The voice was a sharp whisper—loud enough for him to hear, but not loud enough to carry beyond the alley. "Up here!"

Lee looked up and saw the silhouette of a woman standing on a black metal balcony above him. He strained to descry her against the glare: She was very thin and had long blond hair. She looked vaguely familiar—perhaps the mother of an old a former classmate. Perhaps another former teacher, like Marie Wilson.

But she identified herself as someone much younger—indeed younger than him. "It's Dawn Hardin," she said, in the same subdued tone of discretion. "Do you remember me? From that party a few years ago. At Rhonda Glasser's house."

Now Lee was able to pull the resemblance from his memory. It was in fact Dawn Hardin, the young woman he had met briefly at the party—a carefree gathering that had taken place on a placid summer evening that now seemed like half a lifetime ago. He recalled his conversation with Dawn Hardin, the honor student who seemed so ready to take on the world.

And at the same time—this was *not* Dawn Hardin. The woman he had met on that night had exuded health. She had been trim and athletic, but her features had been softened by youthful femininity. Her skin had been unblemished.

The woman now standing on the balcony near the fire escape looked like a much older version of Dawn Hardin, and one that had been struck by some disfiguring disease. She was gaunt, her eyes pale and glazed, and her cheeks angular and protruding, like an elderly woman in the early stages of decrepitude.

What could be wrong with her? Cancer perhaps? Whatever it was, Dawn Hardin was clearly not in good health.

Then Lee noticed the pockmarks on her face. He had seen similar pockmarks on the skin of Malcolm Taylor—on the face and bare arms of the other junkie with whom Malcolm had kept company.

Was it possible that Dawn had fallen prey to meth as well? *No, surely this could not be so.* She had talked so animatedly that night about her scholarship, about her plans to become a doctor. There was no way she could be a drug addict.

Dawn Hardin did not offer any explanation. At least not now. Instead she said: "I heard about you on the news."

And then Lee felt a jolt of fear: Was it her intention to turn him in? Perhaps she had called the police before she hailed him, and was now trying to delay him until they arrived.

Lee shook his head and said to her imploringly: "I did not do it,

Dawn. The things they're saying. I know it must be hard for you to believe. But I'm telling you the truth."

She nodded slowly and said: "I believe you."

They both paused for a moment, neither of them speaking. Then Dawn said: "Wait by the door and I'll let you in."

She disappeared into the room behind the balcony, and Lee waited. *Could he trust her?* His instincts and immediate impressions told him that she meant him no harm. However, the preceding days had overturned so many of his base assumptions. Only last week, he would have passed Jimmy Mack, Deputy Norris, or even Malcolm Taylor on the street without apprehension; and all of these men had attempted to kill him.

There was a rattling at a brown-painted, metal, windowless door at the first floor of Dawn's building. The door creaked open and she stood there, beckoning him: "Come on," she said. "Or are you trying to attract attention?"

Lee gave his surroundings one final look to make sure that they were still alone. Then he walked across the gravelly pavement and followed her inside.

88

"What happened to you?" Lee asked. They were alone in the living room of her little studio apartment, sitting on the floor. This was all she had been able to find in town after her father had thrown her out. A part of her had been inclined to return to Louisville—but there was nothing for her there but more hooking and more drugs. The same downward spiral.

At the same time, there did not seem to be much for her here in Blood Flats: A family that now despised her, and this apartment—where she could sit alone with her craving for meth, rationing out the supply she had brought with her from the city.

Redemption, she thought. *That is what I will find, one way or another. Redemption of my former life. Redemption or death.*

Lee leaned back against the wall and Dawn sat cross-legged, her back against the apartment's threadbare sofa. The air was close and stuffy. A hint of a breeze blew through a double screen door that opened onto the balcony from where Dawn had stood to beckon him a few minutes ago.

What happened to you? The scope of the question was so massive, so personal and so painful that she knew it would be difficult for her to answer him. Although she detected genuine concern in his tone and expression, Dawn bristled as his presumptuousness. Lee McCabe was apparently the same blunt, cocky sort that she remembered him to be. Never mind the fact that she had opened her makeshift home to him, such it was. Whatever his degree of innocence (*and she did believe that Lee was innocent—despite what she had heard on the news*), this still represented an enormous gesture of charity and trust. Never mind the fact that he was now a fugitive wanted for multiple homicides. (*He probably had his own rank on the FBI's most wanted list by now.*) He would still find the space to notice how far she had fallen since their last meeting, and he would still have the nerve to bring it to her attention.

"You first," Dawn said. "Why does half the world believe that you're a mass murderer?"

She listened as Lee recounted a convoluted tale that spanned back several days. A few of the names she vaguely remembered from the news, as murder victims that had been attributed to Lee's actions. When he mentioned the name of Lester Finn she stopped him.

"I know Lester Finn," she said. She folded her arms across her chest, gripping each bony elbow with the opposite hand.

"A friend of yours?" Lee asked, with a trace of accusation.

"No. Of course not. I despise Lester Finn."

"But you do know him."

Dawn shrugged. She could sense him backing her into a corner, interrogating her, though he had absolutely no right to appoint himself as her inquisitor.

"So how does an honor student like yourself become acquainted with a drug dealer like Lester Finn?" he finally asked.

"I'm not exactly an honor student anymore," she said.

She gave him a short history of her drug problem. She did not mention that she worked the streets of Louisville to make money to support her habit. That would be too painful, too humiliating to admit. But she imagined that Lee McCabe had somehow surmised the entire truth.

"That stuff you take," Lee said. "This is the stuff that people are trying to kill me for."

"It's almost killed me, too, for the record."

Lee McCabe appeared not to have heard her. He was lost in his own private rage, she could tell.

"What's your problem, Lee? I get the feeling that I've disappointed you. Well, for what its worth, I've disappointed a lot of people. My father has disowned me, and my mother and sister want to pretend that I don't exist anymore. And I've disappointed myself."

"This is just great," he said. "You screw men for money, and then you buy drugs."

Dawn recalled her first meeting with Lee McCabe, at that party several years ago, when she had been a college freshman with a bright future stretching out before her. Back then Lee McCabe had misjudged her as a snob. Now he was misjudging her again—only in the opposite direction.

Did he have any idea how much she hated what she had become? Did he know about the countless times she had contemplated suicide?

She felt possessed by her own rage—and in that moment her anger was as implacable as the desire for the drug sometimes was, even at its worse.

Before she could stop herself, she slapped Lee McCabe across the cheek. Then she leaned back, folded her arms again, and said nothing.

Lee rubbed his cheek where she had struck him. She knew her own strength was limited and that she could not possibly have hurt him. Nevertheless, there was a red patch across the skin where she had struck.

Lee looked at her, seemed lost in contemplation for a few seconds, then said:

"I deserved that. I was wrong."

"No, you're right, about me, I mean. You're as arrogant as ever, and you have the tact of a pit bull; but I can't fault your assessment of the situation."

"I'm a jackass," Lee said.

"Yes. You're right about that, too."

"I'm usually a lot better than this," Lee said. "I've been having what you might call a bad day—a bad couple of days, in fact. Half the country thinks I murdered two of my neighbors. A local drug lord is trying to kill me. And at least one police officer has tried to kill me, too."

"You're certainly making the news," Dawn said. "There's going to be a special edition about you on CNN this afternoon. Some journalist who claims to have met you."

Lee's surprise was immediately apparent. "A journalist? You mean Brett St. Croix?"

"Might be," Dawn said. "I don't recall. But he's going to talk this afternoon on CNN. On the *Situation Room*."

89

O n the way back to Ben's house, Lee's mind was awhirl with questions. For one thing, why had Brett St. Croix not contacted him? Lee tried calling the journalist several times. Both calls went to voicemail. On the second call, Lee left a message.

"*Call me*," Lee said, in his most placating tone. He knew that he had few bargaining chips to use vis-à-vis Brett St. Croix at this point. "*I'd really appreciate hearing from you.*"

He feared that the lack of contact portended a betrayal of some sort; but he pushed this thought out of his mind. St. Croix had promised that he would help him. Until the journalist proved himself to be duplicitous, Lee would give him the benefit of the doubt.

The condition of Dawn Hardin had deeply disturbed him. He had not given her much thought since that summer, though their encounter had oddly affected him then. And he was no stranger to tragedy after the war, the untimely deaths of his parents, and the past week.

Yet he took Dawn's fall from grace personally, as if it were somehow akin to his own. Perhaps it was. In different ways, the world had beaten them both down. And they had both been so confident only a few years ago.

He also felt guilty for the way he had treated her today. He had had no right to talk to her like that—no right at all.

Before he left, Dawn told him what she knew about Lester Finn's operations: drugs, prostitution, and gambling. More or less what Lee had suspected. The question was: *How to tie all of it together in a way that could exonerate himself?* Once again, Lee was acutely aware of his own limitations: He could handle weapons and conduct combat operations; but he was neither a legal expert nor an investigator. He was out of his depth in these fields.

Maybe Brett St. Croix has already linked all the elements together, Lee thought. *Maybe after the five o'clock broadcast on CNN, there will be no need for me to run anymore. I'll be able to come out of hiding, and Lester Finn, Ron Norris, and perhaps even Sheriff Phelps will be the ones behind bars.*

These thoughts were comforting—so comforting that he dare not embrace them too fondly.

Before he had left, Dawn had volunteered to assist him further, making him feel like an even bigger jackass for the way he had treated her.

"Here's my number," she had said. "Call me if I can help. And despite your acting like a jerk, it's been good to see you again. You've actually made me feel hopeful."

"Oh, come on," Lee said, welcoming the much-needed levity. "There isn't much in the way of hope that I have to give at this moment."

"Well, you remind me that despite all my problems, things could always be worse. I'll never be on *America's Most Wanted*. And you might make the show any day now."

But to Lee, there was something in the young woman's forced cheerfulness and weary expression that told him a different truth: She knew that she was not long for this world; she was coming to terms with her own death.

90

A t four fifty-five Ben and Lee gathered in the family room of the Chamberlain house. It was a bright, many windowed room that faced the backyard—which Lee had invaded just the previous day.

Lee felt tense, despite his anticipation of at least some assistance from Brett St. Croix. *If a famous journalist publicly took up his cause and declared his innocence—that would have to count for something, wouldn't it?*

Ben Chamberlain's television set was an old model—barely adequate for cable. It took a few moments for it to warm up. Ben pointed the remote at the television and flipped through four or five channels until he came to CNN.

The *Situation Room* was the program that CNN had plugged into the five o'clock early primetime slot. The program was produced in a news magazine format; it featured in-depth coverage of whatever stories happened to be most on viewers' minds. Usually this meant something of international or national significance—the latest blood-letting in the Middle East, or a budget showdown in Washington. Local events from throughout the country made the show if they had proven sensational enough to arouse interest beyond a specific area. That usually meant violence of some sort, or a scandal.

Lee took neither pleasure nor amusement from the realization that the facts of his life—both real and fabricated—were now being broadcast to so many people. Even if he did exonerate himself, he would reap no benefits from his fifteen minutes of fame. Regardless of whether he was killed, declared innocent, or captured, the public would forget him as abruptly as it had learned of him.

"Central Kentucky used to be known for horse racing, family farms, and the small-town way of life," a voice on the television said. *"More recently, though, it is meth and murder—not the Kentucky Derby—that have been making headlines in the Bluegrass State."*

They had been expecting Wolf Blitzer. Instead it was another anchor, a man whom Lee had never seen before—not that he had caught much television over the past few years. The anchor standing on the CNN set was young and his manner suggested that he was less than comfortable with his role.

"During the next hour, we're going to learn more about the new front lines in America's war on drugs, and the young ex-marine who is now the target of a regional manhunt."

On the TV screen, the camera shot panned up and away, allowing for a wider view of the set. Lee could see his own picture in the background, displayed prominently on one of two screens on a rear wall. It was the now overly used portrait of him in his Marine Corps dress blues. Opposite Lee's own picture was a montage of what appeared to be a pile of white methamphetamine powder and a collection of syringes and pipes. There was a caption across the photo, in streaked red lettering, probably meant to simulate blood. It read: "Drug Violence in the Heartland."

"This is Mitch Conway," the CNN anchor said. "Filling in for Wolf Blitzer, who is on assignment today." This was followed by an upbeat musical score, and the CNN logo swam across the screen, followed by the logo of the *Situation Room*.

When the opening credits were done, Conway looked at the camera and said: "A few short months ago, Sergeant Lee McCabe was a decorated member of the U.S. armed forces, and a veteran of Operation Iraqi Freedom. But when he came home to Hawkins County, Kentucky, things didn't turn out so well for Lee McCabe the civilian."

Understatement of the year, Lee thought sourly.

Conway continued. "As most of you have heard by now, Lee McCabe is now the prime suspect in multiple homicides in and around his hometown of Perryston, Kentucky."

"*Multiple* homicides?" Ben asked.

"They probably blame me for the deaths of the two men in the gas station," Lee said. And then he reflected that this was not entirely unfair. "I did kill Jimmy Mack. But it was self-defense, like I told you."

On the CNN set, the screen that displayed Lee's portrait rolled into a live feed of Brett St. Croix. St. Croix was in a remote studio, probably a CNN affiliate in Cincinnati. In the bottom right corner of the screen the writer's name floated in white letters, and below that the name of his book about the American armed forces.

Mitch Conway turned to the live image of St. Croix.

"Today we're going to have a conversation with Brett St. Croix, a journalist and author who resides in Cincinnati. Mr. St. Croix is the author of *The Death Factory: How the U.S. Military Turns American Youths into Killers*."

Mitch paused for a moment, perhaps considering the provocative title of the book, Lee thought. Then he went on:

"Mr. St. Croix recently embarked on a field journalism project that was daring by any standard. He went into the woods of central Kentucky where Lee McCabe is believed to be hiding, and he actually interviewed the suspect in person. Mr. St. Croix, I think it's safe to say that your project dispels the popular notion that writers are delicate types who spend all their time drinking flavored coffee in Starbucks."

Brett smiled with the appropriate degree of good-natured modesty at both the compliment and the ribbing. "Well, I've certainly downed my share of coffees in Starbucks. But a writer of current events needs to get out into the field, too," he said.

Mitch consulted a page of what were obviously notes about Brett St. Croix. "And just so our viewers can get a complete grasp of the lengths you went to—I understand that you actually camped out in the middle of the woods in order to find Lee McCabe."

"That part wasn't as bad as it sounds," Brett said. "The weather was nice."

"Tell us, then, how did you find Lee McCabe, when law enforcement has been unable to locate him thus far?"

Brett went through a brief explanation of how he and Lee had made contact. "It's easy to find a fugitive when you make an appointment," Brett said.

"I suppose it is," Mitch laughed. "And tell me, after your meeting with him, what can you tell us about the man—his character, his state of mind, his motives?"

"I would have to say that Lee McCabe is a very determined and resourceful man, despite his youth. As for his character and motives, well, those are difficult for me to judge. And others may be directing him, as other members of the media and law enforcement officials have publicly speculated."

"You believe, then, that Lee McCabe is a hit man for a meth amphetamine trafficking ring?"

The man whom Lee had met in the woods hesitated briefly before answering.

"I would have to conclude that Lee McCabe is indeed working with organized criminal elements," St. Croix said. "But I only interviewed him, in the capacity of a journalist. I did not conduct an interrogation."

Conway looked at the camera and raised his eyebrows. He seemed to be waiting for St. Croix to continue. St. Croix said nothing.

Lee felt as if someone had struck him in the stomach. *What the hell was St. Croix doing?*

"Can we conclude, then," Conway began. "That Lee McCabe actually admitted to the shootings of the people in the trailer park?"

"*I did not say that—*"

"And if so, did he also admit that he shot those people for money, as a paid agent of a criminal organization?"

Brett smiled tightly. "Lee McCabe is far too crafty to actually *admit* to anything. He realizes that he may be caught someday, and he doesn't want to make any statements that could be used in a future case against him. Let's put it like this, I spent about an hour talking with Lee McCabe, and he spent most of that time trying to convince me of his innocence."

"And did you believe him?"

Lee heard Ben crack his knuckle on the other side of the room. He looked over at his host and caught Ben staring at him.

"I kinda get the sneakin' suspicion that this guy ain't helpin' you out so much," Ben said. There was real concern on his face, and Lee was forced to contemplate another dark possibility: *Would Ben now turn against him, swayed by the expert on the television screen?*

"I believe I've already answered that question by my previous statements—which are not verdicts, but a writer's inferences," Brett went on. "Once again, I am a journalist—not a law enforcement officer or a judge. I'm not even an attorney, for that matter. I'll leave conclusions regarding Mr. McCabe's guilt to others. I'm more interested in what makes the rogue soldier tick. That is my area of specialty."

Rogue soldier? Lee thought. He could feel his cheeks and the skin on his neck turning red. Now he knew that the time he had spent with St. Croix would do him no good—the writer had decided to betray him, for reasons that Lee could only speculate about.

"Mr. St. Croix, you were one of the few reporters who obtained permission to interview Timothy McVeigh prior to his execution, is that not correct?"

On the screen opposite St. Croix, the photo of the meth-amphetamine and the drug paraphernalia was replaced by a picture of the Oklahoma City bomber clad in orange federal penitentiary garb. The thin, angular face of Timothy McVeigh stared defiantly back at the camera. In this photo he was in his late twenties. McVeigh would be in his mid-forties if he were alive today.

Lee had been a child on April 19, 1995, when a large, homemade truck bomb exploded a few yards away from the Alfred P. Murrah Federal Building in Oklahoma City. Lee recalled how his teacher had interrupted class so that students could watch live news feeds of smoke billowing from the wreckage. This was a big deal, after all—things like this did not happen in America.

In the hours immediately following the blast, speculation had been focused on Middle Eastern terrorist cells. This supposition had not lasted for long. Relying on the paper trail he had left behind at motels and a truck rental office, police quickly traced the destruction to Timothy McVeigh, an unemployed antigovernment radical and veteran of the Persian Gulf War of 1990-91. McVeigh had been nabbed for a routine traffic violation shortly after detonating his truck bomb.

The attack—the largest on American soil until 9/11—killed one hundred and sixty-eight people. Somewhat ironically, McVeigh would never know about the act of terrorism that dwarfed his own, although he missed it by only a few months. McVeigh was executed in June of 2001.

"Yes, I interviewed McVeigh," St. Croix said. "And I believe I can anticipate your next question."

"Well, please, do go on," Mitch Conway said, doing his best to be a good sport about the fact that Brett was upstaging him.

"You want to know if Lee McCabe is anything like the late Timothy McVeigh. It's a logical question. Both men were combat veterans of wars in Iraq. Both men were the perpetrators of incredible acts of violence."

The CNN host did not bother to remind St. Croix—and the world —that Lee had neither been tried nor convicted for the murders. Lee had no idea of his actual legal status at this time. It was safe to say he was a suspect. But had he even been formally charged with the murders? Perhaps that no longer mattered. The proclamations of his guilt had now been repeated hundreds—perhaps thousands—of times on the TV and the Internet. The media and the masses had pronounced their verdict.

"And here's what I have to say about that," Brett continued. "Timothy McVeigh was an entirely different animal. He was motivated by hatred for what he perceived as an oppressive and dictatorial government. Profit was never part of his agenda. Quite the opposite, in fact.

McVeigh was a death-seeking fanatic who clearly wanted to become a martyr at the hands of the government, just as he was willing to sacrifice the lives of one hundred sixty-eight men, women and children for his cause."

"A bit like—" Conway began before Brett preempted him.

"Yes, a bit like the al-Qaeda operatives that Lee McCabe faced in Iraq. More young men who were willing to kill and die for some dark vision of utopia."

"Yes, but getting back to Lee McCabe—"

"If Lee McCabe is what they say he is—and again, I don't claim to know this based on my interview of him in those woods—then Lee McCabe is no Timothy McVeigh. Lee McCabe is motivated by profit, perhaps, or perhaps by a deeper need for self-validation."

"Self-validation?" Mitch asked. "Could you elaborate on that?"

"Certainly. Lee McCabe came from a lower middle-class background. What awaited him back in Hawkins County, Kentucky, after our government was through with him? A decent-paying factory job? Fat chance. Our corporations have been sending all our manufacturing jobs to places like India and China. College? Again—not very likely. College is for upper middle-class youths who don't have to go in the military in the first place."

"So you're saying that Lee McCabe had few realistic choices."

"Exactly," Brett said. His tone suggested that he was glad that poor Mitch was finally grasping the point. "Let's suppose, just for argument's sake, that Lee McCabe really is a mafia hit man. Is he really any different than the inner city kid who becomes a crack dealer out of desperation? In a way, Lee McCabe is a victim of sorts—a victim of the government that turned him into a killing machine, and the society that left him with no other options."

Lee McCabe himself had by now had enough of all this. He pounded his fist on the arm of his chair. "*Liar!*" he shouted at the television set. "*That son-of-a-bitch! He's sold me out. For what, I don't know. But I was a fool to think I could trust him!*"

Lee stood up, unable to contain his rage. He whirled on Ben.

"This is a pack of lies. You understand that, don't you?"

"I believe you," Ben said. "You're no Timothy McVeigh, and you don't kill people for profit, either. Keep in mind, Lee, I know all about Lester Finn. And I still hold him responsible for the death of my wife."

"And what about me?" Lee asked.

"Even if you aren't as blameless as you claim to be, my priority is taking down Finn."

"I thought you said you believed me!" Lee protested.

Ben smiled. "Hold your horses. I do believe you. I'm only speaking hypothetically."

"That's more or less what Brett St. Croix claimed to be doing!"

"That man is no friend of yours."

"No," Lee said, finally calming himself. "And he was the one I was relying on. The one who was going to put an end to all this."

"It looks like you'll have to move to your back-up plan, then," Ben said.

For this Lee had no answer. He had been working on his back-up plan earlier in the day, with his reconnaissance of the Boar's Head, and his chance meeting with Dawn Hardin. As of right now, he had no back-up plan.

91

Michelle Ackerman watched incredulously as her boss dominated the lightweight fill-in for Wolf Blitzer. She was sitting in her office at Queen City Media. There were no facilities for a television hookup in this building, so Brett had walked three blocks to the studio of one of the major Cincinnati television stations.

When Brett was done speaking, she looked out the seventh-story window of her office. She stared down at the Ohio River. A steamboat was chugging beneath one of the main bridges that connected the states of Ohio and Kentucky. Just above the waterline, the words *Ohio River Scenic Tours* were inscribed on the bow of the steamboat in old-fashioned lettering. This office commanded an enviable view.

Space was at a premium downtown, and first-year employees in the media trades often had to content themselves with cubicles and cubbyholes. Not her, though. Brett had generously made arrangements for her to have an office of her own. This gesture had not gone unnoticed, or unappreciated.

Brett had been good to her—no doubt about it. And while he made his desire to sleep with her transparent, Brett had never insisted on a quid pro quo. Yes, he had tried, tried repeatedly, in fact

—but he retreated with good humor when rebuffed. On balance, his desire was far more pathetic than it was threatening.

She admired Brett as a journalist, for the work he had done, the significant issues that he had illuminated for the ignorant and the unenlightened. This was the source of the bond between them. She shared her boss's convictions.

And what was Lee McCabe to her? McCabe was at best a macho swaggerer—at worse a sadistic killer. He might not be guilty of the murders in Kentucky. (*And then again, perhaps he was.*) But he was guilty—by association if nothing else—of bringing violence and mayhem to the people of Iraq. He was a willing pawn in a war fought for the big oil companies, a war fought for the personal vanities of George Bush and Dick Cheney, and the profits of Halliburton.

Could Lee McCabe have been a guard at Abu Ghraib? she wondered.

Michelle had been in her final year of undergraduate journalism when the Abu Ghraib scandal was exposed. One of her professors—himself an army veteran who was predisposed to take the side of the military—had argued that the incidents at the Iraqi prison were being blown out of proportion. The professor had condemned the individual Americans who had abused their power, but he refused to see the incident as an indictment of America's war aims—much less an indictment of everything America stood for. Abu Ghraib, the professor argued, had to be seen in the context of the overwhelming brutality that was loose in Iraq, the brutality that U.S. forces were attempting to stamp out. So a few rogue soldiers had humiliated a handful of captured insurgents—forced them to take off their clothes and affect demeaning poses. Yes, this was bad. Yes, it deserved punishment and condemnation. But why did these banal indignities provoke such righteous outrage in the world media? The people of Iraq were beset by a far greater threat: Islamic militants who stoned women and beheaded innocent captives. Were the homegrown Arab militants not the greater outrage?

Michelle had of course disagreed. Midway through the professor's discourse, she and three other students had stood and walked out of the lecture hall in a silent gesture of protest. Michelle had not let the matter rest there. In the wake of the Abu Ghraib scandal, she had taken to the streets with her classmates, denouncing the U.S.-led occupation of Iraq. She had carried a sign that showed the face of President Bush made up to look vaguely like that of Adolf Hitler.

When Brett St. Croix had interviewed her for her current position, she had told him the story of the walk-out, and how she had so passionately thrown herself into the antiwar movement. Brett had said that he admired her conviction and commitment. "It's a sign of personal integrity," Brett had said, "that you were willing to take action. Lots of people watch injustice on the news, but few do anything about it."

Reflecting back on that interview, Michelle had no trouble admitting to herself that Brett had also been admiring her legs and breasts, even then. But a part of him had been speaking from a place of sincerity. He had meant what he had said about the need to stand behind one's convictions.

But what about standing behind the truth?

As Brett's assistant, she had access to his file on Lee McCabe and the ongoing violence in Kentucky. There among Brett's notes was Lee McCabe's cell phone number.

As the CNN interviewer moved on to another guest and topic, Michelle realized that she faced a significant moral dilemma: She would have to either help Lee McCabe or leave him to his fate. She would also have to decide whether or not she would betray the trust of her boss. If she aided Lee McCabe in any way, Brett would find out. He was no idiot and he would be able to discern her intervention. This would cause a serious rupture in their professional relationship —probably the end of it.

This was not a decision to be made lightly.

Brett's constant ogling of her body—his continual efforts to get her into bed—these had not gone unnoticed. Despite his liberal pretensions, Brett was, in the final analysis, just another man. And all men were ultimately interested in only two things: Sex and power. Nevertheless, she could not deny that Brett had been fair to her, his obvious carnal desires notwithstanding. He seemed legitimately interested in sharing his expertise, in helping her gain a foothold in the competitive rat race of journalism. And he had secured for her this nice office, she reminded herself again.

By any reasonable assessment, Brett had omitted many important details of his interview with Lee McCabe. Brett had failed to disclose what he knew about the drug trafficking ring that was loose in Hawkins County, and the involvement of the tavern owner named Lester Finn. Not to mention what Brett's own investigation had uncovered at the abandoned furniture factory.

All of these items should have been revealed in the interest of fairness and full disclosure. So why had Brett mentioned none of them?

She was suspicious of her boss's motives; but she did not believe him to be capable of outright fabrications. *And it would be true to say that Brett had told no explicit lies during the CNN interview. He had qualified all his conjectures as mere conjecture, hadn't he?* Moreover, he had openly acknowledged his own fallibility. That was more than you could say for most of the men in power in the world—the ones who ran large corporations that poisoned the land, and their counterparts in government, those who sent young men to wage war in foreign countries. Even if Brett had chosen to betray Lee McCabe, did this outweigh the good that he had done by exposing the innumerable crimes of the U.S. military? Did she owe the fugitive ex-marine more than she owed her boss?

There were also some practical considerations to weigh. Jobs in journalism were scarce nowadays, given the poor economy, and the beating that the industry had taken in the age of online bloggers and free news sites. It was difficult to make a good living in the media-related trades nowadays. And entry-level positions with luminaries like Brett St. Croix had been scarce even in more prosperous times.

If she went against Brett, he would fire her, and likely blacklist her in the industry. The field of professional journalism was tight-knit and incestuous. If she departed from this job in ignominy, she might never find a similar one again. She would have to resign herself to a life inside a corporate cubicle farm. There were even worse possibilities, of course: She might spend her twenties waiting tables or serving flavored coffees behind the counter of a Starbucks, only to settle into a loveless marriage of convenience around the age of thirty. She would exchange her dreams of making a difference in the world for the bland palliative of bourgeois mediocrity.

Once again, she asked herself: *Was this Lee McCabe and his (probable) innocence worth the sacrifice? Worth the personal setbacks she would have to endure? Worth the damage it would do to the reputation of a great journalist like Brett St. Croix?*

She knew that she would be unable to decide until she had spoken to Lee McCabe herself, face-to-face.

She jotted down Lee's cell phone number and left a post-it note for Brett, informing him that she had taken ill and would need to go home to rest for the remainder of the day.

Then she went to her own computer and Googled Hawkins County, Kentucky. If she left within the next hour, she could be there by 10 p.m.

She knew that the course of action she had decided upon was uncertain, and more than a little dangerous. But the futures of at least three people—Brett, Lee McCabe, and herself—would depend on her actions between now and midnight.

She would give Lee McCabe a trial, she resolved. A trial of her own. Yes, she would give this Lee McCabe the opportunity to convince her of his innocence.

92

Lee's cell phone rang at 9:36 p.m. When the female caller identified herself as Michelle Ackerman, an assistant of Brett St. Croix, Lee was incredulous. Without further preamble she asked him:

"Is there someplace nearby where we can meet? The parking lot of a McDonald's, perhaps."

"Are you serious?" Lee asked. "Public appearances aren't exactly my thing lately, with being wanted for mass murder and whatnot. And your boss has only made things worse."

"It would be in your best interests to meet with me, Lee."

Lee laughed. "That's what your boss told me."

"I'm not my boss," the young woman on the phone said. "And my boss doesn't know about this trip—know about my calling you. He thinks that I've gone home for the day sick."

"So basically you're a defector."

"Don't get your hopes up," she said. "But I am working on my own. Let's just leave it at that for now."

Lee weighed his options. Of course there was a chance that this could be part of another betrayal by Brett St. Croix. But he didn't think so. Whatever his many conceits, the journalist would not use a woman—a woman who worked for him—as bait in some sort of a police sting.

Of course, there were other possibilities: Perhaps this woman had no affiliation with Brett St. Croix. Perhaps she was herself a member of law enforcement, or an agent of one of the criminal gangs that was trying to kill him.

"Let me ask you a question," Lee said. "I gave St. Croix some information about a clue I had discovered. And he was going to follow up on it for me."

"Sawdust," Michelle said, perceiving the test. "Now listen, I don't have the time or the patience to play twenty questions with you. If you doubt that I am who I say I am, you can call Queen City Media's automated phone directory. You'll get my voicemail, and you'll hear the voice in the greeting message. You'll recognize it as me. Now, I've had a long and hot drive. And I'm here to help you, just maybe. Do you want to meet, or not?"

Lee decided that he would meet with Michelle Ackerman; but he also decided that he would take no chances. He instructed her to proceed to the parking lot of an agricultural warehouse just outside of town. When she called and asked where he was, Lee gave his actual location: Another warehouse just up the road.

Michelle arrived a few minutes later in an Audi sedan. The young woman who stepped out of the car was a stunner: She was tall with long chestnut hair and the build of a former high school tennis champ. Lee vaguely wondered if Brett St. Croix had slept with her—or had at least tried.

Probably not, Lee thought. *She seems a bit too intimidating for St. Croix.*

The first thing she said to Lee was: "What the hell was that all about?" referring to the redirect of the meeting location. "First you tell me to go to one place—then you send me to another. You think I don't know that was deliberate?"

"You're damned right it was deliberate," Lee said. He was leaning against the side of the warehouse. Michelle had left her Audi running, and he was illuminated in the glare of the headlights.

"That's what you do when you meet with someone who you don't fully trust. That makes it harder for them to ambush you. Now before we get started, I'll have to ask you to kill that engine and to kill those headlights."

She sighed in a show of aggravation, then shrugged and leaned back into her car, and turned off the ignition. Now their only source of light was the moon.

"Satisfied?" she asked, walking over to join him. Lee immediately noticed that Michelle Ackerman was a good two inches taller than he was.

"Not yet," Lee said. "But that's not bad for a start. Now, I'm a very busy man with all the people who are after me; and like I said, your boss has made my circumstances much worse. Suppose you tell me what this is all about."

"I want a follow-up statement from you," Michelle said.

"What?" Lee nearly shouted. "Why?"

"My boss isn't the only one who has appearances to make on CNN," she said. "I want a follow-up statement from you about the direction of the case against you."

Lee was flabbergasted. This woman had drawn him out into the night on a ruse—for this?

"Well, to hell with you then. Go back to Cincinnati. And tell your boss that my revenge is this: I'm not going to hunt him down, and I'm not going to do you any harm, either. Somehow, some way, I'm going to prove my innocence. And when this all comes out, he will be shown to be the liar and the backstabbing son-of-a-bitch that he really is. And you—you won't look much better."

Lee saw a hint of a smile on Michelle Ackerman's lips. *What the hell was she thinking? Did she imagine this all to be some sort of a game? Didn't she know about the lives that had already been lost? About the lives that were still at stake? Didn't she grasp that if he was in fact dangerous, he could kill her right now and no one would be able to do a thing to stop him?*

Angry and confused at the conduct of this strange young woman from Cincinnati, Lee turned to go.

"I have nothing more to say to you."

"Wait!" she called, in a tone that made him obey her.

"What now? Do you want to take a picture of me? Yes, that would be great, wouldn't it? Another publicity stunt for you and your boss."

She waved him silent. "I don't want your picture. You look like you might be handsome if you cleaned yourself up a bit, but you could use a shave, you know that? You're in no state to have your picture taken."

She is *crazy*, Lee thought. "I'm going," he said.

"The Peaton Woods Furniture Company," Michelle said. "That's where you need to go if you want to prove your innocence."

"The Peaton Woods Furniture Company?" Lee asked.

"Do you know where it is?"

"More or less, sure. It's been closed for years, though."

"Exactly," Michelle said. "And the Peaton Woods Furniture factory is now owned by one Lester Finn—or by a shell company that his lawyer has set up. I'm not sure about that. But I can tell you this— the Peaton Woods Furniture factory is the main site of Lester Finn's meth-running operation."

She stood there in the full moonlight and spun a tale that made Lee's anger rise. Apparently Brett St. Croix had carried out his own investigation. St. Croix must have realized that he had interviewed an innocent man. Nevertheless, the journalist had decided to betray him —for reasons that Lee believed he would never fully understand. Something about a book deal, according to Michelle.

"I suppose I do owe you some gratitude after all," Lee said when she was finished. "But you might have come out and told me from the very beginning. Why did you hold out on me, like this was some sort of a test or something?"

"Maybe it *was* a test," she replied. "I'm taking a huge personal risk here—probably sacrificing my career, in fact. I wouldn't do that for just anyone. When I led you to believe that I had deceived you— wasted your time—you reacted honorably, under the circumstances. I know that you could have shot me."

My God, she is crazy, Lee thought.

"Will you go public with what you know?" he asked.

"I'll drive straight back to Cincinnati tonight," she said. "I'll stop by the office and write something up. This is going to be an all-nighter. Then tomorrow morning I'm going to walk into the office of Queen City Media's senior management and tell them everything I know. I'll also denounce Brett St. Croix as a liar."

She uttered these last words with some difficulty, and Lee sensed that this would have many adverse consequences for her. He wondered again, if this attractive and obviously ambitious young woman had been sleeping with Brett St. Croix. Then he pushed that thought out of his mind; he had much larger matters to worry about.

"Thank you, Michelle," Lee said at last. "And I want you to keep an eye out for those bad men. They seem to have a way of turning up and killing innocent people."

"I appreciate your concern for my safety," she said. "That's very gallant of you. But I'm a journalist, remember. I'm willing to take a personal risk in order to get the truth out."

He was thinking of Amy Sutter, of course; and he said a silent prayer that another woman would not have to die in order to preserve his life.

"Is something wrong?" she asked. "You don't look so good, all of a sudden."

He did not feel capable of talking about Amy, though. And anyway, it would take too long to explain. So he gave Michelle Ackerman another reason.

"There's more to it than that. If you get killed, what you know dies with you. So take care of yourself, Michelle. For both our sakes."

rett St. Croix's interview disturbed yet a third viewer. Earlier that day, while Lee McCabe and Michelle Ackerman had watched CNN with mounting disgust at the journalist's prevarications and subtle lies, Alfonzo Coscollino had also watched St. Croix spin his tale.

Alfonzo sat in his customary spot in front of the big-screen, flat-panel Toshiba television, clad in his usual warm-up attire. He lit a cigarette and thanked whoever might be listening that at least his bladder was not troubling him today.

The journalist from Cincinnati was lying through his teeth—that much was clear. Of course the CNN interviewer had only sensed St. Croix's lies and omissions; Mitch Conway seemed to have concluded by giving the semi-famous author the benefit of the doubt. And it would have been bad manners to outright accuse St. Croix of lying, anyway. Didn't journalists maintain a sort of fraternal order among themselves, just as cops and men of *la cosa nostra* did?

Whether Mitch Conway perceived the lies or not, Alfonzo knew that he had an advantage in such discernments, an advantage that few men outside his particular line of work would possess. During his years as an enforcer and *capo*—and his later years as a don—

Alfonzo had been lied to many times. Far more times than he could count. Lying was what men did when they had been caught in an act of betrayal, and their lives hung in the balance.

Alfonzo had learned over the years that the best policy was to assume that men were mostly lying when they spoke to you. If you began with the assumption of a lie, you could then discern the actual facts of a matter from the fragments of truth that they let slip out while attempting to make their lies more credible.

He removed his cell phone from the pocket of his warm-up jacket and took yet another look at the photo that Paulie had emailed to him. The bearded man in the silver Acura with Ohio plates. The one who had been seen driving away from the Boar's Head in Blood Flats.

The photo was blurry. As an independent piece of evidence, it was insufficient by itself. The man behind the wheel of the Acura might have been Brett St. Croix, might not have been. Nor was the Ohio license plate conclusive by itself. This journalist on Alfonzo's television screen obviously hailed from Ohio; but Ohio and Kentucky were neighboring states, after all. On any given day, you could probably find hundreds or thousands of cars with Ohio plates in every corner of Kentucky.

Nevertheless, Alfonzo did not believe that the man in the blurry photo would ultimately turn out to be anyone other than Brett St. Croix. While coincidences were possible, only a fool relied on them to explain away danger.

One thing was obvious: This Brett St. Croix had gotten himself very close to events in Hawkins County, Kentucky—and perhaps close to the family's business as well. The man was clearly a publicity hound, a grandstander. Was he planning an exposé on the influence of organized crime in Southern states? Investigative journalists had caused the family trouble before. They were worse than cops in some ways, because they weren't bound by constitutional restraints.

This Brett St. Croix represented another loose string. Alfonzo closed his eyes, and considered the roster of operatives that the family had in Cincinnati. Cincinnati lay only four hundred miles southeast of Chicago, and the family had long considered the Ohio city to be within its sphere of influence. Cincinnati was the home of numerous trucking companies—a business in which the family was still actively involved.

After a few moments, one name came to mind: Big John Lewis. Not an Italian, but a reliable man who had proven his worth to the family on previous occasions. Yes, Alfonzo, decided. Big John Lewis was the right man for this particular task.

Alfonzo muted the television, lifted his cell phone from the armrest of the easy chair, and selected Big John Lewis's phone number from the device's internal directory. Lewis answered on the second ring. After respectfully greeting the don, Lewis asked, *"So what can I do for you, Mr. Coscollino?"*

In the manner of a patient father, Alfonzo explained the situation with Brett St. Croix, and told Big John Lewis what needed to be done. *These are the questions that must be answered*, Alfonzo explained. *These are the answers that determine whether or not the journalist is to live or to die. Do you understand? Can you do this for me?....Of course you can. I know the Family can depend on you, Big John. You know, it's time a man of your abilities was made a capo. When all this business in Kentucky is over, I want you to come to Chicago. I want you to visit me here in the family home. We need to talk about the future.* Your *future, Big John.*

Alfonzo terminated the call and placed the cell phone into his pocket. He pressed the television remote's mute button, restoring the Toshiba's sound. On CNN, Mitch Conway was now interviewing a stock market guru who was predicting a financial meltdown in the United States and all the major European markets.

The stock market may or may not survive, Alfonzo thought. *But the Family will, because we do what needs to be done. Because we're thorough and we don't leave loose threads dangling—threads that could eventually become nooses.*

He had told Big John to use his own discretion, based on what he learned when interrogating the journalist. Alfonzo believed, however, that Brett St. Croix was not long for this world. Big John was thorough—and he had a bit of a sadistic streak. That sadistic streak had sometimes made him useful in the past.

I may have a leaky bladder and bad lungs, Alfonzo thought. *But I am still in command of this family. And I will do what I must in order to defend my Family from those who seek to destroy it.*

Brett St. Croix would deserve whatever Big John did to him. Alfonzo imagined the pale, pudgy journalist writhing in agony, and he afforded himself a sadistic moment of his own.

94

After his CNN interview, Brett felt too anxious to return to the office, and too restless to return home for the night. He wanted to be among his fellow human beings as he savored his victory—even if those human beings were only anonymous parties who knew nothing of his narrow escape from professional disaster.

And a victory it was. Brett had barely departed from the television station before a text message appeared on his cell phone: a text message from Alistair Jones:

"Bravo! Stellar performance on CNN. I believe that your future in the Fenton, Stafford, & Brown stable of authors is quite secure."

BRETT REREAD the short message several times: *Bravo, indeed.*

There was a downtown hangout that he frequented at least once per week: the Wildwood Bar and Grill. The bar was close to the river. Sometimes Brett liked to step out onto the sidewalk between drinks inside the Wildwood during the summer. If there was a baseball game underway on the riverfront, he could often hear the cheers from inside the stadium.

The interior of the Wildwood consisted of soft reddish lights, bare brick walls, and the pervasive presence of jazz. A live band played every night of the week beginning at eight. This early in the evening, the music of trumpets and snare drums was piped into the bar area via a central sound system.

The bartender on duty tonight was named Nick. He greeted Brett as he entered and took a seat at the bar. Nick knew Brett by name, as did most of the bartenders at the Wildwood.

"What'll you have?" Nick asked. Nick was a thirty-eight year-old man who still wore a gold earring and the latest youthful fashions, despite his rapidly receding hairline and rapidly expanding waistline. Nick had tried his hand at acting during his twenties, giving up his quest after five years of struggling to pay his rent in Los Angeles. The only thing he had gained from his years in LA was an unwanted occupation as a bartender.

Nick sometimes claimed that he would return to LA for another try before he hit forty. Brett knew that Nick would never leave his hometown again; and he would still be a bartender when he was sixty.

"I'll have an order of chicken quesadillas and Samuel Adams," Brett said.

"Fries, too?"

Brett gave the question a moment's thought. "Sure. Why not?"

Nick drew a beer from the tap and set the glass down on the bar before Brett. There was a frothy foam on top that ran down one side of the glass.

"I saw you on CNN this afternoon," Nick said, gesturing to the television mounted above the bar.

Brett nodded. "From national television to this barstool. How far a man can fall in a mere hour."

Nick laughed. "You got a way with words, Mr. St. Croix."

"Well, we all have our strengths. I've got a way with words, and you've got a way with the ladies."

"Aw, I did sometimes when I was younger. Not so much anymore. But anyway, that was a great interview. You dominated, as they say."

Brett smiled in appreciation and took a sip of his beer. He could not tell if Nick was speaking sincerely, or if he was merely angling for a generous tip. *Maybe a little of both.* After all, even a relative dullard like Nick the Bartender would have been able to recognize the coolness of the responses he had delivered, the way he had made Mitch Conway look like a sophomore journalism student.

But Nick would not know the full extent of his coup, partly because Nick was a dullard—and also because he did not know the stakes that had been in play. And how Brett St. Croix, semi-famous journalist and author, had won them hands down.

No one could find fault with what he had said in the interview. As evidenced by the text message, Alistair had found no complaint with the degree to which he had taken Lee McCabe's part. He had preserved his all-important contract with Fenton, Stafford, & Brown. And if Lee McCabe was ever vindicated, no one could claim that he had uttered an explicit falsehood. He had perfectly walked the fine line between prevarication and disclosure.

Of course, there was another possibility that he had to consider: Lee McCabe might surface and publicly denounce him. If this ever occurred, the matter would come down to a contest between his own credibility and the word of a fugitive. True, McCabe might attract some populist sympathy. Americans predictably loved an underdog. At the end of the day, though, Brett believed that he would be able to shred McCabe in the court of public opinion—just as he had trounced Mitch Conway.

But the ex-marine would probably never have the opportunity to challenge him in any public forum. McCabe was most likely headed for prison or death. First the young man had been placed in a difficult position—and then he had compounded his own predicament at every step along the way. Lee should have surrendered that morning at that hillbilly trailer park. This might have meant a few days in jail; but his Iraq war record and simple, plainspoken manner would have worked in his favor.

Instead McCabe had chosen to run. This decision had placed him in far greater peril, and turned the tide of public opinion and mass media attention against him.

These realizations allayed the momentary pang of guilt that Brett felt over his betrayal of the ex-marine. The laws of probability strongly suggested that McCabe would meet a bad end. Brett had no intention of attaching himself to a doomed cause. Why should he jeopardize his own career—a half-million-dollar-book deal—for a dead man? Why throw away a fortune on an almost certain failure?

Nick brought the quesadillas and fries, and Brett watched the television while he ate them. Nick was a news junkie, and he kept switching the channel between CNN, Fox, and MSNBC. There was considerable coverage of the young fugitive from Hawkins County, though no further coverage of the journalist who had interviewed him. This was fine with Brett. Let McCabe take the limelight for now. He would analyze and write about the ex-marine long after the young man had passed from the scene.

As the early evening dinner hour passed, Brett switched from Sam Adams to vodka on the rocks, cut with a shot of mineral water. At nine p.m. he was about to call it a night, when he noticed the blonde woman seated on an adjacent bar stool.

She was two seats down from him, and Brett had no idea how long she had been there.

The blonde woman was probably four to six years younger than he was—though not nearly as young as Michelle. The thought of his attractive but forbidding subordinate filled him with a frustrated heat. He might be a distinguished guest on CNN, but he had so far been unable to find the key that would unlock Michelle Ackerman's defenses. Or her pants.

Perhaps it would be better for him to settle for a more realistic, accessible target. This thirtysomething occupant of the adjacent barstool likely had lost most of her youthful pretensions. (*A process that lay some years ahead in Michelle's future*, he thought sourly.) A divorcee, perhaps, or a single career woman who was just beginning to detect the first signposts of spinsterhood on the distant horizon. In either case she would be vulnerable.

Then, as if the fates had intervened on his behalf, CNN was playing a segment from his earlier interview, as part of its ongoing coverage of the events in Hawkins County.

Brett leaned in the direction of the blonde woman and tapped on the bar. When he had her attention, he pointed at the television set.

"There's no way I would trust that man. He looks like a complete scoundrel."

She looked at the television set, then back at him, then again at the television set. Brett suppressed a grin as disbelief registered on her face.

"That's not—*you*, is it?"

"I am afraid I must confess to that crime. The unsavory gentleman on the television set is indeed me. A true scoundrel, that man." At this moment, the onscreen version of Brett was selectively recounting the time he had spent with Lee McCabe.

"Oh my God!" the woman gasped. "You're somebody famous, aren't you!"

Brett thought: *Bingo!*

"Ah, famous is too strong a word. You give me far more credit than I deserve."

"But look," she said. "You're on TV!"

95

It was easy for Brett to get the conversational ball rolling after that. She wanted to know why he was on CNN; and that lead to a discussion of his previously published book, his numerous travels, his career as a journalist and reputation as an author. She told him that her name was Lena. Indeed, Lena was both a divorcee and a career woman. She sold financial products for Fidelity Investments, a brokerage house that had a large presence in Cincinnati. There wasn't much to it, she said—really she was very low on the totem pole. Just another cubicle job. Lena had a mortgage and a teenage daughter who attended a private school. She did not receive much help from her bum of an ex-husband.

Brett had met women like Lena many times before: fading beauty queens who had married poorly, educated themselves inadequately, and were now reaping a less than bountiful harvest of early middle age. They were looking for lifelines—someone to prop them up and give them a sense of security.

A confirmed bachelor, Brett knew that he had no intention of providing Lena (or any other woman, for that matter) with any such security. In his estimation, women were like the investments that Lena peddled: You didn't buy stock when it was declining in value.

But you could have some fun with women like Lena. Moreover, a quick and easy conquest might patch up his ego a bit after the blows it had suffered from Michelle's repeated rebuffs.

Brett lost track of time as the conversation steadily drifted away from its original focus: Her polite interest in his status as a semi-famous public personality. When he tried to tell her about Rwanda she gave him a puzzled expression. He had to stop and recount the events that had transpired in that African country in 1994. In 1994 she had not been paying much attention to the news, she explained, somewhat apologetically. Lena had been married and having a baby at that time. She was having a baby even though she knew that her marriage was going south.

This prompted a segue into why her marriage went south, beginning in 1994—and Lena forgot all about Rwanda and whatever it was that Brett had done there. It turned out to be a long jeremiad; but Brett listened patiently, buying drinks and nodding at the appropriate points in the story.

It was nearly an hour past midnight—within sight of closing time —when she finally looked at her watch and said: "My God, Brett, it's late, isn't it? And I have to go to work tomorrow." Lena placed a hand on his wrist. "What about you?"

"Actually, I have to work tonight. No, no—I'm not that hardworking. When I'm out and about like tonight, it's my habit to make a final swing by the office before I head home for the day."

She drained her glass. "And look at me—rambling on and on about my problems, keeping you out so late."

"Quite alright," Brett said. He was calculating the odds that Lena would agree to come home with him, in which case he would skip his final visit to the office. This being a weeknight—he realized that the odds were against him. She had clearly stated that she had to go to work tomorrow. His best course of action, then, would be to set his sights on the upcoming weekend.

"I've really enjoyed talking to you, in fact," he said.

"Really? I find that hard to believe. After all, you spend your time running all around the world and talking to all those famous people."

"It's not as glamorous as it sounds," Brett said. "As I mentioned, my last assignment involved camping out in the woods of central Kentucky."

She shook her head in appreciation. "Incredible. You're too modest; but really I have to be going, and—"

"Well, can I call you sometime?"

Lena was all too eager to give up her phone number, Brett discovered. As he walked the blocks between the Wildwood Bar and Grill and the Queen City Media building, he plotted out his strategy: He would wait twenty-four hours before calling Lena. He would invite her out to dinner this Saturday. And with even a modicum of luck, she would wind up in his bed at the end of the evening.

He was lost in these pleasant thoughts when someone called out from the nearby shadows: *"Hey, whatchuu doin' man? Out by yo-self dis late?"*

Brett could barely make out the facial features of the youth leaning against the wall of a building. His skin was dark brown, and his eyes and his white teeth shone in the spare light of a halogen streetlamp.

Another voice laughed, and Brett saw more movement in the same vicinity. Then he noticed that there was another youth, and another. Three in total.

Now Brett realized the nature of his mistake: Rather than proceed down the main thoroughfare, he had taken a shortcut through a side alley. The alley was safe enough during the daylight hours, when the downtown district was heavily peopled. But the wee hours of the night were another matter.

He made a conscious effort to control his breathing. No need to panic. He had dodged worse dangers in Rwanda, after all. And a few days ago he had interviewed a young ex-marine who was a fugitive. Then he had narrowly dodged an encounter with a probable mobster. Those were worse dangers than three punks in an alley. He could talk his way out of this.

"Just passing through, guys. Not looking for any trouble."

"*Well, maybe trouble be lookin' fo you,*" another of the hoodlums said. "*Maybe trouble already find you, huh?*"

Brett couldn't tell if they intended real harm, or if they were simply having fun with a middle-aged man who was an outsider in their world. In any either case, he determined that he would take no chances. The situation could quickly escalate, Brett realized, even if the youths' initial intentions were harmless.

Without turning his back on the youths, Brett maintained his pace as he walked past them. There was a cry of "*Hey, get back here!*"; but they did not seem inclined to pursue him once he had cleared the immediate confines of the alley. He made a sharp right turn onto the sidewalk of a major street, and then—now that he had lost visual contact—broke into a light trot. Traffic was light at this hour on a weeknight. If the hoodlums decided to give chase, there would be no rescuers.

Brett did not relax his gait until the building that housed Queen City Media was in sight. He was winded and he could feel faint patches of sweat soaked into the shirt material beneath his armpits.

The first-floor lobby of the building was even more deserted than the city streets outside. It smelled of lemon and ammonia—the solution that the janitorial crews used to clean and wax the floor each night. In four or five hours the lobby would start filling up with people again; but for now they were all asleep in their beds, most of them in the distant suburbs. Most of them with families. Only single men who were night owls truly thrived in this sort of environment, Brett thought.

Queen City Media leased a suite of offices on the seventh floor. As he rode upward in the elevator, Brett allowed himself to laugh at his encounter with the young punks in the alleyway. *He had overreacted, hadn't he? Hadn't he behaved exactly like one of those middle-class suburbanites whom he so disdained? He had bolted like a coward, filled with terror because the youths had been inner city residents with dark skin.*

I am not completely without bourgeois prejudices, Brett thought, as he slipped the key into his own private office. *But what can you expect of a man, confronted like that on the street at night?*

He was shaking off the last of his residual fear over his encounter with the youths when he saw the man seated behind his desk. And then the floor of the world dropped out from beneath Brett St. Croix's feet.

96

B rett knew at once who the man was—or, at least, who the man represented. Brett reflected, in the brief space of a few seconds, that so many of his decisions had brought him to this moment. He had taken far too many chances, deliberately courted disaster on too many occasions.

What had he been thinking—playing amateur sleuth in the mafia's backyard? He had seen those two men in the dark blazers outside the Boar's Head, hadn't he? The ones who did not belong in a town like Blood Flats, Kentucky. Why had he listened to the voice of his own hubris, the one that insisted that he would be able to skirt disaster this time, too?

The man seated behind his desk was huge, and probably in his early forties. He wore a blazer and a dark-colored tee shirt.

"My name is John," the big man said. "My friends call me Big John."

"Do you count me as one of your friends?" Brett asked.

Big John smirked at the question. "Lena said you were quite a talker. She said it was easy to keep you occupied for the time I needed to conduct my little investigation."

"Lena? You mean—"

"Lena is a gambling addict from southeast Indiana. Funny thing about gambling addicts. They just can't get the first rule through their heads: *The house always comes out ahead in the long run.* They tend to gamble themselves into very deep holes. Lena owes one of our associated gaming interests a lot of money. She agreed to help us tonight in exchange for a significant reduction in her debt."

"But what about—"

"What about that phone number she gave you? That number rings at a Mexican restaurant on the east side of town."

"I'll be damned!" Brett said, unable to believe the intensity of his sudden anger at Lena. She had been deceiving him all along.

"The lying bitch," he observed.

"Don't be too angry at 'Lena'," Big John said. "She has a very sad story of her own—though not the particular story she told you."

"You mentioned an 'investigation,'" Brett said. Perhaps he would be able to save himself by drawing this character out. "What did you mean by that?"

"I mean an investigation of your investigation in Hicksville, Kentucky." Big John held up a copy of Brett's file—the one of that documented his findings in Blood Flats. There were notations of practically every detail: A transcript of his interview with Lee McCabe, notes regarding what he had seen at the Peaton Woods Furniture factory. In short, everything.

"You know," Big John continued. "You really made my investigation very easy. I appreciate the way you documented everything. Very thorough."

And now Brett had an idea of what was coming. "Suppose," he said hastily, "that I gave you not only this file, but my computer's hard drive as well. And further suppose that I would be willing to swear to you that I will never write or speak about the recent events in Kentucky. This can all be buried."

Brett flinched as he uttered this last word. A Freudian slip if ever there was one.

"I'm sorry," Big John said. "I think you already know that's not possible."

Big John stood up from the desk at a speed that belied his immense size. At his full height, he looked even larger than he had while sitting down—probably six feet six, maybe three hundred pounds. And that weight all appeared to be solid.

For Brett, any notion of fighting this giant was out of the question. Then he noticed the object that Big John held in his right hand: It was a pistol fitted with a silencer.

97

L ee was awakened by another phone call from Michelle Ackerman around three a.m. She was hysterical and crying; and Lee was himself mired in the residual delirium of sleep. She had to repeat herself several times before Lee fully grasped the import of what she was saying.

"Brett is dead!" she shouted into the phone. "My God. *He's dead!"*

"Dead?" Lee needed to repeat this, as only hours ago, Brett had been a triumphant face on CNN.

"That's right," she said. *"How can this have happened, Lee?"*

"Slow down and tell me what happened."

"Brett had his faults. He wasn't perfect. But he didn't deserve this. No, he didn't."

"Michelle, tell me what happened."

"When I came back to Queen City Media's offices, I noticed that Brett's door had been left open. He never does that. So I looked inside and I found him. And now the police are here and—"

"How?" Lee asked, desperately hoping that the violence had not spread even further, that Brett St. Croix had somehow expired from natural causes. But he knew better even before Michelle answered him. "How did Brett die?"

"*Shot!*" Michelle said, breaking into sobs again.

"Damn," Lee said.

"Someone must have broken into his office. Either that or they followed him in. They ransacked the place. Smashed his computer, emptied his desk drawers. He must have surprised them, or tried to fight with them. They shot him numerous times...I don't know how many times. I couldn't look. I just walked out, like I was going into shock. But I was able to force myself to dial 911."

It took Lee a moment to absorb this. *Does it have no end?* he wondered.

"Michelle, I don't need to tell you that what killed your boss was no random robbery gone bad. It couldn't have been."

"No," she said, steadying herself. "I've already figured that much out."

"Based on what you told me, Brett got close to the truth, even if he ultimately decided not to use that truth to help me. Lester Finn—or, more likely, the people who Lester Finn is working for—killed Brett so that he wouldn't be able to change his mind about what he chose to reveal."

"I know."

"And that also means that you could be next."

"No—no, you're wrong about that, Lee. They wouldn't have known that I was privy to all the information from Brett's investigation. And these people can't simply start killing off the entire staff of Queen City Media."

"Michelle, these people have proven numerous times that they'll do whatever they want to. They'll kill as many people as they feel necessary."

"I'm going to tell the police," she said. "I'm going to tell them everything I know."

"No! I tried talking to the police, and the police took a shot at me. From what you said, these people made sure that they destroyed all evidence of the investigation when they killed Brett. Did you make a separate copy of Brett's file? Was there any evidence on the company share drive?"

"No and no," she said. "Brett never let me make copies of his files. And he keeps all information about his ongoing projects on his personal hard drive. He was always very secretive that way."

"Then you gain nothing by talking to the police. And you risk even more."

"What should I tell them, then? All I told them in my statement was that I returned to the office and found him. I didn't say anything about my trip, or what I had found earlier."

"Then leave it at that. And then you need to leave town, too. Go somewhere where no one can find you, where no one will even think of looking for you. Don't use your credit card. Pay for everything in cash. I'll contact you after I take care of matters here."

"And how do you think you're going to 'take care of matters'?"

"I'm still working on that part," Lee admitted.

"Which means that you're no farther along then you were before. You can't do this by yourself, Lee. Let me help you. Let me be your voice to the public—as Brett should have been."

"You listen to me," Lee said. "I won't allow you to take that chance. Another woman took a similar chance for me, and she's dead now." He recounted for her the ride that Amy Sutter had given him, and that unfortunate woman's fate.

"Please, Michelle," he said finally. "You've done enough for me. Let me take things from here."

98

Lee spent most of the next day in Ben Chamberlain's living room, wracking his brain for a way to approach Lester Finn. For a way to prove his innocence. Throughout his arduous journey to Blood Flats, he had convinced himself that the answer lay here—that he would find his final battle and his absolution in this town.

But now that he was actually in Blood Flats, he found himself floundering, hesitating. He still believed that a final battle was coming; but he was unsure of how to commence the battle. How should he go on the offensive?

And all the while, the forces of his enemies continued to draw around him. According to Ben, the police presence in Blood Flats was still minimal—their focus was Perryston, and the wooded areas where a fugitive would be likely to hide. As Lee had suspected, the law had not tracked him to Blood Flats. Ironically, his flight through the countryside had reduced the normal police presence in the town where he was actually hiding. But Lee knew that this gap in their dragnet would be short-lived.

"We should just walk into the Boar's Head," Ben Chamberlain said. "Walk in there and call Lester out."

Lee was able to convince his host that such a course would be futile. "His men would simply gun us down," Lee said. "And we'd prove nothing."

Ben grunted and nodded his assent. Lee could see that the older man was growing restless. He had his own score to settle with Lester Finn, after all.

The confrontation, Lee believed, would occur at the factory. It was a location that he desperately wanted to visit—needed to visit. But his instincts told him that he should wait one more day before approaching the reported site of Lester Finn's meth operations. In the wake of discovering Brett's activities, his enemies would be hyper-vigilant.

Tomorrow, Lee decided. *Tomorrow I will visit Peaton Woods. But today I will meet with Dawn again.*

Lee called Dawn early in the evening. She answered her cell phone on the second ring. *Would she have time to meet with him*, he asked.

At present, Dawn knew far more than he did about Lester Finn. The previous day, she had told him about Lester's illegal activities. Now he wanted to get a handle on the man's character. *What made him tick?*

Dawn was more than willing to talk; and she seemed pleasantly surprised when he indicated his intention to talk in person. Really, he could have gotten the information he required via a phone call, and that would have been the wiser course. While hiding out in a hostile zone, a man does not go on social calls.

This represented a lapse in his discipline, he knew. He was being overpowered by something else.

He felt a need to talk to Dawn—partly because of the callous way he had treated her before, and partly because of something else he could not quite define: that long-ago night when he had met and rebuffed her at the party. Afterward, she had haunted his thoughts for the better part of a week. And now he had to reconcile that image of her to what she had become, and everything that had happened since. Dawn's downfall had added to the radical disorientation of the past days; it was another way in which the earth had shifted beneath him.

While she had been clearly interested in him that night, he had judged her to be ultimately unattainable, the sort of local girl who was bound to leave Hawkins County for bigger and better things. Girls like that did not marry local boys who stalled out at blue-collar jobs. They left for college in distant cities, where they met young men who were to become doctors and lawyers and up-and-coming corporate players. They lived in faraway, well-manicured suburbs and visited their families in Hawkins County on the major holidays, their smartly dressed husbands and finely groomed children in tow.

He had, in that instant several years ago, imagined her being with him for a while and then eventually rebuffing him. His status then as a marine meant a temporary source of excitement for a girl just out of high school. A straight-laced teenager's attempt at thrill-seeking. But he would be a mere dalliance for her, he had been sure. An experience for her to have before she began the real business of her adult life.

Or so he had thought. Dawn had, in fact, gone in a different, opposite direction. Her ascension had turned into a fall from grace. Clearly he had done a poor job of predicting her future. What if he had also been wrong about her intentions? And was that question even worth considering now? Did it make any difference? He was a fugitive and she was a hopeless drug addict. Not to mention a prostitute. They could not simply begin where they had left off.

When Dawn answered the door of her apartment, her mood was different than it had been over the phone. She seemed more preoccupied, as if something had happened between the termination of their phone conversation and this moment. She gave him no further clues as she invited him in, though.

In the sparsely furnished living room of her studio flat, they sat on the floor and talked. She made them iced tea and they placed their glasses on cracked vinyl coasters. The cold glasses were wet with condensation in the humidity.

"I met Lester shortly after I became addicted," Dawn explained.

"It was my first summer as an addict, and my finances were already a mess."

She described how Lester had introduced her to the world of prostitution, and how her cravings for the drug had made her acquiesce to everything that life had entailed. The business was demeaning; but it provided a constant, mindless cash flow—exactly what a junkie needs.

"But then," she said. "Then the meth started getting the best of me, and I didn't look like some middle-aged man's secret fantasy anymore. I woke up one morning and realized that I looked like a junkie, and well, I guess Lester and Lester's customers had realized it, too."

"So Lester fired you?" Lee asked.

"Well, not exactly. Lester is always thinking of a way to turn an illegal buck, you know. He had this idea of recruiting a second tier of girls, ones who would be willing to work cheaply in the bad neighborhoods, servicing the more dangerous clients. Stupid, idea, really. I can tell you from experience that there is no money in the bottom end of the trade."

"But that's where you eventually ended up," Lee observed, not unkindly.

Dawn sighed. "Yeah. But I didn't make Lester enough money on my race to the bottom. He held it against me, started smacking me around when we met. So I broke my connections to him. Went out on my own. That didn't go over very well with him."

"But you said you weren't making much money for him, anyway."

"It wasn't so much the money thing as pride. Lester fancies himself a kingpin, you know. And he's never forgotten what he sees as my 'ingratitude,' if you can believe that. From time to time I'll get a phone call from him, and he'll ask me how I like living in the gutter, and if I would like to get down on my knees and.....beg him for another chance."

Lee listened to Dawn with clenched fists. He had not yet met Lester Finn, but he wanted to kill him.

Lee noticed an opened envelope on the floor near Dawn's knee.

Its contents had apparently been removed, read, and placed back inside.

"You keep looking at that envelope," Lee said.

"Yeah," Dawn's voice faltered. "Well, you see."

"What is it?"

"Never mind. You've got enough to worry about."

"Right now I'm worried about you."

She gave him a wan smile. It quickly faded.

"Well, it's like this: I've been wanting to get off the street for some time now. Make a clean go of it, if you will. I know that what I do— the life I've been leading—entails certain health risks. If there was anything wrong with me, anything that couldn't be walked away from, I wanted to know it now, and not be surprised by it later."

"Okay," Lee said, waiting for her to continue.

"So a few weeks ago I went to a health clinic in Louisville and had a blood test done, and—"

She broke down at this point, and it was clear that she could not continue. She picked up the envelope and handed it to Lee, silently inviting him to read for himself what she did not have the strength to put into words. Lee had already surmised what the paper inside the envelope would reveal; but he read it anyway.

The paper said that Dawn was HIV-positive. Lee did not know how to process news like this—did not know whether it was better to say nothing, or to make some inadequate attempt at comforting her. It seemed incumbent on him to say something, though; and so he asked her:

"How did it happen? Was it one of the men?'

Dawn shook her head and ran the back of one hand across her eyes. "I don't think so. I was always careful with my—customers— always insisted that they use protection. But I did something even more dangerous one day. I was low on money and low on meth and I ran into another woman who was shooting it up with a needle. She looked sick and I should have known better. But I told myself that it was only one time, and I wiped the needle off before I used it."

She smiled bitterly through her tears. "Can you believe that? I was a premed student, and I told myself that I could clean a virus off a needle by wiping it with a Kleenex."

"Well," Lee said. "I convinced myself that I could run away from a crime scene, and somehow everything would turn out alright."

Things might have been different, Lee reflected, though he would not have voiced this sentiment. That idea could do neither of them any good now.

"Lee, I'm going to ask you a favor. And it's incredibly selfish of me; but I'm going to ask you anyway."

"What?"

"It's been a long time since I had an evening out. No—I don't want to go anyplace public. I just want to get out of here for a while. I know a place where we can go, where we won't see anyone. We can take my car."

99

She drove them to a roadside place outside the town proper of Blood Flats, a little soft ice cream and hamburger shop. A plain white sign announced the name of the restaurant, *Diane's Tasty-Freeze*, in a cursive writing style that would have looked modern forty years ago. The thirtyish woman who manned the outdoor window counter was therefore almost certainly not the original Diane.

Lee took a seat on one of the picnic tables that had been set up for patrons. He chose the table located farthest from the restaurant. He wore a billed hat that he pulled down over his face. In the failing light, no one would have recognized him unless they were specifically looking for Lee McCabe; and he did not expect Sheriff Phelps or one of his deputies to materialize here at this hour. Nor was there much of anyone else. Much to Lee's relief, fellow patrons were obligingly absent. There was one woman in line at the service window in front of Dawn; but she took her order to her car and drove away. He and Dawn had the place to themselves.

Dawn bought them each a hamburger and fries with a fountain Coke. Two plastic cups of ice cream for dessert. She sat down across from Lee with the overflowing tray.

"Thanks," Lee said, helping himself to one of the sandwiches. "I guess I'm turning out to be a cheap date. You know, it's been a long time since I've been out to eat like this. This is nice, even if I am in hiding."

"You'll make it through this," Dawn said.

"I'm not doing such a great job so far. Every move I make seems to backfire in one way or another."

He knew that even his own considerable problems must seem small compared to hers. His enemies were without, after all; her enemies were within. He had never been good at cheering people up; he wasn't a counselor or a mentor at heart, like the Hunter or Marie Wilson. Nevertheless, he felt compelled to say something, to acknowledge her circumstances.

"I'm sorry," Lee said. "I mean about—"

"I know," she said. "And what I am running through my head right now is all the what-ifs. You know, I tried meth for the first time after a stranger offered it to me in the lobby of my dorm hall at college. What if I had refused him, like I should have? For that matter, what if I had been content to stay in Blood Flats, and live out the cycle of my parents and most of my classmates? I feel like one of those chumps in Greek mythology, who gets punished by the gods for arrogance, for trying to reach beyond their station."

"I'm sure it can't be that," Lee said. "I kind of see it the opposite way. If you were going to be punished for something, you'd be punished for wasting your life. Not for trying to make the most of it."

"Hmm, well, my attempt to become a doctor is going to result in my death. Make of that what you will. I'm not blaming anyone, you know. I walked into this trap—even if someone else put it there."

"That's one of the things the world does, doesn't it?" Lee observed. "The world is full of people who put traps for others to walk into."

Immediately after he said it, Lee knew that this was not the entire story. The world was also full of people like Ben and Marie—and Dawn. The problem was that all too often, the bad ones seemed to be winning.

They were disturbed by a burst of girlish laughter. A group of children—three girls about the same age as Ben's daughter—sat down at the table directly behind them. They had ice cream sundaes. At first Lee considered leaving; but the girls were absorbed in their ice cream and in their conversation. They looked far too young to recognize him. Then he remembered that Izzy had recognized him. But Izzy was an atypical eleven year-old girl.

Lee was about to relax again when he heard a man clear his throat.

Lee had no idea how long the man seated at the adjacent picnic table had been sitting there watching them. He was too far away to overhear their conversation—especially with the giggling young girls nearby—but he was close enough to allow Lee to see his teeth when he smiled. The man stood up, his long grey hair falling behind him. His cowboy boots clicked on the gravel and broken pavement as he approached.

Dawn turned when she saw that Lee was distracted by the man. Lee was somehow aware of his identity even before Dawn said his name.

"Lester Finn!" Dawn pronounced his name involuntarily with a short gasp, as if she had muttered an unholy oath.

"Dawn Hardin. First you were my best dope customer. Then you were my employee. Now you're Lee McCabe's dinner date. You seem to be suffering from an identity crisis." Then to Lee: "Yes, McCabe, I know who you are. You're famous, after all."

"What are you doing here?" Dawn asked.

"I make it a point to keep tabs on all my people," Lester said.

"I'm not your people!" Dawn hissed, her cheeks reddening.

"You *are* my people," Lester said. "Until the day I decide otherwise. And before this is over, I swear I'll see you crawl before me, and beg my forgiveness for your ingratitude. Down on your knees on the floor of the Boar's Head."

"You'll rot in hell before you see me step foot in that dump," Dawn retorted. "Or anywhere near you for that matter."

Lester chuckled. "This from a girl who blows strangers to feed a drug habit."

"Shut your mouth, Finn," Lee said. "If you've got something to say, you can say it to me."

Lee was already scanning the adjacent road and the area around them, looking for the men who would surely be there—or on their way. Perhaps Lester Finn had happened upon them—or he had merely been planning to harass Dawn for sport. In either case, though, he would already have notified his henchmen. Unless he was truly foolish or completely filled with false vanity.

Lee had a small pistol tucked away in an ankle holster beneath the leg of his jeans—another specimen from Ben's extensive gun collection. As he contemplated reaching for it, Lester seemed to read his mind.

"I'm sure you're armed," Lester said. "As am I. But we won't be having a shootout here. That's not what this is about. I've already paid other men good money to take care of that."

"Then what is this about?" Lee asked.

"I merely wanted to say, McCabe, that I respect you on some level, even though you will have to die at the hands of my people. You're a brave man. Foolish and young—yes, definitely. But brave, none-theless. This will have to end as it will in fact end—sooner or later. I'd like to think, though, that in another time and place, you and I might have been friends."

"I don't think so," Lee said. "You're a dope peddler and a whore runner and a murderer, from what I hear. Not the sort of person I usually include in my circle of friends."

"Tough talk from a man who can't even eat dinner in a public place for fear of arrest." Lester said. "Have it your way, though. My previous comments stand as I left them. My father was a marine in Korea. He was also a brave man."

Then Lester turned to walk away, but not before saying to Dawn: "You, though—you're scum. Thought you were some kind of princess, didn't you? Thought you were above people like me. Well, you don't look like much of a princess now."

Lee stood up. Lester heard him. Lester stopped but did not turn around.

"Hold your temper, McCabe. Or maybe you would like to shoot me in the back and see if you can find a place to hide before the law descends on you. You see that woman working that order window? There is a phone on the wall beside her. So if you shoot me, you'll have to shoot her as well in order to save yourself. Then there's the matter of those girls at the picnic table behind you. Would you like to make them collateral damage if we settle this here and now?"

Lee realized that Lester was right. He returned to his seat. Lester resumed walking toward the parking lot.

"You really ought to thank me, McCabe," Lester called over his shoulder. "Not just for the acknowledgement but for the gesture of chivalry. I'm giving you a free pass. This time."

Lester climbed into an old Cadillac. The engine started with a rumble and Lester drove off without looking back at them.

"Come on," Lee said. He scooped their unfinished meal onto the tray. "We've got to get out of here. Now that Lester has delivered his speech and made his exit, his gunmen can't be far behind. His 'people' as he calls them."

THEY DROVE AWAY, back toward Blood Flats. "Let me take you home," Dawn said. "Wherever you're staying."

Lee shook his head. "Too risky. Lester could follow you again. I'm sorry, Dawn. It looks like I've put you in danger."

"You're forgetting that I was the one who wanted to go out."

Lee insisted on exiting the vehicle long before they were close to her apartment. That was a risk, too: If Lester was "keeping tabs" on Dawn, then he likely knew where she was staying.

"I think that this is goodbye for a while," Lee said. "After tonight, there will be no respite for me. I know all about Lester's operations. He knows that I'm in Blood Flats. The time for talking is done. For both of us."

"Good luck," said Dawn.

"Good luck yourself," Lee said. "Thank you again for everything. Now I want you to do me one last favor."

"What is that?"

"Please leave town for a few days, until this is over. Lester is the sort of man who would kill you just out of spite. No—don't argue with me. Do it for my sake, if you want to think of it that way. I won't be distracted worrying about you."

"Okay," Dawn said. "I still have a few friends and relatives who haven't dropped me. I have an aunt over in Bardstown. She'd probably take me in if I asked her, at least for a while."

Lee noticed that there had been a trend of late: Women had been helping him in various ways, and he had been pushing them away with admonishments to be careful. Once again he was reminded of how Amy Sutter had paid the ultimate price for helping him. And once again he hoped that there would be no more like her—that such a fate would not befall Dawn. That somehow she could even find salvation from those ills that had already come to pass.

She was looking at him expectantly now. He tried to see her as she had been on that night, the honor student who had been so beautiful and confident, ready to take on the world. He tried to see himself as he had been: a free man who still had only a nodding acquaintance with death. A young man who had also been eager to take on the world—if in a somewhat different way.

He was unable to hold either image in his mind for long. They had both changed since then, and they were what they were—whatever they had once been.

He leaned across the front seat of her car and he held her briefly, chastely. Then he kissed her lightly on the cheek before releasing her and bidding her good night with a nod. It was a wordless expression and their mutual understanding of all that he could not give her. Of things that she would never, in all likelihood, receive from anyone— though she might have received so much. That part of her life was over now, before it had even really begun.

100

As he drove away from his encounter with Lee McCabe and the ex-princess turned whore, Lester Finn dialed the number for TJ Anderson. He told Anderson to summon his crew: His job had just become a lot easier. Lee McCabe was cornered now, right here in town.

So Lee McCabe was "hiding out" in Blood Flats, of all places. If his enemy was that brazen, then their encounter by the picnic tables would not have dissuaded him from his course. There would be no panicked flight to another location. Lester would kill Lee McCabe, with time to spare before either the Coscollinos or the various law enforcement agencies of the state became aware of his presence. The law would once again learn that it had no power to bend Lester Finn to its will; and the Coscollinos would look foolish for doubting him.

He did not regret his decision to let Lee McCabe live one more day. Killing him right there in the parking lot, before a gallery of witnesses, wouldn't have been a practical course of action. Nor would his Cadillac have been the ideal vehicle for tailing the young man. His vintage Eldorado Biarritz, with its tailfins and apple-red paint job, was about as inconspicuous as a fire engine. Nor could he have called in back-up: TJ Anderson would have never made it to the parking lot of the outdoor dairy in time.

No, he had performed well, in a manner that would have made his granddaddy proud: He had transformed the chance meeting into an opportunity to demonstrate his superiority—over Lee McCabe, that arrogant prick Paulie Sarzo, and certainly Dawn Hardin—who was beneath contempt. He had shown them all that he was the only one of the bunch who had true composure, true class, true style. These were qualities that the Coscollino men could never buy, not even with all their money. These were attributes that you were born with. You either possessed them, or you did not.

Once when he was channel-surfing, Lester had seen a documentary about the rules of medieval combat. Knights of the Middle Ages were bound by a warrior's code of honor. For example, if a knight happened upon an enemy who had not yet donned his armor, he would wait for his opponent to dress for combat before engaging him. That was something like what he had done this evening with Lee. And the memory of that exchange would make the killing of him an even sweeter victory.

101

L ee approached the Peaton Woods Furniture factory late in the afternoon of the next day, as the shadows were just beginning to lengthen.

It was a tactic that he had been taught in the Marine Corps, and it was particularly effective against an undisciplined, irregular enemy—the sort that often comprised the ragtag bands of Arab fighters peculiar to the war in Iraq and other localized conflicts. Such enemies were vigilant throughout the prime daylight hours, and grew wary once again at night. But in the hours between dinnertime and nightfall, their vigilance often lagged. This was the period when men's thoughts turned away from the business at hand—when cigarettes were smoked and conversation flowed freely.

Ben dropped him off a mile away from the factory, on a side road where there was virtually no chance that he would be seen. The older man had wanted to accompany him; but Lee had resolutely refused.

"At least let me stay nearby," Ben had said, running his hand across the stock of the shotgun that lay in the front seat of his pickup truck. "Or better yet, change your mind and let me go with you. If there's a gunfight it will be better to have two of us."

"The idea is *not* to get into a gunfight," Lee had told him. "And if there's two of us, that's double the chance that one of us will be seen." Lee had not wanted to remind Ben that he was past his prime, and his military training was many years in the past. Nevertheless, he said: "Don't forget, I was doing this sort of thing a few short months ago. This is no big deal for me—not really."

But of course, a mission of this nature was *always* a big deal. It was always a matter of life and death.

And now, crouched on the hillside near the side entrance of the factory, Lee felt acutely alone. It was the same feeling that he had felt at the beginning of his flight from the law and the other armed men: In the Marine Corps, he had been part of an organization—he had been one of a band of thousands. There had always been strength in numbers. This time, however, all the numerical strength was on the side of his enemies.

Lee peered through the brush at the two armed men who were posted on guard duty. They carried their weapons discreetly, tucked inside their belts, so that the guns would not be visible from the highway should someone drive past. Nevertheless, their posture lacked the furtiveness that Lee had always supposed criminals should have. It was as if their identity had been inverted, and they now considered themselves to be the establishment. *Well, perhaps there was some truth in that,* Lee thought: It was himself—and not these men—who was on the run and on the defensive because of the recent bloodshed that had taken place throughout the county. The law seemed to be leaving these men to go about their business.

Lee heard the sound of a car approaching on Briar Patch Road. The engine slowed down, eventually chugging to an idle. A horn sounded. Once, then again, with an air of impatience.

One of the armed men looked in the direction of the highway. "It's our friend," he told his companions with a note of heavy irony. "I'll go see to him. You get Lester."

Then one of them began walking casually toward the highway, down the sloping gravel drive, as the other disappeared inside the factory. Lee risked standing up to nearly his full height, reasonably sure that the camouflage would cover him adequately for a moment.

He saw the first guard unlock the padlock that connected the two lengths of chain at the end of the driveway. He waved impatiently at the driver of the blue Ford Escort that stood idling, its driver obviously impatient to be let inside.

The car rumbled up the driveway, stirring dust, as the guard walked back up behind it. Lee eased himself back down into the foliage, taking care to make his movement as slow and as fluid as possible.

When the second guard stepped out of the factory he was accompanied by Lester Finn. Lee thought about his recent encounter with Lester outside Diane's Tasty-Freeze. But that brought back thoughts of Dawn. Dawn, who was now doomed to an abbreviated life under the very best of circumstances.

The door of the Ford Escort opened and Lee was only mildly surprised to see that the driver of the car was Ron Norris.

Norris was wearing civilian clothes, obviously off-duty now. He and Lester Finn looked at each other and it was apparent that the two men were acquainted. Equally apparent was the fact that the rogue cop hated the tavern owner.

"Good afternoon, Deputy Norris," Lester said. "How kind of you to join us. Can I get you something? A beer, perhaps?"

Norris started to raise his fist at the aging hood; then he stopped himself when he became newly aware of the two armed men. So Norris contented himself with mere angry words:

"This entire thing has turned into one giant clusterfuck, Lester, and it's a clusterfuck of your making."

Lester snorted. Lee could tell that the small-time criminal boss was putting on a show of bravado for the benefit of the guards, who would be his men.

"I'm talking about Lee McCabe, Finn. Sooner or later he's going to be apprehended, and on that day he's going to start talking. Tell me, do you have any idea what McCabe saw in that trailer? *Do* you? For all you know, McCabe can name every man you hired."

"If that were the case, I think our young friend would already have turned himself in and started talking, don't you?"

Lee wondered if Lester knew about Norris's failed attempt to gun him down in the field. Probaby not. That was an incident that the cop would have seen no advantage in sharing.

Lester went on: "Lee McCabe knows nothing. Otherwise, he would never have run in the first place. And for all we know, McCabe may very well have finished off what those other men began. Maybe McCabe held a grudge against Fitzsimmons. Maybe he paused to put a bullet of his own in Fitzsimmons's head. Did you ever consider *that* possibility?"

"Jesus," Norris said, shaking his head. "You are so pathetic. Grasping at straws."

"And you're a dirty cop with a predilection for young girls. Ah— that smarted, didn't it? *Deputy* Norris."

Norris moved threateningly in Lester's direction, and the two guards reached for their weapons. The deputy checked himself once again. He realized that his police status would not help him here.

Lee noted Lester's reference to Norris and something about young girls. That would explain the deputy's involvement with Lester Finn. The cop must have been blackmailed, and he would buy his salvation by killing the only outsider who knew what had really happened in Tim Fitzsimmons's trailer that morning.

"Just so you know," Norris said. "The ballistics reports have come back, and they show that multiple weapons were fired inside that trailer, from multiple angles. That's more or less proof that more than one person was involved."

"So the law will conclude that Lee McCabe had an accomplice," Lester said. "And if you were smart you'd be back there working to convince them of that, instead of driving out here to yammer at me. Why don't you make yourself useful?"

The side door of the factory opened once again and now another man stepped outside. He had a stocky build and an olive complexion. His clothes didn't belong in Blood Flats, or anywhere in Hawkins County. Whoever he was, he wasn't a local, Lee decided.

Lester stiffened when the man approached. *Lester Finn is afraid of this guy*, Lee thought.

"Deputy Norris, this is Paulie Sarzo. Mr. Sarzo works with our friends in Chicago."

"Shut up, Lester," the man named Paulie said. "What do you think this is, a goddamned chamber of commerce meeting? I ought to slap you again."

Lee noted that Lester remained silent, though his face reddened. Lester *was* afraid of the stranger. No mistake about that.

"I know who you are," Norris said to Paulie, his voice trembling. "I know who you represent. And I'm telling you both that this has gone too far."

There was a moment of silence as the three men looked at each other. Then the one named Paulie finally spoke.

"You're telling me, huh? Is that it? *You* don't tell me *nothing*," Paulie said. Without warning, he punched Norris in the stomach. The cop doubled over, choking.

Paulie took a silencer-tipped pistol from his jacket. He pointed it at the cop's forehead. "You want out? Is that what you want? I'll take you out of it all right now."

"Paulie," Lester said. "Please. We still need Deputy Norris's cooperation. He's our eyes and ears on the inside, after all."

"He's a dirty cop and he'll sell us out as soon as he gets a chance," Paulie said. He held the muzzle of his pistol to Norris's head.

"Norris won't try to sell us out," Lester said. "You may recall that we have some 'insider's information' regarding certain aspects of Deputy Norris's personal life. Please, Paulie, forgive the good deputy for his poor attitude. Keep in mind that he's used to working on the other side. He doesn't understand matters of respect."

There was a long moment in which Lee believed that Norris was going to die, anyway. This man called Paulie seemed intent on spilling blood. There had been many like him among the insurgency in that faraway land—men for whom violence came naturally and casually.

"You got that right." Paulie reluctantly put the pistol away.

"Oh my God," Norris gasped, sensing his narrow reprieve.

"You never can trust a dirty cop," the Italian said. "And I understand, Deputy Norris, that you are a dirty cop in more ways than one."

Norris righted himself, shaking uncontrollably now, in a tremor that Lee, from his vantage point, perceived to be an equal mixture of fear and rage.

"Perhaps now you understand, Deputy," Lester began. "That 'getting out' isn't so easy. This isn't a bid on a piece of real estate. This is for keeps." Then he said to Paulie: "Norris here is afraid of Lee McCabe, and what Lee McCabe might say should he become a guest of the state or the county."

"Don't worry about him," Paulie said with a laugh. He placed a cigarette in his mouth and lit it. "Lee McCabe is a dead man, one way or another."

"Damn right!" Lester seconded.

"I'm going back inside," Paulie said to the tavern owner. "And when I come back, I don't want to see this piece of trash around here. I'll shoot him, do you understand?"

Lee could not be completely sure about the exact nature of the relationship between these three men; but the basic outlines were clear enough: The man named Paulie was a representative of a crime syndicate that stretched far beyond the borders of Hawkins County. Lester had mentioned that he came from Chicago; and Lee knew that the Windy City had long been home to organized crime. Somehow Lester was involved with such a group; and he had blackmailed Norris into cooperating with him—and them.

These three men might be in cahoots, but there was no harmony between them.

Nevertheless, Lee realized that their shared interests would be sufficient to get him killed. They would kill him—as they had killed other innocents—in order to suit their ends. And possibly they would turn against each other the following day. But this would not bring back their victims.

Lee realized now how naïve he had been, believing that he had left human evil behind him in Iraq. The men before him now were birthed by his own country—two of them were products of his hometown. As long as men like these existed, then any society might be in danger of descending into chaos. These were the wolves who were always at the door, in any country and in any time.

Then Lee had another thought—and one that might be far more useful to him. Paulie, Lester and Norris were presently standing close enough together to be captured in the frame of a single photograph.

He carefully laid down the gun he had brought with him. It was a Sig Sauer that he had borrowed from Ben's collection. Then he slipped his cell phone from his pocket. He had used the device's camera function only a handful of times, and he desperately hoped that he remembered the correct steps. Most of all he prayed that the flash was indeed toggled in the OFF position. A flash in the woods would surely alert these men and get him killed within the next thirty seconds.

Lee moved the cell phone's camera lens in front of one open eye. He needed to have the three of them in one shot—so as to form an indisputable photographic record that these men were indeed in regular communication.

And to whom would he take this photograph? To the sheriff who bore him a lifelong grudge? To the state police, who had now put a cash price on his head?

Well, he would answer that question later.

He clicked the camera button twice. Thankfully, there was no flash. But there were two very audible clicks.

"What was that?" Paulie asked, whirling in the direction of the woods. The Italian's eyes bored into the foliage were Lee was hidden. He had dropped his cigarette onto the blacktop.

"What was what?" Lester asked. "I didn't hear anything."

"I heard something in the woods over there." He withdrew his pistol again, the same gun that he had used to threaten Norris's life a few moments ago.

Lester laughed nervously. "Paulie, you're from Chicago, for goodness sake. You're not used to the woods. The woods are noisy—there are animals, and wind, and—insects. Rabbits all over the place, you know."

"Shut up!" Paulie snapped. He pointed his pistol in Lee's direction. Lee allowed himself only a very shallow breath. In order to draw his own gun, he would have to first set down the camera and then pick up his weapon. That much movement would alert Paulie, who would easily be able to kill him before he could fire on the Chicago mobster.

"That wasn't any rabbit," Paulie continued. "And it wasn't the wind, either. Do you feel any wind, you idiot? That was the sound of metal, like someone cocking a weapon, or—"

Paulie fired three quick shots in Lee's direction. The silenced pistol coughed and the bullets zinged through the leaves.

Lee used an old technique that he had sometimes used to steady himself in Iraq: He saw himself as a small child, in his mother's kitchen, during a brief period of tranquility between his parents. He focused on the feelings of calm and safety that the scene always brought him.

After the shots had been fired, he made a mental inventory of his body parts: No bullet had struck him. He was luckier than he had been when Norris had similarly fired at random.

"Paulie!" Lester shouted. "Please! There's nothing there!"

Paulie looked from Lester to Norris with visible disgust. "Idiots," he said. "I wish my uncle would give me the word to shoot you all."

With that pronouncement Paulie stalked back inside.

After Paulie had gone back inside, Lester turned to the rogue cop.

"You ought to be grateful, Norris," Lester said. "I saved your life a few moments ago. Paulie would have cheerfully shot you."

102

Paulie was alone in his rented room late that night when his Uncle Alfonzo called and scared the hell out of him.

It had not been a particularly pleasant evening anyway. The godforsaken state of Kentucky was too hot in June, and the wall-mounted air conditioning unit that he had to make due with was entirely inadequate. Mostly it just made noise, all the while cranking out stale-smelling air that was almost as hot as the air outside.

Then Lester sent him a whore and she, too, turned out to be entirely inadequate. She was in her mid-thirties, and by the looks of her, she had already birthed a sizable brood of little rednecks. The moment he laid eyes on her, Paulie knew that there was no way he could mount her. Why should he have expected any different? Everything in this part of the world was substandard—why shouldn't the whores be substandard, too?

Paulie had sent her away in tears, striking her across the face when she asked if she had to return the money.

"Keep it!" he shouted. "But get out of my sight!"

An hour later Lester had called him, obviously still intimidated, but at the same time indignant. "What's the idea, Paulie? Striking a girl like that?"

"That wasn't any girl, Lester. That was a worn-out old broad who will never see thirty-five again."

Lester had then launched into a long-winded spiel, explaining that all his good whores were based in Louisville, and why would he maintain any real beauties in Blood Flats, where there were so few customers, and that if Paulie really wanted a good whore, then he should allow Lester to set up something for him in Louisville, but there was still no need to smack a perfectly good whore in the face like that, and—

Paulie had terminated the call as Lester was still speaking, and then his Uncle Alfonzo had called.

"Are you having a nice vacation, Paulie?" the old man asked. Uncle Alfonzo's tone was not light, and his question had been anything but frivolous.

"No, no, Uncle Alfonzo. I mean yes. Or I mean, I'm wrapping this up."

"Paulie, Paulie. You disappoint me. You're doing anything and everything *but* wrap this up. The marine is still free and he can still tell a story that could bring all this crashing down on our heads. I can't let that happen. Do you understand me, Paulie?"

"Of course, Uncle."

"No, I don't think you do. I want you to remember a conversation we had a long time ago, when you were still a punk kid barely out of high school. I told you to go to college, get an education. Help the Family in some nice administrative role. Run one of our many businesses. But no, you were stubborn, Paulie. You didn't like to study and you thought you were a tough guy. You asked me to give you a street role in the Family. And I said, 'Paulie, that's a dangerous path. A road of no return that could get you killed.' Do you remember that conversation?"

"Sure I do, Uncle Alfonzo."

"Don't you 'Uncle Alfonzo' me. Listen: I'm not going to sacrifice the Family for you, Paulie, and I'm not going to sacrifice myself. And don't be thinking that you can just walk away from this. That option of doing something else—you gave that up a long time ago. Now do you understand what I'm getting at, Paulie?"

"Yes, sir."

"I hope you do, Paulie. Because it would break my heart to you know...To see you...fail."

For a long time after the call was concluded, Paulie shuddered as he stared at his cell phone. He didn't need any further explanation to grasp the significance of what his uncle had said. He was aware of the Code. He knew that the life he had chosen carried with it both incredible rewards and constant, deadly risks. He understood his uncle's notions of discipline. He knew that the Coscollino family had eliminated employees who were guilty of incompetence as well as disloyalty. This was not so much a matter or retribution as it was survival. The family could not risk the living presence of a disgruntled ex-employee. Paulie had been involved in the "resolution" of several of these personnel issues.

So far, to the best of Paulie's knowledge, this element of the Code had never been applied to an actual member of the family. But it was not unheard of in the wider world of *la cosa nostra*. As an organization became ever more desperate, so went its methods.

And so he knew that he would have to exercise his powers of creativity. The method that both Lester Finn and the police had been using—pursuing the ex-marine throughout the countryside—that clearly wasn't working. It wasn't working at all.

McCabe had grown up in this part of Kentucky. He knew the landscape intimately, and his military training had made him all the more formidable in the outdoors.

No, pursuit wasn't working; and in all likelihood, even the Family's resources wouldn't yield a successful outcome in this way. He would have to try something different. He would have to find a way to bring Lee McCabe to him.

He would also need some help. Well, help would be here soon. He had already made the necessary phone calls. Within hours he would be tracking Lee McCabe by more sophisticated methods.

Paulie leaned back on his bed, despising Hawkins County and

everyone in it more than ever. His very life depended on killing the young ex-marine. That was the only way to assure his return to grace in the eyes of Uncle Alfonzo.

If he pulled this off cleanly, in fact, Uncle Alfonzo's estimation of him might even increase. He might be moving up within the family in the near future.

Paulie pressed the button on his cell phone that summoned the device's name and contact number directory. He was going to have to make some additional calls before he went to sleep. His resources were already on the way; but he needed to tell those resources to hurry.

103

Ben Chamberlain detected nothing particularly suspicious about the man clad in the Central Kentucky Power and Light uniform.

The only thing unusual about him was his accent. His English bore the vestiges of a childhood in Russia, or some other godforsaken corner of the old Soviet Bloc. This was atypical in Hawkins County but not unheard of; and there were many recent East European immigrants in Lexington and Louisville.

When Ben answered the door, he was greeted by a blond man of perhaps thirty years of age, medium build and height. He wore a blue CKP&L uniform, and a photo nametag that looked official. The nametag identified him as Sergei Dunzhev.

"Hel-lo, sur," Sergei said, displaying a smile that promised prompt and courteous customer service. "I am so sorry to disturb you."

"That's alright," Ben said. "How can I help you?"

"Dere vaz a power sorge in one of the transformers that services this area," Sergei explained. "And ve've had some reports of damage to residential electrical facilities as a result."

"We haven't noticed any problems here."

"Are you sure? No fickering lights? No buzzing sounds in your fooz box?"

"No," Ben said.

"I see," Sergei said. "Der vaz a fire in a fooz box in house just down the road. Very bad. Occurred during za middle of da night. All because of dis power sorge."

"Well, I'll check my fuse box right away," Ben said. "What do I look for?"

This prospect made Ben a bit uneasy. His carpentry skills were strong, his plumbing skills middling. His skills regarding electricity and electrical infrastructure were practically nonexistent.

"You have to measure ohms coming into da fooz box," Sergei said. "If the ohms are too high, you may have risk of fire."

"Ohms," Ben repeated. He vaguely recalled hearing the term *ohm*, and he knew that it was somehow related to electricity. He didn't have any idea how many ohms a fuse box should contain. And he had no idea how to measure them.

Sergei seemed to sense his dismay. "If you vould like, sir, I can very quickly take a measurement of ohms for you."

"Maybe that would be a good idea. How long would it take?"

"Just a few minutes. Very queek."

"And you can do it now?"

Sergei beamed. "I can do now."

Ben had not the slightest misgivings as he opened the door and beckoned Sergei to come inside. His uniform and ID seemed impeccable. Nor was there anything about Sergei personally that gave him uncomfortable vibes. Other than a little trouble with the accent. But then—Ben realized that as a Hawkins County resident, his own regional accent would sound strange to some of his fellow native-speakers of English.

Then he remembered: A wanted fugitive was staying in his house. Lee was sitting in the living room at this very minute.

Lee's face was plastered all over the newspapers and the local news websites. His face had been shown on television many times.

What were the odds that this man would recognize Lee?

About fifty-fifty. And there was no way to tell Lee to lock himself in a bedroom without arousing suspicion.

Therefore, allowing this man inside his home would constitute an unacceptable risk.

"Uh, hold on," Ben said. "Could we do this some other time? My wife is asleep right now. She has migraine headaches. Terrible, you know."

This lie caused him no small amount of anguish as poor, murdered Julie came to mind. However, it was the only excuse he could think of in the space of five seconds.

Sergei paused on the edge of the threshold. "Of course." He removed a business card from the breast pocket of his uniform. It bore the logo of the CKP&L company, his own name, and a telephone number. "Feel free to call me to reschedule. I can come almost anytime, Monday through Friday, between the hours of ten a.m. and seex p.m."

104

The man who called himself Sergei Dunzhev walked back to his truck. Ben had no way of knowing that his real name was Alexei Primakov, and that he was an employee of the Coscollino crime family.

Alexei's smile departed as he started the van, which had only that morning been painted to resemble a service van of Central Kentucky Power and Light. He was one of a crew of more than a dozen men whom Paulie Sarzo had charged with finding Lee McCabe. Unlike the men hired by Lester Finn, these men were not random ex-cons and addicts. They were professionals. Many had been trained by the militaries of various countries.

Also unlike the men hired by Lester Finn, Paulie's operatives were not roaming the countryside with guns. They were tracking Lee McCabe through a variety of more sophisticated methods. These included ruses like the one that Alexei Primakov was currently undertaking. If Lee McCabe had taken refuge in a private household, one of these men would find him.

Alexei drove the van about a quarter mile down the road, where it would not be visible from the house belonging to Ben Chamberlain.

Alexei parked the van and retrieved a laptop computer with a wireless Internet connection from beneath the driver's seat.

It took him only a few minutes to discover that Ben Chamberlain's wife, Julie Chamberlain, had a DOB of 9-10-1970, and that she had died only a few years ago.

Had Chamberlain remarried? Possible—but not probable. There were no online records of such a marriage, and Alexei's tools gave him access to every known public database.

Alexei read further and discovered that the late Julie Chamberlain had been killed by a burglar who was a probably meth addict.

That might mean nothing—or everything.

In either case, though, Ben Chamberlain had been lying. And he had lied for a reason. This warranted further investigation.

SHORTLY BEFORE DARK, Alexei parked the van near the dead end of a gravel road that ran perpendicular to the road on which Ben Chamberlain lived. No one would bother the vehicle here—at least not for a few hours, and a few hours would be sufficient.

Alexei changed into a camouflage-style hunting outfit. He smeared a dark substance from a tube onto the pale skin of his face. There was a 9-mm Beretta in the van's glove compartment. Alexei withdrew the gun and placed it inside one of the pockets of the hunting fatigues. Then he removed a camera with a long telephoto zoom lens from a storage compartment in the back of the van.

He used a compass and a personal GPS system to thread his way through the fields and woods back to Ben Chamberlain's house. He finally arrived at the edge of the backyard, where Lee McCabe had arrived only a few days prior.

He found a position amid the trees where he would have a clear view of the house, but where anyone inside the house would have difficulty seeing him. The angle of the fading sunlight, his camouflage, and the trees all weighed in his favor.

Alexei worked for the Coscollinos, but he was no fighter. He could use a gun if he had to, though gun work was not his specialty. He hoped that he would not have to use the Beretta.

He leaned back and pointed the camera at the house. He had to wait fifteen minutes before he detected any movement in what appeared to be the kitchen window.

Finally a male figure appeared: This was definitely not Chamberlain, but another man who appeared to be much younger.

He snapped three photos in rapid succession. Then he compared the pictures he had taken to a picture of Lee McCabe that he had stored on his cell phone. This was the now ubiquitous shot of him in his Marine Corps uniform.

Alexei smiled. It appeared to be a match. This would mean a nice bonus from the Coscollino family.

And he had not even had to kill anyone.

105

Paulie Sarzo told Big John Lewis the news about Lee McCabe being discovered in town. Big John had driven down from Cincinnati only yesterday.

They were seated around a little table in Sarzo's rented room. Tony Loscatti and two other Coscollino men had rented the adjacent rooms.

They had plenty of men.

They knew where McCabe was.

Now all that was left was to kill McCabe—but to do so in a way that would not cause Uncle Alfonzo any more grief. And that would mean killing him quietly, without drawing additional media attention. Ideally, Lee McCabe would be captured, killed execution style, and then quietly buried in a field somewhere in Hawkins County. Alfonzo had made it clear that he didn't want to see any more public massacres like the gunning down of the college girl in the blue Honda. That would add fuel to the chain reaction that threatened to topple the Family.

They looked at the screen of the laptop computer that lay open on the tabletop. On one side of the screen was the media-circulated photo of Lee McCabe. On the other side was the photo that Alexei had taken earlier that evening.

The photo had been checked and verified by experts who occasionally did freelance work for the Coscollino family. The family had an extensive network of experts in many fields: men—and more than a few women—who would work for anyone for the right price. Experts who conducted all of their trade with online aliases, email addresses, and numbered accounts in banks located in Switzerland and the Cayman Islands.

"It's a match, then?" Big John asked.

"Our guy in Amsterdam says there is a 97% probability of match." Paulie said.

The freelance photo analyst in Amsterdam also worked for the Amsterdam police department. His judgment could be trusted. And even to the untrained eye, the subjects of the two photos looked substantially alike.

"Good enough," Big John said.

"So this is where you come in. My uncle trusts you. McCabe is staying in the house of a local man named Ben Chamberlain. We don't know how Chamberlain is involved in all of this. There's no family connection that we could find, and Chamberlain is twenty years older than McCabe. But we did find out that Chamberlain's wife was killed a few years ago by a meth addict. Maybe one of Lester Finn's customers."

Big John sniggered. "A vigilante. Anyone else living in the house?"

"Yeah, Chamberlain's eleven-year-old daughter. But she shouldn't give you any trouble."

"I should say not," Big John raised his eyebrows and smiled meaningfully but said nothing. Paulie was aware that Lewis had some unsavory predilections. Desires that were unspeakable even on this distant side of the law. Big John made regular trips to Thailand and South America, where young girls could be obtained almost as easily as grown women.

"I'd like to go in there right now," Paulie said. "We have plenty of men to take them both out—even if they resist. But Uncle Alfonzo wants this done discreetly."

"Your uncle is right," Big John said. "If we go in that house we will have to kill this man Chamberlain, too, and possibly his daughter. More civilian deaths. That would turn the cops rabid and give the media freaks a field day. That would mean even more national attention. The kind of attention your uncle doesn't like."

Paulie nodded. A part of him did want to order a frontal assault on the house where Lee McCabe was holed up. But another part of him knew better: There were too many things that could go wrong with such an operation. A shootout might draw not only police and the media, but local vigilantes as well. Kentucky was gun country, wasn't it?

They could get away with killing McCabe in broad daylight. Half the country thought that McCabe was a cold-blooded killer-for-hire, anyway. But all hell might break loose if they ended up killing a widowed father and his adolescent daughter.

Paulie tensed. *This was war, wasn't it? What about the concept of "collateral damage"?* Well, there was no way around it: He could not risk incurring the wrath of Uncle Alfonzo any more than he already had.

"So what do you have in mind?" he asked Big John at length.

"All we have to do is watch that house," Big John said. "It all comes down to surveillance and a well-timed shot from a high-powered rifle. I have several men in Cincinnati who can do that. Then we'll need two cleaners to make sure that there's nothing left for the media or the local citizens to gawk at."

Cleaners were men who specialized in the removal of crime scene evidence—especially murders. In a situation like this, a team of skilled cleaners could quickly make a body disappear. They could also remove any crime scene traces of blood or other bodily tissues, which were inevitable in any hit with a firearm.

"I figure we position one shooter, one spotter, and two cleaners near the house," Big John said. "McCabe is obviously going in and out. We wait until he exits and then we pop him and bag him."

"How long will it take for you to put a team in place?" Paulie asked.

"Give me twelve hours," Big John said.

Paulie felt the blood rush to his head. Big John's proposal was perfectly reasonable. It made sense, and it would conform with Uncle Alfonzo's wishes. He also knew that Big John Lewis had a superior level of experience in these matters. He had conducted many covert hits for the Family.

However, Paulie was also acutely aware that the clock was moving against them. At any moment Lee McCabe might decide to take off for another town or state; and this time they might lose his trail for good. Or worse yet, the police might take him into custody. Then he would be beyond their reach—the worst scenario of all.

Lee McCabe's knowledge of the Family's operations in central Kentucky now extended far beyond the events that took place in that trailer. He had been seen in the office of one of Lester's operatives—the garage owner whom he had killed in a gunfight.

Who knew what Lee McCabe knew? And if he were captured, the government would be eager to listen to his story. Not the local police, perhaps, but the Kentucky state police and the FBI. The few crimes that McCabe had actually committed—the murder of a drug dealer and resisting arrest—would be hardly worth the state's time. They would offer McCabe immunity in exchange for turning state's witness. And this was a deal that McCabe would readily accept.

"*We can't wait!*" Paulie said. He was seized by a sudden urge to personally drive over to Ben Chamberlain's house and gun down everyone inside. "*We can't lose a single minute. I want to kill Lee McCabe right now. Tonight!*"

"Paulie, Paulie. You know better than that. Sooner or later McCabe is going to leave the house for something. Maybe he's got a girlfriend in town, maybe he decides to go for a stroll. When he does, we do it. One shot. He'll never even know what hit him. Just give me twelve hours. Please. It's not much time to put a team in place. Then it will be done."

There seemed to be a condescending subtext in Big John's words.

A subtext that suggested that he, Paulie, would never have been a Coscollino man if he hadn't been born into it. *Did Big John look down on him?* he wondered. This would be a topic for him to contemplate later.

For now Paulie considered Big John's proposal: The potential delay was not the only aspect of Big John's plan that bothered him. He had wanted to have a wounded and bleeding Lee McCabe brought before him, so that he could watch his adversary beg for his life before he personally pulled the trigger. What Big John was suggesting was a military-style surgical strike. Impersonal. Technical.

It was strangely unsatisfying.

"Okay," Paulie said finally. He was willing to forfeit satisfaction if he could be sure that the problem would be taken care of. "Twelve hours, right?"

"Less than twelve hours. Alexei is watching the house as we speak. We sent our other investigators home, but Alexei is good: He's the only one who found McCabe, and McCabe won't be able to leave that house without him knowing about it."

"If Alexei is so good, couldn't Alexei go ahead and take the shot? The clean-up work is a secondary issue."

Paulie knew that this was not completely true; nor was his proposition completely reasonable. But he was frustrated; and he found himself suddenly resentful of Big John Lewis—this man who seemed to know everything, but who was telling him that it would take another half-day or more to kill Lee McCabe.

Big John shook his head. "Alexei is as timid as a rabbit. A first-rate investigator and surveillance guy, but not the man you want behind the trigger when a shot really counts. And this shot will count. I figure we'll get one chance at McCabe—and if we don't take him out then he'll go back into hiding."

Paulie Sarzo pounded his fist on the table. "*No!* If this way fails, then we do it *my* way: We go in there like men and we take them all out if we have to: every man, woman, and child. Leave as much blood as necessary. Screw the news and the bad publicity."

There, thought Paulie. *Let's see you argue with that.*

"Paulie, Paulie. I'm only doing my best to fulfill your uncle's wishes."

"I don't care. We don't know what McCabe knows: But if he leads the law to Lester Finn, then he eventually leads the law to us. And if that happens, 'my uncle' Alfonzo will put someone at the bottom of Lake Michigan."

Paulie stared at Big John, and reminded him of what he already knew.

"And that someone might be me. And maybe you, too."

106

"Now where are you going?" Ben Chamberlain asked. Lee was sitting on the front steps, lacing up his boots. A single light burned overhead in the front hall, casting long shadows. It was past ten o'clock in the evening.

A pistol that Lee had borrowed from Ben lay on the step below where he was sitting. Lee picked up the pistol and stood.

"Call it another reconnaissance mission,"

"A reconnaissance mission," Ben said. "Care to fill me in?"

Something in Ben's tone suggested an air of confrontation. Lee could not imagine why this should be the case; but he was still not fully acquainted with his host—this man who had opened up his home as a base of operations against Lester Finn. Lee also realized that despite their common cause, Ben had his own agenda. His commitment to Lee was based only on their mutual goal of destroying Lester Finn. His outward generosity was not a gesture of charity. Ben saw him as a tool for extracting his long-awaited revenge on the man who was responsible for the murder of his wife. Lee knew that he would forget this fact at his peril.

Lee said: "I've been thinking: I need to gather some concrete evidence that ties Lester Finn to those murders at the Tradewinds."

"Go on," Ben said.

"Then I can go to some outside law enforcement agency. To hell with Sheriff Phelps and Hawkins County. I'll go to the state police. Maybe even the feds. I already have evidence that proves Ron Norris is a dirty cop."

"If you've got that much, then why not go to the police now?"

"No. I've left them a loophole. I can prove that Norris is involved in this, but I can't prove that I didn't kill my neighbors at the Tradewinds. For that I need to get closer to Lester Finn. I need to watch him and see if he'll lead me to the remaining killers. I know that one of the shooters was Jimmy Mack, a local man. I could identify him, but he's dead now. He can't do me any good."

"But can't you see?" Ben asked. "He can do you just as much good dead as he could alive. I've been thinking about what you told me—about the ledgers you found in Jimmy Mack's office. The police would have found those, too. They'll be starting to piece this together."

"Maybe. But I can't count on that. If Norris got to the ledgers before Sheriff Phelps, he probably destroyed them. That's what I would do if I were him. And if Phelps is in on it, too, then there is absolutely no chance that the evidence in Jimmy Mack's office will prove anything. Working together, Phelps and Norris could easily have buried that entire connection. That's why I need to watch Lester Finn. I've got my camera. Sooner or later Lester will lead me to the other killers."

"You really think that you can take on Lester Finn, Lee? Keep in mind that he keeps a small army on his payroll."

"True. But Lester has already proven that he's capable of making stupid mistakes. He approached Dawn and me openly, so that he could make a grand gesture to satisfy his ego. He could have killed or captured me then."

"And you can bet that he still intends to kill you. That's the problem with your whole game plan, Lee. You can't get close to Lester Finn. He knows who you are."

"He does," Lee admitted.

There was an edge to Ben's voice. "So let me do it, Lee. Tell me what evidence you need. I can walk right into the Boar's Head, and Lester Finn will think nothing of it. Let me fight with you instead of standing on the sidelines like a damned spectator."

So that was the source of Ben's irritation. He felt that Lee was somehow slighting him by not soliciting his active involvement. Or he was afraid that Lee would cheat him out of the revenge that he believed to be rightfully his.

Of course Ben wouldn't be able to grasp the real reason that Lee had deliberately left him out of it all: Ben was a good man; but he was also a hothead who was spoiling for blood vengeance. He had made that much clear on the first day of their meeting. He was determined to kill Lester Finn in order to avenge his wife. To kill him at all costs.

And if Ben were to be killed in the course of this, it would be another innocent death on his own head. He would also be responsible—if indirectly—for making Izzy grow up an orphan.

"No," Lee said sharply. "I've already put you and your daughter in enough danger. I'm risking your lives simply by being here. I won't make it even worse by taking you along on a trip that might get you killed."

Ben stepped closer to Lee. "I think I already told you that I have my own reasons for helping you out with this. You talk about taking chances with our lives. I'm taking a chance simply by living in the same town with Lester Finn. That shit he sells already caused the death of my wife. Izzy will be in high school in a few years. I can't keep her sheltered from what's out there forever."

"If I can take out Lester Finn, then the county's number one source of meth will be gone long before Izzy gets anywhere near high school."

Ben's cheeks had gone red. A vein protruded from his forehead. *"My wife is dead, Lee—because I wasn't here to protect her. I'm not going to make the same mistake with my daughter. Now let me help you, damn it! Like I've been telling you!"*

There was a long stretch of silence. Ben stared at the ground, tears of rage gathering in his eyes.

"Son of a bitch!"

Lee stepped back, giving Ben room to vent his fury. How could he explain to Ben that there was a time for a man to fight, and a time for a man to leave the fighting to others? He understood the older man's feelings; but he also knew that Ben was driven by these feelings—a high-octane combination of rage and the desire for revenge. Lee knew from his months in Iraq that men who were driven by these emotions often took foolish risks.

"I'm sorry," Lee said. "But I already have multiple deaths on my hands. I don't want yours on my hands, too. Say what you will about this being your fight; but you were living your life in peace until I came along. If you want to go to war with someone after I'm out of the picture, be my guest. For now, though, I'm going to have to ask you to leave the operations side of things to me. Sorry; but that's the way it's got to be."

Ben started to protest but Lee cut him off.

"I might also remind you that you've got a daughter to take care of. Izzy has already lost one parent."

"I know, I know."

"Don't do anything that might make her lose two, then. Hell, Ben, I know how you feel. But you've got to think of Izzy."

"I love Izzy more than anything in the world."

"I know you do."

Ben sighed. "Alright. We'll do it your way, then. At least let me drive you, though."

"No."

"You don't even trust me to drive you?"

"It's not a matter of trusting you. It's a matter of the way I need to do this. Where I'm going, I'll go alone."

Lee sensed that he had secured Ben's acquiescence, although the other man did not fully agree with him. Lee was anxious to end this discussion before Ben could think of more counterarguments.

And then Ben laughed, though not unkindly. Lee decided that he would probably always have a hard time figuring out Ben Chamberlain.

"I'll be damned, Lee. You know what that reminds me of? You sound like Sergeant Elias in that scene in *Platoon*. When he takes his leave of Charlie Sheen."

Lee forced a smile. "I feel a bit like Sergeant Elias just now."

"And you'll remember what happened to Elias," Ben said. "The evil sergeant shot him."

ON THE WAY out the door, Lee thought about the last part of his exchange with Ben.

He had grown up watching those old war movies from the 1980s: *Platoon*, and *Top Gun*, and the various iterations of *Rambo*. In those days he and his mother had lived on a severely restricted budget; but those movies could be borrowed from the library. Occasionally she would buy him his own copy at a local garage sale, and then he could watch the heroes resolve their problems of war and death multiple times.

It seemed strange now to compare the plots of those films to his own predicament. The heroes of those films had seldom appeared helpless before the forces arrayed against them. Maverick Mitchell and the eponymous hero of the *Rambo* movies had possessed an instinctive knowledge that told them what to do next; such was the province of the fictional hero.

Lee did not know if what he was about to do was right—or foolhardy and doomed to failure. He knew only that he must take action. The forces aligned against him were surely taking action even now. They were drawing nearer, and sooner or later, they would close in. It would be better to die on the offense, he reasoned, than to wait for them to make a victim of him.

107

From the top of the stairs, Isabelle Chamberlain listened to the conversation between Lee McCabe and her father. They could not see her, but she could hear every word of their conversation, and its overall gist made her heart ache.

Lee was leaving, and he was going to place himself in considerable danger.

She could feel a nervous little pit deep in her stomach, like she did the night her mother had died in the hospital, following her injuries from the break-in. Isabelle was both sad and frantic at the same time.

In the few days that Lee McCabe had taken refuge in their house, Izzy had come to deeply admire him. *No—it was more than simply a matter of admiring him. Why couldn't she admit it to herself, even?*

Lee was strong and confident, and she felt so safe when he was around her. He didn't talk much; but when he did he always said something kind. And he was handsome, too—though not in the way of the boys at school who were generally regarded as "cute."

She knew that Lee had been to war—as her father had been—and that Lee had survived many bad things in Iraq. (Izzy could find

Iraq on a world map, though she had only a basic grasp of the politics that surrounded the two American wars in that faraway country.) She knew that Lee was in trouble now. There were people who were saying that Lee had done some very bad things.

But she was sure that Lee would never do anything bad. *He was good—wouldn't any girl fall in love with him? So why did she feel so embarrassed about it?*

It was the age difference, of course. Lee McCabe was a grown man and she was a little girl of eleven. There was no way he would notice her.

Today. But things might be different in the future.

She knew that her mother had been a very beautiful woman—why shouldn't she be beautiful someday as well? She had her mother's dark hair and big brown eyes. She hadn't yet started to develop as some of her friends had, but time would take care of that, wouldn't it?

As she heard Lee McCabe prepare to leave, she allowed herself to indulge in a fantasy that was as pleasant as it was embarrassing: She saw herself as a young woman of twenty, as tall and as beautiful as her mother had been. She was walking down the aisle of her church in a wedding dress, while Lee McCabe waited for her at the altar.

Was this fantasy really such a stretch? Lee McCabe had mentioned that he was twenty-three. He was barely more than ten years older than her. She knew that her mother had been seven years younger than her father.

So it really wasn't such a stretch at all...

But it would never come true if Lee got himself killed.

She wanted to go with him. She didn't dare ask: She knew that there was no way either her father or Lee would agree to such a plan. They would say that she was only eleven years old (*almost twelve!*) and that was true—but this eleven-year-old girl had proved a good match for Lee in their backyard that day, hadn't she? Had Lee forgotten how good she was with a slingshot?

Below her, Lee was bidding her father farewell.

It was now or never. If she hesitated, she might lose him forever.

There was really no question about it; her decision was already made. She walked carefully (but quickly) on her tiptoes so that they would not hear her. She padded down the hall, then turned into her bedroom. From the top drawer of her bureau she removed the slingshot—the same one that she had used to confront Lee on that first day.

She turned to the darkness outside her bedroom window. Did her father know about her secret way of exiting the house after dark? (*If that were the case, it wouldn't be a secret anymore, would it?*)

When she left her bedroom at night, she never went beyond the backyard; but sometimes the very act of climbing down the side of the house was thrilling. And it wasn't dangerous—not really. It was no different than climbing on a ladder, and her dad climbed up and down ladders all the time.

Izzy lifted her bedroom window open and unlatched the screen. Like always, the screen came out easily. She leaned the screen against the interior wall. Warm night air flowed into the room, along with a large moth that had been drawn by the light.

A moment of hesitation usually preceded her first step outside. This was not the case tonight, as she realized that she would have to catch up with Lee. Izzy swung her body into the empty space, bracing her hands against either side of the window frame.

She stood on the roof just outside the window. The pitch was so slight here that she had little trouble maintaining her balance.

The trellis was a few short steps away, at the roof's edge. This was the only part that caused her a little hesitation—that first glance down into the yard. She had never had an excessive fear of heights; but it was two stories down to the ground, after all.

The trellis was covered with ivy. It smelled wet and green. The plants were smooth and moist to her touch. The ivy was thick at this point in June, but there were enough gaps to allow her sufficient handholds and footholds in the wooden latticework.

In a moment she was climbing down the trellis, the leaves of the ivy tickling her cheeks and nose as she descended. Gnats and other nocturnal insects skittered against her face, arms, and legs.

Her feet hit the ground. She picked up her slingshot. (It had fallen from her back pocket on the way down.) Lee McCabe had exited from the front door, so she would have to hurry in order to catch him.

lexei watched a lone figure exit Ben Chamberlain's house through the front door. The figure crept low and moved furtively.

It was Lee McCabe. It had to be.

Alexei examined the moving figure with a pair of night-vision binoculars. It was indeed Lee McCabe.

Then he saw another figure run around from the back of the house: a person who was considerably smaller than Lee McCabe—apparently a child or an adolescent.

The eleven-year-old daughter of Ben Chamberlain, perhaps?

Alexei didn't care about the young girl. One way or another, she was worthless to him. He cared only about Lee McCabe—the man whose death would bring him a large windfall bonus from the Coscollino family.

When he saw Lee McCabe he saw dollar signs.

This could mean the ruination of everything. While Lee McCabe might only be out for a stroll, there was also a chance that he was departing the Chamberlain house for good.

That would mean the end of the bonus that Paulie Sarzo had promised him upon McCabe's death, wouldn't it? And if the Coscollinos decided that McCabe's escape was somehow his fault, it might mean the end of his life. He was responsible for keeping tabs on McCabe until the execution team arrived.

Alexei brought his cell phone to his ear after pushing the button that would call John Lewis, the massive, unpredictably violent American whom they all called Big John.

Big John answered the phone immediately.

Trembling a little, Alexei said: "Meestur Lewis, sir, I think ve might have a problem."

109

"We move *now!*" Paulie shouted. "Now!"

Big John had just terminated his call with the cowardly Russian—the one who could successfully track men for death but could not bring himself to pull the trigger.

Now he did not have to worry about Ben Chamberlain or any other collateral parties. They would intercept Lee McCabe out in the open and then they would kill him.

But not before they had made him suffer for all the trouble he had caused.

Paulie Sarzo slapped Big John Lewis on the shoulder and the big man flinched. Paulie had intended it as a show of camaraderie; but the hit man seemed to interpret it as a sign of disrespect. Paulie pulled back, wondering if Big John was going to strike him in response. Finally Big John smiled; even he would not dare raise a hand against the nephew of Alfonzo Coscollino. But Big John had wanted to, for a moment. Paulie had seen the desire in his eyes.

Never mind—to hell with Big John. Right now his only concern was Lee McCabe. Within the hour he would see Lee McCabe dead. Then he would report his triumph to Uncle Alfonzo and gain a new level of respect in the old man's estimation.

And he would never have to worry about showing respect to Big John Lewis again. Nor to anyone.

He might even be the head of the family someday. It was certainly not beyond the scope of possibility.

He realized that he was getting ahead of himself. But if he succeeded, there was no reason not to believe that such things could come to pass.

He paced over to the wall that separated his own room from Tony Loscatti's.

"Tony! Time to get your ass moving!"

Paulie smiled. Lee McCabe didn't know it—but he was already dead.

110

His heart in his throat, Alexei began to trail Lee McCabe through the darkness. McCabe was moving quickly, and Alexei's lungs strained for air in the heat of the summer night. Compared to his native Moscow and his current home of Chicago, June in Kentucky seemed like a tropical jungle.

"You've got to follow him!" Big John had ordered over the phone, in a tone that brooked no discussion. "Tell us where he goes, and then we'll corner him."

Alexei reluctantly agreed. No one needed to tell him what Big John would do if he refused or simply disobeyed. Before hanging up, Lewis had asked if he was armed. Alexei had responded in the affirmative. He did have his pistol. But he had only fired it a handful of times at a target range.

McCabe broke through a patch of trees at the edge of the road and into an illuminated area of moonlight. Alexei jumped behind a tree as Lee stopped and whirled around. He was sure that the fugitive American could not have heard his steps. At this distance, even his labored breathing should have been inaudible.

He held his breath until the American resumed his forward pace. No, McCabe had probably not heard him, after all.

The night was by no means silent: A chorus of crickets and cicadas chirped incessantly. The damned bugs had annoyed Alexei a few minutes ago, but now he was grudgingly thankful for them. Their songs would provide cover if he were unlucky enough to step on a branch or a pile of crunchy dried leaves from the previous season.

McCabe slowed his steps again, as if a sound had distracted him. This time Alexei was certain that the American could not possibly have detected his presence. He had not even moved yet.

Then Alexei saw what had made the sounds that spooked McCabe: The child (whom Alexei could now recognize to be a young girl) was following Lee as well. She was hiding behind a tree, watching McCabe.

McCabe did not seem to be aware of her position, though he had apparently heard her steps.

After waiting for what seemed like an eternity, Lee McCabe started forward again. The young girl trailed after him, darting from tree to tree.

And then Alexei, in his turn, followed. Perhaps he did not even have to follow the man with the gun. Maybe he could simply follow the young girl, who was doing a very good job of trailing McCabe through the darkness.

He swore under his breath: *Chert voz'mi*—what a coward he was! And to think that his father had been a member of the elite *Spetsnaz* special forces in the former USSR. His father had fought bravely in Afghanistan in the 1980s. And now he, the son of a *Spetsnaz* warrior, was timidly following a young American girl in order to avoid getting too close to another man who carried a gun.

Alexei decided (for the umpteenth time) that he had indeed made a mistake, getting into this line of work. His jobs for the Coscollinos and others like them kept him supplied with all his favorite luxuries; but perhaps it was no longer worth it. No, it wasn't: He should have gotten a regular job, where he wouldn't have to carry guns or face other men who carried them.

Chert voz'mi! He repeated the curse to himself and began walking again.

111

Alexei continued to track his quarry as Lee McCabe proceeded up Pond Mill Road, in the direction of the town proper of Blood Flats.

The girl who was following Lee—who Alexei now assumed to be Ben Chamberlain's daughter—trailed Lee at a somewhat shorter distance.

At intervals Alexei called John Lewis on his cell phone to relay McCabe's progress. Alexei was able to gather that Big John Lewis—along with Paulie Sarzo and Tony Loscatti—had left Blood Flats by car and were heading towards Lee.

Alexei's nervousness was growing. Although he had done many surveillance jobs, his surveillances were always "cold." He gathered information on targets long before the actual hit came. Sometimes there was no actual hit involved at all; the victim might be a person whom the Coscollinos merely wanted to blackmail or manipulate in some way.

This was a first: he was following an armed man who might turn around and shoot him at any moment. And his fear was compounded by the humiliation of the girl—her presence mocked him, suggesting that he was intimidated by mere child's work.

He watched the girl's silhouette as she appeared briefly in the moonlight, then disappeared back into the shadows. She showed no fear and her movements appeared effortless.

Alexei hated her.

He speed-dialed John Lewis again and gave him another report on Lee's whereabouts.

"We're almost there," John Lewis said. "McCabe is obviously heading toward the town, probably to make some sort of a stand. Based on that, he should be making a right turn onto Highway 1634 at any minute."

"What do you want me to do?"

"Follow him, you idiot. What do you think?"

112

Halfway up Pond Mill Road, Lee became aware that there were two people following him.

One was following him closely, the other seemed to be trailing at a considerable distance.

The distant one had already revealed himself several times. Lee had furtively turned around and there he was: a man of medium height and slight build. He seemed to be making some effort to conceal himself; but he wasn't doing a very good job of it. He was walking straight up the road, almost as if he were out for an evening stroll.

His second follower was more skillful: He had not yet seen this person. He had only heard the evidence: the occasional sounds of crunching leaves, and muffled footfalls moving through the long grass at the side of the road.

His first impulse was to immediately take evasive action: there were plenty of woods all around him, and he could easily dive into the pitch blackness of the trees, where it would be nearly impossible for his pursuers to see him.

He decided to wait, though, so that he could figure out the situation.

The two people who were now following him weren't mere assassins. They had already had multiple chances to take clear shots at him. They were most likely working in coordination with some other person or group of people.

Which would mean that they would be directing these other attackers toward him. He had heard his distant follower speak into a cell phone in a low voice. Lee had been unable to decipher any of the words; but the man's voice had sounded tense.

The question was: where would the attack come from? It would be a good idea to figure that out before he took any evasive action. He knew that he did not have much time to make his decision.

The woods were the option that made the most sense: But what if there were more attackers who would emerge from the woods? He slowed his pace and tried to concentrate on the sounds around him. If a group of men were approaching from the woods on either side of him, he would likely be able to hear them. It would be almost impossible for a team of men to move through mid-summer foliage without making any noise at all.

Of course, the chattering crickets and cicadas weren't helping him. Their collective din could mask many other sounds in the surrounding countryside.

Then he saw a pair of approaching headlights. Ordinarily, this would be no particular cause for concern. This was a public highway, after all, and it was a major route between the town of Blood Flats and a belt of residential homes and farmlands to the west of town.

But the appearance of the headlights might be related to the fact that he was being followed.

His wariness increased as the vehicle gradually dropped its speed. A few seconds ago it had been traveling at perhaps fifty miles per hour. Then it slowed: Lee guessed to forty m.p.h.

Then to around thirty m.p.h.

He whirled to get another look at the man following him on the road. The man was talking into his cell phone and pointing frantically in Lee's direction. Now the glare of the headlights illuminated him.

His follower was carrying a gun in one hand and a cell phone in the other.

Lee dove for the adjacent ditch just as the car screeched to a stop. Multiple car doors opened. He heard at least two men shouting angrily.

Shots. They were firing in his direction.

Luckily, though, the shooters didn't seem to have a fix on his exact location. They were firing almost at random; but at least one of their guns was a semi-automatic.

Lee bent low and ran past the car, so that they would have to turn around in order to drive toward him.

He came to a downwardly sloping embankment. He slid onto the grassy hillside. He could not see the men but he could still hear their furious voices. They were shouting reproaches and curses. One man ordered the others to fan out through the woods.

They lowered their voices, speaking in low whispers. But Lee could still hear them talking and moving.

They were moving farther away from him.

113

A lexei saw Lee McCabe turn around and look at him, and he somehow knew that all was lost.

The car bearing Paulie, Big John and Tony Loscatti stopped abruptly. The three men exited the vehicle just as Lee was diving for cover. They were firing at him, but McCabe had the advantage of the darkness working in his favor.

True, they might get lucky. *But it had not been a lucky night.*

Alexei ran forward down the dark blacktop of the highway. This much would be expected of him, wouldn't it? He was no longer so worried about saving his bonus; he was worried about saving his life. He had witnessed a bit of Paulie Sarzo's temper. The nephew of Alfonzo Coscollino was irrational—an overgrown adolescent in an adult's body. And the character of Big John Lewis was even worse.

As Alexei charged toward the unfolding melee, he noticed a flash of movement to his right. Someone darted out from behind a thicket and began running in the direction of Lee McCabe. This person was running in a zigzagging arc that would avoid the gunmen.

It was the daughter of Ben Chamberlain.

Perhaps everything was *not* lost. If McCabe had been staying at Chamberlain's house, then there must be some sort of bond between him and his host. Alexei had no idea why the young girl might have been following McCabe; but surely he would not want to see something unpleasant happen to her.

She might come in handy as a hostage.

Then there was the way that her very presence had so infuriated him, seeming to mock him by appearing to be fearless in a situation that had so frightened him.

Let's see how fearless she really is, Alexei thought.

The girl did not notice Alexei running after her until the last second, such was the commotion in the opposite direction, and her determination to run after Lee McCabe. When she finally turned around and stared him in the face, her eyes grew wide with surprise, then stark, naked terror.

This last facial expression brought Alexei considerable satisfaction.

They were both within sprinting distance of the parked and idling car when Alexei slammed into her. He was not a large man, but the girl was positively flyweight. They both tumbled to the ground, and Alexei dropped both his gun and his phone in the impact.

She struggled but Alexei quickly overpowered her: at least he thought he had overpowered her. She squirmed and bucked wildly in his arms, kicking his shins with both feet.

Then a wall of pain hit him as she sunk her teeth into one of his hands.

The girl would have escaped if Big John had not seen them rolling around in the grass at the side of the road. Alexei looked up at the giant man and saw that he was partially amused. He did not know how long John Lewis had been standing there, watching them.

As the girl wriggled free, Lewis stepped forward and literally scooped her up. She began the same squirming and kicking maneuver in Lewis's arms, but he gripped her around the middle in a massive bear hug. For an instant she was on the verge of passing out. John relaxed his hold slightly and she inhaled frantically.

"That's a good girl," Lewis said. "Now, are you going to continue to be a good girl, or should I pop you in two?" He smiled down at her—

an expression that even Alexei, in his current state, recognized as unnatural and unhealthy. "You know that I can do it, don't you?"

"She's the daughter of Ben Chamberlain!" Alexei cried out triumphantly. "Lee McCabe was staying with her father."

Alexei had by now already surmised that Lee McCabe had neither been captured nor killed. Paulie Sarzo and Tony Loscatti had materialized out of the shadows behind Big John. The headlights of their vehicle illuminated their faces, which conveyed that this mission had not been a success.

But his own catch might just enable them to snatch victory from the proverbial jaws of defeat. Alexei resisted the urge to grin. He was still worried about his bonus—still worried about his life, for that matter. No one, however, could deny that he had done a superb job of noticing the girl and detaining her.

"Take her with us," Paulie said. "You think you can handle that, John?"

"I think I might be able to manage that nicely," John replied.

John Lewis held her tightly with one of his arms. With the other hand he patted her cheek.

The big man saw the girl's mouth open but he did not react quickly enough. It was a danger to which Alexei might have alerted him, seeing as his own hand was now throbbing in pain.

The girl's jaws closed down on the hand of Big John Lewis. The mafia hit man screamed aloud, cursed, and withdrew his hand. The arm that still held the girl squeezed inward. Alexei cringed as Big John moved his free hand at an angle to deliver the first blow.

"You're going to regret that," Big John promised. "You're going to be sorry."

And a split second later, the cries of the hostage revealed that she was very sorry, indeed.

114

L ee stood up from his hiding place on the side of the embankment when he heard the unmistakable cries of a young girl. The sound was completely out of place. Surely the men who hunted him had not brought a child along with them.

It made no sense.

He peered over a hillock, through several clumps of scrub bushes and thickets. He could make out the shape of a large man forcing a much smaller captive into the backseat of the car that had delivered his attackers. The front passenger and driver's side doors slammed shut.

The child—the girl—struggled weakly as the big man finally pushed her inside the vehicle. She let out a final, exhausted cry.

The child was Izzy!

What would she be doing out here?

Then he thought: the second person who had been following him —the one he had not seen.

Could that person have been Izzy?

Yes—that person must have been Izzy. But *why?*

That didn't matter now, of course. Earlier this evening he had been fretting about the possibility that his presence would make Izzy an orphan. Now it appeared that his presence might result in her being killed—or worse.

He bolted up the hillside, just as the vehicle was backing up, changing direction, and then speeding away. He saw that it was a black or dark-colored car—a Jaguar.

With Illinois license plates.

In the distance, Lee saw the two red lights at the rear of the Jag make a sharp turn to the right, up Highway 1634. The men were taking Izzy in the direction of Blood Flats.

His plans to observe Lester Finn completely forgotten, Lee clambered up to the pavement and began to run after the speeding Jag.

115

About an hour later Lee McCabe reached the town of Blood Flats, in pursuit of the men who were also pursuing him.

He paused near the edge of the downtown area, painfully aware that he could not proceed much further with his borrowed pistol. If only this had been fall or winter; his summer attire of jeans and a tee shirt gave him few options for concealing the weapon.

His original plan of surveillance had accounted for the same eventuality. He knew that he might have to stash the weapon. But suddenly a better idea occurred to him.

There was a Food City located in a strip mall that lay just before the town proper. Lee walked along the fringe of the parking lot, past the main entrance and the rows of empty shopping carts that were waiting for shoppers outside. The side of the building was hemmed in by a thick hedgerow of prickly bushes. He thought it unlikely that anyone would go poking around in these shrubs.

After making certain that no one was watching him, he carefully removed the pistol from the waistband of his pants and laid it on the ground between the hedgerow and the wall.

He approached the bright, yellowish glare of the main entrance. He was painfully aware of the fact that Isabelle was in mortal danger —possibly even dead. He had very little time to find her.

Isabelle's abductors would use her as a hostage. Their first step would be to call Ben. *Deliver Lee McCabe*, the men would say, *and you might see your daughter alive again.*

And Ben, given his current state of mind, would likely attempt something reckless. Ben would not call him, because Ben was now convinced that his fugitive houseguest would insist on acting independently. Instead Ben would agree to a meeting with the gunmen, but now he would be the one going alone, with the intent of gunning down his daughter's kidnappers.

As he passed through the Food City threshold and into the bright, air-conditioned interior, Lee wondered if he had been too insistent on acting in a solitary fashion. It was difficult to convince a man that you meant no offense, that your only interest was in keeping him alive so that his daughter would not be an orphan—the daughter who had already lost one parent.

But now that daughter was in grave danger herself.

It would be only a matter of time before the gunmen contacted Ben with their demands. Probably no more than a few hours. Lee wondered if he should preemptively call Ben himself, and tell him what had happened. Then he could try to calm him down.

But how do you calm a man down when his eleven-year-old daughter has been abducted by killers?

"Sir, we close at midnight."

This information jolted Lee from these contemplations. The teenaged female cashier at the cash register looked at him with impatience, but no hint of recognition. If she had seen Lee's face on the television news or on the Internet, she did not recognize him now.

"It's 11:50 p.m." she added. "Ten minutes."

Good, Lee thought. *Her only concern is that she will be able to leave on time at the end of her shift. And I certainly don't plan to delay her.*

"I won't need any longer than that," he assured her.

Lee walked quickly back to the bread aisle and selected a loaf of Wonder bread. Then, so as not to make his actual purpose too obvious, he went to the condiments aisle and picked out a small plastic jar of mustard.

Luckily, he seemed to be the only customer in the entire store.

Back at the cash register, the cashier was busy tapping a text message into her cell phone. Once again, Lee counted his blessings. He pulled a ten-dollar bill from his pocket and handed it to her. She barely looked at Lee, absorbed as she was in tapping out her text message.

Then a man in a Kentucky state police uniform walked through the main entrance.

He was easily six-feet-four and had a crew cut. Lee was acutely aware of the semi-automatic firearm on his Sam Browne belt.

And then the situation went from bad to worse: another Kentucky state cop entered. He was almost as large and equally armed.

Lee was in plain view of the policemen but they had not yet noticed him. This was probably the end of their shift as well, and their minds were not focused on looking for suspects in Food City checkout lanes. Nevertheless, these two men would have seen his photo multiple times. If they made eye contact with him it would all be over.

He would be taken into custody.

Isabelle would die. Possibly Ben, too.

Exercising great care to make his movements slow and casual, Lee pretended to notice an item that interested him on the candy rack. He stooped down and began sorting through several cardboard trays of chocolate bars.

"We close in five minutes," Lee heard the cashier say. Though he could not see her from his current crouched position, he assumed that she was still absorbed by her cell phone.

"Well, all we want are some chips and some pretzels," one of the cops said.

"Aisle twelve," the cashier said. "And we close in five minutes,"

Lee waited half a minute and then stood up. The state policemen were temporarily out of sight; but it wouldn't take them long to retrieve some chips and pretzels from aisle twelve.

The cashier was shaking her head, frustrated that the cops threatened to delay her departure. She cocked her cell phone between her cheek and shoulder. Somehow she had managed to dial someone immediately after she had given the policemen instructions regarding the location of the chips and pretzels.

She took Lee's money and handed him the paper portion of his change in dollar bills. He heard the clink of metal in the register's coin tray. He pulled the two quarters and three pennies from the round tray and slipped them into his pocket.

Now for the whole purpose of his visit. The cashier began to place the bread and the mustard into a translucent plastic bag.

"Could you give me paper?" Lee asked.

"What?" the cashier paused her cell phone conversation.

"Could you give me a paper bag?"

The cashier looked around her for a paper bag. Finding none, she bent down and checked the shelf space beneath the cash register.

"I don't have any," she said.

Lee knew that the policeman would reappear at any second.

"You don't have any?"

"That's right. I don't have any."

Then Lee noticed a small pile of folded paper bags on the adjacent cash register. This register, like the other four behind it, were currently unattended.

"There are some paper bags," Lee said, indicating his find.

"Okay," the cashier said dully.

Her friend on the other end of the cell phone call seemed to say something especially interesting. She said *mm-hmm* and nodded emphatically at the unseen person.

An eternity seemed to elapse before the cashier managed to pull a paper bag from the pile at the register next to hers. Another eternity before she loaded the bread and the mustard into the bag.

"Thank you," she said finally, handing Lee the paper bag.

Lee nodded, took the bag, and walked quickly toward the door.

As he was walking out the main entrance, he heard the two state policemen talking to each other and to the cashier. One of them was apologizing for delaying her past the end of her shift.

Lee had evaded them with a margin of only a few seconds.

116

Once clear of the Food City's doorway, Lee quickened his pace. He wanted to run; but this would arouse the instant suspicion of the police if they exited the store before he was out of sight.

He continued on until the end of the building. He turned the corner and slipped into the space between the hedge and the wall.

The prickly bushes bit into his skin and rustled against his paper bag.

"How much longer do you think we'll be stuck in Hawkins County?" he heard one of the policemen ask his partner.

"What have you got against Hawkins County?" the other replied. *"I've got relatives not far from here."*

"Figures," the other said. They engaged in some good-natured ribbing as they climbed into the state police car, which Lee had barely noticed during his hasty retreat from the Food City. The police vehicle was parked almost directly in front of him, though at a fair distance away.

Nevertheless, the cops would notice him if he moved. They might notice him even if he didn't move.

Lee held his body perfectly still, trying to refrain from breathing. The engine of the police car roared to life. Shortly thereafter the glow of headlights washed over him. And past him.

He did not move until he heard the car's engine grow faint and diminish to nothing.

117

S tanding with his back against the outer wall of the Food City store, the bag of Wonder bread and mustard in his hand, Lee reflected that perhaps his last-minute innovation for concealing the gun had not been so clever.

In the Marine Corps they had taught him how to improvise, but within certain parameters and using the tools they had given him. The innovation required of him since the murders at the trailer park was different: He was proceeding with no rule book, no protocol—no way of knowing if his actions were wise or foolish.

With the state police car gone, he stooped to retrieve the gun from its hiding place. He recalled the banter of the policemen—how one had talked about being stuck in Hawkins County, and the other had claimed that he had family nearby.

These men were undoubtedly part of the dragnet that was drawing closed around him, a dragnet that, so far as he could tell, was still moving mistakenly in his direction without any grasp of the actual killers.

And then he got to thinking: *Why did that car have Illinois license plates, and what is Lester Finn doing hiring men from so far away? Are they locals who are merely using an out-of-state car, or are they authentic out-of-towners?*

Then he recalled the man he had seen at the Peaton Woods Furniture factory, the one called Paulie. He had obviously not been a local. And he would be affiliated with the men in the Jaguar, wouldn't he?

And if they were from out of town, maybe they didn't work for Lester Finn.

Maybe Lester Finn worked for *them.*

Lee had already figured out that the local drug ring dominated by Lester Finn could not be completely independent and self-sustaining. Lester must be relying on a larger network. And those men from Illinois might be affiliated with that network.

This thought chilled him: *Lester Finn might not dare to kill a child in cold blood. But who could say what these men from out of state might do?*

Lee placed the gun in the paper bag along with the bread and the mustard. Then he folded the open mouth of the bag closed and rolled up the top of the bag into a makeshift handle.

Now he could carry the weapon openly along the street. He realized that even this countermeasure was lacking: The weight of the gun was considerable in the bottom of the bag, and it drooped conspicuously. Eventually it would tear. But it might last him until he located the men who had abducted Isabelle.

He had decided that the best approach would be to focus on locating the Jaguar with the Illinois plates. That was the only way, in fact, at this late hour. Someone had to have noticed it. Such a car, with out-of-state plates, would stick out like the proverbial sore thumb in Blood Flats.

Lee walked into the town proper. It was now past midnight and the streets were deserted. He knew that he must look suspicious himself, even with the bag concealing the pistol. And then there was the matter of him being a wanted fugitive.

He came to a pub and two young couples filed out, laughing and stumbling from a few too many drinks. Both of the men were lighting cigarettes.

Lee approached them as casually as he could.

"Excuse me."

They abruptly stopped talking and laughing. One of the men paused, holding a flickering lighter before the tip of his cigarette. He let the lighter's flame go out.

"Excuse me," Lee repeated. "I'm sorry to bother you. But I was wondering if any of you had seen a dark-colored Jaguar around town. The car has Illinois plates."

The four young people looked at Lee as if he had just inquired about extraterrestrials roaming about town.

"Dude," one of the men finally said. He was the one who had yet to light his cigarette. "We ain't seen no cars in the past three hours, lest they been in this here bar."

Then the women laughed, and the other man said, with more than a trace of indignation in his tone: "What do we look like, the local welcome wagon? Do any of us have the word 'information' written on the front of our shirts?"

With that Lee saw that he was going to get nowhere. He thanked them and walked away. He headed toward the next intersection.

As he rounded the corner, he realized that he had aroused more suspicion than any cars they might have seen:

"That guy was weird...Carrying around a paper bag like that late at night."

"He looked familiar. I think I've seen him before..."

"Well, he's gone now, so let's forget about him. Tara, you got any weed left in your purse?"

This was not going to work, Lee realized. To search for Isabelle in this way would be the equivalent of looking for a needle in a haystack.

Time was running out—and Lee was already out of ideas.

118

Alexei knew that he would be unable to sleep. He lay on his bed in his hotel room. The room was stuffy and miserable. He badly wanted a drink.

The abduction of the girl had only made him even more nervous. He had ridden back to this miserable town in the back seat of the Jaguar. The entire way, John Lewis had been manhandling the girl, alternately slapping her and shaking her. Alexei heard Paulie name a location on the other side of Blood Flats where they would take her.

Once in town, Alexei had begged John and the other Coscollino men to let him out of the car. He wanted no part of this, he said. Yes, he was the one who had captured the girl, but participating in her murder was another matter. And he could only imagine what John Lewis had in mind for her.

Then Paulie had drawn a gun and aimed it at Alexei's head. Finally John had calmed down the crazy nephew of Alfonzo Coscollino. He had said that Alexei was a coward, a spineless, womanish man—but nevertheless valuable to the family in his role as an investigator. Let him live, John Lewis had said. Let him out where he can walk back to the hotel. Alexei—spineless and woman-like though he is—is nevertheless trustworthy, John had insisted.

Then Paulie had ordered the car stopped and let him out, cursing at him and issuing threats.

The reprieve had not reassured Alexei. Both his pay and his life were still very much in jeopardy. The Coscollinos might still decide to kill him. And now he was potentially complicit in the murder of a young girl. If the girl died, her death would be sensationalized by the American media.

This would not be like the other deaths in which Alexei had been a bit player. It was one thing for him to provide information about the drug dealers, union agitators, and businessmen whom the Coscollinos later destroyed. But he had tackled the young girl. He had delivered her to her present captors.

This could go very badly for him. Very badly, indeed.

He imagined the taste of vodka sliding past his lips, the warmth cascading down his throat. That was what he needed now.

He looked at his watch. It was past midnight. In a little burg like this, there would be no open bars at this hour on a weeknight, would there?

But perhaps he could find a place where liquor was sold by the bottle. This would do, he decided.

He gathered his wallet and his room key and stepped outside his hotel room door into the muggy blackness of the parking lot. He surveyed the surrounding town and tried to locate a place where he might find his medicine. Then another thought occurred to him: he had heard that some southern states had entire counties that were "dry"—where no alcohol could be sold at all. He shook his head and hoped that Hawkins County was not one of these dry counties. The very concept of "dry counties" struck him as absurd. Such foolishness would never be seriously considered in Russia.

Alexei had walked nearly a block before he saw the sign that read: "All Night Pony Keg." The neon shape of a bottle, plus the words "Beer," "Wine," and "Liquor" told him that he was in luck.

He walked into the dark interior. An older man in a stained and threadbare Skoal baseball cap nodded to him as he entered.

Alexei walked past the cooled glass display cases of beer and wine, toward the shelves in the back of the store. After the day he had had, neither beer nor wine would be sufficient. He was in the mood for something harder.

119

I t was time to give up, Lee, decided. He would call the state police and turn himself in. *Tonight. Right now.*

He knew that this would mean the end of his freedom. He could present the evidence he had gathered thus far to his interrogators at the state level. Perhaps they would be motivated to investigate Lester Finn's connection to the murders in the trailer park—perhaps not.

His own freedom had ceased to be his priority. Nor was he even concerned about bringing Lester Finn to justice. However, he could not allow himself to consider the idea that Isabelle, too, might die so that he could live and go free.

Surrender would be a long shot; but it might just be a long shot that would save Isabelle's life. If he placed himself in police custody, then he would be unable to surrender to the men who had taken Izzy hostage. They might try to get to him another way, of course. (He had heard about criminal organizations arranging murders inside the prison system.) But he would be unable to turn himself in to the gunmen.

As he walked through the business district of Blood Flats, he became suddenly aware of the grocery bag in his hand—the bag that contained the absurd combination of a gun, a loaf of bread, and a jar of mustard.

He looked for a dumpster in which to toss these now worthless items. He would go the law unarmed and unprotected. Hopefully the state police would not attempt to shoot him as Norris had done.

They'll kill her anyway, Lee thought. *I can't save her by giving up.*

The kidnappers would contact Ben first. Ben had a telephone number in the public directory, and Isabelle was his daughter.

The kidnappers would have no way of knowing that Ben was so unpredictable. They would expect him to do what most fathers would do in the same situation: panic, and then proceed to sacrifice the life of a wanted fugitive in order to save his daughter.

Instead Ben would try to make a stand against the men who had Isabelle, and both father and daughter would die as a result.

How the hell do I find Isabelle, then? Lee wondered. *The entire town of Blood Flats has gone to bed, and I have no one to help me.*

He saw a set of dimly lighted windows at the rear edge of a parking lot a short ways down the street. There were no cars in the parking lot, but the establishment seemed to be open. *Billy's Pony Keg.* Maybe the attendant had seen the Jaguar with the Illinois license plates. It was a long shot; but it was the only shot he had.

120

W hen Lee entered the pony keg, the cashier was waiting on a customer. A blond-haired man stood with his back to Lee.

"I think I'm going to need to see some ID," the cashier said to the customer. "That's Kentucky bourbon you've got there. That's the hard stuff."

"But I am thirty years old!" the customer protested.

Lee felt a chill run down his spine. The customer's Eastern European accent was atypical for a small town in central Kentucky. He was wearing camouflage pants and a dark tee shirt.

He recalled a very recent conversation between himself and Ben. About a man with a Russian name and accent who came to Ben's front door, claiming to be a representative of the Central Kentucky Power and Light Company.

"*That's odd,*" Lee had told Ben. "*It sounds like he was looking for some excuse to get inside the house.*"

"*Well, he was driving a van that looked like a power company van. And he had an ID. He handed me this business card.*"

What had the name on the business card read? *Sergei something or other....*

Lee studied the back of the man standing at the counter, arguing with the cashier about bourbon and driver's licenses. Atypical dress, too. Not the sort of thing one usually wore for a casual stroll about town.

Then he recalled the figure that had been tailing him in the dark this evening. *Dark clothing. Blonde hair.*

"Well, maybe so," the pony keg attendant said flatly. "But I still need to see your driver's license."

The customer sighed and removed his wallet from a pocket in his camouflage pants. Then his driver's license from the wallet.

The older man behind the counter held the license up the light.

"Illinois. You're a long way from home, aren't you, Mr. Primakov?"

The customer merely nodded. He handed over his money and received his change. When he turned around he stood face-to-face with Lee.

In a crowd of people, Lee would not have recognized him as the man who had tracked him along the highway two hours ago. Only the peculiar clothes, the blonde hair, and the build looked familiar. Even the Illinois driver's license and the foreign accent might have been dismissed.

But Lee could not dismiss the recognition written on the man's face. He knew exactly who Lee was. There was no doubt: this was a man who had studied Lee's image many times.

121

T he man with the accent was not the only person in the pony keg who recognized Lee. The cashier called out, "Hey, I know who you are. Get the hell out of my store."

Lee heard him fumbling beneath his counter. He knew that the man was retrieving a weapon.

From the corner of his eye Lee saw the barrel of the cashier's shotgun, and he thought: This is going to be like Jimmy Mack's garage all over again. But the greater part of his attention was consumed by the Russian.

Lee's pistol was still in the paper bag, with the mustard and the loaf of bread. If he withdrew it now he would have to kill the cashier or be killed himself by the man's shotgun. There was certainly no time to explain. And he knew that the Russian was probably armed as well.

Contrary to Lee's expectations, the Russian did not draw a weapon. He dropped the bottle of bourbon that he had purchased. It shattered on the floor of the pony keg with a wet splash and the tinkling of broken glass. He shoved Lee out of the way before Lee could stop him.

Now the cashier had a shotgun leveled at him. Lee ignored the weapon, opting instead to run after the Russian. He did not know if the pony keg attendant would shoot him in the back.

Luckily he did not. Lee bolted out the door, in time to see that the Russian had run to the left after exiting the pony keg. Lee charged after him, carrying his absurd package in one hand. He would need the gun when he caught the Russian.

If he managed to catch the Russian.

Lee was gaining. But the other man was fast. They ran down the empty sidewalk.

The Russian paused to look back. This proved to be his critical mistake. Lee summoned a burst of speed. He hit the man with his shoulder. Their joint momentum carried them forward and to the right, where the sidewalk was contiguous with an alley. They crashed into a building. Lee gripped the man with both hands as they rolled into the adjacent alley.

The paper bag was between them. Lee felt something inside the bag crunch. *The gun*, he thought. *I have to get the gun.*

The man reached up and clawed at Lee's chest. His hand caught the pocket of the tee shirt Lee was wearing—the shirt that had until recently belonged to Marie Wilson's younger son, Jeremy. The pocket ripped free, and Lee was vaguely aware that a piece of paper—or perhaps a piece of cardboard, fell to the ground. This was not the act of an experienced fighter. Lee had never been in a brawl before in which his opponent resorted to ripping his clothes.

They tussled briefly on the ground. The Russian may have been a fair runner, but he was no match for Lee as a wrestler. Lee soon had the man on his back with his arms pinned. Lee was sitting on his chest.

Yellow streaks of mustard covered the man's chest, face, and neck.

Lee saw his own gun glinting on the pavement, just out of reach. Through his pants he could feel the hard outline of the Russian's gun.

"Where is the girl?" Lee asked, skipping all preliminaries.

"Vat girl?" the man asked. "I do not know anything about girl. I don't have her."

Lee slammed his fist into the supine man's face. He pulled his punch so he would not knock his prisoner unconscious. This was nevertheless enough to make him delirious.

"Please, sir, I did not do it!" he protested. He moaned. "Oh, I want nothing to do with that girl. You must believe me!"

"I thought you said you didn't know anything about her," Lee said. "I've just caught you lying."

The man was so incapacitated that Lee risked leaning forward to pluck his fallen gun from the pavement. He was careful to keep the man's arms pinned.

He pointed the muzzle of his pistol at the Russian's face, which was now a mess, smeared as it was with blood, mustard, and dirt from the alley's pavement.

"Listen," Lee said quietly. "I know that you were following me earlier tonight. I know that you took the girl."

"I did not take any girl! Look at me! Do you see any girl?"

"Then your friends took the girl."

Lee brought the muzzle of his pistol to the man's eye.

"Okay," the Russian said hastily. "My friends took the girl."

"And you know where she is."

The man beneath Lee took a moment to contemplate this statement, which was also a question.

"Okay," he said. "I know where she is."

"And you're going to tell me. Or I'm going to put a bullet through your head. Simple as that."

"Nyet!" he whimpered. *"No!"* Lee was honestly surprised to see that tears were gathering in the man's eyes. "Okay. *Da.* I will tell you."

"Then start talking. And you'd better not try to bullshit me."

Lee listened as the Russian fumbled out the information he had demanded. Of course, he could not know for sure at this point if his prisoner was attempting to bullshit him. However, the specificity of his explanation suggested that he was telling the truth.

"Now you must let me go," the man with the blood, dirt, and mustard-smeared face said. "You promised."

"I didn't promise you shit," Lee said.

A part of him wanted to shoot the Russian in cold blood. He knew that this man, while obviously not an enforcer himself, was a willing accomplice of men who regularly killed innocents for profit. He deserved to die.

But Lee would not have this pathetic man's death on his shoulders. He had never killed a defenseless man and he would not start now.

At the same time, he could not simply let him go. He would contact his cohorts and warn them.

Without saying another word, Lee slammed his pistol into the side of the Russian's head. He went out like a light. The blow had not been enough to kill him, but more than enough to leave him out cold for a few hours. He would have a nasty headache for a while, too.

Lee removed the unconscious man's pistol from one of the pockets of his camouflage pants. He tossed the gun into a dumpster that filled much of the alley.

Then, contemplating the most direct route to the location that the Russian had told him, Lee started after the men who had taken Isabelle Chamberlain.

122

"The little bitch bit me!" Big John shouted. He was holding his right hand in his left one. He released it and stretched out the wounded palm. It bore a red semicircle of indentations. The teeth marks did not penetrate the skin, but they were causing some moderate swelling.

"Little bitch," Big John repeated, and gave Isabelle Chamberlain a baleful stare.

Isabelle sat in the corner of the cramped, filthy room. She was gagged and her wrists were tied behind her back. There was a welt on her cheek that promised to blossom into a nasty bruise—the result of her encounter with Big John.

Big John turned to Tony Loscatti and then to Paulie Sarzo. "This goddamned hand is going to hurt like a motherfucker tomorrow!" he said.

Tony found this irresistibly funny. He began to guffaw. Then Big John looked at him threateningly, and Paulie whacked him across the back of the head with an open palm. Tony rubbed the spot and glared at Paulie.

"Watch it, Paulie."

The comment stunned Paulie. The younger man had never challenged him before, even when he occasionally cuffed him. But now Tony Loscatti was talking back to him. Almost threatening him. Was there some conspiracy brewing amongst his underlings? Had they gotten wind of the fact that Uncle Alfonzo was less than pleased with his management of the family's affairs in Kentucky?

And more to the point—did they know something that he didn't? Was there already a hit planned on him? Could it be that one of these men standing here with him now would be the one to pull the trigger?

"Frickin' idiot," Paulie said at length. "This isn't a game, Tony."

They were in the storage room of a building that had once been an auto body shop. These accommodations were courtesy of Lester Finn, who had apparently secured the building as collateral against the owner's outstanding drug, gambling, or whoring debts. Or possibly some combination of the three. The place was a dump; but it suited their present purposes well. The body shop was relatively secluded down a rural side road, so no one was likely to disturb them by accident.

Isabelle leaned back against the dirty cinderblock wall. She looked into the single light bulb that burned overhead. Then her eyes moved from Paulie, to Tony, and then to Big John. She appeared to shiver.

Big John noted Isabelle's fear and smiled. "The little bitch ain't biting anyone now, is she?" he asked no one in particular. Big John stuck his tongue out from his mouth and lolled it an obscene, leering manner. Then he grabbed his crotch.

Isabelle pushed herself back against the wall. *The girl understands,* Paulie thought. *She may be young, but she grasps that message loud and clear.*

"You know, Paulie, I ain't never had a girl that young. I've always been curious, though, ya know—about what it would be like."

"Oh man," Tony Loscatti said, laughing again. "That's pretty sick, John."

Paulie, knowing all about Big John's trips overseas, guessed that John's claim of inexperience was far from truthful. Nevertheless, he was more than a little annoyed at the trouble that the young girl had given them. If the threat of up-close-and-personal time with Big John would make her more compliant, so be it.

"Hear that, little girl?" Paulie said. "You give us anymore shit and Big John here is going to get to know you a lot better."

He gestured for Big John to step outside the little building with him. "Watch the girl," he said to Tony.

"I think I can handle that," Tony responded.

Outside, the night was pitch black. Paulie looked around in all directions. The moonlight provided almost no visibility. There were trees everywhere. If Lee McCabe and the girl's father chose to stage an ambush, the hillbillies would have a decided advantage.

And he wouldn't even be able to hear them coming—because of those stupid cicadas or crickets or whatever they were. How did these hillbilly lowlifes sleep at night, with those damned bugs chirping like that from dusk to dawn?

"This is no good," he said to Big John. "You can't see shit from this place. If we tell McCabe to come here, he'll hide in the woods and pick us off."

Big John nodded. "You got a point there. I ain't never done a hit in the woods.."

"We're a little out of our element, tactically speaking."

There was much truth in this statement and once again Big John indicated his agreement. Hunting and killing a man in the woods wouldn't be like carrying out a hit in the city, where either he or Big John would know how to use the environment to their advantage. In the city you could usually see a target approach from a considerable distance, whether he arrived by foot or by car.

This goddamned forest was something else entirely.

"We can't tell him to come here," Paulie said with finality. "Too much can go wrong."

"What do we do then?"

"First I'm going back to the hotel to get the .30-06 from the trunk of the Lexus. Then I'm going to find a parking lot somewhere near town where I can see McCabe coming. Then I'm going to call the girl's father and tell him to bring McCabe, or we start sawing up little pieces of his daughter. And then I'll wait for him to come and I'll take him out."

"You want to take the shot yourself?" Big John asked.

"Yes," said Paulie. He would be able to tell Uncle Alfonzo that he had personally fired the bullet that killed the ex-marine.

"What about the girl's father?"

"If he's stupid enough to come with McCabe, I'll kill him too."

"Alright," John said. "I know you're a good shot with a rifle."

Paulie was going to remind Big John that he was more than a "good shot with a rifle." He was an accomplished marksman.

Instead he merely said: "I'll hide someplace where I can take a clear aim. And the 30-.06 has an infrared scope."

Big John nodded. "Okay. But there's one other thing."

"What?"

"What about the girl?" Big John asked.

Yes, it would figure that Big John would be thinking about the damned girl, wouldn't it?

Paulie thought for a moment. He had an opportunity here to win Big John over to his side. Big John was a good man to have in your corner. He was smart and he was an efficient killer.

If someone within the lower ranks of the family—someone like Tony Loscatti, for example—was planning some sort of treachery against him, Big John might send him word. He might even take care of the problem in advance.

He would give Big John something that he really desired, Paulie decided. In the process he would gain Big John's gratitude—and he would acquire a secret to use against him should that need ever arise.

"I think I know what you really want here, John."

The big man licked his lower lip and said nothing.

"I saw the way you were looking at that girl," Paulie continued. "So here's the deal, I'm going to arrange things so that you can have what you want."

Big John narrowed his eyes at Paulie. Then he allowed himself a tight smile. There would be no more false pretenses about the matter.

"But what about your uncle?" Big John asked quietly. Paulie could see that an inner war was going on within the other man. He was torn between the unexpected opportunity to satisfy his darkest desires, and another force that counseled constraint. "He ain't gonna like the idea that something like that could get out, you know?"

"That's why it *won't* get out," Paulie said. "Here's what we're going to do: First we kill McCabe—*and* her father, as necessary. Then you have your fun with the girl."

Big John raised his eyebrows. "Go on."

"Then we'll take care of her. We can make her disappear. There's acres of forest on either side of us. An easy problem to dispose of. And no one will ever know."

If this doesn't win his trust, nothing will, Paulie thought. The girl had no relation to the family's business beyond her temporary value as a hostage. Big John would understand the risk that Paulie was taking: This would be a bargain between them that went beyond the interests of the Family. Beyond either one's loyalty to the Coscollino organization. A personal bond of loyalty between two men.

"I suppose that could work," Big John said at length.

"I take care of men on my crew," Paulie said. "I want you to remember that."

Paulie didn't have to mention the quid pro quo more explicitly. It was already implied and understood by both of them: Big John would have his fun, yes, and he would be indebted to Paulie in return. He would watch Paulie's back. And if Paulie ever needed a special favor at some point in the future, he would feel free to call on Big John.

"Okay," Big John said. "That works. You cover for me here. And later, someday, I'll be there for you when you need me."

Paulie did some quick mental calculations: It would take perhaps another hour to get ready for the hit. He wanted some time by himself, to clear his head and summon his focus. So far, others had blundered. He would succeed where they had failed.

"I'm going on ahead of you. I'll make the call to this girl's father. Then I'm going to call you, and I want you to bring Tony."

"But—what about the girl?" Big John asked.

"It doesn't look like she's going anywhere. When I call you, you double-check that she's tied up good, then you come and help me out. Remember what I said, John: You'll have what you want; but first we need to kill McCabe."

John Lewis nodded and smiled contemplatively. The big man stared off into the blackness of the surrounding forest, no doubt lost in his own dark thoughts.

123

Even though it was dark, Lee McCabe did not approach the abandoned auto body shop via the road. He knew that the men who had taken Isabelle would be expecting as much.

Instead he followed the road to within half a mile of the building's parking lot, then climbed the adjacent hillside into the woods.

He heard the symphony of insects around him. Now he was grateful for them. Their ceaseless noise would mask any minor sounds that he might make inadvertently. The trail that he found received little moonlight through the overhead canopy of trees, and it was overgrown in places. He knew that he would not be able to avoid stepping on the occasional dry twig.

He was, however, concerned that the Russian had given him false information. Although the information was highly specific, the man whom the pony keg cashier had identified as Alexei Primakov might have spun a lie nonetheless.

There might even be an ambush waiting for him when he stepped out from the trees. *I knocked him out*, Lee thought. *But perhaps I made a mistake by letting him live. I should have at least checked him for a cell phone.*

But there was no way to correct that mistake now.

At last he reached a high spot that allowed him to look directly down on the body shop. It was a ramshackle building that had not been used for numerous seasons, but the windows were dimly lit by electric light.

Something was here, after all. But would he find Isabelle here?

A large, hulking man passed by one of the windows. He was talking but Lee could not distinguish any of his words.

Lee placed his gun in the waistband of his pants. He began to creep down the steep declivity toward the body shop. If one of them saw him now, he would make an easy target. A wrong step—a misplaced hand or foot—would be enough to get him killed.

Another man stepped outside the front door of the building. He was younger and thinner than the man Lee had seen in the window. Dark hair and fancy clothes. Definitely not a native of Hawkins County.

Lee saw the flash of a lighter, then the glowing ember of a cigarette. The man stepped into a pool of illumination thrown by the light inside the building. He wore a shoulder holster that was somehow incongruous with his nightclub attire. The butt of a pistol protruded from the holster.

Lee watched the man enjoy his cigarette. He did not appear to be very alert. Lee's impression was that the man was mostly concerned with escaping the heat inside the auto body shop. The well-dressed man did not comport himself like a guard who was anticipating an imminent attack.

The big man whom Lee had seen in the window a few minutes ago stepped out and joined the other one. He dwarfed the young man with the dark features. But they were both large, formidable men.

"How's the girl doing?"

"She ain't had much to say," the big man laughed. "A gag in your mouth will do that to you."

The younger man laughed at this, and the big man lit a cigarette of his own.

That was the evidence Lee needed: They had clearly been talking about a girl, and the reference to the gag indicated that she was being held against her will. Lee didn't need to seriously consider the possibility that the men might be holding another little girl captive inside the abandoned building: It was Isabelle that they were talking about.

Lee realized that he had to act immediately, while the two of them were both outside the building, where he could eliminate them with minimal risk to Isabelle's safety. There was no chance of using mere reason or threats with these two: They would have to go down.

Lee hunched low and began walking forward. He made an effort to keep his footfalls muffled, but his major concern now was speed. The younger man had been smoking for a while now, and he was nearing the end of his cigarette.

Don't go back inside, Lee thought, as he continued to creep forward. He had to get close enough to make two shots within a tight range. Without the elements of surprise and proximity, the two men would have a definite advantage over him in a gunfight. They might even be able to safely maneuver their way back inside the building, where they could use Isabelle as a human shield.

Then the younger man with the dark features did exactly what Lee had hoped he would not do. He tossed the butt of his cigarette to the ground and rubbed it out with his foot. Lee was close enough to see light reflect off the polished, expensive leather surface of his shoe. He turned to walk inside the building.

It was now or never. Lee took three long strides toward the auto body shop and the two men who stood before its entrance. His last step landed squarely on a metal object—probably an old aluminum can—that crunched audibly beneath his foot. The men looked in his direction, instantly alert. The younger man withdrew his pistol from the shoulder holster with a speed that surprised Lee. The older, larger man had a machine pistol aimed in Lee's direction.

Lee was standing in a patch of light. They both knew he was there now. It would be over, one way or another, in a matter of seconds. Lee quickly fired two shots that knocked the big man back against the wall. Wounded and bleeding, he fired his machine pistol as he went down, its rounds spraying up dirt and gravel in a semicircle.

The younger of the two men took aim at Lee for a head shot. Lee was able to anticipate this at the last second. He dropped onto his chest and stomach. Then he squeezed the trigger three times at his astonished assailant, who was probably not used to exchanging fire with military-trained men. Two of Lee's shots went wild, tearing powdery gashes in the outer wall of the building. One connected. The dark-haired man was knocked backward but he remained on his feet. Lee noticed a bulk around the man's middle—a light-grey bullet-proof vest that had been indistinguishable at a distance.

The gravel around Lee flew up. His attacker was charging toward him, fearless, screaming with rage.

Lee fired two more rounds that destroyed the top of the man's head. He fell backward, going down this time.

Lee clambered to his feet and ran to the downed man. He was dead; blood was spurting from the top of his ruined head. But Lee kicked the pistol well clear of his body just to be safe: He was taking no chances here.

The big man whom he had shot earlier was another matter. He was on his hands and knees now, crawling toward his machine pistol. He had left a visible trail of blood. Lee could see that his belly and chest were stained crimson.

He looked up at Lee and smiled.

"Don't move," Lee said, leveling his own weapon.

The big man smiled and reached for the machine pistol.

Lee shot him in the head.

He ran toward the front door of the building, giving the big man's body only a brief glance. He was safely dead.

Lee entered the auto body shop with his pistol extended in a two-hand grip. His biggest fear at this point was a third assailant. There could be another man who at this moment was holding a gun to Isabelle's head. That would make rescuing her infinitely more diffi-cult, if not, in the end, impossible.

The interior of the auto body shop was not large, but there were multiple rooms and they were mostly submerged in shadows. Lee thrust his gun into each one, ready to take fire and ready to return it. He was running on adrenaline, and he knew that he was probably being careless, exposing himself as he was. But another force was pushing him forward: Isabelle would not join the list of casualties who had died for his sake.

Finally no one shot at him, and then he saw Isabelle, bound and gagged, leaning against a corner in one of the little debris-filled and dusty rooms.

Her eyes opened wide when she saw him, first in fear and then in recognition.

Lee laid his pistol on the floor—he was satisfied now that there had only been two gunmen—and leaned down toward Isabelle. The girl was trembling.

Don't go into shock, he thought. *Please be brave for me until I can get you back to your father.*

He removed the dirty rag that the men had thrust into Isabelle's mouth. She cried out his name, and her words came out tearfully, as if the girl had done her best to hold out until now, but this ordeal, ultimately had been too much. She began to cry freely. Then he reached behind her and removed the nylon ropes that bound her. Luckily, they had not gone to extensive lengths to restrain an eleven-year-old girl, and he was able to unbind her quickly.

She threw her arms around him and wailed something unintelligible.

He looked her straight in the face and asked: "Izzy, listen to me: I need your help. How many men did you see here tonight? How many took you?"

To Lee's amazement, the girl began to calm herself down. It was as if she had had her cry, but now it was time to move on.

"Four at first," she said. "Then only three."

Lee figured that the Eastern European man with whom he had struggled was one of those four men. Then there were the two he had killed. That still left one unaccounted for.

He snatched the pistol off the floor. "Stay right here," he told Izzy.

Lee made another quick search of the auto body shop. He found no one. There were only so many places to hide, and he did not believe that an assailant would have concealed himself for so long without attacking.

"I hadn't seen one of them for a long time," Izzy said when he returned. "He's went off somewhere, I think." She had not moved from her place on the floor, but she was rubbing the areas on her wrists where the ropes had been. "You done kilt the other ones?"

"Yes, Izzy. They're dead."

"Good," the young girl responded. "I'm glad!" And Lee thought: *She is definitely her father's daughter. This is a bloodthirsty clan I've hooked myself up with.*

The thought of Izzy's father made him remember his next task: He removed his cell phone from his pocket and punched in the number of Ben Chamberlain's cell. Looking at his messages queue, Lee could see that Ben had tried to call him no less than half a dozen times over the past hour.

God, don't let me be too late...

"Hello?" Ben said. Lee could tell from the background noise that Ben was in his truck. "Lee, is that you? Where the hell have you been?" He was on the verge of hysteria. "They—they got Izzy! And I'm going to get her back!"

"Stop where you are!" Lee said. "Izzy's fine. She's right here with me."

"Don't tell me to stop!" Ben said. "What the hell do you mean—"

Lee decided that the easiest course would be to actually let Ben talk to his daughter. He handed the phone to Izzy. After father and daughter had exchanged a few words, Lee motioned for Izzy to hand back the phone.

"What the hell happened, Lee?" Ben asked.

"It's kind of a long story. Listen: Wherever that man told you to go, you can't go near there. That's a trap—probably intended for me but they would gladly kill you too for good measure."

"They ain't gonna kill me!" Ben protested. "I'm gonna kill them. But first I want to get my daughter back. Tell me where you are."

Lee recalled Izzy's mention of the fourth kidnapper—who was apparently gone now but who might come back at any moment. And he might bring more men like the two Lee had killed outside. If this was indeed an organized criminal outfit, there were likely more where those two had come from.

"Listen to me, Ben," he said. "We don't have much time."

124

Alexei Primakov awoke in the alley. His head and much of his body were aching from his unsuccessful struggle with Lee McCabe. The American had certainly gotten the better of him.

Still on his back, Alexei lifted himself onto his elbows in the darkness. There was little light in the alley. He thought he heard the sound of a stray cat—or possibly rats—foraging in the space behind him.

The enormity of his failure suddenly dawned on him: Pinned, cornered, and terrified by Lee McCabe, he had betrayed not only Big John Lewis—but also Paulie Sarzo, the half-insane nephew of Alfonzo Coscollino.

Alexei began to shake uncontrollably: They would kill him if they found out what he had done, wouldn't they? And if Lee McCabe showed up at that auto body shop—the one where they said they were taking the girl—how difficult would it be for them to connect the dots? For that matter, they might have already captured Lee McCabe. They might be interrogating him under torture at this very minute!

He would of course deny any contact with Lee McCabe. *Deny,*

deny, deny—that was his best strategy. But he would need to give them something more, something that would demonstrate his worth. And Alexei knew that he was worthless in a fight. His source of value was intelligence, information.

Then he noticed the laminated plastic card that had fallen to the ground during his struggle with Lee. He had torn it from the pocket of Lee's shirt.

He lifted the card from the dirty pavement and turned it over in his hands. Alexei had expected it to be Lee McCabe's driver's license.

He was surprised to find that the face on the card was not Lee's— but that of an African-American man named "Jeremy Wilson." Nor was it a driver's license. The card was a photo ID indicating this Jeremy Wilson's membership at the Hawkins County YMCA.

Who was Jeremy Wilson? Obviously not a close relative of Lee McCabe. But might there be some other connection—a connection that he could use to redeem himself? Maybe, and maybe not. He had no idea of what might be occurring at the auto body shop right now, where John Lewis, Paulie Sarzo, and Tony Loscatti were holding Ben Chamberlain's daughter hostage. He was grasping at straws.

But did he have any other choice?

He shoved the laminated card into his pocket and, despite the pain that suffused his body, managed to walk back to his motel room. By the time he came to the motel parking lot he was actually running.

Then he booted up his computer and went to work, looking for the connection between Jeremy Wilson and Lee McCabe. It took him less than an hour to hit pay dirt. He had completed his research and was congratulating himself on his own ingenuity when his cell phone rang. It was Paulie Sarzo. The nephew of the great don was delirious with rage. He was screaming into the phone so loudly, so hysterically, that Alexei could barely comprehend his words. But the gist was clear enough: Paulie was at the abandoned auto body shop, and things had gone horribly wrong. And Alexei was to get his ass out there, *immediately.*

125

L ee arranged to meet Ben in the parking lot of Diane's Tasty-Freeze, where he had shared the abbreviated meal with Dawn a little more than twenty-four hours ago. The parking lot was nearly pitch-black, the restaurant having been closed for hours. A single overhead halogen light, mounted high on a metal pole with peeling paint, provided the only source of illumination.

He and Izzy were panting by the time they arrived. They had gone through the woods and along several roads, Lee trying to maintain a brisk pace—but not too fast for Izzy. The girl had surprised him with her endurance. Her breathing had occasionally been labored along the way, but not once had she complained or asked him to slow their progress.

Ben was already waiting for them. He had turned off the truck's engine and headlights, but they could see its windshield glinting in the glow of the overhead light.

Ben stepped out of the truck and Izzy left Lee's side, running to her father.

"Izzy!" Ben said, kneeling down to take his daughter in his arms. "Did those men—did they—"

She gave him a puzzled look. Then, thinking the matter over, she said. "One of them hit me a few times. Then they tied me up. Then Lee came and killed them. That's all."

Lee walked over to the two of them, and Ben said: "Are there more of them? More of these men?"

"Yes," Lee said. "There are almost certainly more of them."

"Then let's kill the rest of them. After I get Izzy someplace safe, of course." Ben hugged his daughter again.

Lee sighed. Ben was determined to either personally avenge his wife, or to go down fighting the men who had brought meth into the county.

"Ben, let's you and I have a talk for a moment."

He motioned for Ben to walk with him. Ben ushered Izzy into the cab of his pickup truck.

"I know you want to fight," Lee said when they were alone. They had not walked very far away from the pickup truck. Izzy was clearly visible in the passenger's seat.

"You're damned right I do!"

"But what I need for you to do right now is to take your daughter someplace safe. I don't mean back to your house—or to anywhere in Hawkins County. You need to take her and hide someplace. Go visit a relative who lives out-of-state. Take the girl on a little vacation, for that matter. God knows she could use it, after what she went through tonight."

"You think I don't care about my daughter, is that it? You think I don't know how to keep her safe?"

Lee might have pointed out that he had not kept her safe this evening; but that would only muddy the waters: Izzy had ventured out of the house because of Lee. He could not fathom her exact motivations at the moment; but clearly she had followed him.

"I know you love your daughter," Lee said. "No one's questioning that. But I also know that you're spoiling for some revenge. You want to kill the men who were responsible in one way or another for the death of your wife. You can't kill the junkie who actually took her life, so you figure that you'll kill as many of those other men as you can."

"That's right." Ben muttered through clenched teeth. "And when

I'm done, they'll never cause anyone to go through what I went through. Not ever again."

"But here's what you don't understand: What I found out in Iraq, first trying to kill all the terrorists who planned 9/11—then trying to kill all the ones who killed my men: You'll never get to the end of them. Yes, you might kill a few, maybe many, in fact. But sooner or later one of them is going to fire a bullet with your name on it, and then your daughter is going to be an orphan, plain and simple."

"So what are you saying, Lee? You want me to just give up? You want me to pretend that my wife's still alive, and none of this ever happened?"

Lee reached out and put his hand on Ben's shoulder. The older man flinched momentarily before relaxing. "No, Ben, I know you can never do that. But you have to focus on what's most important now—and that thing is to be there for your daughter, no matter what."

When Lee removed his hand, Ben asked: "But what about you, Lee? Do you think you're bulletproof? You don't look bulletproof to me."

"No, of course not. But I have a lot less to lose—and a lot fewer choices. The government wants to put me in a cell, or maybe in an execution chamber. Those other men are trying to kill me outright. And I would leave no one behind: I don't have a child, I've never been married, and my parents are both dead."

Lee could see that Ben was wavering. A war was going on inside him, and he might go either way. He glanced back at Izzy, then said to Lee:

"I don't feel right about this whatever I do. I hear what you're saying, but I don't feel right about letting another man fight my war for me."

"That's not what I'm doing. This is *my* war, Ben. I wouldn't be involved in your war if it wasn't for mine."

"Okay," Ben said at length. "Okay. We'll do it your way. My mother lives near Lexington. In Somerset. She hasn't seen Izzy in a while. We'll go visit her for a few days—until this thing goes one way or another. We'll just need to stop by the house to get a few things."

"No," Lee said. "Don't go back to that house. Not until this is over. Leave now, and drive through the night. Don't stop until you're well clear of the county. Those men might not have given up on the idea of using your little girl as a hostage. And I left two of them dead tonight because they had taken her. You won't be the only one looking for revenge."

Ben shook his head, and Lee could anticipate his thoughts. There seemed to be no end to the dangers astir this night.

"You're right," Ben said. "We can be at my mother's house well before morning. We'll go shopping tomorrow to get what we need to tide us over."

At last it seemed that whatever else Lee would face—he would not have to worry about either Izzy or Ben getting themselves killed.

As relieved as he was about this positive development, he could not help reflecting that the bulk of his problems remained very much unsolved. He was still a wanted man. And then there was this group—multiple groups—of men who were bent on killing him.

Ben turned to go. "Will we hear from you again?"

Lee did not know what to say. It seemed that he would jinx himself either way.

"You know, when I was in Iraq, I remember this saying that the Arabs had, *insha-allah*. It means 'God willing.' And I guess that's about the best answer that I can think of."

"If you make it, Lee—and somehow I think you will—then you call us. We won't bother you until then. But I am looking forward to hearing from you when this is over."

"'God willing,' Ben. Consider it a promise."

Lee watched Ben walk back toward the truck. After he climbed inside, he spoke with Izzy for a minute. Even across the distance and the darkness, Lee could see the emotion written on her face.

She exited the truck before her father could stop her. She ran over to Lee and nearly tackled him when she threw herself against him.

"I don't want to go to my grandma's," Izzy said, her face pressed up against his chest. "I don't want to hear about you gettin' kilt on the news tomorrow."

"Well, I'm going to do my best to make sure that doesn't happen, Izzy." Lee patted the girl's shoulder.

"Can't you come with us?"

"No. This is the only way."

Izzy began to sob, and Lee could discern that the emotion sweeping through this girl was more than just the trauma of the preceding evening—and more than simply the concern she might have felt for a houseguest. This girl had obviously developed some sort of a crush on him, as girls of that age sometimes will.

"And when I come back, you and me and your father are going to get together and talk about what a mess this all was. We'll be able to do that after this is all over."

She looked up at him: "You promise?"

"I just promised you, didn't I?"

With that she separated herself from him, and ran back to her father, who was now standing patiently outside the pickup truck. Izzy turned back once and shouted: *"You be careful Lee! You come back safe, you hear me?"* And these words were partially choked by tears.

Well, Lee thought. *I suppose it's good to have her pulling for me. It might even bring me luck. I only hope I don't disappoint her by getting myself killed, after all.*

The girl and her father climbed into the truck. Ben started the engine, and Lee was bathed in the glare of the truck's headlights. Izzy was now waving at him furiously, as if she might bring him more luck by doing so. She turned around to continue waving as the truck rolled past him, toward the road.

Despite the much larger concerns looming over him, and despite the necessity of their going, Lee was more than a little sorry to see them go. In an odd way they had become almost like family to him over the short days they had been together. It had been a long time since he had been in any regular living situation that was even remotely domestic—not since before he had gone in the Marines—

before his mother died. He felt the return of that odd and now familiar feeling: He was alone in the world once again.

He waved at them one final time and they were gone.

126

"**Y**ou stupid, cowardly son-of-a-bitch!"

These were among the words that Paulie Sarzo screamed as he pummelled Alexei Primakov—first with his fists, and then with his feet after the Russian fell to the ground. Alexei was currently curled up in a fetal position in the gravel parking lot of the auto body shop where the girl had been held as hostage barely more than an hour ago.

Paulie did not know exactly what had happened—how the Russian had betrayed them—or why. Judging from the marks on his face, it appeared that Lee McCabe had somehow gotten to Alexei, and then forced him to provide the whereabouts of the Chamberlain girl. The Russian was an utter weakling; only a minimal amount of coercion would be needed to compel him to talk.

Now their hostage was gone, Big John and Tony Loscatti were dead, and Lee McCabe had slipped from their grasp once again.

Beating the Russian like this would do him no good, Paulie realized. He was wasting time and energy. He should simply shoot Alexei Primakov in the head and resume the hunt for Lee McCabe. A fresh group of Coscollino men was en route from Chicago; they would arrive by morning.

But the white-hot, molten rage was irresistible. It seemed to fill every cell of his being. Paulie would beat the Russian to death; and then he would continue to beat the inert, bloody pulp of the man until his rage was finally spent.

"*Vait a minute!*" Alexei screamed between two blows from the tip of Paulie's shoe. "*I have more information. Another vay to get Lee McCabe!*"

Paulie paused the beating. His rage was not yet spent; but he was actually winded from kicking the cowardly Russian.

"Go on," Paulie said.

Alexei sheepishly reached into his front pants pocket. Paulie could see that this simple movement caused him great pain: His right hand was swollen; Paulie had broken at least one of the fingers.

Alexei withdrew a small laminated card: It might have been a driver's license or a membership card of some sort.

"*Dis man,*" Alexei said, choking back tears. "McCabe vaz wearing dis man's clothes."

"So what?"

"I researched him. On za computer. He is da son of Marie Vilson, a teacher of Lee McCabe—from long ago. When McCabe vaz a boy."

Paulie prepared to deliver another kick when Alexei continued, frantically:

"Don't you see, Paulie? Lee McCabe was wearing the clothes of dis Marie Vilson's son. Dat means he was at der house. And *dat* means dat Lee McCabe care about dis woman—juss like he care about dat little geerl."

Paulie paused to consider Alexei's proposition: Lee McCabe had indeed proven to be susceptible to concerns about the welfare of hostages who meant something to him. They had taken Ben Chamberlain's daughter, and that had drawn him in like a magnet.

Could the same tactic work again? Well, why not? And it would be a lot easier to abduct this Marie Wilson than it would be to track Lee McCabe from scratch again.

"Okay," Paulie said. "That's not a bad idea, Alexei."

The Russian smiled through torn, bloody lips. Two of his front teeth were broken. "Oh, thank you, Paulie!" he said. "I beg you to give me second chance! I am veely sorry about vat happen before!"

Then he dug painfully inside his pocket again. "I even have the address of this Marie Wilson. Not far away! Easy to find. Very easy!" He held up a piece of paper that was covered by handwritten notes and a crude map.

"Sure, Alexei," Paulie said.

Paulie stepped back from the Russian, who now lay on his back. He withdrew a silencer-tipped pistol from his jacket and aimed it at the Russian's forehead. In what seemed to be only a fraction of a second, Alexei Primakov's facial expression shifted from tentative relief to utter dread.

"*No*—" Alexei said, futilely placing his battered hands upward, as if they could stop a bullet. Paulie fired the pistol twice, and Alexei's brain—the brain that had such knacks for computers and excuse-making—was obliterated by two rounds that shattered his forehead and removed the top of his skull. The body of Alexei fell backward like a mannequin that had been dropped.

Paulie stooped to the ground, and plucked the identity card from the gravel. He also picked up the paper that detailed the location of Marie Wilson's house.

Then he removed his cell phone from his shirt pocket. He had the numbers of the arriving group of men. He called the man who was leading them.

"Don't check in to the hotel yet," Paulie said into the phone. "You have to make a stop on your way into town."

127

Dawn was breaking, and Lee found himself bereft of both shelter and allies. Now that Ben had gone, he was once again without a place to stay. But he was still relieved that Ben and Izzy had gone, even if that meant resuming his solitary existence in the woods.

He would camp out in the surrounding countryside, he decided, and make forays into town as his plan required. He would wage his war against Lester Finn and the Chicago mobsters by himself. But now, once again, fate had dealt him a card that made the struggle even more difficult.

As soon as I make progress, Lee thought, *it seems that I must be due for a major setback*.

He was hiking in the direction of Blood Flats when his cell phone rang. It was an unidentified number with a local exchange.

Who could it be? For a moment Lee considered letting the call go to voicemail. But then he thought: *It could be Ben and Izzy*.

"Lee McCabe!" said the voice of the caller. Lee could hear wind rushing in the background. The male speaker—whoever he was— was obviously in a moving vehicle.

When Lee asked the man to identify himself, Joe Wilson—the

elder of Marie's two sons—appeared slightly offended that Lee had not recognized him by his voice alone.

"Have you forgotten about me already?" Joe asked. "And you were the one who said I should come with you!"

Then Lee remembered: The morning he left Marie's house, he had asked—practically challenged—Joe Wilson to accompany him. And now Joe was taking him up on it, apparently.

"Where are you Joe?"

"Three miles north of Blood Flats," he said. "I'm in my truck. I'm armed, too."

"Don't go into town," Lee said. "Meet me first."

He arranged to meet Joe just north of town, on a gravel road that went down into the woods. Even this was not safe. No roads were safe. The middle of the woods was not safe.

The Joe Wilson he met now seemed a different man from the Joe Wilson who had practically shoved him out on the road that morning. Lee walked up to Joe's pickup truck, an old Ford F-100 that had seen better days.

Joe had a pump-action shotgun in the front seat. He held the gun aloft so Lee could take a look at it.

"I'm ready, Lee," he said. "If you still want me to help you, I'm here and I'm armed."

"What about your mother?" Lee asked. This seemed a ridiculous and insulting to question to ask a thirty-year-old man, implying that he needed his mother's permission for an outing of this sort. But he had met Joe only because of his old connection to Marie. The man was bound to him in no other way.

"What do you mean, 'what about my mother'? Of course she isn't a part of this. This is between you and me."

"Joe," Lee began. "I need to ask you frankly: The other day, you were of no mind to come along with me. In fact, you wanted nothing to do with me. You pretty much shoved me out the front door. What made you change your mind? This is what you might fairly call a one-hundred and eighty-degree turnaround."

Joe ran one large hand across the stock of the shotgun. "You're right," he said. "I did change my mind."

"And now I'm asking you why."

"Well," Joe said—and Lee could sense that the other man was recalling some internal struggle. "My brother Jeremy—*my little brother*—he's been in Afghanistan 'bout a year now. I've got a dead-end job running a forklift on a factory. If he dies tomorrow he's a hero; if I die tomorrow I'm a nobody."

"And how many times have you fired that gun?"

For this Joe Wilson had no immediate answer. He stared back at Lee.

"How many times, Joe?"

"I've fired it."

Lee could see that he had made a mistake that morning—urging Joe to join the battle against Lester Finn and his extended network. The assistance of Jeremy Wilson—Joe's younger brother—Lee could surely have used. Jeremy was military-trained, and a combat veteran. But Joe had barely fired a weapon before; and he would likely freeze or make a careless mistake if he faced targets who fired back at him. Moreover, he was here for the wrong reason. His presence here was about demonstrating his worth—competing with the younger brother who had left town and was playing his own role in the events of the world.

Well, thought Lee, *I can understand that. We all have the need to prove ourselves. But this is not the time or the way for Joe to do it.*

"Go back, Joe," Lee said, not unkindly. He almost said *Go back to your mother*; but he stopped himself. "I appreciate this gesture; but this isn't your fight. And I can't ignore the fact that your mother runs the real risk of losing one of her sons each and every day, with Jeremy in Afghanistan. I could never forgive myself if I was the cause of her losing the other one."

Lee had expected a recriminating or bitter response of some sort; but Joe surprised him with his reply:

"Have it your way, Lee McCabe. You asked me to come and help you. And I did. If you die now, your blood—well, it will not be on my hands."

128

Luke paused in the doorway of the Boar's Head's utility room. He had been planning this day for weeks. And it had finally arrived.

He could hardly believe it. The prospects were heady—and a little scary, even for a man who had been to prison, and recently killed his coworker. He wondered, ironically, if the carp and the crawdads in the reservoir had finished eating Dan's body yet.

Dan had been a loudmouth. An idiot. He, on the other hand, was going to be rich.

That thought banished what was left of Luke's hesitation. He strode into the utility room, an empty blue gym bag in his hand. In a few minutes, this gym bag was going to contain a lot of money.

Lester's money.

As he kneeled down and removed the plywood that Lester had so meticulously placed before the old workbench, Luke could not suppress an involuntary smile. Lester had always dismissed him as a dummy—a mental lightweight.

Lester had never guessed that this impression had been imparted to him by design.

Luke knew that he was no rocket scientist—but nor was he the dullard that he had manipulated Lester into believing him to be. Luke had learned in prison, among other places, that it was sometimes advantageous to play the dummy. This encouraged men to underestimate you, to trust you with valuable secrets because they believed that you would never have the good sense to use such information to your advantage.

Well, in his own case they were wrong. And Lester had been wildly wrong.

The bar opened at noon. Every weekday morning, Luke arrived at the bar an hour early. This he did with Lester's full knowledge and consent. It was his job to prepare the place for the lunchtime crowd, and the post-lunchtime alcoholic crowd. And the tavern owner trusted him, after all.

Lester never suspected that Luke had long since seen him putting cash in the safe. Once Lester had turned around from his furtive chore and looked Luke straight in the face. Luke had been passing through the hall, on his way back to the storeroom. *What are you lookin' at?* Lester had asked. *Nothin*, Luke had replied, and kept walking.

But Luke had filed that observation away. He had some grasp of the scope of Lester's drug profits. He knew that the money was easily in the high six-figure range, possibly in the seven-figure range.

And a healthy percentage of it could be found in that safe at any given time.

So in the past weeks, Luke had made effective use of his daily unsupervised hour in the bar. He had gone over Lester's desk with intricate care, making sure to disturb nothing. Lester was fussy about his possessions. He would detect a single paper left out of place.

At first Luke had been frustrated. There were no numbers written on the desk blotter that could be reasonably assumed to be the combination to a safe. Then he had picked the lock on Lester's desk. His desk drawers had yielded some five-figure bundles of cash (which Luke, exercising considerable willpower, did not take).

A perusal of the various folders and documents inside the desk drawers produced extensive information about the extent of Lester's criminal activities. Luke deduced from the documentary evidence that Lester not only ran meth; he also operated a prostitution ring in Louisville. He also seemed to be working on additional schemes to launder more of his ill-gotten funds.

Luke found these materials interesting. It was a study in what was possible if a person simply decided to organize himself a bit. These materials also made him reflective: Thus far, his own ambitions had been limited to hopelessly small-time endeavors—like the burglary charge that had landed him in prison a few years back. Lester was taking things to the next level, which might explain why he was in Lester's employ rather than the other way around.

And after all these thoughts and all this snooping, Luke still did not have the combination to the safe.

Next Luke had tried a series of obvious numbers on the safe: Lester's date of birth, the phone number to the bar, his personal cell phone number. Luke had even found out the birth date of Lester's sainted mother, whom the barkeep had apparently respected.

Still no luck.

Then he had considered the idea of simply removing the entire safe. He was certainly strong enough. Once he had removed the safe from the bar, he could open it with a welding torch.

This option was tempting. But it would also amount to a gamble.

Luke had already figured out that the safe was a temporary storage place. Lester was emptying it at regular intervals, probably for deposit in a bank account.

That meant that the amount of money in the safe constantly fluctuated. The money built up during a certain period, until Lester emptied it.

If Luke happened to remove the entire safe shortly after Lester had emptied it, he would be left with little or nothing. And once he removed the entire safe and torched it open, there would be no turning back. Even Lester would be perceptive enough to figure out who the thief had been.

Therefore, he had to find the combination to the safe. Then he would need to monitor its contents over time, until it was so full that Lester would have to empty it soon.

Then he would steal the contents and flee.

For a while Luke was beginning to conclude that this plan would be beyond his means, all for want of the combination. He had been on the verge of giving up. Then one day, almost on a whim, he decided to check Lester's computer.

This had not occurred to him previously (a fact which Luke later regarded as highly ironic). Lester was a self-declared technophobe who subscribed to all sorts of harebrained conspiracy theories about the now pervasive devices. Some combination of Bill Gates, George W. Bush, and Barack Obama were using the Internet to monitor everyone's communications, Lester believed. Something crazy like that.

As a result, the tavern owner could barely use the Compaq PC that sat atop his desk. Luke did not believe that his boss even turned it on every day. On those relatively rare occasions when Lester summoned Luke to his office, the Compaq's screen was dark.

He therefore was not expecting much on the morning when he booted up the machine. *Why did Lester even own a computer*, he wondered, *if he never bothered to turn it on?* Lester had once claimed—in a rare moment of self-deprecation—that anything electronic baffled him. Lester's skills were probably adequate for surfing porn and accessing email, and not much else.

Thanks to a computer basics course he taken in prison, Luke did know the fundamentals of PCs and the Windows operating system. He passed the first hurdle when the Compaq started up without a prompt for a password. Then he launched Windows Explorer and began navigating through the file system.

There was only a handful of files in the My Documents folder. And the first one was the most obvious one: A Microsoft Word file entitled *Passwords.doc*.

Bingo! Luke had thought.

It would figure that Lester—who lacked the foresight to protect his computer with a password—had also failed to assign a password to Passwords.doc. Luke opened the file. It was a cornucopia of information.

Luke could see a series of numbers that he discerned to be bank account numbers, followed by another series of numbers that might have been passwords to the accounts. These, too, were tempting targets; but there was no mention of the banks that held the accounts. To track these down would be almost impossible.

Stick to the plan, he had thought. *Stick to the plan.*

At the bottom of the column he found what he was looking for: A dashed number that was without doubt the combination to a safe. His heart thundering, Luke had written down the combination on the back of a business card that he'd quickly fished from his wallet.

Then he had gone to the utility room, cleared the junk away from the safe, and turned the safe's dial to the numbers of the combination. As he had expected, the little metal door came swinging open.

Bingo!

But not quite. There had not been much money in the safe on that day: less than $5,000, Luke had guessed. So Lester must have emptied it only recently. That was okay, he had decided. He would have time to prepare before the safe became full again.

And so Luke had monitored the safe at regular intervals throughout the past four weeks—watching his future fortune grow by increments. It had been a nerve-wracking ordeal. He had had to fight the temptation to check the safe every day—a compulsion that would only increase the danger of exposure. He had also struggled against the knowledge that so much could go wrong: For example, Lester might change the combination and decide to store the new code on a slip of paper inside his shoe, or something odd like that. The tavern owner was a weird and unpredictable bird.

Now, as he opened the safe for what he knew would be the final time, he allowed himself to savor his sense of accomplishment. He had stuck to his plan and it had paid off. This was his jackpot: The safe was practically overflowing with stacks of one hundred dollar bills. *God, how he loved the face of Ben Franklin.*

As he scooped the cash into the gym bag, he contemplated the steps before him: First he would head to Louisville, where he had family and old friends (or old acquaintances who would surely give him shelter in exchange for a little cash.) While in Louisville, he would find a way to place the money into a bank account. While in prison, he had learned that professional criminals—the ones who made really big money—routinely set up offshore accounts in the Caribbean. This sounded like a plan to Luke.

He zipped the gym bag closed and lifted it, savoring its weight. With this money safely sheltered in the vault of some tropical island bank, he would never have to worry about being short of cash again. He would never again have to take orders from a man like Lester.

He stepped out into the hall, just outside the utility room. The clock hanging in the hall—a commemorative NASCAR theme clock that Lester had purchased some years ago—indicated that the time was 11:35 a.m. He was running a little late, but not disastrously so. He doubted that Lester would check the safe first thing upon his arrival. Hours—or even a full day if he were lucky—might pass before Lester opened the safe.

Every minute that passed until Lester discovered the theft would add to his head start.

With this fact in mind, there was one last step that he had to take before he departed. This would make the deception complete. Of course Lester would sense that something was up if he was simply truant from work. Luke removed his cell phone from his pants pocket and dialed the bar's land line. He could hear the phone ringing in Lester's office, and simultaneously in the front area: There was a wall phone behind the bar.

He left brief message telling Lester that he would be out sick today. This was a fairly rare occurrence for him—but not so rare, he hoped, so as to arouse his employer's suspicion.

He exited through the rear door. He had parked in the back parking lot today. He placed the gym bag on the floor of the front seat, on the passenger's side, before taking his seat and starting his car—an old Dodge that he would soon replace with something decent.

As he edged the car out into the early lunchtime traffic, he realized the nature of his mistake: He had erred by waiting so late to commit his heist and depart.

He could have left hours ago, before dawn.

He had waited until the late morning, he now understood, because he wanted to be able to pull back at the last minute—to wait another day.

He knew that Lester would respond with wrath when he found the money missing. It wouldn't take him long to connect the dots and figure out who had taken the money. Soon men would be hunting him—just as they were hunting Lee McCabe.

He started on the road out of town, a road that would eventually take him in the direction of Louisville. Now the enormity of his actions hit him, and the feeling was both terrifying and exhilarating. It was a bit like his murder of Dan at Lester's behest, but there had been no real upside to that. He had killed Dan to satisfy the whims of his (*now former*) boss. This action, on the other hand, would change his life forever, if he could only escape and hide the money.

He would have liked a joint. But since he did not have a joint he steadied himself by focusing on positive thoughts. Once he had the money secured in an offshore bank, he would head for Mexico. He would live in a big house with servants. (*Why not?—he had heard that American dollars could buy a lot down there.*) He would eat well. And he would get laid everyday. Yes, that should be more than doable down in Mexico.

Luke was feeling quite relaxed until he saw the flashing red lights in his rearview mirror, and recognized the markings of a Hawkins County Sheriff's Department squad car. Suddenly his thoughts of Mexico were gone, and Luke was quite certain that he would have to kill again before he even left Perryston.

129

L uke pulled the Dodge over to the curb and stopped. For a split second he had considered gunning the engine and running. But he knew that the ancient Dodge was no match for a turbocharged police car. The hot pursuit would be over in a matter of minutes.

Continuing to look in the rearview mirror, Luke watched the cop step out of his vehicle. It was not Sheriff Phelps, but Deputy Norris.

Luke was vaguely aware that some sort of understanding existed between the owner of the Boar's Head and this policeman. He had also sensed—from comments that Lester had inadvertently dropped from time to time—that there was hostility. The two men did not like each other.

Luke watched Norris approach. Now he looked at the reflection in the driver's side exterior mirror. Norris put on his hat and withdrew a metal clipboard from the cruiser's dashboard.

Nothing about the cop's gait or posture suggested undue caution or preparation for a confrontation of any sort. This might be nothing more than a routine traffic stop.

But there was the gym bag full of money sitting on the floor in plain view. Would Norris attempt to conduct a search of the Dodge's interior? Didn't cops do that at random sometimes, when they perceived a "reasonable cause," or something like that?

Luke's thoughts turned to another item on the floor of the Dodge. This item was beneath the driver's seat, directly behind his feet: a sawed-off 20-gauge shotgun.

Maybe he should pull the gun now, in the few seconds he had.

Maybe he should simply hold tight and see where this went.

The cop was not exactly relaxed; but he didn't seem to be focusing much attention on Luke himself. Norris was distracted. He was actually looking away, into the distance, distracted by something that was going on in his own little mental world. Not exactly typical behavior for a sheriff's deputy at a traffic stop.

"License and registration," Norris said. Then he recognized Luke. "Ah, you're one of Lester Finn's employees, aren't you?"

Luke was about to reply, *So are you*, but he stopped himself. Norris might be a dirty cop, but he presently had the power to crush Luke's entire future. Unless he used the shotgun.

"Uh, yeah," Luke said, giving the copper the dunce act. He leaned over and withdrew the Dodge's registration from the glove compartment. Luckily, this car was his, free and clear and not stolen.

"What's in that gym bag?" Norris asked. "Bricks?"

"Naw," Luke said. "Just some old books I'm getting' rid of,"

"You don't strike me as much of a reader. You did some time in the state pen, didn't you?"

Luke gave Norris a contrite stare. "Long time ago. I'm straight now. No more jail for me."

Norris sniggered, as if he was thinking that the Pope would just as likely stay out of Catholic churches.

"Say," Luke said. "Why did you pull me over?"

"Your license plate sticker is three months expired," Norris said. "But I tell you what I'm going to do: I'm going to let you off with a warning, since your boss is such a fine, upstanding member of the community, and you're making such an effort to turn your life around and walk the straight and narrow."

The sarcasm did not go over Luke's head, as the deputy had

doubtlessly thought it would. But he wasn't going to let the deputy know that.

"Gee, officer; I really appreciate that."

"Think nothing of it, jailbird," Norris returned Luke's license and registration. "And get yourself a new plate sticker. You can buy it down at the DMV. Next time I'll ticket your ass."

"Yes sir!"

Norris sighed and began a perfunctory trek back to his cruiser.

Luke put the Dodge in gear and cautiously edged the car back out into the flow of downtown traffic. He permitted himself a smile. His luck had seemed to have run out for a moment there; but in the end he had escaped.

Maybe this was going to work after all.

130

L ester Finn was in a foul mood. First the sick call-in from Luke; and then Paulie Sarzo had refused to return his calls.

This latter development worried him considerably. For days the Italians had been glued to him like the proverbial flies to manure. Now they were ignoring him. Shunning him. The most likely explanation was that they were taking matters into their own hands, running their own operation. But there might be another explanation, as well: Perhaps they were planning to eliminate him.

Lester involuntarily reached for the pistol he kept below the bar when the front door of the Boar's Head swung open. He had half expected to see one of the Coscollinos's hit men, ready to gun him down with a silencer-tipped weapon.

But it was only the most infinitely corruptible member of Hawkins County's Finest.

"Norris," Lester said. "I'll have to ask you to come back in ten minutes. We open at noon today."

The sarcastic barb allowed Lester to release some of his internal tension. The last week had frayed his nerves and left him jumpy. First the botched murders at the trailer park, then the whole issue of Lee McCabe. Perhaps he had made a mistake the other night, in the parking lot of Diane's Tasty-Freeze. He should have put a bullet in McCabe's head right then and there, while he had the chance.

Now the county was filling up with dangerous outsiders: made men and government men. Lester had noted the increased presence of the state police, and he suspected the involvement of the FBI.

And damned Italian gangsters who disdained him. *Who called him a hick!*

A showdown of some sort was brewing. The entire situation was going to come to a head soon, he believed. Lesser men might not live through it. But he would survive.

Nevertheless, it left him with a lot to think about. And the message from Luke left him short-handed and with even more to do.

Norris ignored Lester's attempt at humor. "If you don't get a handle on this situation very soon, Lester, you aren't going to have any bar to open or close. You aren't going to have jack shit. You'll be spending what's left of your miserable life behind bars—if you're lucky."

"You're talking awfully confidently for a lawman who's taking bribes, aren't you?"

"I never wanted your money," Norris said indignantly. "I'm involved in this because you blackmailed me, you son-of-a-bitch. Don't think that I've forgotten that for even one second."

"I'm sure the jury would appreciate that distinction," Lester said. "As would your new neighbors in one of our state institutions. I don't need to tell you what they do to former cops in prison. You'll be getting it from both sides. It will be a contest to see who kills you first, the guards or your fellow inmates."

Lester could see that he had struck a nerve with his last comment. Norris visibly bristled. *Good*, he thought. *Let Norris worry. I'm sure as hell worried.*

"Alright," Norris said through clenched teeth. "So we both have a stake in seeing this thing out to—some sort of satisfactory conclusion. That's why I'm here. I want an update. A status report."

"And I can't tell you anything right now. McCabe is still alive, as far as I know. What I can tell you is that our friends from Chicago have more or less taken over, and they have considerable resources to throw at the problem."

Norris looked at the ground and shook his head. "You think that's a solution? You screwed up big time, when you got involved with those thugs. If it weren't for them, the FBI wouldn't be in Perryston, and the state boys would have forgotten all about this by now."

Lester felt his stomach churn. So the FBI *was* involved.

Over the past several days he had been trying to mentally channel his granddaddy, who would certainly have known what to do. Yes, the old man would have set everything right by now, he was sure. But Lester had been unable to gain any insights from his dead grandfather, if such a thing were even possible.

"Listen to me, Norris," Lester said. "One of my employees, an idiot named Luke, called in sick today, and I'm short-handed. I have to open the bar in less than ten minutes. We can discuss this other matter later. Until then, I can assure you that everything is under control."

Norris laughed, but there was no humor in it. "'Under control?' You can't even control your own employees. I just stopped your 'employee' Luke on the main drag out here for expired tags."

"What are you talking about?"

"I pulled your man Luke over not ten minutes ago. He didn't look sick to me. And maybe he's not such a dummy, Lester. Maybe you are. Luke had a big blue gym bag full of something that looked like bricks or bundles of paper. When I asked him what it was he told me it was books."

131

"Norris, get the hell, out! Go!" Lester shouted, the color draining from his face.

The lawman departed. There was no more need for the pretense that as an officer of Hawkins County, Norris commanded special respect. He had given himself to too much sordidness. And Lester was in no mood to cater to pretense of any kind. If Norris had not departed willingly, he was prepared to wave the deputy away with a gun.

But before Norris left, Lester did have the foresight to confirm the direction in which Luke had been traveling.

He bolted into the utility room, and threw the plywood camouflage away from the safe's hiding place in a mad scramble. His hand was shaking as he dialed the safe's combination.

After Norris's revelation, Lester had required no less than a few seconds to connect Luke's truancy to some sort of treachery. Luke had been lying to Norris about the contents of his gym bag, that much was certain. No way the big dummy would be driving around town with a bag full of books.

When Lester opened the safe, he saw that his worst suspicions were in fact real: Luke had somehow divined the safe's combination.

And he had stolen a great deal of money. A crippling amount of money.

The big idiot's act of betrayal could not have come at a worse time. With the way things were imploding around him, Lester had been thinking about making a run for some idyllic overseas location. Thinking about it a lot, in fact. The recent aloofness of the Coscollinos was an omen that he could not afford to ignore.

He didn't bother to close the empty safe. He speed-dialed TJ Anderson, so far the most capable and reliable of the thugs he had recruited in Hawkins County.

But there was a marked shift in TJ's attitude. His new right-hand man answered him warily, with a hint of suspicion.

In his current state of mind, Lester was in no mood for subtlety. He asked TJ what the hell was up.

"I got a call from that little dago—what's his name? Sarzo. Yeah. Way he talked, you been demoted, Lester."

No! No! Lester thought. Everything was going wrong at once.

"Listen to me, Anderson. And listen to me good. I'm the one who pays you—not the wops from Chicago. That means you take your orders from me—and only from me."

"Yeah, but those Italians can sure put a bullet in me, Lester. I know better than to mess around with those guys."

"We'll talk about them later. Right now we have another emergency."

Lester told TJ only what he needed to know: that Luke must be apprehended. TJ asked Lester: What about those Italians? Lester had to promise Anderson an additional bonus when Luke was caught.

"Just find Luke," Lester said. "I'll make it worth your while. Leave the Italians to me."

Luke had talked a lot about Louisville; he had mentioned having family and friends in the city. And based on the bearings Norris had given him, that would be the direction in which he would be heading. There was only one main highway that could take you from Blood Flats to the Louisville-bound interstate. And the big dummy could not have gotten very far. Not yet.

Lester was relieved when TJ Anderson finally agreed. He seethed at the perfidy of the Coscollinos; but right now, he knew, he had to focus on the money. He had to keep Anderson on track.

Not that Lester planned to stand by and rely solely on the competence of others. The bungle at the trailer park had convinced him of the folly of that course. He would join in the pursuit himself. He would savor the expression on the big idiot's face when he was caught, his deceitful scheme cut short.

Lester smiled to himself, in spite of his anger and his considerable anxiety.

He was going to get his money back.

And Luke was going to pay for his sins.

132

L uke saw the four-wheel drive pickup heading his way, barreling down the highway. He recognized it immediately as the truck belonging to one TJ Anderson, the new favorite among Lester Finn's band of enforcers.

And he knew that Anderson was coming for him.

He didn't believe in coincidences. Somehow Lester had been tipped off. Perhaps Lester had entered the bar a few minutes after his own departure and had decided to check on his money before he did anything else. Maybe the stupid cop had told him. *Of course—it was probably the damn cop. Why hadn't he figured on that?* He already knew that Lester and Deputy Norris were working together. So why didn't he assume that the cop would contact Lester, upon discovering one of his employees in a suspicious situation?

Luke's anxieties about the truck were confirmed when the vehicle suddenly switched lanes and accelerated even faster in his direction.

Then he saw that there were two men in the back of the truck, both of them holding rifles.

Damn! To come this close to freedom—this close to the good life and Mexico and constantly having different women and all the rest of it....Only to have his ambitions crushed and his life extinguished at the last minute!

He was not going to let that happen. Not without a fight.

Luke pulled the steering wheel sharply to the right, down a narrow road that barely consisted of two lanes. He had long ago forgotten the road's name, but he remembered it from his youth in Hawkins County. He also knew that this particular road had a distinct advantage as an escape route: a number of gravel tributaries branched off from it. If he could turn down one of them before the men in the truck were close enough to see him, they would not know his exact whereabouts. They would have to use the process of elimination, going down each gravel road until they found him.

And by then he would be gone.

The Dodge nearly skidded off the pavement as he rounded the bend, its tires screaming in protest against the blacktop. As soon as he had made the turn he gunned the accelerator again. The gravel roads were appearing now on either side of him; they bore quaint names like Cemetery Pass and Weeping Widow Hollow.

He did not take the first of these turns, nor the second or the third. That would be obvious. He made the Dodge roar down the first dip in the main road and over the hillside. Then he jerked the steering wheel to the left, shooting down a gravel-covered lane called Wilma Jean's Walk.

The Dodge's undercarriage scraped the ground as the road became more and more uneven, rutted as it was with holes and depressions where the spring rains had washed away large amounts of gravel. He drove over a particularly deep gulley that cut directly through the road, and for a second he was sure that he had lost a tire —but the Dodge kept going. He was deep in the woods now. Dappled sunlight made kaleidoscopic patterns across the dashboard.

Then he saw, directly in front of him, that the road abruptly ended, and he realized the depth of his own stupidity.

He had chosen a dead-end road for his escape route.

He put the Dodge in park and frantically tried to think. The engine rumbled in the silence of his surroundings.

The first thing he needed to do was to kill the engine. If Anderson and his men were nearby now (and the odds of this were high) then the Dodge's motor would give them an immediate fix on his location.

The car was all but useless now. He could not drive it forward. And he could not go back the way he came, where they might be waiting for him.

His only chance, he decided, was to make a run for it through the woods. He pulled the gym bag from the floor beside him. The damned thing was heavy. When he had been back at the Boar's Head, the weight of the gym bag had seemed like a blessing. Now it seemed like a curse. He would not be able to run very fast while carrying it. But leaving it behind was out of the question. If he lost the money, all the risks he had taken thus far would be for nothing.

The gym bag in hand, Luke ran from his car and made a course straight into the adjacent woods. He leapt over a ditch, and his feet nearly slid on the carpet of leaves that that covered the embankment on the other side. *Why did this country have to be so damned hilly?*

Up the hill he went, waiting for the sound of Anderson and his men, waiting for a shot to pierce his back and leave him writhing on the ground, unable to move or speak but still conscious in the throes of an unspeakable pain.....

Finally his feet landed on level ground. He had made it to the top of the hill, the burden of all Lester's ill-gotten money notwithstanding. He was almost home free now. He could make his way through the woods, maintaining a careful distance from any roads whereby Lester's men might track him. When he got far enough away, he would simply peel a few hundred dollar bills from one of the bundles in the gym bag and pay cash for another means of transportation.

He was holding the gym bag in his left hand. The lack of a counterweight made him suddenly conscious of the very essential item that he had left in the Dodge.

The shotgun.

He needed the shotgun. And the package of shells that were in his glove compartment. Despite his head start, there was a chance that he would encounter Lester's men at some point in his journey. He also needed some means to protect himself from more random, opportunistic theft. He was carrying a small fortune—*no, not such a small fortune*—in the gym bag.

Cursing his own forgetfulness, Luke placed the gym bag behind a massive oak tree and began a hasty descent back down the hillside. There was still no sign of TJ Anderson. It would be all right. He had time to grab the shotgun from beneath the driver's seat.

An eternity seemed to pass as he navigated his way downward, sliding much of the way, but remaining on his feet.

He leapt across the ditch again, experiencing an explainable but nevertheless discomforting feeling of déjà vu.

All his life, people had dismissed him as a big dummy. Lester and his late coworker had only been the latest in a long series. Even his own father—a small, cruel, alcoholic man, had called Luke an idiot, a dummy, and a fool. But he had not laughed on that day when finally, at the age of fourteen, Luke had had enough, and he had thrashed the old man within an inch of his life.

That had brought him minimal satisfaction—especially when the old man, still recuperating from his beating, had threatened to strangle or shoot him in his sleep. So he had left home and dropped out of school, eventually drifting into a life of petty crime.

His size and physical strength had always sufficed to save him when his limited understanding of the world caused him to feel overwhelmed. That had certainly been the case in prison, where he had survived by playing dumb most of the time, and occasionally exploding with brutality when someone pushed him too far or outright threatened his life.

He had never been sure of the actual gap between the *pretend* Luke—the one who presented a dumb face to the world for protective purposes—and the *real* Luke. He was not as dumb as he pretended to be, he knew; but he certainly tended to end up on the losing side of things. A man who couldn't steer his circumstances to some sort of advantage couldn't be very smart, he figured.

This thing with the money, it was the first time in his life when he finally seemed to gain the upper hand. He was thrilled by the size of the fortune, of course; but there was also the sheer satisfaction of outsmarting Lester.

It could not unravel for him at the last minute.

He pulled open the front door of the Dodge on the driver's side. He reached beneath the seat and felt the walnut stock of the sawed-off shotgun.

That was when he heard the rumbling of a vehicle—a low, deep rumbling, almost diesel-like. The sort of rumbling that could only belong to a big, jacked-up four-wheel drive pickup truck. That was no 4-cylinder passenger car coming his way.

Luke pulled the shotgun clear of the seat and took aim at the pickup truck. The last thought to go through Luke's mind was the futility of the gesture—the stupidity of it, really. A single sawed-off shotgun was no match for a truckful of men with various semiautomatic weapons.

One of the gunmen in the truck cut him down with two shots. Luke's neck—and most of his face—exploded in dark red ribbons of blood, bone, and flesh.

The shotgun fell to the gore-streaked surface of the gravel road. The one shot that Luke had managed to discharge did no harm to the men inside the truck, and almost no harm to the vehicle: One of the truck's headlights was shattered.

The two gunmen leapt down from the back of the truck, doing their best renditions of rebel war whoops. The shooting of Lester's rogue employee had been an unexpected diversion.

TJ Anderson exited from the driver's side of the cab. He silenced the gunmen with a sharp word and a harsh stare.

Anderson stepped over Luke's ruined body and poked his head into the front seat of the Dodge. He looked first on the passenger floor, the most obvious location for the money. When he found nothing there he looked in the backseat, which contained a small suitcase that Luke had evidently packed for the journey, but absolutely no bundles of hundred-dollar bills.

Finally he popped the lid of the trunk. He rooted through the random garbage strewn back there: beer cans, soda bottles, and empty, crumpled bags from McDonald's and Hardee's.

But absolutely no money. Lester had told him over the phone that Luke would have the money in a gym bag.

Then Anderson heard another vehicle: He didn't have to look up to know that it was Lester Finn himself. Lester had been communicating with him via cell phone throughout the pursuit.

"Good!" Lester shouted, practically jumping from his car. The old tavern owner's long hair looked wet and matted behind his head. He held a weapon of his own—a big revolver that appeared to be a .44 magnum.

Lester strode forward. He gave Luke's body a brief, contemptuous stare, and nothing more.

"The money!" Lester said impatiently. "Let me see the goddamned money!"

TJ Anderson sighed, while the two men on his own crew sniggered at Lester Finn. They would take the old criminal's money but they brooked him no respect.

"Lester," TJ said simply. "I believe we have a problem."

133

Lee McCabe watched his tormenters confer in the cul-de-sac of the gravel road. He had happened late upon this scene—just in time to see the big man frantically carry the gym bag back into the woods. Lee watched him place the gym bag behind the tree before scrambling back to his vehicle. Then the shootout had occurred, or rather the slaughter. The lone man had had no chance. He might just as well have turned his own weapon upon himself.

Lee watched from the hillside opposite the one that the dead man had gone up, then descended, coming back the way he had come, and then into the deathtrap.

Now, as he heard Lester scream and curse at the man called Anderson, he began to piece the situation together. The gym bag had apparently contained money, no doubt a mother lode of Lester's drug profits. And Lester, obviously, wanted it back.

"He must have dropped the money somewhere along the road," Anderson speculated. "Or maybe someone was working with him. Hell, the money might be on its way to Louisville or Lexington now, for all we know."

This provoked more screaming and cursing from Lester Finn, until finally Anderson said. "Now hold your horses, Lester. And don't you be threatening me or abusing my men. We did what you asked. We stopped this man for you."

"But don't you see?" Lester shouted back. "You also killed him. And he is the only one who knows where my money went."

"We'll find your money, Lester. We'll find it and then you'll give us a percentage. Like you promised."

Lester had no immediate response to this proposal. Lee knew what the tavern owner was thinking: Anderson and his men would look for the money; and if they found it Lester would never see it again.

But these men did not know where the money was, of course, any more than Lester did. By the time they had arrived, the dead man had already returned to his abandoned getaway car. He had already hidden the money.

"You do that," Lester said at length. Finn apparently realized that the dead man and Anderson had unwittingly conspired to back him into a corner. "You just do that. And I'll give you a ten percent commission when you find it."

"Mighty generous of you, Lester."

"Twenty percent if you find it within three hours!"

If Lester detected the sarcasm in Anderson's voice, he certainly gave no indication. "Alright! Get your asses in gear and let's find that gym bag!"

Lee continued to listen. He had no trouble hearing the shouting men. This might be good news, very good news indeed.

Over the past hours, a new plan had begun to form in his mind: He would capture Lester Finn and extract a confession from him. Force Lester to tell him—at gunpoint if necessary—the names of all the men who had carried out the killings at the Tradewinds.

The problem, of course, was that Lester would be difficult to capture. From what Lee had observed, his movements outside the Boar's Head were random and unpredictable—and he was always armed and surrounded by associates when in his bar.

But the missing money. Lee could retrieve the gym bag after the men had gone. Then he would contact Lester Finn and give him an ultimatum: If you want the money, meet me alone. Then Lee could extract the confession. His cell phone had a voice memo recorder.

Did this idea have a chance of working—*or was it simply the ill-thought product of a desperate mind?*

No, I can make that work, Lee thought. *I can pull it off. Lester Finn will be the desperate one. He'll agree to anything in order to get that gym bag back. And he'll reason that if he retrieves the money without the help of his men, then he won't have to deliver on his promise of a finder's fee. I can use Lester's greed against him.*

Lee he was feeling better about his prospects. He would only have to wait until Lester and his men cleared the area, which they would surely do soon. Then his cell phone—the device that was central to his plan of trapping Lester—began to ring inside his pocket.

L ee did not have time to curse himself, to reflect at length on his mistake. Throughout his journey, he had alternately set the cell phone's ring to the silent/vibrate mode. He should have checked it. But he had neglected to take this one simple step. And he would likely die as a result.

Lester's men immediately swung their guns in his direction. And they almost as quickly picked out his form among the bushes. Lee did not even draw his gun.

"Who is that?" Lester screamed. He gestured for his men to hold their fire. Lee supposed that Lester did not want to add the death of yet another uninvolved civilian to rap sheet. "Stand up and show yourself. As you can see, we're very well armed down here."

Lee knew that if he identified himself, they would instantly kill him. And yet, running was no option either.

Maybe this is finally the end of the line, Lee thought. *Maybe I should pull my gun and go down fighting right here. I could take a few of them with me.*

But Lee knew that under the circumstances, he would be able to take no more than one of them down. If he was lucky.

"Your man put the money in a blue gym bag!" Lee shouted. "I saw him! I've been tracking him since he was in town!"

"Who the hell are you?" Lester shouted back. "Wait a minute —you're—"

"He gave the money to an accomplice!" Lee called back.

"Hey, that's Lee McCabe over there!" one of Lester's hired guns shouted. "Shoot him! Take him out now!"

Lee tensed his body, ready to make what would be a futile attempt at escape on foot.

Then Lester pointed his gun at the man who spoke. "Not yet, we're not!" Then back to Lee: "Stand up slowly, McCabe. Keep your hands in the air! And don't even think about running or pulling a gun. We'll shred you like paper."

This was no reprieve from death, was it? Lee did not want to walk into the midst of these men, who would likely torture him until he revealed the location of the money.

Nevertheless, there was no choice but to do as Lester commanded. Slowly, Lee pushed himself up from the earth, then shakily stood on his feet. He kept his hands in the air.

"That's good, McCabe! That's good," Lester said, "Now come down here! Keep walking!"

When he stood among them, TJ Anderson snatched his pistol— one that Ben had given him—from his waistband. "Give me that!" Lester snapped, and snatched the pistol from TJ's hand. He shoved the pistol into his own pocket. Lester held a .44 magnum revolver in his free hand. He aimed the giant revolver at Lee's nose, so he could see down the barrel. The inside of the gun looked vast and cavernous at such close proximity.

"You know what I want!" Lester said. "Start talking, McCabe. Tell me where I can find my money, or I'll blow your fucking head off."

Lee was terrified. This was, he realized, perhaps the closest he had ever come to dying helplessly at the hand of a man who had taken him prisoner. This was the way that so many of the jihadis' prisoners had died in Iraq. To Lee it seemed a horrible way to die, and he had always hoped that he would not meet such an end.

His only chance would be to bluff Lester. But he could not push the tavern owner too far. The man's base emotions—his vanity, his rage—obviously overrode his self-interest. Otherwise, he would not have wasted the chance he had had at the Tasty-Freeze. A man like this was so unpredictable. At any second he might kill Lee out of sheer spite, even though he would curse his own actions seconds later.

Lee forced himself to laugh. "Or you'll 'blow my head off?' Isn't that exactly what you've been trying to do all week?"

Lester's cheeks clouded with an unmistakable flush of rage.

"Now on the other hand," Lee went on. "Maybe if you were willing to offer me something—say my freedom and enough money to get me out of the county—out of the state—then maybe we could work something out. A strategic alliance, so to speak."

"Lester," said TJ Anderson, interrupting them. "This fella could be lying, you know." He pointed the barrel of his gun at McCabe, so that now Lee had two guns aimed directly at his head. "You said that you tracked him out here; and you're on foot and he was ridin' in a car. How to you explain that?"

"I hitched a ride," Lee said, knowing how unlikely this aspect of his story was.

"Ain't nobody goin' to give a wanted man a ride," TJ scoffed.

"I still have friends in the county," Lee said.

"Ask me, Lester," said Anderson. "Mr. Lee McCabe here is telling you a tall one. I say we go ahead and put a couple rounds through his skull, then we get busy findin' your money, which is probably somewhere in between this spot and your bar."

Lester smiled at Lee. "What do you think, McCabe? TJ's got a point. I do need you dead; and we're wasting time with you."

"Don't do it, Lester," Lee said. "Not if you want to find your money. I am the only man alive who can tell you where it is. But I'm not going to tell you so you can shoot me five seconds later. You have to give me my life. And my freedom."

Lee realized that what he was asking for now was a far cry from the plan he had devised only a while ago—in which he was going to capture Lester and set the terms of their negotiation. But once again, the ground had shifted beneath him.

"What color was the gym bag that Luke was carrying?" Lester asked.

Luckily, Lee had noticed the color.

"Blue," he said without hesitation.

A smile spread across Lester's face.

"Good, McCabe. Very good."

"Could be a lucky guess," TJ suggested.

"TJ," said Lester. "You may be right. But with Luke dead now, and the money missing, I'm going to need to take a flexible approach to this situation."

"Lester," TJ protested. "Paulie Sarzo wants him dead. He's made that pretty clear."

Lester turned his head to face TJ. The gun that he held before Lee's face did not waver. "Is that what this is about, Anderson? What the wops from Chicago say?"

TJ merely shook his head. "You're making a mistake if you don't kill him right now."

"We'll see about that," Lester replied. "Mr. McCabe, say goodnight."

Without further warning, the pistol shifted rapidly before Lee's eyes. He saw a blur, then felt a sharp blow against his temple, followed by a flood of unimaginable pain that seemed to vibrate and resonate throughout his entire head. He stumbled forward, and then the world went out of focus before plunging into total darkness.

135

Dawn Hardin did not do as Lee had instructed. She did not go to stay with her aunt in Bardstown. She remained in the little efficiency apartment that she had rented near the center of Blood Flats.

Lester Finn did not molest her further—not after that night when she and Lee encountered him in the picnic area outside Diane's Tasty Freeze.

What was the point of running to Bardstown? She had grown fatalistic. The results of the blood test had given her one more obstacle—one more millstone to struggle with. She was not yet twenty-three, and she had ruined her life.

Her cravings for meth were growing uncontrollable. She had rationed her supplies; but she had exhausted the last of the drug the previous night.

She sat in her living room, shaking uncontrollably, chills and cramps buffeting her body.

Where was Lee? Where was he?

A few minutes ago she had called his cell phone number; but there had been no answer. It would have been comforting to hear his voice—to know that he had made it out of the county, if that was what he had decided to do. Simply to know that he was still alive.

But Lee had not answered his cell phone, and she had not left a message. What would she say to him? Would she ask him why he hadn't called her? It wasn't like she was his girlfriend, was it? This idea caused her a bitter laugh. After the news she had given him, that was pretty much ruled out, wasn't it? Even if Lester Finn, and the charges against Lee, and all of their other problems dropped off the face of the earth tomorrow.

Even if her family accepted her back now, things would never be the same at home.

No way out. No solution.

She could not bear the claustrophobic solitude of the apartment any longer. She walked down the main staircase of her building, and out into the little alley where she had seen Lee walking a few days earlier. The sun was hot; but it seemed to reduce the trembling chills that were troubling her so.

Dawn stepped out onto the sidewalk. From this vantage point she could see much of the town's center: the war memorial, a little park where she used to play when she was a child. Where her father used to take her and her younger sister, Liz.

She did not recognize Lester Finn's car until the garish red Cadillac was almost on top of her. Her first impulse was to dart back into the alley, as Lester would surely see her and stop to harass her.

But Lester's attention was fixed on the figure in the passenger seat. A figure that was slumped against the passenger's side window.

A large hat—a fedora of some sort—had been pulled down over Lee's face. Dawn caught only a fleeting glimpse of his chin.

She felt two emotions surge through her: Terror for Lee, and rage at Lester Finn.

Was Lee dead? No—it wouldn't make sense for Lester to kill him and then bring his corpse back into town like this. But Lee was clearly incapacitated.

Lester would be taking him to the Boar's Head, of course. Where else? Dawn knew immediately what she would have to do—not only for Lee, but also for herself. There was more than one way to find redemption.

136

A CLOSED sign hung in the front window of the Boar's Head. There would be no business at the bar today. Today Lester needed the space for more important matters.

He stood behind the bar in his customary spot. He was smart enough to know that his situation was on the verge of unraveling. He still believed that he would triumph in the end, though his margin for error might be growing thinner: He was smarter than his enemies, he resolved, smarter than his opponents believed. Their underestimation of him would be their downfall.

Lester Finn was alone in the Boar's Head, except for one party, who could not add much to the conversation. Lee McCabe lay at Lester's feet behind the bar. A chain with one-inch steel links was wrapped around Lee's body. The two ends of the chain were joined by a padlock. The key to the padlock was attached to Lester's key ring.

"What do you say, McCabe?" Lester asked, in a tone that suggested a casual conversation over beers. "How's your head? Are you ready to tell me where that gym bag is?"

Lee McCabe made an indecipherable sound from the floor. The ex-marine was in pretty bad shape, after a few close encounters with the pointed toes of Lester's cowboy boots. The earlier blow to his head did not help him either, though he had (much to Lester's surprise) begun to awaken during the drive back to the bar.

He had told TJ to take his crew away and await further instructions. Now that TJ was in communication with Paulie Sarzo, he could no longer be trusted. If Lester managed to extract the needed information from Lee McCabe, he might be able to retrieve the money without further assistance from Anderson. Then he would not have to pay Anderson the commission. He could simply kill McCabe and tell Anderson that his prisoner had been lying, after all.

Then he would get the hell out of town. Out of the country.

But Lee McCabe would have to talk first; and the young man didn't appear ready to talk yet.

That would change with the right sort of persuasive techniques.

"Come on, McCabe," Lester said. "I haven't got all day; and this can't be much fun for you. Tell me where the gym bag went. And don't change your story again. First you said there was an accomplice, then you said that Luke left the money in the woods."

A few minutes ago, McCabe had tried to lure Lester into going for a walk in the woods. McCabe had claimed that he had made up the story of the accomplice in order to mislead Lester's men. The money, he said, was actually in the woods. And while he knew where the gym bag was located, he could not adequately describe the location. He would need to see the terrain; he would need to guide Lester to the exact spot.

The oldest ruse in the world. He would either have led Lester into an ambush, or tried to turn the tables with his hand-to-hand combat skills. Lester had no doubt that Lee was a skilled hand-to-hand fighter, given his physical condition and military training. He had no intention of placing himself in circumstances where the young ex-marine would have an advantage. Any advantage at all.

Lester did not intend to play games with McCabe much longer. The young man either knew where the money was located, or he was lying. Either way, Lester would discover the truth soon enough.

He had laid a towel across the surface of the bar, and here he had assembled a variety of items that would serve his task: a nine-inch butcher knife, a pair of kitchen shears, an ice pick. Lester smiled: In a few minutes, McCabe would likely be feeling more articulate—more cooperative.

Lester was proud of his ingenuity and resourcefulness. He had created a complete interrogation kit from a collection of randomly gathered items. *I could have been a professional inquisitor during the Middle Ages*, he thought. *I seem to have an instinct for this sort of thing.*

At the same time, he realized that an activity like this was beneath his dignity, a job better suited to one of his underlings. That was the way it was supposed to work: the man at the top gives the orders, and the pawns carry them out. But now there no underlings whom he could trust.

Oh well, I suppose it can't be helped, Lester thought. He lifted the butcher knife and said to McCabe: "Where should we start, McCabe? How about we start with one of your fingers?"

At that moment, Lester's cell phone began to ring. He laid the butcher knife back down on the towel and answered the call. It was Dawn Hardin.

When Dawn said that she wanted to meet, Lester's first inclination was to refuse. He didn't have time to dally with junkies today. Then he reconsidered: It might be amusing to bring Dawn Hardin here. It might serve his purposes. She had been his pawn in the past, and she could play that role today—albeit in a different way.

"Sure, I'll meet with you," Lester said. "But you have to come right now. I don't have much time. Now listen to my instructions, because I don't intend to repeat myself......"

Perfect timing, Lester thought as he terminated the call. If Lee wouldn't talk to save himself, perhaps he would feel like talking after Lester had sawed off one of the junkie's ears or fingers.

137

D awn sat inside her car in the parking lot of the Boar's Head for almost five minutes before she summoned the composure to open the vehicle's door. She felt multiple forces at work against her: For one thing, her urge for the drug was nearly overpowering, threatening to block out every other thought—no matter how hard she tried to will the cravings away.

"Once an addict—always an addict." Hadn't she heard those words on the streets innumerable times? Had she really believed that she would be able to conquer meth simply by taking a sentimental journey back to Blood Flats? From the first moment she stepped inside her parents' house, one fact was evident: Home had changed irrevocably. There was truly no such thing as going back.

She felt guilt over Lee's predicament. He could be dead right now, and it was partially her fault—at least indirectly. Her habit did finance the forces that had created this mess, the ones that were attempting to kill him.

And for all she knew, Lee might be dead already. That thought filled her with dread. Strange that it should affect her so deeply— after all, she barely knew Lee McCabe, and she certainly had ample problems of her own.

And finally, she sensed a dreadful finality about the task on which she was about to embark.

Is this a suicide mission? she asked herself.

No—it could not be a suicide mission. If she died without accomplishing her aim, her death would be in vain—one more wasted opportunity to end a lifetime of wasted opportunities.

She looked inside her purse one final time before she stepped out of the car. The .38 special was still there.

Her plan was simple, if desperate: She would walk inside the Boar's Head. She would catch Lester unawares. She would kill him with the revolver. And then she would free Lee McCabe.

Beyond that, she had no idea: She knew she would be tempting fate to even imagine a successful outcome, one in which both she and Lee emerged from this ordeal alive and free.

The gravel parking lot was dusty and heat-baked; sunlight reflected off the remnants of a broken beer bottle. Dawn closed her car door but did not lock it. Maybe she would be making a fast escape from here in a few minutes. Perhaps the two of them would be fleeing together, having defeated Lester. Was that really too much to ask for? Didn't fairy tales come true once in a while?

She glanced down at her forearm—it was scrawny and scarred with meth scabs. The drug had done that to her, and still she wanted more of it. Truth be told (*and, oh God, how difficult it was to be honest about this*) she believed that she wanted the drug even more than she wanted to see Lee alive and safe again.

The big double mahogany wood doors of the Boar's Head were closed. A CLOSED sign hung in the tinted window, in front of the curtains—just has Lester had said. "I'll leave the door unlocked for you, though, honey," her tormenter had promised. "Just walk on in. Don't bother knocking."

138

"That's far enough," Dawn heard Lester say.

After the full afternoon brightness of the parking lot, her eyes did not immediately adjust to the semidarkness of the Boar's Head. She could only make out outlines and shadows— Lester Finn standing behind the bar on the other side of the vast room of dark wood flooring and empty tables.

Then her eyes adjusted to the minimal light and she saw that Lester Finn was pointing a gun at her.

"Drop that purse, Dawn," Lester said. "Come on, I'm not fooling around with you."

Now she faced two options: She could either drop the purse, which contained the .38 special, or she could attempt to pull the revolver before Lester could gun her down.

The latter option had the appeal of the dramatic last stand. Realistically, though, she knew that she had no chance of succeeding. And she could not help Lee by dying here in Lester's doorway.

So she dropped the purse on the floor.

"Step inside," Lester ordered. "And close that door behind you."

Once again she saw no choice but to do as Lester commanded.

"Now come here, honey."

As she approached Lester, she began to take in the rest of the situation: she could hear Lee McCabe groaning and moving about on the floor behind the bar. Then she noticed the crude torture devices that Lester had laid out on a towel: The most salient of these was a large butcher knife.

"Oh, Dawn," Lester said, a malicious smile spreading across his face. "How nice of you to join us. I have my two favorite young people here: You and Lee McCabe. This is a bit like our little get-together the other night, isn't it? Except that now the circumstances are much different."

He continued to hold the gun on Dawn, but he looked briefly at Lee McCabe on the floor. "You two thought you had me beaten the other night, didn't you? Thought that you were going to mock Lester Finn and get away with it. Well, I don't see either of you laughing now. Oh, don't cry Dawn. I can see your tears, but the time for crying is long past. Tears won't change matters now."

Lester passed through the little partition door that separated the bar area from the main customer area. Still, the gun in his hand never wavered.

"I want you to join us, Dawn. And Lee, I was going to go to work on you first, but maybe I'll start with her. Let's see how tough you are when she's bleeding and screaming in a few minutes, begging for you to tell me where my property is so I can make the pain stop."

Dawn could not grasp the entirety of what Lester was talking about, but one thing was clear: Lester intended to torture her as a means of extracting information from Lee.

"Dawn? Is that you?"

"I'm here, Lee!"

"Damn it! Why didn't you do as I told you? Why didn't you leave?"

"Dawn's a girl with a will of her own," Lester said. "Despite her many weaknesses, she had pretensions of grandeur. But we're going to put those pretensions to rest in just a moment. Come here, baby. Keep walking."

She was only a few paces away from him. Another step, and he would be able to reach out and grab her. Then she would be completely within his control, given that he had the gun.

She heard Lee struggle behind the bar, trying to break free of whatever binds Lester had placed on him.

This momentarily distracted Lester. The gun did not waver, but he turned his gaze away from Dawn and looked down at Lee.

"You can just stop that," he said. "You can stop that right now. Or it will only make things worse on her."

Dawn realized that this would be her only chance to act. It was now or never. If she hesitated, Lester would have complete control over both of them, and this sadistic game would proceed according to his wishes.

She didn't intend to let that happen.

Summoning the last of her strength, Dawn plucked the butcher knife from the towel atop the bar, and in one fluid motion drove the tip of the blade at Lester Finn. She aimed for the carotid artery, relying for the last time on the knowledge that she had so painstakingly acquired in high school and college—in her aim to be doctor, a saver of lives.

Lester saw the glint of the blade from his peripheral vision. He swung the pistol at Dawn and fired, but not before the butcher knife severed the main artery in his neck.

Dawn felt an impact in the center of her chest, a massive, all-encompassing blow that drove out all other thoughts and considerations. She was unaware that she had dropped the knife, did not hear it clatter to the floor. She was vaguely aware of falling, but this was a dreamlike sensation. A dark tunnel was closing around her field of vision. She thought briefly of Lee, and seemed to have a sense that despite all of this, somehow now he would be all right. She had made it so. This was not redemption for everything; but it was as close as she was going to get.

Nor was she aware of Lester, as he dropped the gun immediately after firing it. The tavern owner staggered against the bar, blood gushing from his neck. With both hands he grabbed his wound. The blood ran in rivulets between his fingers.

And behind the bar, Lee McCabe heard the sounds of a struggle, of a gunshot, and the sounds of both his captor and his would-be rescuer falling to the floor.

139

N ow what? Lee called out Dawn's name, but there was no answer. Nor did Lester Finn cut him off with a sarcastic rejoinder or warning. He might have been alone in the tavern—and he did not want to consider the full implications of this.

He called out Dawn's name again, hoping against hope that she would respond, but he was answered only by silence.

Lester had bound Lee's hands and ankles with twine before wrapping the padlocked chain around the length of his body. With a bit of effort, Lee was able to wriggle three fingers free of the twine. Then he used these freed fingers to attack the knots. Soon he was able to free his hands.

The chain was another matter. Lester had wrapped it tightly around him. The links were cutting off some of his circulation, in fact. He was therefore unlikely to wriggle free of it. However, Lester had obliged him by placing the padlock near the small of his back, just below where his hands were bound. He would have to retrieve the key, though.

Moving his body like a primitive, slithering invertebrate, Lee scooted himself across the floor, toward the partition that separated the bar and the customer area. When he was through the partition he saw Lester Finn. He also saw a great deal of the tavern owner's blood.

He could also see Dawn's body on the floor, also covered in blood and very, very still. He could not think about that right now. He would will himself not to think about it. He would focus only on finding the tiny key that was attached to the dead man's key ring.

As his hands were bound behind his back in the tangle of chains, Lee had to roll over on his side and scoot himself backwards toward Lester Finn's body. Then he had to dig in Lester's pocket, which was still warm as if Lester was yet alive. But clearly he was dead. It appeared that Dawn had severed one of the main arteries in his neck.

As a pre-med student, she would have known exactly where to strike, Lee thought. It occurred to him that Dawn's desire to be a doctor—a desire that had so intimidated him when he had first met her several years ago—may have saved his life today.

He found the correct key and managed to fit it into the padlock. The padlock fell to the floor and he pushed the chains off easily. He was free.

Lee sat up and unbound his ankles. Then he looked at Dawn.

He was no doctor; but he had seen enough combat casualties to know that he could do nothing for her. She had likely been dead even before she had struck the floor.

The fact that Dawn had not suffered a prolonged agony did nothing to alleviate his grief, his shame. Yet another person had faced death in his place. And Dawn had been much more than that. She had been—well—there was no time or space for such reflections now. Later on, if he managed to live through this, he would have to think about it. Why this woman had so willingly sacrificed her life for his. She must have known that she had little chance of leaving the Boar's Head alive.

He found his borrowed gun behind the bar. He knew where he was going next. He was beyond caring about the consequences.

But what about Dawn's body? He might not be able to pay his respects in any conventional way; but he knew that he could not leave her like this. He stepped over to one of the tables that was arranged for large dining parties near the back of the main barroom area. It was covered by a light blue tablecloth. Lee grabbed the edge of the tablecloth and yanked it toward him, sending six sets of plates and silverware crashing to the hardwood floor. Most of the plates shattered and the silverware made a noisy cacophony.

He laid the tablecloth across Dawn's body, covering most of her. Both the gesture and the makeshift shroud seemed hopelessly inadequate. Just as she had deserved a better life than the one that had found her, her body deserved a better treatment than this. But this was all he had to give her.

Lee stared for a long moment at the bony frame beneath the tablecloth. Then, choking back his tears and his rage, he proceeded to leave the Boar's Head.

140

Hal Marsten was trembling as he approached the entrance of the Hawkins County Sheriff's Department office.

So much had happened in recent days—none of it good.

First there was Mamma's illness. Then those horrific murders in the trailer across the road. Afterward, he had been visited by that hood Lester Finn, who had shown up in the middle of the night, issuing threats like the Devil himself.

Lester had threatened to kill Mamma if he told the police the truth about what had taken place in Tim Fitzsimmons's trailer. And for a number of days that threat had held his silence.

But then the doctor had located him in the waiting room of the hospital one evening in Lexington. Even as the doctor approached, Hal had been able to decipher the awful significance behind his stare: Mamma was either passing, or she had already passed.

Hal had made it to her room in time to say goodbye, though she did not seem to recognize him through the haze of her medication. *How do you say goodbye to the woman who gave you life*? he had wondered. And then it was over, and there was nothing more that he could do for Mamma, at least not in this world.

With Mamma's death, the threats of the hoodlum with the long grey hair and the mocking eyes were partially nullified, and so he would have to go and tell the truth; he would have to help Lee McCabe, if he could. According to the news, a number of law enforcement agencies were still seeking the ex-marine. Given Lester Finn's involvement, it was likely that criminal elements were seeking McCabe as well.

Hal opened one of the double glass doors of the sheriff's department, and he passed from the humidity and heat of the sidewalk to the coolness of the inside. Hal quickly scanned the room for Sheriff Phelps. He wanted to find the sheriff before Deputy Ron Norris became aware of his presence.

Lester Finn had suggested that he was capable of silencing Deputy Ron Norris, the officer whom Hal had telephoned with his testimony. Hal wasn't sure if Norris was in cahoots with Finn, or if Finn had somehow been able to blackmail or otherwise threaten him. Either way, Hal was unable to overlook that fact that he had called Ron Norris, and a visit from Lester Finn had immediately followed. The cop might be dirty or he might be cowardly; he was definitely unreliable.

The sheriff's office seemed to be deserted. Hal saw what appeared to be three deputies' desks but these were unoccupied. Were all the deputies out looking for Lee McCabe, he wondered? Or had some other, unrelated emergency befallen the town?

There was a woman about his own age in a little glass-enclosed office at the rear of the room. Hal recognized the tangle of consoles and wires that surrounded her as police dispatch equipment.

The woman stood and walked to a service counter that was adjacent to a half-door entranceway. She slid the glass panel open and addressed Hal.

"Can I help you, sir?"

Hal could see that her name tag read "Rita Dinsmore". She remained patient and silent as Hal wavered, trying to judge if this woman could be trusted, or if she would be another Ron Norris.

"I'm here to see Sheriff Phelps."

"Sheriff Phelps is in out in the field. Can I help you?"

"No!" Hal said, more emphatically than he had intended.

"Well, can you tell me what this is about? Is this an emergency?"

"I'll come back when I can talk to the sheriff."

"Can I have your name, at least? The sheriff can contact you when he returns."

Hal shook his head. "I'll be back later."

The woman named Rita Dinsmore was looking at him as if he were slightly unhinged. But *she* had not been threatened by Lester Finn, had she? Nor was it likely that she had just lost her mamma or witnessed a murder within a few paces of her front door. So she was confused by his actions. Well, let her be confused.

"I'll be back," Hal said. And without another word to the woman named Rita, he turned and walked out of the sheriff's department.

HAL WAS out in the parking lot when he heard someone call after him. The person did not know his name, but merely addressed him as "Sir!"

Hal turned, more than a little suspicious. The man who was walking out of the sheriff's department was not dressed like a member of the Hawkins County Sheriff's Department. He wore a suit and tie. His bald head and somewhat delicate features didn't remind Hal of a police officer, either. This man looked more like an accountant.

"What do you want?" Hal said guardedly. This man didn't look like the sort of person who would be in league with Lester Finn; but Hal didn't intend to take any chances. Not after all that had happened.

"I saw you walk in and ask to talk to Sheriff Phelps," the man said.

"Yeah, what about it?"

"It seemed to me that whatever you had to say, it was pretty important."

"What if it was? Who are you, Mister?"

The man reached into the pocket of his dress slacks and withdrew a leather badge holder. "I'm Special Agent Jack Lomax," he said. "I'm playing a hunch—and it's simply a hunch—but I think that you and I might be able to help each other. You wouldn't refuse to talk to anyone but the sheriff if this was a routine matter."

Hal stared in awe at the FBI badge. This man might be trustworthy after all. Lester Finn might be able to exert influence on a local cop like Deputy Norris. He would not be able to reach a special agent of the United States FBI.

"Well," Hal said. "I guess we could sit and chat a spell."

"Excellent," Special Agent Lomax said. "I'll grab a meeting room where you can talk to my partner and me in private."

141

L ee exited the Boar's Head via the rear entrance. In his pocket
were the keys to Lester's apple red Cadillac.

Lester Finn, his primary tormenter—was dead now. But
there was still the matter of the meth operation at the abandoned
furniture factory. Not to mention the Chicago mafia.

The simplest course of action, he knew, would be to call the state
police right now, from inside the Boar's Head. The scene inside would
speak for itself.

Or would it? Deputy Norris's actions toward him clearly demonstrated that there was corruption within the county sheriff's department. Was it a stretch to speculate that this corruption might extend
to the state level, as well?

He would not go to the authorities until he had irrefutable proof.
He had hoped that the proof would come from Lester's forced confession. That was impossible now. And Lee did not know if Lester had
left any tracks that tied him to the meth operation or not. How careful
had he been? And who within the law enforcement hierarchy would
be working to erase these tracks, so that their involvement would
never be discovered?

No way to know. There were too many wild cards. Once the police become untrustworthy, the rest of your base assumptions about the legal system collapse, Lee thought. They collapse like a house of cards.

He would have to get inside the meth operation at the old furniture factory. He would need to collect photographic evidence; and then he would immediately contact the state police. If he did half of their work for them, they would not dare to bury the evidence that he had collected, would they?

A CLOSED sign hung in the window of the Boar's Head, and there was no one to report the Cadillac stolen. He would need an hour—two at the most. Then he would end it. No more running. No more innocent deaths.

Lee was about to open the door of Lester's Cadillac when he heard the police siren. The siren sounded once, as the police will sometimes do when they simply want to get an errant driver's attention.

Deputy Frank Norris had pulled his squad car in behind the Cadillac.

"Put your hands behind your head," Norris said through the squad car's loudspeaker.

142

T his would be his last chance—absolutely his last chance— to kill Lee McCabe, Norris realized. He could not believe this windfall of finding the ex-marine in town.

Of course, the issue of Lee McCabe's presence at the Boar's Head raised another set of questions. There would be no reason for him to be here.

Could McCabe be secretly working with Lester Finn? Even Norris —who regarded himself as cagey and suspicious by nature—found this impossible to believe. McCabe and Finn had absolutely no shared interests. Their only mutual interest was that each would want to see the other one dead.

That might mean that McCabe had come here for a showdown with the tavern owner. Yes—that had to be it. Wouldn't McCabe's swaggering, confrontational nature make him prone to such a step? Of course it would.

And McCabe was walking out of the bar, obviously alive and unscathed.

That might mean that—

Yes, that might mean that Lee McCabe had killed Lester Finn!

What other explanation could there be, when you added up all these circumstances?

Oh, please, oh please, let it be so, Norris thought.

The last step, then, would be for him to gun down McCabe. Kill him right here in the rear parking lot of the Boar's Head with no witnesses. And even if there was someone watching from a nearby window—well, that was a chance that Norris was willing to take. McCabe was a wanted fugitive, the chief suspect in multiple homicides, and he was surely armed.

Norris could kill him, and worry about the details later.

Norris stepped out of his vehicle with his Remington shotgun at the ready. There would be no mistakes this time, no margin for error.

The ex-marine reached behind his back, and Norris knew that in less than a minute, one of them would be dead.

LEE HAD no intention of trusting Norris in a second arrest scenario. Twice already, the deputy had taken potshots at him. Norris had already wounded him once. To submit to the lawman now would be suicide.

Lee noted the auto-loading shotgun in the deputy's hand. Lee himself was out in the open, with no cover. If he allowed Norris to level the shotgun at him, then the deputy could shred him to ribbons at will. Even Norris would not be able to miss with that gun at this proximity.

Lee drew Ben's Sig Sauer and aimed it at Norris. He shouted for Norris to drop the shotgun; but the deputy's face was fixed in a fatalistic grimace. He had no intention of allowing Lee to disarm him; nor would he submit to a draw. The deputy would know the consequences of Lee's survival. He would expend his last breath to make sure that Lee did not survive.

Lee fired the Sig Sauer just as a Norris was swinging the shotgun in the direction of his head.

He shot Norris twice in the chest. The deputy dropped the shotgun and it fell to the pavement. Norris was thrown back against the police cruiser. He made a frantic attempt to cover the holes in his chest with his hands. But it was clear to Lee that the lawman's wounds were fatal. He slumped to the ground, sliding down against his patrol car.

"Damn you, Norris!" Lee cursed silently.

Now he had stepped over the line, he realized: He had gunned down a sheriff's deputy in broad daylight, in the middle of town. Now it would be even more difficult for him to exonerate himself. But he still had the photos of Norris with Lester Finn and Paulie Sarzo stored away on his cell phone. Thankfully Lester had not taken his cell phone when he had clubbed him over the head; Lester had only been concerned about retrieving his money.

There was nothing to be done with the deputy's body or the patrol car. He would have to leave them here. He would have to move quickly, all the while fighting time, fatigue, and the enemies that were still chasing him.

One final battle, Lee thought. *Then it's either over, or I'm over.*

143

W hen Sheriff Phelps saw the body of his deputy lying on the blacktop outside the Boar's Head, he was seized by an unbearable loathing for Lee McCabe.

Barely thirty minutes ago, a call came into the station via the 911 line. A citizen had witnessed a gun battle between Lee McCabe and Ron Norris. According to the witness, it had been a mostly one-sided affair. Lee had put two rounds in the fallen deputy. Norris had not fired a single shot.

Norris had not been the ideal deputy; but he had been loyal and mostly dependable during his years in the department. Whatever else McCabe had done, with this murder he had committed the unthinkable: He had murdered a police officer, a crime that would surely send him to the lethal injection chamber.

I wonder, thought Phelps. *I wonder if I will be able to stop myself from doing the state's work myself.*

He did not like to even entertain such notions. In all his years in law enforcement, he had never gone vigilante. In fact, his only real lapse in professional conduct had occurred when he had stopped Lee McCabe on that rainy spring night, when the young man's smugness had nearly driven him over the edge.

And now Lee McCabe might drive him over the edge again.

The paramedics were loading Norris's body into an ambulance, though the deputy was already gone.

The horror of Norris's death had been compounded by the horrors inside the Boar's Head. Phelps did not yet know what to make of the bodies of Lester Finn, and a young woman who had yet to be identified. Phelps thought he had seen the young woman around town in years past; but she had obviously been in the advanced stages of meth addiction.

There had been some sort of a three-way shootout, apparently. Phelps was not surprised to find that Lester Finn was somehow involved in all of this—but exactly what had been his connection to Lee McCabe? Were the two men heading rival drug-trafficking factions? That was usually the case in homicides like this. The young woman might have been working with Finn—or she might have been a meth user who had gone to the Boar's Head to buy drugs, only to find herself at the wrong place at the wrong time.

All questions that would have to be answered later, after McCabe was taken off the board.

His radio crackled. It was Rita from dispatch.

"Sheriff," she said in that scratchy voice of hers. "Lee McCabe was just seen heading north on Briar Patch Road. Driving an apple-red Cadillac."

Briar Patch Road. This was a rural stretch of highway outside of town that had fallen into decay in recent years. Several decades ago, this part of the county had shown nascent promises of industrial development, and Briar Patch Road had once been home to a small industrial park. There had been a handful of new and hopeful companies out there: a machining shop, the Peaton Woods Furniture Company, a few others. All of these were now defunct, their decaying hulls a reminder of the county's subsequent economic decline, as big manufacturing had abandoned rural America, lured by the dollar-a-day wages of nations like India and Pakistan.

Phelps knew a route whereby he could reach the northernmost

stretch of Briar Patch Road. Then he would be able to head south and intercept McCabe as he drove north.

"I'm going," Phelps told Rita.

144

Lee drove north on Briar Patch Road, assembling the final details of his plan of attack. Quick in—quick out. Yeah—like it would really be that simple.

He had taken Norris's shotgun. He knew that he might find himself in a gun battle with multiple men, and he knew that these men would be heavily armed. This was an incriminating step, of course. But he was already deeply implicated, and he needed the extra firepower.

The countryside blurred by on either side of him. Only a few miles to the abandoned furniture factory. He would stop a half-mile short of his destination, where he would abandon this ridiculous, highly conspicuous car of Lester Finn's and travel on foot.

Lee heard the sirens before he saw the approaching police car. The Hawkins County Sheriff's Department cruiser was barreling toward him; he saw it as it crested a distant hill. The cruiser was traveling perhaps eighty miles per hour. Its rooftop flashers were on, as were the alternating strobe lights on either side of the front grill.

He had come too close to the final step to be apprehended by the police. Of course, there was a possibility that he could persuade the sheriff's deputy to investigate the factory, wasn't there?

Then he saw the driver of the cruiser: It was Sheriff Phelps himself.

Had the sheriff already found Norris's body? Undoubtedly he had: their gunfight, after all, had taken place out in the open. Someone must have heard something, saw something. Phelps would be aware that his deputy was dead. And even though he had not been positively identified as Norris's killer, he would be the logical suspect.

Then there was the matter of the gun on the seat beside him—a police-issue Remington shotgun with Norris's fingerprints all over it —no doubt with a serial code that could be uniquely traced to the Hawkins County Sheriff's Department and the dead deputy.

How would Phelps handle him now—that he was identified as a cop killer? Well, how had he and his fellow marines felt about the jihadis who killed U.S. marines with car bombs and IEDs? When combined with the antipathy that Phelps already felt for him, it was likely that the sheriff would offer no quarter. Phelps would gun him down exactly as his deputy had tried to do on three separate occasions.

The police cruiser was closing fast. He would not make it to the Peaton Woods Factory, which lay less than a mile in the distance. And he could not risk a surrender to Sheriff Phelps.

At least not until he had time to create additional options.

Lee swung the steering wheel of the Cadillac abruptly, turning the car into a driveway to his right. Tires screeched on the pavement then skidded on gravel. The Cadillac fishtailed, and Lee pulled the steering wheel again to keep the car on the driveway. One of Cadillac's wheels briefly caught in an earthen rut alongside the gravel, but a quick maneuver with the steering wheel righted the vehicle's course.

The sirens were growing louder. Lee knew that within seconds, the police cruiser would swing into the driveway as well.

He had pulled into the private roadway of an old machine shop —another one of those many local businesses that had been shuttered during the previous decade. The large grey building that dominated the lot still bore a sign that read: *Kinney Machine Works*.

But no business by that name had operated on these premises for years.

Lee threw open the door of the Cadillac and bolted toward the building. He noticed that one of the building's side entrances—a set of rusting, metallic double doors—was partially ajar. That sort of thing happened when buildings were left abandoned like this for years at a stretch. Nature and bored, restless teenagers often pried open these spaces that had once been so carefully guarded.

As Lee struck the metal doors it occurred to him that while he had the Sig Sauer, he had left the shotgun in the front seat of the Cadillac. All that additional risk for nothing. He briefly considered going back for it but thought better. And the final images of Lester's now dead employee were still in his mind: The big man who had stolen Lester's money had also gone back for a forgotten gun, only to die in a hail of fire.

Lee ran into the near total darkness of the machining plant, knowing that Phelps would be following right behind him. It was a cavernous space, filled with hunks of discarded machinery, miscellaneous trash, and the odors of putrefied industrial materials—a smell that was simultaneously organic and chemical. The sole source of illumination was a faint, dirty light that filtered through a series of frosted windows placed high above the main area of the factory.

He would have to hide someplace. Perhaps he could negotiate with Phelps, in order that he not become the killer of two members of the county's sheriff's department.

As Lee turned left where the factory layout formed an L-shape, he heard Phelps clatter through the metal double doors. The likelihood was high, he knew, that only one of them would walk out of this building when this was done.

145

As Phelps had expected, Lee ran into the wing of the factory where the darkness was the most pronounced. There did not seem to be any windows in that far corner of the building.

That's what I would have done, Phelps thought. *McCabe is running to where I'll be more visible, and he'll be against the darkness, practically invisible.*

Phelps knew that the more lighted area of the building's interior would be behind him as he approached. McCabe would therefore have a profound advantage if this situation deteriorated into an all-out shootout. The young man would have a better chance of seeing him than vice versa. So Phelps ran the risk of dying without even glimpsing his killer.

He heard the pounding of feet ascending in the darkness. These were metallic thumps. Then he heard another series of footsteps, almost directly above him, though high in the air.

There must be a mezzanine, Phelps thought. Like many factories, the machine works was likely equipped with a metal catwalk that was suspended above the plant floor. This would have been used by maintenance employees of the company that had previously occupied the building.

In any gunfight, the man who held the higher vantage point held a distinct advantage. But the man who was also gifted with the cover of total darkness—and an opponent who was standing in the open with light behind him—that man was not merely advantaged. That man could be an executioner at will.

My God, Phelps thought. *I've walked into a deathtrap.*

LEE SAW Phelps standing in the middle of the floor below him. Although the light was dim, he could clearly make out the silhouette of the sheriff. Phelps had his gun drawn; but he clearly had no idea of where Lee might be.

He had caught the sheriff in a most disadvantageous position. From the floor, the overhead mezzanine space would be completely invisible—as dark as the inside of a cave. Phelps, on the other hand, was backlit by traces of ambient light.

Lee stepped carefully on the metal grille of the mezzanine, and moved behind a steel support pillar. This would provide him with cover if Phelps decided to try his luck with a random shot.

I could kill him now, Lee thought. *Just like that day at the gorge. What difference would it make, really? I'm already a cop killer. And Phelps probably plans to kill me, anyway.*

Lee realized that he faced a choice—and a gamble. He would either have to kill Phelps, or somehow engage him—try to negotiate with the lawman and win him over to his side.

He remembered an object that he had placed in his wallet that day at the gorge. And he had an idea. But he was still weighing his grim alternatives—not yet sure what he was going to do.

Either choice could result in his death. Either choice could result in him losing his freedom forever.

PHELPS HEARD a slight movement above him. Probably McCabe was maneuvering himself into an even more advantageous position. Phelps could see the lowest portion of the steel support pillar: McCabe might be taking cover behind it—which would make him even more difficult to shoot.

I'm a dead man if I don't take cover, Phelps thought.

Behind him was the rusting hulk of an old machine—a manual lathe by the general shape of it. He ducked quickly and crouched behind the base of the machine. He scraped his knee and shoulder against the teeth of the device's exposed gears.

Crouched on the floor behind the old lathe, the scent of oil was cloying, and the floor here was covered with prickly metal shavings. But he was out of immediate danger. Not that McCabe couldn't fire some shots in his direction and hope for a ricochet hit. Then McCabe could descend from the mezzanine and finish him off, if he were still alive.

Stay calm, Phelps told himself. *Maybe you weren't cut out for this sort of thing—not really, you weren't. But now you're here, alone with the killer of a man in your charge—the probable killer of multiple citizens who trusted you to protect them.*

"I didn't kill Norris in cold blood!" he heard Lee shout from the dark space above him. "You've got to listen to me, Phelps!"

Oh, I'll listen, all right. Maybe I can talk him into making a mistake, Phelps thought.

"But you admit that you killed Norris?"

"I killed him," Lee responded. "I killed him because he had previously tried to gun me down twice, and he was preparing to kill me in cold blood in that parking lot!"

Phelps snorted. "Norris was a non-violent man, McCabe. Until you ended his life. He wouldn't have tried to kill a man in cold blood. Why would he do that? Do you think I'm an idiot? Why don't you drop that gun and come down here. Save us all more bloodshed."

"Norris was dirty, Phelps. And I can prove that to you."

"Then drop your weapon and come down here. We'll talk. You'll have your chance to prove whatever you want. The law will give you a trial, McCabe—a lot more of a chance than you gave Norris."

"First I need some options," Lee said. "I need to know that you won't gun me down in cold blood, like your deputy was trying to do."

Phelps felt a fresh surge of anger, driving his fear into the background. How he hated that man up on the darkened mezzanine. How he wished that man had never been born.

And are you sure of all the motives behind that sentiment? he asked himself. But this thought, too, was quickly driven away.

"You gave up your options when you went on the run, McCabe! You gave up your options when you started killing cops!"

I can't promise that I won't kill him on sight, Phelps thought. *After all he's done. After Norris and the other deaths. May God forgive me; but I'm not feeling like a lawman just now. I'm feeling like an avenger.*

Lee McCabe was the wrong man to become a cop killer. The wrong man to ask him for mercy.

Phelps saw something fluttering downward from the mezzanine in the near total darkness. When it passed through a stray shaft of light, he was able to identify it as a piece of paper—perhaps an index card. Or maybe a photo.

"Take it!" Lee shouted. "You think I'm a cop killer? Look at that photo. You'll see that I had a chance to kill you a few days ago—if I had wanted to."

So it was a photograph after all. The picture was lying only a few yards from him. But since it was beyond the cover of the dilapidated lathe, it might as well have been a mile. From his position on the mezzanine, Lee would have a clear shot at him.

"Nice try, McCabe!" Phelps called back. "But you should realize that I know better."

Phelps heard Lee mutter a curse. Then he saw another object fall from the mezzanine. It struck the floor near the photograph with a metallic clank.

It was a pistol.

"There!" Lee yelled. "Now I'm unarmed!"

The pistol, now harmless to Phelps, lay on the dusty concrete floor. This did not make the situation completely safe, of course. Lee might have more than one weapon. That was an old gunfighting trick —throwing one weapon from a hideout, only to open up with another gun when your opponent let down his guard.

But Phelps did not believe that Lee had another weapon. He looked around behind him, in the little area that had been the workspace of the now unemployed lathe operator. Two workbenches formed an "L" shape. These workbenches would have contained the raw materials and additional tools that the lathe operator had needed to produce his output.

Phelps saw a long thin object lying on the floor. He leaned back, extended his arm, and clutched the grainy wooden handle of an old shop broom. As he lifted it and swung it in his direction, he saw that the head of the broom was nearly stripped of bristles—no wonder it had been left behind when the factory was closed.

He pushed the head of the broom toward the photograph with one hand, retaining his grip on his pistol with the other. It took him three attempts to pull the photo close enough for him to grab it. And all the while, he exposed himself to McCabe's aim if the wanted man did indeed have a spare weapon.

Phelps removed the flashlight from his belt and examined the photograph. When he saw the photo of himself and Lori—the one that he had believed to be burned to ashes—he felt his heart move within his chest.

He recalled how this photograph should have been burned with the rest, that evening in the brazier.

He did not need to have the scenario explained to him, but Lee nonetheless shouted an explanation from the mezzanine.

"You see? I took this from your cruiser when you stopped by the gorge. I was there the entire while. I had a clear aim at you. I could have dropped you any number of times!"

To this Phelps had no immediate response. It reminded him of an episode in the Old Testament—in which David demonstrated his loyalty to Saul by cutting off a corner of the older man's cloak. Saul had accused that younger man of the worst sort of treachery—had declared him outlaw and pursued him. But David had confirmed his innocence by coming close enough to kill his tormenter, and then deciding to let him live.

"I'm coming down now," Lee said. "And if you gun me down, Phelps—well, then damn you to hell!"

146

When Lee approached Phelps in the almost-darkness, the sheriff did not draw his gun on him. To Lee's surprise he holstered his weapon.

To Lee the sheriff looked oddly crestfallen—and in some indescribable way—broken. Lee's gesture had somehow tipped the balance of power in his own favor. But it had to be more than just the photo, he knew. Phelps was a man uniquely haunted by his own internal demons. That had been obvious for years.

"Show me," Phelps said. "Show me what you have."

Lee removed his cell phone from his pocket. He showed Phelps the picture of Norris, Lester, and the Italian gangster in a conference outside the Peaton Woods Furniture factory.

"Where did you take that picture?" Phelps asked.

"Just down the road." Lee briefly related the events of that day— and what he knew about Lester's drug trafficking activities in the county.

When he was finished, the sheriff nodded silently. He seemed— grudgingly—to have reached some sort of decision.

"I believe you," Phelps said. "If that means anything. But you understand that I can't just let you go. And you don't want to run any longer, do you? The state police—even the FBI—you've got a lot of people looking for you."

"That's why I came down from that mezzanine," Lee said. "I'm tired of running. I only want it to end. But I have to be sure that I'll get a fair shake."

"I'll do what I can," Phelps said. "You have my word."

It occurred to Lee that Phelps did not seem altogether pleased at the prospect of assisting him. However, the sheriff did indeed seem convinced of Lee's fundamental innocence. And he had given his promise.

"And I had to be sure that you wouldn't murder me in cold blood —like Norris tried to."

"I haven't shot you, have I?"

"That's very reassuring."

Lee noticed a blinking light on his cell phone: a voice message from a call that had come in while he had been evading Phelps. Fearing a repeat of the incident that landed him in Lester's custody, Lee had placed the cell phone on silent mode.

Who would have called him? A man in his situation didn't receive casual phone calls. But Dawn was dead, Sheriff Phelps was here with him, and he didn't expect to hear from Michelle Ackerman again.

"I need to hear this message," Lee said.

Phelps nodded. "Go ahead."

The number from which the call had come scrolled across the display screen. It was a number from the 312 area code. Any number in Hawkins County would have had an area prefix of 502. There were only a few other area codes in the state; and none of them was 312.

"That's a Chicago area code," Phelps said, as if reading his mind.

Lee pressed the play button on the messages menu. The first voice was unfamiliar. It was cocky and brash and it exuded challenge. The voice of the guy in the bar who was always looking to pick a fight.

"Hey, McCabe, I guess you're too busy to answer this phone call. Your schedule must be packed nowadays, huh?" A throaty, humorless laugh. *"Yeah, even the governor knows who you are, hero. Well, I got two friends*

of yours here, though they may not be particularly fond of you for very much longer...."

Lee's heart sank, as he had an idea of where this might be going. He was ready to quit now. He had just given up, ready to let justice—whatever that might mean—take its course. He would accept their jail cell temporarily, if it came to that, and wait for the men and women of goodwill who worked within the system to sort out the truth. He had enough evidence of his own to spell it out for them now, didn't he?

But no—that voice on the phone was about to tell him that the violent part of his journey had not yet ended. Somehow he knew.

The message continued to play. "It seems, Lee McCabe, that you were once very close to a local teacher by the name of Marie Wilson. Now I find that very charming; a southern white boy like yourself being mothered by a woman of her complexion...And that's why I've arranged for a little reunion. You see, I've got both Mrs. Wilson and her son here, and I think they'd really appreciate a visit from you."

There was a pause, and then the sounds and commotion of the unknown man proving that he did in fact have Marie and Joe Wilson in his custody. Lee heard the shuffling of feet, and then the gut-wrenching sounds of Marie and Joe crying out in pain. Apparently their captor was kicking them.

Lee heard Marie call out: *"Don't you come here, Lee! He'll just kill us all!"* She cried out again, more sharply this time, as the man struck her. Lee heard the blow reverberate.

Now the voice of the man again: "You've got thirty minutes to call me, McCabe, or I kill Marie Wilson's boy. Another thirty minutes and I kill her. Your choice, tough guy." The message terminated.

Lee bent down and picked up the pistol that he had dropped before Sheriff Phelps's feet. "This changes things, Sheriff. I'm not going in with you. At least not until I make sure that Marie and Joe Wilson are safe."

Phelps shook his head emphatically. He placed a hand on Lee's shoulder. "No, Lee, you don't understand what's going on here."

Lee stood up and tucked the pistol into his belt. He brushed

Phelps's hand away. "What the hell do you mean, Sheriff: *I don't understand?* I understand everything: This man is holding Marie and Joe Wilson as hostages, all because Mrs. Wilson befriended me. I don't know who he is, but I have no doubt he'll kill them if I don't return his phone call."

"Well, Lee, I do know who he is—or at least who he's working for. I told you that was a Chicago area code. That man would be with one of the Chicago mafia outfits. He's not some bungler like Lester Finn. If you go to him, you'll be walking into a trap that you won't escape from."

"Don't be so sure. I escaped from you, Sheriff. And your friends in the state police as well."

Phelps sighed. "So you did. But our aim was to capture you, working within the constraints of the law. Whatever Norris might have done on his own, the rest of us were only out to apprehend you. This man is different. He's determined to kill you, and you know as well as I do that that means different rules of engagement. And you can bet that he knows what he's doing. You can bet that he's killed many men before."

"I'm not going to leave Marie and Joe to their deaths," Lee said simply.

"I'm not suggesting that you leave them," Phelps said. "I'm telling you to go back to being what you are: a civilian. Let me take care of this. There are two FBI agents in Perryston right now. They originally came here to help apprehend you. Now they can help Marie Wilson and her son. The important point for you to realize is that you can't do this—what you're planning. You can't pull it off, Lee. You have to give me that gun and come with me right now, and I'll take care of Marie and Joe Wilson."

Lee stared back at Sheriff Phelps and realized the nature of his decision: He would have to entrust the lives of Marie and Joe to this man, this man who had long held an unearned vendetta against him, this man who, only now, after so many years, was offering such a paltry olive branch.

And what if Sheriff Phelps failed? What if his FBI agents arrived too late, or if they did not agree to help, or if they turned out to be as false as Deputy Norris? The events of the preceding days had not predisposed him to trust law enforcement agents, though he still regarded himself as fundamentally law-abiding.

It would be all too easy to do as Phelps said, and no one would be able to hold such a surrender against him, not after all he had been through both at home and in Iraq.

But if he took that path in error and Joe and Marie suffered the consequences of his mistake, there would be no chance of atonement.

"No," Lee said. "I'll accept your help, Sheriff, but I won't give up my freedom until I know they're safe."

"Lee, we want the same thing here. You should know that this is personal for me as well. Mrs. Wilson had already started teaching in my day, you know. I care for her as well."

"Then come with me, Sheriff. Come with me and we'll stop this together."

But Phelps merely shook his head regretfully and said, "No, Lee. Not without backup. Now I need for you to give me that gun."

"No," Lee said. He was about to depress the call return button on his cell phone when Phelps grabbed his arm.

Lee shoved Phelps backward, so hard that the older man toppled over his feet and sat down hard on the concrete floor.

"Goddamn you, Sheriff!" Lee shouted. "*What do you what me to do? Trust you? You?* Just look at yourself: You've spent half your life nursing a grudge and feeling sorry for yourself, all because my mother jilted you twenty years ago. You're pathetic. You know that? You were angry at me simply for being born, simply for being who I am. Do you think my mom never told me about it? Don't you know that she warned me to stay clear of you?"

"Your mother," Phelps began. "I mean Lori."

"Shut up about my mother. My mother's dead. Leave her out of this. It's only about the two of us now. Don't you think I remember the way you treated me at that traffic stop? How can you expect me to trust you now?"

Phelps merely sat there where he had fallen. He made no move either to stand up or to reach for his own gun. He did not even seem inclined to offer Lee any further verbal response.

Disgusted, Lee ignored the lawman and pressed the call return button. The call was answered by the same man who had spoken in the voicemail.

"Lee McCabe," the speaker said in a mocking, openly menacing tone. "I'm glad you could be troubled to call. I was getting ready to put a bullet into one of these people."

"Harm them," Lee said. "And I'll kill you." He knew that he was speaking on pure adrenalin and anger now, and that such words could serve no purpose. In fact, such outrageous claims might even work against him. But he could not help himself. "I swear it, you son-of-a-bitch."

The man on the other end of the connection was not amused, nor did he seem to be the slightest bit affected by Lee's threats. "You know, I might just decide to teach you a lesson about respect before this is over," he said.

"Tell me what you want me to do in order to get my friends," Lee said. Then, more calmly: "If you need to be angry at someone, be angry at me. But leave them alone. The woman is a schoolteacher who never harmed anyone, and her son has never hurt anyone, either. They're innocent."

"You're breaking my heart, McCabe. Now listen to me. I believe you'll know where the Peaton Woods Furniture factory is. That's where I want you to come."

"I'll be there in a few minutes."

"Hold on," the voice continued. "Because the lives of these two people depend on you following my instructions very carefully. To the letter. You are to come alone. I repeat: alone. If I see any evidence of anyone else with you, then I kill these two immediately, no questions asked, no negotiations. Is that clear?"

"Yes," Lee said.

"You are to approach from the main road and walk up the driveway with your hands behind your head. Don't even think about trying to sneak up on the factory from the rear or one of the sides. We've got all those directions covered, and we'll take you out before you even get close. Do you understand?"

"Got it," Lee said.

"Then get your hillbilly ass moving."

Lee heard a click as the man terminated the call.

Now Sheriff Phelps was standing up. His uniform pants were dusty and oil-stained. The lawman's right hand was within reach of his sidearm.

"Are you going to shoot me, Sheriff?" Lee asked. "Since my father is no longer around, are you going to take your anger out on me again?"

Phelps shook his head slowly. "No, McCabe. I'm not going to shoot you."

"That's mighty big of you, Sheriff." Lee walked past Phelps without another word or gesture of acknowledgement. He did not care about Phelps now. He needed to focus on the confrontation ahead of him.

Lee had no doubt that Phelps, for all his failings, had uttered two correct assertions: The man who had made hostages of Marie and Joe was mafia, and he knew what he was doing. Lee could imagine what was waiting for him at the Peaton Woods Furniture factory: He would almost certainly be walking into a loaded trap. They would either take him prisoner and shoot him later, or they would simply shoot him on sight.

In either case he would be a dead man, which meant that Phelps had been right on that point, too.

If only it could be anyone but Phelps here, today, Lee thought. *Because I could really use some backup.*

But he did not want to ask Phelps for anything; and the disgraced lawman was probably not feeling inclined to help him now, anyway.

He made his way quickly out of the machine shop, wondering what he was going to do. He would be walking into a trap but there was no way around it. He could not reasonably hope for success but he could not go back, either. It seemed that the die was cast.

When he exited the machine shop, a light summer rain was falling, sending steam rising from the pavement. Briar Patch Road lay ahead of him, at the end of the abandoned factory's driveway. He walked past Phelps's parked cruiser. Its red and blue lights were still flashing.

When he reached the road he placed the Sig Sauer in the back of his pants, near the small of his back. *The man had not said anything about coming unarmed, had he?*

You can't give up, he thought to himself. *The lives of two innocent people depend on you. And what about your own life? You want to live, don't you? Why don't you hurry up and think of something? You've made it through some pretty bad scrapes so far, relying mostly on your own wits.*

He tried to think as the steam rose from his own body as well as the pavement, but there was the driveway of the Peaton Wood Furniture factory already.

He was only mildly surprised to see the two men with guns waiting for him. One of them was vaguely familiar. A local man, no doubt.

"That's far enough at that speed, McCabe." There were two muzzles pointed at him: A twelve-gauge shotgun, and a Tec-9 with a perforated, air-cooled barrel.

"Put your hands over your head and walk this way, real slow," the taller of the two commanded. Through his open flannel shirt the man's prison tattoos were visible, and then Lee realized who he was: TJ Anderson. The man who had appeared to be the leader of Lester's crew—the crew of men who had shot the man who stole the money.

This Anderson was another Hawkins County man who had done time behind bars. He had found work in Lester Finn's private army. But Lester had no men any longer; and so Anderson had probably been all too glad to sell his services to the Chicago mafia, if that was in fact the force that was now pulling the strings.

Lee did as he was told. The pistol was still wedged in the small of his back; but he would never have time to reach for it. The two men would gun him down if he made any move for his weapon.

Lee raised his hands and began his dead man's walk, watching the two men and the muzzles of their guns loom closer. The gravel crunched beneath his feet, and for a second he vaguely considered employing it in a diversionary move: he could kick gravel in their faces, roll to the ground, and then take shots at them from a prone position.

The idea was idiotic. Pure suicide. He discarded the notion almost as quickly as it occurred to him.

TJ Anderson looked at the other gunman and then back at Lee. A toothy, malevolent grin spread across his face.

"Stop right there, Lee McCabe," Anderson said. "And fold those hands behind your neck."

147

P helps watched McCabe walk past him and toward the exit of the machine shop. The young man seemed intent on making a suicidal, vainly heroic last stand. The organized crime lords who were behind the abduction of the Wilsons would kill him, of course. McCabe was walking into a slaughter that would accomplish nothing but his own death. Worse yet, he would eliminate any chance that the Wilsons could be rescued unharmed.

Phelps realized that whatever the past issues between himself and Lee McCabe, he had a sacred duty to prevent the young man from taking his intended course of action. It was his duty as the chief lawman of Hawkins County—even if this was a role that, in his deepest and most secret heart, he no longer desired.

All the collected baggage of the past—his treatment of Lee at the traffic stop, his own doomed romance with Lori Mills, his hatred of Tom McCabe—none of that had any real significance now. If he had to use force to arrest Lee McCabe, so be it. He would subject the young man to peril in order to save his life if it came to that.

He now fully grasped a fact that he had been circling warily around for so long: He had made a grand mistake in the planning and the execution of his adult life. Eager to seek redress for the still-born ambitions of his youth, he had allowed himself to drift into a job for which he was fundamentally unsuited. A real lawman, he knew, would never have allowed a civilian to brush him aside. A real lawman would have taken control of Lee McCabe and the situation, the baggage of the past be damned.

That did not change the nature of the duty that he had to fulfill right now—nor the fact that he alone could fulfill it in this time and place. He was starting after Lee McCabe when his cell phone rang. It was Lomax.

"Phelps? Where are you?"

"Just outside of town," Phelps answered, walking as he spoke. "I'm about to take Lee McCabe into custody."

"Wait! Do you have sixty seconds first?"

"No—but I'll listen to you while I walk." Phelps responded.

"Please do, sheriff: I just received a call from Washington. An FBI team in Chicago got a warrant to intercept the cell phone messages of Alfonzo Coscollino, the acting head of the Coscollino crime family."

"And?"

"The Coscollinos were ultimately behind those deaths at the Tradewinds, though their local man, Lester Finn, was certainly involved. Not Lee McCabe, as everyone had previously thought."

"I know. Lee McCabe is innocent. I spoke with him a few minutes ago."

"What? I thought you said that you were on your way to arrest him."

"It's a long story, Lomax."

"I just interviewed a local man by the name of Hal Marsten. He witnessed the actual murders at the Tradewinds. He saw four men enter that trailer before Lee McCabe appeared on the scene. It seems McCabe was trying to help."

"I know," Phelps said. "Yes, I know that now."

"But the Coscollinos are actively searching for Lee McCabe. When you listen to the recordings of their phone conversations, they paint a pretty clear picture: Lee McCabe didn't murder Fitzsimmons and White, nor was he in the employ of the Coscollinos or Lester Finn. They corroborate Hal Marsten's statement: McCabe was an innocent bystander after all. Hell, he may even have been trying to stop the killings. The Coscollinos seem to believe that McCabe may have seen the real killers, which is why they're so eager to have him dead. Then the whole country will believe that justice was done."

"Lomax—" Phelps interrupted. He stepped out into the hot, misty weather. Lee McCabe was nowhere in sight. Had he already arrived at the Peaton Woods Furniture factory?

"There's one more thing," Lomax continued. "And it's important. Paulie Sarzo, a nephew of Alfonzo Coscollino and a member of the family's inner circle, is in Hawkins County as we speak. He's been personally charged with making sure that the hit on McCabe is carried out successfully. And from what we can tell, he's brought a small army with him."

"I was afraid of something like this."

"And there's one more thing."

Phelps quickened his pace. He briefly considered taking his squad car and then quickly decided against it. What awaited him was not a police action, but something more akin to what he would have faced during his long-ago days in the military.

Phelps stopped to remove his Remington auto-loading shotgun from his rear of his squad car. With one hand, he continued to hold the cell phone to his ear.

"Phelps?" Lomax asked. "Are you still there?"

"I'm still here. Based on what you've told me, Agent Lomax, I believe that Lee McCabe is on his way now to a confrontation with elements of the Coscollino family. Perhaps with this one you mention."

"Then stop him, Phelps! McCabe is going to throw his life away for nothing. There is going to be a raid on the Coscollino home in Chicago within the hour. And I'm calling in backup to Hawkins County as well. No need for either one of you to play Wyatt Earp."

Phelps was on Briar Patch Road now, the Remington in one hand and his cell phone in the other. "It gets worse. We've got a hostage situation. Some friends of McCabe—an elderly woman and her son."

"That does make it worse," Lomax agreed. Phelps could picture the accountant-like federal lawman rubbing his balding head on the other end of the call. "Where are you, exactly?"

"The old Peaton Woods Furniture factory on Briar Patch Road. West of town. With Darla in the hospital, I'm fresh out of deputies now. Why don't you send in some backup? Whatever you can muster in federal resources. I know you also have the contacts at the state level."

"What about Norris?" Lomax asked.

"Norris is dead," Phelps said. "He was working with the Coscollinos."

A few more paces and the Peaton Woods factory would come into view, Phelps knew. He had to terminate the call with Lomax.

"Send whatever you can in the way of backup over here," Phelps said. "Though I would imagine that this is going to go one way or the other long before anyone can get here."

"Hold out as long as you can," Lomax said. "Wait for me. Give me thirty minutes."

"I don't have thirty minutes," Phelps said. "I don't even have five minutes. I may be too late already, in fact. And anyway, how would you get a state or federal team in place that quickly?"

"Who said anything about waiting for a team?" Lomax said. "I'm coming myself."

Phelps started to protest, to tell Lomax to focus on coordinating the men who would be needed after the approaching standoff. It would be one of two basic outcomes: If Phelps were victorious, a backup team would be needed to take away the men he had either subdued or killed. But if Phelps perished (the more likely of the two scenarios) men would be needed to finish the job he had begun. They would have to fight the same battle and win it. This work they would have to do alone. Lee McCabe would be dead by then, too.

But before Phelps could say this, the FBI man had already hung up; and Phelps could already see Lee McCabe in the distance. McCabe's form appeared and disappeared through patches of trees and shrubs that were now overgrown tangles on the grounds of the former furniture factory. McCabe was approaching the two men who beckoned him up the driveway, marching toward certain death.

148

During her period of recovery, Sheriff's Deputy Darla Johnson had kept abreast of the developments in the county. She called Rita Dinsmore at regular intervals from her hospital bed. Norris she had never trusted for some reason that she could not fully articulate; and she did not want to trouble the sheriff. So she relied on Rita for regular updates.

"Today," Rita told her this afternoon. "All hell has broken loose." Rita spoke through tears. "We've lost Ron Norris. And we might lose the sheriff today, too. Pray for him, Darla. I need you to pray for him."

She intended to do more than pray. When Darla heard that Sheriff Phelps was on his way to face gunmen from the Coscollino crime family, she began to disconnect her IV, and the other assorted tubes and lines that tethered her to her bed in Hawkins County General Hospital.

This startled the nurse who happened to be making her rounds at the time. The nurse poked her head into Darla's room just as she was shedding her hospital gown.

"Deputy Johnson?" the nurse said. "What do you think you're doing?" The nurse's tone suggested that whatever Darla's authority outside the walls of the hospital might be, within these confines she was just a civilian at the mercy of another system.

"I'm leaving," Darla said. "Checking out. Police business." Darla was searching for her uniform in the locker at the foot of the bed. She was entirely naked except for a pair of panties. Her body still bore numerous contusions and scratches from her accident. The deputy's right forearm and left calf were both bandaged. And then there was the large bandage affixed to her forehead.

"You'll do no such thing!" The nurse began walking imperiously in her direction, until Darla held up a hand and stared back at her with an expression that brooked no argument.

"I'm leaving," Darla said, wiggling into the jogging pants that her mother had brought for her. Then she slipped a Hawkins County Sheriff's Department tee shirt over her head. The police uniform she had been wearing when the accident occurred was not in the locker: It had been irrevocably damaged in the accident, and during the subsequent ministrations of the paramedics and emergency room doctors. They had cut the uniform from her body, in fact.

"And anyway, I'm fine," she told the nurse.

"You don't look fine."

"Well, I'm fine enough," she insisted. Darla winced in pain as she kneeled and laced up her gym shoes.

"You'll have to wait for Dr. Singh at the very least," the nurse said. "No one checks out of the hospital without a signature from the attending physician."

The nurse picked up the wall phone beside Darla's bed and began dialing Dr. Singh's extension. But she hung up with a gasp before she had pressed even the third digit.

Darla Johnson had walked past her and out into the hallway.

149

TJ Anderson pointed the barrel of his Tec-9 at Lee's forehead. The ex-con retained his sadistic smile, as a cruel child might when torturing a small animal. Lee could smell TJ's breath—a mixture of tobacco and alcohol, and the oniony stench of whatever he had eaten for lunch.

Lee felt his bowels turn to water. So this was how it was going to happen: He would not die in a firefight; he would die like a lamb going willingly to the slaughter.

I have to do it now, Lee thought, feeling the heft of the pistol against his lower back. He might have a few seconds at the most before they discovered the gun or simply shot him.

"Waste him, TJ," the man bearing the shotgun said. He was about Lee's age, and very eager to prove himself capable of violence. "Blow his brains out right here." And then he added, somewhat reluctantly, "Or let me do it."

"Oh, this pleasure is going to be mine and mine and alone," TJ said. "McCabe, I hope you're ready for a little walk in the woods."

Then he told his accomplice: "Now search him. This man wasn't stupid enough to walk up here without bringing a weapon."

The younger man walked behind Lee, and smiled when he saw

the Sig Sauer wedged in Lee's waistband. He was reaching for the gun when Lee heard the first deafening boom.

THE YOUNGER OF the two men stumbled against Lee, his body thrown forward by the impact of a shotgun blast. He knocked Lee to the ground in his own dying fall. On his way downward Lee could see Sheriff Phelps standing in the open with his Remington auto-loader. The lawman had apparently approached from the side, avoiding detection, as Lee's captors were absorbed in the handling of their prisoner.

TJ Anderson was shocked but quickly recovered. He swung the Tec-9 in the direction of Phelps. Another second and Phelps would have been dead. But before Anderson could get a bead on the sheriff, the Remington erupted again. Anderson was knocked off his feet, then fell backward into the grass. His chest had been torn open by the blast.

With some effort, Lee pushed the young man's corpse off his own body. Then he picked himself up from the gravel drive, the reports of the gunshots still ringing in his ears.

"I have to thank you for that, sheriff. I may be dead in another five minutes, but you've surely bought me some time." He turned away from the sheriff, and looked at the main entranceway of the factory. It was probably unlocked, but almost certainly guarded. He took a step in the direction of the double doors.

"Wait a minute, McCabe," Phelps said. He grabbed Lee's shoulder and Lee flinched and shrugged his hand away. Phelps spun Lee around. "Goddamn it, McCabe. Can't you get it through your head that we're on the same team here? Forget all that shit from the past."

"Sheriff, if you'll recall it was you who was so intent on keeping the past alive. Those aren't my memories."

Phelps looked at the ground. "You may be right, McCabe; but neither one of us has the time for you to be right just now. The man who called you is most likely Paulie Sarzo. He's a high-ranking member of the Coscollino crime family. Very dangerous and no fool. You can bet that he's got backup men inside the factory." Phelps regarded the bodies of the two gunmen. "He wouldn't be foolish enough to rely on these two alone."

"Fine sheriff. Thank you very much and I forgive you. That business at the traffic stop from a few years ago? Bygones. Now if you'll kindly get out of my way, I need to right a bad situation that I'm responsible for. At least two good people have died for my sake this week, and I don't intend to add Marie and Joe Wilson to the list."

"Listen to me, Lee: If you go in there by yourself, he'll kill you, kill the hostages, and the three of you will die for nothing. There's a better way."

Lee's first inclination was to argue—to resist the sheriff to the bitter end and then resist him some more.

But Lee realized that to resist the lawman now would defeat his purpose. It would indeed mean suicide for himself and almost certain death for Marie and Joe Wilson. So he would have to cooperate with Phelps, whether he wanted to or not.

"Let me see that number on your cell phone," Phelps said. Lee shrugged and took his cell phone from his pocket. Phelps retrieved his own cell phone, keyed in the number, and pressed the call button.

"Paulie Sarzo?" Phelps asked. "This is Hawkins County Sheriff Steven Phelps. It's over Sarzo. You've reached the end of the line."

AFTER PHELPS HAD TERMINATED the call, Lee shook his head incredulously.

"You've been authorized to offer this guy a deal of some sort?"

"No," Phelps said. "But this is the best thing I can think of right now. Not perfect, but better than going in guns blazing. Right now I've got an FBI agent in my office who's calling in the cavalry. Our priority at this point is to stall the man inside that building and keep your hostages alive. Then when Sarzo sees the score, he'll cave. Because he knows that there is some kind of a deal waiting for him at the end of this, and as soon as he sets down his gun, he'll be thinking about calling his lawyer."

"And you think that he'll submit, just like that?" Lee asked.

"I know you've only recently come home from a war against an enemy that fights to the death. But organized crime isn't al-Qaeda. These guys don't believe that seventy-two virgins are waiting for them on the other side. They want to live to fight another day, cut a deal with the prosecutor, and do their time. Then they start up their operations again and the cycle continues."

Lee stepped back from the bodies of the two fallen gunmen, as the smell of the blood was already beginning to reek. The sheriff was confident that Paulie Sarzo would be unwilling to go down fighting. After Iraq, Lee found it difficult to believe that any enemy wouldn't insist on a battle to the death.

150

From a former foreman's office in the abandoned hulk of the Peaton Woods Furniture factory, Paulie Sarzo stared at his cell phone and wondered what he was going to do.

First he attempted to call TJ Anderson. He was not really surprised when the call went to voicemail. The lawman and the ex-marine must have overpowered or killed Anderson. The sheriff would not have told a lie that would be so easy to verify.

Anderson was nothing, he was a pawn of negligible value—even if he did seem to have more promise than the other Hawkins County screw-ups. His loss did mean that the enemy had gained a small tactical victory; but Paulie had planned for temporary tactical losses. He had implemented a system of redundancy: From where he stood in the foreman's office, Paulie could see the remainder of his men: a man behind a lathe who held an AK-47, three more on the overhead mezzanine who carried Tec-9s. And he knew there were still others whom he could not see from where he stood. But they were all here, at his disposal.

The larger question was the sheriff's claim about the federal authorities raiding the family mansion in Chicago and taking Uncle

Alfonzo away in fetters. Alfonzo, who swore that he would rather die at his age than spend a single night behind bars.

A large part of Paulie dreaded the possibility so much that he did not want to confirm it, though a larger part of him knew that there was no way to avoid it. Such a defeat would mean the end of everything.

He turned as he heard one of his hostages move around where they sat, hands bound behind their backs, against an adjacent wall. He commanded them to hold still and waved his pistol at them. The old woman sighed. She seemed about to plead with him until he silenced her with a preemptive stare. The old woman's adult son glared back at him.

Paulie was tempted to kill his intractable male hostage now as a precautionary measure, and as a way of relieving his stress—restoring his full sense of control and power. But that would make the old woman hysterical. He would have to shoot her as well, and then he would have no more hostages.

He had to investigate the sheriff's story. He had to discover the truth now.

Paulie didn't call Uncle Alfonzo. If the sheriff was lying, he would only look foolish and weak before the head of the family. And if the sheriff was telling the truth, then he would be too ashamed to talk to the patriarch. Uncle Alfonzo, for his part, would be seething with rage—at the authorities, of course, but also at the nephew who had let him down.

He touched the web browser icon of his Samsung smart phone and was relieved to see that his 3G Internet access functioned in this remote backwater of central Kentucky. But soon his relief turned to dread—a sinking feeling of disbelief—after he executed a query for the Family's name on Google's news search engine.

What the hick sheriff had said was true—or basically true. Federal authorities had indeed carried out a raid on the Family's mansion in Chicago.

The Family's involvement in the Kentucky-Tennessee-Ohio meth trade was now a matter of public knowledge.

Uncle Alfonzo was in federal custody—or would be, soon.

His life was over.

This wasn't the end, of course: the Family's attorneys would likely be able to negotiate a bail arrangement for Uncle Alfonzo, basing their argument on humanitarian grounds: Alfonzo was old and his health problems made him an unlikely flight risk. But this wouldn't be enough to keep his uncle out of jail in the long run. The government sent old men to prison every day.

More to the point: this would be the end of the road for him. If Uncle Alfonzo didn't order a hit on him, he would be forever banished from the family. And who could blame Alfonzo? He, Paulie, had been responsible, after all.

Or rather, the ex-marine Lee McCabe had been responsible. And now this sheriff, who had apparently switched sides and was now working with McCabe, wanted him to surrender, on the flimsy promise of a nonexistent deal.

Did the hick sheriff take him for a fool?

He accepted the fact that this was the end of the line. However this ended, it would not end well for him. There was still a small chance of escape—into a rootless life as a fugitive from the law and the family. This prospect did not appeal to him, and he was consoled by the greater likelihood: that he would be dead within a few hours. But not before he killed the ex-marine who had placed him in this predicament. Paulie knew it was time to play his last card. He would go down fighting.

He assessed his two hostages, the bargaining chips that would bring Lee McCabe before the barrel of his gun. In all truth, he held no ill will toward this pathetic old woman and her son. She stared wearily back at him from the corner of the abandoned office. She would give him no trouble—even if he had not bound her hands behind her back.

Her son was another matter. The young man's rage was palpable. The glint in his eyes indicated that he wanted to kill Paulie.

Paulie hit the return call button and the sheriff answered on the second ring.

"No deal, Sheriff. We end this here. We end this now."

151

"We have no choice, then," Lee told Phelps. "We've got to go in now."

"Can't you see that's exactly what this man wants?" Phelps asked. "No, listen. We do this my way from here on out. It won't be long until I'll have backup here. Then we carry out a coordinated attack. We'll have superior force."

"How long until your 'backup' arrives, Sheriff?"

"I don't know, exactly," Phelps admitted.

"Then I can't take the chance. He'll kill Marie and Joe before then. Like you said—this man is no fool. He can figure out what we're doing. He can guess that you've called in reserves. That's what the police always do—just like the military."

Lee did not wait for a response from Phelps. Before the sheriff could respond, he bolted toward a side entrance of the factory. He did not doubt that this door would be unlocked. The men inside were waiting for him. They wanted him to enter their death chamber.

Please, Lee thought, as he placed his hand on the knob of the metal door. *Please see me through this.* He did not know exactly to whom he was imploring—the being that he perceived as God, the souls of his deceased parents. It was not a question that he could even begin to untangle at the moment.

Lee stepped inside the door of the factory and all hell began to break loose. He heard the report of a gun that he recognized as an AK-47. The floor around him erupted in a shower of miniature explosions, as concrete chips ricocheted against the bare skin of his arms and face. Concrete dust filled his lungs and eyes.

Lee turned and caught a brief glimpse of a gunman on the overhead mezzanine. He was holding the AK at shoulder height, firing almost randomly in Lee's direction without bothering to take much of an aim. For a split second Lee contemplated the odds of taking him out with a precise shot from the Sig Sauer but immediately thought better of it. The man was high in the air, partially enclosed by the metal framework of the mezzanine. Moreover, a semi-automatic pistol was no match against an AK-47 under the best of circumstances.

And there were other gunmen as well. Lee was aware of movement throughout the vast, cavernous room of the Peaton Woods Factory floor. Light streamed in through the frosted glass windows that surrounded the factory at the second-floor level, and Lee could see men scrambling in his direction, guns going off in a mad effort to eradicate the intruder.

He spotted a metal enclosure a short dash away: a storage bin that had probably been used to store raw materials in the days when Peaton Woods was a going concern. It formed a cubicle of sorts: three makeshift steel walls erected against the far concrete wall. This represented his only means of cover, his only chance of living through the next thirty seconds. He ducked and ran, as rounds continued to burrow into the floor and walls around him. He ran in a zigzag pattern, as he had been trained to do under fire.

Lee took a tumbling dive into the storage bin, which was filled with decayed sawdust, unidentifiable grit, and cobwebs. Bullets were now dinging against the sides of the bin, and Lee knew that he was trapped in an ultimately suicidal situation. He would be able to go down fighting but that was all. They would surround and overwhelm him with their numbers and collective firepower. Or he could surrender and submit to a summary execution. Either option would lead to the same ending.

Then there was a momentary cessation in the firing as the outside door of the factory creaked open again. From his vantage point Lee could see Sheriff Phelps burst into the kill zone with his Remington raised at the ready. The sheriff took aim at the man on the mezzanine and fired. Pellets pinged sharply off the mezzanine's framework; but some of them had also struck home. The untrained gunman had obviously never been shot before, nor was he prepared for it. He screamed and dropped his weapon. The AK-47 fell to the grated floor of the mezzanine walkway, then bounced through the railing and fell to the factory floor, smacking the concrete with a bounce and a shattering sound. The gunman fell to the grating of the mezzanine, shrieking and clutching his wounded legs.

Phelps prepared to fire at additional assailants; but they had the advantages of number and cover. The sheriff's thigh exploded outward in a red blossom as he was struck. Phelps was simultaneously driven backward by a bullet that struck his chest.

The sheriff fell backward, the Remington falling from his hands as he struck the floor. Lee cursed silently, fighting the urge to bolt from the cover of the storage bin and retrieve him. That would serve no purpose. The gunmen already knew his location, and they would take him down before he could complete two full steps in Phelps's direction

He tried to ascertain if the sheriff was still alive, and if the wound to his chest was fatal. It was impossible to tell: the sheriff had fallen behind a pile of old pallets that obscured his body from Lee's vision. Lee could see only the sheriff's legs, which were still and covered with blood.

152

Paulie Sarzo heard the first shots in the factory and cursed, then pounded his fist against the nearest wall. His fury blinded him, swam through his head in a red current.

His hired hillbilly gunmen—not to mention some of his own Chicago men—had apparently disobeyed his orders, or had otherwise blundered. He had commanded them to capture Lee McCabe and the lawman alive.

Paulie did not want to see McCabe and Phelps die in a gunfight. There should be no easy way out for these two interlopers, who had brought down everything that he had worked for—who had made it impossible for him to regain his status in the eyes of Uncle Alfonzo, and his position within the Family.

If he died as a result of this debacle, he would not go to his grave without personally carrying out his vendetta. He would look into the faces of each of these men and watch them die. And these deaths would be long and slow. They would be symphonies of protracted agony.

And then there were his two hostages. Paulie supposed that they were useless to him now. Their entire purpose had been to lure Lee

McCabe to this factory. McCabe was here. He had might as well kill them, before they caused any trouble.

The old woman and her son flinched as Paulie raised his pistol in their general direction. *The young black man's expression was a little less defiant now, wasn't it?* He had never before looked death in the face. That much was clear.

Then another plan crystallized in his mind—one that would make his revenge on Lee McCabe complete: If McCabe loved these two so much, then he could watch them die in the final moments of his own life.

But first, Paulie knew, he had to rein in the operation on the factory floor. Otherwise, Lee McCabe would beat him once again by claiming a quick and merciful death.

He would not allow that to happen.

153

J oe Wilson watched the Italian gangster run out of the office shortly after the gunfire began.

He could not believe his luck (if it was possible to consider oneself "lucky" in the context of the current situation). For the past hour, Joe had been patiently picking at the knotted nylon ropes that bound his hands behind his back. Then he flexed the muscles of his arms to make his skin slick with sweat. Next he went to work on the knots for a few more minutes. Then he flexed his arms once again, repeating the steps.

The painstaking process had nearly driven him mad. The mafia man (and Joe had now surmised that their captor had to be a member of some out-of-state, organized criminal outfit) would surely have killed him had he discovered the subterfuge. This man seemed to be a sadist of some sort. Best case, he would have inflicted horrible pain on him (and likely his mother) before binding him so tightly that escape would become completely impossible.

Joe shifted his left arm backward one final time. For a second he feared that this action would backfire and retighten the last remaining knot. But then his left hand slid free of the nylon ropes.

He had to restrain himself from crying out with relief.

"Thank God," he whispered. He quickly brought both hands in front of him, and then proceeded to peel the ropes from the hand that was still bound. Marie saw this and closed her eyes in apparent gratitude to divine providence as well.

"Yes, son, we can thank God, we can. But let's get out of here first. You see that door back there? I'm pretty sure that's an exit."

Joe nodded as he untied his mother, though he had no intention of escaping through the back door himself. He helped Marie to her feet and walked over to the door. There was a knob button and a deadbolt that locked the door from the inside.

Joe knew that the door would lead into the woods, but his knowledge of that fact left many questions unanswered.

"Mama, if we go out that way, that man is simply going to track us down and shoot us. He'll be back in a few minutes."

"So what do you want to do, son? Stand here and wait for him to come back?"

"No," Joe unlocked the door and cautiously opened it. As he had anticipated, the door opened onto a small patch of overgrown grass, and then the surrounding woods. The wall of trees was broken by a trail that looked easy to ambulate.

Joe stepped outside into the humid air and looked in all directions. Gnats flitted at his perspiring face.

"I want you to go, Mama," he finally said. "Walk down that trail as fast as you can, and wait for me. I'll be along as quick as I can."

Marie stared at her son in disbelief. "What are you talking about, Joe?"

"Lee McCabe is out in that factory," Joe said. "He came here for us. I'm not going to leave him to face those men alone."

"Weren't you listening, Joe? Lee has got Sheriff Phelps with him. He's going to be just fine."

"You don't know that, Mama. You can't know that."

Marie was shaking her head, refusing to believe what her son seemed to be contemplating. "Listen to me Joe, Lee McCabe is a trained soldier, just like your brother and your papa. He can take care of himself."

"And I can't take care of myself?"

"Oh good Lord, Joe." She placed both hands on his cheeks. "If this is about you trying to prove yourself, you can forget that right now. I'm proud of you, son. Your father was proud of you. And you're going to be a fine man when you.."

Marie abruptly stopped speaking, as if she recognized the inadvertent admission in her last sentence.

"That's what I mean. *Don't you see?* 'I'm going to be'. Well, I'm thirty years old and it's time for me to *be* something rather than just becoming something. If I leave now, the only thing I become is a coward."

"This is crazy, Joe." Marie was practically frantic now. "Don't do whatever it is you're planning on doing. You don't even have a gun on you. There wouldn't be anything you could do for Lee McCabe, anyway."

Joe shook his head. "I was watching that crazy man," Joe said. "I saw him put a spare gun in that desk over there."

Joe walked over to the empty desk, which was the only piece of furniture left in the room. It was a rusted aluminum hulk that had lost most of its original coat of grey paint.

He pulled open the top left drawer of the desk. A few short years ago, a middle manager at the Peaton Woods Furniture factory might have used this drawer to store file folders or pens—or perhaps a paper bagged lunch. Now the drawer held something entirely different.

The gun that Joe lifted from the desk drawer was a machine pistol of some kind. Joe was no expert on guns; but he guessed it to be a Tec-9 or something similar. He held the gun up in the air. Its heft felt powerful and deadly.

"Please, Joe," Marie pleaded, tears in her voice. "Don't do this. I'm begging you."

"I've got to, Mama. I won't let Lee McCabe die for me. I couldn't live with myself. I love you, Mama, but you'll have to understand."

154

Two gunmen rushed at Lee from across the floor. They both carried machine pistols: one held what looked to be a Steyr TMP, and the other gripped an Ingram MAC-11. Their muzzles flashed as they charged in Lee's direction, in an apparent attempt to overwhelm him with speed and firepower. Their sense of aim was no better than that of the fallen man on the mezzanine. Nevertheless, Lee had difficulty getting a bead on one of the men amid the barrage. The walls of the storage bin clattered and thundered in the shower of rounds.

Lee squeezed the trigger of the Sig Sauer twice and one of the gunmen went down, writhing. This caused his companion a moment's hesitation. Lee squeezed the trigger two more times, and the second man went down.

There were more coming at him from the other side of the room. Another man had taken the fallen man's place on the mezzanine. They knew that there was only one of him now; and they knew that sooner or later he would have to submit or perish. They were surging forward with a pack mentality, urging themselves and each other along with a stream of yelps and curses.

Lee squeezed the trigger of his pistol again and it produced nothing more than an empty click. The inevitable had happened: he was out of rounds and the gunmen were still coming. His only choices were surrender or suicide now.

Lee's predicament had not gone unnoticed: There was a renewed whooping and shouting as the men realized that their job had suddenly become quite easy. This was not going to be a battle any longer, but a slaughter. They were going to have some fun with this intruder who had caused them so much trouble.

Then Lee heard another voice amid the chaos: a booming, stentorian voice that was instantly familiar. The voice spoke with absolute, unquestioned authority. It heaped abuse on the ragtag band of gunmen, calling them inbreds, and motherfuckers and sons-of-whores. It commanded them to hold their fire as he made his way into the room.

Lee's battlefield instincts told him to take cover; but what difference did it really make now? He could not resist a look.

Paulie Sarzo strode imperiously across the factory floor. His face was reddened with rage. He continued to rant, screaming at the men on all sides of him. The factory, which had been filled with the sounds of a war zone less than a minute ago, was silent—except for Sarzo's screaming.

Then Lee heard another voice—which was also familiar. He saw the lone figure of Joe Wilson running after Sarzo, following him from the same direction. Joe held a gun aloft.

Sarzo stopped and turned around. He looked incredulously at his former hostage, who was now armed and free and brandishing a weapon at him. Then, suddenly, the full implications of the situation seemed to become clear to the Chicago gangster.

Sarzo drew a pistol from the shoulder holster he was wearing. Joe aimed his weapon dead at the Italian. Lee watched as Joe pulled the trigger several times. However, no shots were fired. It appeared that the trigger was moving as it should have, so it was not a matter of the safety being on.

My God, thought Lee. *Joe is attacking Sarzo with an unloaded gun.*

Paulie Sarzo looked at Joe Wilson and smiled. With almost

theatrical deliberateness, he raised his own gun and fired a quick succession of rounds.

Joe's body twisted as the bullets slammed into him at nearly point-blank range. One of the shots struck Joe in the forehead, and Lee knew that it was all over. Joe was thrown backward; his body fell upon the floor with a dull thud, blood pouring from his multiple wounds.

Sarzo walked calmly up to Joe's body and spat on his chest. He kicked the body hard. There was no reaction. Sarzo fired three more rounds into Joe's corpse. The lifeless body bucked from the impact of each shot.

Lee let out a scream of rage. He stood, abandoning his cover, and ran at Paulie Sarzo.

Sarzo leveled his pistol at Lee and pulled the trigger. Now he was the one who was out of bullets. He looked at the now useless pistol and cursed.

Paulie dropped the gun and ran at Lee. The two men collided in the open floor. Both men cried out at the instant of the collision; and to Lee, it felt like hitting a freight train. The Italian had the advantage in weight and strength. He drove Lee back the way he had come, into the little storage bin.

Lee frantically attempted to keep his balance. But his feet caught on a tangle of debris, and he fell backward to the ground, Sarzo on top of him.

Lee did not have time to prepare for the blow that struck him on the side of the head. The pain saturated his every thought, so that for a few seconds, he and the pain were the only entities that existed in the entire universe. He saw stars, and his grip on consciousness itself began to waver.

Sarzo reached inside his pocket and withdrew a thin cylindrical object. A second later a blade appeared. It was a switchblade.

Only one of Lee's hands was free; the other hand was beneath Sarzo's knee. With his free hand, Lee scooped up a handful of the sandy, pulpy grit that covered the floor of the storage bin.

Lee flung the mixture in Sarzo's face. He tried to blink, but Lee's maneuver had been unexpected. Sarzo reflexively dropped the switchblade and ran one hand across his eyes. Lee kicked the knife out of Sarzo's reach, toward the opening of the storage compartment, just as the gangster was clawing for it.

This provided Lee with a very brief window of opportunity, as Sarzo's attention was diverted. Lee drove his fist squarely into the heavier, stronger man's front teeth. He felt several of the teeth give way, felt cuts from the shattered enamel.

The blow disoriented Sarzo, and Lee wriggled out from beneath him. Then he delivered another blow, this time striking Paulie in the side of the jaw. Lee struck him again. Sarzo went down and Lee was atop him.

Lee thought about Joe Wilson, who was definitely dead. And for all he knew, Marie might be dead as well. He raised his fist and brought it down on the gangster's clenched, bloody face. He felt tissue and cartilage give way beneath the impact. This man who was now at his mercy would also likely be responsible for the death of Sheriff Phelps. He still harbored much bitterness against Phelps; but Phelps's death was nothing he desired. It would only add to the weight of his soul's debt—another person who had forfeited life so that he might live.

From inside the red blur of his rage, Lee heard the distant sounds of more people entering the factory, and the mass gunfire—which had been still for so long now—started again. He imagined that this would be the backup that Phelps had mentioned, arriving ten minutes too late to save at least one life.

Lee straddled Paulie Sarzo's body and systematically pummeled his face, summoning his rage for what had happened to Dawn, to Amy Sutter, to Joe Wilson, to all the good men who had died in Iraq —all those he had known. He even thought of his parents, who had not died by the gun, but had nonetheless died before their time. They had been taken from him, too.

Lee's own head was swimming with blind, animal instinct, as he imagined the swarthy gangster to be a conduit that could drain all of these feelings away from him. His fists were nearly numb now from striking multiple blows. They were wet and slick with Sarzo's blood, and his own blood as well.

Then, as he raised his hand to strike again, he felt another hand on his wrist, restraining him. The sudden restraint jolted him from his vengeful daze, and he looked into the face of an early middle-aged man who seemed utterly out of place. He was wearing a black flak vest that bore the insignia of the FBI and a name badge that read "Lomax"; but this man had the overall bearing of an accountant or a loan officer at a bank. He certainly did not fit the image of the reserve forces that Phelps had promised, and Lee had a strong urge to yank his arm away, to resume his beating of Sarzo, whose head now lolled backward in a state of semi-consciousness. Lee realized that he might easily have beaten the man to death, and at this moment he still very much wanted to; but the thoroughly calm Lomax would not relinquish his wrist.

"Come on, McCabe," he said. "It's over now. Stand up. Clean yourself up. I'll take Sarzo into custody."

And with this statement Lee's consciousness shifted again. For a solid week the law had been pursuing him, based on the erroneous belief that he had murdered Tim Fitzsimmons and Jody White. Lomax's words conveyed the understanding that a great miscarriage of justice would now be righted, if he would only be willing to cooperate with this accountant-like man in the FBI flak vest.

He stood up from the semi-inert body of Paulie Sarzo. The gangster let out an anguished, furious groan as the FBI man took over. Lomax forced Sarzo into a sitting position, then produced a set of handcuffs to secure him.

"You've been cleared, McCabe," Lomax said, as if anticipating Lee's own thoughts and questions. "We know that you're innocent of the murders in the trailer park. Hell, maybe you're even a bit of a hero now. But you were still a damned fool to run from the police like that. What got into your head?"

"It's complicated," Lee said.

"I'll bet it is."

It was, after all, just as Sheriff Phelps had said. Before today Lee had never heard of the Coscollino crime family, who had changed his life so radically and ended so many others.

Lee struggled to his feet. He noticed his Sig Sauer lying in the sawdust.

"Why don't you leave that where it is?" Lomax said. "You're not under arrest, but I don't want you to walk out into a room full of police brandishing a gun. Never a good idea, you know."

"So it's safe now?" Lee asked. "You've killed them…You and the other FBI men?"

"We had some state and local help," Lomax said. "Sheriff's Deputy Darla Johnson killed about half of them. I know it's a cliché; but I'm going to nickname her Annie Oakley."

Lee stepped past Lomax and his fugitive, into the main area of the plant. He saw state police in flak jackets and helmets, and a woman in a Hawkins County Sheriff's Department tee shirt and sweat pants who had to be Darla Johnson. Johnson leaned against a steel support pillar in the center of the room. She slid down against the pillar to a resting, seated position, her rifle cradled in her arms. There was blood on her clothes, and she seemed to be in a fair amount of pain.

There was a team of paramedics bearing stretchers. One of the paramedics detached himself from the group and double-timed it over to Johnson. She acknowledged him with a nod. Then she issued some instruction that Lee could not hear but nevertheless understood the gist of: Darla wanted the paramedics to attend to another officer first—one who had fallen in battle.

She was referring to Sheriff Phelps, of course. The lone paramedic nodded back at Darla, then quickly assisted another paramedic who was attending to Sheriff Phelps. Lee could see that the sheriff was badly wounded, but very much alive. Phelps arched his back and grimaced in pain as the two paramedics moved his body carefully onto a stretcher. One of the paramedics was fitting an IV into the sheriff's arm, preparing him for transport to an ambulance.

155

W hen a pair of men from the county coroner's office went to retrieve the two bodies in the Boar's Head, they did not fail to notice that one of the corpses had been covered with a blue tablecloth.

"You imagine that soldier covered her up, Sam?"

"Maybe. I understand that he knew her before all of this. Maybe he was soft on her, who knows?"

"It's hard to imagine any man being too soft on her. "

"What the hell are you gettin' at?"

"Well, just look at her."

"What do you mean? She's dead."

"You see those needle tracks on her arm? Those scabs? This was one heavy-duty meth-head. That's what I'm sayin'"

"Fine. You're very observant. But she's dead now, so why don't you cut her some slack?"

"I wouldn't want to have encountered her in a dark alley. That's all I'm saying."

"I'm sure she would have felt the same way about you."

"Asshole."

"Yeah, yeah. Look: I feel the same way. But this woman was probably incapable of reading at a third grade level. She was obviously a meth whore and that's all she would have ever amounted to."

"Now who's the asshole?"

"I'm just saying: Some people simply aren't meant to rise above the bottom. But I don't want to think about her. I don't want to think about why she ended up like this. It's depressing. Now let's do our job and bag her up and then take care of the old guy, too. I promised my wife and daughter that I would be home in time for dinner."

"Okay, okay." They went about the grisly work that had become so routine for them. This scene was bad enough; but these two men had seen far worse: Some traffic accidents were much, much worse.

"Tell me, Sam: Is Janey still planning to go to medical school?"

Sam smiled beneath his sanitary mask. His daughter Janey was a straight-A student and the apple of his eye. "She sure is. And if she keeps her grades up she'll get in, too." Sam regarded the dead woman one last time before he zipped up her black body bag. "Strange, isn't it? How some people turn out."

156

In the days immediately after he regained his old life, Lee McCabe refused to return the calls of the many reporters, bloggers, and curiosity seekers who were so anxious to talk to him. Their attentions were another form of pursuit—not as deadly as the one he had just endured; but equally unwelcome for the time being.

However, there were two people whom he did want to see immediately: Lee drove out to Ben Chamberlain's house and Izzy answered the doorbell.

"*It's Lee!*" she squealed, opening the door. Ben Chamberlain appeared seconds later and the three of them embraced in the doorway.

"I'm glad you made it," Ben said.

"I'm glad, too," Lee said. "And I can never repay you for what you did." He looked at Izzy. "Either of you. Izzy, you were very brave that night. You're going to be hell on wheels when you get a bit older."

"I whooped 'em," Isabelle said. "I whooped 'em good."

"Yes, Izzy," Lee said. "You surely did."

ON THE THIRD day of the aftermath, when his voicemail was still full of unreturned messages, Lee was seized by a sudden impulse to visit the man who had counseled him and offered him shelter during his first night on the run.

Out there in that cabin, Lee thought. *He probably doesn't get much of the news.*

He knew the general area where the Hunter's cabin should be. He drove to the general vicinity, then stopped and asked a farmer who was taking in hay for specific directions.

"James Hunter?" the late-middle-aged man asked. "The old Hunter cabin was not too far from here. Yeah, I can tell you how to get there."

The farmer seemed busy and in not much of a mood to talk. He did not seem to recognize Lee from the news. Lee produced a pocket notepad for the farmer to draw him a rough map. Then he thanked the farmer and bid him good day.

"'*Was* not too far from here,'" Lee said to himself as he started his car again, preparing to drive where the map took him. "Did he really say 'was' and not 'is'"?

Lee decided that he had either misheard the man's statement, or the farmer had misspoken.

The map took him back a long country road, a one-lane path of packed dirt and gravel. Once another car approached and Lee had to pull to the side so the other driver could pass. There were wide, empty, uncultivated fields on either side of him, and steep hills covered with impenetrable woods beyond that. Really this area was not so different from the landscape in the rest of the county, but its complete lack of human habitation made it seem even more wild and remote.

Finally the road became so rough that the car could reliably traverse it no farther. Lee put the vehicle in park, removed the keys and hiked the rest of the way.

When Lee reached the spot where the map ended, he did not find a cabin. At first it appeared that the vast field before him was completely empty. "That farmer misled me," Lee said aloud. Then he noticed an irregular spot in the high grass and brush—a place where the vegetation seemed to be sparse.

He walked out through the field. When he came to the spot that had caught his eye, he found what appeared to be the charred remains of a foundation. This had been a wooden structure, as there were no stones, and the fire that had destroyed the building had purged it completely.

Lee shook his head. For a second he feared that somehow the Hunter had also become a target for the Coscollinos. But no: this cabin—if it had in fact been a cabin—had burned many seasons ago. Little patches of grass, chicory and other weeds had sprouted among the ashes.

"What the hell?" Lee asked. A strange ending to the strangest week of his life. Well, he had made a reasonable attempt to find the Hunter and thank him, to tell him how things had ended. The Hunter's cabin must be out here somewhere. Perhaps he would seek it out on another day. Perhaps not.

Lee was preparing to step back into this car when he noticed an old man walking up the path in the same direction from which he had come. He had come so far today, it was worth verifying the farmer's map with a third party.

"Excuse me," Lee hailed. "I wonder if I could bother you for a moment. Do you know where I might find the cabin of James Hunter?"

"I think you were just lookin' at it," the old man replied. "Or what's left of it. Hunter's cabin burned after—you know."

"No, I don't know," Lee said. "You see, I came out here looking for James Hunter, and no one seems to be able to tell me where to find him."

"He ain't to be found, you see. James Hunter died about four, five years ago. Quite a man he was—but never the same after that accident killed his wife and daughter. Ah yes, I remember Jim Hunter." The old man stared wistfully into the distance. "They say he shot hisself, and set that cabin on fire just before he did it. Rigged it so that cabin would be his funeral pyre."

"Th-thank you," Lee said. "I understand."

But Lee did *not* understand. He turned away and let the old man pass. He leaned against the roof of his car, trying not to draw the logical connections between his encounter in the woods, and the evidence and the testimony before him now. Because these connections were far from logical.

I'm going to need some time, Lee thought. Some time to think about what this means.

And now, after all that had happened, Lee imagined that he would have plenty of time to think.

L ee did not drive directly home after that. He drove out to the road where Lester had captured him. Where the big man named Luke had met his end.

He not given Lester's stolen drug money much thought that day. At the time, it was potentially a tool that might be used to turn the tide against Lester, with no significance beyond that.

Now it might be very much more, indeed.

After parking his car, Lee hiked up the embankment and into the woods. The large tree—a massive oak that was perhaps a hundred years old, stood out from the other trees in the forest.

Lee looked behind the oak tree. The blue gym bag was right there. Exactly where Luke had left it.

Lee unzipped the gym bag. There had been a small amount of light rain since that day, but the gym bag was waterproof. The stacks of one hundred dollar bills inside the bag were completely dry.

What to do with so much money? It was an intoxicating amount. More than enough to change lives—for the better or for the worse.

Lee had no intention of turning the money over to the state. The state had come into the fray only at the last minute—and only after so many innocent people had died. No, there was no branch of the government that deserved any of this money. Lee knew that other people would see it differently; but they would be viewing the situation abstractly, impersonally. For Lee, the losses of the past week were intimate and personal. He could not frame the situation in dispassionate terms.

This much money would be more than enough to make him comfortable for the rest of his life. And who could argue that he had not earned it?

But this money had also been purchased with the deaths and miseries of countless innocents—not only those who had died this past week—but also those who had become addicted to Lester's meth. And the miseries of their families as well. When you added it all up, this money was tainted. It was a cursed thing.

This was not logical, he knew; but his earlier experience at the ruins of the Hunter's cabin had caused him to question the nature of logic itself.

The best thing might be to burn it. But no—that would be a waste.

Is there some way to make this money pure, Lee wondered. *Some way that will be directly connected to its evil roots?*

And then he recalled one of the emails that he had received just yesterday, from another person he had met along his journey.

Maybe, Lee thought. *Maybe that could be the right way.*

Lee zipped the gym bag closed and carried it out of the woods.

EPILOGUE

Another month and a half passed before Lee's meeting with Phelps. It was the season of late summer, when the brutally hot days passed seemingly without end, and an August sun baked the wooded hills of central Kentucky.

The two of them arranged to meet at a Denny's near the main interstate, where neither would be recognized by practically every diner in the restaurant. They had only coffee; neither one was in much of a mood for more substantial fare. It was an awkward meeting at first; but the two of them did in fact have much to talk about. Lee had some idea of what the sheriff most wanted to discuss; but he knew that the older man would beat around the bush for a while first.

"You were right all along about the significance of the sawdust," Phelps said. "I have to hand it to you, putting the pieces together like that. When we cleaned out the factory, we found that they were storing the meth in an old lumber storage room. Most of the packages that they sold were covered with traces of sawdust."

"Well, you forget, Sheriff: I can't take credit for that: Brett St. Croix was the one who figured that out."

"Speaking of journalists," Phelps went on. "Or rather, speaking of

Dawn Hardin: Some journalist at CNN learned of her story. He was fascinated by the fact that Dawn fell so far, so fast, all because of meth. They're going to do a documentary about her, so that her story will be a warning to others." Phelps took a sip of his coffee, pausing to reflect. "Maybe it will prevent some future kids from falling into the same trap. I suppose that this way, her life—as well as her death—will have some meaning."

"I think they both had meaning already," Lee said. "But yes, I suppose that's a good thing, what you're saying."

"There's more. A charity has been set up in Dawn's memory: the Dawn Hardin Foundation. The foundation will help young people who have been abused, turned to drugs, the street life."

"Really?" Lee asked, displaying his best poker face.

"Do you know who Michelle Ackerman is? Brett St. Croix's assistant?"

Lee nodded. "I may have spoken to her once or twice."

"Well, she presented the Dawn Hardin Foundation with an anonymous gift of more than nine hundred thousand dollars. All in cash. All in one hundred dollar bills. She's refused to name the source of the money. There are some sources in the state government that have some suspicions concerning the money's source. But they're going to let it go. They don't want to be seen as taking money away from a charity. The state already took a beating after they initially mishandled this case. And Michelle Ackerman has already vowed that she will raise hell if they don't leave it alone."

Lee shrugged. "Strange things happen, don't they?"

"That they do. I think you already know that Alfonzo Coscollino committed suicide rather than submit to arrest. There's an article on the homepage of the *Chicago Tribune* this morning: 'The Fall of the Coscollino Empire'. Records retrieved from the raid on the Coscollino mansion gave investigators a lot of threads to follow, and they're following every one of them: drug trafficking from Illinois to Tennessee, prostitution rings in twelve cities, even loan sharking and murder-for-hire rings."

Lee took a drink of coffee. "Wish they had made that raid a few weeks earlier. A lot of innocent people would still be alive now."

"I know, Lee. I know. But the FBI isn't infallible or omniscient—any more than the military is, any more than you and I are."

"How much do you want to bet," Lee asked, "that those two FBI agents who worked with you get a promotion and a pay grade increase out of this?"

"Cynical, aren't you?"

"Hell yes I am, after this past week. Aren't you?"

"Sure I am. I'm a citizen first and a public official second. Even as a county sheriff, I was skeptical of the FBI's agenda. But I have to admit that Lomax and Porter came through for me, even if they were too late to save the lives of Dawn Hardin and Joe Wilson. The Coscollino family is out of business now, and that will save lives in the future. It's an imperfect set of outcomes, I know. But these are the only outcomes we have."

Yes, there were many outcomes to all of this, Lee thought. *Too many outcomes that will take me a long time to forget.*

But already he could feel the healing process beginning. Despite all this tragedy—despite the dour, defensive face that he knew he was showing to Phelps—Lee was starting to free himself from the pall of what had occurred. He had no other choice, or else he would end up like the Hunter, a man whose face and voice still occasionally appeared in his dreams.

"I'm retiring from law enforcement," Phelps said. "Effective at the end of my current term."

Lee recalled Phelps's actions at the Peaton Woods Furniture factory. He had to grudgingly admit that the sheriff had saved his life.

"Who will take your place?" he asked.

"I plan to leave the people of the county in capable hands. Darla Johnson will be the next sheriff of Hawkins County. She was always the best of my deputies, and she's decided to run. Needless to say, I'll be giving her my full public endorsement."

"Good," Lee said. He recalled Darla Johnson's actions in the factory that day. He later heard about how she had gotten up from her hospital bed to join the assault at the abandoned factory. The people of Hawkins County could certainly do worse.

"You know that I loved your mother, right?" Phelps said abruptly.

"If I don't know, then I'm the only one in the county who doesn't."

"But that's past now." Phelps leaned forward and removed his wallet from his back pocket. He took out the photograph that Lee had let fall from the mezzanine that day.

"I believe this is yours," Phelps said, extending the photo. "You should have this."

Lee reached out to take the photo, but stopped himself. "No, thank you, Sheriff. I—I would rather not remember her that way."

He was somewhat taken aback by his own reaction; but it made sense, in a way. It occurred to him that his mother—like everyone else, had been various people throughout her life. She had not stayed the same. The Lori McCabe he knew had been married some of the time to his father—and had always loved his father—often contrary to her own best interests. She was the woman who had prepared his meals as a child and who had succored him when he fell down on his bike, or ended up on the losing end of a playground brawl.

This young girl in the photograph—she had existed in a time when he had not. She had no place in his memories. On some level, perhaps that girl belonged more to Phelps than to him, or even to his late father.

Sheriff Phelps was looking at him, and Lee wondered exactly what it was that the lawman saw—or fancied that he saw: the son of the woman he had loved, or the son of the man who had taken her away? But this distinction was impossible: both of those people were one and indivisible in him. And Lee knew that Phelps must been seeing both: the future that might have been his, and the future that would never be his—the one that he had lost.

No, he and Phelps would never be close. The past would always stand in their way. But through the events of the past June, they had reached the one thing that was possible for them: a truce bounded by a mutual respect.

"Okay," Phelps said, returning the photo to his wallet. "As you wish."

There was not much more for them to say, and soon it came time for Lee to excuse himself. Phelps held out his hand as Lee stood up.

"Peace?"

Lee shook the sheriff's hand. "I believe we've come as close as we are going to come, Sheriff. Goodbye. And good luck."

"Good luck to you, Lee."

PHELPS DID NOT WALK out of the Denny's with Lee. He stayed behind at the table, and through the window watched Lee McCabe's car pull up to the stop sign before the highway. The younger man gunned the engine and his car sped away.

Why had Lee McCabe said "Goodbye?" Perhaps McCabe grasped the conclusion that he had been gradually acknowledging in recent weeks: It was time for him to leave Hawkins County, finally—after all these years. Time to go somewhere else and make a fresh start.

He pulled the photograph of him and Lori Mills from his wallet again. He decided that he should burn it to ash like the rest of the old photos, and then he thought better of it. This photograph had found its way back to him through a series of occurrences that could only be described as extraordinary. Perhaps the Fates wanted him to have it, after all. It was a talisman that told him where he had been, but not necessarily where he wanted to go. He had his memories; now he would have to see if he had a future as well.

He tucked the photo back into his wallet, looked through the window of the restaurant out across the wooded hills, and began to contemplate the choices that lay ahead of him.

LEE HAD three more visits to make. And then his absolution would be complete.

First he visited Dawn's grave. She had been two years younger than him; and Lee reflected that her entire lifespan was now encapsulated within his own. He might live to be an old man of eighty or ninety; but Dawn's life would always be contained in that short span of twenty-odd years.

He laid a small bouquet of flowers on her headstone. On his way out of the cemetery, he passed by a family—a young couple and two small children. They were going to pay their respects to the grave of a long-dead grandparent or great-grandparent—for there was no air of fresh tragedy about them. Both the man and the woman hailed Lee, calling out to him in a friendly manner as he walked by. But Lee turned away, his face suddenly moist and hot, feeling oddly shameful and protective of his grief.

Next he drove to the Wilson farm and Marie stepped out onto the porch. Without saying a word she stepped closer and wrapped her arms around him.

"It's alright," she said, hugging him tighter. Lee could feel the wetness of her tears through his thin summer shirt.

Lee knew that it was never going to be all right—not completely. Joe Wilson was dead. Joe was never going to come home to his mother's house again; he was never going to have a future, nor children of his own. The story of Marie Wilson's elder son was over now; it had been terminated by those shots fired in wrath at the abandoned furniture factory.

And finally he drove to Warwick, on the other side of Hawkins County. He sought out Amy Sutter's parents. He spoke simply and to the point. He told them that Amy had saved his life, and that he would be eternally grateful for what their daughter had done.

It was over now, he decided. His cell phone chimed and he saw that he had received another text message from Michelle Ackerman. She had been in regular contact with him in recent weeks. Sometimes asking how he was doing, sometimes talking about the work of the Dawn Hardin Foundation.

"I would not mind if you gave me a call, you know." Her message read. "In fact, I wouldn't object to seeing you again."

Lee understood the subtext here and it made him hopeful, even as he saw the numerous obstacles to him and Michelle pairing up. He was a decorated former marine, a combat veteran; and she was a left-leaning journalist who had protested the very war in which he had so distinguished himself. As a couple, they would be as self-contradictory and internally conflicted as America itself.

Still, he thought. *She is one hell of a woman: Not only beautiful but smart and gutsy as well. I can't simply let an opportunity like this pass without at least checking it out. And I also can't forget the risk she took for me: I suppose that I would have to add her to the list of people who saved my life in one way or another during that week.*

I will not feel guilty, Lee thought, *for the hope that I am feeling, or even for the yearning that I feel for that woman in Cincinnati. Even with all this death around me.*

He knew that he would always honor the sacrifices of Joe, Amy, and Dawn; but he could not make their deaths the central theme of his existence. It was now his job to go on. And go on he would. He would move through that darkness that the Hunter had talked about —the darkness that he now knew to be the inextricable and constant burden of life on this earth.

As the one who had lived—the one who went onward—a man could do no less for his fallen friends.

THE END

NOTES AND DISCLAIMERS

Blood Flats is a work of fiction. The characters contained herein are entirely products of the author's imagination. Any resemblance to actual persons—living or dead—is purely coincidental.

While this novel is set in Kentucky, I took considerable liberties regarding the geography of the state. There is no Hawkins County. (The fictional Hawkins County—for readers who wish to place it on a map—would be located in the central part of Kentucky, to the east of Louisville, in the 502 area code.) Perryston, Blood Flats, and Warwick are likewise fictional names. All highway names are fictional. If you look for the Chickasaw Creek on a map of the Bluegrass State, you won't find it, though a creek by that name does exist in Alabama.

Two historic battles are mentioned in this novel, one real, one fictitious. To the best of my knowledge, there was no Battle of Perryston in the U.S. Civil War (though the Civil War generals mentioned in this book were real.) There *was*, however, a Battle of Perryville. Keep this fact in mind if it shows up in the form of a multiple-choice question on a U.S. history exam.

In regard to twentieth-century history, I was more faithful to the facts: The "Highway of Death" described through Phelps's viewpoint was an actual battle that occurred during the first Gulf War of 1990-1.

This novel is not intended to be a commentary on the actual state of law enforcement in Kentucky. The law enforcement institutions mentioned in this book are portrayed in a wholly fictional manner. The hierarchy of the Kentucky state police that I describe is loosely based on the real organization's structure. The prison locations mentioned in the book are likewise real. However, none of the specific law enforcement officials in *Blood Flats* are representations of actual persons.

While writing this book, I made efforts to make my depictions of U.S. military weapons, operational tactics, and other details as accurate as possible. That said, I recognize the gap between research and experience. I have never been a member of the U.S. military; and actual veterans will no doubt be able to find inaccuracies in specific elements of my depictions.

The methamphetamine epidemic of the rural South is real. However, there is no Coscollino crime family. While there are no doubt real drinking establishments named the *Boar's Head*, no actual establishment was used as an inspiration for the one in this book. Feel free to visit any bar of this name that you may encounter as you travel through Kentucky; you will not be greeted by Lester Finn.

MORE THRILLS FROM EDWARD TRIMNELL

Available on Amazon/Amazon Kindle Unlimited!

The Consultant: Barry Lawson is an ordinary American trapped in North Korea. The regime has a mission for him. Will he escape, or perish within the most tyrannical state on earth?

The Eavesdropper: What would you do if you discovered that three of your coworkers were planning a murder? A thrilling workplace mystery.

VISIT ME ONLINE!

Thanks for reading *Blood Flats*. Visit me online at EdwardTrimnellBooks.com.

Made in the USA
Las Vegas, NV
22 June 2021